I0561684

# THE
# BLACK ROOM

## doors one—eight

# Jasinda Wilder
## with Jade London

Copyright © 2016 by Jasinda Wilder and Jade London. ALL RIGHTS
RESERVED.

THE BLACK ROOM: DOOR 1
THE BLACK ROOM: DOOR 2
THE BLACK ROOM: DOOR 3
THE BLACK ROOM: DOOR 4
THE BLACK ROOM: DOOR 5
THE BLACK ROOM: DOOR 6
THE BLACK ROOM: DOOR 7
THE BLACK ROOM: DOOR 8

No part of this book may be used or reproduced in any manner
whatsoever without written permission except in the case of brief
quotations embodied in critical articles and reviews.

This is a work of fiction. Names, characters, places, and incidents are
either products of the author's imagination or are used fictitiously. Any
resemblance to actual events, locales, organizations, or persons, living
or dead, is entirely coincidental.

Cover art by Okay Creations
Interior Formatting by Champagne Formats

ISBN: 978-1-941098-62-2

●

I open my eyes to utter darkness.

Where am I? Dear god, where *am* I?

I cannot see a thing. Nothing—this darkness is blacker than any-thing I've ever known.

I can feel nothing, hear nothing, and I am aware of nothing.

No sounds, no smells.

I cannot even hear my own heartbeat.

There's just…nothing. Absolutely nothing. Nothing at all. No one.

Not even me.

Me.

Me?

Who *am* I? My mind is a total blank.

I don't understand…where *I* should be there is only blackness.

There is no breath. No sense of being. No fibers of awareness.

Only darkness.

There is only darkness.

• •

I feel my lashes resting against my cheek; the first sensation.

I am awake.

I *am*; the second sensation.

I breathe in, a slow exploratory breath. I blink again just to feel my eyelashes sweep like the flutter of moths against my face.

And then, a tiny, dancing flicker of light appears. Orange and yellow, wavering side-to-side, jumping upward, then going still. Only the flame, though, no candlestick, no details revealed in the dim pool of illumination.

I stare at the candle flame. Involuntarily, I reach out for it, and discover that I do in fact have hands. And a body. The stiffness and tingling I feel in my hands and legs becomes an almost-painful pins-and-needles.

I feel the heat of the flame. But now it is no longer teardrop shaped. It has become a dim small orange orb, nearly dead, as if starved for oxygen. The candlestick reveals itself, but I fear to touch it, fear to lift it higher. What if the flame goes out? I'd be left in the darkness again, doubting my existence. So I merely stare at the flame and gently bend my knees, then flex my fingers and wiggle my toes.

I'm lying down; the third sensation.

I begin to move cautiously, testing the limits of my motion, testing the strength in my limbs. I stand up and feel dizzy, but more from the disorientation of near-total darkness than from physical weakness.

Questions begin to bubble deep within my consciousness, but they are too weak and too deep to rise to the surface. The questions barely even register, and that's fine with me. I have so much to do to simply rediscover myself in this place of darkness.

I'm standing upright now, firmly balanced on the heels and balls of my feet. I'm aware of something warm underfoot, warm but not hot. Cool, but not cold. The floor is not carpeted, nor is it made of marble or tile; it's just…a floor. A solid presence underfoot, featureless yet reassuring.

Once again I reach for the candle flame and my fingers brush through the flame. It is hot, and I jerk my hand back. Of course it's hot—it's a flame. I reach for the candlestick but, instead, I grasp hold of something thick and cool and round—the candle. The flame illuminates the white wax, some of it melted and dripping down one side. I lift the candle up, but I can see nothing beyond the tiny pool of light—only more darkness.

I turn around, but I can see no evidence of the couch or bed I was laying on mere moments ago. I step out hesitantly, but feel nothing. I can see nothing. Maybe there never was a bed; maybe I had been lying on the floor? But it doesn't feel that way. I don't know for certain. My memory is fuzzy. Each moment now seems unique, as if each thought, each second, each sensation is its own entity, separate from the one before. As if…

I don't know. My thoughts won't coalesce.

It's as if time does not exist here. There is no forward or backward, now or then. There is nothing but…*now.* Only now.

I try to corral my thoughts, but it's like trying to hold water—impossible.

My thoughts are just out of reach and I cannot quite grasp hold of them with any real firmness or understanding.

There is only now.

So, in the now, I take another slow, questing step. Not forward, because there seems to be no forward or back, either. No directions, only…*here*.

And *there*.

Another step, cautiously. A third. With confidence, I take more and more steps, perhaps as many as a hundred, and then I fetch up against a wall. The candle flame flickers, dances, gutters, and I hold my breath, remaining absolutely still. It jumps up once more, and dances merrily. I breathe out in relief, blinking my eyelids, curious about what lies in front of me. The wall, like the floor, is cool but not cold, warm but not hot, featureless but real nevertheless. I touch it, running my fingertips over it. It feels slightly pebbled, as of paint over drywall, perhaps. It's just a wall, but it's *something*.

I follow the wall, trailing my fingertips along it as I walk, holding the candle up high. It doesn't provide enough light for me to see beyond my own feet, or to even *see* my feet. Only my hand and the candle are visible to me: long fingers, slender but strong, fingernails short and un-painted, neatly rounded. Feminine hands, real and familiar; *mine*.

I continue walking beside the wall, counting my steps.

Fifty paces, and then my fingertips touch an irregularity in the wall. A protrusion of some sort.

It's the frame of a door.

My breath catches, because this…this is *real*.

I stop directly in front of the door, and now I feel my heart beat. It is a steady pulse and then, as I examine the door, it begins to beat a little harder. Thumping quickly, just enough to get the blood flowing, as if I've jogged a few steps.

Holding the candle close to the door, I scrutinize the frame and the black door itself, taking in every detail I can. But there is nothing much to see, just the wall, and the doorframe, black-painted hinges. A lintel. A handle.

The door handle is a simple, modern lever. Black metal. It curves upward and then swoops back down, tapering into absence, like a com-ma turned on its side.

I notice one more thing about the door.

In the center of the door is a simple numeral:

# 1

Stark, bare. Made of silver metal, it offers the only bit of color, the only hint of something other than the blackness of the room, and the dull, dim light of the flickering candle flame.

To the right of the door is a wall sconce. Elaborate, black wrought iron, it sprouts from the wall like some kind of organic metallic bloom. Inside the sconce rests another candle. This one, however, is several times the size of the one I am holding. It is not a torch, per se, but a proper candle, writ massive. I touch my flame to the thumb-thick wick, and there is a crackle and a sparkle, a spit and a sputter. And then the huge candle bites and flutters into life, casting a bright glow, illuminating the door, the door handle, and the number.

I reach out to touch the handle, but my heart begins to thunder in my chest, anxiety growing in the pit of my stomach like a heavy knot curling and tightening.

*Not yet…*

*Not yet…*

It's a gut feeling. Thoughts echo loudly in my brain.

I back away, shaking my head. I touch my chest just over my heart, feeling the pounding subside as I step away.

I walk away from the door, moving in the direction from where I had just been, the wall now on my left.

I take another fifty steps. Another door.

This door is also black and identical to the first door, the difference being the doorknob and the silver numeral:

# 2

This time the doorknob is very plain, unadorned, and unremarkable. It is just a knob. Round, black, no keyhole, no locking mechanism.

Beside this door, on the wall, is another sconce containing a massive candle identical to the previous one. I light it.

I've seen two doors, now.

Curious about what else I might find, I continue another fifty paces and reach a corner, a right angle. I take fifty more paces and encounter another door. It, too, has a silver numeral affixed:

## 3

The knob is made of old glass, antique, delicate, rattling loosely when I touch it.

I move on. Another fifty paces. Another door.

## 4

This knob is brass, gleaming and ornate, with a swirling, dizzying, knot-work design on the face.

Another fifty paces, another corner. Then another fifty paces. Another door.

## 5

This door handle is a little frightening: a single snarling lion's head in burnished bronze, a heavy bronze ring pull clutched in its jaws.

I keep walking, and the emerging pattern has now become obvious. Fifty paces, a door with a sconce beside, fifty paces, another door, another sconce. Fifty more paces, a corner. If basic geometry applies in this place, there will be eight doors.

# 6

Door number 6 is bizarre. The door itself is like all the others, painted black, the same size and shape, the same silver numeral in the center, a wall sconce to the right. But the latch is not a knob, or a pull, or a lever. It is a slab of wood fastened to the door by a thick, rough iron nail or pin. The slab is seated by a hook fastened to the wall beside the door, so that to open the door you must lift the latch, and pull. The hook, it appears, moves up and down. If I understand the basic mechanism, there would be another lever on the other side of the door, so that you would pull the lever down to lock the door, and lift it up on this side to unlock it, releasing the door. Old...*very* old. The wood of the mechanism is not black, but worn smooth with age, made of oak or pine, unpainted. Not polished, not sanded, but worn smooth by generations of hands.

I am curious what lies beyond this door, but I don't open it. I want to know first what the other doors are like. Assuming there are two more doors, that is.

# 7

This door hurts to look at, and I don't know why. This door is not black. It is green. Old, deep, dark green. The paint is chipped in places. The knob is old brass. Scuffed, scarred, and scratched. There is a keyhole in this one, and it is marred by the scuffmarks of a key scraping at the edges of the keyhole countless times over countless years. I push through the visual pain and touch the knob, finding it warm, unlike the others, which were all cold. This knob is...somehow familiar. As I grasp hold of it, it feels as if I've grasped this knob a million times before. It's as if I should have the key: a plain brass key with jagged teeth, the kind one would see on any keychain.

I force myself away from door 7. To step away is painful, even more painful than looking at it. Moving away sends an ache cutting through my chest and into my abdomen. I want to just stand there and hold the knob, simply for the comfort of it.

The last door is unlike the others, as well.

There is no numeral. The door is plain silvery metal, with a utilitarian metal knob. No keyhole, no lock. The door is dented and pock-marked, could lead to a janitor's closet at a school, or into a hospital room.

I do not touch this door, or the knob. I'm not sure why, but I dare not. And I don't want to.

I follow the wall another fifty paces to the corner, and there is the first door, fifty steps away, lit by a flickering orange flame. I finally take a moment to look around the room and I see all the other doors, and the sconces, which light the room with an orange glow. The room is a large square.

I walk back to the center of the room, guiding myself by the orientation provided by the doors and the meager candlelight.

I can now see there is a bed in the middle of the room. A simple cot with a white sheet fitted around the corners. No blankets, no flat sheet, no pillow. Just the mattress. Opposite, a few feet away, and within reach of the cot is a small square table. Empty; it is where the candle had been.

I sit on the bed, breathing slowly through my nose. In the dim light I stare at each door in turn, one through eight. When I come to door 7 I skip over it; I don't want to look at that door, I don't want to think about that door.

The only light is that cast by the candles.

There are no windows.

Just the doors, the sconces, the bed, and the table.

And above? Complete blackness. It goes on forever, perhaps. Or maybe just for ten or eleven feet. In any case, it does not matter to me.

Where am I?

Why am I not scared?

What do I do?

The answer comes easily:

Try door number 1.

I stand up, leaving the candle on the table. Padding on bare feet, I walk toward door 1—I feel the featureless floor beneath my feet, and I see the candle flickering in the sconce.

I stand in front of door number 1. My fingers hover over the latch. My heart pounds again, telling me I shouldn't be touching this door. I shouldn't go through this door. Don't do it. Don't do it. Don't do it. This is fear, harsh and acidic and biting.

I must; this compulsion is stronger than the fear.

*Open the door.*

*Open the door.*

*Step through, now.*

*You must.*

I am powerless to stop my hand from reaching out.

I touch the handle.

I depress the lever and hear the soft *click*. The door is weightless, swinging open easily.

This door does not lead outside but, rather, into what I think is another room. There is only more darkness on the other side, but this time the darkness is leavened by a faint reddish glow. The walls are black, but the floor here, once I pass over the threshold, is carpeted. Thin, tightly woven, dark in color. Above, there is a low black ceiling. I notice an opening ten or fifteen feet ahead of me, where the hallway takes a ninety-degree turn to the right. The reddish glow comes from that opening.

I walk toward it, but stop halfway down the hall. I turn: door 1 is still open. I can see the plain white cot. The table. The short white candle.

Reassured, I continue down the hall.

I hear noises now. A dull throbbing, as of drums in the distance, a bass line thudding rhythmically, steadily, rising and falling.

I follow the noise, drawn to it as if a string was tied to a sharp point just on the inside of my belly, behind my navel. My feet are silent on the carpet, but any sounds would be muffled by the drums and bass.

Then I hear a voice. Male. Deep. Rough. Grunting rhythmically, gasping, snarling. Underneath the male voice there's an underlying thudding, a quick thwacking coming in flurries and in singles and doubles. It sounds like a fist hitting a punching bag.

Nearing the turn now, I slow my steps. I come to the corner.

With no thought of turning back, I look around the corner.

The opening leads to an expansive room, lit crimson by the glow from some source I cannot yet see. The ceilings in this room are high, rising out of sight. The walls, or the wall I can see opposite, is made of bare gray cinderblock bouncing back to me the sound of the pulsing music, and the sound of grunting, along with the thwacking, thudding, punching noises. The room echoes with a cacophony of sounds.

Now that I face the room, I can hear the music more clearly. It is punishingly loud, jarring my eardrums, banging against my ribcage and slamming into my stomach in a barrage of bass-driven waves. It is violent, angry music. Guitars chug like chainsaws distorted down to a guttural snarl. Drums like the heartbeat of a beast, wild and relentless and maddening. Bass notes are woven beneath it and through it, like the wind in a thunderstorm, powerful and undeniable, but somehow almost lost in the madness of the thunder and lightning. The guitars are shrieking now, like banshees in a fantastical Irish midnight, howling, driving, crazed and chaotic.

I dare another step forward, repelled by the music, but drawn to it as well. More powerful than anything else, however, is the scent of sweat and the sounds of violent exertion.

Something thrills inside me.

Three tentative steps forward bring me completely into the room. It is mammoth. Bare concrete floors, steel rafters bathed in long shadows, cinderblock walls. In each of the four corners is a large floodlight with a red filter, the sort that would be used to illuminate a stage. Each light is aimed toward the interior, casting the deep crimson glow I first noticed.

The music comes from everywhere and nowhere; I can see no speakers, no stack. It is all pervading and it is so loud it rattles my skull and shivers my gut and sets my teeth to clenching.

There is no turning back now. I am mesmerized by the assault on my senses.

And then I see him.

A man—more than merely a man, he is a…*presence.*

He dominates the room.

He *is* the room.

I cannot breathe, cannot move. I am locked and frozen in place. Hypnotized.

He is over six feet tall, thickly muscled, heavy slabs of toned tissue defined by deep grooves in his flesh. These are not the muscles of a bodybuilder or a vain gym rat. This is the body of a warrior. Sleek, lean, corded, hard. Plates of muscle sheathed in darkly tanned skin, not black but very dark. Black hair cropped to a few inches of naturally spiked growth.

His body is covered in scars…so many scars.

Burns, cuts. Ribbed, veined, gnarled scars. Puckered holes. His back ripples as he moves. He's facing away from me, crouched low, hunched over, elbows tucked in to his sides, head pulled down between his shoulders, body twisted to face the punching bag edge-on. He's wearing a pair of skin-tight black trunks, not underwear but the sort of thing a kick-boxer would wear in the ring. They're molded to a pair of thighs nearly as thick as my waist, and to an ass so tight and hard and round you could use it as an anvil—you could bend metal bars over that ass.

He moves like lighting, like the wind, like a striking viper. Crouched, always moving. Dancing. Lithe, quick, powerful. His fist strikes faster than my eyes can track, and the bag is sent jerking and swaying, and then three more lightning-fast punches, *onetwothree*, and then his knee lifts and his leg scythes, and the *thwack* of his foot impacting the bag is deafening, even over the music. It happened so fast, that kick. So hard. The bag is still dimpled from the impact.

He seems oblivious to me, so I can't help but move closer.

He moves like a predator, each step oily-smooth and balletic and graceful. He breathes out sharply with each punch, each kick. Grunts, snarls. He's hitting the bag as if he hates it, as if to murder it with each punch, over and over. No mercy, no quarter, no rest. Only vengeful, snarling fury.

I don't know when, I don't know how, but he senses my presence. I see it in the way he tenses his shoulders, a brief, infinitesimal pause between blows.

He continues his abuse of the heavy bag, which is suspended from the ceiling by a thick iron chain.

And then, after one last, vicious, uppercut blow of his fist, he turns. A thick mat of dark curls covers the massive breadth of his chest.

His eyes bore through me, and they are as dark as the rest of him, as dark as the shadows and infinitely more dangerous.

His eyes fix on me.

He is a silent predator, and his steps carry him toward me. I am a gazelle caught in the open, and if he catches me, I will be gutted.

I know this.

Yet I am powerless to move.

I tremble as he approaches.

My heart throbs in my throat. My knees knock together. I want to turn and run, but I'm rooted to this spot, as if I am chained here.

I can almost hear the tinkle of the iron rings at my wrists. Almost feel the cold metal at my ankle. If I tug, I would feel the chains, the manacles.

I can only swallow over and over and over as he prowls closer to me.

He's inches from me, staring down at me with brown/black shadowy eyes, furious, hungry eyes.

He smells of sweat, pungent, sour, and male. Unspeaking, unmoving, he merely stands in front of me, blocking out the room, the light, invading my senses. His presence is all consuming. Devouring. His hands remain at his sides. His chest is heaving and it's feels like he's consuming all the oxygen in the room. His nose has been broken so many times it's permanently crooked. His lips are split and scabbed from a recent fight.

He lifts a hand, slowly, inquisitively, as if giving me time to flinch away; I don't—I cannot.

His hands are rough, coarse-looking. Scarred. Callused. His knuckles are split open, bright red blood trickling down his wrists, around the blade of his palm and between his fingers and pooling in the web of his thumb.

I cannot move away.

I try to swallow, try to speak, try to breathe, but I can't. I'm utterly captivated, terrified, struck mute.

And turned on.

I'm throbbing all over. Tingling. My core is alight, my thighs clenched together, desire pooling within me, boiling.

His fingers curl in slow motion and move toward my throat. I could move away. I could step out of reach.

But I don't.

His hand encircles my throat.

His grip tightens.

My lips part, and a tiny gasp squeaks out.

He doesn't *quite* cut off my oxygen, and he doesn't *quite* hurt me, but he's close to doing both.

A hint, a ghost of a smile teases at the corners of his lips. Feral. Primal. Predatory.

Hungry.

"Beg." His voice is a guttural slur. Accented, deep. *"Beg."*

• • •

"Please…" I hear myself gasp.

What am I begging for?

Mercy?

A kiss?

"Please…" I repeat.

But a man such as this does not know mercy, does not possess the tenderness or the softness for a kiss. He stares down at me that ghost of a smile playing on his lips.

"Please…*what?*" He snarls.

I don't know. *Please what?* I don't know.

His fist around my throat is unrelenting, pinching off my oxygen. I can't breathe. I'm going dizzy. I see stars.

His gaze leaves my eyes and rakes down my body. And now, only now do I suddenly realize I am utterly nude. My own gaze follows his, but I know what he's seeing. Golden skin. Taut, tan. Large breasts, firm and full, swaying and lifting as I attempt to breathe. Wide dark areolae, the size of silver dollars. Erect nipples, thick and dark, begging for his lips…

…or teeth.

Flat belly with a bit of abdominal definition. Not a six-pack, but a stomach that reveals time spent exercising. My core is bare. Shaved clean. Tight. Thick, prominent labia. Moisture gushes as he and I both look at my core. The tip of his tongue slides over his lower lip, as if he can almost taste my essence. I leak, then, thinking of his tongue on my core. Juices slip and drip. I rub my thighs together, because I ache. I *need*. My thighs are strong, too. Firm, powerful. Muscular.

Right down to my toes, his gaze flows over my body. My toes are painted a deep, lush crimson, and the same color as the light in this room.

His empty hand, the one not clutching my throat, lifts now too. The knuckles on this hand are split and bleeding. God, those hands are unlike anything I've ever seen before and they are as large and hard and viciously powerful as the rest of him. This hand wraps itself around my hair. Gathering the platinum mass in his fist, he jerks my head backward, tilting my face upwards, baring my throat. I almost expect him to bury his teeth in my throat, like a lion devouring a gazelle. He releases my throat, and I suck in a heady breath. Now that I can breathe, I am nearly hyperventilating. Gasping, panicking, needing. My breasts bounce with each intake of breath.

He steps closer yet, crushing his body against mine, his chest like a cliff face. My breasts crush flat against him, and the curls on his chest scratch and tickle. I am weak in the knees, trembling. Staring up at him. He is violence coiled, fury and potency and virility sheathed, poised to unleash.

Hand fisted in my hair, body pressed against mine, he merely stares at me. Into me. Contemplating? Deciding where to bite first? I cannot move my head, so hard is his grip. My hair stings at the roots, my neck aches from the angle. I'm gasping in long, deep, ragged breaths, each one smashing my breasts harder against him. His eyes are cruel, enjoying his power over me. Relishing the ache in my eyes.

And then he moves.

He does not kiss me; I knew he wouldn't. He is not a man who kisses. He claims. He takes what he wants.

He wedges a hand between our bodies and curls two fingers inside me. No warning, no slow build up. Just thick, callused fingers inside me, drawing a whimper of equal parts pain and pleasure. Pain, because I wasn't ready, pain because his fingers are large and strong and rough. Pleasure, for the same reasons. Weak in the knees before, now I am made utterly boneless. I sink onto his fingers. Bury them more deeply inside me.

His cruel, hungry eyes watch mine, gauging my expression.

"Fuck my fingers," he commands. "Ride them."

He does not move them, does not stroke me to completion, does not curl his fingers inside me, seeking my G-spot. He holds them motionless, maintaining his iron grip on my hair, keeping my head tilted painfully backward.

I ache.

Fuck, do I ache.

I do not understand this. I do not understand myself. He is causing me pain, and I relish it. I find heat from it. I do not know who I am and I can remember nothing of myself beyond this room. Beyond this now. But I know...I *know* I am not used to such treatment. I am not accustomed to being used so roughly. To having such demands made of me. I am used to kisses and tenderness and love.

I don't know how I know that, but I do. It is as true and real and undeniable as the bones beneath my skin.

But this...

*Him...*

It is something new. Forbidden. Dark. Dangerous. I shouldn't be here. I do not belong to this man. I should not do what he demands.

I should pull away. Leave this room. Go back out into the larger room with the cot and the doors and the candles. Leave him to his punching bag and heavy metal.

But I don't.

I want his roughness. I want him to use me. I want him to force me to his will.

I want him to *take* me.

He jerks my hair, eliciting a shriek of pain from me.

"Fuck my fingers." He repeats his command, and curls his fingers once, just so, perfectly, and a lance of heat and ecstasy rips through me. His thumb presses against my clit, and the lance drives deeper, harder, hotter. "Come on my hand."

I gasp, whimper, shiver, unable to move, refusing to comply—let him make me. Dangerous, foolish. He will not spare me his violence because I am a woman.

He curls his fingers again, rubs the wide pad of his thumb against my clit, sending thrills of pleasure through me. He builds me up. Works me to nonstop whimpers, fucks me with his fingers and his thumb. Fucks me with them until I am writhing, mewling.

"Please..." I beg. "Please."

I want to come. I need to come. I have ached since the moment I entered this room and saw this man. Just the sight of him made me ache.

Now I ache for a whole other reason. In a whole other way.

He withdraws his fingers from my core. Releases my hair. Steps back several paces.

*God, no. Please, no. Don't stop now.*

I can't make the words come out. I follow him. Naked, trembling, near release, desperate. Confused by my own desperation. By the suddenness of this. By the ferocity of my need.

He puts his fingers in his mouth, and they glisten with my juices. He takes his time licking them one by one. His trunks are tented and, my god, he's massive. I can see the outline of his cock clearly imprinted on the stretchy fabric: as thick as my wrist and probably eight inches long, at least. Those trunks are so tight, his cock so big, so thick, so hard I can see the outline of the circumcised head, the broad mushroom shape visible near the waistband. He's almost spilling out of his trunks, and I can see his cock bending as it continues to lengthen.

He sees me staring. "You want it?"

I nod. Pant. "Yes. Fuck, yes."

"Say it."

"I want it."

He teases me as he hooks his thumbs in his waistband and tugs down just enough to bare the tip. "What do you want? Say what you want."

"I want your cock." I don't recognize my own voice. Bold, but quiet. Strong, feminine, musical.

"Then come and get it." He crosses his arms over his chest.

I take a few steps toward him, my legs shaking and my heart pounding. In spite of my fear, my pussy aches and all I can think of is release. My mouth waters at the sight of him. His physique is powerful, rippled with corded muscle. The scars add to his hard and dominatingly masculine presence. From the thick hair on his chest to a days worth of stubble on his chiseled jaw, from his bloody hands to his massive cock, he is completely hypnotic. He waits and watches, his stance wide, feet splayed, arms crossed, chin lifted, his eyes glittering, missing nothing.

I'm drawn toward him, and my hands reach out. My fingers curl automatically into the elastic waistband, and I slide the tight black trunks down. Inch by inch. Baring his big, beautiful cock. When the trunks reach his thighs, his penis springs out and sways, freed of its prison. Impatient, he rips the trunks off and stands proudly naked. He resumes his pose, arms crossed, feet spread wide apart. But now his cock stands tall at attention. Fully erect, it is a monster of a thing.

My core weeps with desire.

My fingers twitch, eager to grasp and claim his magnificent cock.

The hunger within me, already roaring, crackling, sparking, is now fanned into a wildfire. My heartbeat matches the frenzied crescendo of the music, which I now realize is still pounding loudly all around. Vicious, violent music.

I curl my fist around his cock and stroke the length of it. Never taking my gaze from his eyes, I know he likes the way I am caressing him. But he remains motionless. He is so thick my fingers do not meet as I grasp him. Now, even with both hands fisted around his length, stroking him down to the root, there are still several inches of flesh above my fists. I have never, in my life, seen such a huge, beautiful, perfect cock. I am breathing hard. I feel delirious, dizzy, aching, but these feelings only fuel my desire. All I can think of is his cock and my pussy, and I know I will do anything he asks…and more.

He remains perfectly still and silent, never taking his eyes from me, and I dare not look away.

I don't know what to do next, because I want so many different things. But, above all, I want to pleasure him.

I want to drop to my knees and crack my jaw trying to fit him into my mouth. I want to climb up onto his body and impale myself on him. I want to jerk him off like a girl playing with a dick for the first time. I want to feel him spurt his seed down my throat. Into my pussy. Onto my hands. All over my breasts. Onto my face.

My god, who am I? Who is this woman who wants these things, desires things that were alien to me until I walked into this room? Something about this man brings out primal needs I have never felt before. It's as if he is able to expose the wanton whore buried within me.

He remains standing, unmoving, watching me as I slowly, deliberately glide my hands up and down his erection. His eyes are glittering and dark. His biceps twitch and flex as he reacts to my touch. He takes a deep breath, his chest swelling.

I step backward and begin to sink to my knees, but he stops me. "No. Not yet," he says in a deep guttural voice.

Then, moving like lightning, he grabs me around the waist, lifting me off my feet effortlessly, then swings me around and roughly sets me down, shoves me backward. I slam up against the cinderblock wall, my breath leaving me in a rush. Before I can regain my breath, he's on top of me. He's everywhere all at once, huge and hard. He thrusts his hand between my thighs and his fingers curl up into me.

Pressed against me, his breath is hot on my face. His fingers are thick and hard inside my pussy. He pinches my nipple with his other hand, hard enough that I gasp in pain. But the pain sends heat boiling in my belly, and his fingers are there, inside me, ready to relieve the ache.

This time he doesn't need to tell me what to do.

Mad with need, I grind myself on his fingers, rubbing my tits against his rough hand. I can't get enough. I gasp in pleasure as his thick digits rock within me.

But it's not enough.

I need clitoral stimulation. I grab his hand, pull it away from my breast and shove his two middle fingers against my aching clit. I press my hand over his and force him to touch me the way I need. Force him to the speed the circling rhythm I need. With his fingers inside me, and his fingers against my clit, I am in a frenzy. I feel his erection between us, nudging my belly. I ride his hand, fuck his fingers, and I grasp his cock with both my hands as he continues the rhythm I've set. I'm close, groaning and whimpering with need.

I grunt, unladylike, wanton, whorish, as my orgasm rifles through me. It's quick, and violent. He doesn't relent, but forces me to a second orgasm within seconds. I cling to him through them, stroking his erection with one hand, grasping his shoulder with the other.

He's unleashed something within me and all I can comprehend is the unbearable need for more.

I grind against him, and then I lift my leg and hook my foot around the back of his knee. I'm ready for more, of that there is no question. But what? I don't know, I just know I need *more*—

...of everything.

I want to climb him like a tree and fit him inside me. I grab hold of his shoulders and lift myself, but he has other ideas. He prises me off him and sets me on my feet. He stares at me with a mixture of hauteur and heat. Then he wraps my hair around his fist and presses his other hand against my shoulder, shoving me to my knees. The concrete floor is rough underneath me and his hand pulls painfully at my hair. My heart is hammering like a drum, I wait for his command.

"Open your mouth." His voice is like thunder in the distance, quiet yet disturbing.

I open my mouth wide, and stare up at him. On my knees, hands on my thighs, mouth open, eyes unblinking, I wait for his instruction. As I look at him, I am aware of his cock throbbing in front of my face. Thick and dark, a trimmed thatch of black curls at the base. His balls are heavy and taut, the veins clearly visible. A dot of moisture glistens on his tip. I want to lick that droplet away, but I dare not move.

He thrusts his hips forward, taking his cock in his fist, and then he nudges the broad mushroom head between my lips. His thickness brushes against my teeth. I taste his skin. Taste pre-cum. My jaw aches, stretched wide open. Soft springy flesh sheaves iron hardness as his cock slides against my tongue. He pushes into my mouth ever so slowly. He goes deep, and I don't think I can take it all.

But I do.

I begin to choke and gag, my eyes watering, and then I remember to breathe through my nose. This allows me to open my throat and take more of him. I taste him on my tongue and feel him at the top of my throat. I relax my throat and take him until my nose touches his belly. His fist remains in my hair, gripped mercilessly tight. He holds me there.

I am almost smothered by him, and I'm completely helpless.

Trying to remain calm, I breathe slowly through my nose and I feel my heartbeat slow just ever so slightly. Feeling more confident now, I slide my hands up the backs of his massive thighs and grip the steel curve of his ass.

He pulls me back by my hair, and then adjusts his grip so he's got it clutched close to my scalp. Pulling me back all the way, he lets me release his cock; the only thing connecting us now is the long string of saliva between my lips and his cock. His chest heaves, and his breath gusts heavily. And then he pushes himself back into my mouth slowly, deliberately, using his hips to guide him. He goes deep once he knows I have opened my throat again and am breathing through my nose.

I'm more relaxed this time but, still, my first thought is that he's so fucking big. But he tastes clean; a combination of sweat and man, and the taste is anything but unpleasant. He defines masculinity in every sense of the word.

He doesn't pull out this time; instead he begins to thrust in and then pull back. I barely have time for a cleansing breath before he's pushing back in. Again, and again, and again.

He's fucking my mouth.

He changes his rhythm, and now his thrusts to the back of my throat are slow and hard before he pulls out. He begins to grunt, like he did when he was punching the heavy bag and, apart from the few words he has spoken, it is the only sound he has made. I hold on to his ass and take each thrust, waiting for the moment when he comes.

He thrusts, faster and faster. Holding my head in place, he fucks my mouth as if he owns it.

And then he slows. And now, instead of moving his hips, instead of fucking my mouth, he pulls my mouth down onto his thick, hard cock. He sets the rhythm, and then lets go of my hair. Gently, he rests his hands on my head.

My jaw is aching and my knees burn.

But I can tell he's close, and I want him to come. I want to feel him come. I want to taste his cum; I want to feel him lose control. But most of all I want to know I have the power to make him come. Will he grunt when he comes? Will he shout?

He's moving faster, but he's holding back. He's making me work his orgasm.

And then I feel it start. The thrusts become harder, but he has less control. There is less precision in his movements. Faster now. He releases me entirely, letting me suck him off my own way.

I pull his cock down, adjusting my position so I'm pushing my face forward onto his belly. I open my throat and let him fuck deep.

I feel him begin to lose control.

And then, right when I know he is on the verge, his thrusts wild and furious, his cock throbbing and thickening yet more, he pulls away. He literally rips his cock out of my mouth and then stumbles backward, his chest heaving. Every muscle in his body tenses. His eyes are dark, intense and focused like lasers on me as he fights for control.

I stagger to my feet. My knees can't take any more, but my body is alive and alert.

I wait.

I want.

I wonder.

He prowls toward me once more, cock swaying with each step. Will he fuck me now? Will I finally feel him inside me? His expression is unreadable, dark, closed, hot with desire, but I cannot read his intentions.

He stops inches from me. "Close your eyes."

I don't know why, but I refuse to do as he's commanded. Instead, I glare at him, defiant.

Not knowing what to expect, I'm curious when he circles around behind me. I hear him breathe in sharply and then he presses his nose to the back of my neck. He inhales. Deeply. One long arm snakes around me. His palm flattens against my belly then slides up. Up. Up. He clutches my breast, kneading it, squeezing it in his powerful hand. Then he does the same thing to the other. Just when I think I know what he is doing, he flicks my nipple with a fingertip, *hard*. I gasp at the sudden assault on my sensitive nipple, and then again when he flicks the other one even harder. I feel him bend at the knees. Yes. God, yes. His cock slides between the round spheres of my ass, and I feel him nudging my entrance. I sink back against him. I widen my stance, ready to take him.

I'm ready, more than ready. I'm giddy with anticipation but I don't show it.

His hand clutches my breast, and now the other hooks around me, and his fingers dive between my thighs. He spreads my labia wide open, flattening his fingers over my clit, smearing my essence all over me. And then he thrusts his fingers inside me and, using that grip, pulls me backward. I have no choice but to step backward with him. He's standing up now, his cock a thick ridge between my ass cheeks. One step backward, then another. In that way we cross the room to a corner.

Now what?

He slides his fingers into me, spearing in and grinding against my clit at the same time, ripping a whimper from me. Several hard, fast, powerful thrusts of his fingers, and I'm riding the edge, knees bending, hips flexing, pushing my pussy against.

And then he stops, abruptly. He's no longer pressed up against me.

He's gone.

I don't have time to wonder, or ask, or even turn to look for him. He's there again, and now he moves with that whip-quick speed. His hands pass in front of my face. I only have time to see that he is holding something. And then the world goes black and I feel something cool against my eyes—a blindfold. He ties it tightly behind my head.

"You want to leave?" His voice whispers in my ear.

"No." My voice is steady and firm. I don't know what he has in store for me, but I'm shaking with need.

He's gone, again. The music continues to pound jarringly all around. It's too loud and too aggressive, yet now I find it suits my mood perfectly.

I smell him before I hear him moving. And then I feel him standing in front of me. He takes my hands, one at a time, and raises them above my head. Something cool and soft is wrapped around my wrists, binding them together. Tightly, gently, softly. I feel tension in my arms and then I feel myself being tugged up onto my tiptoes. I'm just slightly off balance, and the strain on my arm sockets is just this side of painful.

At first I'm confused about what happens next.

Suddenly, and faster than I ever thought possible, and with unerring, unhesitating precision he wraps what feels like a series of ropes or cords around my thighs, waist, and ankles in a specific sequence, never tying the ropes tightly, never pinching or hurting. And then, somehow, I'm no longer standing; I'm suspended completely.

Arms raised over my head.

Blindfolded.

I could not be more helpless.

My feet are bound taut against my buttocks so that my thighs are spread apart and my core is bared for him.

My pulse thunders; I am truly afraid, now. The bravado I felt a few moments ago has disappeared completely. I should have left when I had the chance.

I have the presence of mind to realize that it doesn't hurt, the way he has me tied up. But I'm breathing hard and fast, gasping for breath, nervous, fearful.

I feel him.

I smell him.

I smell *me*. Pungent, rife, the scent of desire.

I feel him, feel his heat, his hardness. Feel him nudge his cock against my entrance. Teasing me with it. Slipping in, just a little. Just the crown. Fluttering, not thrusting. And then I feel his fingers, swiping at my clit. He flicks my nipples. His fingers delve into my pussy, gathering my essence, which he smears over my lips. I taste myself. Then I feel his cock again, fluttering against me, nudging, teasing, and then... god, oh god, he's sliding it in, an inch, maybe two inches.

Fuck...oh *fuck*, he's huge. But it hurts *so* good. Already I feel split in two, and he's only partially inside me. I know there's so much cock left to fill me, but he stops. I feel him push against me, leaning closer. I feel his breath on the skin between my breasts. He licks my breast around the areola, flicking the nipple and the heavy underside with his tongue.

And then he bites down, sudden and hard enough to make me scream in surprise and pain.

At the same time, he slams fully into me, hard, fast.

Oh, holy fuck, I can't breathe for the fullness. I ache and burn at the same time. If I had breath left in my lungs, I'd whimper or cry out from the perfect pain of it.

And then he pulls out. Suddenly, so fast that I'm left swinging in the air.

Nothingness.

Darkness.

The only sound is the music crashing like the screams of a vengeful god.

I continue to swing back and forth, my nipple throbbing from his bite. My pussy is stinging and aching from his thrust but even worse, from the absence of his extraordinary erection.

The tension of the ropes around my wrists loosens, and my upper half is released from the strain, while my lower half remains as it was, swinging gently.

I can hear him adjusting the ropes and then he lowers me until I'm horizontal, lying suspended in the air on my back. My head hangs down between my shoulder blades. My long hair is loose and I can feel it graze the floor. My breasts have fallen aside by gravity; the only movement is the gentle swinging motion, and the only sound is the blaring, jarring music.

My senses are heightened and I am aware that he is quietly walking around me. He cups my breast as he passes by, a quick squeeze. And then he's between my thighs, his trim waist wedging them apart. He positions his cock at my entrance. Places his palm against my belly and gives a shove that sends me swinging back and forth. I expect what happens next just moments before it happens, moments before our bodies crash together: his cock impales me on the back swing, our flesh meeting with a loud *slap*.

I cry out.

But then he's pulling out. Moving around me. Trailing his finger up my body as he circles me. My head lolls backward, upside down. Fingers touch my face. My cheeks. Deceptively gentle, he traces my features. My eyes. My chin. My lips. Then, more insistently now, his fingertips pry open my mouth. I smell man, musk and sweat mixed with the strong scent of my own liquids—the effect is intoxicating. Then I feel the round, springy flesh of his cock's head against my lips, and I taste myself, and him. His cock enters my mouth, all the way. Slowly, gently.

And then, as his sac hangs against my nose, he thrusts once, hard, deep into my throat, and I'm swinging again. A gentle swing, this time, and he lets my motion do the work of allowing his cock to enter between my lips.

He moans, and apart from a few words and the grunt, it is the only sound he's made so far.

I should not be as thrilled as I am by that noise, but the animal sound of it sends desire coruscating through me, along with a sense of power.

It was just a low, soft grunt of male pleasure as his cock glided between my lips, pushing into my throat. I have to swallow at the intrusion, and he groans again at the rippling of my throat muscles on his organ.

I mirror his moan, a sound in my throat and my mouth, a hum around his flesh, buzzing through his engorged hardness.

He pulls out abruptly, and I hear him breathing hard.

He is gone again and I'm left swinging.

The music stops abruptly, and the silence is deafening. A quivering, pregnant silence. It's as if the sound provided a cover, a blanket for me, but now I feel more exposed than ever.

Where is he?

While I wait for him to reveal himself, I ponder his control. It is nothing less than exquisite, and to approach the utter edge of orgasm and then turn away at the last second demands more than control—it demands skill.

The silence is deafening and time stands still.

I shake with need, trembling in the ropes. I'm desperate for his touch and I want his cock more than anything I've ever wanted. It's time to bring an end to the teasing.

Come. Just come already. In my mouth, in my pussy, on me somewhere, anywhere. Just give it to me, for god's sake.

I don't hear him approach; I only know of his presence when I feel him between my thighs.

His tongue drills into my pussy in a sudden assault, lashing against me, quick and rough, he slathers his saliva on my clit, and then uses his dripping mouth to spear my entrance. He licks my labia, sucks my clit between his teeth and ravishes me in ways I have only ever dreamed of. He brings me to the edge of orgasm and then pauses just long enough for me to begin thrashing in my prison of rope, desperate for that release. Oh god, oh god, oh god. I want to come so bad I can think of nothing else.

But this is too much. Too fucking much.

And then he plunges his tongue into my cunt and I scream, and scream, and scream. I'm coming so hard I see stars, so hard I buck and writhe in the ropes, and he lets me swing, keeping pace with me somehow while he continues his assault on my pussy with that mouth of his.

I come, and come, and come.

I lose count.

I lose all sense, and all I can think is that I never want this to stop, coupled with the feeling that I can't take anymore.

And then, on the blasting, blistering, shredding crest of another climax, he slams his cock into me.

Overwhelmed, exhausted, wrung out, I break apart.

• • • •

I regain myself, and my first thought is that I wish I could see him.

I wish I could see *us*.

My blindfold is still firmly tied in place, and I cannot see a thing. All I can do is feel and smell and hear, but those three senses are more alert than they have ever been. He's buried deep inside me, impaled fully, his balls at my opening. My thighs remain tied apart, as wide as they can go.

I'm imagining what we look like together, and I so badly want to watch him fill me. I want to see my pussy swallow his cock, see that massive organ penetrating something as small and tight as my cunt.

I begin to feel tension building on my wrists, and I feel my upper torso being lifted. I'm not completely vertical, but almost—it's as if I'm reclining on a couch of nothingness.

Even as he remains fully impaled inside me, he remains perfectly still. I want motion. Friction. I want the slide of that god-sized organ in and out of me. I want his groans, his grunts, and his breathless murmurs.

But I am left wanting.

His hips are crushed against the tender insides of my thighs, but he remains motionless. Pushed deep. Throbbing within me. And then I feel his palms carving a pathway up my calves, over my knees and up to my thighs. I feel him angle his body away, and now his touch glides against my clit. A thumb, gentle, exploring. Pressing ever so gently. Teasing. Then harder. Faster. Until I'm gasping and writhing—and then, of course, he stops.

He pulls out completely and I feel a pressure on my clit, soft, warm, thick…his cock tip nuzzling against my clit. Oh…oh fuck. This. Yes, *this*. He's using his cock like a dildo, massaging me and bringing me writhing and screaming and whimpering to orgasm yet again.

Holy fuck, how many times can I come? He's determined to find out, I think.

Wanting more, I arch my spine and flex against the silk of the ropes binding me, reaching for another orgasm, and it doesn't take long. I'm coming and coming as he works me into a frenzy. And then, again, just as I'm riding the crest of the orgasm, he slams his cock into me.

But this time he does not stop. It's not just one lone pounding thrust.

It's a million spearing plunging drives into my quavering cunt.

Wild and primal, almost angry, he hammers his cock into me. Again and again and again, without mercy. And I ask for none; because this is perfect pain, perfect pleasure. I didn't know this existed. I've never felt anything like this before.

Have I?

I have no idea.

All I know is this moment. I don't remember anything before I entered this red, glowing room, before hearing the pounding music, and seeing and tasting this man, this beautiful, feral man. Who was I? What do I even look like?

I do not know the answers to these questions, but it doesn't matter.

Nothing matters.

Nothing exists.

I am consumed by this experience, and *that* is what matters.

I'm buried under the avalanche of his presence. Eyes closed behind the blindfold, I can still see him in my mind's eye. Every line, every curve, every muscle. I can see his dark eyes glittering as they rove over my naked body, now glistening with sweat. I can see his hands cupping my buttocks and pulling me into his thrusts, his powerful fingers digging into the plump swells and jerking me to him. I can see his abdomen rippling and flexing as his hips piston. I can see his thighs tautening, tensing. I can see him in my mind, so clearly it feels as if I know him. As if I've experienced this with him countless times before.

This bondage feels familiar. But I don't know why.

I don't know him.

I don't know *me* anymore.

I don't know anything.

I only know this. Just this.

His huge cock sliding in and out. Stretching me with every thrust. Burning beautifully from the way his size spreads me apart. Core aching from the nonstop pounding. Clit throbbing from having come so many times, pulsing with the need to come yet again.

All I can do is feel this, feel him.

Relish in the unforgiving grip of his hands on my buttocks, the merciless ecstatic thrusting crash of his shaft into me again, and again, and again.

I hear myself crying out with each thrust.

But he remains silent as he fucks me.

"Take off the blindfold," I whisper. To speak loudly would be to ruin the sanctity of this moment, somehow.

"No." One syllable, grunted.

"Please."

"No."

"I want to watch us."

That gives him pause. He falters in his rhythmic thrusting, and then stops altogether. "You want to watch?" He sounds...curious, maybe a little amused.

"Yes," I breathe.

He moves away and I'm left swinging, aching, wondering in the silence.

I hear motion, then I hear a scraping sound followed by long moments of strange sounds I do not recognize, and then I feel him next to me. I'm raised up vertically once more, arms high over my head. The blindfold is untied, and he's behind me. Mirrors surround us in a reflecting, disorienting ring. Everywhere I look I see us.

Him.

Me.

Him, a god, mammoth, perfect, dark, gorgeous. Cock ramrod stiff and straight, jutting up proudly, thick, hard, long, wet from my pussy. His ass, cannonball-round globes of iron hard muscle. His back, a rippling field. Broad shoulders, trim waist. Thatch of dark spiked hair. A maze of scars. Hands loose at his sides, the blindfold, a thin strip of red silk, dangling from one hand.

And me, trussed up, knees bent, legs folded, heels against my buttocks, crimson ropes wrapped around my body in a complex, elegant system of knots and tension. Arms high. Wrists bound. Breasts lifted, nipples pert and thick and begging for attention. Pussy bared, spread open, wet. Dripping.

The ropes disappear overhead in a pulley system. There are several of them and their loose ends are knotted together. He has only to pull one or another and I will lift or lower according to his desires.

"What do you want to watch me do?" His voice in my ear, a bass murmur.

"Everything. Touch me. Fuck me. Come for me."

"Come where?"

"Anywhere," I gasp.

Gasp, because his fingers have found my clit. I watch, and it's beautiful. Erotic. A dance of light touches. A flick, a scrape, a circling. Pinching. Sliding into me, drawing out, his fingers coated in my wetness. He smears my essence over me, and I'm already so drenched that each motion of his fingers on me squelches noisily. I cannot stop watching.

"Watch yourself come," he says.

And I do.

I come beautifully. My cheeks flush pink. My body arches, writhes. My big breasts bounce and jounce and sway. My thighs try to close and they strain against his ropes. My mouth hangs open, my brows draw down. My hair, long fine thick platinum tresses hanging to mid-spine, gleam and shimmer in the red light. My pale skin reddens, and sweat appears on the Cupid's bow of my upper lip and on my delicate temples. Sweat rolls down between my breasts as they sway side to side with my arching, writhing movements.

Then he circles in front of me and adjusts a rope so my front half lowers down, forward this time instead of backward, so facing I'm belly-down. My hair drapes over my shoulders and around my face in a blond curtain.

I turn my head to see us in profile. Him, dark, swarthy, all hardness and angles, like a magnificent statue carved from marble. Me, softness, curves, pale golden skin. Breasts hanging, now. He cups them in his hands, and I catch my breath at the feel and the sight of his rough hands on my sensitive skin. They engulf even my large breasts.

I watch, in profile, as he takes his cock in hand and rubs the crown against my lips. I watch my tongue flick out, and lick him. For a moment I turn to look in a different direction and I see his ass, his back, his shoulders blotting out everything. I return my attention to the profile view and I see his cock, my mouth.

Yes, god, yes.

I watch, enraptured, as he feeds his shaft between my lips. I watch as it vanishes into the warm wet sanctuary of my mouth. I see his body tense from the pleasure and his jaw tighten and flex. His brow is furrowed, his stomach a hard plane, his buttocks flexing as he pushes in.

A thrust.

A second.

I watch each one and I can see my face clearly, the focus, the desire completely evident. I like this. I shouldn't, but I do. It feels as if what I'm doing is forbidden. Wrong, somehow.

But it is so right.

He doesn't fuck my mouth for long.

He steps away and moves around behind me.

I watch in the mirrors as he positions himself, his palms cupping my ass. His arm moves, his hand lifts, and I tense in the second before impact. *SMACK!* His palm strikes my left buttock. Hard, *so* hard. I cry out from the pain, the sting lingers. Almost immediately, his other hand lifts, descends, and cracks across my right buttock, and now both sting painfully.

I have no time to catch my breath before the next blow, which is just as hard. The impact makes me jolt forward, swinging, my breasts swaying pendulously. I gasp, gagging on my cries, but the sting is delicious. Especially now, especially when he slides his cock into me and spanks me again as he thrusts. The burn of being stretched accompanies the sting of his spankings. The lines blur, pain and pleasure combine, becoming something else. My ass is reddened. I watch the way my buttocks ripple with each blow of his hand, each slam of his cock. The way my breasts sway and then jounce as he fucks into me.

God, he's not even touching my clit, and I'm ready to come again.

Another spank, another ramming thrust, and I'm on the edge.

One more, and I'm over it. Heat blooms inside me. My muscles contract, everything going white with exquisite blossoming painful pleasure, his unending thrusts driving the orgasm higher and higher. And then I feel him moving harder yet. Less controlled.

My eyes open and I watch him in profile. I watch him pull out, inches of cock pulling out, glistening. And then his ass flexes, his hips piston, and I'm filled again.

"Don't—don't stop this time," I gasp.

He doesn't answer. He just keeps fucking. And I keep watching.

No more spanking, just his hands on my hips, pulling me into him.

I'm watching us, feeling something massive well up inside me. Yet another orgasm, but different from the others. Stronger. Deeper. Sharper.

I'm full of anticipation. I'm waiting for him to come and I want to feel him come. But he has unreal stamina. He can hold it off indefinitely,

I think. He continues to pound into me, pushing me to multiple orgasms, until I'm weak and dizzy from them.

When the next wave crashes over me, I lose myself to it, knowing it will break me, somehow.

And it does.

The orgasm crescendos through me like a tsunami, slamming through me so powerfully I cannot help but scream at the top of my lungs, ripped apart by an agony of ecstasy.

It drowns me.

I feel faint and I succumb to the feeling. I feel it wash over me, pulling me under, pulling me down into a place of security and relaxation.

When I waken, I'm no longer bound, no longer suspended. I blink, momentarily disoriented. A low crimson light bathes the entire room, including the cinderblock wall behind me. Looking up, there is only darkness shrouding the thick iron rafters over my head.

I'm on the floor, in a corner of the room, resting in a nest of blankets and pillows. It's not a real bed, but somehow it is more comfortable than that. Warm. Infused with a distinctly masculine smell.

I sense him.

And there he is, prowling toward me, naked, arms swinging easily at his sides, his gait that of a predator stalking prey. His cock is still rock hard so I surmise I must not have been out for long. He lowers himself to the nest of blankets and levers himself over me, nudging my thighs apart with his knees. Possessive, familiar, demanding.

"I don't come while you're in the ropes," he says as his eyes search mine.

"No? Why not?" I'm curious about his response.

"The ropes are foreplay." He plants a fist in a pillow beside my head, then reaches between us, finding me wet and waiting. "The ropes are for fun. For you. This…"

He curls his fingers against me, drawing a gasp from me.

"This, *sweetness*… it's all for me."

I shiver, because the promise in his voice is ripe, potent.

Unbound and no longer blindfolded, I am free to touch him. To drag my palms over his shoulder. Down his back. Cup his ass, feeling the hardness. I hook my leg around the back of his knee and bury my fingers in his hair.

He glides into me, slowly. And this time, somehow…this time it is different. It feels different. The position, maybe? I don't know. The way he does it, the way he fucks into me. It's not for me, this time. Not to tease me, not to fuck me, not to push me toward orgasm. It's for him. Slow and deliberate, as if he's memorizing each sensation.

I breathe in his masculine scent and slide my hands all over him, wherever I can reach. Throat, neck, shoulders. Chest, back. Hips. Buttocks. I move with him, slow sinuous lifts of my hips against his lazy thrusting.

Gradually, the tempo increases. Increment by increment, his motions become more needy. More desperate. Less precise, less controlled. His eyes never leave mine. A world of hidden emotion whirls behind those dark eyes. His brow is furrowed, the bridge pinched, carving a sharp line between his eyebrows. His jaw is tensed. I know nothing of him, nothing of what he's feeling. Just that he's here and his feelings are here, and both are more than I could ever fathom. Complexities in layer upon layer.

I feel him beginning to breathe more heavily, feel him fighting for control, fighting to hold back, and I want to kiss him. I want to bite his lip and suck his tongue into my mouth.

I know, somehow I just *know* I cannot, should not do that. I fight the urge by raking my fingernails down his back, pushing up into his manic, frenzied thrusts. I clutch his ass and pull him harder against me, murmuring and whimpering and crying out, partly because I cannot help myself, and partly to encourage him.

"Yes, yes, yes!" I breathe. "Harder, god, please, harder."

He doesn't give it to me harder. He slows. Gentles. Eyes on mine, never once wavering. That gaze is impossible to hold for long, the intensity impossible to match. But yet I must not look away; I know this, too. So I don't.

I hold his gaze and the intensity increases exponentially with each and every second that passes.

He moves, pumps, thrusts, wild and furious once more. Fists beside my ears, burly biceps blocking out everything.

I know what he's about to do when his movements falter and slow. When he trembles. Pulls out.

I curl my fingers around his length. Keep my eyes on his. Stroke him. Slow. Soft. Delicate. He shakes above me. His breath shudders between his pursed lips. His eyelids begin to flutter, but his gaze does not leave mine. I wrap both hands around him; twist them around his thickness as I stroke him from tip to root, as slowly as I can.

He thrusts into my hands, wanting it faster, but liking it slow.

A grunt.

Yes, *god* yes.

Soft, slow glides of my palms and fingers down his thick, wet, throbbing cock. Wet noises of skin smearing essence on skin. His back arches, bows outward. He pistons into my touch, grunting raggedly.

*"Fuck—"* he groans, a drawn out syllable. *"Fuuuuuuuck...."*

I turn my eyes downward now, greedily. I cup my palm around the crown and squeeze, rubbing his tip with my thumb. Twisting my hand around the broad, wide head, my other hand pumping him slowly near the root.

Hand over hand. Twists of my palms. Fluttering, quick movements of my hand around the head. I watch the fat mushroom sprout above my fist, wet with pre-cum. I watch inches of hard shaft grow as I squeeze hard and plunge my fist down to the root. He's groaning, gasping, shaking. Not moving at all. Trembling. Holding back. Making me force it out of him.

Somehow, I just know how he likes it. I instinctively know how to touch him and I know what drives him crazy, what teases and tortures him. And I do all of it. As I continue to give him what he needs, I marvel at the feel of him. Marvel at the control required to hold out for so long. Minutes pass as I toy with him, touching and stroking and pumping his beautiful cock, as much for my own enjoyment as his own. The feel of him in my hands, the pleasure of touching him, the beauty of him as he struggles against the need to come, these things are all I know. I know nothing *but* this. This is all there is.

All there ever was. All there will be.

When I know, intuitively, that he's riding the razor edge, I cease the toying and the teasing, cease the slight touches and the fluttering strokes, the gentle glide of fist over fist. I begin a rhythm. Slow, purposeful. Hard, the way he likes it best.

I lay on my back in the nest of blankets with him levered above me, trembling with exertion. Sweat on his brow. Tension in every line of his body.

I stroke his gorgeous cock the way he likes it until he's thrusting with me, into my hand, grunting, groaning, cursing under his breath.

He pushes into my fist and holds there, spine arched in, shoulders bowed, head ducked, and his face resting between my breasts, hips flexed.

I watch him explode. The first spurt of seed gushes out of him as from a cannon, a thick white jet splashing hot on my belly. Now I stroke him hard and fast. He curses, shouts, and comes. Another jet, harder than the last, shooting up onto my chest in a warm wet line between my breasts. Again he ejaculates, this time in a thick pool just above my pussy. An endless river of cum pours out of him, coating me.

After what seems an eternity of orgasm, he finally finishes and holds himself trembling above me, sweating, gasping for breath, eyes fixed on me, as ever. As if to break our gazes would be a mortal sin.

And then, abruptly, he rises. Stalks away, hand passing through his hair as if angry.

"What?" I ask.

"You shouldn't be here." The words are quiet, spoken so softly I barely hear them. But they are razor sharp in the silence.

"Why not?"

He doesn't turn to look at me. Just stands facing away, catching his breath, naked, a carving of raw masculine beauty and power. "You just shouldn't. You don't belong in a place like this."

I stand up. His words cut me to the quick. I like it here. I like him. I know him, but I do not know him. It's a confusing thought, but I can't shake sense out of it and can't shake the truth of it. I both know him and I don't. How can that be? What does it mean? What is this place? *Why* don't I belong here?

I move slowly, cautiously, up behind him. I skim my hands around his ribs and down to his stomach, and then brush my breasts against his back. He sucks in a deep breath.

"Don't." He spits out the word.

"Why not? What's the matter?"

"You have to go. You can't stay here."

"But I don't want to go." I hate the childish, petulant tone in my voice.

A hesitation. "But you *have* to." He grabs my wrists in his hands and pushes them away from his body. "It's time."

Physically, he is so much more powerful than I am, but somehow I get the impression that removing my hands from his body takes all the emotional and psychological strength he can muster.

I do not resist him.

I release him and take a few steps past him, toward the dark doorway that will take me back to the beginning, to the black door room.

More than anything I want to stay here, with him, in this room. I don't want to go, yet I know there's no point in arguing.

I turn in place, and he's still standing there, watching me. He's still breathing hard, but not from sexual exertion. This is…the breathlessness of self-restraint.

He's erect again, somehow. Fucking hard as a goddamn rock. A thick silken iron shaft, long and thick.

"Once more…please?" I sound breathy. I sound desperate.

God, that cock. I want it. I fucking *want* it, I want him one more time.

I step toward him, feeling bold, feeling decisive; I don't stop until I'm wrapped around him. My arms tangle around his neck and I lift myself up, hooking my legs around his waist. With bated breath I nudge his cock against my entrance. He furrows his brow again, clearly waging some internal war, and then I feel his hands on my waist, lifting me, attempting to move me off him.

But for once I am too quick for him and I sink down and impale his hot hard shaft inside me, all the way, so deep, so perfect. Oh, the beautiful ache, the sweet burn. He growls, an animal snarl. I do all the work, now. I writhe on him, grind on him and ride him like the wild mustang he is. His hands grip my ass and assist my motions, almost begrudgingly. The angle has him so deep, but the way we're positioned sends his shaft sliding against my clit, giving me delicious friction against the hypersensitive bundle of nerves. Immediately, I feel the boil in my belly, the throb in my bones, the bliss as I near orgasm. I'm panting, gasping. Whimpering. It's building quickly and bashing through me so hard it almost hurts.

And now it breaks, an atomic bomb of a climax, ripping a scream from me as I lift up as high as I can and sink down as hard as I can, his hands helping me, lifting me then slamming me down.

My mind goes completely blank and I don't have any thoughts or intentions or desires but experiencing this one last orgasm.

Without thinking about it, I kiss him. Hard.

I slam my lips across his mouth; thrust my tongue between his teeth, taste blood on his lips as the crashing kiss splits them open.

A moment, then, of kissing. A breath-long kiss as I come so hard I weep.

He rips me away with a curse and a vicious snarl. There's no time to react. He moves with that viper-fast speed, seizing me, throwing me to the ground so hard my knees sing with pain. My palms scrape on the cement, and my lips throb from the kiss.

"I'm sorry," I breathe, "I—"

He's behind me, on his knees, grabbing my hair in a vise-like grip, tugging my head back sharply. He stabs his cock into my pussy, a rough hard thrust that sears my breath away. Words dissolve on my tongue. Protests die. I'm on my hands and knees, ass in the air, and he's fucking me so hard I'm rocked forward with each thrust, so hard my tits hurt from the jouncing sway.

I know two things: I've never been fucked so hard in my life, and he's punishing me for the kiss.

But the trick's on him, because I realize a third thing: I've never enjoyed a fucking so much.

I can't remember anything but this room, anyone but him, any fuck but his.

I don't come again.

But I'm not meant to.

It doesn't last long.

And it's not meant to.

My hands and knees scrape painfully on the cement floor. His grip on my hair borders on agonizing.

But I don't feel that.

All I feel is his thrusting. His fucking.

There is no control. No technique. No holding back. No tenderness. This is raw and primal. He's taking my body and using it with no thought or consideration for anything. Flesh slaps against flesh, his hips ram against my ass. Each violent thrust fills me to the brim, stretches me wide with a sharp burning ache, squelching wetly. I can't even catch my breath long enough to scream, or even gasp. All I can do is suck in desperate panting breaths as he pulls back for a fraction of a second and then my breath is forced out of me at the brutal impact of his cock.

Impossibly, he becomes even wilder, fucks even harder as he nears his climax.

None of the usual terms apply, then. Hard; rough; fucking; climax; orgasm….none of those words express the violent, animal way he uses my body.

It's not something to enjoy. It's something to experience.

He doesn't pull out, this time. He fucks through the orgasm, jetting hot gouts of cum into me in thick wet waves that fill me to the brim and squirt out with each next thrust to drip down my thighs, and still he fucks, still he comes.

He continues to fuck me until his cock goes soft inside me, and I'm quivering, shaking, gasping for lungfuls of oxygen, aching all over, the insides of my thighs wet and sticky with his cum, which still drips out of me.

He releases my hair, and I collapse forward.

He does nothing to help me.

I feel nothing, then, but the throb of my pussy and the cold cement against my cheek, my breasts, my hips, and the hot sticky drip of his cum oozing out of my cunt.

I fight the dizziness, the darkness, and it takes a supreme effort to avoid being sucked under. I fight it so hard, fight desperately, wretchedly, as if to succumb to this darkness means death, means nothingness; I'm more afraid of the nothingness than I am of death itself.

Then I see him and I feel his arms scooping me up. His eyes on mine, sad and regretful; yet these words do not capture the depth of what I see in his eyes—I'm not sure there *are* words for what I see.

"You can't stay," he says.

He sets me on my feet in front of the doorway.

Standing behind me he whispers in my ear. "You have to go, now."

Without a backward glance, I step toward the door and I twist the doorknob.

There is no in between, no waiting, no putting it off. My feet obey some unheard command.

I step through the doorway and his hands fall away, his heat diminishes, his presence cools and becomes cold and then…

There is nothing…

…nothing.

…nothing.

Silence.

Perfect, utter silence.

A drowning quiet.

I hear myself breathing; the first sensation.

I ache all over; the second sensation.

I open my eyes; the third sensation.

Once again I'm in the room of black doors.

The white cot is under me. To my left sits the small square black table and on it the thick white candle, flickering, casting a dim light. Rivulets of melted wax drip down the sides of the candle to pool and harden on the silver candlestick.

I look around and see seven pools of orange-yellow light. Seven doors. Five black, one green, one silver.

It hurts to see at the green door; simply looking at it cuts my heart and soul and mind into bleeding ribbons.

I don't know why, and I don't know what it means.

I have no thoughts, no memories, and no ideas about that door, only an abiding sense of agony.

So I let my eyes slide away from the faded, chipped, old green door with its brass knob.

My gaze travels to the silver door but it doesn't cause pain, only… revulsion. There is something wrong. That door is *wrong*.

As I consider that thought, something else strikes me.

Seven pools of light?

I count—and yes, there are only seven doors now.

Not eight.

The first door I passed through is gone and only a blank wall stands where the door used to be. No sconce, no frame. Nothing but an empty wall.

I'm on my feet and suddenly standing before the spot where that door used to be, though I don't remember walking toward it. I touch the wall, finding it cool, smooth, and slightly pebbled.

Where is that door, the door that leads to him?

Where did he go?

What has just happened?

I slide my palm along the cool wall, and my feet carry me fifty paces to door number two. My heart thunders in my chest, beating rabbit-fast, so hard it almost hurts. My palms sweat. This isn't quite fear, though. Anticipation? Nervousness? I don't know.

But my thoughts are banished.

The candle is forgotten.

Also forgotten is the cot, the six remaining doors, and the missing door.

He, the boxer, is…not forgotten, but tucked away in a quiet corner of my hazy mind.

It's hard to think, here in this space. Nothing makes sense. I have no grasp on time. How long have I been standing here in front of the door marked *2*? Forever, possibly. Or as brief a time as a single heartbeat. I really don't know.

What came before this room? I don't know.

Why does not knowing not bother me?

I don't know that either.

I know nothing except one thing: I'm about to twist this sleek black modern doorknob and step over a new threshold.

That's the only thing I know. The only thing I need to know.

I *have* to open this door. I *have* to go through. I don't know why, but I am compelled. I *must.*

My hand rises.

My sweaty, trembling palm meets cool metal. My heartbeat pulses so fast I can barely breathe.

I turn the knob.

I push the door open, and it swings inward on silent hinges.

Light bathes me.

Heat warms me.

I step through.

Unafraid.

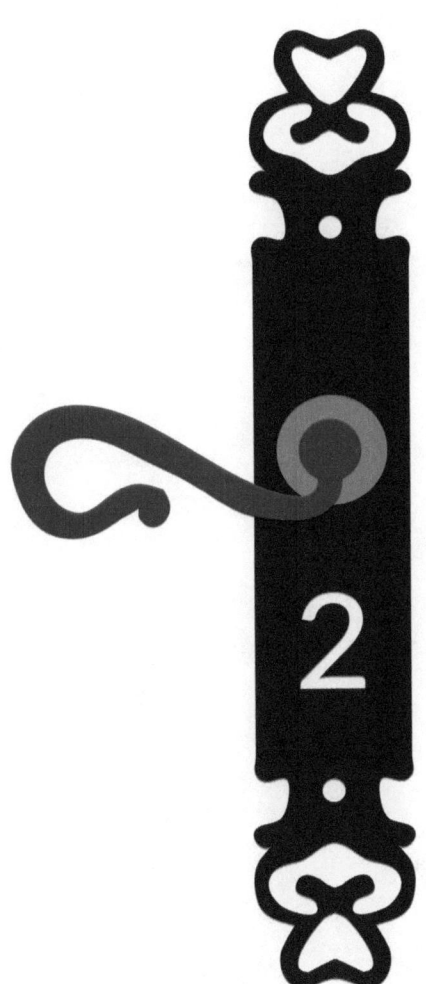

●

I leave utter darkness and step into brilliant light. The light does not blind, but occludes all else.

The transition is seamless—there is no shock, no adjustment, no wincing at the blinding illumination. I see no shadow behind me. No silhouette. No distorted rectangle of light cast upon the floor. I barely have time to consider these things, these oddities, because from the moment I enter this room I feel a sense of calm, and a welcoming warmth.

As I step over the threshold, a sense of clarity pervades and the world crystallizes into a single shining moment.

The light recedes and I find myself inside a large, modern apartment. A high-rise. To my left are floor-to-ceiling windows, and far, far beyond is a glass city. Seen from my tilt-shift perspective, I cannot even see the ground, so dizzyingly high off the earth am I. It is still daytime, mid or late afternoon. Brilliant, warm sunlight bathes the room in natural warmth.

I pull my gaze from the spectacular view and notice that I am standing in a large, ultra-modern bedroom. Across the room is a door, solid wood and painted white, its only decoration a black doorknob. The door is almost closed but not quite, open only an inch or two.

To the right of the door is a massive flat-screen TV mounted to the wall. Sleek, black and slightly curved, it is a silent presence in the room. Below it sits a slim, modern, handcrafted bureau, undoubtedly made of some expensive wood and easily six feet long. With its chunky squared-off handles and clean lines, it is an expensive piece of functional art.

As well, I glimpse a darkened doorway leading to a bathroom, large and beautiful with a marble floor and porcelain fixtures.

Taking center stage in the room is a bed. Like the bureau, it is an ultra-modern masterpiece: a gargantuan headboard mounted to the wall and crafted from the same wood as the bureau. The black wood is relieved by an upholstered white wool insert, connected by a series of brass rivets to the black frame. A luxurious black and white duvet with a diamond shape embroidered in the center, covers the bed. The expanse of the duvet is accented by an assortment of black and white throw pillows. A black footlocker, fitted with leather straps and of the same design as the headboard and the bureau, sits at the foot of the bed, the brass rivets gleaming in the light. Large but minimalist black bedside tables are positioned at either side of the headboard, each with a stand meant to hold a smart phone and a watch, the appropriate charger cords vanishing neatly behind the tables. No clocks. No knickknacks.

The entire room is covered in plush white wool carpet, my feet sinking into the luxurious pile.

I smell food.

Bacon is cooking: I hear it sizzling over the sounds of music and voices. Other scents, less easy to identify, drift my way. Eggs maybe, or toast? Definitely breakfast food.

What time is it anyway?

I glance out the window, wondering if I'd somehow misjudged the time of day. But no, the shadows are long, too long for dawn, or even early morning. The light is golden, hinting at the approaching dusk.

My curiosity gets the better of me. I walk across the room and pull open the door leading to the adjoining space. I leave the bedroom and find myself in a short hallway, and then I walk past another partially closed door through which I can make out another bedroom and en suite bathroom. Past that doorway, and then I enter an expansive seating area.

The place is huge, expensive. From the doorway, the first thing I notice is a great room decorated in more minimalist black and white modernism. A black couch, a white love seat, and a crimson armchair—the color draws my eye immediately, as intended. The couches are centered around a low glass coffee table on which are stacks of huge art books; a white coffee mug with the Harvard University logo on the side sits on a black leather coaster.

An exposed brick wall opposite the open doorway seems at odds with the modern decor of the rest of the apartment, but nevertheless adds something to the otherwise unrelieved modernism of the décor.

The view in this room is to die for: miles and miles of city, glittering high-rises and, far below, a grid of streets crisscrossing and stretching as far as the eye can see. The vehicles below, cars and cabs and trucks, look so tiny they don't seem real. A jetliner floats across the vista, leaving a thin white contrail.

I leave the bedroom and find myself in a short hallway, passing another partially closed door, through which I can make out another bedroom and en suite bathroom. I enter an expansive seating area centered around a low glass coffee table on which are massive art books.

Across from the seating area is the kitchen, with a large island in the middle. Around the marble countertop are four stools made of thick black iron with pale pine seat tops, which can be raised or lowered by a screw mechanism positioned under the seats.

But my real attention is drawn to the people in the room. The man standing at the stove is…simply breathtaking. A few inches over six feet, he is facing away from me, clad in nothing but faded blue jeans. I can't see his feet, but somehow I know he's barefoot, his back is defined with sculpted muscles sheathed in dark golden skin. He has thick, curly black hair, messy, unruly—just-fucked hair.

He reminds me of someone, but whom?

All I know right now is that he is *gorgeous*.

He's got his back to the room, and as he prepares the food he's talking with the two other people—a man and a woman, both in their twenties—seated at the island. They are all laughing together.

They are all drinking wine, and the mood is relaxed and easy. Clearly they are all friends, and they're waiting for breakfast.

The scene is…domestic. Pleasant.

The guy at the stove turns around with a plate of food in his hands. God, he's fucking gorgeous. Black hair, thick and messy with one long curly strand hanging down in front of one mocha-brown eye. Liquid chocolate eyes, like hot cocoa made from pure milk chocolate, wide-set and almond-shaped, open and emotive in their expression.

I can do nothing but stare at him, basking in his utter masculine perfection. Dark stubble, somewhere between a couple weeks of growth and a new beard, trimmed and shaped at the neckline. Scruff, delicious and scratchy…I can almost feel it scraping rough against my upper lip, against the insides of my upper thighs as he—

I shake that sudden, dirty thought away.

I shiver. I tremble. I'm damp between my thighs just looking at him.

He looks up and sees me, "Hey, you're up. You're just in time for breakfast."

The two people at the counter turn to look at me when they realize I'm in the room. The first thing I notice about them is that they are just as gorgeous, just as striking, as their friend, the dark-haired, dark-eyed god.

The woman has dyed red hair, a deep, lush crimson falling in loose waves down her back. She is clad in a Little Black Dress, short, revealing, tight, expensive, and deserving of the capital letters. Stilettos dangle from her feet, equally black and expensive. She looks as if she's dressed to go out for an evening at the club, yet despite her expensive clothes and sophisticated beauty, she has the air of a girl next door.

"God, I'm *so* glad you're here," she says to me. "I was getting tired of their lame jokes and stupid sports talk." She's smiling and laughing as she says this, a playful look in her eyes.

"Oh, come on," The other guy responds, "our jokes might be

lame, but you were laughing just as hard as we were."

He's pale and blond with eyes as blue as the noonday sky. With a strong jawline and full lips, he looks like a Hollywood actor, an A-list heartthrob. He shoots me a glance and passes his long fingers through loose, shaggy blond hair. His gaze is friendly, but assessing.

"Hey," says the dark-haired god, "while you guys are jabbering, the food is getting cold. Let's eat." With that he plates up eggs, bacon, waffles and coffee.

"I'm changing this god-awful music," the blond guy declares, looking pointedly at the girl.

"Whatever…" she says. "You know you love it."

"If by love," the blond man says, "you mean *hate*, then yes."

I have to agree about the music choice. The sound system is playing something light with a pop beat. There is nothing creative about its artificial drums and synth keyboards, and the warbling female voice repeating a trite, meaningless hook phrase.

I'm standing on the border between the sitting room and the dining area, unsure, hesitant.

The woman slides a stool out with her foot. "Sit down, silly. Food's not gonna eat itself."

I walk toward them, drawn overpoweringly. A familiar feeling pulls at me—a tug, sharp and insistent, as if we're all somehow connected.

I know these people, I know this place.

I feel…at home.

I sit at the island between the woman and the dark-haired god, feeling the cool wood under my bottom, and that's when I realize I'm naked. I'm curious, but not concerned. No one seems bothered by my nudity, and neither am I.

I tuck into the meal with gusto, more famished than I'd realized. Everything is delicious: eggs just the way I like them, with lots of cheese, salt, pepper, garlic, and cayenne. Bacon just this side of burnt. Coffee as black as the midnight sky.

Conversation resumes and the talk turns to a show of some kind.

"You *have* to see his YouTube video. You won't believe it."

"Yeah, I've heard of this guy. I want to see him, for sure. Plus he's super cute," says the girl. The guys just roll their eyes.

The meal is over and the girl looks at her iPhone. "Oh, my god! I've gotta get going or I'll be late. The show starts in an hour and I still have to re-do my make-up. I'll be back, I promise," she says, looking at me.

There's something in the way she looks at me, something in the way her eyes flick and flutter down my body, linger just a touch too long…I shiver, and she doesn't quite hide a grin.

And then she's gone.

The blond man clears the dishes, and then announces he's going to take a shower. He disappears into his bedroom, and the sound of water running can be heard.

The dark-haired man wanders over to the seating area and sits down on one of the plush couches. His long legs are stretched out, his feet resting on top of one of the art books, his ankles crossed as he sips his coffee. He looks over at me, gestures for me to come and sit beside him.

I slide off the stool, clutching my mug of coffee in one hand, palm against the side, ignoring the handle. Heat leaches into my hand, burning my skin, but I don't mind, somehow. His eyes follow me as I cross the dozen or so steps from the island to the couch. I see him follow the swing of my hips, the sway of my breasts. Unless I am very much mistaken, the zipper on his jeans has tightened rather significantly.

I sit beside him, cross my legs and rest them against his thighs, cup the mug in both hands and sip slowly.

I glance over at him. Barefoot and shirtless, in faded blue jeans, there's not a single ounce of fat anywhere on his body. My eyes follow the ridge of muscle slicing down into that sexy V-cut that disappears under the waistband of his jeans.

I look at his eyes and I can tell he's not exactly happy.

He seems distant, and I hate it. I want to fix it, close the emotional space between us.

"Hi," I say, unsure of where to even start, or why he's upset.

"I thought you weren't speaking to me." His voice is a deep bass, smooth as silk.

I'm lost. "I...why wouldn't I be speaking to you?" I feel as if I've missed something vital.

It's his turn to look confused, and he peers down at me quizzically, "Our conversation last night? You were pretty pissed at me."

I don't remember being angry—I don't even remember last night. Besides, how could I be angry with someone so ruggedly beautiful?

I shrug, hoping to deflect the fact that I'm lost. "Not anymore," I say simply.

He frowns, but I don't think it's from displeasure, but more from a deepening confusion, or disbelief.

He has something else to say, and I'm waiting for him to say it.

"If you aren't angry anymore, then what we discussed last night... you've thought about it some more?"

I don't remember what happened ten minutes ago. How do I tell him I don't remember last night? I remember...

Nothing.

Apart from the bedroom, and this room. Apart from him and his friends and breakfast at sunset, I remember nothing.

"I..." words elude me. "I must have had too much to drink last night. I don't really remember what we talked about."

A groan of frustration. "We only had a couple glasses of wine. How can you not remember?" He passes a hand through his hair, a gesture of irritation. "It was the worst argument we've ever had, and you're telling me you don't remember?"

I shrug. "I'm sorry. I must have...I don't know. I just don't know."

"You're sorry?" His tone is disbelieving. "*You're* sorry?"

"Shouldn't I be?"

He laughs then, a short ironic burst. "No. I thought for sure you'd be gone when I got back from work. I thought...I was pretty damn sure we were done."

"It must have been serious, then. Refresh my memory. What did we argue about?"

He shakes his head. "No. Ohhh no. I'm not bringing it up again. If you've forgotten, then it is best left that way."

I'm doubly curious now. A dumb idea that sparked an argument so bad I broke up with him? What could he have suggested? "Just tell me," I say. "I won't get mad this time."

He shakes his head. "I don't think so."

"I will be mad if you don't tell me."

Another low laugh. "You're impossible. I'm damned if I do, damned if I don't." He sets his coffee down, walks over to the kitchen and comes back with the wine.

We drink in silence and I try to think of something to say, try to figure out what he could have said to make me so angry and...why don't I remember it? Except for the past hour or so, my memory is a complete blank. Not just hazy, but...gone. All I know is this moment, this man, and this apartment.

I'm coming up with nothing. No memories, no ideas.

We hear sounds coming from the bathroom. The blond guy is complaining, loudly, "Shit, man, why'd you use all my hair gel?"

"I never touched your hair gel. Don't know if you've ever noticed but I don't use that shit. Talk to our red-haired friend, maybe."

A few more sounds of drawers slamming and then the blond guy comes into the living room.

He sees the two of us on the couch, neither speaking, both looking upset. He squeezes in to sit between us. "What's with the long faces? Let's get this party started!" He grabs the remote, his expression playful.

He flips through the channels before settling on something titled *SpecialDelivery*.

"Now we're talking," he says, then twists to look into the kitchen. "Where's the wine?"

The guy with the black hair rolls his eyes, "Right in front of you, dumbass."

More wine is poured and whatever it was he chose on the TV has started. I'm confused, at first. It's poorly acted, has zero production value, and features far too many close-ups on a woman wearing way too much makeup…

Darkness has fallen outside and the vast city is bathed in twinkling lights. Inside the apartment, the lights are dim, giving a warm, comfortable ambience.

My head feels a little fuzzy from the wine, but I'm comfortable and warm all over, sandwiched between two gorgeous men. I feel like I should address the elephant in the room, the issue between me and the dark-haired man, but I'm too comfortable and he's resting his hand on my thigh. He pours me more wine, which only makes my head spin even more pleasantly, and it makes the issue seem distant and unimportant.

On screen, a woman is at her front door, draped loosely in a sheer robe. A deliveryman stands on the other side of the threshold, dressed in brown shorts and a brown shirt. There's a flatly delivered line about needing to inspect the package and then, somehow, the deliveryman is in the house, and the woman is tossing her robe aside, and the man's hands, as if magnetized, go to her tits, which are absurdly gargantuan. She moans as if his nipple-twisting grip is somehow erotic. His hands move from her tits to her shoulders, and he shoves her down to her knees. Eyes wide and sultry, she opens his pants to reveal a cock so big a horse would be jealous. A few idle, toying strokes and she opens her mouth so wide her jaw must be cracking and, impossibly, she fits his the head of his cock into her mouth. Even more impossibly, she takes more. Gagging, she deep-throats him, and then he takes her by the hair in a rough two-handed grip and jerks her face to his belly, and she moans as if that feels good.

"You go girl," says the blond guy.

I roll my eyes. Are they seriously enjoying this? It's stupid.

It's idiotic, but the two guys find it funny….and I can't help but notice that both of them are fighting serious erections behind their jeans.

Their eyes are riveted on the screen as the woman lets him fuck her throat, moaning all the while, and then she takes control. She strokes him, then cups his balls and takes them into her mouth, using both her hands on his saliva-wet shaft.

The blond-haired man turns down the television sound a bit and gets to his feet saying, "Well, I'm going to go take a nap—I'll be working late tonight." He adjusts his zipper, glances at the other man and then me. "Have fun, kids," he says, winking at me. He leaves the room then, closing his bedroom door behind him.

Alone, now, we turn our attention back to the porn, and soon I feel his hands begin to wander. Starting at my ankles, they drift upwards, caressing and massaging my calves, and then he begins to knead my thighs. I suppress a gasp and try to surreptitiously slide a little closer to him. His touch moves closer to where I want it, and he nudges my thighs apart a little.

He gives me a long, searching look. I return his glance, noticing that his zipper is even tighter, the front of his jeans visibly tented. He attempts to relieve the pressure without directly touching himself, and I'm tempted to help him out, but I'm enjoying his discomfiture.

I'm going to make him wait a bit, draw this out.

Back on screen, the actress has moved from her knees to sitting on the edge of a counter in the kitchen. The actor is between her thighs, giving her head. Enthusiastically.

She's got her heels hooked around his back and her hands on his head, jerking him against her just as roughly as he did to her.

I'm sure it's not meant to be comical, but the actor has somehow removed what were rather tight brown shorts, and is now on his knees wearing the shirt and the boots and socks, but no pants. Bare white ass, bright white socks, chunky boots, and a brown shirt…the guy looks like an idiot. Who does that? Nobody.

But the way he's eating her out looks…phenomenal. I almost buy her enjoyment of it. She's propped herself up with one hand now, and has the other cupped around one of her big heavy tits. She's pinching herself, kneading, bouncing, playing with her own breast with as much enthusiasm as the actor had earlier.

This is so stupid.

But yet…

I can't stop watching.

And my core aches a little.

My breasts feel heavy, my nipples sensitive. Even as I realize this, I feel my nipples hardening.

He notices. His tongue touches his lips and his hand burrows between my thighs…and they part for him. Quickly, easily.

On screen, they've moved to another room. Either we missed it, or it was a quick cut. Now she's on her hands and knees on the bed, and he's finally naked. He's shoving that mammoth horse cock of his into her pussy, slapping her ass at the same time, which makes her tits jiggle and bounce. The camera goes close, then focuses on the slide of the actor's cock into her wet channel, on the juices coating it, on the way it stretches her pussy. She's fingering herself as he fucks her, moaning a little too loudly and breathily to be believed.

And then her bedroom door opens and a second actor stands at the threshold, doing a half-decent impression of indignant anger, or jealousy, or something. He demands to know what's going on. I miss the explanation the other actors give, because fingers have found my clit and my slit, and when I come back down from the sudden ripping zing that sizzles through me at the unexpected touch, the new actor is on the bed, too, and he's unbuckling his pants and pulling out his cock. And, yes, he too is hung like a horse. Although, given the build of the actor, *hung like a rhino* might be more apropos. They are not handsome men, these actors, nor do they possess any real acting skill. It's the somewhat improbable size of their cocks that got them the job, I suppose.

Oh—

Oh my…

Oh my *god*.

The actress is taking it from both of them. Behind her, the first guy, the deliveryman, is delivering a serious fucking, hard and fast and rough and brutal, while in front of her, the new guy is ramming his cock down her throat. The fucking from behind pushes her forward, so she's forced to deep-throat the other guy, who shoves his cock at her, pushing her backward once more. Back and forth, like a Ping-Pong ball.

I'm trying to tell myself how unpleasant this all looks.

I'm trying to tell myself I'm not at all curious.

Beside me, on the couch, there's a lot of shifting going on. His hands pluck at the front of his jeans. His hips flex. He winces. He finally shoves his hand in his pocket and adjusts himself.

How long can I pretend I'm not horny too?

Not long, is the answer.

I sit up and try to act casual, although I'm not sure there's any point; we're playing a game, but I don't know the rules, and I don't care. I just know, deep down, that this is how he and I do things. We tease each other. We pretend. We don't speak of what we're doing… and I'm not sure why. All I know is that it's fun. I snuggle closer and lean against him. He pivots a little and tugs me against his chest, and we fall backward.

On screen, things have shifted again. Now both men are on their knees, and the woman has a hand around each impossibly, absurdly huge dick, stroking, kissing, sucking, and licking each one in turn. Paying lavish, loving, exuberant attention to each. Never neglecting one for the other. She pulls them closer, fits both in her mouth at once. Damn, she has a big mouth—that's a *lot* of dick.

Who would do that, in reality? I mean, really. Come on. It's stupid. The scene on screen seems improbable—it's hard to imagine anyone, let alone me, doing something like that.

We're horizontal now, his head resting on a throw pillow on the arm of the couch, and I'm wedged between him and the back of the couch, more on top of him than anything else. I trail my fingers down his bare chest, tracing the outline of his pectorals and then fingering the grooves and ridges of his abdomen. Slowly and teasingly, I work my way closer to the waistband of his jeans and, once I'm close, I palm his belly again. Then down once more, a little closer, just close enough to hook a fingertip under the edge of his jeans. His breathing hitches as I get close to his dick, and his stomach goes concave.

On screen, the actress is riding one man, taking his cock in her cunt while the other is on his knees behind her, fucking her in the ass. She's moving desperately, moaning and whimpering breathlessly, thrashing her hair everywhere. Taking a double fucking and making it look… almost hot. Well…she is a pro, I guess.

And no, I do *not* wonder what that would feel like. There's no way on earth I could take that much cock. Or take it that hard, especially not in my ass. No way.

…Or could I?

I glance back at the gorgeous man beside me and I rub my hand over the top of his jeans, pressing against the thickness of his bulge, then move down his thigh and back up again. He's straining to remain in control. He looks—really looks—at me, saying nothing, yet he frowns and clenches his jaw, then looks back at the TV screen. There's an odd expression on his face as he looks from me to the double-penetration happening on screen.

Ah. The penny drops. Maybe *that's* what he was getting at, earlier. In fact, I'd wager anything that that's it.

But he remains silent, not saying a word.

Still, the idea takes hold in my mind and I find myself becoming turned on by it with every passing moment.

Between the man beside me and the porn on TV, I'm horny as hell. I attempt to casually, almost accidentally, nudge open the snap of his jeans. He looks at me, and I grin and shrug, as if to say *Oops, how'd that happen?*

His hand is on my waist, just resting there in no man's land, not near my ass, not near my core, not near my breasts. He's being careful and precise; this is not an accidental hand placement.

His gaze fixes on me then, and my acting ability flees. I abandon the game, for a moment at least. Keeping my eyes on his, I pull the tab of the zipper all the way down.

Commando.

Bare skin beneath the denim, black pubic hair trimmed close to his skin. His cock springs free. He's long and thick, dark, heavy, veined, circumcised. It is every bit as massive and perfect as the rest of him. If this man were a porn star, all other men, such as the guys on TV, would be out of business. He'd dominate the industry. No woman would ever want to see another man on screen. And no actress would ever want to work with anyone else. He's that perfect.

But…there isn't actually much porn available meant for women. What would that be like, I wonder? Hot guys, naked, jacking off on screen? Lots of close-ups of ripped abs and big cocks, and the guy on screen pleasuring himself slowly. That would sell, guaranteed.

Shit, I'd watch that.

God, where is my head going? Why am I fantasizing about female porn when I've got the real thing right here?

Back to reality.

I look at him, wait for him to say something, but he remains silent.

On screen, she's on her back now, head tipped back to take one cock down the throat, hips lifted to take the other in her pussy, which is splayed open, nothing left to the imagination. There are lots of grunts and groans, lots of *fuck yeah* and *oh baby* going on, lots of sweating skin and close-ups of sliding, glistening cocks, and her spread open pussy.

As we both watch the screen, I trace the thickness of his cock with a thumb and forefinger. Toying, playing.

He's barely breathing, his eyes are glazed and he stares into the middle distance.

He's waiting.

Finally, unable to resist any longer, I wrap my fist around his cock and stroke the considerable length of it; he's so large my middle finger and thumb don't meet.

He turns to look at me again, and then glances between the screen and me.

"That's what you asked me last night, isn't it?" I ask, gesturing with my chin at the TV, where the two men and the woman have shifted positions yet again.

"*Ménage à trois.*" His voice is low, a grating rumble. "Yes."

"Threesome." I try the word.

He looks as if he's waiting for me to express disgust, to get up and leave. But that's not going to happen. I just stare at him as I rub my thumb around the tip of his cock.

His jaw flexes and tenses, his eyes narrow. "You're not saying anything."

I shrug. I pulse my fist along his root, then back up. A quick glance at the screen shows the actress fisting one man's cock, and deep-throating the other. My nipples throb at the sight of those images.

He notices my reaction.

"You aren't serious, are you?" he demands. "Last night, you—"

"This isn't last night," I cut in, because I don't know *what* happened last night. Or today, either, for that matter. I don't know anything. I don't even know how to explain why I feel so turned on watching this stupid porn flick… or why I feel so curious about it.

This isn't me. Is it?

Could it be?

He watches my hand lazily gliding up and down his length. Toying, playing, teasing. "You better not be playing some goddamn game," he murmurs, his voice hard with warning. "Don't fuck with me about this. I don't want to if you don't."

I shake my head. "Number one, I'm not playing a game. Number two, either you do, or you don't. You can't change what you want based on what I want."

"It's just…your sudden change of heart has me nervous."

"No games." I kiss his shoulder. "I swear."

"You have to say yes. I need to hear you say it." He grabs my hand, stopping my hand mid-stroke.

"You haven't asked." I'm being coy. Coquettish.

"Do you want to have a threesome?" He growls the questions.

I pause a moment before answering. "Will the other man be as sexy as you?"

"I think you already know my friend is good looking," he says with a grin.

I slide down and pull his cock away from his body. I breathe a hot breath on him, and then flick my tongue over his tip.

A wild scream from the TV has us both glancing over at it: full-on double penetration. One man on his back, thrusting into her ass as she lays on him reverse cowgirl style, the other kneeling in front of her, pounding away at her pussy.

God, that looks…

…Equal parts terrifying and fascinating. I tamp down on my curiosity—no way I could do that. No way.

But the other parts of the onscreen three-way…god, yes, I'm curious.

I'm more than curious. I *want* that. I'm not sure what I'm capable of doing myself, but I want to try. If one cock feels good and tastes good, what would two gorgeous cocks be like?

I shiver, thinking of it. My imagination runs wild and I conjure up a dozen different ways I could play with two cocks…

The possibilities are endless.

He glances at the screen, and I follow his gaze—she's getting ready for a facial. Both cocks are aimed at her face, her mouth and eyes are open and her hands stroke both cocks in unison.

"Yes," I whisper, as curiosity and inflamed lust blast through me. I lean in and run the tip of my tongue along the side of his dick. "Yes."

"Shit," he says with a gasp. "I didn't think you'd actually agree."

A thought just occurred to me, "Or did you mean me and another woman?"

"That could be fun, too."

My thoughts disappear when he bends, lifts me in his arms, and carries me into the nearest bedroom. "Let's go wake up our friend. Nap time is over."

The bed is huge and the blond guy is turned on his side, sleeping deeply. I'm laid gently on the bed, right near the edge, on the far side from Rip Van Winkle.

"We'll take pity on him, wake him up slowly." Then he sinks to his knees, places my knees over his shoulders and then, without a word, he begins his assault. Ohhhh, god, yes. His scruff feels every bit as delicious against the tender skin of my inner thighs as I had imagined: scratchy, rough, yet somehow soft and tickling. Abrasive and amazing. And then his tongue spears into me, laps against my clit, and I can barely breathe.

For the next several minutes, he pleasures me with his nimble, eager tongue. He laps and licks and sucks with mind-altering skill. It's not until he slides two fingers into me that I can come, but he waits until I'm gyrating my hips and jerking at his hair to give me that, and when he does I come apart in his hands and on his face with utter abandon, screaming and whimpering and cursing.

I'm floating, dizzy, wracked with after-shock spasms.

As I lay on the bed, recovering from the incredible orgasm, I'm aware of something. I feel the bed shift ever so lightly.

My heart palpitates. I sit up on the bed, but my man is beside me, mouth on my breasts, whispering, but his words are muffled against my skin.

"What are you saying?" I ask.

"Telling you how fucking sexy you are." He cups my breast in his hand, letting the flesh mound and overflow. "These big beautiful tits of yours drive me wild."

I smile, then, and reach down for his cock, stroke the hard length of it.

I feel someone moving behind me, look over my shoulder to see that the blond man has woken up.

"Holy shit, what a way to wake up," he murmurs, his voice low with anticipation.

For the second time, my brain is fried by a vision of raw masculine sex appeal:

The blond man slides off the bed to stand in front of me, lifts the hem of his t-shirt and strips it off. He's lean and toned and razor sharp, rather than bulked up and heavy with muscle like my man is.

I flop back against the mattress, flush and shivering with equal parts nerves and excitement and fear and lust…

And the lust quickly wins out.

Blue eyes rake over my body, and I find myself arching my back, posing.

I stare back at him as he unbuttons the top snap on his jeans, touching himself as he does so. He pops his fly open and I get a glimpse of his cock as he kneels on the bed.

But only a brief glimpse, because on my left, my man is flicking my hardened left nipple with his tongue, lifting the breast to his mouth, cupping, kneading, and stealing my attention.

On my right, the blond man is reaching a reverent hand to my right breast. His eyes are on mine. There's no hesitation, it's just as if… he's giving me a moment. I'm silent as he cradles my right tit in his hands, and now…

A mouth on each breast.

Oh god.

Oh shit.

Tongues toy and flick at both thick, pebbled, sensitive nipples.

At the same time, an unfamiliar hand skates down my right thigh then slides back up. I gasp, and writhe my hips as long, strong, fingers ply my opening, gentle, quick, sure. He pinches my clit and then his fingers slide in, finding my wetness and smearing it over me. God, I'm so wet. I'm dripping.

Who's touching me where? I lose track, can't follow the hands as they tweak and twist my nipples and caress my clit and slide in and out of my cunt. Whose mouth is lapping at my breast, and whose mouth is licking at my clit…?

I close my eyes as a blistering blast of ecstasy shudders through me.

Together, the two men wrench me into a wild and furious orgasm, one I can't help but scream breathlessly through.

● ●

When I return to my senses, I realize both men are still wearing their jeans; there's entirely too much clothing, since I'm the only one naked; I decide to rectify that.

My left hand tugs the faded blue denim down. He lifts a knee and kicks away the jeans. Naked. Glorious, hot skin covering hard muscles. I spend a moment devouring his beauty. Then I find his erection with my fingers and begin stroking. A slow rhythm, I'm toying with him again.

A few moments later I focus on the blond god to my right, help him out of tight black jeans, exposing a long, thick cock. Similar to the one in my left hand, a little shorter, a little less thick, but his has a slight inward curve to it. He's just as magnificent and mouth-watering with his beautiful cock standing straight up, flush against his belly. I give him an exploratory caress and watch his face as my fingers slide down his length. He closes his eyes involuntarily, and then they open once more and he watches as I cup his balls. Heavy, tight to his body, sparsely dotted with blond pubic hair, unlike the trimmed thatch of dark hair at the base of my man's cock.

Different, these two men, but equally delicious.

I keep my right hand busy, sliding slowly up and down. Twisting at the base, gliding up, curling around the soft, springy head. I rub my thumb around the tip and he moans low in his throat, flexing his hips at the same time.

Now that I know I've got his attention, I turn my face to the left. Dark eyes, hooded, heavy-lidded, are fixed on me, watching every move I make. I lean close to him and as I grip his manhood to draw him closer he lifts up on his knees in front of my face. Now his cock is within reach of my mouth, and I keep my eyes on his as I stroke him, then I part my lips and take him into my mouth. He groans, eyes fluttering.

"Shit, shit," he murmurs. "Take it all, baby."

I widen my jaw, open my throat and take it all—there's so *much*. I taste his skin and the musk of leaking essence, of salty flesh. Moving slowly, so slowly, I take my time, tasting every marvellous inch. My eyes flutter upwards and I watch him enjoy it, watch him struggle to keep breathing; he's fighting the urge to fuck my throat. His hands are in my hair, clutching, and his hips are tensed, wanting to flex. I let go of my hold on the base of his cock and reach around to cup his hard ass—god, so tight, that ass. Carved out of marble. I pull at it, encouraging him.

At the same time, on my right, my stroking fist is moving faster and faster, skimming up and down his thick, straining cock. He's flexing into my fist, cupping my breast, kissing and licking my nipple, making it harden, making my core ache. Almost idly, he fingers my cunt until I'm soaked and dripping.

The cock in my mouth throbs and thickens.

Not yet, oh no. Not yet.

I pull away, letting his dick fall free with a *pop*. He moans in protest, but I've got my fist around him immediately, holding, squeezing, and pulling him back from the edge.

I want to taste the other cock, so I turn to my right and find him ready and waiting. I wrap my fist around the head, then squeeze and slide my grip down, slowly, slowly, slowly, touching my lips to the tip as if I'm taking a bite of ice cream. Mmmm, he's leaking too, his salty musk smearing on my tongue. I let his cock glide into my mouth and over my tongue, scraping ever so gently between my teeth. My eyes are fixed on his blue gaze as I take him further into my mouth, and I lower my fist to the base. The curve of his cock forces me to tilt a little to let him slide into my throat. He's so long I have suppress a gag as he buries himself to the root, and I lavish my tongue and lips all over him as I back away, then sink down again. I take him deep, and then back away once more, and I can feel his moan more than hear it. I feel his balls tense; feel his breath catch as his belly hardens.

I don't know what comes next, so I look left, then right. I watch my hands move and watch as the men fight the urge to let go.

I'll give them what they want, but first I get what *I* want.

I roughly shove the blond-haired guy back against the pillows; he goes willingly, blond hair splayed around his face. He reaches for me, sliding his hands over my hips, cupping my ass. For just a moment I let him touch me, let him feel my skin, let him toy with the juicy round-ness of my ass, and then I kneel astride him. His eyes glitter, his jaw sets, his tongue runs over his lips in anticipation. I grab his cock, lift it and fit the head to my slit. As I roll the head in circles over my opening, I roll my hips and grind against him.

"Oh, fuck yeah," he groans. "I bet you're tight. Tight and wet, aren't you?"

I smile for him, a sultry, flattered smile. "I don't know—am I?"

I sink down on him, flush and deep. Oh fuck. Oh fucking hell, he feels good. That curve has him sliding against me just right, the tip hitting me just right deep inside my channel as his shaft grinds against my clit.

"Am I tight and wet?" I ask.

He gasps. "So fucking tight, baby. So wet."

I writhe on him and roll my hips in grinding circles while he's deep inside, giving him a hint of what awaits.

But first…

"You want more?" I ask, my voice low, playful.

"Yeah." He clutches my ass and tries to make me move. "I want all of it. Give it to me, baby."

I lift up and pull him out of me, then I swing my leg over his torso so I'm facing away from him, on all fours, ass in the air.

I back up, pressing my dripping slit to his face. "Then start licking. Make me come again, and I'll let you fuck me."

"Jesus," he groans, and spears his tongue against my clit. "You're fucking soaked."

I drop my head and whimper as he fucks my clit with his mouth. I take a moment just to relish the feel of his tongue whipping in circles around my clit, flicking it, feeling his day-old stubble against my tender skin. "That's good," I murmur, writhing against his tongue, "Just like that. Don't stop. Jesus, don't stop."

"What about me?" a deep, amused voice says, in front of me.

I open my eyes, look up and smirk as dark eyes reflect heat and impatience and need. He's got his cock in hand, and he's masturbating slowly. Mmmmm. I like watching that. He sidles closer, stroking, his big fist roughly pumping his length. I part my lips and lick my upper lip, eagerly anticipating the taste of him, the feel of him between my lips.

Closer, closer…

There it is, finally, the big, round head brushing soft and springy against my lips, and then I lick his cock from root to tip. I gasp when from behind something frightfully delightful begins to happen to my clit; as that happens I sink my mouth around the cock in front of me. Mmmm. This is good. Oh, so good. A tongue at my pussy, a cock in my mouth, and god, god, god—an orgasm building.

I release his cock and lift my eyes up to his. I'm coming—I'm coming so hard I'm liable to accidentally bite down, and I wouldn't want to do that to such a lovely organ. I grind my pussy against the lapping tongue, moaning, pushing backward, spine bowed inward, head dropped between my shoulders as a raging climax blasts through me. As soon as the peak passes, I sheathe my man's cock between my quivering lips, sucking hard, burying it in my throat, swallowing around the shaft until he's groaning and pumping helplessly.

He pulls out of my mouth abruptly. "I don't want to come down your throat."

I blink up at him, still shaking from my orgasm. "No? Where do you want to come?"

He grins wolfishly. "All over that lovely face of yours."

"That sounds messy," I say, not feeling anywhere as disgusted as I maybe should be.

"I would clean up every inch of your gorgeous body. You know that."

Behind me, someone looks ready for me to hold up my end of the bargain. Blue eyes are fixed on my ass as he rises up onto his knees. His palm caresses my buttock, the other clutching his erection.

"Put it in," I say to him, over my shoulder.

My blond hair cascades over one shoulder, momentarily obscuring my view of the man in front of me. I pretend, just for a split second, that it's just me and the blond god behind me. I hold my breath as he searches my pussy with his fingers. He quickly finds my opening, scissors two fingers inside me, then fits the broad head of his dick to my slit, grunts low in his throat, eyes narrowing in pleasure as he slowly slides in. He takes his time, centimeter by centimeter, gliding deep. I gasp, lost in the fullness.

"Fuck me hard," I whisper. "Don't be gentle."

He growls as he sinks up to the hilt into me and, for a moment, a split second of time, our breathing matches, both of us panting shallowly as he thrusts deeper, hips flexing until he's so deep there's no more depth for him to plunder. I keep my eyes on him, letting him read me, letting him see me.

He pounds.

Once.

*Hard.*

Strong hands grip my hips, pulling me backward into roughening thrusts.

"Oh fuck, yeah, just like that," I groan. "Don't stop..."

I'm rocked forward by his thrusts, into a hard body in front of me. Something at once hard and soft nudges my cheek, my chin. I open my eyes; see a hint of jealousy in the dark brown eyes. I grin up at him, tease him. I play up my noises, my responses to what the blond guy is doing. I push back into the fucking, moaning even louder. His eyes narrow, a hard smirk spreading on his face as he realizes my game. He wraps a fist in my hair, gathering the thick sheaf of golden locks around his fist, and pulls my face toward his cock and shoves in deep, so deep I gag. He backs out, a thick string of spit dangling from the tip of his cock to my mouth. I manage a deep breath, and then he's back in my mouth, pulling at my face. I moan for him, hum around his cock, bobbing vigorously, going down on him for all I'm worth, sucking hard, letting him fuck deep into my throat.

And, oh god, I'm still getting good and fucked from behind, too, and now it's taking all my effort to divide my attention. The cock in my pussy slams and drives, sinks deep and holds there for a pulsing thrust or two, and then he's backing out and thrusting shallowly.

I'm not ready for him to release yet, I realize, and he's close. Do I want him to come inside me?

The answer is easy: No. I realize despite all the playing around, only one man will come inside me, which is why his threat to come on my face is idle.

Maybe in private…

A thought for another time?

I push the blond man away and he takes the cue, backing up on the bed. I slide forward, gasping as his cock slips out of me.

This is all about me, I realize.

They're waiting…

And I make them wait even more.

Make them ache.

Blond hair to my right, black to my left. Two huge, hard cocks, waiting eagerly to bury inside me. Where do I want them? Such amazing choices I have.

I wonder how my cunt tastes, smeared all over another man's flesh?

I twist to my right. Reach for the curved shaft and bring it to my lips. I inhale, catching my own scent, then take his cock between my lips and taste my essence and his, mixed, mingled. Why the *fuck* does that make me throb? It shouldn't, but it does.

None of this should be so erotic, but it is. None of this should feel so fucking good, but it does.

There's something darker, though, lurking inside me. Deep, beneath the lust, beneath the hunger for everything, the desire for all I can handle, is the need to be fucked and used and taken until I'm twisted up and done and about to faint—beneath all that dirty, slutty neediness, is something dark.

I want to make *him* jealous.

I *liked* that gleam of possessiveness in his eyes as he accepted the fact that the cock now in my mouth has just plundered my pussy. *He* wanted to be there. *He* wants to be the one inside me. *He* asked for this, he wanted this threesome, but now that it's happening, maybe it's not what he wanted. Maybe he's more jealous of me than he thought he'd be.

And maybe everything I'm doing is a calculation on my part, at least on some level, to twist the knife of jealousy a little deeper.

I want to make him crazy.

I change things around so both men are side by side in front of me. I go down lustfully on the long, curved dick, swallowing it, tasting the pre-cum leaking, tasting the throbbing thickening as he nears orgasm… and I use both hands on my man's thicker, straighter cock. I plunge both hands up and down to the same rough rhythm as I'm using with my mouth. Double grunts, tandem gasps. Two sets of hips thrusting. Fuck, oh god. I *like* this. I wrap one hand around the cock that's in my mouth, just beneath my chin, and continue the rhythm then switch my mouth to the left. I take the thickness between my jaws, feeling it almost crack as I struggle to accommodate his girth. God, so thick. So wonderfully, perfectly, beautifully thick. For the space of three swallowing fucks of my mouth, I take him.

And then I switch again.

Back and forth, back and forth, pumping with my fists nonstop, shifting my mouth back and forth until both men are gasping and grunting and thrusting, sweating, muscles tensed and hard as they both hold back.

And then I stop, as they're both at the very edge.

"Not yet, boys," I say. "I'm not done with either of you, yet."

"Shit," my man says, voice thick and frustrated. "I'm so close it hurts."

"Fuck...me too. I can't hold out much longer." Another voice rough with need, fraught with frustration.

I've got them both on edge.

Hell, *I'm* on edge.

I've kept them waiting long enough, I think.

I slide off the bed and lean forward toward them, bending at the waist, using one hand to prop myself up. I reach with my other hand for something long and curved, pulling the blond haired, blue-eyed, hard-bodied man toward me with a hungry grin, and a smile full of promise.

I pause a moment, though, before I take his organ between my lips.

Then I reach for the dark curly hair and pull his face toward mine. I whisper in his ear, "Take me..."

He's off the bed and standing behind me in a flash. Hands caressing the length of my spine, dragging his nails down my back, clutching my hips, kneading the globes of my ass, parting me. I feel him nudge. He flexes against me.

He presses into my cunt, his cock thick, stretching me wide, stretching me to burning. He slides in slowly. *Deep*.

And god...so gentle.

I gasp, whimper, feeling an unbelieavable bliss, my mouth falling open. A whine escapes my lips, and then I remember the man in front of me. I open my eyes just in time to see him rub himself against my cheek. Soft, so soft against my skin. He's glistening, damp with our combined essences. He drags his slick cock across my cheek toward my mouth. I gasp again as another thrust has me rocking forward, waves of tightening heat billowing through me.

I stroke the cock in front of me. Caress it. Massage the curved length. Toy with it, take it from him, rub the head against one cheek, then the other. Nuzzle it. Then, teasingly, I kiss the tip. I open my mouth to let him push in, a slow penetration.

He groans, eyes closing, head lolling back.

There won't be any putting him off, this time. He clutches my shoulders, groans as I take him oh so gradually deeper, and deeper, and deeper.

Moments blur, then. Sensations tangle and merge. I twine my fingers in those of the hand on my shoulder and push his hand into my hair. I grasp his hand and show him what I want him to do, namely, pull me onto his cock, use my mouth, and let go of control.

He takes direction well, it seems. He tugs at my face, hesitantly at first, then with more authority, more control, and more assertion.

I lose track of everything, then. I let all the sensations move through me, in me, and over me. I take it all: I move with them both, pushing back into the wonderfully rough thrusts, then forward to swallow heat and thickness, a mouthful of thick throbbing, pre-cum leaking cock. I'm overwhelmed, taking so much my senses are pushed to overload.

And then I feel my ass being spread apart by rough, insistent hands. I feel pressure on the tight rosebud knot of muscle; hear a *crack* sound, a squirting sound, and twist to see my man spreading lube on the fingers of one hand. I'm not ready, I'm not ready—oh my fucking *god*…

It's the most amazing thing I've ever felt.

Just his finger, the long middle finger sliding slowly into my asshole. Oh….*fuck*.

I go cross-eyed from it. Delirium blasts through me, a sudden, unexpected orgasm crashing through me, lightning hard and lightning fast, tightening my cunt around his cock, my asshole around his finger. I'm so full, every orifice stuffed, crammed. Pussy, mouth, and asshole, all being used beautifully all at once, and all I can do is ride the sensation through, gasping, moaning, writhing, impaled and fucked to within an inch of my life and maybe a bit beyond.

As the crest of climax sears through me, he adds a second finger, more lube, and now the feeling of being stretched beyond capacity is all consuming.

"More…" I beg, not recognizing my own voice as I whisper my plea against the soft, veined, iron-hard, saliva-wet side of the shaft throbbing beside my mouth. "Oh fuck, that feels too good. So fucking good."

"You want more?" He's whispering in my ear, fucking my pussy and fingering my asshole, moving his fingers in and out to the rhythm of his fucking. "You want all of it?"

"God yes…god, fuck yes." All I know is I want more, even as an orgasm rips through me.

Then a sudden absence of everything, cold, empty, still, as both men withdraw.

I'm dizzy from the climax, dizzy from need, delirious from the pulsating, crashing aftershocks and manic lust.

I'm lifted.

Settled on my back on a hard body.

I twist my head to one side and open my eyes to see dark olive skin and black scruff, lips whispering against mine. "This is what you want?" he nudges against my asshole with the tip of his cock.

"Oh…" I can't make words emerge. Can't make sense of anything.

I'm a riled-up, orgasm-loose, hot, horny, sweaty, needy knot of wanton bliss. I feel bodies and hands, feel a stomach beneath me, hands on my pussy, at my clit, on my breasts, toying with my tits and pinching my nipples, fingers plunging into my cunt, a cock nudging my asshole, a big hand moving mine to help me wrap fingers around a wet, throbbing shaft. Sensation is confusion, too much of everything, man all around me, hardness and essence and muscles and hands and cocks and breath and moans.

"Say yes," I hear him murmur in my ear. "I need to hear you say yes." Familiar words. Why? I don't remember.

I hear the wet squishing slurp of lube and a hand sliding up and down a wet organ. I use my heels to lift myself up a little, so I can reach around and touch the slick, lubed-up cock. I moan as fingers, three of them now, spread the lube on my asshole, pushing in. I want to cry out, but I'm breathless, unable to do anything but take the fingers and writhe onto them. Different fingers, a different hand is at my pussy, spearing in, curling to find a spot high inside, pressing against my clit, ramping me up toward another building climax.

"Say yes, honey. Or say no." His lips move against the shell of my ear, breath straining, whisper lilting.

"Yes...*Yes*..." I sink back down onto his body, ass to his stomach. I lay back, rest my head on his shoulder, turn my face to inhale his scent, touch my lips to the side of his throat, feel his hands on my body, on my skin, one cupping my breast, tweaking my nipple, the other three fingers inside my ass, three-knuckles deep. "God, yes. *Fuck* yes."

I reach out and clutch a cock, stroke its curved length. I force my eyes open, and meet a pair of blue eyes. "Soon," I whisper, all the promise I can manage at that moment. I pull him closer. "Soon."

"Oh fuck," he grunts back, pressing the head of that long, lovely shaft against my clit, "I can't wait. You're so fucking tight, you feel so fucking good."

"Ready?" The voice in my ear demands my attention.

I nod. "I'm—oh *shit*...I'm ready."

• • •

Not ready. I'm not ready. I said I was, but I'm not.

Because fuck, fuck, *fuck*, what happens next is too much.

Any capacity I might have had for rational thought is eradicated. I can't see straight, I can't think straight; I can only revel in sensation.

Slowly fingers slide out of my ass, but before the muscles can contract they're replaced by his cock. Just the tip, at first. A nudge in. Spreading me apart. I doubt, for a moment, that I can take him; he's too big, too much. But then he flexes his hips ever so slightly and I gasp, whimper, and take more. An inch, now. God, I'm being split apart. An ache, a burn, sweet, delicious pain-laced perfection. Something soft and thick rubs against my clit, and I focus on that for a moment, force my eyes open and watch as he grinds his lovely, curved cock against my clit, teasing my slit with it, and holy shit, that's beautiful. He has his hands on himself, my legs spread open for him, his cock nudging my cunt, and he's leaning over me and sucking my tit into his mouth. The tugging blast of pleasure of this somehow lets me take *more*, more of the impossibly massive cock that is somehow fitting into my asshole.

I clutch the cock that's in front, knock his hand away, and stroke him. I fit him into me. I gasp and writhe as I feel him slide into my pussy. And now…

*Ohhhhhh* god, oh god, oh god. Too much. It's too much. I'm so full it hurts, but not in a bad way. It's madness, utter carnal madness. I can't breathe, can barely function, can barely move for the fullness.

There's only a tiny, thin sliver of skin separating the cocks inside me. I'm crammed so full nothing else exists but the fullness, as if I'm about to split open from the inside.

A breathless moan escapes me, turning to an all-out shriek as the man beneath me, *my* man, buries himself fully into my ass. I've taken all of him, an impossible feat, and if I was going to split apart before, *now*, oh god, now I *am* bursting apart, because they're both buried all the way.

I'm crying, gasping, writhing, needing…I don't even know what I need, don't know what to do, or even how to exist in this moment of all-pervading fullness.

I flex my hips just a little, to test my ability to move.

Ohhhhhh Jesus, holy hell that's it, that's what I need.

"Fuck me," I hear myself say. "Oh god, please, fuck me. *Please*…"

And they obey, both of them. In unison.

I roll my hips and feel the cock in my ass tug outward just a little, the cock in my cunt slipping out a bit more, and then as I roll my hips again, they both fuck into me, and I'm crying out, taking it and screaming as they fuck me, both men moving now, thrusting into me, fucking me full of so much cock it should be impossible. There is so much of everything, a mouth on my ear, biting my earlobe, teeth on my nipple, a rough hand cupping my other breast and kneading it with familiar possessiveness.

My world is grunts and groans and muscle slipping and grinding against me, cock sliding in and out of me, splitting me open, mouths on my skin, hands on my hips and hands tweaking my nipples.

"Fuck…"

"Oh god—"

"Jesus, you're so goddamn tight—"

"Oh…oh god…don't stop, don't fucking stop—"

I don't know who's talking, who's saying what. I don't know anything.

I feel the curve inside me, open my eyes and watch him move, watch his long hair sway and curl in front of his eyes, watch his carved abdomen rippling as he fucks me, his thighs pulsing with each thrust, hips flexing, and it's his hand on my breast, the other gripping my hip and holding me in place.

I turn my head, see the beautiful profile beside my face, familiar dark scruff up close, swarthy skin, eyes closed in bliss, focused, and his body beneath me is a perfect hard cushion, moving, writhing, thrashing as he buries himself deep.

I'm everywhere, with my hands. Clutching biceps, sliding along thighs, burying in hair, smoothing over abdomens, cupping a flexing ass, touching everything I can reach, my body undulating, arrhythmic.

Time out of time, then. Pleasure without end. Ecstasy in never-ending seconds, stretching out into infinity.

I come at least once, maybe twice, or maybe it's one long, unending orgasm. I don't know. I just know my whole body is wrenched and wracked and twisted with searing bliss, tightening heat, climaxes shattering me and splintering me, and I come back down only to feel another wave blast through me.

I feel a change, then.

An impatience in the thrusting body above me, driving with unadulterated need.

I meet his eyes, and then reach between us. He pulls out, rises up on his knees, and takes his glistening cock in his fist.

I knock his hand away; take him in both of mine.

He throbs in my fists.

I cup his sac in one palm, feel his balls tighten, slide my middle finger along his taint and press hard. I stroke his length, pulling him closer, feel him straddle me to get close enough that I can take him in my mouth, and pump my fist at his root, and suck on the thick head. He grunts and moves, writhes, curses, and fucks my mouth.

"Shit, I'm close. Fuck, yeah, just like that. Suck it, baby, god, suck it so good, yeah, just like that."

"Mmm-hmmm?" I hum the question. "Mmmmmm."

He thrusts wildly, lost to it now. I feel him thicken in my mouth. Feel his thrusts stutter, falter.

Beneath me, my man fucks my ass with a wild, pounding vengeance, hard, rough, and I writhe against him and take it and grind against him. I reach up behind me with my free hand to bury my fingers in his curly, inky locks, clutching his hair viciously, pulling at him.

Above, I have heavy balls in one hand, my middle finger against his taint, pressing, pulsing in time with the sinking, bobbing movement of my mouth on his shaft. Not deep, this time. Just enough to suck hard, a few inches in mouth, my fist stroking the rest of his length hard, fast and crazy, moaning, humming. I open my eyes to watch him. He's a wild man, primal, sweat coating his body, muscles tensed, everything hard, all raw masculine beauty, blond hair sticking to his forehead and chin and neck, abs flexing as he moves.

"Ah god, fuck," he groans, "I'm coming. God, take it, baby, oh fuck, right there, just like that…"

He explodes in my mouth, one hand clutching my hair and pulling me roughly into his thrust, and I groan as he slides to the back of my throat, hot cum sluicing down my throat. I swallow and he pulls out, cum filling my mouth, and then he pulls out abruptly, entirely, and I watch him fuck into my hands and watch a thick white jet of sticky wet cum splash onto my tits, and then he spasms again and more cum pools on my breast, slides wet over my nipple and I can't breathe to swallow the mouthful, so I let it gush out of my mouth and down my chin and throat and he watches this, raptured, still thrusting into my fists, cum no longer spurting out but seeping, smearing, so I don't pump his length any longer, but caress and twist and jerk, milking every last twitch out of him.

And god, shit, I still have another cock moving, fucking me, another hard male body beneath me, insistent, rough, hands all over me, clutching my tits and squeezing as his thrusts become wild and frantic, and I feel something huge building inside me from the fucking my ass is taking, an orgasm the likes of which I don't know if I'll survive. Fingers in my pussy, now, at my clit, fingering me, for my benefit alone. I press my hand to his, show him how I like it: gentle touch, moving fast, circling my clit but never quite touching. He catches on fast, and keeps it up as I begin to undulate in earnest now.

There are grunts in my ear, my man's hands grasp both my tits, his hips flex beneath me, shoving his cock into my ass and pulling out, hard and fast now. I would never have believed I could take a fucking like this, but now I can't imagine anything else, I'm not sure there's ever been anything else.

I turn my head to the side, finding scruff at my lips.

Kiss.

Breathe—try to breathe, at least—as his mouth stutters against the side of my neck.

His whisper is only for me.

So quiet I nearly miss it, beneath my own moans.

"I'm going to come in your ass," he murmurs.

Why does that make me even more wild?

I don't know, but it does.

I'm out of control now, so wild. I can't get enough of him.

I writhe all the harder, impaled by him, on him. I ride him, feeling complete, replete, flush with ecstasy..

He clutches me against his body, one hand on my hipbone, guiding my undulations, the other sliding up and down my torso, carving over my breasts, between them, and he's grunting. I'm moaning.

It's a fraught moment, then.

"Oh god," I cry out, my voice louder than I'd intended. "Yes...god yes, fuck me, fuck my ass so hard, baby...come for me, let me feel it—give it to me. Don't stop, *don't stop*—"

He buries his face in the intimate, tender spot behind my ear, and his hand wraps around the delicate column of my throat.

Everything falls way as the pressure of his hand on my throat increases.

Increment by increment, as he fucks harder and harder.

I suck in a rough breath, clutch his hair with shaking hands, feet planted in the bed beside his knees, pushing myself up, bracing against his movements.

"I'm—shit, shit, I'm coming," he gasps, breathing the words so quietly, so intensely I strain to hear them, but I feel them in my bones.

All the universe shrinks down to this.

To him, beneath me, inside me, hands all over me, fucking my asshole so hard my whole body shakes from the force of his thrusts, our bodies meeting with loud slaps, his hand on my throat, the pressure not quite cutting off my breath, yet somehow not being able to breathe, somehow his hand on my throat sends me over the edge.

I come with a hoarse scream.

And that, my scream, my orgasm, brings him with me.

I feel it, I feel his cock throb and pulse, and then heat fills me, and his fucking slamming grinding thrusts lose all semblance of rhythm or control. He pushes in, deep, coming and coming and coming, and my orgasm is a vortex of dizziness and darkness and wicked delirium dragging me down, everything I am focused on writhing, pulsing, thrashing on top of him, focused on the feel of his perfect cock inside me unleashing again and again and again, and then there's only his breath and mine, gasping in ragged tandem.

I'm sucked under the veil of darkness.

Sweet, cool, oxygen fills my lungs, a kind of secondary climax.

Voices.

Nothingness.

For a space of a single thought, this nothingness, this succumbing to the darkness is…

Too familiar.

Frightening.

As if I've fallen into a blackness like this before.

*Not yet*, comes the thought, bubbling up from some secret corner of my soul.

*Not yet.*

● ● ● ●

I blink, and I breathe, and I stretch—languid, euphoric, feline. I'm wrapped up in softness, surrounded by heat.

I awake to a white ceiling above. Cityscape light from the windows lights the dim room. I can see skyscrapers with countless yellow rectangles of light, a helicopter scudding and thudding in the distance, a dark sky and even darker clouds. The moon, a slim crescent in the night sky.

"That was unexpected," comes a deep voice.

He's leaning in the open doorway, a glass of red wine in each hand. Back in his jeans, no shirt, barefoot. So fucking sexy.

"What was unexpected?" I ask, sitting up and scooting back to lean against the headboard.

I don't bother with the pretense of modesty; I don't clutch the flat sheet to my chest. I just let him look.

He saunters toward me and extends one glass to me. I sip; the wine is rich, thick, bold, dry.

He gestures to the bed. "That." A long sip. "Us. Him. The whole… thing."

"Not what you thought it'd be?" I ask him.

He shakes his head; his hair is wet, recently washed. "I felt more jealous than I thought I would."

I hide a knowing smirk in the wineglass. "I know. I noticed."

"Noticed?" He quirks an eyebrow. "You *noticed*? Honey, you were pushing that button for all it was worth."

"I wouldn't say that," I mutter, knowing he's right.

"You liked seeing me jealous." It's not a question.

I shrug. "Sure I did. It was hot."

"Me being jealous was hot?" he sounds utterly disbelieving.

I nod. "Super hot."

There's a gleam in his eye. Anger? I don't know. I can't read it. Playful? Mischievous? A little of all that, maybe.

" So, where is our blond friend?" I ask. "Is he still here?" God, am I really still pushing his buttons? I need to stop.

"Yeah, but he's just getting ready to go to work."

Right then I hear the soft chime of the doorbell. He goes to answer it and I watch him swagger out of the bedroom, tight ass cupped perfectly by expensive denim. A few seconds later I hear three familiar voices talking together, discussing the show the red-haired woman just returned from.

I finish the glass of wine and realize that what I want more than another glass of wine is a hot shower. I'm crusty from recent activities and, god, a shower sounds beautiful. I grab the rest of the wine, and pour the last of it into my goblet. I take my glass into the shower with me and turn on the water so hot it nearly scalds me. I luxuriate in the large shower, taking my time washing my hair and scrubbing my skin.

The shower is equipped with a lot of gels and soaps but, curiously, there is also a matched set of high-end color-safe shampoo and conditioner for red hair.

I'm hit by a burning, gut-twisting emotion. Jealousy?

I think so, yes.

I'm a natural blond, so there's only one person I can think of who might need this kind of hair product.

And I'm pissed.

But do I have any right to be, considering what I just did?

I use the shampoo and conditioner anyway, because it's quality stuff. I rinse, shut off the water and step out. I towel off my hair and my body, wrapping a huge bath towel around me. As I leave the bathroom, I can hear them.

His voice, low and deep.

Her voice, breathy and excited, yet sultry and sexy at the same time.

Then I hear an amused huff of laughter.

"Yeah?" she asks, her voice low, just above a whisper. "Like this?"

"Yeah, just like that," he says, his voice tight, buzzing with pleasure. I know that tone in his voice. I know what it means.

Jealousy burns bright, followed by anger.

But I also feel that damned specter of curiosity.

I walk on silent feet to the bedroom door, which is open, just a crack. I peer out.

He's leaning back against the front door. I can just barely see him; his head is tipped back, eyes closed. His jeans are tugged down around his knees and I can see his abs and his hairy, powerful thighs, but nothing in between. I can't see any more than that because the red-haired woman is on her knees in front of him.

She's giving him a blowjob.

One hand is clutching his ass, the other is in front of her face, near her chin, and I can see her arm moving, her wrist sliding up and down.] Her head bobs. Crimson hair, loose, wild, a profusion of scarlet waves.

My gut twists into a knot. He's got his fingers buried in her hair, and he's pulling her against him, encouraging her to take him deeper. And shit if she doesn't do exactly that, letting go of his cock for a moment to brush her hair out of the way, and then she grasps him again and bobs harder, deeper. I can hear her gagging on his dick, hear the wet slurping, sliding sounds. He grunts. She moans.

I watch, because I can't look away.

And then his eyes slide open lazily.

His gaze is directed at me.

A smirk curls the corners of his mouth.

Bastard. He's getting back at me.

What follows is an almost out-of-body experience. My hand lifts. I watch it rise up, watch my fingertips, all five of them, touch the white wood of the bedroom door. I gently push it open. The hinges squeak, ever so softly, but it's enough.

She pauses, just for a second. She knows I'm here.

I walk across the thick rug over to them.

I am naked but for the towel wrapped around my torso, tucked under my armpits. My hair is wet, stringy, and sticking to my shoulders.

My eyes are narrowed and my breath is coming in long, deep gusts. I'm angry. I'm jealous. I'm confused.

I'm less than a foot away from them, right behind her. His eyes are on me, his hands in her scarlet locks, pulling her against him as she sucks him eagerly, ferociously.

She doesn't slow in her movements, even though she must surely know I am standing right behind her, watching her suck my man's cock.

Or is he even my man?

Now I doubt it.

Suddenly, I don't know anything.

Or rather, I realize I never did. I only *thought* he was my man. Now seeing her again, and knowing she has an established presence in this home, I wonder.

I cast my thoughts aside and my eyes follow his fingers as they descend from her scarlet hair down to her shoulders and to the thin straps of her dress. I watch in rapt attention as he slides them aside and off her shoulders. The fabric falls, exposing her breasts. She does a little shimmy, and it falls to pool around her waist. She's not wearing a bra.

God, she's still sucking his cock, and she's making quite a show of it. Slow. Deliberate. Teasing. Backing away, then sliding down. A lot of tongue. She's using her hand as much as her mouth, too. God, she's good. He's struggling mightily, his eyes narrowed to slits, his head resting back against the door, breathing hard, abs tensed, trying to hold back.

And then he moves and pulls away from her. His shoulder blades touch the wall, his hips are thrust forward, and his cock juts hugely and proudly away from his body. God, that cock—he's wet with saliva. Glistening.

Her fingernails are painted silver, glittering like the lights outside the windows. Her fingers are thin, delicate and long. They wrap around his thick cock at the base, and slide up slowly to the tip, her palm engulfs the broad head, and then she squeezes and twists around the head and plunges her fist down. He thrusts into her hand, hissing.

"Fuck..." he growls. He reaches out and grabs her hair at the back of her head and jerks her face to his cock, shoving himself into her mouth. It's a rough, violent, commanding gesture. I expect her to fight it or to say something, but she doesn't. She only opens her mouth wide and takes his dick—all those long thick inches—right down her throat, and she moans in obvious pleasure as she does so.

But her eyes, oh...her eyes are on me. Gray, storm-cloud gray. Cunning. Not malicious, necessarily, but cunning. Wickedly intelligent eyes. Knowing eyes. Teasing, mischievous, sex-hot eyes. They don't just flick over me and return to him, oh no. They *peruse* me. Roam. Search.

The girl next door definitely has another side to her.

She's devouring me.

And she's every bit as hungry and salacious as the blond man who was here so recently—here in this apartment...

...And in me.

She's looking at me with open interest and I suddenly feel naked.

She's missing nothing. Not my legs beneath the towel and certainly not my cleavage. A droplet of water from my wet hair slides slowly down my shoulder. Hungrily, her eyes follow its path down my throat, over my clavicle, between my breasts. She regards my face with interest, taking in my platinum hair and my glistening eyes.

I'm momentarily confused.

Why is she looking at me like that?

Why does her gaze make me feel so shaky and so unsure of myself?

Why does her stare heat me up in a way I have never experienced before?

It's not the same way I feel when a man looks at me. It's similar, but not the same. I feel the heat between my thighs. The fire in my core. The hunger. But it's different. Softer, but somehow *more*....

I watch her lips wrap around his cock; my lips twitch, remembering, knowing how that feels. Her fingers slide and caress his thickness; my fingers twitch, remembering, knowing how that feels.

She switches hands, her right hand releases his cock and her left hand takes its place. Her right hand stretches out and snags the bottom edge of my towel. She tugs hard, enough that I'm pulled forward two short steps, enough that I'm within touching distance of them both.

They are both looking at me. Waiting? I don't know.

He reaches out and untucks the edge of the towel.

Her fingers tug at the same time, and the thick white terrycloth falls and pools at my feet.

I'm naked.

Wet.

Droplets of water dip down my shoulders, between my shoulder blades, between my breasts. Yes, wet like that.

But also...*wet.*

One of his hands remains buried in her hair, and the other, now that my towel is gone, caresses my boobs. One, then the other. Caresses, cups, kneads. And then he tweaks my nipple. Flicks it. I gasp, and my breath catches. He bends down and to the side, a slightly awkward movement, and captures my nipple in his mouth. He sucks hard, and then releases it with a *pop*, and his tongue laps against my nipple.

I'm about to step away, but I feel a hand trail up the inside of my leg, from ankle to thigh, a light, teasing touch. Soft, gentle, feminine. I shiver and my nipples, already hard, sharpen into diamonds. My cunt, already wet, drips.

Oh god.

Why does this feel so good?

She does it again.

I look down, and watch. She's still got those plump lips wrapped around his cock, and one hand is still slowly and even lovingly caressing him near the root, but the other is at my ankle, the opposite one now, and is tracing a path upwards along my leg. She's tickling the side of my knee, the back of my knee. Up, up the back of my thigh, reaching between my legs to carve delicate fingertips over the back of my thigh, the inside, and then up over the outer edge of one side of my labia. She moves back down the other lip, down the inside of my thigh, around the back, down my knee, tickling the backside. Cupping my ankle now, palm against my skin, and roaming, sliding up my flesh, up the back of my knee, up the back my thigh, and then she's cupping my ass cheek, small hands and long, delicate, soft fingers clawing into the fat and muscle of my ass. She pats it lightly, as if testing the bounciness, and then she goes to the other cheek, cups, claws, caresses, and skates down the back.

All the while, his mouth and hand are on my tits, alternating between them.

Holy shit.

I'm completely off balance.

Dizzy, flush with ache and pleasure and confusion. I have to steady myself, and the only place to put my hands is on him, and on her. So I do. I rest my hand on his waist, and on her shoulder, and regain my balance.

And god, the disparity in the sensation of touching them both is heady. Soft, warm skin and delicate, bird-like bones contrasted with solid muscle and hard bone and hot flesh.

I close my eyes and give in to the sensation.

My left hand flutters through thick sheaves of hair, soft skin, and slim shoulders, all unfamiliar. My right hand seeks the familiar: ridges of abdominal muscles, the hard round bubble of his ass, hairy thighs.

My left hand slips down and finds a warm slope of downy soft flesh, and a pebbled nipple. My throat closes, and my core clenches, and my heart trips, then hammers in my chest. I cup her breast, and the feel of this woman's tit in my hand is utterly unfamiliar and alien, yet it makes me shiver and shudder. I don't let go, I knead it the same way I like my tits touched; sure and firm, but gentle. I tweak her nipple the way I like mine toyed with, twisted, flicked, and pinched, and I hear a soft gasp and then her fingers find my inner thighs and slide up the seam of my pussy. She hesitates.

And then she delves in.

And the way she touches me…

I'm lost—

She just…*knows*.

She swipes and flicks and circles my clit with surety and familiarity, as if she's masturbating herself. She knows *exactly* how I like to be touched, and it brings me to orgasm within seconds, heat rifling through me, twisting and knifing through my core. I gasp and rock against her fingers, and then she slips two fingers deep inside me and scours me for my wetness and smears it all over me. She begins touching me all over again with my own wetness, an unnecessary but delirium-making lubrication.

And all the while, he is worshipping my tits. Lapping them. Cupping them. Flicking my nipples, licking them. Kissing my flesh.

And me?

I toy with her breasts as if they were my own.

But now, I'm hungry.

And not just for his ass, his abs, and his thighs.

I open my eyes and she backs away, his dick falling free from her lips. My hand wraps around the thick mushroom head of his beautiful cock, and I stroke him. Her hand is at his root, and she strokes him. And he's…god, he's gone. Rapturous. In heaven. We don't stroke him in unison. Our hands bump and collide, nudge, she meeting mine on the upstroke, mine meeting hers on the down stroke.

She leans toward me, her lips parted. Her eyes are on mine and I don't look away; her gaze is a storm cloud glittering with lust.

Her lips touch my labia, and I cease breathing. I stare down and watch as her tongue slides out from between her lips and spears into my cunt and flicks my clit. A lick, just one, and I'm helpless. I lean forward, against her mouth, and she grins. She laughs, knowing exactly what I'm feeling.

I have no idea what comes over me, but I find myself burying my fingers in her hair—god, her hair is softer than silk and a perfect shade of scarlet, and so thick. I pull her against my pussy.

And she, willing, eager, hungry, lascivious, goes where I direct her. Her mouth mashes against my pussy and her tongue slides into me, and curls to lap up my dripping juices. She strokes my clit, and now she tongue-fucks me with the same familiar skill as she finger-fucked me. She eats me out the way I would beg a man to eat me, but I don't have to say a word, don't have to nudge or breathe hard to indicate she's doing it right. She *knows.* She laps and licks, sucks and spears and slurps and I'm dizzy and delirious and wild, gripping her hair in one hand to hold her face against my cunt, and stroking his big glorious perfect cock with my other as I come and come and come like a wildfire blazing out of control.

I feel him thickening, throbbing and thrusting uncontrollably into our hands.

My eyes go to hers, and she knows as well as I do how close he is. She pulls me down, and I go to my knees. His fingers knot into my wet hair. Eager, now, I reach out and find her slit, and she widens her thighs to allow me access. I find her cunt wet and ready, her clit thick and plump and hard and I flick it as I would my own, reaching curling fingers into her slit to smear her wetness all over her throbbing clit. She moans, now, and the sound is so brazenly needy, so erotic, that I have no control over myself, no way to resist the urge to lean in, lean close, and take her mouth with mine. And fuck, *fuck*, she tastes like me, but her mouth is soft and her lips are wet and I also taste him, and that, Jesus, that's what does me in, the taste of his cock and my cunt on her lips.

I kiss her and shove my tongue between her teeth and taste her tongue on mine, a vicious and horny and somehow sweet kiss, and then she breaks away to bury his cock between her lips, one hard hungry thrust, and then she backs away and glances at me to indicate to me it's my turn, so I take him next. I open my throat and part my lips and fit his hot hard wet cock into my mouth and taste his pre-cum and her saliva, and I take him deep and hard for a moment.

And then I back off, and she takes over.

We trade, again and again, his fists in our hair, my fingers in her pussy, hers in mine, my lips around his huge throbbing dick and my mouth crushing against her swollen lips and I don't know what's what or who's who. My only awareness is the combined taste of him and her and me, and the feel of her tight cunt around my thrusting fingers. Then I feel him tense and hear him growl, and his fists jerk in our hair, twice.

I've got him down my throat as he begins to let go, and then he pulls out quickly.

I watch his big rough hand clench around his cock and he takes over jerking himself, but she's not having that, oh no, she goes after him with eyes wide and lips parted, and she takes his first spurting gush on her mouth, on her face, and then he pivots slightly and I take him in my mouth and swallow the hot salty musk of his cum rather than take it on my face, and then he's backing away and I'm watching her take him down her throat and watch her swallow, and as she's swallowing his cock and his cum, she's bucking into my hand, moaning around him, choking as she tries to moan and come and swallow all the same time.

I shove my fingers deep inside her and feel her clench around me as she comes. I slide my fingers out of her and smear them in hard fast circles around her clit until she's helpless to do anything but fall backward to the floor in the foyer, and I—god, what has come over me?

Who am I? Who is this person doing these things? Why do I fucking love this so much? Why am I going utterly mad, utterly haywire for the taste of cunt on my tongue, the feel of pussy around my fingers? I twist away from him and go to my knees and bury my face between her thighs, lap at her slit with my tongue like a dog drinking from a bowl of water.

"Fuck...*fuck* that's hot," he grunts, his voice guttural. Big hands grab her; grab me, lifting us to our feet. "Let's take this somewhere more comfortable."

My knees are shaking, she's leaning on me for balance, and he's got his arms around our waists, one of us on either side, leading us to his bedroom. My hands reach for him, roaming his chest, fondling his flaccid but still impressive cock. As my fingers slide up his chest I feel feminine hands collide with mine, and my fingers caress hers, tangle with hers, all this on the hard muscular wall of his chest.

And then we're in his bedroom, all three of us crawling across the rucked, rumpled sheets, and she's falling to her back, crimson hair splaying across the white sheets. Her creamy thighs are parted, spread open for me.

For one brief moment I find myself wondering who I am. Why do I feel these things, why do I feel this hot hunger for a woman, when only an hour ago I was glutting myself on cock and male muscle?

I am a puzzle to myself.

But I don't fight it.

The mystery only heightens the eroticism.

I feel him somewhere behind us, near the foot of the bed, and I'm vaguely aware of a rustling of clothes. I can hear him breathing. But, for now, he is a silent presence.

She's on her back, heels digging into her ass cheeks, head on the pillow, hair a scarlet halo on the white fabric. She has big breasts, not as big as mine, but large all the same. Firm. Real. High and tight. Her taut pink nipples are centered on small, dark areolae. Gravity has allowed each breast to fall to the side ever so slightly. Pale, pale skin, milk white and flawless, long limbs. Those fingers, delicate, small, are roaming her body, skating up her thighs, palms lifting and releasing her tits. Spine arching. Eyes wide, cheeks flushed pink, lips parted, tongue running over her upper lip, then her lower lip, tasting the corner of her mouth

She's staring at me and then glancing behind me, over in his direction.

I crawl on my hands and knees toward her, a little more nervous now that we're in the bedroom. I was lost to the heat of the moment, there in the foyer. But now I'm a little less sure of myself.

She lifts her hips, and my eyes are drawn to her slit.

Plump, pink labia, the tip of a prominent clit peeking out. Tight.

Wet. God, so wet.

Something inside me shifts. Deepens. Sharpens.

My nerves fade away.

I crawl across the mattress toward her, and she reaches for me. She slips all of her fingers into my hair, tenderly, gently, affectionately, as if she knows me, likes me, as if we've done this before a thousand times, as if this isn't new and alien. She's slow and careful and insistent as she guides me between her thighs, guides my face to her core. She pushes my damp hair away from my face and smooths it over my shoulders and down my back, and then she cups the back of my head with both hands and brings me to her.

I begin slowly, tentatively with a questing lick with my tongue, up the outside of her pussy and along the seam of her tight lips. She gasps, a soft sound. And then I lick again, and again, still tasting the outside, exploring the length of her slit with the flat of my tongue, and now, licking from bottom to top, I stiffen my tongue and slide it against her clit, which is hard and begging for me. As I circle my tongue around it, she moans, grinds her hips against my face, and I hear a male grunt behind me. I feel the bed dip.

He's directly behind me—I feel his heat, his hard body.

I'm on my knees, my chest against the mattress, and my ass in the air. He takes full advantage of my position, smoothing big rough hands over my buttocks, caressing the globes softly, reverently, then strokes down my thighs and back up, cupping my hips. Down again, and now his hand slips between my thighs and nudges them apart. I open wide for him, moaning against her clit as he dips a long thick finger into me. I flick my tongue against her clit, and then suck it between my teeth using my lips and tongue to create suction, bringing her to writhing, arching madness. I'm moaning too because his fingers are inside me, scissoring, and then gliding out, spreading my essence over my clit.

A moment of absence, and then I feel his hair soft against my inner thighs and his lips kiss my flesh, my thighs, and then his tongue mirrors what mine is doing, as if he can somehow see what I'm doing. Licking when I lick, sucking when I suck, flicking when I flick. It's hard to eat pussy while I'm coming, but that only makes it all the hotter, because I'm totally out of control, helpless, lost to this. I'm swiping my tongue around her clit in crazed circles and rocking my hips to grind my pussy against his mouth and I'm coming and she's coming, we're both screaming and thrashing, and now he's pushing me forward and throwing me to my back beside her.

"Let me watch you kiss," he commands. "Touch each other some more."

I twist my head, heart pounding, cunt throbbing, gut twisting, the aftershocks making me shudder. She's in the same straits, barely able to breathe, eyes heavy, her hair sticking to her temples, and her breasts heaving.

She's the first to move. She slides closer to me, brushes her palms over my breasts on her way to cupping my cheek with a soft, tender hand. Then she pulls my face to her own.

Kissing a man is a study in the exchange of power. It's a battle. Dominance versus submission. Kissing her is...a vastly different proposition. She kisses me to show me...something. To let me see something, feel something. To take something from me and, in so doing so, give me something in return.

Her lips are the softest, warmest things I've ever tasted, wet, willing, pliable, and plump. Eager. Moving on mine with ravishing passion, as if kissing me is delirium and madness and wonder all at once. I forget everything; forget me, him, us, the blond man from a few hours ago, so there's nothing but her and me and the kiss.

I'm reminded of reality by the feel of a finger in my pussy, a thumb at my clit. By the way she gasps suddenly against my lips. I open my eyes and see him on the bed between us, his mouth on her pussy and his fingers inside me. I don't know how he keeps everything straight, how he moves in such perfect synchronicity, his right hand tweaking her nipple, his left hand at my cunt, his lips on her clit, moving surely, unerringly, unhurriedly, driving both of us to the wrenching cusp of orgasm before shifting it all around and moving his mouth to my core and his fingers to hers and pinching my nipple so hard I whimper. And then, right when I'm a breath away from tumbling over the edge into orgasm, he switches it up again, and judging by the hiss against my lips, she's as deliciously frustrated as I am.

Again and again, he brings us both to the edge and then switches, until we're wild with need, buzzing, humming, and snarling with pent-up sexual energy. How long does this go on? I have no idea. I have no concept of time, only sensation. Only feeling. Only mouths, and fingers, and tongues plunge and push and pull and the edge is right there, right there—

We both come at the same time, and we can't keep kissing for the rip of orgasm blasting through us, our lips both frozen together, fused, breath coming in ragged gasps, and I twist toward her, clasp against her, feel her soft skin and full breasts against mine, my nipple brushing and rubbing hers, sending my orgasm higher and wilder, her tongue sliding along my lower lip and her whimpers and shrieks blending and tangling with mine. He's rapacious as he devours our cunts, back and forth, and back and forth, using his fingers and his mouth. He's all over us, milking every last shred of ecstasy out of us.

I'm still gasping, still shuddering, still whimpering when I feel him slide up between our sweaty, trembling bodies, hard, angular muscle sandwiched between softness and curves; he twists toward me, palms my face, claims my mouth. I feel movement, break the kiss for a breath and catch a glimpse of her hand on his cock, sliding leisurely up and down its stunning length.

I rest my cheek against his and catch my breath and watch her fondle his cock. Watch the way she twists her fist around the plump head, plunges down to the root and flutters fast shallow pumps at the base and then alternates to long slow glides.

God, why is that hot? Shouldn't I feel jealous? I do, a little. But not because she's doing that to him, no, but more so because I want to touch him, too.

So I do. I slide down his body and take his balls in my hand, cup them, caress them, and suck them into my mouth. I cup them in my palm again and massage them gently. I take his cock between my lips and feel her hand pumping him, and then we find a rhythm together, me sucking while she plunges both fists around his thickness.

He's gasping, grunting, cursing. Thrusting into my mouth, into her fists. Hands in my hair, on her back and waist and ass.

"Fuck, fuck." His voice is deep, bass, guttural, and rife with need. "Stop, Jesus, *stop*."

We both stop, and his hands go to my face. He pulls me up and settles me on his stomach. Eager and with a heady sense of need, I lift up and reach down to guide his cock into my cunt, sinking down on him, burying him to the hilt inside me.

"Fuck, you're so goddamn tight and wet, baby," he mutters. Then, reaching for her, he pulls her toward him. Guides her leg over his torso, brings her slit to his face. "And you…god, babe, you taste like fucking sugar."

I ride his cock, and she rides his face.

She angles and grinds, and I lean forward, wrap my hands around her big, bouncing tits and flick my thumbs over her nipples and kiss her neck and she reaches behind her body and somehow finds my clit with her two middle fingers, and everything is sensation, him fucking me, her fingering me, her tits heavy and hot and soft in my palms.

Between his thick, pounding cock and her sure, quick fingers, I come hard and fast, grinding on him in wild circles, cursing nonstop, and clutching her tits with all my strength.

I lift up, letting him slide out. I nip at her earlobe and tweak her nipples. "Your turn to fuck him," I hear myself say.

She shudders, at the cusp again. I move off him, and she slides down his body, impales him into her in one smooth motion, letting her head droop forward and a gasp rush out of her as he fills her, and god, I watch the way he splits and stretches her, watch his cock disappear into her slit.

That shouldn't make me hot and bothered, but it does.

Part of me says this should all feel wrong, but it doesn't. It feels right.

It feels…familiar.

He pulls me toward him again, and somehow I'm ready for yet more. I throw a leg over him, reversed this time, so I'm facing his feet. I position my knees against the mattress and lean forward so he can press his firm lips and nimble tongue to my core. Leaning forward, I plant my fists in the mattress, gasping and writhing as he takes his time now, leisurely, luxuriously, slowly driving me towards yet another climax. I've lost count, now. Too many. So many. I ache deliciously from them, and as another ramps up inside me, I find myself gasping, on all fours, rocking back into his mouth, tits swaying against his stomach, and this motion brings me closer to her, brings her breasts to my face, and I suckle her thick, hard nipple into my mouth and she whimpers as I bite down gently. I redistribute my weight so I can worm a hand between her body and his, and I find her clit with my finger.

This doesn't last long, though. Without warning, she rises up, lets his cock flop free, rotates to ride him reverse cowgirl, wasting no time getting him back deep inside her. I'm treated to the sight of him buried balls deep in her cunt, her slit stretching to accommodate his enormous size, and she's riding him for all she's worth, slamming up and down, rough and hard and unrelenting.

Her asshole is bared to me and without thinking or considering I spit on my fingers and smear the saliva around the knot of muscle and slip my middle finger inside, slowly, carefully, millimeter by millimeter, until she rocks forward and whimpers and relaxes for me, and then I can slide my finger all the way in to the last knuckle.

And now, god, fuck, oh god, he's lapping at me hard and fast and my climax is building and my core is throbbing and she's clenching around my finger and he's fucking her with all he's got while eating me out, and we're all grunting and cursing and shouting *oh shit, fuck, right there, god don't stop.* We're all moving and writhing and fucking, and she's coming apart on top of him, fucking him so hard the wet squelching and the slapping flesh on flesh is all I can hear even over my own breathless whimpers of climax.

I fit a second finger inside her as she comes, and she's half-crying from the force of her orgasm, gasping, almost sobbing.

I end up on the bed, on my back, a voyeur, watching raptly as my man fucks this other woman.

Then he throws her off and bends her forward over the bed, positioning himself behind her and slamming hard into her cunt. His eyes fix on me as begins to fuck. Hard, rough thrusts. Hands gripping her hips, yanking her back into him. Brown eyes hooded and unblinking, assessing my reaction as he fucks her in front of me. She watches me too, arms outstretched, mouth open wide, brows drawn down, body rocking forward with each powerful fuck of his trim hips.

I can't move, can't breathe. I can't look away. They're both watching me watch them. God, he's fucking her so hard, so goddamn hard it has to hurt. He's not fucking her to get her off, but I can tell she will. I can tell by the expression on her face, the way her eyes widen and her lips tremble and her body is wracked, curling back into his thrusts, spine arching and bowing up to shove her big round ass into his driving hips.

Fuck, I can feel it. Watching him fuck her, I can almost feel what she's feeling. The burning stretch of my pussy around his cock, the thickness of it gliding in and out of me, filling me, the way his hips slam against my ass with a loud clapping sound, the sweet slide out, the sweeter mad crash back in. Fuck, I'm hot all over again, writhing, watching. My fingers find my clit; I'm masturbating, watching him fuck her to mindless orgasm. He grabs her hair, wraps the crimson length of it around his big hard fist and jerks her head back, roughly, forcefully, mercilessly, then fucks her even harder, grunting like an animal as she thrashes and screams and fucks him back just as hard, their eyes never leaving me.

With one hand knotted in her hair, the other lifts in the air, draws back, and swings down and cracks her wickedly across her ass cheek, sending it quivering, making her scream even louder in equal parts pleasure and pain. God, now he's spanking her with each thrust, one cheek and then the other, again and again in time with each ramming crush of his cock, and she keeps on coming, screaming herself hoarse.

My fingers fly, and they're watching that, watching me bring myself to yet another orgasm, this one rising up slowly and heavily.

And then, as I begin to whimper and whine and arch up off the bed with the searing fury of my climax, he pulls out of her pussy. He wraps his fist around his cock and jerks himself. Three hard yanks of his cock, and a jet of cum spurts out of him to splash across her back, up her spine, and then another jerk and another gush pools on her ass and dribbles down the seam of her ass, and then one last spasm and more dripping cum on her ass.

I come so hard I black out.

I return to awareness slowly.

I smell him, first.

He's clean. Smelling of soap and aftershave and man.

I feel him, second.

Muscles. Body hair. Flesh against my flesh.

I'm on my side, and he's spooning me, breathing steadily, deeply. Awake, but relaxed. His hand explores the length of my body from knee to breast in a line, and then scours back down. He caresses my thigh, teasing in, just a little, then up to my hip, cupping my hipbone. Fingers move teasingly toward my core, but then he backs off and slides his hand up my belly, tracing the line of my diaphragm. He tickles the underside of my breast, and then slides a fingertip in a ring around my nipple, which hardens and slowly stands to attention.

Something else hardens, as he realizes I'm awake.

Something big, a thickening between the globes of my ass.

His lips brush the shell of my ear. "You're a dirty girl, aren't you?"

I writhe my ass against him, sliding his cock between my ass cheeks. Good god, how the fuck are either of us horny *again*?

"Yeah," I breathe. "A very dirty girl."

"We did some bad things today, sweetness."

"Lots of *very* bad things." I angle my hips, lift my thigh, reach between my legs for his dick, fit the head to my slit, and then with a sigh, sink him in. "You tried to make me jealous, with her, didn't you?"

He laughs, a rough scraping chuckle. "Yeah, that backfired a little."

"A little?" I laugh, sarcastically. "I got off harder watching that than I did when you fucked me."

"I noticed." He slides his arm around my hips, and that arm becomes an iron bar pinning me against him. "Might have to fix that."

"I thought you were going to come inside her," I say.

He grinds into me, and I arch my spine to press my ass back against him.

"Never," he growls. "Only you."

"Only me?"

A laugh. "That's how it's always been with us, right? We fool around with other people, but I only ever come inside you."

His palm cups my breast as he starts to lose control.

"That's right," I breathe. "All your cum, just for me."

"You want it?" He's breathless too, his hips pistoning hard and fast now.

"Yeah, baby," I gasp, tilting my head back to rest it against his shoulder. "Give me that cum. Give it all to me. Let me feel it."

"Fuck…" he presses his hand over my pussy, slides a finger against my clit. "I'm close already. So fucking close…"

I twist my head and find his mouth.

Instead of kissing me, he bites my lower lip. His fingers pinch my nipple hard enough that I forget about kissing because it hurts and steals my breath and then his fingers slide down my body to massage my clit and I'm coming, coming fast and coming hard.

My cunt squeezes around his cock, and that's all it takes for him to find his own release, grunting in my ear, breath huffing on my cheek and his voice loud, body thrashing, cock slamming into me and filling me with his thickness. I feel him twitch, pulse, throb, and then he thrusts into me and flutters, pushing deeper and deeper, grinding harder and harder into me as he comes, and I feel a hot wet rush, a blast of cum filling me and spilling out and he's still going, still thrusting, still fucking, still coming.

I lose my breath for a moment, lose thought, dizzy, overwhelmed. Something about the feel of him like this, intimate, just us, the way he goes limp behind me even as he remains hard inside me, his arm laying heavily on my ribs, mouth pressed in a long kiss against my shoulder.

I let myself lie in his embrace, and just breathe. Feel him. Feel us. Something in this silence between us is...alive. I feel him. Not just his body, but *him*. His soul. His essence is wrapped around mine.

Something binds us together in this darkness. A deepness. The meaning is secret, beautiful...and fleeting. I reach to find it, seek to drown myself in it, but it flees. I'm left gasping, near tears from the beauty of it, and from the absence of it.

I'm facing away from the windows, facing the bathroom.

I see another door, one I hadn't noticed until now.

Was it there, earlier, when I took a shower? I don't know. It's hard to remember.

And now I can't seem to look away. It's a black door, plain and unadorned, except for the handle, which is a modern black knob. It's partially ajar, opened just a sliver, just a crack.

I feel his awareness behind me.

There's a sudden strange tension, a palpable heaviness to the moment between us. Sadness? Perhaps.

A knowing.

A farewell.

His lips touch the side of my neck, the hollow behind my ear, my jawline, my cheekbone. "You have to go, now." His tone indicates there will be no refusal.

"I don't want to."

"I know."

But I stand up. My legs are shaking, trembling. Aftershocks still wrack my body. Cum leaks out of me and drips down the inside of my thigh. I feel him behind me, his hands on my waist. I walk forward, and he moves with me.

We stand at the door. I twist the knob, slowly, reluctantly. It opens toward me, swinging on silent hinges to reveal darkness. Blackness. Nothingness.

A familiar blackness, a familiar nothingness.

I don't want to go through.

I want to stay here.

I don't know what's on the other side. Or do I? I can't remember. I only know him, behind me. His body. The passion, the all-consuming erotic need. His touch.

I only know shuddering in the darkness with him, and sometimes the breath and the heat and the slide of someone else's skin against my own, against his, many limbs tangled together in a secret moment out of time.

I want to stay here and feel more of that. I want to feel more of everything.

But despite my wishes, my feet carry me forward involuntarily. His hands press against my waist, pushing me forward and pulling back in equal measure. He wants me to stay, but he knows I can't, and he doesn't know how to verbalize it either, anymore than I do.

One step, two.

Three.

The threshold is before me, and he is behind me. There is no in between, no waiting, no putting it off. My feet obey some unheard command, a pulling, a pushing.

I step through, and his hands fall away, his heat diminishes, his presence is enveloped by darkness and cold and then…

Nothing.

&#42; &#42; &#42;

Silence.

Perfect, utter silence.

A drowning quiet.

A longing, deep and unfulfilled, soul-deep, a bone-deep *need* for something I cannot have; the first sensation.

Pang of loss, gnaw of guilt, acid bite of shame, burning heat of lust, a deep delicious soreness in all the right places—all of these sensations roil and coil and mingle together, wedded; the second sensation.

I open my eyes; the third sensation.

I'm in the room of black doors.

The white cot is beneath me and, to my left, a small square black table on which is the thick white candle, flickering merrily, rivulets of melted wax dripping down the sides to pool and harden on the silver candlestick.

Beyond me, I can see six pools of orange-yellow light and six doors: four black, one green, and one silver.

I lay still. The only sounds are my heart thumping in my ear and my breath, soughing in and out slowly. This is all that exists, within and without.

How long do I lay in the warmth of that candlelit room, not thinking, not feeling, barely even existing?

I don't know.

Time out of time.

But no, that isn't right either. There is no time. If you cannot measure the passage of time, then there is no time. The only measure of anything is the infinitesimal shortening of the candle, and the pool of hardening wax around the base of the silver candlestick.

I feel tiredness in my bones, lethargy in my muscles, and an overwhelming unwillingness to get up.

I close my eyes once more and feel the heaviness of sleep pulling me under, and then I'm floating as I drift along the edge of consciousness into that place of not sleeping, but of not quite being awake.

And then sleep pulls me down, and I am helpless to resist.

Everything fades. Memory of anything, knowledge of anything— it all fades away to nothingness along with my knowledge of my body, my mind, and myself.

Only darkness remains, only the vague point of *I*, floating in eternal nothingness.

Floating away.

Drifting.

That infinitesimal point of *I*, the dot that is *I* begins to brighten and come into focus.

Hardens. Expands.

The darkness is not my friend. I won't let it swallow me.

I—

I am.

I am.

The point of *I* becomes a pinprick of light.

And then it grows.

Flickers.

Dances, wavering and jumping, twisting and leaping, guttering, flaring.

A candle flame.

It calls to me.

Breathes upon me, into me.

I cling to that life, that light, that breath. I let it push through me. Let it diminish the darkness, until I can feel myself once again. Feel the fullness of my body, the expanse of my mind, the presence of my sense of self.

The darkness wants to pull me down. It desires me. Seeks me. Hunts me.

There is something alive in the darkness of unseeing.

My eyes flick open, and I sit up and touch the floor with my feet. I scan the pools of light and blackness in between.

Eventually, when the languidness has faded, I rise off the cot.

Six doors.

The second door has disappeared and my memory, fuzzy and hazy and vague, tells me little. I focus, think, strain to remember.

I remember very little.

Only him.

Wishing I could be his. Knowing I'm not.

Nearly kissing him. A tease, an almost-kiss.

I remember a different version of him. But there is confusion, even there. Despite the rushing chaotic bliss of lust, acquiescing to the hunger within, even then…

Questions without form, without substance. Just the knowledge of them, the idea of them.

Questions unanswered.

Unasked, even.

I focus on remembering—

The first door…

The boxer. Big. Rough. Dominant. Possessive. Virile and primal. The ropes. His violent refusal to kiss me. It doesn't come rushing back; instead it flits and meanders through my mind, out of sequence. The way he fucked me, there at the end. As if it was the last time he'd ever see me, hold me, touch me, fuck me.

The second door…

It only just happened, but it feels like a thousand years ago. The memory is slippery and hard to grasp. Two men—the blond man and *him*, light versus dark, lean and lithe versus broad and massive. A flurrying glut of sensation. Revelling in debauchery. Slipping and sliding down into delicious, all-consuming sin, two men fucking me into delirium. Then her, the scarlet goddess, her mouth on my core, the hunger for her burning inside me, secret at first but then wild and undeniable. Then just him, just us, being filled, taken. A connection, deep and dark and fraught, and so briefly felt.

I scan the room and the remaining doors. I skip over the cutting pain of the green door and the revulsion I feel regarding the silver door.

Number three, then.

My legs move, my feet carry me across the empty space. I halt in front of the door. Black, with the large, silver numeral 3 at the center. Lower down, on the right side of the door, a handle. Trembling, I reach out my hand and touch the handle. It's glass knob. Delicate. I wrap tentative fingers around the faceted glass, and the knob rattles under my touch.

Twist.

Push.

The door creaks and squeals on protesting hinges.

＊＊＊＊

Darkness. Heat. Humidity. The scent of bodies. Soap. Oils. Perfume. The heat of the room allows the scents to comingle, almost becoming cloying.

I can see nothing.

Something presses against me on one side: a body. Soft, warm. The flesh gives in a way only a woman's flesh does. Then I feel other women, jostling and bumping in front of me. To my left, to my right. All around.

The sound of breathing.

Hoarse, fearful breaths.

A whimper.

And then sudden light, brilliant and blinding. A pair of doors opens, and the windows are uncovered.

A man's voice, rough, slurred, and accented. "C'mon, c'mon, girlies! Step on out here, now! Don't be shy, ya'll. Step out, step out."

There is motion as those around me begin to shuffle forward unwillingly, bumping into each other, holding onto whatever is near for balance; a hand grabs my shoulder, another my arm, someone pushes at my spine, small hands, trembling fingers.

"Now ya'll make a line, right here. Right here. Stand still, now. No fidgeting, no talking."

I blink in the blinding light. I squint, closing one eye. The sun is glaring through a window, beaming directly at me, flaring across my vision. I can see only silhouetted shapes and forms. A hand clutching a cane. A hat, broad-brimmed, low-crowned. The swirl of a coattail. A boot. Spurs jingling. I smell sweat, now. Leather. Dust. There's a hint of swirling cold, as if a door had just been shut, and the cold still lingers.

I'm shuffling forward with the others, my feet bare on the smooth wooden flooring. A hand grabs my arm, roughly jerking me to one side and then stopping me in a precise spot, squeezing my arm. *Stay put,* that squeeze said. He strides away, a shotgun tucked under one arm.

I'm still blinking, but I can see a bit more clearly now as my eyes begin to adjust. A line of men stand abreast, opposite, with a bank of windows behind them. They're all dressed warmly. Thick wool coats swirling around leather boots. Snow clings to the soles and heels of the boots. Cravats are tied under necks. Gold chains arc across chests and disappear into watch pockets. I see fine leather gloves, someone clutching a crystal-topped walking stick, another a riding crop, a third a lever-action rifle.

I count seven men, ranging in age from white-haired and weathered to barely old enough to shave, most in between somewhere, but the quality of each man's dress speaks of wealth. Their demeanor and posture shout power, dominance, utter surety of their place in life. Every pair of eyes gleams arrogantly.

To my left and my right are women, and we are also standing in a line abreast. The women, unlike the men, are all of an age: young, nubile, beautiful, none over twenty-five. There are twenty of us, and I stand directly in the middle. We are each of us clad identically in a thin cotton robe. Not even a robe, really, so much as a knee-length bolt of thin, rough-spun cotton with holes for the arms, tied closed with a length of rope. It obscures our bodies, yet does little to cover us, or to keep us warm.

Fear hammers at my heart. No one is speaking, but the silence is fiercely thick with anticipation. Ripe with the fear felt by the women beside me. Lust burns in the eyes of the men. Boots scuff as weight shifts, hands in gloves curl into fists and release, or are tucked into trouser pockets. We women only shiver and tremble.

Boot heels click sharply on the wood floor, calling everyone to attention. A man enters the room from my left, striding with focus and arrogance between the lines of men and women. A woman follows behind him. She stops just inside the door and stands, waiting. The man has a burlap sack in his hands, which clacks and clatters, swinging back and forth as he swiftly strides across the room. He stops at the far end of the line, then reaches into the sack. He withdraws a small square of slate and shoves it into the hands of the first woman in line, then reaches into his trouser pocket and comes up with a chunk of chalk. He scrapes a single vertical number *1* on the slate. Then he steps to the side, reaches into the sack for another piece of slate and hands it to the next woman. He repeats the process, this time scratching out a *2* with a quick flick of his wrist. And so on down the line. I am number ten.

When he reaches the end of the line, he tosses the sack aside, shoves the chalk back into his pocket and brushes his hands together.

He is tall, immensely tall, six foot six, perhaps, but thin and wiry. Elegant. Expensively dressed in a three-piece suit, a gold pocket watch peeks out of his waistcoat pocket, a brown derby hat on his head. He wears a graying brown beard trimmed in the Van Dyke style, the ends waxed and twisted into points. His eyes are cold, hard, and emotionless. Diamond blue and diamond sharp. Calculating.

He stands at the leftmost end of the line, between the men and the women. He withdraws his pocket watch, flips it open, consults it, and replaces it.

"Let us begin." His voice is cultured, smooth. "You have all put in your thousand just to be here. The first to put in another five hundred gets first pick."

"Here." The oldest man, white haired, white goatee, craggy features, weathered skin. "Five hundred." He withdraws a stack of bills from an inner pocket and extends it to the man in charge.

It's clearly pre-counted and accepted as such, for it is not recount-ed. It is pocketed immediately.

"Very well." A hand sweeps to gesture at us women. "Take your pick, sir, and place your offer."

The older man steps forward, crystal-topped walking stick thump-ing. He's on the far right of the line of men, second from the end. His step is spry, strong, and quick, despite his obvious age; the walking stick is affectation. A foot away from the woman at that end, number one, he stops. He eyes her up and down. Blinks once, as if in dismissal, then moves to the next; another dismissal. He walks past the third wom-an without pause; the same silent disregard. At the fourth woman, he stops and nods to himself. He reaches a large, gnarled hand for her robe tie. He pauses with the end of the rope in his fingers, then glances at the man in charge, as if for permission.

He receives a nod and then, with a single sharp tug, the rope is untied and her robe falls open, baring her naked body. His eyes narrow, flitting up and down, perusing her carefully. He drops the end of the rope, takes the slate from her, then steps back one pace.

I cannot look away. I dare not speak. I can only watch in numb, disbelieving horror.

The white-haired man crooks his finger. "Step forward."

The girl hesitates, and then steps forward. Her arms hang at her sides, her hands clenched into fists. White-knuckled.

She has long straight black hair, hanging down to mid-spine, and as she stands, waiting, I can see her hair shaking. She's clearly terrified.

He flicks his finger again. "Off with that. Lemme see you, girl."

She ducks her head, and her shoulders lift as she breathes in deeply. She lifts her chin, vying for courage then shrugs away the rough cotton, and it billows to pool on the floor at her feet. She is thin. Narrow hips. Strong, though. High, round buttocks. Long legs.

He twirls his index finger at her. "Turn."

She pivots in a slow circle. Small breasts, tips upturned. Pale, pale skin. Her ribs show, but not from malnutrition, due rather to her lithe, svelte frame. As she pauses facing us, her eyes scan ours, left to right. A tear trickles down her cheek.

"Back around," comes the gruff order.

She crosses her hands in front of her groin, and the man steps forward. He grabs her wrists and shoves them aside effortlessly. He reaches, curls his fingers between her thighs, roughly shoving them inside her, right here in front of everyone. She cringes, whimpering.

*Click-click.* The sound is unmistakable, loud in the silence—a gun being cocked.

"No touching until you have made your payment, if you please, sir. And you, girl—I believe you were informed of the rules before you were brought in." His gaze rakes to include all of us.

"I shall repeat the instructions, so there can be no misunderstandings. You will not speak. You will not move. That means no covering up. No cowering. Do as you're told immediately. The buyers are not allowed to touch you until they have bought you, but if they do, you will allow it until such time as I see fit to stop them. Is that clear?"

He glares at us, and a few girls mutter responses: *yes; yes, sir.*

He cuts his glare to each of us in turn. "I did not hear all of you. Do you understand the rules?" he bellows.

There's a louder chorus of agreement. I feel apart, separate, numb, disoriented, but I do not speak. Immediately, that unnerving diamond gaze fixes on me. He steps toward me, sharp quick steps. He lifts his hand in which is concealed a small revolver. He touches the barrel to the underside of my chin; the mouth is a cold round **o** digging into the soft flesh just back of my jawbone.

"I didn't hear you, darling," he says in that low voice, razor sharp, the term of endearment becomes an epithet, a threat. "Do...you... *understand?*"

I wobble, gasp. "Yes—yes, sir." The hammer is cocked, and I can see bullets in the chamber.

He steps away, turns, gestures with his empty hand at the woman still standing at the door: she's dressed in a voluminous gown of jade silk, the bodice cut indecently low, propping up a broad expanse of cleavage. Her skirts bell out from her waist and trail behind her. Her blond hair is pulled back from her temples and over her scalp and is fastened at her crown; the rest is loose, falling around her bare shoulders. Her eyes are as blue and hard and calculating as the man running this sale of human flesh. Despite the difference in their hair color, her eyes mark her as his sister.

"If anyone sees fit to break these rules, you shall be sent to my sister here. She runs a brothel, as you should know. And the clientele at that establishment—well, let us merely say they are not quite as… savory…as the men standing before you. I shall leave the details your imaginations. Suffice to say silence and cooperation is, by far, the better option of the two choices left to you."

He holsters the gun beneath his left breast then gestures at the white-haired buyer. "My apologies for the distraction. Have you decided, sir?"

The man nods, stroking his white beard. "I have. Two thousand for the shy little thing here." He holds up the slate. "Two thousand for Number 4."

A quick nod, the Van Dyke beard twitches. "Accepted and agreed."

A bundle of cash is counted by one, handed over, and then re-counted by the other.

The girl, bought and sold, kneels shakily to retrieve her robe. That gnarled hand grabs her by the arm and lifts her to her feet. "Oh, you won't be needing that." The leer in his voice is unmistakable and it makes my flesh crawl.

"But…" her voice is quiet, achingly delicate, tremulous. "It's—it's cold outside."

He doffs his coat and drapes it over her thin shoulders. "Wouldn't want you to be cold, now, would we?" He pinches her nipple, twists it viciously, until she whimpers in pain and tries to curl away. "That wouldn't do at all." Then he tugs the edges of the coat closed and buttons it up.

It's comically big on her. Hanging well past her ankles, trailing on the floor. The sleeves sag several inches past her fingertips.

He prods her into motion and guides her to the doorway leading outside. She picks her way on bare feet across the threshold onto hard-packed snow. The door closes behind them, sending a gust of icy air into the room.

My nipples pebble in reaction to the sudden blast of cold, nearly poking through the thin muslin.

Opposite me, in the middle of the line, a pair of eyes drifts down and fixes on my visibly prominent nipples. Brown eyes. Hard, not quite cold, but…blank, perhaps. Studiously so, maybe. Familiar eyes, in some strange way. Black hair swept back beneath a black, wide-brimmed, low-crowned hat. Full beard cropped close to his jaw.

His eyes slide back up to find mine.

I cannot look away. I don't dare.

Around me, one after another, the women are sold. Purchased, then hustled outside. Some leave completely naked, some with their robes on, others covered in a cloak or coat. All weep piteously, but quietly, as they're sent with their new masters. Their *owners*.

There is one man left—the man with the brown eyes.

Myself and a few other women remain and the seller moves to stand beside me.

"Quite a prize, this one," offers the man in charge. "Minimum bid is two thousand. If you cannot or will not meet that, then I'm afraid you, my boy, are out of luck. Entry fee is non-refundable, you'll remember."

The man looks at me and his fingers twitch. The rope knot flies apart. A sweep of his hand, and the robe drifts to my feet, baring me completely. My knees shake. My nipples throb and ache. I desperately wish to cover my core, to cower, to hide. But I do not. I stand, shoulders back, shaking, fists clenched at my sides, my eyes on the man who, I am positive, is about to purchase me.

Opposite me, brown eyes rake down my body. Slowly, taking time.

Beside me, a hand grips my shoulder and forces me to turn in a slow circle. "I chose this one myself. The high bid, I freely admit, is meant to deter you. If I don't get my price, I might claim her for myself."

His voice in my ear is a low murmur, boiling with lewd promise and provocative threat. He inhales deeply, and his palm slides across my hip, daringly close to my core. "Lots of curve to this one. Imagine the delights to be found in all this—" he cups my breast, and I cannot suppress a shudder of revulsion— "sweet, lush, firm flesh. Imagine the fun you could…"

"Six thousand." The offer comes brusque, rough, and harsh.

"Six? But sir, I —"

Brown eyes flash dangerously; his hand brushes his coat aside and hovers over a gun butt. Threat is woven through that deep voice, deadly and unmistakeable. "Six thousand. Now get your hands off." A thick stack of cash flies to thump at the seller's feet.

The seller bends, retrieves the cash, straightens; he doesn't stop to count it. "Very well, very well." A moment of taut silence. "Do you wish—?"

"What I wish is for you to leave us. Now." This is a command, snapped in a voice that brooks no disobedience.

The seller, the guard, the madam, and the remaining women all leave, and now I'm alone.

With him.

Sold like so much meat.

Possessively, his eyes roam my body, rake over my form. He takes in my breasts, my slit, my hips. He moves toward me, boots clomping noisily, spurs jingling, coat tail billowing behind him. He circles to stand behind me.

"You belong to me, now." He speaks with authority. He's close, smelling of wood smoke and leather and wool. His voice is a deep, rasping grumble, rough, rocky, but his speech is articulate and educated. "Do you understand?"

I shake, tremble, and manage to nod. I clear my throat, find my voice. "Yes. Yes, I—I understand."

"Good. Then there won't be any trouble." His boots thunk noisily as he crosses the wooden floor and kneels to retrieve a pile of neatly folded clothing near the far wall, beneath the bank of windows. He walks back to me and hands me the pile. "Get dressed. We have far to ride, and it's not getting any warmer."

I dress quickly. Flannel underwear. Wool stockings. A thin, fine wool slip, tight against my skin, the hem reaching my knees. Another underdress, this one looser and longer, made from thicker, coarser wool. This is followed by blue-gray calico dress, ankle length, snug at the bust and hips, blossoming into voluminous skirts from my waist. There is a thick wool coat with a deep hood. Warm, fur-lined boots, a little too big. Thick mittens.

Once I'm dressed, he nods and moves toward the door, clearly expecting me to follow. I walk behind him, noticing the holsters tied low on both thighs, revolver handles visible when his coat flaps open.

Outside he mounts a huge black horse, its flanks covered with white patches; he's gripping the reins of another, smaller paint, holding it for me as I make my way across the snow. I mount, settle my skirts over my thighs, and accept the reins.

He eyes me. "You run, I'll catch you." Reins in one fist, the other gloved hand on his thigh. "Won't go well for you, if I have to give chase."

"I won't run," I tell him.

Besides, there's nowhere to run. There is nothing around us but trees and snow and mountains off in the distance. It's a frozen hellscape, and I have no clue where we are. So, no, I won't be running away. He's my only hope for staying alive, it appears. Staying here clearly isn't an option, nor would I choose that even if it were. I'll take my chances with this man.

"All right then. Stay close and keep up."

He rolls his spurs lightly against his horse's flank, and it glides into a smooth trot. My horse follows automatically, trotting just behind the other horse.

Twenty or thirty minutes of riding, and it becomes obvious we're in the foothills of a massive mountain range, and we're headed up into them, angling for a notch between two sky-spearing, snow-capped, craggy peaks. It is bitter cold and the light is fading.

So far, we've stuck to a path meandering through the forest. Not a road, nothing so grand as that. More of a narrow dirt track, once a deer path, perhaps, now used by people. In places, the trees are close together and the branches snap and ricochet against us.

Trees carpet the waist and shoulders of the mountains, and surround us in thick, impenetrable ranks of pine and spruce and fir, the mountains only visible sporadically when glimpsed between the thick branches covered in rustling branches and needles.

We begin to gain altitude and the horses are laboring under the cold and snow and terrain. We are close to breaking through the forest's edge. Before us I glimpse a wide frozen lake, snow-blanketed, and beyond it is miles and miles of wide-open foothills bellying up to the rise of the mountains themselves. This new landscape is comprised of a series of rolling hills with open fields dotted here and there. Trees, birch and aspen, stand in profusion, their branches devoid of leaves. They are silent sentinels, marking our progress.

The sky above is clear blue, cloudless, a wide cerulean dome overwhelming by virtue of its expanse. It is bitterly, bitingly cold. I tug the hood of my coat over my head, burrow back into it, and rub the tip of my nose with a mitten. Despite my warm garments, the cold seeps into my bones.

We angle around the lake and, as we ride, I notice that my new owner's head is never still, but always moving and scanning, and occasionally he twists around to glance at me or further behind us. The skirt of his duster is draped across his horse's hindquarters, the edges pulled away to leave his guns free. He sits straight, spine flat and ramrod stiff, yet his body moves loosely and easily with the rolling walk of his mount's gait. Broad shoulders and back, he holds his reins comfortably in one hand, which is resting on the pommel of his saddle.

"Where are we going?" I ask, finally summoning the courage to raise my voice.

"Home."

"And where might that be?"

He gestures with the reins, pointing at the notch between the peaks. "Other side of those mountains. Three, four days ride, maybe. Depends on how much snow is in the pass." He twists in his saddle, glances at me. "Why? You eager to get there?" There's a thinly veiled hint of salaciousness to his words.

I shrug, trying for an indifference I do not feel. "Only curious."

He doesn't quite smile, but the ghost of a smirk touches the corners of his lips. "Only curious." And with that he swivels back around to face forward, and says nothing more.

Home.

Three or four days in the wilderness, in the dead of winter, in the company of a man who owns me.

Tears prick hot behind my eyes, but I force them down. They will do me no good out here, and they will only freeze on my face.

Besides, something tells me tears will not move a man such as him.

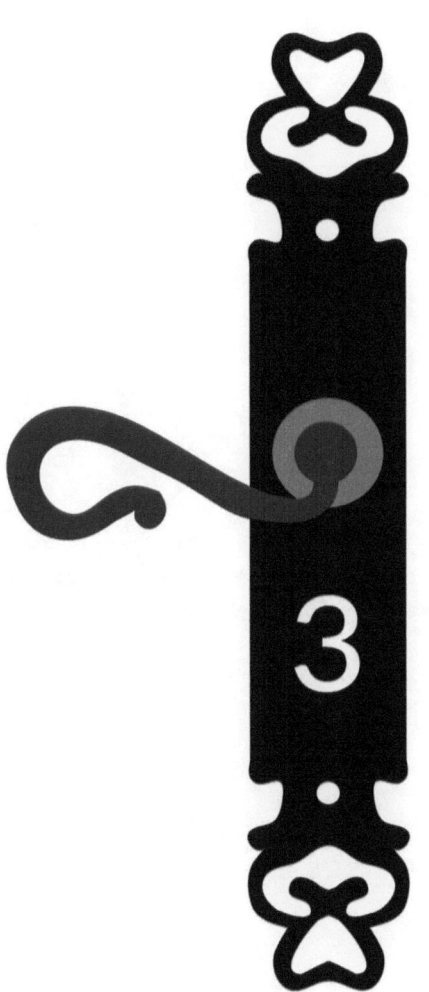

●

The small fire crackles merrily, a small bloom of hot yellow flickering bravely against the onslaught of cold and encroaching shadows. I extend my hands to the flame, warming my numb fingers. My ass and thighs ache from untold hours in the saddle. Cold is a state of being, a fact of my existence; a chill has sunk into my bones, its claws biting into my very marrow. Even my warm clothes cannot keep out the relentless, penetrating, frigid air.

I am too cold to be afraid of the man sitting to my left, a man who has not spoken a word in so long that I'm beginning to wonder if I've forgotten what speech sounds like. I am too cold to be curious about where we are headed—the place he calls "home". And I'm so cold now I am no longer afraid of the journey, or of the unknown.

Being cold is just about all I think about...but with nothing else to do but ride and keep up with this man all day I had nothing to do *but* think. My thoughts often strayed back to that miserable room and those wicked men. Thompson, the man in charge, was the worst—him and that sister of his. While I do not like being out in the freezing cold, it's better than spending another day in their company.

We crossed the open plain, riding hours past nightfall, until we reached the tree line at the foot of the mountains. He seemed to know exactly where he was going, leading us unerringly in a specific direction. In places I could tell that the path had disappeared, but he was undeterred. He'd veer around any obstacles, big or small, only to return to our original heading.

"How do you know where we're going?" I had asked, eventually.

He was passing by a thick, towering fir tree as I asked the question, and he reached out with a hand and tapped a finger against the bark. There was no other answer, just that single terse gesture. As I passed that same tree, I saw what he'd referred to: a blaze gouged into the bark with a knife, hard-angled gashes forming the initials CK, with the down-stroke bar of the K elongated to form an arrow, indicating direction.

"C-K?" I had queried.

He continued on several paces after hearing my question, his shoulders swaying with the huge animal's gait. He hadn't turned to face me, instead speaking as he ducked under a low hanging branch.

"Conrad Killian." He'd fairly grunted it, his voice so low and deep it sounded like an avalanche heard up in the high mountains.

He hasn't spoken since.

Now, hours after that exchange, we're sitting side by side around a tiny but hot campfire. The fire is so small I could almost cup it both of my hands; he could probably cradle the entire campfire in one of his broad paws.

Our fire is built in the lee of a downed pine tree, the roots up-ended out of the earth, acting as a reflector for the fire's heat, and a block against the ever-present wind. The horses are tied a few feet away, munching noisily out of nosebags tied to their halters. We'd eaten a small meal of some dried, jerked meat, and hard, crusty bread. Nothing fancy, assuredly, but better than nothing. Mercifully, the snow that threatened earlier on never really materialized.

And now…?

We just sat.

He did not stare into the fire as I did. Rather, he sat angled away from it, leaning a shoulder against the bulk of the downed tree's root ball, glancing now and again into the darkness, scanning, alert, listening. His hands were busy with a pile of rawhide sliced into long thin strips, which he was plaiting into a rope, his thick, blunt fingers nimbly braiding the half a dozen or more strands together. His rifle stood near to hand, butt in the dirt, barrel leaning against the roots, and his gun belt was spread out just beyond it, handles facing him for easy access. He didn't seem particularly worried about anything, just…alert. Ready for anything.

"You oughta sleep." His words abruptly broke the silence. "Even longer ride come sunup."

He stands up, setting his busywork project aside, and walks over to retrieve my saddle—or rather, the saddle of the horse I'm riding on this journey. He hauls it one handed over to me and sets it down a few feet away. He stalks back to the pile of gear and brings me a horse blanket and a thick gray wool blanket rolled up into a tight cylinder and tied with a length of rawhide. He tosses the horse blanket near the fire, and then unties the knot on the blanket roll and passes that to me, too.

"Saddle makes a decent pillow," he explains, as he resumes his seat just outside the pool of light of the fire. "And the horse blanket will help keep out the cold underneath you."

"What about you?" I ask, wrapping the wool blanket around my shoulders.

Really, I don't much care what he'll use for a bedroll, because he did *buy me* after all, but it is wickedly cold out here.

He eyes me with the ghost of a smirk on his lips, the expression on his face sarcastic. "I won't be sleeping." He shakes out the pile of strands and resumes braiding. "These parts, you best keep watch."

Something about the last statement combined with his constant watchfulness stirs the fear in my gut. "What's out there to watch for?"

"This is the wilderness, sweetness. There's more to watch for than I've got words." He gestures at his rifle and gun belt, "Nothing's gonna bother you. Not while I'm here." He doesn't say this arrogantly, just with a total surety of his own abilities.

There's nothing to say to that, so I lie down on the cold hard ground, settle my head against the icy leather of the saddle, wrap the blanket tight around my body, and close my eyes.

Yet, despite my exhaustion, sleep is not swift in coming.

I crack my eyes after an indeterminate amount of time spent trying to sleep. His eyes glint brown in the firelight, and they are fixed on me.

He glances down at his plaiting, then back at me. "What's your name?"

"Now you ask?" I can't help the vitriol in my voice. "After purchasing me like a prize steer and then hauling me across the wilderness without a word?"

"Don't owe you any explanations, sweetness. Got my reasons for what I do, and that's all you need to know." A pause, a glance at his work, and then he looks down at me. "You don't want to tell me? Ain't no hair off my chest. I'll just call you Susie, then."

"Susie?" I remain bundled under the blanket.

"Had a dog named Suzie, when I was a boy. Sweet little thing. Dumb as a hammer, but sweet." He doesn't look at me when he says this, but there's humor in his voice.

He's baiting me.

And damn him, it's working.

"I'm Hannah," I tell him. I shouldn't tell him my name, but I do. "Hannah Tavistock."

He just nods. "Hannah, then." Another long, but not entirely uncomfortable silence. Another glance at me. "Can't sleep?"

I shake my head. "I'm tired, but I just…" I shrug. "Just can't."

"Happens. 'Specially out here." He sets his plaits down. "You read?"

I nod slowly, and he rises, crosses to his saddlebag and digs out a small but thick leather-bound tome. He moves to stand over me, extending the book to me: *Collected Works of The Great Thinkers*.

At my lifted eyebrow, he scowls at me. "Don't give me that look. Bet I've read more books than you have. That book there has got Plato, Euripides, Sophocles, Shakespeare, Bacon, Aristotle, plus some translations of them A-rab thinkers—Averroës, Avicenna, Al-Kindi, Al-Farabi. More than I can remember.

"Not much to do 'round the fire at night on those long drives 'cept read. Come across a fellow with a book you ain't read, you trade."

I sit up, taking the book. "Thank you."

I try to get comfortable, and then I choose something to read. He plaits, and I read, and we pass the time like this.

At some point, I begin to get so tired I can hardly keep my eyes open. So I lay down, rest my head on the saddle, and fade effortlessly into sleep.

He shakes me awake while the sky is still lead-gray. "Time to move on."

I was in a deep sleep, so I sit up slowly, stretching the kinks out of my body, and reminding myself of my situation.

By the time I've made it to my feet, he's got the horses saddled, the gear packed away, and the fire buried. Last to be packed is the blanket, rolled up tight and tied off, fastened behind his saddle. He produces a canteen from somewhere, hands it to me and I drink deeply. I find the water icy, achingly cold, recently drawn from a nearby stream. In fact, I hear it burbling now, a small, faint trickling not far away. I remember hearing it, last night, but only now does its presence register.

We mount up, and as he leads us away I glance back and see that the campsite has been struck so well I wonder if it was ever there in the first place.

We ride, and after an hour or so he hands me a few pieces of jerky and another hard-tack biscuit.

The hours pass, both more swiftly than I would have expected and more slowly. We don't stop for lunch, just eat more jerky and biscuits in the saddle.

Besides those four words spoken to wake me up, he says nothing else the entire day.

We're climbing now, moving steadily upward, leaning into our saddles. Here and there, the horses have to scrabble and jump to get over the rocky ground. In other places we have to angle around an outcropping. Either way, it's slow going.

Up at this altitude the trees grow stunted and twisted, thinner, shorter, few and far between. By sunset, the valley is spread out beneath us and I can see the stream glinting silver in the fading daylight, gleaming between the gaps in the trees. We're following the water's path, roughly, keeping it to our left as we ascend.

The air up here is thin, and I don't feel able to gather a full breath. It's hard on the horses, too.

We're approaching a clearing in the trees when he tugs his horse to a stop, gesturing for me to do the same. Hooves crunch quietly in the sparse snow and the leaves beneath, and then all is silent but for the ceaseless soughing of the wind.

Slowly, quietly he withdraws his rifle from the scabbard on his saddle and tucks the butt to his shoulder. I squint into the clearing, but I can't see what he sees.

A long tense moment of silence, and then I hear him let out a soft breath—

*BOOOOM!*

The rifle bucks against his shoulder, and I start in the saddle; the horses are unmoved, unsurprised. I watch as a shape bolts across the clearing, runs half a dozen steps toward the far tree line, and then crumples. A deer, I think. Three hundred yards away, easily, if not farther.

He replaces the rifle, rolls his spurs against his horse's side, and we're moving again, trotting across the wide clearing. Golden-red sunlight bathes the field of snow, highlighting a jutting outcropping of jagged stone, as if the bones of the mountain itself protrude through the skin of dirt and ice.

He halts beside the corpse of the deer and swings down out of the saddle. He lifts the heavy body easily and tosses it across the back of the horse, right over the saddlebags and blanket roll. The red seeping wound, just behind the deer's front foreleg, drips blood onto the horse's rump. Instead of riding now, he grabs the horse by the reins and leads us out of the clearing and back into the forest. He's scanning now, but with purpose, as if looking for something in particular. He's eyeing the tree trunks carefully, I think. He spots it at the same time that I do, another CK carved into the tree, another arrow pointing the way.

He follows his own marker, which brings us to a place where the mountain bellies outward in a thick bulge of lichen and moss-covered stone, a sheer vertical face of stone a hundred of feet high, and extending out of sight in both directions, mimicking the subtle curve of the mountainside. Following this outcropping brings us higher and higher yet, and now we're out of the tree line altogether, exposed to the air, with the bulk of the mountain beneath us and the valley spread out like a map in every direction, sunset bathing it golden and red and orange. It's a breathtaking vista, but we don't stop to admire it.

We spend another fifteen or twenty minutes following the outcropping, and then he stops. The mountain is on our right and, on our left a steep embankment, which falls hundreds of feet away to the stream far below.

He walks directly toward a spot on the side of the mountain. A cave. The opening is high enough to admit the horses and, as I enter, I see that the cave is no small hole carved into the side of a mountain, but rather the opening of what I think must be a massive series of caverns. The cave is huge, some thirty feet wide, ten or fifteen feet from floor to ceiling, extending back into infinite darkness. Sounds echo and fade after long seconds. Each scuff of a foot, each whicker of the horses bounces and distorts sound in the space. The sunlight is fading so the only light is what's provided by the opening of the cave, which is little enough. He seems to know what he's looking for though, digging in his saddlebags for a match, and then rummaging on the cave floor.

The match flares, and the flame touches a curling piece of tree bark, catches, spreads to a pile of tinder—all small twigs and chunks of bark. Within seconds, the fire is flickering bright yellow, and immediately he places a few smaller branches on it, setting it to burning higher and hotter. I notice, now, the stack of logs and branches along one wall, another smaller pile of tinder material beside it.

"You must use this cave a lot," I remark.

"Not just me. Trappers, miners, traders, the old mountain men from when the Europeans were first exploring this area. The Spanish and the French explorers both knew of it. 'Course, the Utes have used this cave for hundreds of years."

"So did you leave this wood here? Or did someone else?"

He shrugs. "Traveler's courtesy, I suppose. Use the wood, then leave more behind. It's a handy spot, for a lot reasons. One of the last sheltered places to spend a night before you try the pass, or the first after you've crossed it."

Once the fire is going, the horses are unsaddled and given feed bags, he hauls the deer out beyond the cave mouth, draws a knife from his belt, and drags the blade from throat to rectum, scoops the guts out, sets them aside. He makes short work of the rest of the skinning process, stripping the deer of its hide, and cutting huge chunks of meat away. He drags the skinned, gutted corpse of the deer off into the woods, far enough away that scavengers won't bother us. He returns with blood-red hands, meat, and the animal skin.

He builds up the fire a bit more and then places a few thick, flat-topped stones at the edge of the fire, in among the coals. Once the stones are hot, he sets the meat on them. The smell of roasting venison fills the cavern, and my stomach begins to rumble.

While the meat cooks, he sets the deer hide on the ground, then places a corner of it on his knee and begins scraping at the underside with his knife, carefully and thoroughly removing every last speck of fat and flesh from the hide. I watch as he works.

Later we eat, and the meat is delicious, juices trickling down my chin, bursting with flavor.

Night is thick beyond the cave, and I can just barely make out a narrow strip of sky speckled with twinkling stars, and the scrap of the waxing moon.

Much later, as I'm drifting into sleep, Conrad stiffens, and then gingerly sets aside the hide he's still working on. Noiselessly, he buckles his gun belt around his waist, ties the holsters to his thighs. He sits down and lays his rifle across his lap, angling himself so the act of lifting the rifle will bring the barrel to bear on the cave mouth. He's utterly still. The horses' ears twitch and swivel. One of them whickers, a low murmur.

We hear the answering grumble of a horse, from beyond the cave.

"Hello!" A man's voice calls from the mouth of the cave. "Might I share your fire, friends?"

Conrad tugs back the hammer of his rifle—*click-CLICK*. "Come on in, but do it slow."

"No need for that. I'm friendly enough, if you are." He sounds genial and friendly.

Perhaps a little too much so. My gut twists and I sit up, scooting closer to Conrad, wrapping the blanket around my shoulders.

Hooves snick and clack on the stone of the cave floor. Leather creaks, and then the newcomer comes close enough to be lit by the firelight.

He's tall, but still an inch or two shy of Conrad. Lean, hard. Blond hair shows beneath a hat brim, and he's clean-shaven with the exception of a few weeks growth on his top lip—he must be trying to grow a mustache. Late twenties, early thirties, a bit well dressed and well groomed for the wilderness. His gaze is icy blue, reflecting intelligence and something darker, harder, frightening, and unwelcome. A single holster sits on his right hip, the belt sitting a bit higher on his waist than Conrad's, and his holster isn't tied around his thigh. He has a rifle tucked under one arm, which he slides into a sheath on the saddle. His horse is a lean, lithe-looking dun, and there's a massive pack mule behind them, long ears flicking and twitching.

He doesn't approach the fire right away. Just stands there staring, assessing. Eying Conrad, his rifle, and his revolvers. He's looking at the deerskin and the leftover meat still laid across the roasting stones.

"Bitter cold," he says, after a minute. "Be glad to warm up."

Conrad eyes the man, his gaze hard, not exactly welcoming. His rifle is still cocked, and I notice he's shifted his position so he's ready to propel himself to his feet. Does he expect trouble? Or is he merely prepared for it? No way to know.

"Sit you down, then," Conrad says. "You're welcome to the venison, if you're hungry."

"Sure am, and my thanks."

The stranger unties and unloads his pack mule, unsaddles his horse and gives both animals nosebags of feed. He rummages through the gear on the pack mule, and comes up with a leather pouch, and a clay jug, then takes a seat opposite Conrad and I, his back to the cave mouth. He eyes the meat and then nudges the roasting stone back into the coals to warm it, then he lifts the jug toward us.

"Home brew from back east," he says by way of explanation. "Care for a drop?"

Conrad shakes his head, and I assume I'm not included in that invitation, so I say nothing. I wouldn't have taken it, anyway. I don't have a good feeling about this man.

Silence, then, as the man removes the stone and makes short work of the meat, careful to keep his hands and mouth clean, and then he washes it down with a long swig from the jug. Then he tugs open a leather pouch, and proceeds to roll a cigarette. He extends the bag to Conrad who nods and takes it, sniffs at the opening, seems satisfied, then rolls his own smoke.

More silence except for the crackle of flames, and the spark of fire licking at the tobacco, along with the occasional murmur of the livestock.

"Where'd ya'll come from, then?" the newcomer asks.

Conrad blows out a plume of smoke. "The Thompson ranch."

A nod, and a pair of blue eyes fix on me, as if he knows what kind of business happens on Thompson's ranch. His gaze is speculative, calculating. "Thompson runs some rare fine stock, I've heard." His words speak of cattle, but his eyes speak of woman flesh.

Conrad only rolls a shoulder. "If you say so." He blows out another stream of acrid smoke, and then peers at the other man. "What's your story?"

"Oh, not much to tell. Hail from Tennessee. Heard there was more fun to be had and more money to be made out west, so I'm making my way over the Divide. Thinkin' California."

"Heard talk about California myself," Conrad says. "Mostly Spanish out that way, ain't it?"

A laconic shrug. "Depends on where you go, is what I've heard." The blue gaze flits from me to Conrad, then back to me. "Name's Charlie Markham."

Hesitation. "Conrad." A gesture at me. "This is Hannah." A flick of fingers sends the cigarette butt end over end into the fire.

"Pleased to make your acquaintances, the both of you." He stretches out, rests his head on his saddle, and tugs his hat over his eyes. "Now, if you don't mind overmuch, I'm in need of rest. Long ride up, as I'm sure you know."

Conrad glances at me, at Charlie, and then returns his attention to the animal skin. "Long day ahead tomorrow, Hannah. You best stretch out, too."

Within minutes, snores emanate from Charlie, long rattling rips of snorting inhalation followed by grumbling exhales. No way I'm going to sleep with that noise going on, but I lower myself down beside Conrad anyway. A little too close, if I'm being honest. My head is near his thigh, and he shifts now, settling lower against the cave wall, stretching his legs out and crossing them ankle over ankle; his thigh brushes my head. I can feel the motion of his hands as he scrapes the deer hide. Something about his proximity makes my belly lurch and my pulse thrum.

He bought me for a purpose; I know what that purpose is. It's obvious, after all. But he hasn't tried anything yet. He hasn't even touched me. Barely even looked at me, much less spoken to me. But I can't forget the ravenous burn in his eyes the day he purchased me.

I hate with every fiber of my being knowing that I was bought and sold, that I had had no choice in the matter. He controls my future, whether I want to belong to him or not, whether I believe in my heart that I am Conrad Killian's "property" or not. I can go nowhere without him. My other choice would be to try to make a run for it, but my chances would be slim to none. And the little bit I know of him tells me I wouldn't get far enough away to even freeze or starve. He told me he'd chase me down, and that if he had to chase me it wouldn't go well for me. What would that look like?

I'm not sure I want to find out.

At some point, he's going to fuck me.

And I won't have a choice in that either.

Complicating matters is the fact that he's not unattractive, and my body responds to this. My body is aware of him. I don't dare dwell on what my heart thinks, or what my mind is telling me. Best to leave those considerations for when it's safer to dwell on them; like never, if I know what's good for me.

But…just laying on a cave floor within touching distance of him has my body buzzing, my mind whirling, my heart flipping, my entire existence upended and confused. Because…part of me wants him, and part of me hates him.

I'm glad for Charlie's presence, though. Having him here puts off the inevitable, for a while, at least.

But I don't trust Charlie. Not even a tiny bit. He might be playing the role of a newcomer from back east, but he knows exactly what happens at Thompson's ranch. And something in his eyes…I don't know what it is, I can't quite place it, but it's a gleam that makes me uncomfortable. And there's a false note in his genial, friendly voice. I wouldn't trust him as far as I could throw him.

For the second night, sleep doesn't come. I manage to relax a little at best, a floating not-quite-sleep, hovering just over the edge of consciousness. My eyes crack open at one point, and while Conrad has set aside his plaiting and has let his head rest back against the cave wall, he's no more asleep than I am. His gun belt is still around his waist, holsters tied down, and his rifle is across his knees, one hand on the stock.

Resting, but alert.

He doesn't trust Charlie either.

Dawn arrives, frigid and gloomy. The sky is leaden, the sun obscured by a thick layer of gray clouds. Fat flakes of snow swirl in the air, whirling in eddies at the entrance to the cave, and beginning to drift on the knife-sharp wind.

Conrad is packing his gear, Charlie doing the same. Saddling, tying down, adjusting.

Conrad hands me two canteens. "The stream is fifty yards in a straight shot from the cave mouth. Fill these both for me, please."

I tug on my hood, wiggle my fingers in my mittens and take the canteens. I find the stream easily; ice is beginning to form near the edges. I find a spot, then remove my mittens and fill the canteens. I pick my way back through the trees and up the slight hill, back to the cave. It's not so cold this morning, and the air is fresh.

As I approach the cave I can see that the animals have been moved outside in preparation for departure, but voices stop me—the words in particular catch my attention.

"How much, Conrad?"

"For what?" This is gruff, disinterested.

"Don't play stupid. Thompson ain't sold a cow or a horse in his life."

A silence, except for the creak of leather being adjusted. "If you say so."

"So my question is…*how much?*"

"Nothing of mine is for sale, Markham."

"You just bought her, so you can't be too attached. I'll make it worth your while. How much?"

"Not for sale."

"You bought her."

"And I'm not reselling."

"Double what you paid."

"Clear off, Markham. You heard me."

"I want her." His voice is hard, sharp, threatening.

"Don't rightly care what you want. I said clear off."

"Come on. Triple, then. How much would that come to? Six

thousand? Ten? I got means, Conrad. I can make this worth your while. Don't need to be a problem. It's just one girl. Thompson's got more."

I creep closer. I can see them, now. They're separated by a dozen feet or so, facing each other. Conrad has one hand resting on his horse's rump, but the other is loose at his side. Charlie is just standing there, looking angry and spoiling for a fight. The air is tense, thick, still.

Conrad lifts his chin. "I said no. Ain't gonna change my mind. Clear off."

Charlie raises his hands, then backs up a step and digs in his saddle-bag, moving slowly, deliberately. He withdraws a stack of cash. "Look. Everything I got. Count it. It's all yours." He cuts his eyes to the side and sees me. He grins, a slow leer spreading across his face. He turns back to Conrad. "Come on, man. Be smart. Last chance."

"Don't want your money, don't give a shit about your last chance. I said clear off. Hannah is not for sale."

"Not again, you mean." This time he cuts another glance at me, insulting, derisive.

Fear blasts through me as Charlie fixes his gaze on me. Dressed as warmly as I am there's not much of me to see, but his eyes seem to undress me, raking over me, making me feel naked. I resist the urge to huddle deeper in my coat; I refuse to give him the satisfaction.

Conrad jerks his head at me. "Time to go, Hannah. Mount up."

I'm forced to walk past Charlie to get to Conrad; I skirt wide, avoiding Charlie by a good five or six feet, and even still my flesh crawls from the leer on his face, from the itching burn of his hungry stare.

I mount up, adjust my skirts, and tug my mittens back on to warm up my tingling fingers. Conrad mounts then, too, and swings around, not sparing a single glance for Charlie.

We're almost around the curve of the mountain, almost out of sight when I hear Charlie shout.

"You're making a mistake, Conrad!"

Conrad ignores the shout, and I don't turn around either. But my spine prickles.

"Don't pay him no mind," Conrad murmurs to me, after a while.

I do, though. I pay Charlie Markham a lot of mind. His leer is burned into my mind. His hunger for me is obvious, and there's a gleam of something dark and malevolent in his look.

His last warning echoes in my mind for hours. *You're making a mistake, Conrad.* Not a warning, not a threat, but a statement of fact.

Conrad seems unconcerned with the likes of Charlie Markham.

I, however, do not possess that peace of mind.

•  •

The higher we climb up into the pass, the harder it becomes for me to breathe. The temperature drops markedly and the snow drifts higher and higher, making it difficult for the horses. On one side of the trail the ground falls away and around us the mountain peaks tower over our heads, their craggy bulk leaning menacingly into the gray sky. We're long out of the trees, so there's nothing to stop the wind from whipping around us and battering us and carving up our faces with icy knives.

It takes all I have within me to stay atop my horse and keep breathing. I want to weep. I want to stop. I want to bury myself in the snow and go to sleep.

But we don't stop, not even to share jerky and hardtack while riding. We straddle our horses, duck our heads out of the wind, and continue moving.

Countless hours of sheer hell.

And when the snow gets too high, even for the horses, Conrad dismounts, and then gestures for me to do the same. He leads the horses ahead of me, breaking a trail. I stumble through the snow behind him, focusing on the swaying rumps of the horses.

Darkness falls, and finds us back among the trees, on the other side of the pass.

Finally, Conrad stops near two huge fallen pines, their trunks crossed and their branches drooping, creating a natural enclosure. The branches break the fall of snow, and their bulk helps to reflect the fire and stop the wind. Another tiny fire, and this time it feels too small, too little light against the encroaching darkness, too little heat against the onslaught of the dropping temperature.

He seems to read my thoughts. "Can't risk a bigger fire. The Utes don't generally bother me, as long as I keep to myself and pass on through. But still, best to not take chances."

"Cold." It's all I can manage through my chattering teeth.

He sits with his back against the tree trunk. He extends his arm toward me. "Lean in, then."

I eye him warily. "Not that cold."

He chuckles. "Suit yourself." He glances down at me. "I won't hurt you."

"You own me. You could do anything you want to me."

"So I do, and so I could. Don't mean I'm going to hurt you, though."

I don't move any closer, but I want to. His body would be a further block against the wind and the icy cold. He would be warm. Solid. Something to curl up against.

I curl up on the hard ground near him, but not too near, shivering. I let my eyes close and let sheer exhaustion pull me under.

When I wake up, he's in the same position he was when I fell asleep: sitting up, rifle near to hand, resting but alert. I don't think he has slept in more than two days.

I'm curled up against him. My head is on his thigh, and one of his big, gloved hands is on my back. Proprietary. Comforting.

I don't remember moving in the night, and now that I am awake I hate myself for not immediately shifting away from his touch. I am a traitor to my own freedom, to my own dignity. To my own self.

But his body is warm against mine, and the dawn is cold.

Another day's ride, another campfire in the darkness, another night spent fighting the urge to get closer to him, just for the warmth. Only for the warmth.

By midday the fourth day we crest a rise, the mountains lie miles behind us, and before us the land rolls away in gently rolling tree-carpeted hills. Everything is blanketed in snow. Ahead is a U-shaped valley, a long narrow piece of land sandwiched between high rocky hills. There's a frozen lake partially surrounded by a dense cluster of aspen, and in the far distance, nestled in the belly of the U of the valley, is a small cabin. The ground above the cabin is utterly inaccessible, surrounded by sheer cliffs. There's only one way into the valley—via the mouth. Horses roam the valley freely, pawing at the snow, looking for the grass beneath.

As we descend toward the mouth of the valley, it becomes obvious that distance played tricks on my sense of scale: the valley isn't so small after all, it is easily three or four miles across and a dozen miles deep. It takes us the rest of the day to make the entrance, and then Conrad nudges his heel against his horse's flank, clicks his tongue, and breaks into a trot. My horse follows automatically, and now we're winding between occasional copses of trees, passing the lake on our right, then suddenly we're surrounded by horses, dozens of them, then more and more. Too many to count. All paints, white and brown and red and black, patched and smeared, most small and lean and lithe like my mount, a few others a bit larger. All have thick and shaggy winter coats, but even my untrained eye can see that these horses are prime stock.

Conrad is silent, but somehow the herd knows he's here. There's no whooping or hollering, just him leaning forward, wind buffeting his hat brim, and then he snarls a gruff *hiii-ya!* and his big black and white horse blasts into a wild gallop. I'm left behind, but I don't mind. It's a glorious sight, a hundred or more head of horses milling and wheeling and galloping, snow bursting from scything hooves, shoulders roiling, heads bobbing, manes fluttering, tails whipping. And him, leaning forward in his saddle, shoulders broad as the mountains around us, his hat in hand, thick black hair wind-blown. It is a sight of complete and utter freedom, wild and powerful.

When I catch up, he's dismounted in front of the cabin, surrounded by the horses. He whispers to them, rubbing between their ears here and a nose there, nudging. It's as if he's one of them, greeting old friends. They nudge him with their noses, brush against him, whicker and whinny at him. He moves through the clustered herd to the porch, leading his mount. He unsaddles his horse, tossing the saddle on the porch. Then he leans into the horse's face, whispers something, and then gives the animal a friendly, playful shove on its front flank. A toss of its head, and the horse is gone, absorbed into the herd.

"Unsaddle her," he says to me. "Leave the saddle with mine and come on in."

I do as I'm told, and as soon as the saddle and the saddle blanket are off, my horse is prancing away, nipping at a pair of white and brown mares, tossing her head, looking for all the world like a young girl excitedly greeting friends she hasn't seen in a while.

I set the saddle with his, and hang the reins on a nearby nail.

The cabin is tiny. Crafted from thick pine, it's sturdy and solid. There's an outhouse a stone's throw away, and a couple of lean-to shelters scattered a hundred feet from the cabin, up against the side of the hill.

Instead of a wood and metal latch such as you might see on most log cabins of this type, there is an actual doorknob, out of place in this otherwise rustic dwelling. It's familiar, somehow. Glass. Delicate. Fragile. Multifaceted. I reach for the knob, but before I can grasp it, the door swings open. Conrad stands in the opening, gesturing brusquely for me to come in.

"An odd choice of doorknob," I say as I enter.

He shrugs as he brings the gear inside the house and stacks it in a corner. "The only keepsake from my life before I built this place," he says this gruffly, brusque, dismissing the topic. He sweeps his arm at the interior of the cabin. "Welcome home, Hannah."

It isn't much. A dozen paces across, perhaps twenty paces deep. Low ceiling, maybe a foot over Conrad's head. Dark, as there is no window. A fireplace on the back wall, a bed on the left-hand wall when facing the fireplace, a table on the right. A couple of chests in the corner near the fireplace, their hasps secured with padlocks. A shotgun on the lintel above the door. Not much else.

He's already got a fire going, using wood stacked beside the fireplace. A big fire, hot and orange and blazing brightly, illuminates the room and quickly banishes the cold. Conrad is shucking his coat, his gloves, untying the holsters of his gun belt and unbuckling it, hanging it off the back of one of the two chairs at the table. His rifle rests on the bed.

I don't know what to do.

I stand in the center of the cabin, watching him as he kicks off his boots with a contented sigh, tossing his hat on the bed, ruffling his fingers through his hair. He plops into a chair, the one with his gun belt hanging from it. Even at rest, in his socks, in his home, there is a weapon within easy reach.

There is a pot hanging from a hook in the hearth, its round bottom licked by the fire. He nods at the pot. "Give that a stir."

There's a thick stew in the pot, just beginning to steam. I realize he must've made it before he left, and then let the cold keep it fresh for his return. I stir it; watching the ice crystals melt on the carrots, potatoes, and chunks of meat. The broth slowly begins to liquefy.

I still have all my cold weather clothes on, and I feel him behind me, standing inches away. He tugs my hood back. Reaches around in front of me to unbutton the coat, and then pulls it off me. I'm frozen stiff, now, and not from the cold. I cannot move, I can barely breathe. He grabs one of my wrists, peels off the mitten, and then does the same with the other. He takes me by the shoulders and pushes me into the empty chair. Sits me down in it. Kneels in front of me. His eyes are brown, molten, and inscrutable. Watching my expression, he unlaces one of my boots. Tugs it off. Then the other.

I'm biting my lip, now, unable to look away from him. Unable to feel anything but his hands on my ankles, subtly sliding upward. His fingertips are on my calves, burning through my skin even through the thick wool stockings. I want to pull away from him, but I don't dare. And I can't. Can't.

His eyes don't leave mine as his fingertips slide up my leg, to my knee. Under the layers of skirts. Higher. To my thigh. To the gap of skin above the top of my stocking. And now my skin is on fire, burning where he touches me. I'm shaking, I realize. Breathing short fast shallow breaths. He curls his fingers between the stocking and my skin... and pulls down. He gently slides the stocking off my leg, caressing my thigh and knee and calf with both hands as he removes the garment. It's hard to breathe when he does the same to my other leg.

He remains on his knees in front of me, my calves in his palms. His eyes search my face, flick to my heaving breast, then back up to my eyes. And then—god, and then his palms skate up my legs once more, trailing fingertips and palms along the backs of my knees, making me shiver and shudder. He continues his trail up the backs of my thighs, carving around to the top, up to my hips. Dancing over the flannel of my underwear, skimming over my core.

Now?

He wants to do this right now?

I'm not ready.

I know this is why he purchased me, and it's why I'm here. I'm not ready, but I don't think I have a choice. He said he wouldn't hurt me, but what if I refuse him right now?

He is a dangerous man, and this is a remote, wild place. He can do anything he wants, anything at all. His word, his desire, is law.

His eyes, those brown indecipherable pools, never waver from mine as he hooks his fingers into the waist of my underwear and drags them down my leg. Not impatiently, though.

No.

Slowly. Deliberately. Teasingly.

He removes them, tosses them aside.

Then he presses his hands to my knees and shoves my thighs apart.

I resist—I can't help it.

I squeeze my eyes shut, prepared for his anger. I refuse to open for him.

"Hannah." His voice is gentle. Not angry. Not scolding.

He rifles under my skirts, glides his palms over my thighs, rests them near the crease of my hips.

"Hannah." He says my name again, more insistently.

I force my eyes open and glance down into his. I look at him.

He presses his thumb to my clit, brushes the pad of his thumb in a slow circle. "It won't be tonight." Another slow circle, his eyes on mine, watching my expression shift as I feel the thrum of heat billowing through me. "But I want you prepared for it."

"I...Conrad, I..." I don't have any idea what to say or why I even opened my mouth. "I'm not—I'm not ready."

"You will be." He withdraws his touch, and I hate the way I ache, then. He stands up. "Might as well take off a few layers. No point in modesty."

I can't help but flash back to that awful room, alone with him and Thompson, Conrad's eyes on my body, raking over my naked curves. He's seen me nude; a few layers of wool won't make any difference at this point.

I stand up, reach behind my back and begin unfastening the tiny buttons up my spine. And then his hands are there, doing it for me. His breath is hot on the back of my neck. Sliding the heavy weight of my thick blond hair over one shoulder, out of the way. The dress loosens as he unfastens the buttons, and then it's pooled on the floor at my feet and he's lifting up the top-most underskirt. Setting it aside. Then, the next layer. He stops when I'm just wearing the thin wool slip. It's molded to my torso and hips, leaving little to the imagination. He stands back, then, openly staring, admiring, taking me in.

"You are a lovely woman, Hannah."

"Thank you," I whisper.

He gestures at the chair, turning away to the fire. "Sit down. The food's ready."

He folds the layers of petticoats and underskirts and the dress, and then sets them on one of the chests. There is a mantle above the fireplace, on which are two hand carved bowls and two tarnished, battered, scratched silver spoons. He ladles heaping portions of stew into each bowl, then retrieves a canteen from the pile of gear in the corner near the door and sets it on the table.

He sits down and begins eating, then stops when he realizes I'm still standing in the center of the small cabin, hands clasped in front of me, knees knocking, barely able to breathe.

Conrad rises, stands in front of me. Cups my cheek with his rough paw. "Hannah." His voice is surprisingly gentle. "Sit, please. Eat some stew. Try to relax."

My cheek throbs where his hard, scratchy palm touched me. I sit down gingerly; take the spoon in hand and ladle a bite of stew into my mouth. It is delicious, hot, lightly seasoned with salt. I sit bolt upright, on the edge of my chair. I'm ravenous, but I don't dare scarf the food like I want to. Don't dare relax.

We eat in silence, as we rode in silence, as we sat around the fire in silence.

When we are finished, he opens the front door, scoops a handful of snow from the porch and uses it to scrub out the bowls and spoons, replacing them on the mantle when they're clean.

He glances at me. "Time to turn in. Been a long ride."

I don't know what I'm supposed to say to that, so I say nothing. I remain seated at the table, watching him. He banks the fire, and now the cabin is a cove of shadows cast by the embers, nothing to see but shapes as my eyes adjust. Conrad stands in front of the bed and unfastens his trousers. Steps out of them. He unbuttons his shirt, shrugs it off, then folds both garments and sets them on the floor. Sitting on the edge of the bed, he toes off his socks.

Naked.

My pulse flutters, my breath catches.

He is the epitome extraordinary masculine beauty.

Hard slabs of muscle are sheathed in sun-tanned skin, leathery and weathered, but glistening with a light sheen of sweat. He has several scars and a thick mat of hair covers his broad chest, tapering down to a narrow trail leading to his groin. I can't help but look. Huge, heavy balls. Thick cock, long even when flaccid. His eyes fix on me, stare at me as I remain seated, my back straight, several feet away, hands folded demurely together on my lap. My hair has fallen over one eye, obscuring half my face in a blond sheet. My breasts rise and fall as I fight for calm. My nipples are hard, poking at the fine thin wool of my slip.

There is one bed.

Without needing to ask, I know I am expected to share it with him.

He said it won't be tonight, but considering his nudity and our situation, he's probably changed his mind.

God, he's fucking gorgeous.

His hair is a shaggy, hat-messed thatch around his neck and in his eyes, a wild black mane of tangles and curls, sweeping against his tan skin. His shoulders are heavy, hard, round. Biceps nearly the size of my thighs. Chest, arms, shoulders, stomach, all rippling with muscle and ribboned with scars—cuts, burns, bullet holes, stab wounds. He's been through hell.

Even at rest he exudes confidence and danger in equal measure, leavened with a sort of preternatural calm. He never hurries and he always seems relaxed. I've never seen him move quickly, never seen him rush. But somehow, I just know he could, if needed, burst into a frenzy of violence. He wears those revolvers as if they're extensions of his body, and he carries the rifle with the same air—as if it is part of his arm, a limb equally as important as an arm or a leg.

He lies down, stretches out on top of the blankets, leaving a space between himself and the wall, then turns to stare at me. "Gonna sit there all night?"

I shrug. "I might."

A chuckle. "Not very comfortable, I don't imagine." He taps the bed. "Built this bed myself. Straw under a layer of deer hide, all wrapped in canvas. Cotton sheet, brought over from Denver. It's comfy, I swear."

"I'm sure it is."

He eyes me. "I won't bite, Hannah."

"It's not your teeth I'm afraid of, Conrad."

Another laugh. "I told you I'll leave you be, for tonight."

"Then why are you naked?" I ask.

"It's how I sleep in my own home. You can keep the slip on, if you feel better about it." He pats the bed beside him. "Come on."

I rise, slowly, then pad on bare feet, knees weak, to his bed. There's a footlocker at the end of the bed, battered wood bound with thick iron straps, a padlock through the hasp, unlocked. I crawl over the foot-locker onto the bed, rather than attempting to climb over him. I lie on my back as close to the wall as possible, and then fold my hands on my stomach. I'm stiff as a board, tense and barely breathing.

A few moments of silence.

"Jesus, Hannah. You're all wound up tighter than a spring." He rolls to his side, facing me. "Breathe. What are you so afraid of?"

Bitterness, anger, and fear bubble up out of the cage I've had them in, all the way here. "You *own* me. You *bought* me. I'm in bed with my *master*. I'm here against my will. You are going to expect sex, whether I want it or not." I finally risk a glance at him, not bothering to mask my emotions. "And you ask what I'm afraid of?"

He sighs. "Have I mistreated you in any way, thus far?"

I'm forced to respond honestly. "No."

"I touched you, a bit ago, but you didn't exactly seem to mind, unless I was reading you wrong. For as much as you're afraid of me, I don't think you minded. Am I wrong, Hannah?"

I swallow the knot in my throat. "No, Conrad. You're not wrong." I meet his eyes. "But that doesn't change my other points."

"Yes, I gave Thompson money, and now you're here. And no, you didn't have much choice. Still don't. *But*—" A pause. "I never received a bill of sale. No record of ownership. The deal was marked by nothing more than a handshake and an exchange of cash. So…stop thinking about it like that, in those terms. I don't technically own you. Not that any law would recognize it, anyhow. Think of it more like…you were a mail-order bride, only I went and got you in person. You're not a slave.

I don't consider you my property. Human beings aren't objects." His voice hardens. Darkens. "One man can't own another."

"Yet you attended a sale of human flesh, and spent a large sum of money in exchange for the life of a person."

He doesn't look away, doesn't shrug. Just stares at me, looking into me. "Yes. I did."

"And I have no choice about being here."

"For now, that's true."

"Then how am I not, in some sense, your slave?"

"Because I'll make you a deal." He stretches out a hand, rest it on my waist, just above my hip. There's less than a foot between our bodies, and it feels at once like a mile and a hair's breadth: too far, and not far enough. "Give me a month. If you're unhappy, if you hate me, if you hate it here, I'll take you back to Denver and set you up."

"Deal." I don't even have to think about it. I know it's too good to be true, but I accept anyway. Mostly because, once again, I have little choice.

He smiles, a very small, very guarded smirk. "Yeah?"

I nod. "Yes."

He nods. "Good. Good." He rolls onto his back and I can't help the fact that my eyes are drawn to his cock, to the way it flops to one side as he moves. "It's not so bad here. *I'm* not so bad."

"I suppose we'll see, won't we?" I close my eyes, trying to let myself drift off to sleep.

A long, drowsing silence.

I can't help the question from bubbling out. "Conrad?" He grunts a query. "Why?"

"Why what?" His voice is sleep-thick.

"Why me? Why like this?"

"Different questions, different answers." He rolls toward me again and reaches out, brushing a lock of hair away from my eyes with just the tip of his forefinger. The touch is exquisitely gentle. "Why you? Because from the second they led all of you women out, I saw only you. If anyone had bid on you, I'd have outbid him. I never even looked at any of the others. Don't know why, rightly. Just…something about you. You're beautiful, yes, and I want you, yes. But…there's something more. Don't have words for it, exactly. Something in me recognizes something…kindred…in you."

My throat closes. "And the other question?" I don't look at him; I stare at the wall, the ceiling, anywhere but into his eyes. Anywhere but his face. If I look at him directly, I'd…I don't know what, and don't want to know.

But I *do* know what would happen. The connection I cannot deny would deepen, and I am afraid of what that would mean.

He sighs. "That there is a sight more complicated." He is quiet a while. Awake, staring into the past. His carefully cultured voice and precise articulation softens and curls into a slow drawl, not thick, really, but noticeable. "There was the war, and…the things I did, the things I saw…it takes a toll on a man's soul. On the ability to relate to folks in a normal sort of way. I marched south with Sherman. Damn near deserted a few times. Probably should have. Might be—might be able to sleep a sight better if I had.

"I met a woman down there. When things ended, I just sort of stayed around Atlanta, what was left of it, leastways. There was this girl. Daughter of a smith. Pretty as could be, and had a smart mouth on her. Lordy, she could flay a man to bits with just her words when the ire took her. We married, and after a bit I got restless, 'cause I've never been one for settling in a place very long. She was game, packed a valise and put on a bonnet and rode shotgun with me. I was thinking Oklahoma, all that land down thataway. We hitched up with a wagon train of other folks headed out in similar directions. We split off on our own after a while, separated from the rest of them. After a few weeks on our own we got hit by a Sioux war party. Just me and her, no one else for hundreds of miles. I held 'em off for…oh, days. Had a good spot where they couldn't surround me, and I had my Springfield and plenty of rounds, and she would reload for me. Then they…they got my wife. Stray round, I guess. I went a little crazy, took after 'em with my pistols and a knife. They let me be, after I'd laid out enough of 'em.

Respected warrior an' all that shit, you know how they are. Nearly died, myself. A half-breed tracker saw the buzzards angling for me, kept me from crossing the Styx."

He sighs. Scrubs his face with his hands.

"Don't rightly remember much after that. Wished I'd have died. Took up drinking whiskey like it could bring her back—that or put me in the ground with her. Somehow, after a length of time I don't remember and don't care to…I ended up in this valley. There was this little herd of paints running free. Miles of green grass, the lake, the mountains. Something about this valley made me want to put down the bottle and…" he shrugs, "I dunno. Live, I guess. So I did. Built this cabin. Caught some of the paints and broke 'em. Rode 'em down to Prescott, sold 'em for a bundle. Turns out I've got a knack for horses, and this stock is prime, pure. Made a bit of a name for myself on account of my paints. I've had a few dustups with the Utes who claimed this valley and the horses in it, but I taught 'em respect the only way they understand it. But I never—I just don't know how to…" he sighs, a deep, frustrated breath. "I'm not the go-courting sort. Wouldn't know who, or where, or how to go about it. But it's lonely out here. Lonely on the trail. I need a companion. Someone to talk to. More than someone to just warm my bed…I need someone to share my life with. And you…you stood there defiant. Chin up. Giving no quarter. Even when Thompson took your robe and left you bare, you…you didn't back down. I respect that."

There's not much I can say to that story, so I don't say anything. But I do relax a little. And when he falls asleep and shifts a little closer to me, his knee touching my thigh, his breath hot on my shoulder, a hand splayed possessively over my hip…

I don't move away.

• • •

I wake slowly. The air beyond the bed is cold, enough so that I can see my breath. But there's a fire going in the fireplace, a merry yellow flicker of freshly lit kindling and as yet untouched logs.

Conrad is beside me, asleep again, on his back.

The blanket is draped low over his stomach, baring his magnificent chest. And an inch or two of his massively erect cock.

Despite the cold air, he's warm. I'm close to him, barely an inch between our bodies. I'm on my side, one hand beneath the pillow, the other between our bodies. He's billowing heat. And I'm cold. My nipples pebble into diamonds from the cold. But just from the cold, though. Not because of him. Not because of his hard body and obvious erection. And god…what an erection. The top couple inches are exposed, the plump, bulbous mushroom-shaped head, the flesh stretched and straining. The length of him that's not bared is outlined by the blanket, giving me an impression of his girth. And, holy hell, the man is absurdly well endowed. Enough that my breath goes shallow and my mouth goes dry and something shifts inside me, low in my belly. An ache blossoms between my thighs.

I turn away from him, onto my back, clenching my hands together, reminding myself how I got here. And why I'm in this bed with this man.

And what he expects from me.

The hell of it is, if it weren't for the little fact that I had no choice in coming here, that I had no say about belonging to this man, regardless of whatever excuses he may make about bills of sale and technicalities…if it weren't for that…I'd want him.

Fuck, I *do* want him.

I just don't *want* to want him.

I want to hate him. I want to stay angry with him. But I can't. He's quiet, unassuming. Absolutely gorgeous. Competent, capable. Dangerous. He's never mistreated me or said a negative word to me. He's attractive, not just physically, but his quiet presence and his confidence make him more so. Damn me, but I *enjoy* being around him. I feel safe with him. And his touch last night—I shudder, remembering— it was skilful, knowledgeable, and gentle. He knew how to touch me to elicit a response.

I'm still ruminating on all of this when he grumbles in his sleep; a low rumbling as he rolls toward me, draping his arm across me, a thigh over my thigh. He presses his lips against my shoulder, not in a kiss, but simply from how closely he is pressed against my body. And suddenly I can't breathe. His hand curls against my hip, flattens, curls. Descends to my thigh. My slip has ridden up, bunching over my thighs. He's almost snoring so I know he's asleep, but his hand seems to have a mind of its own. Slipping lower, under the hem of the slip, and up to cup my bare hip. He uses my hipbone as a handhold to pull me closer. Automatically, my body rolls to cradle my spine against his chest, curling to fit my body into the comma of his, leaving his hand flattened against my belly. Low. *Very* low. His erection is nestled between the globes of my ass, a hot naked rigid of flesh pressed hard between my ass cheeks.

I can't breathe.

Can't move.

Somehow, my palm has found its way on top of his, and I'm struggling to keep my hips still.

He remains asleep and I, comfortable and aroused and confused, drift as well.

I wake again, rolled the other way, facing the room. He's sitting on the edge of the bed, hunched forward. His right arm is moving. My breath catches and my mouth goes dry and my thighs clench when I realize what he's doing. I remain perfectly still and silent as his hand moves harder and faster.

He's so caught up in the moment that he doesn't realize I'm awake. Doesn't feel me shift behind him.

What am I doing?

*Don't do this*, I tell myself, but I'm a helpless prisoner in my own body. My mind has lost the war with my body.

I sit up, legs curled beneath me. I press up against his spine; he tenses, freezes. His hand stills on his cock, gripped low at the base.

"Hannah, I didn't think you'd—"

I reach up with my right hand and press my palm to his lips, silencing him. My left hand curls around his waist. I lean against him, resting my chin on his shoulder and watch as my right hand steals across his thigh, and my fingers wrap around his erection. He gasps, a sharp inhalation that turns to a long deep moan as I slide my hand up to the tip, squeeze once, and then glide back down. His head falls back to rest on my shoulder, and he releases his grip on his cock, clutches his knees instead.

My hand is small, and his cock is mammoth. It takes me an extraordinary amount of time to stroke him from root to tip, and I do so slowly, caressing his length. Pressing my breasts against his shoulder blades, I bring my other hand down from his mouth, and now wrap both hands around him.

Stupid, stupid, stupid me, I turn my face into his neck. Inhale his masculine scent, the tickling brush of his beard against my cheek. I close my eyes and focus on feeling his hard body between my arms, his chest and back expanding and contracting with each breath, growing deeper and faster the more I stroke his cock. And god, that cock. Thick in my hands. Hot, hard. Skin softer than silk sheathing a rod of iron. The veins expanding under my palms, his belly against my thumbs as I reach his root. I reach down and cup his balls, heft their weight and massage them ever so gently, then my hands go to his erection, wrapping my fingers around the broad plump head and I rub my thumb against the impossibly soft and springy tip, directly over the tiny hole at the very top.

I don't care about much of anything right now, except that I like the feel of his cock in my hands. I enjoy the way he can't catch his breath, can't stop himself from gyrating his hips. I enjoy drawing this out, caressing him for the raw pleasure of the sensation, not for him, but for me. Because I like his cock, I like touching it. I don't really care what he wants right now. I'm not trying to make him orgasm. I'm touching him for me.

He groans, a loud sound in the small cabin. Shoves his hips up, thrusting into my hands. He's close.

I open my eyes and watch, now. No hurry, I don't jerk him faster. Don't jerk him at all, but continue to caress him slowly, for my own enjoyment. Watching as he thrusts into my hands, shuddering now, wanting it faster, wanting it harder, but holding back.

He moves like a striking serpent. Twisting in place, he wraps his arms around me, falls to the bed, and rolls to his back once more, except now I'm on top of him. His huge hands grip my ass, which is generously proportioned enough that even his large hands cannot cover it all. He tugs me against his body. His eyes are on mine, hard and fierce and fiery. He scrapes his fingernails up my spine, drawing my slip with it.

"Lift up, Hannah." His voice is a murmur, barely audible, but rumbling powerfully.

I press my hands against his chest and lift up a little, and he peels the slip up and off. My naked breasts fall against his chest, and his gaze goes there and remains there. After tossing the slip to the floor, he tucks my hair behind my ears. He grazes my shoulders with his palms, and then cups my breasts. His palms are work-rough, callused, and the sandpapery scrape against my sensitive, erect nipples is delicious. So much so that my eyelids flutter and a soft breath escapes my lips, and then his fingers pinch my nipple and I gasp.

He hauls me further up his body, so I'm straddling his stomach, pressing my bare core against his belly, thighs spread wide. My tits brush his face, and he nuzzles between them, one then the other, and then he suckles my nipple and flattens it between his tongue and roof of his mouth. He sucks hard. I moan and thrust my chest forward, tip my head back, helpless against the erotic thrill that bolts through me. And then his hands, oh...fuck, his hands. They skate down my spine and cup my ass. Clutch it, then he spreads me apart. His fingertips slide dangerously close to the tight knot of muscle in my ass, but skip over it.

With no warning, no teasing, no build up those fingers delve into my cunt, spearing inside me, three of them, thick, rough, spreading me apart. Sliding in and out, just a little. Fingers curling inside me. His mouth moves from nipple to nipple, licking, teasing, suckling, and I feel something inside me clench, tighten to piano-wire tautness. Feel something hot spread through me. Wetness suffuses my pussy, and now the in-and-out of his fingers makes a wet squelching sound.

He pulls them out of me and smears my essence against my clit, and now a whimper slips out of me, a lip-between-my-teeth groan. A circle of his fingers, slow at first. Then faster. My hips begin to move on their own as he builds me up, tightening the wire inside me, adding heat to the fire within. Faster, faster. My hips gyrate, slide against his hand.

"Are you there, Hannah?" His voice breaks the silence, rough and low and unexpected.

I nod. "Yeah...yeah, I'm there."

He keeps fingering my clit, then dives into me and gathers wetness and spreads it against me, circles, delves in, coats his fingers, smears them wet against my clit. I'm about to bite through my lip, and my moans are grating past my lips nonstop, and my hips are flying hard and fast, pistoning against his hand.

"Close, now?"

I arch my back up, and then press it concave, fighting the orgasm, on my hands and knees and grinding against his fingers. "God yes. So fucking close. So fucking close."

"Come for me, Hannah. Let me feel you come."

I can't help it. I don't even try to fight it, anymore. My fingers dig into his chest, claw into his flesh and muscle and rake down, my hips fly and grind and swivel and my core tightens around his fingers and I can't see, can't breathe, can't do anything but fall apart on top of him, crying out wordlessly, a hoarse whimper as an orgasm blasts through me, detonating inside. Everything is heat and pressure, pleasure and the ache twisting into ecstasy, his fingers gliding perfectly, unendingly, unhurriedly over my throbbing clit.

And then I feel him.

His cock nudges my slit, and my hand moves between us to grip his thickness and I guide the broad soft head to my entrance, resting my forehead on his chest as I lift my hips. I'm a breath away from sitting down on him and spearing him into my cunt.

He grips my hair in his hand and tugs my head backward, tilting my face up to his. "Look at me, Hannah."

I open my eyes and meet his molten brown gaze. He is on fire. He is lust embodied. His hard body is huge beneath me, one hand caressing my ass and my spine and my thighs, wherever he can reach, and the other is gripping my hair, forcing me to look at him. He tenses his muscles, hard and mammoth. I'm panting through clenched teeth, raw need clashing inside me, battering against the rush of post-orgasm bliss. I *need* this. I have to have him inside me. Nothing else matters. I don't even remember anything else. There's never been anything but this moment in time, his cock teasing the slit of my cunt, his hand on my skin, and his grip on my hair rough yet careful.

The connection…it's sparking and igniting, catalytic, raw, primal. No words are needed to encapsulate or describe or enumerate this thing between us. He feels it as fully as I do. It cannot be denied, now.

He lets go of my hair, and his hand leaves my flesh, and I'm free to do as I please. I could climb off of him, and he wouldn't stop me. I know this. He's letting me choose.

There's no choice, though, and the ghost of a smirk on those damned lips of his tells me he knows it.

I sit up straight.

Pause.

Slam my ass down onto his hips, hammering his cock into me.

"Oh—my fucking *god*—" he snarls, eyes widening. "Fuck...oh *fuck*. Hannah—Jesus. You're so goddamned tight. So wet."

"And you're huge, Conrad. You barely fit. It almost hurts, you're so fucking big." The words fall out of my mouth, unbidden. Each one a truth. I ache. I burn. He's nearly too big, perfectly so. Seated deep inside me. "You feel so good inside me, Conrad. So good I can't handle it. So fucking good."

He's not moving. Just thrust deep, motionless, thick inside me. I can feel every ridge, every vein, every goddamned perfect inch of him. I need him to move. I need him to fuck me.

But he doesn't.

He just fixes those big brown eyes of his on mine and smirks, a not-quite-smile painting the corners of his mouth. I can't help a shuddering flex of my hips, and he moans with me as his cock grinds inside my cunt.

That's all it takes, that slight movement of mine. It pushes me over the edge, has me falling forward, palms flat on the wall of his chest. Hips swiveling slowly, because as much as I want it hard, fast, now, more—I'd rather savor it, take my time with it.

He glides his hands over my cheeks, brushing my hair away from my face, then down my spine, his warm touch making my flesh tingle. Then he moves to my hips and then my ass, cupping the heavy globes and pulling me apart as he thrusts, pulling my ass cheeks apart so he can fuck deeper.

It's too much.

Too much.

He's too much. Too big inside me, too hard. Too thick, too long.

And he's moving, now, and I'm moving with him. We're utterly synched, even our breathing matches, his hands lift me up and pull me apart, and his dick drives into me, spearing deep, all the way in, and I moan and he groans and snarls and pulls out, and I lift up, using my thighs to pull away, and then I feel it rising inside me. Another orgasm. Bigger than the first one, hotter, harder, deeper.

It's there, hovering within me like a balloon on the cusp of popping, like a bubble about to burst. He lets go of my ass and grips my hips, pulls me against him. God, god. His cock, my god. I focus on feeling it as it slides in and out of me; focus on each wet slide in, each smooth glide out, focus on the way he fills my pussy, stretching me apart. He thrusts in and I whimper as he plunges deep, and I squeeze down with my pussy, clamping my walls around his thickness.

He's moving slowly, so slowly. Teasing me. Driving in and out with maddening, deliberate slowness, looking up at me, staring at me as he fucks. And I can't look away from him, can't stop my hips from swiveling, rocking on him, can't stop myself from sitting up and finding my balance and grinding on him, then lifting up and sitting down on his cock. I cup my breasts with both hands and rock, lift up and crash down, harder and harder, and he has no choice but to move with me, fuck harder with me. I feel him throb inside me, pulsing with each thrust.

Turns out he does have a choice.

I'm riding the edge, teetering on a knife's edge of near-climax, pinching my own nipples as I ride his cock, reaching for the orgasm, moving harder and harder, gasping, crying out, feeling him move with me, hear him grunt and snarl, moving harder and faster and I'm there, and I know he's there too—

And then somehow I'm on my back and he's out of me and off the bed.

Chest rising and falling rapidly, cock standing straight up against his belly, slightly curved back toward his body, balls heavy and tight against him, ripped abs tautening with each breath. Brows furrowed, fists clenched.

"What—" I'm disoriented, off-balance, frustrated. "I was—Why'd you stop?"

"Wasn't ready for that."

"I don't understand. I thought this was what you wanted." I move off the bed, toward him. Stop a few inches away. "I was enjoying it—"

"It is, and so was I. But it's been so long since—" he cuts off, jaw clenched, teeth grinding. "It's been a long time."

There's so much going on behind his eyes, deep inside him, but I can't read any of it, can't fathom any of it. I can't fathom *him*.

He pushes past me to sits on the bed like he was when I woke up; sitting on the edge, knees wide apart, hunched forward over himself. "Go back to the beginning. The way you were when you first woke up."

Confused, I do as he says. I climb back onto the bed, settle behind him, feet tucked under my butt, sitting on my shins. I press up against him, crushing my breasts against his back. "Like this?"

"Yeah." His voice is tight, quiet. "Touch me. Please."

I slide one hand around his waist and find his cock, still glistening and slick with my essence. I grasp him, low at the base, and then rest my cheek against his back, between his shoulder blades. I close my eyes, and stroke his length, tamping down the ravaging urgency of a few moments ago, the need to finish coming. He rumbles, a sound of grudging pleasure emerging from deep in his chest.

I caress his cock, fondle its unbelievable length, top to bottom, again and again. As slowly as possible. I brush my thumb over the tip and squeeze the head. I roll my palm over the top and glide my fist around him to the root.

He groans again, a long, drawn-out sound of relief and pleasure, and it's so palpable I can feel it, and it makes me want nothing more than to make him enjoy it all the more. I shouldn't. I know I shouldn't. I know this changes nothing. But I'm utterly lost to this right now, even though I know I'll have a debt of emotions to sort through when it's over.

But for now…

I bring my other hand around his waist and stroke him hand over hand, long slow downward gliding touches, one hand and then the other, and then I pump him with both hands until he starts to flex into my hands, and then I stop.

I slide off the bed and fall to my knees on the floor in front of him, between his legs. He stares down at me, brows scrunched together, expression characteristically intense but unreadable. I cup my hand around the head of his cock, summon saliva and let it spill out of my mouth and into the cup formed by my hands and onto his cock. Then I smear it onto him, massaging the saliva over the head of his cock and down his length, and now I can stroke him faster and faster, plunging my hand up and down his cock until he's grunting and grinding into my hand, his fists planted in the mattress, head tipped back, spine arching in now as he begins to lose control.

When it's obvious he's seconds away from coming, I slow down and back him away from the edge, don't stop to think about what I'm doing or why…and sink my mouth onto him. I taste my own spit, my own essence, his pre-cum, his flesh. He groans again as I wrap my lips around his cock, and the groan turns into a sigh as I take more and more of him.

One hand just beneath my lips, I lift up until I'm kissing the tip of his dick, and then sink down, and he moans the whole while, ecstasy so bone-deep, relief so soul-felt that it makes something inside me swell, burst, and I bury more of his huge cock in my mouth until he's at my throat.

His hands settle on my head, tangle into my hair, slide beneath the thick blond locks to cup my scalp in his powerful hands, but his touch is gentle, not insistent nor forceful. Affectionate, more than anything. As if what I'm doing feels so good he can't help but try to show me, can't help but hold on to me in some way.

"Oh…god, Hannah."

"Mmmmm."

"Don't stop."

"Hmmm-mmmm."

I move a little faster, then, and suckle. Suck. Caress my hand down his length from below my mouth down to the root, back up, sliding just the head and first few inches of his cock between my lips, sucking, swallowing, swirling my tongue around the tip.

"Fuck...oh fuck."

"Mmmm-hmmm?"

He likes it when I hum, judging by the way he grunts and thrusts and thickens in my mouth.

"So good, Hannah...I've never felt...oh fuck. Don't stop...don't stop."

"Mmmmmmmmmm." Stroke, suckle, sink down on him, take him to my throat and back away.

He's moving, now. Involuntarily, his hips flex and thrust, and his cupped grip on my head tightens, and I know he's close again. Closer than ever.

"I'm gonna come, Hannah. I'm gonna come so hard—"

"Mmmm-hmmmm?"

"Oh fuck, fuck yeah. So hard." He's struggling to remain still as the orgasm wells up in him, rifles through him, and I feel his cock thicken, feel his balls tighten, his abs go taut, hear his breath catch. "Can you take it, Hannah?"

"Mmmm-hmmm."

Oh god, can I take it? I can take it all, every last little bit. I look up at him as he comes. I watch him. His face distorts in rapture, his mouth falls open and his brows lift, and his lips tremble, and his tongue slides around the corner of his mouth. An expression I can read, finally: euphoria.

"Oh god, Hannah, I'm coming...fuck, oh fuck. You feel like heaven, you feel so perfect, make me feel so good. Oh god..."

There it is. He thrusts, shoving his cock deeper into my mouth and grunts, and I feel it spurt out of him, taste it on my tongue and I swallow, stroke his length and suck and swallow, bob up and down on him, sink him deep and slide him out. His cum is hot and wet and thick and salty and smoky as I swallow it, gulp after gulp as he comes and comes into my mouth. So much cum, too much. I can't swallow fast enough, and it leaks out of my mouth, squirting out around his cock and dripping down my chin.

He pulls out, then, and I take his slick, wet, sticky cock in both hands and stroke him hard and fast until he collapses backward onto the bed, hips lifting up off the mattress, and he spasms helplessly as I ply his length to milk every last drop out of him, lick the beads of cum away as they appear. Finally, then, finally he's finished, cock slackening, hips sinking to the bed, gasping.

I fall backward onto my ass as he sits up, chest still heaving. He reaches out a hand, and I take it, letting him pull me up to the bed to sit beside him.

He stares at me, his expression inscrutable once again. His thumb scrapes across my chin, beneath my lip, wiping away the errant drops of cum, and then his forefinger tugs my mouth open, and I taste his thumb, and his cum, eyes on his, and I swear his cock twitches already as he feels me lick the cum away.

"Your turn." His voice is a raspy murmur as he slides off the bed, to his knees, mirroring my position from moments ago.

He doesn't dive right in. He toys with me first, nudging my thighs apart. A teasing touch at first, from my knee along the inside of my thigh, skimming across my core, and along the other leg, down my inner thigh to my knee. He feathers a light kiss to my inner thigh, and another, closer. Closer. I sigh as his lips brush over my pussy, and then his tongue smears down my slit, licks my labia, one side and then the other, light tickling teasing touches of his tongue, tracing my opening, licking the shape of my cunt from top to bottom, side to side, before finally flicking his tongue-tip to my hardening clit.

Now his fingers are there, fingertips grazing the lips of my pussy, tracing around the outside, teasing, teasing, teasing, and his tongue is gliding up the length of my slit, over and over, but not against my clit, not even into my cunt, just licking the seam as he traces it with his fingertips.

Learning.

Exploring.

Tasting.

And then, simultaneously, his long middle finger probes my entrance and glides into my wetness and warmth, and his tongue stiffens against my clit. I make a whimpering cry, and I feel my cunt squeeze his finger as heat and pressure build like wildfire in the pit of my belly. The spasm is imminent, and he's only just begun.

My hands find his hair, so thick, so soft. I bury my fingers into it, tightening them into a knotted grip as he suckles my clit between his teeth. His finger glides in until his knuckles bump against me, and then he withdraws and adds a second finger.

He curls them inside me, finds a spot that makes my eyes cross, rips a gasp from me, forces my hips into motion, and then—oh shit, shit, shit, his tongue is a mad wild fevered starving thing, flying around my clit suddenly so fast I can't breathe, my lungs burn and my eyes squeeze shut and I fall back onto the bed and arch my spine, and all this only crushes my cunt harder against his face and his fingers massage that perfect magical spot and his tongue flits and flicks in crazed circles.

He sits back, hauling me partially off the bed, and my legs wind around his neck and shoulders. I'm shamelessly grinding against his face, now.

And then it's too much to take and I can't even keep my legs tight. I go limp, spine arched to shove my tits toward the ceiling, cunt fused to his mouth, his hands under my ass, supporting my weight, his tongue working madly. And then, seconds from the orgasm peaking and blasting through me, he slides me back onto the bed and shoves my legs apart, and I'm bucking with need, wild with it, growling wordlessly, writhing, desperate for him to lick me, touch me, fuck me, anything, anything to make me come. I hold my legs apart and he slides those two thick fingers back inside me and presses the fingertips of his other hand to my clit in slow circles, sliding his fingers in and out of me and circling my clit in sync, slowly, slowly, until I'm whimpering nonstop, writhing into his skilful touch, crying out as he increases the pace, working me faster and faster.

I'm so wet, so ready. His fingers squelch in and out of me, wet sucking, slurping sounds echoing in the small cabin as he finger-fucks me, but it's his touch to my clit that has lightning searing though me, the way he doesn't press too hard or too light, swiping around the hard throbbing little nub of nerves so perfectly it's like he just *knows* how to touch me, how to make me scream.

And god, fuck, scream I do.

His relentless touch speeds to frantic fucking and circling, and my hips are gyrating, rolling, bucking, and I'm crying out, sobbing. He withdraws his fingers from inside my cunt, flattens his palm over my belly, and smears his fingertips around my clit hard and fast and perfect, holding me down.

Everything inside me breaks, then. Explodes. Heat, pressure, and piercing ecstasy plow through me. I scream so loud my throat aches, but it's not enough to relieve the painful shearing rupture of ecstatic bliss. The pressure of the pleasure is too much, I'm breaking, cracking, thrashing under his touch but held down and even though I've come, he doesn't let up, and the climax continues to build, continues to tear me apart, smashing me into pieces. I'm bucking against his hand, spine bowed off the bed, tits jouncing everywhere, and then—

And then—

Whiteness suffuses me.

White heat.

A billowing magma-hot climax takes over. It's too much, too much, too much.

I feel myself let go, hear his voice— "Look at me, Hannah. Look at me when you come."

I wrench my eyes open as I fall apart, as I come with a potency like the heavens breaking open, and I feel a spasm ripple through my cunt, watch a spurt of something wet stream out of me and coat his naked chest, and I come, and I squirt again, and he doesn't stop as wave after wave after wave of climax hits me, freight-train hard, unending, until I'm weak and ragged and breathless, and finally it ends, finally I collapse to the mattress, gasping hoarsely for breath.

And that's when he levers over me, and my gaze trails from his intense brown eyes down his damp chest to his erection, massive, thick, and straining for me.

I'm utterly spent, unable to even move a hand.

And he's nudging my knees aside with his, carving his palm over my hip, across my diaphragm, and cupping my tits. He's gripping his cock in one fist and touching me everywhere with the other, and now the wide tip of his cock is nudging my slit, and I cannot believe myself, cannot believe that I'm ready for this. I'm not, but I can't stop it, can't stop myself from wanting—*needing*—to feel him inside me.

It's different, now.

"Hannah…" He breathes my name as he enters me.

Hypersensitive from climax, the sensation of his cock gliding into my cunt is the most incredible thing I've ever felt, I'm so sensitive I feel each ripple of skin as it slides between the lips of my pussy and into my channel, and I can't help squeezing around him, clenching down as he fills me.

"Oh fuck, Hannah. Tell me you feel this."

"I feel it," I admit. I don't want to feel it, much less admit it, but I do.

I feel him, *him*, the man, and his soul. Not just his body. A stranger, almost, but I feel him as he enters me. I feel him needing this. Not just the physical, not just the release. If it were just that, he'd have been sated after I sucked him dry. And if it was just physical for me, I wouldn't be even more in need of him now than I was before he ever touched me. I don't get it. I don't understand it. I don't know where it came from, or how it happened.

But it did, and I can't deny it.

I cup his taut ass and pull him against me. I slide my other hand up his back to curl around the back of his head, pulling his face to mine. He hovers an inch above me, staring down into my eyes, and I swear the veil parts, just a little, and I can almost see into his soul, into his heart. I can see the loneliness like a specter haunting him, see the heartbreak from the story he told me, how he lost his wife. I can see his need for someone…anyone. For a connection, a human connection.

We move in unison, move together as if we've always moved like this, slow and deliberate and languorous and delirious, eyes locked, bodies moving, sweat beading and dripping and trickling, hands moving and exploring.

I feel him, feel it inside me, something like an orgasm but so much more. So, so much more.

When it comes, I can't help the sob that rips through me.

His cum fills me, I clamp around his pounding thrusting beautiful perfect cock, as I come apart yet again in a way I've never felt before, orgasming not just with my body, but with my soul and my heart and my mind—he feels it, too, and I see it in him, see it in the way his face moves, softens, in the way his eyes search mine, the way his palm cradles my cheek and his mouth slams down on mine.

He kisses me.

● ● ● ●

He kisses me as he comes.

His tongue tangles with mine, slipping and sliding, searching the cavity of my mouth, tracing the line of my gums, my teeth, ravaging my mouth, fierce and wild and demanding. And as his tongue plunders my mouth, as his lips slant and devour wet and hungry on mine—in unison with all this, he comes.

He grunts into my mouth, into the kiss. I feel his cum fill me, hot wet jets spasming out of his cock and splashing hard inside my cunt, and still he fucks me, slow pounding thrusts, unhurried, deliberate, *hard,* rough, primally brutal, and dizzyingly perfect, pushing my own climax to new shattering heights, and he keeps fucking until his cum squirts out around his cock and trickles along my labia and down my inner thighs, so much cum, so impossibly much because he's *still* coming, and it's filled me and is overflowing and dripping down my taint and into my ass.

And all the while he is kissing me.

Fucking me and kissing me.

Groaning against my lips, sucking my tongue into his mouth and groaning as if his entire being is being consumed as he comes inside my cunt, as if he can't believe what he's feeling—

I know I can't.

It's unreal, how this feels. To come, and come, and come, to taste his mouth and his tongue, and swallow his groans and suck down his moans, and clamp my cunt around his cock and feel his cum in me dripping out of me and down my thighs, to feel him, *him*, all of him, so much of him that it overwhelms me, overflows my soul and mind and heart exactly the way his hot wet thick sticky cum overflows my cunt.

When he can't come anymore and neither can I, he finally stops kissing my bruised lips, and his eyes are fraught, open, wild, haunted, hunted, delirious, vulnerable.

In a split second, like this, with his eyes on mine, his secret inner self is bared to me.

And then he's off me and across the cabin, hands braced on the smooth-hewn logs of the wall, his back heaving as he gasps for breath, ass taut as he presses against the wall with all his power, as if he's trying to push over the wall.

Every line of his body is tensed. Every hard plane of muscle speaks of turmoil.

I leave the bed and move softly, carefully across the room to stand behind him. I'm still in denial, I think, still refusing to think about how and why I'm here. It's easier to pretend that all this can mean something, that we could both move beyond the fact of my situation, the fact that he owns me, that I am stuck here in this tiny cabin in the far rugged wilderness of the mountains until and unless he sees fit to take me somewhere else. I could be stuck here forever, living with him.

In this moment, I think of none of that.

I think only of the agonized conflict written on his body.

Think only of the need to soothe it.

I press my breasts to his back and smooth my hands up and down his chest. "Conrad. What is it?"

"I got...lost, there for a while." He's speaking barely above a whisper.

"I didn't mind." I'd hope that'd be obvious, that he can read my body well enough to know there's a lot more to how I felt about what we just did together than "not minding."

"Let me ask you something, and I want you to be completely honest."

"All right."

He doesn't turn to look at me. He remains as he is, palms braced against the wall, head hanging between his arms. "Why'd you touch me? Why'd you do...all that, with me? I thought you weren't ready. Thought you didn't want to. That you're afraid of me."

I stand behind him, run my hands over his back, shoulder to shoulder, from neck to buttocks, in random soothing circles. It's easier to let the truth out if I'm touching him, somehow. "I did it because I wanted to. I woke up, and I saw you touching yourself, and...I don't know. I wanted to touch you. I'm not afraid of you anymore. You haven't given me reason to be."

"Not yet. Give me time, though." He laughs, a bitter sound.

"What is it, really?"

He straightens, turns around. "I told you, I got lost."

"What does that mean?"

"I haven't had sex with anyone since my wife died. And that was three years ago. So I had a good bit of pent up...frustration, I guess you could say." His expression shutters. "I knew where I was, and I knew you were you, but—" He clicks his teeth together to stop the words, to keep them back, keep them inside.

I remain as close to him as I dare, a hair's breadth separating our bodies. "Don't shut down now, Conrad. Tell me." I force him to look at me. "It's not like I can go anywhere."

"I knew I was with you, but...I felt *her*. I don't know how to put it better than that. I miss her so damn much, and—I just felt her. That was why I had to stop, when you were on top of me." His eyes search mine as he speaks, and I see a hint of apology in them. "That was how she liked it best. And when it was you, it—was too difficult to keep the past and the present separate. You, and her."

"Do I look like her?"

A shrug. "Not really. You're tall, curvy, and blonde. She was short, petite, and she had auburn hair. Wasn't much to her, physically. But she was one of those people who just…filled a room." He leans back against the wall, staring at the ceiling. Seeing her. "Wasn't afraid of anything, or anyone. Never afraid to speak her mind, no matter the circumstances. She—she told me it was a mistake to break away from the wagon train. I didn't listen. And it got her killed. Even as she—as she died, she never blamed me."

"I'm sorry, Conrad."

He straightens, and his face drains of emotion. "Nothing for you to be sorry for. It's done and in the past. Only thing to do is move on. Which is what I'm trying to do."

"I can't replace her, Conrad."

"I'm not trying to. Nothing against you, Hannah, but no one ever could replace her."

"Then why am I here? What is it you want from me?"

"I was desperate, Hannah. Utterly alone for three years, except when I went south to sell my stock. And even then I discovered it's entirely possible to be alone in a crowd. I couldn't stand being alone anymore. But I'm not—good. Or safe. My life isn't safe. I'm not the man I was. I can't stand cities. Even little towns are too much for me. I need the space, the wide open spaces, and the solitude. Just…not alone. I need one person to share the silence with."

I touch his chest with one hand. "I understand."

"Do you?" His eyes are sharp, his voice hesitant.

"As much as I can, yes."

"So you'll stay?"

"I didn't realize I had a choice."

"I told you, already. I didn't know how else to find anyone to bring here, to be with me, so I resorted to Thompson. You're free to go whenever you want, and if you do want to, I'll take you. Get you somewhere civilized, give you some money to set up a life for yourself. If that's what you want."

He doesn't give me a chance to respond, instead sidles past me and begins getting dressed.

When he's dressed, he shoots me a glance. "Got work to do."

And just like that, I'm alone.

I climb back into the bed, let myself drowse.

I must have fallen asleep, because I'm jolted awake by the sound of boots on the porch. The door creaks, and snow skirls in through the opening, eddying in the wind. A body darkens the doorway, and my heart skips a beat, thinking it's Conrad.

Then he enters, and my blood runs as icy as the air outside.

It's Charlie.

Dressed in furs, which are coated and matted with snow, rendering him all but invisible.

He has a shotgun in his hands, and his eyes—the only part of him visible—are the palest blue, icy, hard, vicious. Wicked. And as they land on me, sitting up in the bed, naked, blanket across my thighs, nipples pebbling in the sudden blast of cold, his gaze goes wild with lust.

"Get dressed, girlie. We're leaving."

"Conrad will return any moment. You'd best leave." I endeavor to sound calm.

He grins, an evil curl of his lips. "I don't think so, honey. He's on the other side of the valley. Won't be back for some time."

"He'll come after you, you know. It won't go well for you when he catches up."

Charlie's evil grin just widens. "Maybe so, but by the time he catches up, I'll have had my fill of you, and he'll be welcome to what's left."

He crosses the room, boots tromping on the wood floor, leaving snowy footprints. He tugs off his glove and reaches for me. I recoil, but he's faster. He pinches my nipple with frigid hands. Then he gathers a handful of my hair and hauls me off the bed, tossing me across the room. I fall to the floor; scalp aching, hip stinging where I hit the floor. Fear has me scrabbling to my feet, backing away from him, but there's nowhere to go.

He levels the shotgun at me. "Quit draggin' this out, girl. I'll shoot you and fuck you right here on the floor as you bleed out. Don't think I won't. I'd rather have you intact, though, so I can enjoy your…charms for that much longer." He thumbs back the hammer of his shotgun, the sound deafening in the silence—*snick-click*. "Now. Get dressed, or I'll drag your carcass out there naked."

I dress quickly, because the venom in his dead gaze tells me he means every word he says. As soon as I'm done, he pinions my arm in a bruising grip, shoving me outside into the blistering, blasting, and knife-sharp cold. The wind has risen to a howl and the snow blows horizontal, obscuring everything. There's a snow-matted horse tied to the rail of the porch, and Charlie unties it, and then tosses me up into the saddle, just behind the pommel, and he hops up behind me. Shotgun in one hand, reins in the other, he hauls the horse around, kicks it in the side to get it moving. The horse bolts forward into a jolting canter. I can see nothing through the blowing snow, but Charlie somehow knows where he's going, or the horse does. I grip the pommel with both hands, cling to the horse with my thighs, and try to keep my seat, try not to think about what Charlie's going to do to me.

Chill slices into my bones, bites my nose, my cheeks, my fingers, my toes. Fear is a heavy lead ball in my gut, rising up into my throat.

We ride, and ride, and ride. As we begin an ascent, I know we've left the valley. In among the trees, we get some shelter against the driving snow, but not against the razor cold. I don't recognize the landscape around us from the ride down, which makes me think he's not going back the same way. Once you've left the valley, options open up a good bit as far which direction to go. And with the blinding, driving snow filling our tracks as fast as we're making them…my hopes of rescue dwindle down to nothing. Conrad may not even know I'm missing.

Time loses meaning. Nothing exists but cold and snow and the sway of the horse. Even fear recedes to a dull knot in my gut.

Until, suddenly, Charlie tugs the horse to a stop, just inside a clearing between the trees. Not even a clearing, really, just a few yards of empty space between the pines.

"Shit." Charlie's voice is a frustrated hiss.

I peer through the snow, and my heart leaps, skips a beat.

Conrad.

On foot, his hat angled down across his face, coat pulled back to reveal the handles of his revolvers. His hands are loose at his sides, but his body is coiled, tensed. He's a rattlesnake bunched into a ball, seconds from striking. A panther in the tall grass, all fur and muscle and deadly grace.

Charlie swings off the horse, casual, unhurried. Shotgun held one-handed, barrel tilted toward the ground.

"Must be pretty green," Conrad says, barely audible in the thick, hushed snow-soft silence, "to think you could sneak into my valley, into my *home*, and take what's mine without me knowing."

Charlie flexes his empty hand, curling the fingers into a ball and releasing them. "Come on, Conrad. You ain't really gonna shoot me over a woman, are you?"

"You know my last name, Charlie?"

An odd question, and Charlie tilts his head in confusion. "No. Should I?"

"Killian. My name is Conrad Killian." He says it like it's supposed to mean something.

The silence is somehow tenser, now, with that name out in the open.

Charlie rolls his shoulders. "I suppose I'm not entirely surprised. Ain't that many men named Conrad out this way, after all."

"So, you got two questions to answer for yourself, Markham. One, can you swing that shotgun up before I clear leather? And two, is it worth it to try? If you've heard of me, you've heard the stories."

"And they're all true, I suppose?" Charlie sounds skeptical.

"Some are, some aren't." Conrad is utterly calm, to look at him, to hear him. "That's what you'd best sort out for yourself, and fast."

I can see Charlie thinking about it. I can see his finger tracing the trigger guard, contemplating his chances.

The horse underneath me senses the violence in the air, scents the roiling tension. He whinnies, dances back a few steps. I clutch the reins and pat the horse on the neck and whisper to it.

Long, long moments of silence. Nothing but the snow blowing, and the two men facing each other.

I feel it happening before I see it. Hear it, before my eyes can make sense of it. Thunder blasts, deafening in the tiny clearing. My horse screams, rears, dances backward, and I have to cling to its neck and lean forward and jerk the reins hard to one side to keep my seat. I feel vibrations against my ribcage, but it's not thunder, it's Conrad's guns, drawn faster than the eye can track, crashing rounds out so fast, one after the other, the individual blasts meld and ripple into a single ear-numbing roll of thunder, stabbing spears of flame flashing.

Charlie jerks several times, six or eight slugs slamming into his torso even as he levels his shotgun. Conrad doesn't move, doesn't lower his guns, doesn't dodge. The shotgun booms, but the spray of shot goes high and wide, scattering snow from branches over Conrad's head and far behind him, snapping branches and sending pine needles exploding in a puff.

Charlie topples forward face first in the snow, and red stains the white in a spreading bloom.

Conrad passes one of his revolvers so he's clutching both in one hand, snaps open the chambers, digs in his pocket for shells, thumbs them in, closes the chambers and replaces the firearms in their holsters. Not a word to me, he just turns in place, disappears into the trees on the other side of the clearing, and then reappears sitting a horse, a small white and brown paint mare.

"Gotta move," he grunts. "We're well outside the territory I've claimed as mine."

"So?"

"So the gunfire will be drawing company, and I'm in no mood for getting in a fight with the Utes. Too damn cold."

I'm not inclined to argue, so I nudge Charlie's horse into a trot behind Conrad, and follow him as he winds his way through the forest.

After a while, I can't keep the questions in any longer. "Conrad? What stories?"

A silence. "After my wife died, I told you I started hitting the bottle."

Another pause. "Made me mean. Sort of earned myself a reputation as a gunfighter. Part of the reason I steer clear of society, these days. Too much temptation to pick up the bottle again, and too many people might recognize me. You develop the kind of reputation I did, it makes the young bucks come after you, think they can prove themselves by trying to take me on. Not what I want for myself anymore. Not the kind of man my wife would have wanted me to be. Can't rightly put down the guns, not out here. So I keep to myself. Charlie's the first man I've had to draw on in quite sometime, not counting the dustups with the Utes."

"How'd you know?"

"That he'd taken you?" He pats his horse. "Horses have keener senses than we do. They scented his horse, made 'em nervous. That horse ain't one of the herd, and they knew it. Made 'em antsy. And when my horses get antsy, I pay attention. Saved my life more than once, knowing when my horses don't like a situation."

We ride once more in that silence that is so uniquely ours, comfortable, but with layers of meaning. Now it's the knowledge that Charlie's corpse back there ended up that way because of me. How easy Conrad made it look. How inhumanly fast he'd drawn those revolvers. Faster than thought. The guns were drawn and bullets were flying before Charlie could even aim his shotgun.

For me.

Over me.

Because of me.

Should I be more upset about Charlie's death? More affected?

No. I'm not. Not at all. He was going to do...terrible things to me. And Conrad saved me. Came after me, and shed blood on my account.

All of this is weighted and tangled by what we did, just few hours ago. I'm still sore, aching from it.

I have to bite my lip, remembering. I can see his body in my mind. The hard angles and heavy muscle. The thick member jutting tall and proud, straining, a droplet of pre-cum beading at the tip.

I'm daydreaming, thinking of him, thinking of getting back to the cabin and getting him naked. Getting my hands on his cock. Getting it inside me again, stretching me out, filling me, making me ache and writhe and tumble over the edge…

I'm woken from my daydreaming by Conrad abruptly halting his horse at the edge of the clearing.

Fifty paces away, in a line abreast facing us, clad in thick furs, armed to teeth with rifles, bows, hatchets, a few spears, a wicked looking club made from a thick bone with a knobby, craggy rock tied to the end—

Twenty Ute warriors.

Grim, silent. Deadly threat exudes from each one.

"Hands up, Hannah. Let the reins dangle on your horse's neck and hold on with your legs. Don't say a word. Don't take your eyes off them." Conrad murmurs this low, so quietly only I can hear him, and even then I have to strain to catch his words. "Just keep riding straight between them."

He follows his own instructions, raises his hands shoulder high, gripping his horse with his knees, letting the reins drape over the paint's neck. Clicks his tongue, wiggles his heel against her side and scoots his butt forward in the saddle to get the paint walking. I do the same, and our mounts move side by side toward the line of warriors. No one speaks. No one moves, save our horses. We sway in the saddle, and I keep my eyes on the line of warriors. Their dark eyes glitter, pierce.

The one holding the club shifts on his horse and tightens his grip on his club.

Conrad's hands sink lower by a few inches; each of the warriors visibly tense, hands tighten on weapons, eyes narrow, breath is held.

The only sound is the soft crunch of hooves in the snow. The sky overhead is gray, heavy. The forest behind us is a thick dark presence, with the valley spreading away below us to our right. I can see the cabin, a tiny dot in the far distance, and a needle-thin string of smoke trickling up from the chimney. A herd of horses wheels in the snow, like a living cloud of flesh and muscle and fur blowing in the wind. The snow has stopped, for now, though more is on the way. Breath puffs in white clouds from our mouths, from the horses, from the warriors.

We're so close now that I can smell their horses, hear the heavy breath of the mounts, see the black mouths of the rifles and the keen jagged edges of their hatchets. The pits and divots in the bone of the club handle, the rough-spun fibers of the hemp rope binding the rock in place. Eyes follow us, gimlet and gleaming and cunning. Ready to pounce at the mere suggestion of violence.

Why don't they attack? What do they want?

Fear knots in my throat as my horse's front flank nudges one of the warriors' horses— the one with the club. The one whose eyes never leave me, not for a second, not even to blink.

We're parallel, now, me and that warrior. He's on my left, head pivoting on his neck to watch me. He's handsome, in an exotic, frightening way. Sharp features, deep-set eyes, cunning, intelligent, cold dark brown eyes. Not wicked, like Charlie. Just—the eyes of someone utterly unlike any I've ever seen. Alien. Those of a warrior through and through, a killer, but only when necessary. Not for sport, or for pleasure. Someone well acquainted with the dealing of death, as a fact of life. He's assessing me. It's difficult to read such alien eyes, such unfamiliar features, but there might be a glimmer of lust there, too.

His eyes remain fixed on me.

My horse is uneasy, head bobbing, shaking. Ears back, swiveling. Blowing skittish breaths. This isn't one of Conrad's horses, not as well trained. Not as calm or steady.

And then a bare hand darts out, quick as snakebite, and snares my reins. My horse halts, and I'm left trembling. Helpless. The warrior touches the tip of the club to my chin. He's not smiling, not quite but almost.

Conrad says something I don't understand—in Ute, I realize. In a calm voice, but hard as stone. It's a demand, despite the numbers arrayed against us.

The warrior continues to stare me down, and I want to look away, but I don't. I don't dare. I hold his eyes and try my damnedest to keep my fear tamped down, to keep my face calm, my expression schooled into blankness. The stone of the club is ice-cold against my chin, setting my teeth to chattering, but I don't dare move a muscle, not so much as an eye blink. I'm not even breathing.

"Give horse." The warrior's voice is higher than I expected, smooth as a frozen pond.

"Conrad?" It's all the query I can manage, and it's weak and tremulous.

"Climb down, nice and slow."

I shift in preparation to dismount, but the warrior grunts a negative. He jerks his chin at me. "Not you, horse." He twists in his saddle and jabs the club at Conrad. "*You* horse."

Conrad swings down, lithe and easy. His hands remain visible, away from his weapons. He begins loosening straps to remove his saddle from the paint.

The warrior grunts again. "Give saddle."

"No way." Conrad flips the girth strap free, lifts the saddle off, rifle in the scabbard and all. "Horse, but no saddle."

"Give saddle." More insistent, now.

Conrad's eyes swing past the warriors, to the wheeling herd of paints. "I keep my saddle, and I give you two more horses."

The warrior squints over his shoulder. His jaw flexes, tightens, tenses, and then loosens. He splays his palm out, fingers spread apart. "Five horse."

"Two." Conrad hefts the saddle to his shoulder. "Only offer I'll make."

"Three horse."

Conrad starts walking toward his valley. "Fine. Three horses. Tomorrow, though."

The warrior spits, an angry, volatile gesture. "*Now.*"

"Only you, then. And leave your club." Conrad stops, fixing his cold brown gaze on the warrior.

The warrior is silent for so long I worry he'll refuse, and he still has my reins in his grip. I haven't taken my eyes off him. His skin is leathery, dark from the sun. That club, though; there are ochre-brown stains in the creases of the stone, bits of something stuck in clumps here and there—blood, and hair, and bits of skull.

And then, roughly, abruptly, he tosses his club to a companion and releases my reins. A subtle shifting of his weight has his horse backing up, and then the horse wheels in place and the air is filled with flying snow and the thunder of hooves as the warrior and horse gallop past us and down toward the valley.

Conrad gives me a glance loaded with meaning—*start moving*, that look says. I nudge my horse into a walk, and the other warriors watch us go, Conrad on foot, carrying the saddle on his shoulder through the shin-deep snow like it's nothing.

Once we're out of sight of the Utes, I glance at Conrad, who seems to be in no rush at all. "Shouldn't we hurry down to make sure he doesn't steal your horses?"

Conrad shrugs. "They're honorable people, in their own way. We made a bargain, and he won't go back on it. It's one thing to attack me and kill me in a fight, take my horses as spoils. That'd be honorable to him. To agree to a bargain and then go back on it? Take more than we agreed to, or shoot me in the back? It wouldn't ever cross his mind. His honor as a warrior and a man is everything to him."

"Why bargain at all? They could have killed us easily. I don't think even you would have survived against those odds, not like that."

"Not a chance in hell. If I've got cover, *maybe* I could fight off that many. But they had the drop on us. We'd have been dead before we hit the ground. I'd have taken a few with me, but—no, we didn't stand a chance."

"Exactly. So why did he bargain with you?"

Another laconic shrug. "Who knows? Just the way they are, I guess—inexplicable, sometimes. That particular warrior has had his eye on my stock for a while, and this was a chance for him to get his hands on some of my horses without having to pay for them, or fight for them. He knew I'd barter, since the odds were against me, and because you were there. Best I can guess as to why."

It takes us quite a while to reach the valley with Conrad on foot, but when I offer to let him ride, or to walk myself so the horse carry the extra saddle, he just snorts in derision and continues on without further response.

It's nearing dark by the time we come to the herd of horses and the Ute warrior. He's on foot, his horse wandering free, pawing at the snow for grass beneath. The warrior is squatting in the snow, watching the horses, toying with a length of rope. Conrad sets his saddle down in a patch of bare grass beneath the shelter of a nearby pine and moves to stand a few feet away from the warrior.

Conrad whistles, once, sharply. The warrior eyes him, then returns his attention to the horses, who are approaching Conrad now, clustering around him, nuzzling him with their noses, bumping him with their shoulders. Conrad shoves them away, roughly but playfully, and a few trot in circles, shaking their heads.

The warrior rises to his feet, reaches a bare hand out toward one of the animals, a tall, lithe, brown stallion with white patches on its rump. The beast whickers nervously, but approaches, sniffs. Dances back a few steps, shakes his head.

The Ute eyes Conrad in question.

"He's not fully broken yet," Conrad says in English. He moves through the crowd of horses to single out one, a stocky white mare with a single black patch on her chest. Conrad pushes her toward the warrior. "This one's fully broken. Lots of spirit, and quick on her feet."

The warrior nods, works his fingers into the mare's mane, but his attention is still on the stallion. "That." He gestures with his free hand.

Conrad shrugs. "It's your choice, but he's got a lot of vinegar in him. Still a bit wild."

This gets a grin from the warrior, teeth flashing white, and he thumps his chest with his fist. "Wild." Gestures at the horse. "Wild." Then he fits his fingers together to form a single fist. "Is good."

Conrad nods. "One more then."

The Ute is silent a while, burying his fingers in the mare's mane, gaze raking over the herd, assessing, deciding. A smirk twitches on his lips, and he gestures at the largest of the herd, the big black stallion that Conrad was riding when we…met, shall we call it.

Conrad shakes his head. "Not that one."

The warrior glances from the black stallion to Conrad and back, and then shrugs, eyes the herd once more before approaching a small mare, all brown and white blotches. The little horse dances away, stops after a few paces, and turns back to look at the warrior, then trots away again when he tries to approach again.

Conrad laughs. "She's not broken at all. If she'll let you catch her, she's yours."

I'm surprised at the strange camaraderie between the two men, considering the thick tang of violence in the air only a few short minutes ago.

The Ute digs in his furs, comes up with a chunk of carrot. Sidles up to the little paint casually, rope dangling from one hand, carrot in the other. The paint nickers, edges closer to him, smelling the carrot. When she's within touching distance, he puts his hand to her neck, and she dances away, but he's kept the bit of carrot. She approaches again, and he rubs her neck with his hand, then with the rope, carefully, gently. He traces her neck and her shoulder with the rope, which he's doubled so one end forms a loop. Then he drapes it over her neck, and lets her have the carrot. And then, while she's munching, he fits the two ends of the rope together, creating a makeshift halter. She dances away when she feels the rope around her neck, and he lets her dance, rear up, prance on her hind legs, pawing at the him with her forehooves. She settles down again, and he pulls on the rope. She follows, and when he stops she keeps approaching, nuzzling the warrior's furs with her nose. He lets her, holding the rope only loosely, and she noses aside the flap in his furs, nudging her nose in until she finds something, coming up with another chunk of carrot, which she crunches loudly.

While she's eating, the warrior loosens the rope, and then in a series of knots too intricate for me to follow, makes a true halter out of the rope, complete with a set of shortened reins.

"I'll be damned," Conrad says. "I've been trying to catch her for weeks."

The warrior flashes a cocky grin, and then, in a single lithe movement, latches onto her mane and leaps onto her back. The little paint goes crazy, whinnying, rearing, bucking, flinging in circles, dancing like mad, trying to dislodge the warrior, but no matter what she does, she can't dislodge him, despite the fact that there's no saddle nor even a proper bit or bridle. It goes on for longer than I'd have believed, had I not seen it with my own eyes, until the horse is blowing and exhausted, and finally settles. And that's when he dismounts, circles to stand by her head and pats her cheek, rubs her ears, whispering to her. And then he mounts her once more, and this time she allows it, only trotting around nervously, unsure of the weight on her back. Once she stops fighting, he dismounts again and leads her to his original horse.

He glances at Conrad. "Give more rope."

There's a long coiled length of rope tied to Conrad's saddle which he retrieves and tosses to the warrior, who then cuts it into two shorter sections and one long one. He fashions halters from the shorter sections, and fits those onto his new horses, and then uses the final longest piece to tie all three halters together, so he can control all three horses at once.

Mounting his original horse, he gathers his reins and the lead for the others, and then pauses with a long hard glance at Conrad. "Good horse. Very fine."

Conrad nods. "I know."

"Maybe I kill you, take all."

Conrad shrugs, that insouciant, devil-may-care gesture. "You can try." A twitch of his hand flicks his coat back, exposing one revolver. "You won't succeed."

A grin from the warrior, equal parts pride and respect. "Maybe no kill." He lifts the lead rope. "Horse make foal. I bring."

Conrad just nods and lets his coat fall back into place. "Okay."

The Ute glances at me. Another of those fierce, wild grins. "Strong woman. Strong medicine."

And then he's gone, kicking his horse into a gallop, the others following in a spray of snow and flying manes. We both stand and watch until the Ute warrior is out of sight.

The big black horse has moseyed over, standing near Conrad, nosing at his pocket. When the warrior is out of sight, Conrad lets out a long, relieved sigh, visibly relaxing, and leans against his horse.

"Shit." He wipes at his face with both hands. "Well…that was fun."

"I don't know how you stayed so calm. I was scared witless." I move to stand beside him, leaning against the horse, brushing my fingers through his thick winter coat.

"Hell, I was scared too. But you can't let 'em see that. Especially not one like him." He gestures at the path the departed warrior made in the snow. "He'll scent the fear on you as easily as a wolf might. You show that, you're dead. They have no respect for cowards."

"He said I was strong medicine. What did he mean?"

He glances at me, pride gleaming alongside the heat blooming in those brown eyes. "That you were brave. Strong. That you'd give me… good luck, I guess you could call it. Medicine for them isn't luck, exactly, but similar. Good fortune might be closer, but you can earn medicine in a way you can't good luck or fortune. Great deeds, signs from nature, prowess in battle, that kind of thing."

"And I give you strong medicine by being strong?"

"Yeah, I guess so." His gaze tells me he's done talking about medicine.

"Is it odd that all that craziness has left me…" I squirm as he pivots, pinning me against the side of the horse, "—all worked up?"

He presses his lips to my cheekbone, then to my throat, and then tugs my coat open a little, exposing my skin to the cold air, and his mouth. "Not odd at all. Adrenaline will do that."

I cling to his shoulders, tilt my face to the sky, baring my throat for him. "Does it do that to you?"

He snags one of my wrists and presses my hand to his groin. I suck in a breath at the thick hard ridge in his pants. "You tell me."

"Seems like it does."

He tugs down the bodice of my dress, baring my breasts to the icy air. His breath warms them, and then his mouth and his tongue set them on fire. He backs away, letting the cold air lick at my wet skin, making me shiver, making my nipples harden into diamonds, and then he returns his mouth to my breast, licking my nipple, suckling on it until I gasp, a sharp tug lancing between my breast and my core. The horse is warm behind me, radiating heat, and Conrad is in front of me, blocking the wind and exuding his own warmth. And then his hands begin to explore, causing heat to bloom inside me, and now I don't even feel the cold, because all there is to feel is Conrad, his mouth on my tits, his hand cupping a breast to lift it to his mouth, the other gathering my dress up in front so he can dive under the layers of skirts to reach my thighs.

I relinquish the last of my balance, leaning fully back against the big black stallion, gasping as his fingers find my inner thighs and delve upward.

"No underwear," Conrad notes, a lust-hot note to his voice, laced with amusement.

"I was in bed, waiting for you, when—when Charlie showed up. He made me get dressed in a hurry. Didn't really have time for them."

His fingers find my slit, finding me damp already. "Turned out to be…" his fingers slide in, up, curl, scissor, withdraw, squelch back in, "…rather fortuitous for me."

I want to touch him, bare his cock, but his fingers are banishing all capacity for thought. His fingers slide in and out of me, finger-fucking me, then he presses the rough pad his thumb against my clit, and as soon as he does that I explode, fall apart into spastic release, my scream echoing off the trees and startling the birds into flight. He doesn't stop there, though, but slows his finger-fucking and removes his thumb, giving me a few seconds to catch my breath and come back down, and then, before I'm ready, he's smearing my juices onto my clit and using the tips of his two middle fingers to stimulate me, smearing my wetness against me and circling hard and fast, relentless, the perfect touch, just the way I need to be touched in order to—

Fuck, oooh fuck, oh fuck—

I come apart again, and again, and it seems he's greedy for my orgasms, stringing them out of me one after another until I'm sagging and limp against the horse, knees shaky and weak.

"Conrad," I gasp, leaning my forehead against his hard shoulder. "Enough, I can't stand up after all that."

He tugs my skirt up around my hips, baring my wet pussy to the cold air. "Can't stand up, huh?"

I shake my head, fumbling for the fly of his pants, tugging at it until it loosens enough for me to shove those stupid pants down, freeing his massive cock. "I can barely think or breathe, let alone stand up."

He grasps me by the backs of my thighs and lifts me up, tilts me against the horse, wedging me between his hips and the huge animal. "Then I'd better hold you up."

He flexes his hips, nudging his cock against my slit. I shift my hips, and the head slips in, splitting my cunt open bit by bit, sliding in ever so slowly. And then his mouth covers mine, and his tongue flits against mine, and the fires of my lust, already blazing, flare to new levels of intensity, so hot I don't know what to do with it…the insane need this man incites within me, from just a touch, just a kiss.

"You can breathe for me too, if you want," I whisper.

He breaks the kiss just long enough to whisper into my mouth. "I think I will."

And then he resumes kissing me, as if kissing me is the end of everything, the start of everything, the meaning of everything. He kisses me as if—

My thoughts are broken as Conrad plunges fully into me, spearing his tongue into my mouth as he thrusts his cock into my cunt. Fully penetrated, split open to an aching burn, held aloft by his strong hands, I can't think for a few seconds, can't form any thoughts. I can only feel, and revel in it, drown myself in the delirious euphoria of this man's primal sexual power and prowess.

God, oh god.

He's not even thrusting, just holding still and letting my pussy adjust to his size. Letting the sensations rifle through me and boil up within me.

Forehead to forehead, lips mere centimeters apart, I can taste his breath, still feel his lips on mine, though he's not kissing me, only breathing against my lips and starting to roll his hips in tiny teasing flutters.

"Hannah—" There's a strange, vulnerable note in his voice.

"What, Conrad? Say it. Say anything."

He thrusts, then. One full wet sliding withdrawal, hands cupping my ass cheeks, spreading me apart and slamming up and in. I scream, startling one of the horses, but not the big stallion that is currently my warmth and my wall.

"I shouldn't have kissed you."

My gut twists. "Why—oh god, *Conrad*—why not?"

He slants his lips across mine, not quite kissing, teasing. "Because I can't stop now."

I close the distance between his mouth and mine. I take this kiss, demand it from him, suck his tongue into my mouth and breathe in his breath and caress his lips with my own, kissing him for all I'm worth, with everything I have, until neither of us can breathe, until he's thrusting desperately against me. I kiss him as he fucks me, and I keep kissing him.

He tries to break away, but I refuse to let him. I allow him the briefest of breaths, and then I kiss him again, slamming my mouth over his and clutching his head with both of my hands, burying my fingers in his hair and jerking him closer, handling him roughly, fiercely.

I kiss him until fucking becomes something else.

Until it becomes something…more.

Finally, I allow the kiss to pause and I speak into his mouth, words clashing with his gasps. "So don't, Conrad. Don't ever stop."

And he doesn't, he doesn't—his tongue mimics the motion of his cock, thrusting in and out of my mouth. "Hannah, Jesus—Hannah."

"Come inside me, Conrad." I pant the words. "Give me all your cum. All of it. Fuck me hard and don't ever stop, Conrad."

He pounds into me, and I feel his hands on my ass squeezing roughly, and a fingertip nudges my asshole, working against the knot of muscle gently but insistently. I exhale, and relax to let him in. I wiggle my ass against his hand, and whimper as his finger slides into me, bit by bit, until I'm pierced by him everywhere—mouth and cunt and asshole.

I explode again, biting down on his lip with an involuntary shout of ecstasy, slicing release blasting through me in spasming waves. I scream so loud the whole valley echoes with my voice. I come, and come, and come.

Clamping down with my cunt, I grip his thrusting cock with my vaginal muscles until he grunts in surprise, and then I feel him prepare to come, feel his thrusts falter. He fucks into me once, hard, and remains pushed deep, his hips slapping against my ass, cock filling me until he can't go any deeper, and he begins to grind there, deep as he can go, shouting against my tits as he comes.

"Yes, Conrad, fuck me! Fuck me so hard, Conrad—" I shout with him, shout *"YESYESYESYES"* to the sky as he fucks me so hard it hurts, and I love it, can't get enough of it, writhe on him and tell him to fuck me harder, harder, *harder*.

I feel his cum gush into me, a flood of hot wet seed filling me and overflowing, and god, fuck, yes, I love it, love the way his cum spurts out around his cock and drips down my taint and he's still orgasming, grunting and snarling and thrusting so hard his balls slap against my ass.

I cling to him as he stills, legs wrapped around his waist, arms around his neck, face buried in his hair, inhaling his scent.

When he sets me down, finally, my legs quiver and nearly give out. Cum slides wet and warm down my thighs.

It's several minutes before either of us can walk, and then we take our time meandering back to the cabin in perfect silence.

＊＊

My eyes are glued to his broad shoulders and tight ass as he clomps up the porch steps, kicking his toes one after the other against the front of the steps to knock the snow off his boots. I climb up behind him, and then stop beside him.

He's motionless on the porch, silent.

Finally, he swivels his head to look at me. "Hannah, I—" he stops, sighs. Glances at the door. "You have to go."

Confusion and sadness war within me. I shake my head. "No, Conrad. I'm staying. I'll stay."

His head moves from side to side. "You can't."

I rip my eyes away from him.

The whole world narrows down to an octagon of glass, delicate, fragile, gleaming in the glow of the fading sunset.

The doorknob blocks out everything: him, me, the valley behind us, and the horses. I sob, once. "I don't want to go. I want to stay with you."

His bearded cheek nuzzles against mine. "I know. But that's not how it works, honey."

"I know." My voice is faint.

I feel my feet carry me forward. My hand—bare, cold—grasps the doorknob. The frigid glass turns in my hand. Twists. I hear the latch click. Feel the creak of the hinges. Feel the door open.

I feel him behind me; feel his heat, feel his solid presence.

Perhaps I only imagine it, his voice is whispering—

*Hannah...Hannah.*

Without looking back I step through into darkness, into the familiar nothingness...leaving it all behind.

$$ * * * $$

Silence.

Perfect, utter silence.

A drowning quiet.

A memory of cold, visions of a thick black beard and piercing brown eyes, and the feel of strong hands on my bare skin; the feeling of belonging, however briefly—the first sensation.

My lips sting from a recent kiss, throb from raking, biting teeth; the second sensation.

I open my eyes, and hate the silence and the loneliness; the third sensation.

I'm in the black room. Alone.

White cot under me. A small square black table to my left, on it a thick white candle, flickering merrily, rivulets of melted wax dripping down the sides to pool and harden on the silver candlestick.

Five torches flicker and cast pools of orange light on five doors: three black, one silver, one green.

I don't want to be alone.

I hate the silence, but I have no words, no voice to speak, and there is no one to hear me, so I remain silent.

I close my eyes to block out the darkness, and to pretend there are no doors. All I want is warmth, a warm body next to mine.

I float in nothingness, and try to remember.

Black hair soft against my cheek.

Tan skin, hard muscles. Flesh sliding against mine. Rough hands that were somehow exquisitely tender.

Is he a boxer, all hard edges and alpha male power and dominance? An elegant, urbane, yet brawny and masculine sophisticate—with a lithe and muscular blonde friend? Or is he a reclusive gunfighter, tall on his horse, hands faster than lightning, utterly at ease in the wilderness?

All of them, and none of them.

I don't want to wake up.

I don't want to be alone.

I want him back.

Any version of him. I just…*want him.*

So I find myself on my feet, drifting across the black room. I stop in front of the fourth door. I trace the numeral 4 with my finger and I wonder what version of him I will find behind this door? Who will he be?

This doorknob is made of solid brass. Polished, elegant. Ornate filigree knot work graces the face of the knob, thin wires of twisted brass curl and knot and overlap in delicate patterns.

I press my palm to the filigree, and the brass is warm under my hand.

I twist the knob and the door opens away from me on silent hinges. As I step over the threshold a burst of darkness washes over me, and through me.

$$\text{✳ ✳ ✳ ✳}$$

Light, a blast of sunshine refracting through the glass, temporarily blinds me.

Through the windows directly in front of me I see the pink-orange of a sunset, the sun beginning to settle beneath the horizon.

I'm in a long hallway and tall windows line one wall, extending away to my left. I blink against the light, turn in place; see the wall beside me, the door, and the brass knob. There's another door at the far end of the hallway, a tiny rectangle in the distance, and another nearby, to my right, a few feet away, the door standing open, revealing the top of a set of stairs.

A woman appears in the open doorway. She's tall and thin, wiry, with iron-gray hair bound in a bun so severely tight my own scalp aches in sympathy. She's wearing a black dress with a white apron, sensible black shoes, and she has a rag in one hand.

"Here you are!" she hisses, shaking the rag at me. "I've searched the whole house for you! What on earth are you doing up here? You know very well Master Killian allows no one up here, child. You'll be sacked if you're caught, and you've only just started."

I gape at her, trying to catch up. "I—I'm sorry, ma'am." The words pop out, unbidden.

"Sorry won't keep you your job if Master Killian finds you up here."

"I didn't mean—I mean—"

She flutters her hands at me. "Just go, girl."

At that moment, the door at the far end of the hall swings open, and a huge male body fills the frame, back-lit by the sun. The silhouette is imposing and it's clear the man is tall with broad shoulders and a trim waist.

My heart begins to pound, and the woman beside me lets out a curse under her breath, so softly I barely hear it. And then she's in front of me, shoving the rag into my hand. "*Go, child!*" she hisses.

I back up and prepare to turn and flee through the door.

A deep, powerful male voice cracks through the silence. "Mrs. Cartwright."

The woman starts, and then shuffles forward. "Yes, sir, Mister Killian?"

"I thought I'd made myself clear. No one is allowed in this portion of the house."

"I know, sir." Mrs. Cartwright gestures at me. "The new girl, sir, she got lost. I was just explaining to her—"

"It should have been explained the moment you hired her."

"I know, sir. I'm sorry—it won't happen again. You have my word."

I turn around, and take two small steps toward the door.

"I didn't dismiss you, girl." His voice is hard and cold.

I halt in place, turn slowly back around, my heart hammering. He snaps his fingers, stabs his index finger at the floor in front of him.

"Well, what are you waiting for?" Mrs. Cartwright hisses at me, gesturing at the man standing in the doorway some twenty or thirty feet away. "Go! If he summons you, you go."

Summoned, like a dog.

I move past Mrs. Cartwright, and it takes me many long steps to reach Mister Killian.

He is enormously tall, towering over me. Dressed in a three-piece suit: slim, tailored, creased navy-blue pinstripe trousers, a matching vest with polished gold buttons, a suit coat over that with a gold chain dangling in a perfect U-shape from pocket to pocket. Pristine white shirt buttoned up to the neck, a narrow red-and-blue striped tie, the knot a precise wedge. An inch and a half of white shirt peeks through at his cuffs, gold cufflinks inset with massive crimson rubies glitter in the light. His black hair is swept back, oiled and gleaming. He is clean-shaven. Glittering brown eyes regard me, missing nothing, gimlet and cold and hard, radiating wealth and power, dominance and arrogance.

"I don't believe we've met yet," His voice rumbles so deeply I feel it in the pit of my stomach.

"This is Hannah Tavistock, sir," Mrs. Cartwright says from the other end of the hallway. "She came with several letters of reference. She was most recently employed with the Orwells—"

"I was speaking to her, Mrs. Cartwright." His eyes flit up, look past me, and he continues with one word. "Dismissed."

"Shall I show Miss Tavistock her duties downstairs, sir?"

"I'll send her along shortly. You are *dismissed*, Mrs. Cartwright." His voice is sharper than razor blades, colder than ice.

"Yes, sir." Mrs. Cartwright's voice is tiny and meek.

His eyes, brown as polished oak, striated with seams of gold—fix on me. "These are my private quarters, Miss Tavistock, and as such they are strictly off-limits. I manage them myself, and I carry the only key." He brandishes a thick brass key. "Which raises the question of how you got in here."

It's hard to summon words, to find my voice. "I—I don't know, sir. I'm sorry, I—"

"Were you snooping, Miss Tavistock?"

"No sir! I would never, I just—"

"I am not known for my forgiving nature, as you should know."

"I'm sorry, Mister Killian. I wasn't snooping. I got lost—"

"You wouldn't lie to me, would you, Miss Tavistock?" His gaze is utterly unfeeling.

"No sir, I'm telling the truth, I swear—"

He steps closer, and now I can smell him, cigar smoke and whiskey and expensive cologne. "You didn't get *lost*, Miss Tavistock. These quarters are on the third floor, and occupy one entire wing of the house. It is virtually impossible to get so lost you find your way past several locked doors, and up two flights of stairs."

"No, sir, I—"

He holds up a hand, and I silence myself. He pinches my jaw between thumb and forefinger. "You didn't get lost, did you?"

"No...sir..." My heart hammers, my knees shake, my hands tremble.

"What is it you were looking for?"

"I—"

He speaks over me. "Because I don't think you'll like what you find if you sneak into my private quarters, Miss Tavistock."

His heat is stifling, his presence overwhelming; his eyes pin me in place, his fingers on my chin are like iron. He is refusing to allow me to look away.

There is a beast in his brown eyes.

It lurks, prowling behind the veil of indifference and arrogance.

I try to step away, but I can't.

Try to look away, but I can't.

He is all pervading, terrifying, consuming.

I feel like a tiny creature caught in the open, caught by the gaze of a predator.

His eyes never waver from mine, his grip on my chin remains unbreakable, and I remain frozen; even if he were to allow me to move, I couldn't. Couldn't. Wouldn't.

His body is hard and huge, blocking out the light, blocking out the world.

I tremble, wondering what he wants. What he's going to do.

His finger and thumb release my chin.

His body presses against mine, and I'm forced backward. My breasts are crushed against his chest, and my traitorous nipples harden. He feels it, I know he does. He feels them poking into his chest. They're so sensitive, like this, so hard, pressing against my dress and crushed against his body.

His scent is intoxicating.

His body is all consuming.

He steps forward again, and I'm pressed up against the window, the glass at my spine. He is in front of me, blocking my escape.

All of my senses are attuned to him.

My nipples throb.

His eyes finally break away from mine and skate down my body. I look where he's looking, see what he sees.

I'm wearing a uniform: a black skirt, the hem just above my knees; black lace stockings; a black button-up blouse with the top three buttons undone, baring an indecent amount of cleavage. A cascade of thick honey-blond hair cascades down the front of my left shoulder.

I suck in a deep breath and my chest expands, the buttons imprisoning my breasts straining.

I'm not wearing a bra.

One wrong move, and my breasts would pop free.

Bare.

Exposed to his gaze.

My nipples poke through the thin cotton of my blouse, protruding visibly.

His eyes rise to meet mine. Hot, burning, the coldness gone, but the arrogance remains. He is totally sure of his power. He returns his gaze to my breasts.

His fingers lift...

He pinches my nipple *hard*, so hard I whimper, cry out, but he doesn't release me, doesn't lessen the painful sting of the pinch. Then his other hand lifts and I try to squirm away, but I can't because the glass is behind me and he's in front of me and my nipple aches, throbs, stings. I can't breathe for the ache, and then he latches onto my other nipple, both of them in his grip now. The fiercely painful pinches steal my breath but, oh, oh, oh the hurt, it lances through me, fills me, the ache sinks into me, consumes all of me.

Oh, the ache.

I feel the ache everywhere—

Between my thighs. God, I ache.

He won't let go.

He's pinching so hard but I don't dare cry.

Pinching so hard I feel it in my pussy.

The pain, the ache…why do I not stop him, why do I not knock his hands away or cry out, why do I only endure it and gasp? Why is that gasp no longer one of protest or pain?

Why is that gasp so erotic? So breathy, so sultry?

Moisture pools between my thighs, dampens my panties.

His nostrils flare, as if he can scent my arousal.

Still with that powerful, painful pressure on my nipples, he speaks to me. "I'm having a party tonight, Miss Tavistock."

"Yes, sir…" I manage.

He increases the pressure on my nipples, and the ache that spears through me sends dampness trickling down my thigh. I'm so wet from the ache that I'm literally dripping.

"I want you in attendance."

I blink, and try to think past the ache. "Yes, sir."

He releases my nipples suddenly, and the absence of the stinging pressure turns my gasp of relief into a moan.

And then he reaches up with one long, thick index finger and touches my upper lip. He trails it down to my lower lip, tugging open my mouth, then down to my chin. I have ceased breathing.

He continues his path down the column of my throat, each millimeter of flesh he touches sears and tingles. His finger now rests on my breastbone.

His gaze goes to mine, demanding I meet his eyes. With those eyes he pins me, pierces me and sees into me.

He drags his finger down between my breasts to the button, to that one lone defense of any remaining modesty.

A smirk curls at the corners of his lips, and then vanishes, a shadow of amusement flitting across the rugged, masculine beauty of his features.

A single sharp tug—

The button clatters to the floor, and my breasts spill free, bouncing, jiggling, nipples standing hard and erect.

He traces one wide, dark areola with his fingertip, circling it.

He pinches my exposed nipple, harder than the last time. So hard I do sob this time, but it's a confused sound, as rife with eroticism as with pain.

"You will appear—" he says, pinching my other exposed nipple now, too, and I ache so fiercely between my thighs that I might implode, "—just like this."

I can't speak. I try, but the pain, the ache, the throb, the pressure on my nipples and the pressure between my thighs is too much. Too potent, too fierce.

He increases the pressure, and my knees buckle. "I expect you to answer, Miss Tavistock."

"Y-y-y-yessssss—" I stammer.

But I can't complete the phrase, because now he's alternating pressure, pinching hard, then relaxing, hard, then relaxing, alternating from left nipple to right, so the ache and the relief travels through me, whirling and pounding and pulsing along that sharp hot line connecting my tits and cunt.

"Yes what, Miss Tavistock?"

"Yes—yes…" It's so hard to think with the throbbing, with the wild fiery ache of his fingers pincering my hypersensitive nipples, hard to think with the pulsating heat between my thighs.

He releases my nipples, and then his thumbs brush them gently, flicking them gingerly. Then he rubs each of them in sync, the broad rough pads of his thumbs rolling against my singing, stinging nipples, soothing and pleasurably stimulating them.

I can finally breathe, and when I do it's to cry out, my breathy scream echoing off the glass and the walls as heat sears through me, piercing the bubble of built up pressure, and my knees give out, my legs crumbling, lightning hitting me, wave after wave of something primal slicing through my entire body, seizing me, and he continues rolling his thumbs over my nipples. I need....god, I need—

What do I need?

Pressure. Between my thighs. I need it. I need release from this ache.

"Yes...*what*, Miss Tavistock?" His voice is barely above a whisper. It's an intimate murmur. His finger touches my chin, lifting my face.

I shake my head, all capacity for thought blasted away.

He presses his lips to my ear. "'Yes, Mister Killian,'" he whispers. "Say it."

I'm sagging, and I realize he's all that's keeping me from falling to the floor, his knee is between my legs. I'm sitting on his knee. Oh...*god*.

I feel myself grinding against his knee. Seeking release from the ache, from the throb, from the lightning searing through me, lightning that won't quite allow me to find what I need, to find the release.

I grind on his knee in harmony with the rolling of his thumb over my nipples, gentle, insistent, precise, teasing each sensation out of me.

"Yes..." I gasp. "Yes...M-m-mister...."

Then one of his hands is doing the work of two, dancing from breast to breast, thumbing and flicking each nipple in turn, and his other hand is descending. Finding my knee. My thigh. Tracing upwards. His rolling thumb moves faster, and my hips move harder, grinding my cunt on his knee. I'm shameless, needing the release. Needing it. All he's done is pinch my nipples and I'm soaring, hovering at the edge, and he won't let me fall over, won't let me find release. I need it so bad it hurts, I ache all over, my gut aches, my cunt aches, my nipples, my thighs, everything aches from the need to come...

And now, yes, god yes, he's skimming the gusset of my panties, running three fingers over the soaked cotton. Right over the seam of my dripping pussy. He drags a fingertip over my inner thigh where my cunt nears my asshole, and through the slippery wetness leaking out of me.

"Say it, Miss Tavistock." He teases the elastic of the leg-hole of my panties, darting under, ever so slightly. " Say, 'Yes, Mister Killian.' Three words, and I'll give you what you want."

He traces the seam of my cunt again, over the cotton, pressing one fingertip in a little, through the fabric. I writhe, grind, needing that touch. Needing it so fucking bad.

"And you want it, don't you? You want it so bad." He whispers this in my ear. "I can feel it. I can smell it. You're soaked, and I've barely touched you, Miss Tavistock."

"I—"

He squeezes my nipple, and I cry out. "Say it, Miss Tavistock." He teases the other side of my cunt now, edging in under the elastic of the gusset. "Say it, and I'll do things you could only imagine. Things you couldn't even fantasize about."

I try. I do, really I do. I work my lips, but the ache is too fierce for thought, and I do want it, god, fuck I want it. He's teasing me, teasing me closer. He knows exactly where my clit is, but he's not giving it to me, not touching me there, not letting me grind on his thigh the way I need to to find release.

"Last chance, Miss Tavistock."

His hand emerges from beneath my skirt, and before I can suck in a preparatory breath, he's pinching my nipples again in that alternating pressure pattern, and instantly I'm teetering on the edge—if only…if only he'd touch me, or let me rub my cunt on his thigh just so—

But he doesn't.

"Too late." He releases my nipples, yanks his thigh out from between mine, and steps back.

I sag, nearly falling, but I catch myself.

My hands go to the edges of my shirt, to cover my bare tits.

He grabs my wrists. "No covering yourself." He pulls a large pocket watch from his vest, flips open the gold-chased cover, consults it, and replaces it. "Be in the card room downstairs in five minutes."

And then he's gone, breezing away in a whirl of cologne and masculinity.

I was seconds from climax, and he's gone.

I ache.

I'm mad with need.

My nipples pulse, and my cunt sings. My thighs are sticky from my own wetness, and my panties are soaked.

I gather my strength, force myself to my feet, and move down the hallway, trying to ignore the fact that my tits are exposed.

I walk out of the hallway and down the narrow staircase. Along a wide hallway that overlooks a staircase in the center of the house. The staircase is circular, mammoth, ascending from the first floor all the way up here to the third.

I hear voices, male and numerous.

I make my way down the stairs, trying to move smoothly, slowly, trying to avoid letting my tits bounce, because each bounce, each jiggle make them ache, so full, so heavy are they, so sensitive from Killian's touch.

I make my way down to the first floor and follow the familiar voice down another hallway, this one wide with waist-high wainscoting of dark oak, thick velvety carpet underfoot, high ceilings ornately painted to resemble the night sky—stars in gold paint on a navy-blue ground. A pair of ten-foot high French doors, partially open, stand at the end of the hall. I can hear male voices beyond, loud and boisterous.

I see him through the gap in the doorway, and he sees me. "Ah, Miss Tavistock. Come in, please."

He moves toward the doorway, and the voices cease as he shoves them wide open and then ushers me inside.

All eyes are on me. How many men are here? I scan the crowd, counting nine, and Killian makes ten. They are all of an age, late twenties or early thirties, handsome, expensively dressed in three-piece suits. All of them are staring at me, at my exposed breasts, at my erect nipples.

They're looking at me like starving men, as if I'm something to eat.

I step into the room.

Killian closes the doors me and moves to stand behind me. He reaches around in front of me and pulls the edges of my shirt apart, exposing me more completely.

"Gentlemen, please find your places at the card table." At his command, the other nine men find seats around a large round table. "We don't play for money, this evening, my friends. No, tonight we play for something much more…interesting."

His lips touch the shell of my ear. "Take off your panties, Miss Tavistock."

I tremble. Shake my head.

"No?" He sounds pleased. "Very well, then. I shall do it myself."

He sinks to his knees behind me. Slides his palms up my thighs, along the black lace stockings. Up, up, up under my skirt. He finds the elastic waistband of my panties.

Slowly, he slides them down.

I shake, nearly hyperventilating, aching. His touch is electric.

The eyes on me are wild with lust. More than a few men shift in their chairs, adjusting their crotches.

He lowers my panties inch by inch, until they're at my knees. Then, he drops them so they fall around my ankles. He cups my calf, lifts my leg, tugs the panties free, and then does the same for the other side. I'm bare, now, beneath my skirt. The air is cold on my damp slit.

It feels as if each of the men can see beneath my skirt, can see my bare, bald pussy.

He stands, lifts my panties, and dangles them from one finger. "This is the prize." He clutches my panties in his fist, balls them up, and holds them to his nose. He reaches under my skirt, swipes a finger into my slit, between the throbbing lips of my cunt, smearing my wetness on his finger. Holds it up, to show how it gleams in the light, wet, glistening. "They smell of her, still. They're wet, gentlemen. Wet from her desire." He pops that finger in his mouth, and then withdraws it slowly.

I hear a few groaned curses from the seated card players.

Killian paces past me to the card table, tossing my panties into the center.

"Win a hand with a full house, her apron comes off. Win with four of a kind, you get her stockings. Straight flush, her shirt. Win a hand with a royal flush, her skirt. Win the final hand, you get those," he says with a gesture at my underwear.

The men smile and murmur between themselves.

"Are we agreed?"

There is a chorus of *yes*, and *agreed*.

His lips touch my ear once more. His whisper tickles, a buzz of sound only I can hear. "When the game is over, Miss Tavistock, I'll make you come so hard your screams will wake the dead."

The game of strip poker is well under way, the table is full of chips. The whiskey is flowing and they're only on the third hand. The men are all drinking like fish, except Killian, but they are all focused on the game and the unusual winnings.

I'm carrying a small silver tray laden with a bottle of whiskey and an ice bucket. My job is to move from chair to chair, man to man, refilling their glasses, and offering more ice. But it's more than that. In this game of strip poker, I'm the only who will be losing any clothing.

My apron is gone, and so are my shoes.

Each time I bring a man a drink, I must endure his eyes on me. Killian seems able to follow the card game without ever really taking his eyes off me. He sees the way the men all look at me, and he allows it.

I pour a measure of whiskey into a crystal glass, and then gently drop in an ice cube. The man whose glass I'm refilling is short and stocky, muscular, goateed. He leans back in his chair as I refill his glass, and then he tilts his head to the side, eying me. He spares a glance for Killian whose face remains impassive, giving nothing away.

I feel a hand on my knee. Sliding up my thigh. Cold, clammy, gripping a kneading handful of my bare ass under my skirt. I shudder, twisting out of reach. I look over at Killian, who I know saw it. His eyes are narrowed, but he says nothing. Does nothing.

The others notice what is going on and they observe Killian's lack of interference.

A few minutes later, it happens again. A lecherous smirk, fat fingers breezing up the back of my thigh, under my skirt, massaging, kneading, cupping my ass cheek. Again, I look at Killian to stop it, but he doesn't.

The game continues as men pitch in chips, calling and seeing and drinking. And as the game heats up, hands continue exploring my ass and thighs.

Then things change. One of the men left his glass near the middle of the table, shoved away in frustration when he was forced to fold. To retrieve the glass I must lean over the table to reach it, which means my skirt hikes up in back, exposing my ass, and my breasts rest against the table. As I straighten up, that man cups my breast in his palm, and wraps an arm around my hips, one hand firmly grasping my ass, the other pawing at my tits. I struggle to get away, but he just laughs and gropes until he's had his fill, and then he releases me with a self-satisfied leer.

I feel sick to my stomach, and fight the urge to run. I eye the door, but it feels a thousand miles away. I can't run. I feel trapped, yet some instinct won't let me leave. I can't. It is forbidden. I have to see this through; I'm not allowed to leave. I cannot simply walk away.

As I continue moving around the table, refilling and replacing the glasses, I now endure not merely lecherous glances, but hands on my flesh. All the raging desire I'd once felt is gone. All the need, banished.

And then…

The man who first groped my breasts wins the hand with four of a kind.

"C'mere so I can collect my winnings, girl," he purrs, reaching for me.

"I don't think so," Killian rumbles. "Miss Tavistock. Come over to me, please."

Feeling bizarrely grateful, I circle the table to stand near Killian's left hand. He pushes back his chair, takes a long sip of his whiskey, and then sets his glass on the table on top of his cards. He curls a hand around my hips, low. His eyes are on on mine, searching, piercing. My heart hammers as he stares up into my face and, once again, everything somehow falls away and vanishes. The world narrows to his eyes. I feel his hand curl around my hip, feel him skate his touch down my leg to my knee. Feel him dive under my skirt. That hand, those fingers, strong, thick, warm, and rough, scraping against the lace of my stockings, skimming up the back of my left thigh. Both hands, now. His hands encircle my thigh, finding the upper edge of my stocking. Teasing a finger along the garter. Then...he stops. There is that ghost of a smirk, and then it's gone.

Oh, that smile. It means nothing good for me.

He leans forward, cradling my calf in his hands and then lifts my leg, placing my foot on his knee. Nine pairs of eyes stop playing to watch, and I feel each stare acutely. Then Killian traces a fingertip from ankle up to knee, and my thoughts begin to scatter. Surely there is some manner of sorcery in his hands, in his touch, in his capacity to banish all logic or capacity for thought by simply touching a finger to my flesh.

With my foot on his knee and my leg bent, the hem of my skirt is lifted, baring my core. Exposing my pussy for Killian's gaze, or for anyone within sight line.

He begins tracing a pattern on the side of my knee and then follows a path across the inside of my thigh. He stops a hair's breadth away from my cunt, and his eyes gleam with something fierce, something wild, and that smirk flits across his handsome face once more. I'm barely breathing, waiting for his touch. Waiting for that forefinger to dip into me, to slide along the seam of my pussy, to delve into my wetness.

But no.

A flick of his fingers releases the clasp of one garter. Another flick, and the second is unfastened. Now my stocking is free and it begins to sag as his hands wrap around my thighs, intimate, possessive, rolling the lace down as he moves down my leg. When the garment is removed, he folds it in precise thirds, placing it on the table. It's hard to breathe, hard to swallow. Rather than removing my other stocking, he returns his hand to my now-bare leg, still propped up on his knee. Both hands cup my ankle and calf, and then begin to caress their way upward, tickling the back of my knee, cradling the width of my thigh, and then finally cupping my ass cheek.

The silence in the card room is stifling.

Every man is watching us in rapt attention, the card game now on hold. I know I should care, but with Killian touching me…I don't.

God, no, I don't.

Not with Killian's eyes on me, not with his touch on my skin. Not when his fingers brush the back of my thigh yet again, then dance across the inside, grazing my core. I bite my lip, because I can nearly feel the intention in him, can almost feel his touch to my pussy before it happens.

Yes…oh god, yes. There it is, the tip of his index finger tracing the outside of my cunt, grazing my labia, and my eyelids flutter, my stomach twists, and I force myself to remain silent. No sounds. No gasp, No whimper. Not one sound…no matter what he does. It's so difficult to obey my own instruction, especially when he fits that fingertip just inside me, right near the top, finding a certain tight, hard bundle of nerves, and then presses his fingertip to it.

I swallow a moan, because his fingertip is deliciously rough, and the touch is gentle yet firm.

And then he stops, withdrawing his hand from my core, and nudges my foot off of his knee, replacing it with the other. In no hurry, he caresses my calf, my thigh, toys with the garter, pulls it back and lets it snap against my thigh. He unhooks the garters one by one, and rolls the stocking off my thigh. Again, he folds the stocking into precise thirds and then hands the pair to the winner of the hand.

He flicks a finger against his glass. "Top me off, if you would please, Miss Tavistock."

I do so, and he gathers his cards off the table.

I get a look at his hand: It's a straight flush, which beats a four of a kind, I do believe.

But he never showed his cards.

And now the winner of the last hand is shuffling and dealing, and the game has begun again.

More refills, more hands groping my now-bare thighs, my ass. My tits.

And Killian allows it all.

The hand is won, this time with a straight flush, which means that the winner gets my shirt.

I'm summoned to Killian's side yet again. He moves his chair back, and this time he turns so his body faces me. He takes the tray from me and sets it on the table. He pulls me to stand between his thighs, and his hands now skate up my legs and lift my skirt, baring my backside briefly, and then he gathers up my thick blond hair in his fist. A sudden sharp tug leaves me staring at the ceiling, head back, throat exposed. And I feel his breath on my chin as he presses his lips to my throat. My skin pebbles from the heat of his breath. One hand fisted in my hair, the other palms my breast, nudging the shirt off my shoulder, one side, then the other, until it hangs off my elbows, still fastened by three buttons.

His finger traces a path down between my breasts, over my sternum, and hooks behind the top button of my shirt. A jerk, and the button pops off. Then the second button flies off, landing on the floor. A third time, and this button lands on the table just to my left. I stifle a gasp at each popped button. My shirt is open completely now.

His quickening breath is hot against my skin, and I'm blinking down at him as he touches his lips to the underside of one breast. Here? Now? With all these men watching?

Yes, oh yes.

His mouth latches onto my nipple, his tongue flicks, and I'm fighting the groan, fighting the sigh. He slides his mouth across my skin to the other nipple, leaving the one wet and hard and exposed to the cool air. I miss the moment when he removes my shirt, because his suckling mouth is the only sensation in my universe, making my core throb.

He nudges me away from him, blinking up at me slowly, his expression carefully neutral. My nipples are wet from his tongue, hard, sensitive, standing erect.

I'm clad in nothing but a short skirt and a garter belt.

A nod from Killian and they're dealing another hand.

Now I must move around the room naked from the waist up, every sway, every bounce, every movement watched and catalogued by nine men…and Killian.

The touching is non-stop, now. There are hands all over me. Everywhere. I should be desensitized, but I'm not. I should be repulsed…

But I'm not.

I feel them all, and though none of them are Killian's hands, I still feel every touch.

My body is on fire.

Again and again, the men show me that they want to make my body their own, yet I can't fight my responses. Shudders at first. Then shivers. I should feel revulsion, but…I don't. I love the feeling of being worshipped, hands desperate for my skin, eyes devouring me, lust burning…all for me.

Over the next several minutes Killian never touches me, never allows me to refill his glass, he simply observes the men and my reaction to them.

The next hand is won, this time another four of a kind, and my garter belt goes to the winner. Killian removes it almost idly, absently, one-handed, without any extra touches. I expect him to finger me, fondle me in some way, and he doesn't. It leaves me feeling off-kilter.

When he's given my garter belt to the winner, he addresses the gathered poker players. "Final hand gentlemen." He reaches forward and snags my panties from the center of the table. "The winner gets these."

By now most of the men are intoxicated, yet their eyes on me are hungry. Some almost desperate.

Except Killian.

The final round of play begins, but Killian is casual, appearing only vaguely interested, except when his eyes find me. And then, when his gaze rakes across my body, a glint of something deep and dark and potent flickers behind his gaze, flitting briefly across his expression. His fingers twitch, tapping the surface of the table. He swirls the liquid in his glass, an absent-minded gesture.

I've had almost all I can take of the hands gripping my ass, fondling my tits, tweaking my nipples, some daring to come close to my core. I can't take much more. I try to keep moving around the table, offering drinks and replenishing ice, but the wandering hands follow me everywhere.

I'm having trouble following the game, except to know that Killian isn't winning, but it doesn't seem as if he's trying very hard.

I'm all roiled up inside, twisted, short of breath, aching all over, throbbing from being so sexually tense for so long.

"Ha!" A man shouts triumphantly, leaping from his chair and tossing his cards face up: ace, king, queen, Jack, and ten of hearts.

A royal flush.

I'm right beside him when he wins, refilling his glass for then umpteenth time; I've lost count.

He's not ugly. Far from it. Blond, tall, sharp features, lean and hard looking. Ice-blue eyes. Clean-shaven. Bespoke suit cut to fit his trim body like a glove.

I turn to face him as he turns to me. I shake all over. His pale, piercing eyes are steady on mine, a smile on his thin lips.

"Lemme see you shimmy out of that little skirt, darling." His voice is smooth, easy, the words rolling with a slight lilt.

I can't move.

Not even to cast a beseeching glance to Killian.

As the winner of the hand with a royal flush, he's won both my panties *and* my skirt. He sidles closer to me, until the tips of my breasts brush against his chest. He leans toward me and buries his nose against my neck and inhales. I'm utterly frozen, not even breathing, my heart skips and then hammers like a tribal drum. He sinks slowly to his knees in front of me, his nose trailing down my centerline from breastbone, between my tits, over my belly, and then he's kneeling in front of me and staring up at me with those ice-blue eyes.

Killian is silent, watchful. I feel his gaze, feel his silence.

I also feel the gazes of the eight other men, each hungrier for me than the last.

And Killian? His gaze is the hungriest of all.

The man kneeling before me lifts his hands, almost reverently, and finds the zipper pull of my skirt, tugging it down as far as it will go. He gathers the material in his hands, and tugs, once, sharply. I gasp at that rough jerk of his hands, and my mouth falls open as my core is exposed.

He palms my hip, slides his touch to cup my ass, pulls me closer to him, and his nose buries in my slit. A long, shuddering inhalation, and I know what he smells: my essence, thick and pungent, my desire, ramped up by Killian's touch.

There is something about his touch, the electric sting of his hands on my flesh.

I have no control over my response.

"Charlie." Killian's voice, a sharp, snapped warning.

It's all it takes. Charlie, the blond man kneeling in front of me and sniffing my cunt, rises, clutching my skirt, and backs away.

He snags my panties off the card table, and saunters for the door, pausing halfway out. "Good games, gentlemen." A glance at Killian. "Conrad…you've really outdone yourself this time, my friend. You've ruined me for poker, I do believe." Another glance, this one at my nude body, a longing, appreciative look. "And you…you've ruined women for me, darling. I don't believe I'll ever find anyone quite so…unassumingly and stunningly sensual as you."

Then he's out the door, and the others are grumbling. Eying me, edging closer to me.

Killian catches my eye. That smirk, that damned smirk. He pats his thigh, and it works like a command on me, has me circling the cluster of men to stand by Killian's side, and he wraps one long arm around my waist. He pulls me to him and settles my ass across his lap.

He moves the chair away from the table and repositions me so my back is to his chest; I'm sitting on him as if he were a chair, his knees between mine. One hand, on the arm of his chair, is clutching his tumbler of whiskey, the half-melted ice clinking against the glass as he lifts it to his lips and sips.

He tilts the glass to my lips, and I taste the smooth fiery burn of expensive whiskey.

With his other hand, he explores me in full view of the other men.

No part of my body is untouched as his hand travels along one thigh, to the crease between hip and thigh. Up my side, tracing the outer edge of my breast. A fingertip circles my areola, a fingernail flicks against my nipple, then two fingers pinch, twist and tweak until my nipple is diamond-hard and aching. I clench my jaw, fighting the sensations and the heat building low in my belly.

My attempts are wholly ineffective.

His touch dances down my torso, to my thighs. Tugs my legs to either side, so my knees are hooked around the outside of his thighs. I'm spread wide open, and I know I'm wet.

So wet.

He flicks my nipple, and then pinches it, *hard*, the way he did earlier, upstairs, and damn him, damn him, *damn* him—I can't stifle the gasp that flies out of me. I *feel* it, then, the gush of hot slick wetness spreading through me.

He smears two fingers through that moisture, spreads it all over my clit, and I'm gone, gone, gone, head lolling back against his shoulder, eyes closed, abandoned to this, to his touch, regardless of who may be watching—that is now irrelevant. No one else even exists, because his touch is sorcery.

He offers me more whiskey, and the fiery weight of the liquor hits my stomach like a freight train, blazes through me, lightens my head, scatters my thoughts, sends me flying, floating. His fingers circle my clit slowly, lightly, and gently. But, god, it's not enough. I need more. I need him to touch me harder and faster so I can finally find the release I need so badly. God, I need it.

I hear the tumbler thunk onto the table, and then I feel his fingers pincer my nipple, and the sound that emerges from my mouth is pure sexual relief, a throaty groan scraping past my vocal chords unbidden as he clamps down hard and twists. He lets go, then flicks the throbbing little nub gently, and then pinches it again, all the while oh so slowly smearing two fingers around my clit, never quite touching it directly.

My hips grind on his lap. I feel his erection beneath his slacks, a thick hard ridge. But he doesn't unzip, doesn't bring his cock out. Doesn't even move his hips to grind back at me.

He brings his hand to my other nipple and gives it the same treatment, alternating hard sharp pinches and gentle, tender tweaks and caresses and flicks, and his fingers on my clit never speed up.

I can't reach the edge like this, and I think he knows it.

"Open your eyes, Miss Tavistock." His voice murmurs in my ear.

I force my eyes open, and eight men are gathered around, watching intently.

His lips touch my ear. I feel his words as much as hear them. "Do you want me to let you come?"

I nod.

He finds my clit with index finger and thumb, rubs it between the pads, and I cry out wordlessly, arch my back and writhe my hips as he brings me to the shuddering shivering edge of orgasm—

And then stops.

"I didn't hear you, Miss Tavistock."

"Y-y-yes—"

"Yes what?"

"Please?"

A single swirl of a finger against my clit. "Remember what I asked you to say upstairs?" I nod again, and he removes his fingers. "A simple nod will not do, Miss Tavistock. Let me hear your voice. Do you remember the phrase I asked you to say upstairs?"

That touch, a single finger pressed to my clit, but not yet moving. Teasing.

"Yes, I remember." I manage the words, because I have a moment to breathe, a second the gather my thoughts.

"Then say it, and I will let you come."

He glides two thick fingers into my cunt. "I'll stop if I don't hear the words."

And indeed he does stop moving his fingers and thumb, but doesn't pull them away.

I swallow hard, wet my lips with my tongue.

"Do you want me to let you come?" he asks, once more.

I reach back behind my head and clutch at him with both hands. "Yes, *please*, Mister Killian."

"Very good." He spears those fingers deeper into my cunt and curls them, somehow unerringly finding my G spot at once and massaging it just so, and I spasm even before his thumb starts moving against my clit. "*Now* you may come, Miss Tavistock."

His thumb works against my clit, rubbing it in slow gentle deliberate circles, and his fingers inside me drive me even wilder, and then when he speaks, when he gives me permission, I fall over the edge.

The pent-up pressure breaks through me like a tidal wave, bursting in a flood of heat. I'm screaming, writhing on him, I can hear my voice going hoarse from the throaty, breathy screams of orgasm, feel my body thrashing. And when the climax hits me, he adds a third finger inside my cunt and uses I don't know which and don't care which fingers of his other hand to swirl with sudden mad wild ferocity against my clit, driving me instantly from mad to utter nymphomaniacal abandon.

I come so hard it hurts.

And I keep coming, still or again, I don't know, his hands working tirelessly and feverishly in me, pushing me from one level to the next, like a reverse version of Russian nesting dolls, each orgasm more potent than the last, until I'm incoherent and spasmed with my spine arched, tits thrust to the ceiling, hips flexed as far as they'll go, his fingers squelching wet and fast, in and out of my slit, swirling against my clit with the flat of three fingers, and now the orgasm shatters, and me with it.

My eyes fly open, mouth open and jaw trembling.

My entire body is a live wire, a conduit of searing aching burning ecstasy bashing through me as if I've clutched a power line and thousands of volts are coursing through my body.

One final wrenching spasm—

I feel something give way inside me, and a thin powerful stream of something wet spurts from my cunt, splashing on the floor and on the shoes of the man directly in front of me, and it doesn't stop, because I can't stop coming, cannot stop the crashing chaotic madness of my climax, can't stop the squirting of my orgasm.

My audience is rapt, watching me come. Watching Killian make me beg, make me come, make me squirt.

Limp now, exhaustion dragging at me, I scan each face. The man directly in front of me has his hands clasped in front of his trousers. He shifts uncomfortably, and I see why: he came in his pants, watching me come.

I feel an odd sense of pride in that.

Killian's hands leave my pussy, slide over my skin to smear my own essence all over my thighs, my belly. He cups my tits, thumbs my nipples, murmuring something in my ear that I am too delirious from exhaustion to even comprehend. Encouragement, perhaps. Or praise. I don't know, I don't care.

Darkness seizes me, and I drown in it.

I wake alone, in a strange room, in a huge comfortable bed.

Naked.

Sticky from my own juices.

Aching all over.

Light bathes me, the pale pink-orange glow of sunrise.

The sheets are white silk, slippery and cool. An entire wall of windows is on my left, overlooking the grounds of an expansive estate with its manicured lawns, topiary bushes carved into the shapes of lions and griffins, a hedge maze, rolling hills of tall grass waving in the wind. A flock of starlings lifts from the trees to wing across the sky.

To my right, I see that I am in a massive suite of rooms. There is a sitting area with a grand piano, a long, polished bar stocked with several crystal decanters of various liquors. A clothes closet is visible through an open doorway, and a bathroom through another.

I hear the scuff of a footstep, and I sit up in the bed.

"You were magnificent last night, Miss Tavistock," Killian's smooth, cultured voice, quiet and powerful, comes to me from across the room.

I look up, and see him in all his glory. He looks fully rested, and judging by his damp hair I assume he has recently showered. He's wearing black tailored slacks, a crisp white button-down, unbuttoned and baring a wide swath of his body that could be carved from living, tanned marble. He's in the process of fastening cufflinks at his wrists, platinum inset with black pearl.

"I was shameless. I made a mess."

He gives me that ghost of a smirk. "I rather thought it was beautiful." He finishes with one cufflink, and then fastens the other. He glances down at me. "I am hosting another party this evening."

"Am I to be the entertainment again?"

"You will be delivering a different but similar performance, yes."

"Another audience to bear witness to my inability to resist you?"

"Something like that, yes." He buttons his shirt, steps into his slacks, and shrugs on his suit jacket. "The card room at nine this evening, if you please."

He saunters away without a backward glance, stopping briefly to snag a folded tie from a side table and drape it around his neck. There is another folded pile of fabric on that same side table.

"Wear that," he commands, tapping the fabric. And now he shoots me an amused look. "And nothing else. "Feel free to have food sent up, have a massage, or just rest. You've earned it."

And then he's gone.

I leave the bed and tip toe naked across the room to the table. I lift the garment he indicated. It's a dress…sort of. I step into it, pulling it into place.

It is made of translucent crimson gauze with thin strips that fall over my shoulder, widening to wedges that drape over each breast. I am swathed in fabric, but in no way are my breasts concealed. Tucked in at my waist, the opaque skirt blossoms to hang to my feet, a slit from floor to navel so that when I walk, my core is exposed. There is no back as such, the garment open down to mid-buttock.

It is a farce of a dress, meant solely to display my curves and nothing more.

Evening arrives, both entirely too soon and not soon enough.

I feel a sense of excitement, yet I am anxious, and curious.

At the stroke of nine p.m., I am standing at the closed doors of the card room. I knock twice, gently. Killian opens the doors, a slow, small, appreciative smile curving his lips and lighting his eyes as he sees me standing there.

Eight men—plus, to my surprise, one woman. Nine players, plus Killian. I scan their faces, seeing the same men as last night, but one is missing. The man who won my stockings is not here—I don't know his name, I never bothered to learn it, or anyone else's. The only names I know are Killian—*Mister Killian*, as he seems to prefer, and Charlie, the blond man standing front and center, pale blue eyes on me. My panties are in the breast pocket of his suit coat.

The woman is obviously here to play cards with the men. She is a few inches shorter than I am, or she would be were she not wearing a pair of black heels. Her hair is a vivid, violent, artificial red, falling in long, loose, luxurious waves down past her shoulders. She wears a dress almost as revealing as mine, strapless, cups mounding her breasts into a shelf of cleavage. If she were to breathe too deeply, her nipples would be visible. The dress is black and is molded tight to her stunning curves and it falls to the floor. It is slit up along each thigh form two narrow panels, leaving her legs bare from the hip down, baring an indecent amount of hip, even showing a bit of the crease where her leg meets her hip. When she shifts her weight, the panels slide aside slightly, and it is obvious she isn't wearing panties, and that she is shaved bare between her legs.

Her eyes lock onto mine, and though her lips remain still and straight and expressionless, a glint in her eyes speaks of some private smile meant only for me.

There is a raised dais against the wall, draped in a shade of crimson silk matching my dress. On that stage is a chair. Thick dark wood, wide armrests padded with buttery-soft leather. Braided strips of scarlet gauze are tied to the front legs of the chair and to the armrests.

My stomach flips and my heart flutters at the sight of the chair.

"Gentlemen, and lady…Miss Tavistock." Killian gestures at me, and there are murmurs of greeting, smiles, some hesitant, others eager.

He then places his hand on the small of my back and guides me to the dais, and the chair.

It isn't any kind of normal chair, I realize. The seat bottom, upon which I am to sit, is foreshortened, providing barely enough room for me to perch my buttocks upon. And it is tilted upward.

"Sit," Killian commands.

Legs shaky, stomach flipping, heart skipping, I sit down. And as I do so, I begin to understand the general nature of what will occur tonight.

The angle of the seat bottom tilts my hips up, so that to remain seated I must lean back against the padded seat back and flex my hips. Add to this the lengths of gauze, which I assume will be tied around my wrists and ankles…

Trussed up and displayed, wearing a see-through scrap of gauze which leaves my pussy exposed—

"We are engaged in a poker tournament, gentlemen." Killian's voice booms authoritatively, cutting conversation short. "But one like none you've ever participated in before, I assure you. We do not play for money, as those of you who were here last night can attest. We play for various…prizes, shall we call them, all concerning the lovely Miss Tavistock, here." He indicates me. "The winner of each hand will be awarded the opportunity to bind one of Miss Tavistock's limbs to the chair…plus—"

A pause, and Killian eyes each man in turn.

"Plus," he repeats, "You'll have one minute on the clock with her, once you've tied whichever limb you've chosen. The only caveat to your one minute is that you may not touch her with any part of your body except your mouth and tongue."

There are murmured exchanges between the men.

But Killian isn't finished. "As we will be playing significantly more than four hands this evening…" a glance down at me, to assess, perhaps, "…once all four lengths of gauze have been tied, the prize becomes two minutes, and you will have the use of your hands."

I'm stunned at his pronouncement and struggle to keep up, as it is obvious he has something else to add.

Killian falls silent and watches the players discuss the rules amongst each other.

"A final note," Killian announces, cutting through the chatter. "Should you bring Miss Tavistock to climax—" he grins at me, then at the others, "—well, I'm sure Miss Tavistock will find a way to demonstrate her appreciation."

Another silence, this one slightly more stunned.

"Are we agreed?" Killian asks, spreading his hands out, palms up. "Everyone?"

There is a rowdy chorus of agreement.

Killian twists to look down at me. "Miss Tavistock? Do you agree to these terms?"

"I do." The strength of my own voice shocks me, my agreement even more so. It is as if the words were torn from me, unbidden, as if some deep, dark, curious, naughty part of me overthrew the more rational side in a silent, sudden *coup d'état*.

I shouldn't have agreed, but I did, and I cannot take back my agreement. The padded bottom of the chair is comfortable, even if the position is bizarre. The armrests are soft under my forearms, and the seat back provides support and cushioning. This chair, devised for a rather specific purpose, feels crafted to my dimensions, and it fits my body perfectly.

For now, I sit with my knees touching, but I know that won't last long. I'm eager to see how the evening progresses and I admit to a not so small sense of excitement, even if it accompanied by trepidation.

The men—and the woman—are beginning to take their seats; some are over at the bar pouring drinks, others are chatting quietly in small groups. Tonight, it seems, my job is to sit here and allow them to tie me to a chair, and put their mouths on me.

I shiver at the thought. I scan the eight men and find none of them unattractive. They are varied in physique, ranging from tall and lithe

and sharp-featured—like Charlie—to short and stocky and blunt fea-
tured, to classically handsome, to ruggedly attractive, bulky with muscle. All are young, masculine, powerful, self-assured men.

And *her*.

If the men are lions and bulls, she is a panther. Sleek, something
beyond beautiful. Beyond sexy. Dripping in allure, bathed in raw sex
appeal. And she knows it and she plays to it. She sits at the table and
crosses one knee over the other. The motion bares her entire leg and
the curve of her ass. As she shifts forward to collect her cards as they
are dealt, her breasts all but spill out of her gown. Her long hair covers
one eye, and an idle toss of her head twitches it aside, a casually elegant
gesture. She doesn't appear to be wearing makeup, but such is her beauty that to wear makeup would only mar what seems to be near-perfec-
tion. No rings or bracelets or baubles, save a necklace—a long platinum
chain woven of fine, thin, delicate links. The pendant is a teardrop ruby,
bright red, vivid, nearly the same red as my dress, and the silk covering
the dais, and her own hair.

"Let's get started," Killian says. "Please take your seats at the table."

The first hand goes quickly. The winner is a lean young man, the
cuffs of his suit coat shoved up to his elbows. He has reddish-gold hair
and plump, expressive lips, a strong jaw. Eager gray eyes. A smile for
me, and a hint of nerves.

He ascends the dais to stand in front of me. He seems about to
speak, but then shakes his head, and closes the remaining inches between us. He kneels in front of me, beside my legs, which are still
pressed together, closed. Removing the length of gauze tied to my left-
hand armrest, he glances at me, at my eyes, and then at my breasts.
There is a hint of something like an apology in his gaze, and then he
ties the gauze around my left wrist, swiftly, adeptly, with the familiarity
of someone well used to tying knots. Someone with his own yacht,
perhaps?

When my wrist is tied, he glances at Killian, who has an hourglass
in his hand. He flips it over, and then sets it down. "You have one minute, starting now."

The young man in front of me seems unsure. He hesitates then leans toward me, touching his nose to my shoulder. His lips touch my skin, near my throat. A clumsy but sweet kiss. Then his nose brushes against me, cheating perhaps, but no one notices except me. I say nothing, and watch as he kisses my shoulder again, this time using his nose to brush aside the strap of my dress. Clever boy, he is. Another kiss, nudging the strap further toward the round of my shoulder. And though his kisses are clumsy but sweet, my skin still reacts, my body responds, my breath shortens, his lips leaving electric stings where they touch. A bit further again, another kiss, and now the strap slides off my shoulder, and the gauze floats away, slowly, ethereally, baring my left breast. He sucks in a sharp breath, a quiet one, so quiet that only I can hear it.

"Thirty seconds," Killian announces.

And now the young man kneeling in front of me spends several of his precious seconds merely looking at me, at the breast he has exposed. And then his tongue extends from between his lips and touches my nipples. It is my turn to suck in a breath, as a flutter of something warm and soft ripples through me at his tender, hesitant touch. Another lick, this time more strongly, more assertively. And then he presses his lips to my breast, breathing out as he does so, bathing my pebbled flesh with his warm breath, and then he's kissing my tit, moving his lips and tongue as if he were kissing my mouth, and my muscles tighten and I have to suck in another surprised breath at the intensity of sensation he's able to elicit, simply from one little kiss to my breast.

"Time," Killian says.

The young man backs away at the announcement, leaving my breast wet and glistening where he kissed me.

A single backward glance at me, and then he's back in his seat and the men on either side of him are congratulating him, pounding him on the back, slapping his shoulder, shaking his hand.

I wonder what it would be like to be alone with someone like him, like that young man? So tender, eager, sweet, inquisitive. Different, surely, than someone like Killian. A wholly different experience, I think.

Rather than the dominating power and commanding presence, taking what he wants and still somehow giving me what I need in the process, someone like that young man would be…eager to please. Pliable. He would do anything I asked, probably. And oh…god, the things I could ask him to do…

I daydream as the next hand is played.

I could tie *him* up. Take my time with him. Toy with his cock, get him hard and suck him right to the edge, and then stop, and kiss him everywhere else, make him wait. Tease him. I could draw it out for hours, probably, using him like a toy to get me off as many times as I want before letting him come. I could pin him to the bed and ride his face, and he would eat me out so desperately, so eagerly, clumsily perhaps, hesitant with inexperience, but I could show him how I like it. Slow, at first. Lick the outsides, my thighs. Use his lips, kiss me there. A little tongue. Make him bring me to orgasm without using his fingers. Just his mouth.

I'm shaken out of my daze by a hand on my thigh.

The man kneeling in front of me this time is *huge*. An inch or taller than Killian even, nearing six-five easily, probably more. Broad as a barn, so massively muscled that the sleeves of his suit coat are bulged and stretched. Shoulders like mountain ranges. Brown hair cropped close, stubble thick enough to almost be a beard. Brown eyes, puppy dog eyes. Playful, glittering with lascivious mischief.

"Hands off, if you please," Killian says, "except to tie the binding."

The hand leaves my thigh and trails down to my ankle. He draws my leg aside, opening me, and then ties the braided strip of gauze around my ankle.

His eyes flit over me, from my face to my breasts, to the hint of my pussy visible now that one leg is pulled aside.

"Think I'll borrow from the last guy's playbook," he says.

"One minute," Killian announces, as he flips the timer.

The man leans closer to me and wedges his huge body between my legs, then he noses aside the second strap of my dress. No games, with this man. No hesitancy. He nudges my dress off my shoulder, and now it pools around my waist, leaving me bare from the waist up. He makes a sound low in his throat. "You are fuckin' gorgeous, honey."

My mouth works, and I clutch the arms of the chair. "Thank you," I manage.

Anything else I might have said is lost as he flicks his tongue against my nipple. A quick flick, and his tongue stiffened. I gasp, and he chuckles. "Gonna have to up my game so I can win another round." He licks the other nipple, and then alternates swiftly. My grip on the armrests tightens until the leather squeaks and my fingers ache, because this man's tongue is nimble, quick, talented. "I want those extra minutes. I think I could make you come all over my face."

"I—" I can't help arching my spine to thrust my tits against his face. "I think—*oh*—I think you could, too."

A minute has never felt so long, nor gone by so fast all at once. He laps at my tits, suckles my nipples. Bites them, not quite hard enough that it hurts in a bad way, but just enough that it spreads those deep, delicious pangs of heat through me. He nuzzles the undersides, kissing them there, all over the roundness underneath, and then the sides, only to return his attention to my nipples, always right at that moment when I began to want the stimulation again.

"Time."

Immediately the man backs away, licking his lips, then wipes his palm across his face. He flashes me a quick grin. "Till next time, sweetheart," he says with a wink.

And oh god, oh god, my tits ache. Throb. My nipples are wet and hard and tingling.

I find myself daydreaming now about that giant of a man, how huge his cock must be. So big it might actually hurt to get him all the way inside my pussy. It would be a good kind of hurt, though. That burn when he stretches me apart…? I wiggle my hips, stifling a moan. That burn would be so sweet, so deep, and when he finally filled me all the way, I'd be so split apart I wouldn't be able to breathe, wouldn't be able to move, could only straddle him and let him fuck me slowly, until I'd gotten used to his size, and then I'd be stretched around him and taking him and the angle if I was riding him would be just right, so perfect that I'd come in seconds—

God, a third round done already?

Must be, because there's another man in front of me. He's medium height, average build, but god, he's the most blindingly, perfectly beautiful man I've ever seen. So gorgeous it seems impossible. Blond hair swept back, except for a few loose tendrils framing one side of his face. He's got chiseled features and piercing green eyes.

He wastes no time. His grip on my ankle is rough and brusque as he ties my other ankle to the chair leg. And now, god, now I'm spread wide open. The chair legs are so far apart that I'm split open, my hips thrust forward by the angle of the seat bottom. It is an erotic position, meant to display my cunt in all its wet glory. I feel the eyes of nine men and one woman raking over me, watching droplets of desire dripping out of my cunt.

And the green eyes belonging to the man in front of me, ooohhh…he likes what he sees.

He kneels between my wide-stretched thighs, and presses his lips to my inner thigh, near my knee. He showers me with a series of kisses, his tongue flicking as his lips suck, moving upward, moving closer. Another kiss, suckling a little harder this time. A touch, a kiss, a suck, inch by inch he moves up my thigh. He's taking his time nearing my pussy. I stifle my moans and resist the urge to thrust my hips at him. The kissing, his lips on my tits, the air on my bare cunt, all the eyes watching this display, watching this man kiss closer and closer to my pussy…it's making me crazy, and I feel something burgeoning inside me, not an orgasm, but something else. I'm *liking* this display. I'm *reveling* in my power, knowing an audience is watching everything, missing nothing.

These men all saw me come last night, watched me come so hard I squirted all over someone's shoes. They know what to expect tonight and I don't want to disappoint anyone, least of all myself.

I open my eyes and find the man from last night, whose shoes I made a mess of, standing right there in front of me, wearing the same shoes. I can see from here that he hasn't cleaned them; dried spots are still splattered across the glossy black finish.

The kisses being planted along my inner thigh are not really kisses anymore. They're too fierce, too harsh, and too rough for that. This last one, so close now that the stubble on his cheek brushes the lips of my pussy…this last touch of his lips to my flesh is sharp, stinging, and as he moves his mouth, I see he's left a hickey, a brownish-red blotch on my flesh. I hear Killian call the thirty-second mark, and instead of using that mouth on my clit, he moves to the other leg, the velvet, tender flesh of my inner thigh, and he latches on again, sucking hard. It *hurts*, and I cry out as his mouth leaves my flesh with a loud *smack*. Another love bite, a match for the first.

He stands up, smirks down at me. "Don't need the last ten seconds. I think I've left my mark."

Oh…my god. I'm dizzy. He saunters back to his chair with an arrogant swagger.

I have one free hand left, and I bring my fingers to the love bites on my thighs, one then the other, rubbing gently, soothing.

But god, and shit—that touch to my thigh, my fingers…so soft, so warm, and I'm so—*worked up*, maddened from the relentless, fruitless stimulation, the teasing, and I'll only have this hand free for so long…

And my clit is throbbing…

I tease myself, and instead of touching my clit I slide my middle finger inside my cunt, working it slowly in and out. I do this with my eyes open, watching my audience, looking at each pair of eyes. I watch them in turn as they watch me finger myself. I feel an intense thrill rocket through me, rather than the bite of shame I'd have expected, a sharp hot wild zing that makes each sensation as I finger-fuck myself that much hotter, that much more potent.

They are all torn—do they play the cards in their hands or do they watch me? All of them are helpless, watching me glide my finger in and out of my tight wet pussy. One of the men sets his cards down and commits to watching. Then the others follow until no one is even pretending to be thinking about cards.

How could they be?

My cunt is soaked and dripping. My fingers squelch in and out of my slit, and juices spill out of me as my fingers—two of them now, middle and ring—fuck in and out hard and fast, and then I stop, pull them out, drag them through the wetness and smear it on my clit, those two fingers moving in slow circles now, slow, *slow*, bringing me back down a little, away from the edge. When the heat builds again to a deafening, blinding, all-consuming roar, I let myself go a little faster, pressing my fingers flat against my clit, up and down, pausing to slide them inside my channel at random intervals.

I'm watching my audience, gauging their reactions…enjoying their obvious arousal and discomfort.

One of the men shifts his weight, adjusting his cock behind his pants.

Another clears his throat, and takes a slug of whiskey.

I hear myself moan, now, a high breathy whine. And then a whimper. Another whimper, which turns into a drawn-out groan.

My eyes rake over the card players and settle on the woman. She's sitting perpendicular to me, twisted in her chair to watch. She leans back, and then she slides lower, her ass against the edge of the chair. Her eyes are hooded, but she's watching me carefully. Her hand steals under the table, and perhaps I'm the only one watching her, or able to see, or maybe she doesn't care. She nudges aside the front panel of her dress, baring her pussy. Bald, tight, plump pink lips, a prominent clit.

She touches two fingers to her clit, her eyes fixed on mine, lower lip caught between her teeth, eyes hooded, brows lowered, spine thrust forward. She doesn't play around, doesn't draw it out. She fingers her clit hard and fast, obviously so turned on it's not going to take her long. So I watch her, and she watches me, and we both bring ourselves to the edge. I moan loudly, which covers her quiet exhalation. No one is looking at her, no one is paying attention to her, and she loves it, the not-quite danger of masturbating while sitting at a table with nine horny men.

I can't fight off the climax any longer. All I can do is buck my hips against my fingers and cry out loud and watch as the woman comes at the same time as me, back arching so sharply she nearly slides off the chair as her climax blasts through her, wrenching her upright and then back down, thighs clamping around her own hand, and I'm mirroring her movements, thrashing against the bonds. The fact that I can't move the way I want to frustrates me but also, somehow, makes me come even *harder*.

I'm screaming in short sharp gasps, coming and coming—

"Royal flush," Killian barks, and tosses his cards down. "I believe that wins me the hand."

And then he's stalking up to the dais, eyes hard and hot, his expression angry. His slacks are tented at the zipper. He ties the remaining gauze around my wrist in a series of abrupt gestures.

"That wasn't part of the game, Miss Tavistock," he grumbles at me.

"It wasn't excluded, either," I say, gasping from the aftershocks of my orgasm, staring up at his irked features.

He isn't angry, I realize, but so wild with lust and need that he's barely containing it, restraining it.

"Since I make the rules," he murmurs to me, although I can tell the other players can hear him, "I'm going to forfeit my one minute in favor of something else."

He reaches into his suit coat pocket and produces two long pieces of scarlet silk. He passes the silk around my thigh, high up, as close to my hip as he can get it, and then ties one end to the framework of the chair supporting the seat bottom and the chair legs. He pulls at the silk wrapped around my thigh, tugging it taut, spreading open my pussy even more, binding me more tightly to the chair. He repeats the same process on my other thigh.

And now I'm spread open, wet cunt splayed apart, my slit on display, and a hint of my asshole as well. I can't move my hips at all. Not an inch.

Killian makes an announcement to the assembled players, "You may now touch Miss Tavistock with your hands, but I want to see who can make her come. And, friends, if you do make her come, she will reward you...*handsomely.*"

Desire pounds inside me, pulses through my veins in place of blood.

I don't think showing appreciation will be a problem.

God, no.

I want to be touched.

And...I want to touch.

All those zippers, burgeoning with cocks. Each one different, each one begging to be licked, sucked, *appreciated*—

I drift mentally once more as the cards are distributed and they play another hand. They drink more whiskey and endeavor to keep their expressions blank. I tune them out, and try to imagine which of these men will win my appreciation first. And how he'll win it, and how I'll show my thanks. The big guy, maybe? That tongue of his was nimble and talented, and those thick, strong fingers...oh my, the things he could do to me. His cock would be so enormous...it'd barely fit in my mouth. I'd have to stretch my jaw wide, and it'd be a struggle just to fit him past my lips.

A chorus of male groans shakes me from my thoughts, and I tear my gaze away from the huge man of whom I was daydreaming. The woman is approaching me, a sultry sway to her hips, a smile on her lips that reminds me of nothing so much as the expression on a cat's face in the seconds before it pounces on a helpless, unsuspecting mouse.

She ascends the dais, stopping to stand in front of me. She steps out of her shoes, and sinks to her knees before me. She glances back at Killian. "The time?"

Killian flips the hourglass and sets it on the table with a thump. "Two minutes."

His gaze is hot on me, a smirk on his lips, as if he knows what's about to happen.

Her fingertips trail up from my knees to my core, light tickling, arousing touches. Again, she drags her fingers along my thighs from knee to labia, and then a third time. Then her index finger traces my seam from top to bottom. I gasp, then, when she does that, and she grins at me. Sliding her index finger down my seam once more, she presses a little more firmly so her fingertip just barely penetrates me. This time, though, when she reaches the apex of her downstroke, she rotates her wrist and drags her finger back up, sliding a little deeper in. Then down again, and deeper. Mere seconds have passed, and I'm throbbing, tingling, heat building, need pounding low in my belly. And now, god, she adds her middle finger and pushes those two digits into my cunt, slides them out, then in, and out, and in, and then—

She rotates her wrist again so her palm is face up. She curls her fingers in a come-here motion, striking my G-spot perfectly, and I shudder all over.

My thighs tremble, and I'm straining against the bonds, wanting to thrust, silently begging her to pay attention to my clit, to touch me where I need it most.

But she knows, oh, she knows.

Another curling stroke to the delightful, delicious little spot high inside me, just behind my clit, and then she leans forward and touches her lips to my labia. She licks the outside of my cunt, one side and then the other, still teasing. How many seconds left? Thirty? Fifteen?

I'm gasping at each slow swipe of her hot wet tongue, my hips trying to thrust, trying to grind against her face, because the throb, the need is overwhelming. The teasing has me groaning, whimpering, needing just one single flick of her tongue against my hard, begging clit—

"Thirty seconds, Arelia."

A hot huff of air, the woman—Arelia—is laughing. Then another breath, this one slower, deliberate, and the heat on my saliva-wet pussy is nearly too much and nowhere near enough.

"No more—" I gasp.

Another of those silent laughs, a brief blast of hot breath. "You want to come?" Her question is for me alone.

"Fuck yes. *Please.*"

"You'll be repaying the favor in kind, you know."

"I know…I know."

"Very well, then." She prods my clit with her tongue, a teasing touch. Then a lick, a slow pressing of her tongue flat against my hard clit. "Come for me, Miss Tavistock—*now*."

As soon as the final word drops from her lips, she sucks my clit between her teeth and then stiffens her tongue and lashes me wildly, and I devolve into screaming and thrashing against the bonds as I'm slammed with a flurry of blinding waves of climax, and she doesn't stop, doesn't let up, doesn't slow, just swirls her tongue around my clit hard and fast and wild until the force of my orgasm has me sobbing, gasping for breath, nearly ready to beg her to stop.

She doesn't quit until I go limp in the restraints. Then she stands, turns, and winks at the men. "That, gentlemen, is how it's done."

"Miss Tavistock?" Killian ignores Arelia's comment. "Are you ready? Arelia has earned a reward, I do believe."

I can barely breathe, barely form words, but I manage a nod, and Arelia's smile is predatory. She glances over her shoulder at the table of men. "Gentlemen? Can you please tip Miss Tavistock's chair onto its back?"

Two of the men, the giant and the one who gave me hickeys, climb onto the dais, grasp the chair to which I am bound, and tilt it backward. The sense of vertigo is dizzying as I'm tipped over, and then I'm on my back, bound to the chair at ankles, thighs, and wrists, utterly helpless.

Amelia circles the chair, steps over me with a foot on either side of my face. I'm staring up her dress at her pussy, and then she's lowering herself to a crouch, gathering the skirts of her dress up around her hips, and baring herself from the waist down. She's a breath away from me, now, her pussy millimeters from my lips. I lift my head, swipe my tongue against her folds. She lets out a breath, grips the chair for balance, and slides a hand between her thighs, using two fingers to spread her pussy apart, exposing her clit for me. I lick at it, swirl it, suck it between my lips. I stiffen my tongue and push it into her channel, and then swipe at her clit once more. She gasps again, a breathy sound, and then I feel her hand abandon her pussy and delve to mine. Then she shifts, leans forward, and now I'm feeling her tongue as I'm giving her mine, and the sensation is all-consuming, devouring, making it impossible to concentrate on her while she's licking at me. She reminds me by rolling her hips, grinding her cunt against my lips, and I go back to swirling her clit with my tongue while she does the same.

I hear footsteps shuffle nearby, and realize the men have clustered around us to watch.

I'm moaning against Arelia's pussy, nearing climax now, and she's writhing on top of me, whimpering, a sultry, erotic sound, the high-pitched shrieks of a woman in the throes of climax, and that sound only turns me on even more.

"Jesus Christ," I hear someone say. "I'm about to embarrass myself in my pants."

"You ain't the only one, buddy," comes a response.

The ache explodes inside me, my second orgasm in less than five minutes, and I'm quaking through it, shrieking, lashing Arelia with my tongue, kissing her cunt as if I'm French kissing her mouth, and she's screaming into my pussy with equal fervor, and I hear male hisses of frustration.

And then Arelia is moving off me, and two sets of hands are righting the chair, and she's in front of me again, reaching up with a palm to wipe my lips, cheeks, and chin clean of her juices.

I'm wiped out now, limp in the bonds, exhausted, delirious. Arelia takes her seat, accepts a new hand of cards, and takes a slug of whiskey. She glances around at each of the men in turn, a pleased little smile on her lips.

"Shall we play, gentlemen?"

More surreptitious—and not-so-surreptitious—adjustments of cocks behind zippers, and then the play resumes, players tossing in chips and tossing in cards, accepting new ones, sorting hands, glancing at each other.

I float and drift through the next hand, eyes closed, relishing the welter of fading sensations.

And then I hear the grunts and curses of the losers, and I open my eyes.

It's the giant, all six and a half feet of him, miles of muscle and an impossible amount of sex appeal. Rugged, hyper-masculine, every curve is hard, every angle is hewn from granite. But his eyes are intelligent and playful and wise—and wild with lust.

"Think you can come again for me, honey?" He murmurs to me, placing a knee between my thighs.

"Not quickly," I admit.

He grins. "Fine by me."

He leans in and, rather than going straight for my pussy, he takes my nipple in his mouth, circles it with his tongue, nips it with his teeth. He does the same on the other side. Then he adds his hands, one huge rough paw cupping my breast, rubbing his thumb across my nipple, pinching it, twisting and tweaking until I'm short of breath and my core begins to throb again, impossibly. Lips and fingers, all over my tits, until I can't keep track, until all sensation narrows down to his mouth and his hands on my breasts, until I feel as I could perhaps come just from this incredible stimulation to my breasts.

But then he fits a finger inside me, sliding it in ever so slowly. I'm wet, so his finger glides in easily, and even his finger is thick enough to make me tremble and clench.

"Oh, baby, your pussy is so tight," he groans, leaning in. "So fucking tight. Squeeze me, baby, let me feel you clamp down around my fingers."

I clench, involuntarily at first, because now he's feathering light quick fast licks against my clit then sliding two thick hard fingers in and out of me, and I can't help clamping down.

"Yeah, honey, just like that. Now come for me. You're right there already aren't you?" He curls his fingers and nips at my clit, and indeed I'm there, riding the edge, drawing it out. "I can feel you getting ready to come. You're close, aren't you?"

"Yeah, god—yes, I'm close."

"Are you going to squirt on my face?" He licks my clit wildly, then, and stops right as I'm about to come. "Gonna make a mess all over me?"

"Shut up and eat me," I gasp.

"Oh…you've got a mouth on you, don't you?"

"Make me come and I show you what my mouth can do."

He doesn't have to try hard, then. I'm so close, so turned on by his skilled fingers and by his hard body and dirty words that all it takes another fat swipe of his tongue and a curling of his fingers inside me, and I'm coming apart around him, not squirting like I did last night, but gushing onto his mouth, coming so hard I see stars, so hard I the clenching of my cunt around his fingers is a crushing force.

He licks me through my orgasm, slow swipes of his tongue, too slow, too deliberate, too much and yet not enough all at the same time, and it makes me wild, makes me thrash against the bonds.

Instead of going limp, this time, I'm fired up, eager to taste him, feel him. "Untie me," I rasp. "Let me touch you."

"Afraid I can't do that," he says. Then stands up, his zipper straining to contain him. "But I can do this."

He unfastens his trousers and tugs them down around his hips. His cock springs free.

Holy *shit*.

I think I'm glad all I can use on him is my mouth, because that cock is an honest-to-god monster. Roughly the same width and length as my entire forearm.

He steps close, and his broad, velvety glans brushes my cheek.

I gaze up at him, a smile on my lips. "Oh my. However shall I show my appreciation?"

He grips himself, wrapping his hand around his girth at the base. Paints my lips with droplets of pre-cum. "Open your mouth and I'll show you."

"No hands," I say, flicking my tongue to tease the tip, wiggling my tongue against his frenulum, that tight little knot of skin on the underside of his cock beneath the glans and above his circumcision groove. "If I can't use my hands on you, then neither can you."

He grins. "Deal." A thrust of his hips has him nudging against my lips. "Now shut up and suck my cock." The smirk on his mouth makes it a joke, or a tease, and in truth, something about his dirty way with words stirs the fire inside me.

I open my mouth as wide as it can go, and take him into my mouth.

I barely fit the head past my teeth.

Dear god.

He grunts as I suction around the head, and his hips flutter. "Is that all you can take?"

I don't answer, at least not with words. I show him, instead. Stretch my lips, my jaw. Take more of him, and more, and more, and when he's at the back of my mouth and I'm relaxing my throat to take more, there's still so much of him left to take. It's impossible, god, so impossible. I have enough freedom with my upper body to lean forward, and I do. I take him into my throat, until my eyes water and I'm gagging on his cock, and he's hissing through his teeth and his fists are flexing at his sides, hips quivering.

"Jesus Christ, girl," he murmurs. "I didn't mean take *that* much."

To prove a point—which point, I'm not sure—I do it again. I back away, spit him out of my mouth and lick the tip, once, quick, a tiny flutter of my tongue over the hole, wiggling the tip of my tongue in it, and then draw a deep breath and angle forward and breathe through my nose and keep my eyes up on his, and slide his massive shaft between my tingling lips and down my throat, fluttering my tongue along his length as he glides in and in and in.

He hisses again. "So fucking tight…"

Then I back away again, not all the way, just enough that the soft, springy, fat head is left in my mouth, and god, that's a massive mouthful all by itself. I focus on that, now, bob forward on it, swirl my tongue around the head as I back away. I take him fast, then, sucking and fluttering my tongue and bobbing as fast as I can, non-stop, faster and faster, until he's grunting and his hips are pivoting, and he's cursing under his breath, fists clenched.

He has to grip the back of the chair, then, as I stop entirely, back away so he flops free of my mouth, and now he's thrusting helplessly, seeking my mouth, bobbing for me, and I tease him, moving so his thrusts miss my mouth.

"Fuck, woman," he snarls. "Quit teasing me."

The moment he speaks, I deep throat him, hard and fast, and now I feel his balls swinging and slapping my chin.

"Oh…fuck yeah, just like that. Take it all, babe. Swallow my cock."

So I do. Again and again, I back away until I'm kissing the very tip, and then take him as deep as I can, setting the rhythm as I fuck him with my mouth.

Until he starts thrusting, and then I change it again.

I let my head thump against the chair back, spitting him out. "If I let you fuck my mouth, will you be gentle?"

He reaches down, wraps my long blond hair around his fist until his hand is coiled tight against the base of my head, gripping tightly but not painfully. The playful smolder is gone, now. His puppy dog brown eyes are narrowed, fierce, brows drawn, jaw clenched.

"Probably not," he growls. "But I won't hurt you."

Not the answer I expected, but one that has me trembling nonetheless.

"Open that sexy mouth of yours for me, Hannah."

I part my lips, not quite all the way—intentionally. He grips himself at the root, gives his monster cock a single rough tug, and then touches the tip to my lips, gives his hips the tiniest, most subtle of thrusts. Just enough to push the glans past my lips, and then he's pulling away, holding my head in place. Taking control, now. With a shudder of exertion, raw self-control I'm realizing, he slides in again, ever so slowly. Backs away. Slides in, thrusting with his hips and holding me in place with his firm grip on my hair.

He's close, I realize. Holding back. Tensed, muscles locked up, brow beading with sweat. Tremoring, pulsing that long thick cock into my mouth, an inch at a time, with exquisite control.

"Fuck," he snarls, again. "I can't hold out much longer."

"Mmmmm," I hum on him, and then he thrusts his hips forward and pulls me onto him by my hair. "Mmmm-hmmmm," I encourage, then.

"Like that?" His voice is a low murmur, meant only for me.

I've forgotten there's anyone else here.

I don't care that there's an audience.

Or that I'm tied up.

In this moment, all I really care about is him coming. Feeling him lose control. I may be powerless, helpless, even bound to a chair, but I'm still in control of his orgasm.

To prove that point, I meet his eyes and hum again, a long breathy erotic sound. As if his cock thrusting into my mouth is the hottest thing I've ever felt. And in that moment? It's not entirely an act.

He grunts, and his fist jerks, and my throat is filled with his cock, but I'm expecting it, and my hummed whimper around his cock is cut off, turned into a gag as he ruts into my mouth. Out again, and now he's shaking all over, denying himself the climax.

"You ready for it, babe?"

I lean forward, seeking his cock with my lips. "Give it to me. Come for me."

He grunts, a snarling, primal sound, and shoves his thickness between my lips. I moan again in encouragement—*mmmm-hmm… mmmmmm…mmmmmm*—as he thrusts, and then I can't make any noises because he's lost to it, falling over into orgasm, and I feel his cock tense and throb and thicken, growing impossibly larger in my mouth, and he fucks so deep his balls slap my chin again and he backs away, using his grip on my hair to tilt my face up and flexing his hips, jerking me toward him, losing all control now. Even in utter abandonment, he doesn't thrust fully. He gives me hard half-thrusts, enough to fill my mouth and nudge my throat, and he's jerking me onto him now, all pretense of thrusting abandoned, shoving me onto his hot hard throbbing cock over and over.

And then, with a shout, he comes.

And holy shit, I cannot take it all, can't swallow it all. He overflows my mouth, fills me with cum in spurt after spurt of hot salty tangy seed. I swallow what I can, but it's too much, and he's still coming, still shooting his cum down my throat even as it dribbles out of the corners of my mouth and down my chin, and then he pulls away and slides his fist on his cock, aiming one last dripping spurt onto my tits. I'm gasping for breath, swallowing another mouthful, and then letting the rest spill out of my mouth and down past my chin to my throat, dripping down to join the thick, milk-white pool on the slope of my breasts.

He shakes his head, staggering backward. "You…you are fucking incredible." He rubs his thumb across my chin, wiping away his own cum. "Thank you."

"You made me come first. All over your face, just like you wanted."

He tucks his softening cock back into his trousers, zips, rearranges his shirt and suit coat, and steps off the dais, takes his seat, but not without several backward glances at me.

There are a plethora of jealous looks shot at him as he settles into his seat and accepts his cards for the next hand.

Killian's eyes burn on mine, but not with jealousy. With some kind of wild, voyeuristic pleasure. From this angle, I can see his crotch, and I can see that he's bulging out of his pants.

He pounds the hourglass on the table for attention. "Winner of the next hand unties her hands. Make her come again, and she's got the use of her hands."

Charlie, the blond man who won my panties last night, has a hungry, devilish grin on his face.

My heart palpitates then, because I just know he's going to win this hand, I can only imagine what he'll do to me, how he'll make me feel, and what I'll do to reciprocate.

• • •

The next hand is quick—Charlie wins, and wastes no time taking his place in front of me on the dais.

"Been anticipating this since last night," he says to me. "Pictured what I might get you to do you if I got the opportunity."

"Oh yeah?" I try to sound casual, even though I'm trembling with eager anticipation. "What'd you come up with?"

"More than you could possibly imagine. More than we could do right now. I'd need a week to accomplish everything."

Wasting no more time, he kneels down and winks at me before beginning to lick my inner thigh. He runs his hands up my thighs to my hips, then skates them back around to my cunt, pulls my labia apart and goes for my clit with a fanatic fervor, his tongue taking me to the brink within seconds, then stopping. He's teasing me, flicking licks at my clit, teasing little flutters that have me trying to flex my hips, but they're bound and I can't. He doesn't let up, doesn't give me what I want and what I need. He builds my desperation one teasing little flick at a time until I'm gasping with frustrated need, until my belly is heaving with my efforts to flex against the bonds, and then, finally, he suckles me into his mouth and flicks with his tongue and sucks and sucks and sucks and flicks. I whine and whimper and whisper *"yes, yes yesyesyes—"* as bliss builds and expands and contorts—

And then, when I'm literally a single eye blink from coming, he stops, and I growl in frustration.

He spits on the fingers of his left hand, keeping his eyes on mine. I'm writhing in the restraints, desperate for his tongue to finish me. He leans in, licks me twice, slow fat licks, and just enough to build the orgasm back up to near breaking, and then he stops again. He places his saliva-wet fingers to my taint and smears the slick wetness over the knotted rosebud muscle of my asshole. Then he presses his thick middle fingertip against me, smearing his saliva as lubrication. I gasp when he slides his finger into my ass, filling me. My desperation ramps up, now. The finger in my asshole takes everything to new levels, and ratchets up the hot unsteady pressure of my burgeoning climax into something unexpected, something wild, something dark. He flicks his tongue against my clit, and the pressure becomes volcanic, and I can't hold still, can't keep quiet. I try to move, to thrust, needing him to give me *more*.

And oh god ohgodohgod does he give me more.

He gives me a sudden onslaught of *more*. He lashes his tongue against my clit, a sudden frenzy of stiff-tongue side-to-side licks, and he moves his finger in and out of my asshole, starting slow and then faster and faster, and then when everything already building begins to break, he slows it all, slides that dirty beautiful finger so it's buried as deep as it'll go, and then he brings his other hand up to my cunt and works two fingers into my clamping, spasming channel, and now—shit, shit, oh god...I'm so full. Wrenched apart, utterly used in every way by him. Tongue to my clit, two fingers in my cunt and one in my asshole, all plunging and ravaging, going from stillness to rampaging wildness in an instant, thrashing me into a furious, volatile state—

And then he stops again, as I'm once again a mere breath away from coming.

"Fuck you," I snarl, after I've stopped screaming in anger and frustration. "Finish me."

He pulls his two fingers out of my pussy, touches them to his lips, licking my juices away. Sidles that one finger left inside me in and out, in and out, building my orgasm back up just with that motion. He uses his free hand to untie my wrists, never ceasing that in-and-out slide of his finger, harder and faster now, only that stimulation. Closer. Closer. My hands are free, and I use them to catch at my hair and pull it, growling low in my throat as tectonic power builds inside me, just from that finger, in and out, in and out. He slides it out, pauses, leans close, spits, works his saliva onto his finger and my skin, and that extra lubrication is all I need, all he needs to be able to fuck my asshole with that finger for real, now, and oh—*shit*—he's added a second, stretching me even farther, so it's almost painful, but the spasm-inducing ecstasy building inside me turns pain to added pleasure, more and more…

He watches me, working that finger in and out, going faster as the climax builds, taking his time, faster, and faster, until I'm gyrating against the bonds and ready to beg him for his mouth on my clit, for his fingers inside me. God, his cock—I want his cock inside me.

But somehow, I know that won't happen.

My eyes flick open, and go to Killian, who's watching raptly, idly stroking himself over his trousers. *He* will be the only one to fuck me with his cock.

And suddenly I realize…

He'll do it in front of everyone. With an audience. Getting me worked up, making me flush with orgasm after orgasm, letting his friends eat me out and mouth-fuck me until we're all wild…and when it's all built up to his satisfaction, he'll take me.

How and when, I don't know. And I don't want to know.

I want the surprise.

Charlie's fingers are ramming in and out of my asshole hard and fast now, and I'm letting loose with a hoarse, breathy scream as the climax starts to shatter. It's a cracking, at first, glimpses of white heat searing through me, tremors seizing me, my body contracting, my cunt clamping spastically.

I can't control the breathless yelps, now, can't stop them and don't

THE BLACK ROOM—door four

try. But I need more. I need—

My fingers find my clit and start to rub, but he bats my hands away and grabs both my wrists. "Play with your tits," he growls. "For now, your pussy is mine."

I pinch my nipples as hard as I can, eliciting another round of breathy shrieks, and the pressure of the pinches only serves to up the ante of my cresting orgasm.

I'm struggling against my bonds so hard now that it hurts, but I can't break them.

And then, when my climax reaches its cusp, when I'm wild and blind with the vaporizing heat smashing through me, seizing me, pushing me into insanity—

Charlie savages my clit with his ravenous mouth and he shoves those same two fingers back into my pussy, finds my g-spot, and then everything stops.

Everything comes part.

I fly into pieces.

I'm coming so hard I can't breathe, so hard I can't scream, so hard I can't do anything but ride the tsunami as it roars through me, wracking me, and he fucks me with his fingers all throughout it, driving me wilder and wilder, tongue thrashing my clit, devouring me insatiably, until the orgasm is enough to make me lightheaded and dizzy, enough to steal my breath and leave me panting, sobbing, gripping his head with both hands and riding his face, smashing myself against his frenzied mouth, grinding on him.

I fall back against the chair, shaking my head as if to deny the power of what I just experienced.

But Charlie is on his feet, unzipping his slacks, freeing the clasp, baring his cock.

Oh, it's a beautiful thing, Charlie's cock. He's hardening as I stare at him. Long, thick, with a subtle curve inward toward his belly. His glans is wide and bulbous, and his shaft is ridged with those veins and ripples I love to feel sliding over my lips. He watches me, hands at his sides, now that he's bared his cock.

I cup my breasts, lift the heavy, overflowing mounds of flesh and fit his thickening, hardening cock between them, and slide up and down, sheathing him between them, lowering until he breaks up out of the mounded flesh, and then I take him into my mouth, working up as much saliva as I can and letting it spill out of my mouth, onto his cock, onto my tits. He's fully erect now, the plump soft head exposed as he thrusts up between my tits. With the up-thrust, the underside of his dick slides against my lower lip, and now all I have to do is tilt my face down and open my mouth, and he slides in against my tongue. He growls—god, what a sexy, animalistic, masculine sound—and pumps his hips, fucking my tits slowly. I spit on him again, and now he fucks faster, harder, and I give the tip of his beautiful cock a long wet kiss every time it peeks up between my mounded tits, sucking hard until he withdraws again.

He takes his time. No hurry. Fucks my tits long and hard and slow, until he starts to falter in his thrusts, and then he backs away. "Use your mouth now."

I fuck Charlie with my mouth, the way he seems to like it, slow, purposeful. No tricks, nothing wild. I just sink him into my mouth as slowly as I can, tongue flat against the underside of his cock, over and over again, cupping his balls and fondling them, stroking him at the base with my other hand, pumping him faster as he begins to lose control, but never speeding up the slow bobbing rhythm of my lips sliding around his shaft.

"Oh fuck—*fuck*—" he grunts, and pulls out of my mouth. "Take it on your big beautiful tits."

I wrap both hands around his thick, throbbing cock and stroke him, slowly, taking several seconds to plunge my fists from tip to root and back up, until he's flexed and tensed and growling, holding back until the last possible second. He's wet from my mouth, so my fists slide easily, smoothly up and down his ridged, veined, velvet-and-iron length, and then finally his eyes flutter and he curses under his breath. I point the tip of his cock at the valley between my breasts, still stroking at the same deliberately, agonizingly slow pace. He grunts, and I watch his body spasm, watch the tip of his cock spurt his thick white cum all over my tits, a gush, another, more and more, until my tits are coated in his cum. It drips down between my tits, over my nipples, down my belly.

When he finishes his orgasm, I take his still-hard length into my mouth and suck the last drops out of him, clean him with my tongue and lips until he pulls free with a grunt.

And then he's backing away, leaving me cum-soaked—

And empty. Aching.

More orgasms than I can count, and I'm empty. I've taken all the cock I can handle, but none of it has left me satisfied, not in the way I need. Not the way I want.

I need to be fucked properly. I need Killian. I can see it in his eyes, I can see how he's built this up between us until this moment.

God, oh god. I need him.

All the eyes are on me.

On my untied hands.

I could throw off the rest of the restraints, and take what I want.

Instead, I lean back in the chair and watch as the next hand is dealt.

"Last hand, boys," Killian says.

There are murmurs, grumbles from those who never won. I feel bad for them, those poor unlucky bastards.

The hand progresses, and Killian's eyes are continually drawn to me.

So I toy with him.

Slide my finger in lazy patterns on my tits, dragging my fingertip through the sticky coating of cum, circle my nipples, and smear it all over myself. Toy with my cunt, play with my clit with my other hand.

Bite my lower lip and send smoldering looks his way. Inviting him.

Begging him.

From the moment he brought me nearly to orgasm simply from playing with my nipples, I've wanted him.

He ups the ante at the table, and I play with the knot in the length of gauze binding my thigh. The others call his bet, and I untie it. I flex my thigh closed and open, and then I untie my other thigh. I rub my legs together, both to tease Killian and to try to alleviate the ache between them.

As they start showing their cards, I untie my ankles.

Two of the players have folded, leaving eight to show. They go around the circle, showing their hands, and I stand up. I stretch lazily, and then toss off the ridiculous excuse for a dress. I descend the dais completely naked and walk toward the card table. I put a sway to my hips, and a bounce in my step so my tits jiggle for them. They're all watching me with unadulterated lust on their faces.

I walk slowly around the table and stop behind one of the men who hasn't won a single hand. He's a little older than the others, a touch of gray at his temples. Patrician, aristocratic, inscrutable, classically handsome. A sour note on his face; poor luck, I suppose. He's already folded, tapping his cards with an impatient fingertip. I tug at the back of his chair, and he slides it backward. I move between him and the table and sink to my knees. I remove his pocket square from his suit jacket pocket and wipe my breasts clean with it, fold it, then place it on his knee.

"Miss Tavistock." Killian's voice snaps out. "What are you doing?"

"Rewarding the less-than-fortunate," I reply.

The men are both silent, so I continue.

I free the cock of the man in front of me. He's frowning, as if not quite believing what's happening. I cup one hand under his balls and massage them, fondle them, and caress his short but thick member. I neither draw it out nor make it fast, but let it take the amount of time he needs to reach climax, using only my hands, gliding one hand over the other down his length, stroking with both at the same time, massaging his balls while pumping his length. I squeeze the head on the apex of an upward glide, and twist on the down stroke.

He is silent through everything, but his eyes never leave mine, flitting between my face and my tits; his whiskey glass is empty, sitting on the table near his hand, only a golden smear of liquid at the very bottom. When he's close, he begins to breathe heavily and his hips twitch, and then his breath catches, and I know he's about to come. I wrap my lips around his head, and stroke his length with both hands and take his cum in my mouth, and when he's finished, I spit it into his whiskey glass, and then lick the last drop off his tip with my tongue.

Then I move on to the next unfortunate card player. I treat him to the same reward: a through hand job, then I let him come in my mouth, and then I spit out his cum and lick him clean.

Five times I do this, in total. Fondle five different and each equally beautiful dicks, take load after load of cum on my tongue. Each man comes differently, tastes different, feels different in my hands. After each one, I give Killian a long, begging look.

When there's no one left I haven't given an orgasm to except Killian, I cross to the bar and grab the mostly-empty bottle of whiskey and pour myself two fingers worth. I take a big slug, rinsing my mouth out.

They've stopped playing, with only Killian's cards left to go.

There are eight sated men, some sitting with their cocks still exposed, others with that dazed, breathless expression men get after they've had their cock sucked.

I love that look.

Killian tosses his hand of cards onto the table. "Straight flush. I believe that's the winning hand, unless I'm mistaken."

No one objects.

I remain where I am, halfway across the room, drinking my whiskey. Relishing the hot burn down my throat, letting it sear away the aftertaste on my tongue.

The silence is thick, palpable.

"My turn, Miss Tavistock," Killian rumbles.

I shiver at the ferocity in his voice, the raw lust, and the pure hunger.

He crooks his finger at me, and I cross the room in a slow sashay, as if I'm in no hurry. I stand in front of him, my tumbler of scotch in hand. He twists in his chair to face me, then grabs me by the wrist and tugs me between his widespread knees. He looks at me first, a long, roving, caressing look. He doesn't have to use words for me know how beautiful I am to him. His gaze says it. His tented zipper says it. But his hands begin to tell me, too. They caress my legs, my thighs, my ass. He spends a long time there, kneading, smoothing his hands in affectionate, possessive circles over each taut round globe. Then he moves up to my waist, to cup my tits. He thumbs my nipples and pinches them. Oh yes, that again. God, yes, please. He gives me that delicious pressure, that sharp hard pinch and the ache in my belly strengthens as his powerful fingers pincer my swollen, erect nipples. Just when I'm beginning to think I can't take the pressure any longer, he releases them, and a blast of bliss shoots through me, and this time he doesn't stop me there, but presses the heel of his palm to my cunt, rolling it over my clit, pressing just hard enough that I shudder and my knees tremble, and the first of what I suspect will be several orgasms shivers through me.

As soon as I begin to mewl and gyrate, he takes my drink from me and sets it aside. Then he wraps his hands around my waist and lifts me effortlessly onto the table, placing my ass on the edge of the table and laying me back onto the cards and chips. He grabs my thighs and shoves them up and over his shoulders, and then buries his face between my thighs, devouring my cunt with all the ferocity of a starving man. The orgasm I was in the middle of shatters into something else, into something frenetic and primal.

He is masterful and unrelenting, tongue-lashing me through two more waves of climax, until I'm thrashing and clawing at him and digging into his back with my heels and grinding my cunt against his mouth.

After he finally allows me to stop coming, he helps me to sit up and then helps me off the table, to my feet.

"Take out my cock, Miss Tavistock."

I kneel in front of him, reach up, open the slide-and-hook clasp of his bespoke slacks, and tug down the zipper. He's bare beneath, no underwear, just a huge, beautiful, perfect cock springing free, bouncing and swaying as it is released. God, so fucking beautiful.

Not too long, nor too short. Not too fat, nor too slender. Huge, gorgeous, just long enough that I know from a single glance it will fill me and overflow me, that he'll be able to fuck me, bury himself in me and fill me until I'm gasping from it, without being too much. Just thick enough that he'll stretch my pussy open, just thick enough that when he fucks into me, I'll feel every movement with hypersensitivity.

So beautiful. I want to worship his cock. Not just make him come, not just bring him to orgasm. Not just reward him for giving me two—or was it three?—orgasms. His cock is perfect, and deserves to be worshipped. There's a subtle upward curve to it, the kind of curve that means when he fucks me, he'll hit my G-spot with every stroke.

He toes off his shoes and steps out of his slacks. I remain on my knees as he shrugs off his blazer. He slides my hands up his body to unbutton his shirt. He doesn't remove it entirely, leaves it open to bare his torso, his rippling six-pack abs, his broad, hard, wide pectorals. A smattering of dark hair across his chest. His cock, standing straight up, curving back so the tip touches his belly just beneath his navel. Plump, heavy balls tight against his body, begging to be licked, cupped, fondled.

I reach for his cock, clasping my hands around it, biting my lower lip, anticipating the taste of him, the feel of him in my mouth, the stutter of those lovely veins and ridges over my lips, the velvet-soft head springy on my tongue, the salt musk of his pre-cum—

He stops me after I've stroked his length only twice.

"No," is all he says, and lifts me to my feet. "That's not what I want from you, Miss Tavistock."

He sits in his chair, hands clutching the armrests, cock rigid against his belly. Waiting.

I sip on my whiskey again, making him wait. What else could he possibly want?

He will have to take me, if he wants me.

He growls at me, and then grabs me by my hips. He twists me so I'm facing away from him, then wraps his huge hands around my hips and pulls me backward toward him. I'm settled on his thighs, straddling him. He takes my tumbler out of my hand, steals a long sip, returns it to me, and then slides his hands under my thighs, just below my ass. He lifts me.

Everyone is watching. Nine pairs of eyes, all on me and on Killian.

Watching for the moment of penetration.

I reach down between my legs, touch my clit, a few swift circles to send the heat billowing through me, and then I reach a little further down and find his hard length. I caress his cock, reverse-grip, the circle of fingers and thumb facing downward, and angle him toward my slit, nudging his broad tip against my opening. I have to set down my glass and brace myself with a hand on the table, bite my lip and focus on remembering to breathe as I feel him begin to fill me.

I look down and watch him slide into me, watch my labia thin out as they're stretched apart by his thickness. I watch my cunt swallow him, inch by inch.

When he's fully penetrated me, I push off the table and lean back against him. He angles backward in his chair, scooting his ass forward, leaning back so now all my weight is on him, so I'm forced to rely on his cock impaling me and on his hold on me. I can't move, because I have no leverage. He cups behind my knees and pulls my thighs backward so they touch my torso, splitting me apart, baring me, exposing us, so everyone gathered can see where his cock fills me. I cup my breasts, toy with them, pinch my nipples, gasping, waiting.

And then he thrusts, using only the power of his hips and abs. His cock spears into me, his tip slams against my G-spot and I clamp down around him, throwing my head back to gasp in shock at the sudden onslaught of utter rapture. God, oh god, oh god—it's perfect. Everything that's gone before now has only served to make this moment all the more incredible.

Everyone watches as Killian grinds into me in slow, measured thrusts, watching his cock pull back to appear thick and long and hard and glistening wet from my dripping cunt, and then he flexes his hips and stomach and drives up into me, disappearing inside my pussy, splitting me apart.

They all watch me use one hand to spread my pussy open and touch two fingers of my other hand to my clit, driving myself wild with my own touch, adding to the ecstasy of being filled…of being so beautifully, perfectly fucked.

Killian is a master of his body, and a master of mine. He knows exactly how to drive me wild, how to use me, how to make me need him, want him. He knows how to fuck me.

And he does.

Slowly.

Filling me with measured strokes of his perfect cock, gliding in and out of me so smoothly there's no differentiation between the in-stroke and withdrawal, just a ceaseless smooth wet glorious fucking, until I'm breathless and teetering on the precipice of climax, and god, I need him to fuck me harder, I need him to force the orgasm from me, to fuck me rough and wild until I can't help but come.

But he doesn't.

He fucks me slow and smooth, until I can't take it anymore, until I'm feral with the need for *more*, until I'm wild with desperation to move, to grind on him.

He doesn't allow it.

He clutches my thighs and holds them tight against my body, and when I begin to fight him, he pauses while plunged as deep as he can thrust into me, brings my legs together and bars his forearm behind my knees. I can't even touch myself like this. All I can do is claw at his forearms and be fucked the way he wants to fuck me.

Which is slowly.

In front of nine watching people, each becoming more and more aroused the longer this goes on.

Arelia is touching herself again, and Charlie is torn between watching Arelia masturbate and watching Killian fuck me.

Killian holds me in place, flexes his hips to drive into me, plunging deep, god, so deep—

But I can't come like this, can't come without clitoral stimulation, and he knows it.

This isn't about me coming anymore.

Nor about him coming. But he will, *hard*, and we all know it.

This is about the fuck.

He continues his unhurried pace, gradually allowing me to open my thighs until I'm spread far enough apart that I can reach my clit again, and he allows that also, while pulling my thighs farther and farther apart until I can't spread any further, until he can't drive any deeper, and now I'm teetering on the edge again, fingers flying around my clit, and I'm gasping, whimpering, rolling my hips to take him deep and slide him out and grinding against my own fingers.

And then, just as I'm starting to come, he stops.

He grabs my wrists and pulls them away from my clit. "You won't come until I tell you to."

He pulls out of me entirely, and then sets me on my feet. He stands behind me and twists me to face him. Again, he picks me up by my waist and sets me on the table and lays me back. He pushes my thighs apart and tucks my feet into his armpits, and then effortlessly slides into me. I watch everyone—upside down, from my perspective—as he fills me while standing up, watch the men whose eyes are on my tits as they bounce with every stroke of Killian's driving cock. He's fucking me harder now, lifting up so his cock is tilted away from his body, stretching himself, each thrust angled down, and god—ohhhhh god, oh fuck, this angle, it's so good, the way his cock glides stiff and thick through me, tip grinding against my G-spot, pushing bursts of rapture through me, and I can tell he loves it just as much because he's not quite able to measure his thrusts anymore, can't contain his power anymore. He's fucking in earnest, now, driving into me, balls slapping against my ass as he pounds in, hard, making my tits bounce.

Oh, so good.

I meet each set of eyes as I'm being fucked on the card table, and being watched only makes it hotter, makes me wilder. I bite my lip and groan, writhe to meet Killian's thrusts, and watch the men watch me. And Arelia, the woman has gone wild herself now, thrashing on her chair as if she's the one being fucked, moaning, and I can see hands moving beneath the table, fists stroking cocks as if they can't help it anymore.

The giant is directly to my left, impossibly huge cock stiff in his fist, and I can't look away as he slides his big fist up and down his length, and I remember the taste of him, the feel of him, and Killian is stroking my clit with his fingers and fucking me in that hard, pounding rhythm designed to drive me out of my mind, and the huge man to my left is groaning, eyes on my tits—

He comes, spurting a mess into his palm, and I watch as he oozes cum onto his hand.

God, oh god—

Killian pulls out of me as I'm on the verge of coming, leaving me momentarily empty, aching, trembling and weak and desperate for the orgasm he keeps denying me, and unable to stand up for the waves wrenching through me, the precursor to climax. He sets me on my feet, hands on my hips, bends me forward over the table, tits smashed against the smooth, cool surface, arms outstretched, my face contorting as the climax continues to build within me, and then my expression twists even more as Killian spreads my thighs apart and guides his cock into me, nudging the head between my throbbing, tingling lips. He flexes there, flutters, teasing, tiny little thrusts just enough to glide the head in and out of me. Then each tiny trust becomes more, and he fills me more, hands gripping my ass cheeks and spreading me open, cupping and clutching, kneading and caressing. And then, without warning, Killian fucks deep, hard.

I scream, loud, piercing, because that hard rough thrust is exactly how I want it, how I need it, and now he's finally giving it to me. I writhe helplessly on the table, toes scrabbling and curling just above the floor, his hands big enough to grip my ass and hold me up, his cock so thick, so long, and so hard that I'm impaled and kept aloft by it, unable to touch the floor for purchase. Killian is in complete control. I can't touch myself, even though I try.

I twist on the table, trying to reach my clit, looking back at Killian. His necktie is undone, still draped over his neck, his only remaining piece of clothing. He whips it off, pins my wrists in one hand, wraps the cool silk around my wrists, binding them behind my back, all without missing a stroke. There are groans and grunts, and I scan the men briefly, watching their fists fly, dirty voyeurs all, finding such erotic pleasure in watching me get fucked.

And god, what a fucking.

Hard thrusts, hips slapping loudly against my ass, pounding deep, smashing into me, filling me, stretching me, crashing wave after wave of pleasure through me, but still not enough to make me come. Not hard enough, not fast enough, not rough enough.

But now I'm tied up again, helpless again, hands bound behind my back, and his hands return now to my ass cheeks, no longer caressing them with possessive affection, but with rough appreciation. With need.

His palm circles one taut, quivering, bouncing globe, and then he smacks me, a hard, powerful spank, and I cry out, a whimper of equal parts pleasure and pain and anticipation. And then he spanks my other cheek, hard enough to rock me forward, the smack coming in sync with his thrust, which is rough and unfettered now. No more games, no more teasing.

He spanks me and fucks me, a thrust and a smack, one side and then the other. My ass stings, burns, but the sting and the burn are so beautiful, spreading through me, filling me, touching every nerve ending and making my whole body more sensitive, and he's unrelenting. I'm in heaven, drowning willingly in a sea of ecstasy, screaming, whimpering, crying, sobbing, writhing back into his thrusts and tilting my hips to meet his spanks and watching my audience lose all semblance of composure and loving their eyes on me, loving that they can't get enough of watching me, watching Killian take me, use me, fuck me.

The burning tingling heat of his spanking and the pounding perfection of his thrusts and my helplessness, and all the eyes watching me and the sounds of fists on cocks and Arelia's fingers squelching wet in and out of her tight, pretty pussy—it's all too much. Too much.

I can't touch my clit, but I don't need to, god, oh god oh god, I can't take anymore, because this climax is an earthquake building up inside me, denied for what feels like forever, not just a clitoral orgasm now, or even a G-spot orgasm…it's everything.

I can't keep my eyes open, can't breathe, can't think, because it's building, building, building, it's everything inside me, impossible, volcanic, tectonic pressure pushing at every wall, spasming through every nerve, erasing and eradicating everything.

And then something warm and wet touches my clit, and a sobbing scream breaks through me. Arelia—god, oh fuck, she's on her knees on the floor beneath me, licking my clit, and I can see her cupping Killian's taut heavy balls and massaging his taint, and he's grunting, gasping, gagging on his growls as she manipulates him to new heights as he pounds away inside me.

Oh god, fuck, oh shit—it's billowing and breaking and going nova and I'm going to shatter, going to just utterly snap into a million pieces—

But he's not done with me, hasn't told me to come, and I can't, I can't, I can't, not until I hear him tell me to.

I hear him spit, feel wetness smeared on my asshole, feel him wiggle a finger inside me, and now—*now* it's entirely too much, the tongue on my clit, the eyes on me, the erotic sight of Arelia beneath me, her small delicate palm cradling Killian's huge heavy balls, her finger massaging his taint to make his orgasm all the more powerful, and Killian himself, god, the man is a machine, a primitive, primeval rutting beast, fucking me with every ounce of his power, hard beautiful perfect cock slamming in and out of my aching cunt—

It breaks, then.

"Come for me," he growls. No qualifier, not "Miss Tavistock" or even "Hannah", just that order, snarled between grunted half-breaths. "Come like you've never come before."

And I do...

God, it's as if the whole universe cracked and shattered inside me. It's an orgasm so powerful I can't even scream, so potent my lips fly open as if to utter curses and encouragement, but I have no breath for words or screams, no sound comes out, my lips just quiver, tremble, eyes wide, my body thrashing, convulsing, spasming.

It's not pleasure, it's not pain, it's both and neither, the two sensations mingled and merged; it's...

It's the essence of the universe, the meaning of human sexuality itself distilled into a single moment, a singularity of ecstasy and agony and perfection and screams and bliss, all of this inside me.

I lose myself in that moment.

I *become* the moment.

I own it. It is mine, and mine alone.

Nothingness devours me, and I succumb to it even as I glut myself on the feel of his hands cradling me against him, caressing me all over.

I succumb.

• • • •

I wake suddenly, completely, my face against his warm hard chest, his hands combing through my hair.

I look around: we're in his room, on his bed.

He skates his palm down my bare waist, over my naked hip, along my thigh. Just touching.

I tilt my face to look up at his. He gives me that subtle hint of a not-quite smile, just a sly curve of the corners of his mouth. "You're awake now." His voice rumbles under my ear.

"Yes," is all I say.

His eyes search me, and I'd have to be blind to miss the mask of sadness in them. His gaze flicks up, to the doorway across the room. To the knob, ornate polished brass with exquisite, delicate filigree knot work on the face. Then back to me.

"Time for you to go, Miss Tavistock." He says, his voice heavy and slow.

I nod against his chest, because it's the only possible response.

He stands up, carries me across the room. Sets me on my feet in front of the door.

We are both naked, still.

He spins me in place so I'm facing him. Fingers brush errant golden locks away from my face; a rough palm cups my cheek. He smiles then, a real, full smile, blinding in its beauty.

He touches me, not sexually, but as if to memorize the feel of my body under his hands. Everywhere, arms, waist, hips, breasts, shoulders, thighs, calves, ass, my back, up to my face, then he buries his hands in my hair.

This moment, it is strange, unreal, disorienting. This is not Master Killian. This is…

Someone else. I don't know whom.

As soon as I begin to grasp the shape of him, the hint of tenderness beneath the voyeur and the exhibitionist, the dominating alpha male—he steps back, tilts his chin up, and the ghost of that man is gone.

"You have to go now." His gaze flicks over my shoulder, toward the door.

I take a step backward, unable to tear my eyes away from him. He's so beautiful, so male, so powerful.

I press my back up against the door and fumble for the knob. It feels warm under my palm.

A twist. A push.

As I step backward over the threshold, into complete darkness, I never look away from Killian.

Some part of me screams, raging against the pull of what lies beyond that door, against the inexorability. I don't want to go. I want to stay. I want to unearth that fragment of a different man. I want more of that, more of him. The tender, and the alpha. Either, or both. God, please, both. I don't want to go. Don't want to go. I fight it, but my feet carry me regardless of my desires. It's like falling, toppling from a great height into an abyss. I can flail and scream and hate it, but I cannot stop it. I fall into the darkness, but I do not look away from him.

My last vision of him is his hard, huge muscular body, his dark hair and molten brown eyes, and his cock, rigid and perfect, begging me to return, to touch, kiss, lick, caress, suck, love—

But I can't, I can't go back now, I'm through the doorway, into the darkness now and it swallows me whole, pulling me down, down, down into the timeless tidal dark of nowhere, of nothing, of every-thing, of silence and peace...

...of naught.

Silence.

Perfect, utter silence.

A drowning quiet.

Him, *him*—Killian.

His name is branded onto my mind. His body, his beauty. That hint of the man beneath the hard mask, the ghost of a man who could be, a lover buried deep beneath the alpha. Him—the first sensation.

Hating this darkness, hating this silence, hating this solitude; the second sensation.

There is no sense of waking up, no borderland between being awake and being asleep, no drifting or floating. There is just...blackness, darkness, nothingness, and then—I'm here, in this black room, the doors, the pools of flickering, guttering, dancing, orange-yellow light. The doors. Five remain. Four have disappeared.

My body works on its own, bringing me to my feet, carrying me across the open space to the fifth door. It is identical to the others, black and plain with a thick silver numeral 5 in the center, reflecting and re-fracting the light of the torch.

I am sure in the knowledge that I *must* open this door, I *must* step through it, I *must* seek him, seek the man on the other side, whoever he is, whatever version of him it is. I *must* find him, Killian, beyond that door: the third sensation.

The doorknob on this fifth door is utterly unlike the others. It isn't a knob, even. It isn't on the right side of the door, but a little lower than midway down the middle of the door. Nor is it a lever, or a knob, not glass or brass or plain metal. It is a mammoth, life-like lion's head, jaws open and snarling, caught in mid-roar, lip curling, curving teeth bared. In the lion's jaws is a gold ring nearly the size of my own head and as thick as my wrist. It is loose in the lion's mouth, stopped from being pulled free by the snarling beast's huge front incisors.

Unlike the other doors, this one does not open inward when pushed open—this time I must pull on that ring.

I wrap both hands around the cold gleaming gold of the ring and pull with all my might. The door is supremely heavy, it feels huge and stubborn. I lean back, pulling, straining, and finally it gives, sliding open on silent hinges.

Beyond is a courtyard bathed in silver moonlight, a hint of the star-washed night sky. A fountain gurgles in the center of the space, the water spouting a dozen feet in the air and falling in a perfect umbrella of glass-smooth water. In the far distance, a forest of columns forms pools of shadow. There is an archway in the middle of the columns and, beyond that, is the bulk of a tall, crenelated tower dotted with small rectangles of warm yellow light—windows, lit from within. Cobblestones lie underfoot.

All is silent but for the splashing of the fountain.

My feet are bare on the cobblestones; they're cold, sending a dull ache up through to my lower back. The wind begins to skirl, long cool gusts tugging at the fabric of my dress, pulling it taut against my thighs, plucking at my hair. I look down and examine my attire: I'm wearing an elegant, lovely silver gown, the hem sweeping along the cobblestones, trailing behind me, and belling at the hips and nipping in to hug my waist. The bodice is stiff but well made, cupping and lifting my breasts into an expanse of pale décolletage. The dress is breathtakingly exquisite, crafted from the finest, softest silver chiffon, so thin, so finely woven as to be nearly sheer, but it is not. It's an airy, floating fairy tale gown, one made for whirling across a ballroom floor in the graceful steps of a waltz.

I take a step toward the fountain, leaving the door behind me. I hear it close with a soft *thump*, and lock behind me. The door is set in a wall of dark, polished marble, the black wood lacquered to a gleam, another gold lion's head in the center, the ring still swinging.

As I step out into the courtyard I stop as I emerge into the brilliant silver glow of a full moon and the scintillating spray of twinkling stars. The ethereal scene is equalled only by the impressive scale of what I am seeing; everything is *massive*.

Above and behind me is another tower, made from man-high blocks of limestone, soaring a hundred or more feet into the air. All I'm able to see from this vantage point is a wall that is long and high and, except for narrow arrow slits, unbroken. I crane my neck and look up, and see the underside of a balcony, the hint of an ornate railing, the glow of candlelight.

Facing the fountain now, I'm close enough to touch the water. To my left is the hulk of a building extending out of sight. It is topped with a series of short towers with crenelated arched bridges connecting them, balconies here and there, some darkened, some glowing with light.

To my right is another wall. Some fifty feet high, made from the same mammoth limestone blocks and crenelated at the top, with short, steep stairways leading down to the ground at regular intervals, the wall extending away from me out of sight, beyond the forest of columns and beyond the archway, meeting the farthest, tallest tower in the extreme distance. From here, that tower looks to be a toy but the distance, along with the height of the wall, tells me that tower is *enormous*.

I extend my hand under the spray of water, and my fingers are wetted as the glassy water falls through my fingers; the water is cool, but not cold. I step across the cobblestones toward the archway and as I near the columns, I realize that the archway is in fact a tunnel, leading underneath the wall itself, which separates the courtyard from whatever lies beyond it. Torches light the interior of the arched tunnel, but to either side, in that forest of thin, fluted columns, all is silent, and still, and shadowed.

As I take in the impressive scene before me, stretching in all directions, I feel as if I've stumbled into a fairy tale.

Then, out of the corner of my eye, I am certain I see something move in those shadows. My heart begins to hammer in my chest, spurring me to hurry through the tunnel.

Heart in my throat, nerves singing now, the tunnel leads me out under the night sky once more, the wall to my right and the soaring, hulking weight of the structure to my left. Before me is a long narrow, shallow stairway dwindling away into a vanishing point. The building—a castle, I suppose it's properly called—continues forward on my left, a massive, a sky-blotting mountain growing only larger as the stairs descend toward the central tower. I descend the stairs, and the castle rises on my left becoming a mammoth wall, and on my right the wall angles away into the distance, with a steep hillside plunging away from the wall and toward the stair, the face of the hill dotted with trees and flowers and meandering lines of sculpted shrubs and manicured grass.

I descend the stairs, and look around me. Tiny shapes move slowly along the wall to my right,. They are spaced far apart, but within shouting distance, each one near a staircase. Something silver glitters on each shape—they are guards, I realize, armed and armored. But they are too far away for me to see any details.

Down, down, down, the breeze of my passage plucking at my dress and my hair. Some instinct in my gut keeps me moving; I feel some need to reach the bottom of the staircase, and that farthest tower.

I don't know how long it takes me, but eventually, as I approach the bottom, the tower attains its full, imposing height, easily five or six hundred feet tall, dotted with windows, which I now can see are not mere tiny slits, but huge breaks in the wall. Not only tall, this tower is wide, extending in a broad curve away from the stairway in both directions, so wide the tower could be an entire castle on its own, never mind the boggling, impossible expanse to my left, the top of which is now far, far over my head, out of sight.

As I reach the bottom of the staircase there is nowhere to go except into the tower in front of me, or back up whence I came. To my left, I can see blocks of limestone twice my height and impossibly huge, and to my right, the steep hillside chasing up to the wall, now a good quarter mile distant, looking tiny and quaint, the guards on it ant-sized.

The stairs end in a broad curving landing made of gold-veined marble tiles. The entryway to the tower is a vaulted arch soaring twenty feet high, with a pair of god-sized doors set in the vault, dark thick ancient wood bound by black iron straps as wide as my waist and thick as my wrist, fastened with rivets the size of my fist. A pair of lion heads with rings in their jaws adorn the center of the doorway, but these gold-sculpted beasts are life-sized, and so artfully fashioned it seems as if they could open their jaws and roar at any moment. The rings here are thicker than my forearm, so heavy I can barely lift one, even with both hands.

There is a shelf in the wall directly to my left, with a sliver of a stairway leading up to it, and standing on the shelf is a guard, huge, imposing, clad head to toe in armor plates scaled like a fish, his helmet crafted to make him appear like a lion, his eyes dark and glittering behind the visor. In his left hand is a shield, the flat bottom resting in front of his foot, rising in a rectangle wider than he is, and then tapering to a wicked point a foot over his head. He could easily hide behind that shield and weather any attack safely, or tilt the top of the shield forward and impale his enemy; it is both a weapon and protection.

In his right hand is a spear. A dozen feet tall, wrist-thick, made of polished black wood, the butt end rests on the ground. The end of the spear is bright polished iron, and the head of the spear is a narrow, viciously sharp, three-foot long arrowhead, the tip so sharply pointed it almost vanishes.

On my right is another shelf in the wall, and another guard, identically armed and armored.

Neither man acknowledges my presence, and neither speaks to challenge me. They could be statues; for all that they show signs of life. Their eyes, though, shift and glitter behind their visors, searching, roving, moving. I know they see me, of that I am certain

There is no doubt that this place—a castle, a fortress—is a place of great danger, yet I feel as if I belong here, as if I am expected. As if I am known.

I approach the huge doors and grasp one of the thick golden rings in both hands and pull hard, expecting the door to resist my efforts. Instead, it swings open easily, as if weightless. It is heavy, though. Impossibly heavy, but swinging on perfectly weighted and balanced hinges.

I walk in, and close the massive door behind me.

I am in an antechamber, a mammoth, empty, echoing room that must occupy the entire footprint of the tower, columns ringing the perimeter and supporting the ceiling overhead, which is dizzyingly high, another vaulted, fluted feat of architecture and engineering, all the vaults and flutes leading toward the center of the ceiling.

Across the flagstones, and through the ring of smooth columns, I can see torches flickering on each one, lighting the open space. On the far wall is another tall, narrow, vaulted archway, with two guards on either side, each attired in the same way as the men outside. They do not register my presence, and they do not bar my way as I move through the arch, which leads to stairs leading to my left, circling the circumference of the outside wall.

I ascend, passing the first set of windows after only a few dozen paces, windows that are as tall as I am and twice as wide, and closed in with thick, wavy glass. Up, and up, and up, the stairs ascend. They are wide and deep, yet shallow, carrying me up so easily that climbing them is almost like walking on flat ground; such is the scope and scale of the tower. When I pass another set of windows, I realize that I've climbed what must be a hundred vertical feet.

I come to a landing and a doorway, but the stairs continue to ascend. A compulsion I do not understand carries me upward, past the doorway, and then as I climb another circumnavigation of the tower's perimeter, another doorway, directly above the last. And then a third doorway. Another, and another.

The higher I go, the harder my heart pounds; yet I know I must continue on. What awaits me, I do not know, but I must go, and I must climb these stairs. I know, deep in my heart, that when I leave these stairs I will meet my fate. I will learn where the purest distillation of truth dwells.

After what seems like hours of ascending stairs, I finally I walk through another doorway.

The room beyond, like the one at the base of the tower, is so huge it defies description. Dizzying, disorienting. A ring of columns ten feet from the door, and then another ring ten feet beyond that, and then a third, each successive set of columns thicker and further apart than the last, until by the fifth ring the columns are too broad for me to wrap my arms even part way around.

The ceiling is relatively low, considering the scope of the room, but as the columns become larger, the ceiling rises higher and then, when the columns stop, the ceiling vanishes entirely, becoming a stained-glass dome of utterly unbelievable scale. A hundred feet across? Two hundred? I don't know. It's too far overhead to know. I am faint with disbelief, overwhelmed by the immensity of this room, of this tower.

Directly beneath the center of this dome, an immense, flat-topped pyramid soars toward the roof. Built from blocks of pure white, gold-veined marble twenty feet to a side, the steps of the pyramid ascend on all four sides. A pair of guards stands at the bottom of each side of the structure. At the zenith of the ziggurat is a throne, too high up and too far away to make out any details.

I approach the pyramid, heart hammering. My legs are weak and trembling, not from exertion, but from nerves and fear.

As I stand at the base of the pyramid I am finally addressed by a guard. His voice is a guttural snarl, so deep I feel it in my chest. "He's expecting you, girl. Go up. Now."

The stairs up the pyramid are steep, the treads narrow. Moonlight hits the stained glass far, far above, shifting to a hundred different colors, bathing the dais atop with an array of shades of muted blue and red and silver and gold. In the sunlight, this spot must be...incandescent, prismatic. Unbearably bright and beautiful.

At night?

It is simply magical. A place of dreams and ethereal peace. Breathtaking.

When I reach the top I am out of breath, and I now feel more fear than ever before. Why am I afraid? I don't know why, but I am, and that indefinable fear has me in its grip, choking me, throttling me.

The dais is perhaps thirty paces across in both directions with a simple, comfortable chair in the center, situated beneath a rosette in the glass far overhead. The chair is a throne, but it's also…just a chair.

The moonlight is bathing the man seated upon the throne as if it's his own personal exquisite spotlight.

And the man himself…

In this moment, in this light, in this place, he is a god.

Clothed in spotless white—a simple tunic and matching trousers—his feet are bare. Simple clothing, and their very simplicity serve to highlight his raw masculine beauty and power. His hair falls in a thick cascade around his shoulders, held back from his face by a simple iron band.

No gems, no precious metals, only plain iron; the arrogant authority exuding from him is enough to name him King. His face is in repose, waiting, eyes closed, at peace. Across his knees is a naked blade, one hand clutching the hilt, the other resting on the blade with familiar comfort. His shoulders lift and descend in regular, even intervals as he breathes slow and deep, soughing softly.

The sword has a blade that is wider than my palm, over four feet long from tip to hilt. The blade itself seems to glow in the moonlight, the glittering whorls chased in otherworldly designs across the metal. It shines as if diamonds had been crushed and turned to paint. The cross guard is a pair of foot-long wickedly-sharp spikes, the hilt plain black leather bound in silver wire, the weighted pommel as thick as my fist and carved into the same fierce roaring lion as on the doors. Despite the beauty of the blade, however, it is clearly no showpiece, no useless, ceremonial thing. The edge is nicked and pitted, honed so razor-sharp it seems to cut even the shimmering, multi-hued light of the moon. This is a blade that has shed blood, seen war, taken lives, and won a throne.

And the man wielding the blade? For all his beauty, for all his regal grace, he is a wild beast poised upon a throne too small and too flimsy to contain his vigor. He is at rest, but he is coiled like a predator.

Without armor, without helm, without shield or bow or mail, he is yet more deadly than any of the guards I've passed on my journey thus far.

When I stand before him, at last, he takes a single deep breath, holds it, and lets it out slowly. His eyes open, molten, vivid, piercing, tumultuous, feral golden brown. A lion's eyes.

"Kneel, girl." Two words only, but from those lips, in a hard, arrogant tone which brooks no disobedience, it is a command. The stars themselves would kneel at his feet, should he command it.

I kneel.

I feel his gaze upon me. Assessing. Judging.

"You are a prize, won in battle. Your king gave you to me as a peace offering." He tone is lofty, disdainful, and my heart squeezes. "I have no need of another wife, nor another soft body to warm my bed. So tell me, lovely little thing—why should I keep you?"

●

What to say?

I want him to keep me. *Don't send me away.* But what words will convince him? What action will sway him?

I am no queen, no elegant concubine. Who am I? What worth have I?

I don't know; I have no answers.

All I do know is that I cannot speak, and don't dare even shake my head, or shrug my shoulders. I remain perfectly still, my eyes averted.

Conrad rises from his throne, sets the sword across the arms of the chair, and then circles the chair to descend the back of the ziggurat. He doesn't gesture for me to follow, doesn't speak a command, but I know I am meant to accompany him. And, of course, I do.

I stay a few steps behind him, down, down, down, across the echoing throne room, my gown whispering quietly on the flagstones. We arrive at a doorway in the opposite wall from that through which I had entered. This is a simple wooden door, rounded at the top, with a plain iron ring pull. A silent guard stands on either side of the door. These guards, however, are unique. No armor, no shield, no spear. Each one is easily seven feet tall, mountains of muscle sheathed in ebony skin, heads shaved bald, each wearing a pair of white breeches, bare foot. Each one holds a single battle-axe, the hafts taller than I am myself, the blades half-moons tapering to vicious points at the top and bottom. A weapon wielded by such mammoth men could cleave an armored foe in half with the ease of a sharp knife through soft cheese. The butt-ends are planted on the floor between their feet and each guard holds his axe extended to arm's length, so the blades cross to block the door.

As he approaches, the guards pull their weapons back in front of their bodies in a crisp, sharp movement, in perfect unison, allowing access.

A single tug, and the door swings open toward us. I expect him to breeze through in front of me, but he surprises me. He holds the door open for me, gesturing for me to pass through first.

"After you." His eyes fix on me as I hesitate, and then timidly step across the threshold into a large, but cozy room, which I take to be his personal bedchamber.

Only twenty paces deep and perhaps twice as wide, it occupies but a tiny fraction of the tower's total area. The bare stone walls have been lined with thick velvet curtains to ward off the chill from outside, and to reflect the warmth back inside. On the flagstone floor is a single hand-woven rug that is a breathtaking work of art, a crimson background woven with gold thread to depict a battle scene. The primary figure is the man holding the door behind me sitting atop a white charger, wielding that same glittering sword in triumph over a field strewn with fallen enemies.

There is a bed, huge, wide, on a high, four-post frame crafted from thick dark wood. The head of the bed is butted up against a wall; the doorway directly opposite the entrance leads out to a balcony overlooking his castle—and, from this height, much of his kingdom as well. Against the wall to the right of the balcony doorway is a suit of armor on a stand. Black steel, so black it seems to absorb the light and swallow it. It is covered in scales, like the armor of the guards I had seen when I first entered the castle, but of infinitely finer quality, the thousands of tiny snake-scales interlocking, allowing him full freedom of movement, yet complete protection from all but the fiercest of blows from all but the mightiest of foes. A snarling lion's head forms the helmet, done in the same ultra-black metal, with luminous rubies for eyes, the wearer seeing through the open mouth. A shield stands beside the armor, and it is of the same style as that wielded by the guards, but made from the same black steel as the armor itself.

The room is occupied by a fireplace with a roaring fire crackling merry and hot, a plush, cushioned armchair angled in front of it, a small table to one side, on which is an opened bottle of wine and a single dented, stained, old metal cup, the kind of cup a soldier might carry with him on his campaigns.

After closing the door behind him, he crosses the room and spins the chair to face the room rather than the fire. He sits, pours himself a cupful of wine, and regards me with those cunning, arrogant, golden-brown lion's eyes. I stand three feet away from him, spine rigid, belly roiling, knees trembling, skin tingling, fingers clenched into fists at my sides, breath coming short. Nerves, fear…and excitement.

"I have no need of you," he says, the words meant to cut. "But you are lovely indeed, so I will allow you to convince me of your worth."

"How—" I begin, but nerves and fear catch at my voice, and I falter. *Take a deep breath, start again.* "How should I convince you?"

A tiny smile curves the corners of his mouth, amused, sarcastic. "I am a man of action more than words. There is little you could say that I haven't heard before. I have grown bored and weary of my…companions, shall we call them…of late. Nothing they do pleases me. I've felt so few stirrings of desire for any of them that I wonder if the problem is with me rather than with them. A king shouldn't admit to such doubts, I know, but…" A careless shrug. "I care not for the opinions of anyone."

He sips from his wine, and his gaze rakes over me from head to toe, examining me thoroughly, piercing me, as if to pry my deepest secrets out of me, undressing me with his eyes. I feel naked under his gaze.

"You are lovely indeed, Hannah. Buxom, fair of skin and blessed with an abundance of womanly curves." He leans forward. "Is your skin as soft to touch as it looks?"

I swallow hard. "I—I don't know."

He lifts his chin. "Come closer, then."

I step across the room, taking shy, uncertain steps closer and closer until I'm within reach of his big, rough hands. He doesn't immediately reach out to touch me. First, he merely looks at me. His gaze scours every inch of my body, twice, starting at my hair, then my throat, then my cleavage, then my waist and hips, legs, feet, and back up. It feels as if he is assessing the quality of the flesh and curves beneath my gown. I feel naked beneath that scrutinizing gaze, as if he can see through the gauzy material. I shiver, and my skin pebbles.

"I haven't even touched you, and yet you shiver, and get goose-flesh." His voice is a low, amused murmur. "Is it anticipation or fear causing such a reaction?"

"Both," I say.

He stands up, and now he's inches away, so close I can feel his breath, smell the wine, feel his heat. "What is it you fear?"

"You." I can barely breathe, can barely speak. "What you will do to me. What you want from me. Being sent away."

"You do not wish to return home, then?"

I shake my head. "No."

"You wish to stay here? With me?"

"Yes. I do."

He takes a sip of his wine; I watch his Adam's apple bob as he swallows. "Prove it, then."

I don't know what to do, or how to prove this to him. He offers nothing by way of direction, only stands inches away, essentially fucking me with his eyes. His gaze tells me he finds me attractive, and he's said so himself. The way his eyes continually rake over my body, stopping at my breasts and hips, telling me without words that he wants me. But he doesn't move, doesn't reach for me, doesn't touch me.

I swallow hard, and let instinct guide me—

I fall to my knees.

His eyebrow lifts, and he takes another sip of his wine.

I reach up and find the laces to his breeches. I untie the simple knot, loosen the laces, and tug the edges apart. Then I grasp the waistband and pull the breeches down around his thighs, baring his cock. Which is…

Slack, flaccid.

I look up at him, surprised. I'd expected him to be erect.

He smirks down at me. "Takes more than removing my trousers to excite my interest, girl. But I am curious, so you may continue."

Even slack, he's an impressive sight. Thicker than both of my thumbs together, longer than my entire hand, heavy hairy balls. I remove his breeches entirely, and then, more for my own enjoyment than his, I rise to my feet and trail fingers up his waist, lifting his tunic. There's another set of laces at his throat, which he loosens with one hand, the neckline revealing a patch of tanned skin and thick black body hair. Off, then, tugging it up and over, and he passes his wine glass from hand to hand, pulling his arms free, and then he's naked, gloriously, perfectly, incredibly bare. A god of marble-sculpted perfection, the epitome of rugged masculinity. Long, burly arms corded and thick with muscle, and ribboned with scars. Shoulders broad as mountain ranges, a heavy chest matted with thick black hair covering hard slabs of muscle. Abs like a furrowed field. Narrow, trim hips, tree-trunk thighs. He's confident in his nudity, utterly composed and at ease.

I sink to my knees once again, his cock at face level, now.

I cup the soft warm weight of his manhood in my palms, nuzzle the side of his cock with my nose, lifting it, letting it lay against my cheek, over my mouth. Licking my lips to moisten them, I open my mouth, lift my chin so his cock slides across my lips, and then let the tip fall into my open mouth. I chance a glimpse at his face. His brows lower, and his jaw clenches; he's reacting, at least, so I know I'm doing something right.

For a moment, I just let his cock lay in my mouth, on my tongue, breathing onto him, teasing him. My eyes lift to meet his and I take all of his still-slack length into my mouth, close my lips over him. I cup his sac in both hands and massage gently, rolling the tender weight of his balls in my palms, rolling his thickening and hardening cock with my tongue. I pull away, letting him flop free, dangling, swaying. His jaw is flexing, clenching and releasing, and his mighty chest is swelling with deep breaths. He lets one corner of his mouth lift in a small, curling smile, and then covers it by taking a sip of wine.

Other than the slight smile and the fact he has a burgeoning erection, there is no response, no reaction. His cock is curved to one side, tip still pointing at the floor, but I can see him lengthening, stretching, straightening.

I wrap my fingers around him, feel him hardening, filling my hand. I kiss one side of his cock, noisily, down to the root, to his heavy balls, licking one of them, suckling it fully into my mouth and then releasing it. I move back up his length, licking and kissing one side and then the other, cupping my hand around it, stroking him now. I can feel him begin to lose himself in my caresses, but I maintain my languid pace, fondling him with both hands, then taking the thick, broad, soft head into my mouth and sucking, fluttering my tongue all over him, all the while stroking his unbelievable length with both hands.

More confident now, I take him deeper, and then with a glance up at him take him as deep as I can, until my jaw aches and he's in my throat. A moment later I back away. He's fully erect now, the head pointing skyward, touching just beneath his navel, so thick my fingers won't fit around him.

I stand up. Facing him, I let my hand brush against his cock, idly touching him, not really stroking, just...toying. Feeling him. I lean against him, pressing my breasts against his torso while I explore the heavy muscle of his chest.

I'm touching his body for myself now. Roaming his masculine beauty with my hands. Shoulders, chest, waist. I discover his ass, warm and hard and round, and grip it with both hands, fingernails clawing into the flesh.

His body is rock hard, yet his skin is soft. He is billowing heat. I touch him everywhere, the smooth curves of his arms, the ridges of his abdomen, his hairy thighs, his back, roaming the line between his spine and shoulder blades and then back to his chest. All over. Down again, to his cock. I stroke him, just a few slow, idle caressing touches, and then I begin to replace my hands with my lips.

I kiss him everywhere I've touched, biceps, shoulders, chest, diaphragm, waist, thighs. And where I'm not kissing I'm caressing, stroking his hard hot flesh everywhere, avoiding his cock, except now and again at random, pausing almost accidentally to lick him, suck him, kiss the side, fondle his sac, tease him.

I do this ceaselessly, kissing and touching and teasing him until his chest is heaving.

"Enough," he snarls, knocking away my hands and stepping out of my reach. "What is your game?"

I blink at him. "I have no game."

I do, though: I want to force a reaction out of him. I want to make him want me. Make him stop *his* game and touch me.

He grips his erection and strokes himself three times, vigorously, harshly. "Do you intend to finish what you started, girl?"

I shrug, a daringly insouciant gesture. "If you wish me to."

I close the space between us and brush his hand aside, taking his cock in one hand and stroking him. With my eyes on his, my breasts nudging his chest, I stroke him slowly, unhurriedly, gliding my fist gently up and down his length. For a few beats, he only stares at me, and then he tries to project an ease and casualness I suspect he no longer feels, sipping his wine and rocking back on his heels. Moving his gaze to my cleavage.

"It is not often that I am naked and the woman pleasuring me is clothed," he remarks.

"Am I?" I ask. "Pleasuring you, I mean."

"Beginning to," is his grunted response.

I lean closer to him, nuzzle my face into his throat, breathing a long warm breath against his skin. Press my lips to his throat, just beneath his Adam's apple. An inch to the left, breathe, kiss. The hollow at the base of his throat: breathe a hot breath, kiss the soft salty flesh. Up, then, to just beneath and behind his ear, a breath and a kiss. His jaw. His chin. The corner of his mouth. His lips part and his eyes are heavy-lidded, and he leans toward me, perhaps meaning to kiss me, to accept the kiss I'm offering.

Instead of allowing his lips to meet mine, I sink to my knees, darting a smile and a glance up at him. He sucks in a breath, but that is his only reaction. I plunge my fist down his length, baring his plump pink glans, tease a flicking lick of my tongue tip across the bulbous head, then swipe slowly with the flat of my tongue over it once more, and again, and again, until his fingers clench into fists at his sides.

I slide my fist back up, form a cup around the head with my fist, and release a dollop of my saliva into the cup of my fingers and onto his cock. I smear my palm over him, spreading the slick wet warmth of my spit onto his smooth, straining flesh.

Again, I rise to my feet and meet his gaze. Beginning slowly, I caress his length once again, lean into him, kiss his chest, his shoulder, his throat—with each kiss I increase the pace of my stroking. The closer I get to his mouth, the faster I stroke him until I kiss the corner of his mouth, my fist becoming a blur as I pump his cock, his hips flexing involuntarily.

And then I stop.

"You test my patience," he murmurs between clenched teeth.

His chest heaves, his jaw flexes, and his abs tense as he struggles to hold back, to regain control.

I press my palms to his chest and push him backward, toward his armchair. When he feels the chair at his knees, he folds himself down into it, gracefully, spreads wide his knees, grips the arms of the chair and sets aside his wine.

I take a sip of his wine, replace the cup on the table.

I've teased him, toyed with him, brought him close to the edge—and I haven't exposed a single inch of my own skin.

Time to escalate the game.

Facing him, standing between his knees, I gather the hem of my dress in my hands. I pull the silvery soft loose chiffon upwards, first baring my ankles, then my calves, and then my legs and thighs. He licks his lips, swallows. Inch by inch, I gather more fabric and expose the juncture of my thighs. His eyes fix on me there, narrowed, jaw flexing, hands clutching the arms hard enough that his knuckles go white.

Then I turn, bunching my dress up around my hips, and present my ass to him, then drop it back down into place.

A groan, then. The first noise he's made, the first sign of his loss of control.

I lower myself, gliding my ass against his thighs. I turn my head to peer over my shoulder, watching him as I slide my ass against his erection, the thin skin of silk all that separates our flesh. His thick length fits perfectly between the cheeks and I writhe in place, teasing him with the soft slow brush of my silk-covered ass against his hard erection. And then I grip his knees and roll my hips, sliding against him.

He groans again and now, finally, he touches me. His hands wrap around my waist first, then he grips my hips and then smoothly they move down my legs to my knees, where he finds what he wants—the hem of my dress. Up, and up, he pulls my dress, tugging it upward past my hips to bare my flesh. I'm grinding on him now, writhing against him, gliding his thick cock between the globes of my ass, providing him with just enough tension and friction to drive him mad, but not enough to allow him release.

I reach between my thighs, find his erection, pull it forward, away from his body, and angle it against my slit. Rolling my hips, the head of his cock slides between the lips of my pussy, and now he thrusts, seeking more.

I turn to meet his gaze over my shoulder, gripping his cock, keeping it just barely inside me, his thickness spreading me open, stretching me, creating a sweet, deep, delicious burn. "Like this?" I tilt my hips, letting him fill me with another inch of his cock. "Is this what you want… *sire?*"

All I get from him is a snarling grunt, a questing thrust.

I don't allow him to enter me any further, matching his upward thrust by flexing away from him.

Hearing his frustrated groan and feeling the grip of his hands on my hips, I can safely assume he's losing the war against my teasing game. I move away from him and my dress falls back down and, once again, I'm utterly decent, clothed, and he's naked on his chair, aroused, the upper two or three inches of his cock gleaming wet with the juices from my pussy.

Oh, this game, this teasing…I am not immune to it; I've teased myself as much as him. I've felt him inside me, felt him fill me, just a little. Felt his hands on my waist, felt their power, their rough possession. I've felt his gaze, and now I want to feel his touch. Feel his mouth. Feel his weight over me, feel his massive cock filling me completely, over-stretching me to blissful fullness until I'm breathless and groaning and wild.

I have desires. I have needs.

He may be king, but my body doesn't know that, nor does it care, just as his mind and soul may be king, but his body is that of a mere man, one with needs.

I turn in place, facing him. Curtsying deeply, bowing my head. "Have I proven myself, sire?"

He laughs, a dark, amused, sultry sound. "Oh, you temptress."

He rises from his chair, and I can't help watching his dick sway as he crosses the space between us. He notices this, too. Stops when only a hair's breadth separates our bodies. I could touch him, but I've done that already. I could tease him, but I've done that, too. If I've done everything right perhaps now he will touch me, tease me, tempt me.

He touches a fingertip to my chin, drags it down my throat, over my breastbone, and down between my breasts. "I believe you have." He traces the perimeter of exposed flesh, following the curve of the bodice, dipping his finger between flesh and fabric. "I wanted you the first moment I saw you, you know. But now…now it is more than mere desire. Now it is…*need*."

"What is it you need?"

He steps away from me, across the room, to the suit of armor where a dagger in a sheath is strapped around the waist of the armor; he withdraws the dagger and returns to me. He places the cold, wickedly sharp point to the flesh between my breasts. A drop of blood beads, despite his feather light touch.

"What is it I need?" he repeats. "This damnable dress off of you."

And with that, he draws the dagger downward, the razor edge parting the chiffon with terrifying ease. Down between my breasts, over my belly, between my thighs, to the floor, slicing through the fabric without so much as a touch to my skin.

A brush of his hands, and the dress falls open, drifts off of my shoulders, floats to the floor.

And now, just like that…I am naked.

And at his mercy.

After a long, hot, hard gaze into my eyes he pivots, returns the dagger to its sheath, and then remains standing by the suit of armor. He's staring at me hungrily, as if he can't decide what he wants to do to me first. I merely stand and wait. I'm aching, throbbing between my thighs, dripping desire, my eyes devouring his gorgeous, naked form. Waiting, waiting, waiting for his touch.

He does not disappoint.

Four stalking, panther-smooth strides, and he's in front of me. His huge hands go to my waist, above my hips and, for a beat, they remain there. Holding me. Palms fitting to the upper bell of my hips so perfectly, as if his hands were formed to cup me there just so. And then his hands slide down and he grasps my buttocks, caressing the generous swell of them, then smoothing around to the front of my thighs, fingertips now pointing at the floor, dragging his touch upward from kneecap to hipbones, trailing electricity along my flesh. To my belly, then, his touch roams, and from there he teases the mound of my pudendum, all ten of his fingers tickling and teasing and not quite touching me where I am most sensitive. I stifle a sigh when he traces the seam of my cunt with a fingertip. I clamp down hard on the urge to thrust my hips into his touch, resisting the need to beg him to touch me.

That teasing, torturous touch, his middle finger sliding up my slit ever so slowly, dragging along the slick, tender, plump lips of my labia, not penetrating at all, only teasing. Not slipping through the keyhole entrance to brush against my clit, not piercing into my channel. Not giving me what I need.

He smirks at me, a sly, predatory curve of his lips, then steps away from me, leaving me shaking and frustrated. He gestures at the chair. "Sit."

I cross the room, pivot, sit in the chair, knees pressed together, thighs quaking, gut churning, blood racing. He approaches slowly, cock swaying, his eyes raking over my body. He stops, his knees bumping mine.

"So many things I could do to you." He slips his hand between my knees, spreading my thighs open then drags his finger through my cunt, coating his finger with my juices. "I could just…touch you, until you came apart. Or I could tease you, like you did me. Touch, but not let you reach climax."

"You asked me to prove myself," I say, in protest. "I meant only to—"

"Quiet, girl," he snaps, his voice low and snarling and brooking no argument; his is a voice you simply *must* obey. "You've had your chance. Now it's my turn." He grips his cock in one hard fist, straddles my thighs and rubs the silky-soft head against my cheek, across my lips. "I could tell you to finish me. You would look rather fetching, I think, with my seed all over your lovely face."

"Would I?" The thought does not disgust me.

Not at all. I would tilt my face to take his cum on my lips, on my cheeks, on my chin, I would open my mouth and swallow it and lick it away.

I run my tongue across my lips, stare up at him through half-lidded eyes. "Is that what you want?"

He wedges his thumb between my teeth, tugs open my mouth, fits his cock between my lips. He stares down at me, arrogance on his features, then thrusts with his hips, filling my mouth, my throat, and then withdraws. "Or I could just fuck your pretty mouth, and watch you struggle to swallow all of my seed."

I hum a moan around his cock because, right now, with his thick hard warm shaft in my mouth, tongue fluttering against his flesh, tasting him, feeling him, I would like that, too. Watching him come, watching him lose control.

"What else could you do to me?" I ask, when he pulls free, stepping back.

He scoops me up in his arms, lifts me from the chair with effortless ease and fits my thighs around his waist. I curl my legs around him, feeling the hard massive presence of his erection nudging my entrance. I cling to his shoulders, bury my face in his throat, ready for him, aching to be pierced by him, filled by him. He walks across the room, his hands on my ass, pulling me apart for him. He leans forward so I fall backward onto the bed, spine on the mattress, ass in the air, my legs still around his waist. He grips my hips and pulls me to the edge of the bed, lines his cock up with my cunt, notches the broad head into my opening…

But he doesn't push in.

"I could fuck you here, just like this." His voice is husky, raspy, his words whispered harshly; this is what he wants. "I could fuck you until you're so sore you can't walk. I could fuck you senseless."

"Oh god…" I can't help the words from whimpering out of me. "Please…*please*."

He leans closer to me, giving me another stretching, beautiful, teasing inch of his cock. His hands carve up my torso to cup my tits, caressing them, squeezing them, pinching and twisting and flicking my nipples until I'm breathless.

"You would like that, would you?"

I nod, arch my back to shove my tits into his hands. "Yes—oh yes. I would like that very much."

"You know…that's what I want most myself." There's an odd note to his voice, and my eyes fly open to meet his.

"Then fuck me. Please. Fuck me until neither of us can move."

He pulls away from me, out of me. "Not yet."

I groan in frustration, emptiness. "Why not?"

"I want it too much. I've desired you for so long that now I have you, I want to prolong the pleasure of taking you." He pushes between my thighs, wedging his body between them, against mine, his erection against my belly. So close, yet so far. His mouth laves my breasts, laps at them, licks my nipples, suckles on them, cups their weight and pushes them together so he can take both nipples in his mouth at once. "Of all the women in my kingdom, of all the women at my disposal in this castle, none of them make me so crazy as you. I don't know why, or what it is about you. But you will be mine, and I'm going to take my time."

His mouth moves down my torso, his tongue flitting into my belly button, tickling, teasing, and then he's kissing my hipbone and the hollow between hip and thigh, his hands under my ass holding me aloft, lifting me to his mouth. He kneels, then, in front of the bed, pushing my legs apart so my thighs press against my belly, spreading my pussy wide for him. His thumbs stroke my labia, and then gently they pull the tender, swollen lips apart, opening my folds like the petals of a flower. His nose nudges my clitoris, and his tongue flicks against my opening, and I gasp at the first warm wet touch of his mouth. I shiver, quake, and my thighs involuntarily close around his head, but he shoves them apart again and returns his touch to my cunt, opening my petals for his mouth, lapping at my entrance, then flattening his tongue against my hard, needy clit. I'm gasping, writhing because he's devouring me now, hungrily, eagerly, skillfully.

I'm confused, though. I thought I was already his? A prize won in battle…weren't those his words? A peace offering?

My thoughts are scattered as his tongue slathers and slithers into my cunt and against my clit, over and over, wildly, desperately, and then his fingers squelch into my slit and fuck relentlessly in and out, noisily, messily. The juices of my need are dripping and dribbling out of my pussy and down my taint, his fingers fucking me in a delicious rhythm, yet it's still so far from what I want most, but almost…*almost* enough to push me over the edge—

Then his mouth suctions around my clit and the sensitive bundle of nerves scrapes past his teeth and he adds a third thick finger inside me and his pinky prods against my asshole, wiggling and worming and digging until his fingers fill me. Now the rhythm of his fucking fingers and the suckling force of his mouth on my clit is all I need...it's just enough.

I come with a loud groan, my back arching off the bed, my fingers digging into his thick black hair and gripping those silken inky locks with desperate strength as he forces the orgasm out of me and milks the waves until I'm trembling and gasping and whimpering.

He rocks back, stands up, and his fingers are glistening wet and his mouth is shiny, and his cock is still hard and straight.

I gasp for a moment, and then gather myself to sit up. I slide off the bed and sink to my knees in front of him and stare up at him. "Let me give you release, sire."

He doesn't answer immediately. His jaw flexes, his fists clench and release; he's warring with himself. "I spoke an untruth earlier."

"You lied?" I remain on my knees in front of him. "About what? And why?"

He turns with a frustrated sigh and paces away. "You aren't here as a peace offering. I didn't win you in battle."

"Oh?" My mind is blank, no recollections of anything beyond the courtyard and the journey to this room. "Then what is the truth, sire?"

"You are...my captive." He turns in place, some feet away now. "Held for ransom. There was a battle, and my forces did win the day. But the war...? Well, suffice it to say the war is not going as well as that battle did. You are betrothed to your king. And I...stole you. He prizes you above anything, and I cannot afford a prolonged war. I have not the men nor the capital nor the desire to pursue the conflict. If I hold you, perhaps your betrothed can be persuaded to sue for peace, on the promise of your safe return."

"Then why did you—?"

"Because we've met before, you and I. Your husband-to-be, we were both protégés of the same master-at-arms, long ago. We trained together, learned together, fought together, bedded the same tavern wenches and servant girls." He lets out a deep breath. "We received our knighthood together, rose through the ranks together. We were assigned to the cohort of guards protecting the king. He was weak, that king. No sons, his wife long dead—in childbirth with you—as a matter of fact.

"Charles saw this as an opportunity. I opposed the plan, but Charles wouldn't listen. He recruited a troop loyal to him, stormed the throne chamber, felled the king in a single blow, and claimed the crown. Claimed you as his bride. But…it is not so simple. You and I, we knew each other, in the halls of that castle. You were the king's daughter, and I a mere soldier, then. When Charles began recruiting men to his cause, I knew I could not be part of it. The king was not a bad man, only weak from long illness, and without a male heir to take the throne. But he was no poor king. He loved his subjects. He loved *you*. Charles… he's always been greedy. He lusts after more, always more. More power, more wealth, more women. He desired *you* almost more than the crown itself. But you wouldn't have him. Perhaps you didn't want me any more than you did Charles. But Charles was the one with the army, so he claimed you."

"So how did I come to be here, and how did you gain your own crown?" I ask.

"That is a longer story," he says, "but the short of how you came to be here is that Charles grew arrogant, having the superior force and greater numbers. He brought you to witness the battle. To witness my downfall, he assumed. It did not go that way, however. My men won the day, and I fought my way to you. Fought him sword to sword, and won. I hadn't the heart to kill him, though I knew should have. Instead, I took you. Locked you in the tower and tried to tell myself I couldn't touch you. Couldn't have you."

"Why couldn't you have me? You make it sound as if I've been given little enough choice in any of this." I pause to think. "I wish I could remember *any* of this, but I confess I recall nothing."

"I am not the sort of man to force a woman to my bed. She will go willingly or not at all."

"You are playing games with my mind, I believe."

"A hazard of politicking, I fear." He sidles closer to me, and the closer he gets, the harder his cock becomes; his erection had faded some as we spoke, but now it is regaining its fully hardened glory. "I want you. I've wanted you since my days in the castle Charles now calls his own. Since you were a nubile young girl, with barely budded breasts, and desires you barely understood but could scarcely control. How I managed to resist you those years, I still do not know. But now you're here, a woman grown into her body…and I desire you more than ever. And you, it would seem, do not suffer a lack of desire in return."

"I do desire you. I cannot hide it, and don't see any need to."

He stops when he is inches from me, towering over me as I kneel on the carpet-covered flagstones, sitting on my heels, hands on my knees, hair draping to almost-but-not-quite cover my breasts. "If I am to sue for peace, to offer you back to him in return for a truce, then I must return you to him unsullied. Already I have pressed beyond all boundaries. But yet I have not bedded you, not in truth."

"I am not asking you to bed me. Only let me offer you pleasure, as you've given me. We could agree that all that has occurred in these chambers…remain secret, between us. No one else need know."

"*I* would know. I would know the taste of you, and live the rest of my days tortured by knowing your taste—of having had a tantalizing glimpse of what it would be like to have you as mine…but, in truth, not having you. That would torture me beyond comprehension. To know the feel of your hands on me, the sweet sugar of your juices on my lips, your essence coating my fingers…to know the heaven of your lips on my flesh…but not to know the truest, deepest perfection of sliding between your thighs and falling into screaming bliss with you." He grips his cock, strokes himself. "Such would be a perfect marriage of heaven and hell, my lady. It would drive me mad."

I lift up onto my knees, and reach for his erection. "Then let us descend into madness together."

He groans. "Temptress, thy name is cruelty."

I sink my mouth around him, lick him as he slides between my lips and into the wet heat of my mouth, my throat. Back again, until he's free of my lips and throbbing in my hands and wet with my saliva. "Does that feel cruel to you?"

"The cruelest temptations feel the sweetest until they're taken away."

"What if told you I wanted to stay here?"

"It would mean years of war. It wouldn't be fair to my kingdom."

"Surely there must be a way," I murmur, and wrap my lips around him once more.

"Fuck...*fuck!*" he snarls as I take him deep into my mouth, swallow around his thickness, my tongue moving all over him, backing away only to gag myself on his cock all over again. "My seed rises, lady. Be warned."

"You have tasted my climax...now let me taste yours."

I back away and run both hands up and down his length, smearing my slick saliva over him, twisting my fists around his head and plunging them down, staring up at him. I flick my hair behind my shoulders to bare my breasts. He groans at the sight of them, so I lean closer and crush his erection between the heavy globes, rise up and sink down, tilt my chin to my chest and take the plump tip of his cock into my mouth as he appears from between the mounded flesh of my breasts.

I do this until he begins to groan and grunt, and his hips flex, thrusting harder against me.

"Soon..." he growls.

"I'm ready," I whisper. "Let me taste you. Let me feel your seed on my skin."

He's breathless now, cock pushing harder and harder, and I close my fists around his erection at the base and let him thrust into my hands, into my mouth. Let him take my mouth, fuck my throat.

"You want it?" he demands.

"Yes," I breathe.

"Now?"

"Now."

His hips flex forward, and his cock throbs between my lips. I back away until he slips free of my mouth with a *pop*, and stroke him root to tip with both hands, one fist above the other, eyes on his, staring up at him. He reaches up, slips the simple band from his hair and tosses it aside. His hair falls loose into his eyes, his chest heaves with deep, gusting breaths, his cock pulsates in my hands, and his fists flex and tighten at his sides.

Another groan, this one long and deep and tortured, and then he comes.

His thick cock spurts a stream of viscous white cum onto me, drenching my face. I close my eyes and continue to stroke him, feel him come again, feel the hot wet cum splash against my eyes and my nose and my lips and my cheek in thick ropes.

"Taste it, my lady," he grunts.

I lick my lips, and then I feel his cock at my lips and I part for him, taste his flesh, and he groans as I suck hard, swallow the last spurts of his cum and stroke him for more, sucking harder, letting him go and then licking his cock and stroking him. I continue to lick and suck around his plump glans and swallow the droplets until he yanks free with a grunt.

"Look at you, my lady," he murmurs. "Covered in my seed. Your beautiful face is white with it. Would you care to see?"

I feel his fingers wipe at my eyes, and then his fingers touch my lips and I lick his seed from his fingers. Thick wet strands of his cum drip down my face, down my chin. He fetches a hand mirror and shows me myself:

Blond hair, golden as the summer sun, with droplets of his seed in it. My face, even and symmetrical, beautiful, my eyes blue and bright and wild with need, with pleasure, with pride. His cum covers my face, smeared and flowing in white rivulets all over my flesh. It's all over me, sliding down my throat, sluicing down between the valley of my tits. I lick my lips and taste it.

"Beautiful." His voice is low, a deep rumbling growl. "Next time, if such fortune be mine that I get another moment with you...I shall paint your breasts with my seed, and then your ass. And lastly, I will fill you with it. I will fill your sweet little cunt so full with my seed that it will spill out of you for days thereafter. Each step you take, you will feel me sliding down your thighs, and you will know the feel of me on every inch of your perfect flesh."

He moves away, snatches his tunic from the floor and uses a sleeve to wipe clean my eyes, another sleeve to clean to my forehead, the tail to wipe my cheeks and chin, and the front for my breasts, and the back for my throat. When I am clean, his once pristine tunic is sticky and matted with his own seed.

He steps into his trousers, ties the laces, and opens the door, but pauses in the opening. "I'll have servants draw you a bath after you've slept. It appears I have a message to send my erstwhile friend, your King Charles."

"He's not my King," I hear myself say. "You are." I stand naked, and cross the room to stand behind him. "What is your message?"

"I'm challenging him to a duel," he says. "Winner takes all. You, and both kingdoms."

"Will you win?"

"I've always been the better swordsman," he says, turning to look at me. "And now…I have the best motivation there is." His grin is quick and feral. "You."

● ● ●

When Conrad has gone, I am left alone and naked in his chambers. I climb into his bed, tug the covers up to my chin, and drowse.

When I blink awake, it feels as if but a moment has passed, yet sunlight gleams golden through the doorway of the balcony, signaling early dawn.

The guards are beyond the still-ajar door, but they are as immovable as statues. Within a few minutes, however, two women appear on the other side of the guards' crossed spears.

"Milady? His Majesty has requested that we bathe you. Will you please accompany us?" one of them says.

They don't attempt to enter the King's chambers, and the guards give no impression that they even see the servant women. The two maids are of an age, younger than I by some years, and they are dressed alike in floor-length scarlet dresses with white aprons.

I gesture at the sliced open remnants of my gown. "I'm afraid I have nothing to cover myself with."

"A fresh gown awaits you in the bathing chamber, milady," she says. "And the chamber isn't far. Perhaps if you merely held the edges together? We are the only ones afoot at this early hour, save the guards, of course."

I slip my arms into the sleeves and hold the edges of the gown together at the breast and groin, as the servant suggested, which provides
at least a modicum of decency. As I approach the door, the guards snap
their massive axes aside, even though neither so much as twitched to
look at me, and my bare feet made no sound on the flagstones. I follow
the women along the far edge of the throne room, the ziggurat mammoth in the distance. The two servant women walk a step ahead of me
and so massive is the chamber that we walk for several hundred paces
before we reach a tapestry hung on the wall, depicting yet another battle, the king the centerpiece, victorious astride a white charger. One
of the women pushes aside an edge of the tapestry to reveal a hidden
archway, a servant's entrance, it seems. I step through into a low, narrow hallway, which curves away into a descending staircase, this one
steep and sharply curved, bringing us quickly to the level beneath the
throne room.

We emerge in an echoing, expansive kitchen. One entire wall is
occupied by a fireplace of a scale that defies belief, the fire in it roaring
and crackling and billowing a blasting wall of heat. Stone pipes carry
the heat in various directions, up through the ceiling, down into the
floor, along the walls to the ovens in the kitchen itself…too many directions for me to follow. Dozens of loaves of bread bake in one oven, a
large bird rotates on a spit over a smaller open flame, chefs in spattered
white smocks scurry in every direction, carrying out their work with
silent efficiency. Despite the bustle of the kitchen, no one is speaking.
It's as if they each know their exact job and require no input from anyone else to do it.

The women lead me across the kitchen to yet another arched
doorway and another staircase, this one ascending. It is a small staircase, leading perhaps ten feet upward to a chamber above the kitchen,
yet below the throne room…or perhaps adjacent to it. The tower is too
massive and the path I've been led along to get here has crossed too
many gargantuan chambers to keep track of the layout.

I emerge behind the servants in a room which I would consider

small in scale compared to the rest of what I've seen. Perhaps fifty paces across in each direction, a pool of hot water is wreathed in steam,
obscuring all but the impression of thin, fluted columns and rippling
water. This is more accurately termed a bathing pool rather than tub,
I would think. The doorway opens to a small semi-circular area with
a marbled floor, which gives away immediately to steps leading down
into the water. It is a low-ceilinged room, the roof a dome painted to
resemble a starry night, just barely visible through the roiling steam.

"I'll take that ruined gown from you, milady," one of them says.

I shrug out of the dress, and touch a toe to the water; it is piping
hot, on the edge of being too hot, just barely tolerable. I shiver, my skin
pebbling, despite the nearly oppressive humidity of the room. I descend
the steps gingerly, the water rising at each step from ankle to knee to
thigh, and then it's at my breasts, and then I duck under the surface.
When I breach upwards, the servant women are there with half a doz-
en different glass jars. I sit on the steps, the water at my belly, and they
stand behind me, barefoot, dresses hiked to keep the hems dry, and ply
me with scented oils, lathering my hair, scooping steaming water in an
amphora to douse me and rinse my hair, then lather it again. They gesture for me to stand so they can scrub every inch of my skin.

When I am clean, they beckon me out of the water, which I do reluctantly; the water is deliciously hot, relaxing, enveloping. There are,
I realize now, two doorways side-by-side, one leading back down to the
kitchen, the other through which the servants lead me. A short, low,
narrow hall, and then we arrive in another chamber, this one tiny, the
dome of the roof curved down to become the walls.

The tiny room is stiflingly hot, dry as a desert. The heat blasts
against my skin, drying me within moments. The servant women
unfold thick soft towels and rub me all over with them, ruffling my
hair ever so gently. And then, dry now from head to toe, they lead me
through a doorway opposite the entrance and into a dressing room.
This room feels homey, comfortable, cozy, even.

The room is of a modest scale, with a balcony overlooking the
exterior of the castle: there is a wide moat spanned by a drawbridge,

mountain peaks jagged in the distance, and a dizzyingly deep chasm beyond the edge of the moat. Without that drawbridge, there is simply no way into the castle, I realize, the chasm is so massive. I see a river in the distance rushing white to fall over the cliffside, the thin white ribbon of the waterfall providing a sense of scale, turning what seemed at first glance to be a narrow gap between castle and cliff into a void so mind-bogglingly enormous I cannot even fathom how this castle came to exist in the first place.

I turn away from the balcony and find the women awaiting me. There is a wardrobe, a floor-to-ceiling mirror, and a low-backed chair. Nothing else, except the doorway to the sauna and another arched doorway, this one with a closed door.

One of the women opens the wardrobe and removes one of many gowns, this one a deep, vivid crimson. She helps me into it, tugging it down, allowing the hem to unfurl and skirl around my feet, brushing the floor as I stand. The bodice is stiff, and they have to tuck my breasts into it, stuffing and prodding the mounds of creamy flesh into place until my nipples are hidden but the largest portion of my breasts are bare. The other busies herself with my hair, braiding it into several strands and then braiding those together, and then twisting that into a knot on the top of my head.

When I am dressed and coiffed, I am led once more out of the room, through yet another long, low, narrow hallway, up a flight of stairs, out from behind a tapestry wall hanging and into the throne room.

A guard sees me immediately. "He's waiting for you, girl. Go on up." No *milady* from him, it seems. Perhaps the guards are exempt from the requirements of courtly respect, or perhaps I don't rate it. I don't know. Nor do I care.

I see him. Sitting on that throne once more, naked blade across his knees. I ascend the ziggurat slowly, eyes fixed on Conrad.

When I reach his level, I see that he has not dressed, has not changed, has not bathed. He is wearing the breeches he slid on last night, bare chested, hair loose around his broad muscular shoulders.

His eyes are alert, if he is somehow beyond the need for sleep.

"My lovely Hannah," he murmurs. "Scrubbed and perfumed and looking lovelier than ever."

"Conrad." I have no idea what else to say.

"I sent a messenger on the fastest horse in the kingdom, within minutes of leaving your side." He runs a fingertip along the flat of his sword. "I expect him to return soon with Charles's answer."

"What then?"

His eyes do not leave my cleavage. "I expect him to answer my challenge. I have offered him the choice of location for the duel, and the terms." A smirk. "I'll kill him as I should have long ago, and then, my dear…then…you'll truly be mine."

"And until then?" I hear the shiver of anticipation in my own voice.

His gaze finally slides up to mine. "I should lock you in the tower. To protect your…virtue."

I laugh. "Really, Conrad? Virtue? I think that was surrendered last night, when you buried your face between my thighs." I slink a little closer, knees knocking with need, belly tensed, core aching with memory. "Or perhaps I relinquished my virtue when I allowed you to paint my face white with your cum."

He shifts on his throne, his fist tightening around the hilt of his sword. "A momentary loss of self-control. You are a prisoner of war, Hannah, not one of my concubines."

"So…that loss of control. It won't happen again, is what you're implying."

"It shouldn't. I am not Charles. I will not take by force a woman who doesn't wish to be mine."

I reach for the laces of his breeches, loosening them until his erection springs free. "Does this feel as if you're forcing me?" I ask, as I wrap my hand around his thick, hot, smooth cock.

He groans. "You're going to have to stop before I lose control again."

I laugh under my breath as I stroke him. "Lose control *again*?" I have him bucking under my hand. "Conrad…if what you're displaying is control, then I must admit to wondering what loss of control looks like."

He snarls. "You tempt me, Hannah. I'm trying to do the right thing."

"What if what I want what's wrong?" I ask.

He grabs my wrist to halt my touch. "You know how many nights I've sat on this throne, picturing you? All the ways I'd take you, including here, on this very spot? I've dreamed of it. I've fantasized about it. And now you tempt me with the reality."

"I'm not tempting," I whisper in his ear, squeezing his cock, "I'm inviting."

He takes one deep drafting breath and holds it for a long moment, staring into my eyes, jaw grinding. And then his hand loosens, releasing my wrist so I can resume stroking him. Only, instead of continuing to caress his length, I just squeeze again. Release, and squeeze. Release… and squeeze. Until he's groaning and his hips thrust.

And then his sword is clanging to the floor and he's pushing me away as he stands up. His breeches are open, his cock standing straight and hard between the laces. He pants, his belly tightening, his gloriously hard dick swaying in front of me. God, I want it. I want him. I need him inside me. His tongue last night wasn't enough. His tongue only served to heat my arousal to a wildfire, stirring it into madness. Now I've touched him, felt his hardness under my hand, and I need that inside me. I'm desperate for it, suddenly.

Not suddenly, though.

From the moment I stood before him on this ziggurat, I wanted him.

I wanted his touch.

I wanted him to fill me.

I stand still, waiting. There's nothing he could do that I would refuse.

Here, now, on this throne, guards all around…I would take him.

He hesitates another moment, hands clenching into fists and releasing.

And then he strikes, swift as a serpent. His hands seize my waist and he jerks me forward, yanking me clear off the ground to slam against his hard body. His mouth seizes mine, but he doesn't kiss me. He bites my lower lip and sucks it into his mouth, then he leans down to nip at my throat, and then he buries his face between my tits and groans as he inhales.

He spins me around, and the arm of the chair meets my belly. I'm bent over the side, and he's behind me. His hands smooth up my back, over the dress. Up to my bare shoulders. He leans against me, and I can feel the steel rod of his erection against my buttocks, pressing between the globes. He digs his fingers into the bodice, clutching my breasts, and then tugs them free of the confines. Tweaks my nipples, pinching them until I gasp.

Then he's gathering crimson fabric into his fists, and the hem rises slowly. Ankles, knees, thighs…it is almost like descending into the hot water, except more and more of me is being bared to him. There is nothing beneath the dress, only my bare flesh.

He's groaning as he exposes me.

"This," he murmurs. "I've dreamed of this." He pushes the dress up over my back, and my ass is bare for him, my legs parted, my core aching. "You, Hannah, bent over my throne."

I can only moan, and it is all the assent I can give as his hands caress my ass cheeks, spreading them apart. I feel his cock nudging against my entrance. I writhe, lift up on my toes and sink back down.

"Eager for it, aren't you, Hannah?"

"Yes, I want it."

"Yes, what?" he growls, smacking my ass with his palm, making me jump and gasp.

"Yes, *sire*," I whimper.

"You want it?" he grinds against my slit, the plump head of his cock soft and thick, spreading my cunt open as he teases my entrance. "You want me inside you, Hannah?"

"Fuck, yes," I growl, not even pretending to hide my desperation. "Please, *please*."

He sinks into me, then, and we both groan in bliss. It is utter rapture, the feel of him filling me, the way his cock stretches me apart, fills me. I hiss in delight, push back into him, take him deeper, eyes closed, focusing on the feel of him inside me. The way my cunt burns as I stretch to take his thickness, the sweet slide of him going deeper, deeper. His hands on my ass, spreading me apart so he can fuck deeper yet. God, so good.

"Hannah, you feel…so much better than I imagined." His voice is tight, low, a snarling murmur.

His breath leaves him as he sinks fully into me, his hips meeting my ass.

"More," I breathe. "Fuck me."

He pulls back, and I mewl in pleasure at the delicious sensation of his huge, perfect cock sliding between the stretched, taut, sensitive lips of my pussy. He pumps a few times, spearing the head in and out of me, and I gasp at each subtle penetration.

He doesn't fuck me.

He teases me. Toys with me.

Slow, shallow thrusts. Until I'm nearly mad with need, wild with the desperation to feel him fill me, ready to beg once more. And then, finally, when I think he's only going to tease me, he finally slides deep, pushing into me in a single hard thrust.

"Yes, Conrad. Just like that." I roll my hips, just to feel the slick wet slide of that gorgeously hard shaft inside me.

The scuff of a boot on marble snaps both of our attention to the steps.

"Sire…" a man appears, sweaty, exhausted looking, covered in dust, panting. "I bring word from King Charles—" He freezes then, on the top step, his eyes on my swaying tits, on his king buried hilt-deep inside my cunt, his hands on my ass, which I'm sure is red from his hand.

He doesn't pull out of me. "And?"

I need him to move. I'm on the edge, riding the cusp of climax. All I need is a few more hard strokes, and I'll topple screaming over the edge.

The messenger hesitates. "I...King Charles, first of his name, has received your challenge to single combat—" he falters, eyes wide, flicking over me. "He has received your challenge—I already said that. Um...I—he sends his acceptance, and his scorn. But while His Majesty King Charles accepts your challenge, he expects the prompt and safe return of his betrothed, the Lady Hannah, daughter of the former, self-styled king." At the use of my name, the messenger's eyes widen yet more, going from my tits to Conrad and back. "He—he says, if you—if Lady Hannah is returned forthwith, unharmed and unmolested, all will be forgiven."

Oh god. Oh god. He's so deep, his fingers digging into my hip-bones, pulling me back against him, pushing his cock deeper. I need movement. I don't care about the messenger, I don't care if he's watching, or what he sees.

"Conrad—" I breathe. *"Please."*

"Greedy girl, aren't you, Hannah?" he whispers. Then, to the messenger. "Did he provide location or terms? For the duel."

"Yes, sire. I—he—um—"

"Spit it out, man. Have you never seen a naked woman before?"

"Not one I wasn't—um...not like this, sire. My deepest apologies."

"I'd rather have facts than apologies."

"Sire, yes, of course, my apol—um. He's only a few leagues behind me. He leads the head of a troop of his best cavalry, sire. I barely out-rode them, and only then because I ran my poor horse into the ground. The terms, he said, were obvious."

He nods. "Fine, then. Leave us."

"But...sire. I—he bade me return with the Lady Hannah."

"That won't be happening," Conrad says. "As you can very well see. Return, and tell him that."

The messenger pales. "Sire? Tell him...what?"

He rocks against me, driving deeper, sending my tits to bouncing and swaying, and the poor messenger is unable to tear his gaze away. "This. What you're seeing. I don't care how you phrase it, but make it clear to Charles that the Lady Hannah remains with me." He smooths a hand over my ass. "Of her own volition, isn't that right, Hannah?" He slides out, then, and pushes back in, giving me exactly what I need.

"Yes!" I can't help but cry out. It's an answer, but it's also an involuntary response to the drive of his cock. "Oh god, yes."

"Sire, I can't—I don't know what I'm…what am I supposed to say, sire?"

Conrad doesn't answer. Just slides deep, withdraws, and then begins fucking me. Right in front of the messenger, who is frozen in place, staring, eyes wide. I brace my hands against the arm of the throne and push back into him, moaning, mewling, gasping. Taking his cock and loving it, feeling him fill me, stretch me, fuck me. He slams deep, hips slapping against my ass.

"Yes, god, yes, fuck me, Conrad. Fuck me hard, just like that—" I hear myself saying, but I have no control over my mouth, or the words coming out of it.

Nor of the sounds I'm making, breathy whimpers, groans so deep and needy they almost sound agonized, but it's agony so perfect I can't stand it, can only roll my hips and slam my ass back into him and rejoice in the way my tits slap and bounce. I'm being rocked forward now as Conrad fucks me, not holding back, giving me everything he has, every inch of his massive cock over and over again, and I'm begging for more, begging him to not stop fucking me, and the messenger is just stuck watching, frozen, unable to look away as his king fucks me.

"*Leave*," Conrad snarls, pausing in his thrusts.

The messenger starts, pivots smartly on his heel, and nearly topples down the stairs, barely catching himself.

"Now," Conrad breathes, caressing my ass cheeks, "where was I?"

"Fucking me," I answer. "Hard."

"Ah, yes."

Conrad resumes, beginning slowly all over again, giving me his cock in slow, long, gliding thrusts, until I'm driving back into him desperately, unable to find release unless he's fucking me the way I want it, the way I need it, hard and wild and uncontrolled.

"Conrad…" I whimper, "harder, *please*, Conrad…*sire*…harder!"

"Sire, again, is it?" He teases. Then, without warning, he fucks me hard, once. "Like that?"

"Yes, god, yes please. Just like that."

He does it again. "This, Hannah?" Another hard thrust, our bodies crashing together with a loud slap of flesh on flesh. "You like it when I fuck you hard?"

"Yes, oh....*oh*—" I break off with a groan as he begins driving into me hard and fast. "I can't come unless you're fucking me just like that—yes, yes, just—oh, fuck—just like that, Conrad…"

"Touch your cunt, Hannah. Put your fingers on your clit. Make yourself come for me."

I brace myself with one hand on the far arm of the throne and stuff the other between my thighs, find my clit throbbing and sensitive, aching. It doesn't take long. A few finger-trembling circles around my clit in synchronization with Conrad's powerful thrusts, and then I'm coming, screaming loud enough to make the walls echo and the stained glass dome overhead reflect my shuddering ululations of orgasm.

He joins me as I come, his voice merging and mingling with mine, his feral and deep, gasping grunts as he slams into me, and I feel him unleash his cum, feel it splash inside me, filling me, and he comes and comes and comes, grunting through it, growling my name as he spurts his cum deep inside my cunt.

Finished, he bends over me, palms cupping my ass, his breathing harsh and rasping, his chest heaving against my spine, and his breath on my neck. "Better than I dared fantasize, Hannah. Being inside you, feeling your pussy squeeze around me…" his words are hot, drowsy whispers in my ear. "I'm going to need it again, and soon."

"When?" I ask, breathing the question, hoping to hide my eagerness, my desperation for more. He's still inside me, softening, his cum hot and wet and dripping out of me, and I already want more.

"Soon as possible," he murmurs. "But first we go meet Charles for the duel."

"We?"

He straightens, withdrawing. "You and me, and my guards."

"Why me?"

"To throw him off his focus." Conrad grins as I stand up and my dress falls into place around my ankles. "If he sees you, especially if he sees you with me, having received my message, it'll drive him mad. He'll be a crazed bastard with his blade, but he'll be manic enough that he'll make a mistake."

"It is a risk you're running, I think."

He tugs tight the laces of his breeches. "A risk well worth taking, with you as the prize," Conrad says, pulling me close, touching his forehead to mine. "Now that I've felt you, known the reality of your body, tasted the truth of heaven between your thighs, Hannah…no risk is too great."

I melt, a little, and my heart hammers at the proximity of his mouth, the heat of his breath, the strength of his hand at the small of my back.

His breath huffs warm and damp on my lips, his mouth closer, closer…

He's going to kiss me.

Hope blossoms.

I need his kiss. Need it.

More than mere desire, more than the desperation for the pleasure he gives me, more than the wild passion his body incites.

His lips brush mine, feather-soft, questing, exquisitely gentle…

Doors bang open somewhere. "SIRE!" a voice shouts, urgent. "Charles approaches!"

Conrad pulls away with a reluctant sigh. "Soon, Hannah. I swear it."

I let him go, then. He snatches his sword and descends the ziggurat at a trot, calling out instructions. I descend more slowly, watching him. His broad back ripples with muscle, his hair loose and tangled and wild. He grips his sword in one hand, wielding the instrument of death as if it is an extension of his arm. He wears nothing but breeches, bare-chested and bare foot, yet he looks ready to step into battle as he is, and I have no doubt he will emerge victorious.

When I reach the base of the pyramid, an armored guard is waiting. "This way."

I nod, and follow the guard out of the throne room, back down
the main staircase circling the tower itself, and through a small, narrow,
heavily fortified doorway leading across the center of the tower's footprint. A journey through a low hallway, torches flickering to light the
way. Then out into the sunlight, blinking, and I find myself in a vast
courtyard.

The tower is behind me and above me, walls to either side, and
the main gate before me. The portcullis is down, the drawbridge lifted.
Within the courtyard, all is chaos. Horses whicker and whinny, stomping their shod hooves on cobblestones to send sparks flashing, harness-
es jingle, manes whip in the wind. Chain mail glints in the sunlight,
lance heads flash, sheaths rattle, shields shift. Hundreds of men in full
armor, helms on, visors down, sitting astride massive chargers wearing
armor of their own. They are arranged in a V formation, and a white
charger awaits at the front, the horse the largest I've ever seen, powerful
yet quick-looking, stomping a hoof impatiently, head bobbing, tossing.

The guard leads me to this horse then he kneels down and bows
his head. "Mount, if you please."

I reach for the pommel, struggle to reach the stirrup with my bare
foot, but the guard has other ideas. He delicately guides my foot to his
upraised knee, his gauntleted hand gentle on my ankle. I step on his
knee and climb astride the horse, and feel the soreness between my
thighs, and the faint sticky dampness of Conrad's seed—as promised—
still leaking out of me, reminding me of him, a potent physical marker
of his presence.

Conrad was not gentle, not at all, and the soreness I feel is a delicious echo of his power.

Moments of waiting follow, no sound but the impatient horses, and
then a door opens somewhere and footsteps echo on the cobblestones.

Conrad appears, dressed in the armor I'd seen in his chambers. He
wears the heavy metal suit as if it were made of the most finely woven
silk, weightless. His step is light, eager. He carries his helm under one

arm, and his sword is sheathed at his waist, the scabbard wrought of black metal scales and inlaid with rubies.

He sees me astride his horse, and allows a small, brief smile meant solely for me to grace his lips, and then he's serious once more.

He approaches, taking the reins from the attendant groom; he glances up at me, and then around at the gathered troop.

"Are you ready, men?" Conrad calls out.

A moment of silence, and then, as one sound, hundreds of lances smash against shields in a slow, pounding rhythm, once, twice, three times, four and then I lose count…each thunderous crash of metal on metal louder than the last until the air is rent by the noise, until it is so loud I can feel the vibrations in my gut and in my bones. Without cue, without command, abruptly, the warriors cease pounding lance against shield, and the silence is deafening, thick and fierce.

Conrad places a foot in the stirrup, swings up behind me, and slams his helm onto his head. This seems to be an understood cue, for the moment his helm is on, the portcullis raises and the bridge lowers.

As soon as the way is clear, every horse bolts forward, leaping into a jolting trot, which becomes a canter, and then a gallop. Conrad is behind me, the metal of his armor cold through the thin fabric of my dress. He grips the reins in one gauntleted fist, and the other rests against my belly and across my thighs. Hooves beat a staccato rhythm on the wood of the bridge, and then on the paving stones of the road. I turn in the saddle and peer around Conrad, seeing the mountainous bulk of the castle, the spire of the tower piercing the sky, impossibly vast, and the rest of the castle sprawling around it like voluminous skirts.

We gallop in formation, the warriors ahead and on either side. Gray stone and green forest blanket a mountain visible to my left. Falling away, to my right, is a precipitous cliff, the road following the gorge separating the landmass from the island upon which Conrad's castle is built.

The road curves away from the edge, eventually, angling toward the mountain itself, ascending. A forest rises ahead of us, thick and dark, all shadows and plucking branches. The road vanishes into the forest, narrowing as it goes. The troop rearranges as we approach the forest, extending into a single file line except for Conrad and I. Warriors ride to either side of us, two ahead, and two behind. So narrow is the road here that there is scarcely room for that many riders abreast.

We move through the forest, without slowing our pace.

We emerge on the other side of the wood, reform the V formation as the road broadens once more and leads toward a rise. As we reach the zenith of the hill, the troop slows and then stops, and I immediately see why: the hill banks downward steeply, and at the foot is a gathered force much like our own, hundreds of horses and men, armor glinting brightly in the sun, weapons drawn, arranged in a box formation around a single rider.

"Marius, Argan, Dorian, with me. The rest of you remain here." Conrad's voice is hard, loud.

Lances crash against shields once, deafeningly, and the formation parts to allow us through. The three warriors join us, forming a miniature version of the V formation, one ahead and two behind us. We proceed down the hill, at a trot, unhurried.

My heart hammers as we approach the box formation of mounted warriors. Charles's cavalry is armored in bright silver mail, so blindingly polished it seems white in the light of the sun.

Three of Charles's warriors take a step forward and aside, creating a gap their formation. Conrad and I enter the square, and Conrad's three men fill the space left in the line, our three black armored men alone in a line of silver.

Charles waits in the center, helm removed and tucked under one arm, sword out and resting across his knees. His beauty is blinding. His armor is of the brightest silver, catching and reflecting every ray of sunlight. His hair is golden as the sun itself, falling around his shoulders in cascading waves, and his eyes are pale blue, ice cold, haughty. An arrogant smile touches his lips.

"Return to me what is mine, Conrad, and all will be forgiven," Charles says, by way of greeting.

"Forgiven?" Conrad sounds truly puzzled, his words muffled behind his visor. "I spared your life, last we met. An act of mercy I have since come to regret."

Rage crosses Charles's face briefly, but he regains himself, "Give her back, Conrad. Last warning."

Conrad removes his helmet, then. He leans close to me, burying his nose in my hair, and he inhales audibly. I cannot help nuzzling against him. "I do not believe she wishes to return to you, Charles."

Another flash of that rage. "It isn't her choice." He eyes me, his gaze cruel and vicious. "Dismount, Hannah. *Now.*"

I cringe back against Conrad, and then find my spine. "No," I say, putting as much steel into my voice as I can muster. "I was never yours to claim."

Charles spurs his mount forward, hate and madness in his eyes. "Enough of this!" He snarls. "You challenged me to single combat. Come at me, then, and have done. I'll run my steel through your throat, and defile her innocence in front of you as you die."

Conrad is unfazed by the threat. "Pretty words for a man who's never once bested me blade to blade, even as untrained youths." A pause, then. "Besides which, you can't defile an innocence she no longer possesses, Charles. She gave that to *me,* just an hour past. Did you not receive my message?"

A gesture from Charles, then, and a warrior hurls something small and dark and heavy toward us; a dismembered head, dripping gore; the messenger, or what remains of him, at least. My stomach turns and I look away.

Charles smirks. "He never got a chance to deliver it." The smile turns sour, becomes that arrogant, hateful scowl. "Enough of bandying words and insults."

Conrad hands me the reins, swings a leg over his horse's head, and leaps to the ground, all in one smooth motion, then glances at me. "Join my men, Hannah, if you would."

I tug the reins to one side and nudge the horse's flank with one heel, and the great beast swings around into a trot, carrying me across the open square to the three warriors of Conrad's escort. One of the guards takes the reins from me, impassive behind his helmet.

Charles dismounts his horse slowly, leisurely. A snap of his fingers brings a warrior to take the mount, and then the two kings are face to face.

One king in bright silver armor faces his opponent, also a king, wearing the darkest of black. Haughty blonde exquisite male beauty faces off against rugged power, masculinity embodied.

Charles gives a few test swings of his sword, which is a long, heavy, wide-bladed thing, polished to a sheen. It is a thing of beauty, with a massive emerald the size of my fist serving as a pommel, and filigreed, gold-inlaid, braided strands of platinum for cross-guards. Running along the center of the blade, along each flat, are words in gold and silver filigreed lettering, though I am too far distant to read what they say.

Conrad, by contrast, merely draws his own blade and waits, no ceremony, no bluster. His blade is the simpler and plainer of the two, but despite this his blade looks the more deadly. It draws the eye, Conrad's sword. The shimmer of the blade, the twinkling of the razor edge, the ethereal glitter…it almost seems alive.

Charles circles, crabwise, sword held in both hands, tip pointed at the sky. Conrad merely stands in place, pivoting on his heel to track his opponent's movement, his sword held in his right hand with the flat of the blade resting on his shoulder, left hand loose at his side. Casual, at ease, confident, yet there is no mistaking his readiness. He is tensed, coiled, a viper poised to strike.

My heart leaps in my throat when Charles swings. It is vicious flat arc of his blade, sudden and swift. Should it meet its intended target, even Conrad's armor won't be enough to stop its force. Seemingly without effort, without forethought, Conrad steps backward and his blade descends at a downward angle, slowly almost, his left hand rising to grip the hilt and impart yet more force, and then the two blades meet with a resounding crash, Conrad's sword smashing down to blast Charles's aside, knocking the golden-haired king off-balance and he stumbles, the added momentum from Conrad's swing too much by half.

As Charles stumbles, Conrad charges forward, a single leap carrying him several feet, his mail-clad shoulder bashing into Charles with tectonic force. The stumble becomes a fall, and silver mail meets knee-high grass, flattening it as he crashes to the ground. He turns the fall into a roll and finds his feet lithely, only to have to stumble backward yet again as Conrad attacks, sword sweeping downward, forcing Charles to defend while retreating.

The men are all silent. The only sound is the creak of saddle leather, clank of metal as men shift, a horse whickering now and again…and the clang and smash of swords as the kings duel.

The next few moments are blur. Blades meet, sparks fly, armor shifts, grass is trampled, bodies spin and pivot, all happening too fast for me to track. Swords swing and are blocked, advantage is pressed, and then lost. Yet one thing I notice, one constant theme: Charles is outmatched. He is always on the defensive, always just barely escaping or blocking the swing of Conrad's sword.

Charles is out of breath, red in the face from exertion, and his swings have slowed. His parries come later and later, and his return attacks lack force. Conrad is sweating as well, and his breathing is deep and swift, but he isn't visibly exhausted. His step remains lithe and powerful, his sword swings with the same crashing, meteoric force as when the duel first began.

The first missed block leaves Charles bleeding from a rent in his armor at mid-thigh. A second time, Charles is too late bringing his sword up and Conrad's blade smashes into Charles's side, leaving another red-tinted dent in the fine silver armor. A third time Conrad's sword meets silver armor, and Charles is left to wield his sword one-handed, his other hand limp at his side and useless, a deep tear in the armor at the elbow.

Two-handed he was no match for Conrad...one handed? Death will come swiftly, I think.

Conrad leaps, kicking out with his front foot, and his boot smashes into Charles in the center of his chest; the blond king falls to the grass. And this time he does not regain his feet.

Conrad stands over him, the point of his sword dimpling the flesh at his erstwhile friend's throat, drawing blood. "Yield, Charles, and I'll spare your life. You'll spend your days in my dungeon, but you'll be alive. I would not kill a man I once bled with unless forced. We were like brothers, once. So I beg you, in the name of the kinship we once shared—yield."

Charles—his sword out of reach, blood trickling down his throat where Conrad's sword touches his flesh, gasping, out of breath—stares up, full of rage and hate and venom, defiant. He glances at me, then he nods to one side; once, subtly.

I hear the unmistakable sound of metal slicing through flesh, the gurgle of bloody breath. I glance behind me to see the three warriors of Conrad's escort toppling to the grass, their throats slit. The moment I realize what's happening, I kick my horse, but a silver-mailed fist has the reins and the mighty charger's momentum is arrested before he can even begin. And then, in the blink of an eye, something cold and sharp touches the flesh between my breasts.

And Charles grins from his place on the ground. "A fair fight, Conrad? Really? You think I'd allow my fate—*her* fate to be determined in single combat? You are far too honorable for your own good, my old friend. I know, I know...a twitch of your hand and I'm dead. But in the same moment as you spill my blood, hers will run as well."

Conrad looks at me, his face in a snarling rictus. "Damned coward." He hisses between clenched teeth, but steps away.

Haltingly, and with great difficulty, Charles rises to his feet, using his sword as leverage. His horse is brought to him, and he mounts with equal effort. Grimacing with effort, he guides his horse next to mine.

"Climb over, Hannah. Time to go." His voice is hoarse with pain.

"I'd rather die," I say, through gritted teeth.

"Be careful what you wish for," Charles growls.

"Go, Hannah," Conrad says, his voice tight. "It won't be for long."

Charles ignores this, grabs my waist and hauls me onto the saddle in front of him. His hands are gauntleted, cruel and hard, digging painfully into my flesh. He smells of sweat and billows heat; were this Conrad, I would think the smell sweet and the heat reassuring, but this is Charles, and it repulses me.

His heels kick viciously into his horse's ribs, and we bolt forward into a sudden gallop, and then the thunder of many hundreds of hooves crashes around us, dirt flying, armor glinting, leather creaking. Fear hammers in my heart, as well as rage.

I twist, looking back to see Conrad standing alone in the flattened patch of grass, the bodies of his slain men behind him. His sword rests on his shoulder, his helm tucked under one arm. The expression on his face terrifies me, and I know Charles is not long for this world. Somehow, Conrad will find me, and rescue me.

How, where, when—I don't know. But he will.

It is a fact as immoveable as the very earth we stand upon.

For now, however, I am in the clutches of Charles, and I do not think his intentions for me will be pleasurable as those Conrad visited upon me so recently.

Across the plain we gallop, leaving the mountain behind us, racing the wind and the noonday sun.

How long we ride, I don't know. Until I am sore from the pounding of the saddle beneath me, aching from the unforgiving cold hardness of Charles's metallic armor, numb from constant fear and the specter of dread.

We approach a river, a wide ribbon slicing through the plain, dividing it. Beyond the river is a land of rolling hills, with occasional copses of trees, a barn or dwelling here and there. In the far distance, shimmering in the distorted haze is the outline of a castle.

Charles calls a halt at the river's edge. "We're near enough the castle we can pause, I think."

"I would advise we continue with all possible haste, sire," a warrior at Charles's elbow says. "Even the small force he brought to meet us would give us a bitter fight, and we are none of us fresh after so long in the saddle."

Charles glares at the warrior. "Do not think to tell me my business." His gaze turns to me, becoming lecherous. "I have a lesson to teach, I do believe."

The warrior stifles a sigh. "Sire. *Please*. Look to our rear, whence we came. They're behind us, and if we get pinned against the river, it will go ill for us."

My heart thunders, hammers, and my gut twists in fear. The idea of this man's hands on me, his body above me—vomit threatens at the very thought.

But Charles stands in his stirrups, twists, peers back from where we came, and whatever he sees has him cursing under his breath. "Damn you, Conrad," he mutters. Then, loudly, to his men: "We cross!"

One by one, the riders spur their horses into the river. It is wide and runs swiftly, so each man rides with great care, for if they were to fall from their horse in full armor, even the strongest swimmer would drown. It is slow going, waiting for the troop to cross in groups of two or three. Charles keeps a strong grip on me as he nudges his mount into the cold brown water, which rises from ankle to knee to thigh, the horse beneath us blowing as it struggles to carry our combined weight through the swift river, its hooves digging into the soft much of the riverbed, ears flat against its head, eyes wide and whites flashing—and then it is scrabbling and charging up the bank and shaking its mane and snorting and we're clear.

As soon as the last rider is clear of the river, Charles spurs his horse into a mad gallop, and each man leans over his mount, spurs digging.

They're afraid of Conrad, I realize. And afraid of his warriors. They dare not face them in open combat.

We approach the castle after another hour's hard ride, the horses now foaming and blowing. The gate is raised as we approach, and we thunder across a short bridge, under a portcullis, and into a court-yard. The approach gave me plenty of time to compare this castle to Conrad's and as in everything, the comparison does not favor Charles. There is no moat here, no craggy cliffs or vast divides. The walls are high, yes, and thick enough, but compared to the brutal inaccessibili-ty of Conrad's home, this place is nearly indefensible, even to my un-trained eye. The approach is wide, with gentle rolling hills in every di-rection, and the slight rise the castle is built on provides little enough impedance for an attacking force.

But I doubt even that will do me any good in the immediate fu-ture. Charles has me in hand, behind his walls, and Conrad is far behind us with a group of warriors that, though fierce they may be, are not enough in number to cause Charles worry, now that we've reached the walls.

The portcullis lowers behind us, and ice fills my veins.

Charles dismounts stiffly, strips his gauntlets off and tosses them to a waiting attendant, and then his eyes flick to me. "Ah, Hannah. My wayward bride now returned."

I have no response, except to glare at him with all the venom and vehemence I possess.

He grins. "Your spirit is undiminished, I see." His hand darts at me, fists into my dress, and he jerks me off the horse and I fall with a painful impact at his feet. I'm still gasping for breath when he lifts me to my feet, and then his face is inches from mine, his breath foul, and his body odor putrid. "What reason have I to offer kindness or affection, now that your virtue has been tarnished?"

"My virtue was never yours," I cannot help hissing.

"I doubt you ever possessed virtue in the first place. You probably gave it to the first flea-ridden stable boy who made eyes at you." His expression is vile, full of undisguised glee and lecherous anticipation. "I watched you, you know. Watched you flirt and wink and swish your skirts at any unattached male within a mile's radius—all *except* me. Most of all, you were slatternly and free with your charms with that stupid upright bastard Conrad."

"I saw you," I say, feeling the truth of my words, "but I found you lacking in any trait that I should find desirable. Clothe you in the finest silks, clad you in the finest armor, garb you with all the gold and jewels in the world, and it will not disguise the truth of your ugliness. No matter how handsome your face, no matter how many riches you may steal, nothing can change the essential vulgarity of your nature."

He snarls, then a wordless hiss of rage, and his fist closes around my throat. "Keep talking, girl. You'll be witness to my essential vulgarity soon enough."

I gasp for breath, see stars, and yet even this would be better than having to endure his touch.

A shout breaks the moment, and I'm not sure if I'm thankful for the reprieve or not. "Conrad is at the walls, sire!"

"How the devil is that possible?" Charles mutters. "The man is inhuman."

Horses are being led away by a throng of stable hands, and the warriors, exhausted from a hard ride followed by the same grueling trip in reverse, stripping off armor and wiping away sweat, groan as one man. They replace gauntlets and pouldrons and breastplates, and re-belt swords, catch up shields.

"How many men?" Charles asks, leaving my side to limp toward the stair leading up to the walk around the walls.

The man on the walls returns immediately. "Two hundred, perhaps. But more approach from the west, following the river."

"They must have forded upstream where the river is shallower," Charles says to himself. "Can we ride out to meet Conrad before his reinforcements arrive?"

"It is unlikely, sire." This is from the same soldier who advised haste at the river's edge.

"How he got reinforcements here so swiftly is what I'd like to know," Charles growls.

"The only possibility with any merit is that he sent them ahead of himself in anticipation of..." the soldier trailed off, uncertain how to finish.

"In anticipation of my treachery, you mean to say? Don't mince words, man, for that is what it was."

"As you say, sire. But the fact remains—we are as ill prepared for a siege as we are open battle. We've taken in no supplies, so the stores we have will last a few days at most."

Charles takes his gauntlet from the attendant and slides it on. "A siege? To hell with that. I've no patience to weather a siege even if we did have the stores laid up. Put archers on the walls and have them ready with bent bows. We'll ride out to meet Conrad, strike in a swift skirmish, and retreat, and then the archers will lay waste with a hail of arrows—and promise them a hundredweight of gold to the man who puts an arrow through Conrad's eye."

"A worthy strategy, sire," the man says—he seems to be Charles's second-in-command. "And the lady Hannah?"

Charles eyes me, thinking. "Put her up on the wall in full view of the field of battle, and have a man behind her with a knife to her throat. Choose someone with little compunction about pulling the blade on my command. If Conrad looks to win—" Charles sneers at me. "Well…the sight of her blood running down the walls should sway him readily enough."

The man pales at the order, but doesn't argue. "As you command, sire." He eyes Charles warily. "Are you sure you're able to ride out, sire?"

Charles turns a baleful eye on the man. "I am. Have no worries on that score. Ready the men."

A matter of minutes sees fresh horses—saddled but lacking armor—brought out, the warriors mounting, forming up. There is no chatter, no excitement, no words of encouragement or inspiration. I hear hooves in the distance, a faint rolling thunder.

A dark, hairy hand closes around my arm, and I'm shoved into motion. The owner of the arm is—I shiver, shudder; if I thought Charles turned my stomach, this man is a thousand times worse, infinitely worse—vile, repugnant. Stinking of a body long unwashed, of booze and onions. He is enormous, twice my height and nearly double my width, heavy with as much fat as muscle. He is clad in ringmail and leather, with a longsword on his right hip and a shield on his back, and a curved, wickedly sharp dagger in his fist. The leer in his eyes tells me all I need to know of his intentions. Death, I fear, will be the more welcome of alternatives.

He hustles me up the steep stone stairs to the walkway, the crenellations thicker than a man and twice as high, providing cover for the archers. When we reach the wall, he pushes me into an opening between crenellations, his fist knotted in the fabric of my gown just beneath my breasts, and he presses the edge of his dagger to my throat. I barely breathe, do not dare move. His blade is so sharp even the slight touch of it stings and burns, and I feel blood trickling down my throat.

I'm afforded a clear view of the battlefield, however. The portcullis rises—I feel the grinding of the gears beneath my feet, and then I feel the clumping of hooves, then see the three man-wide column of soldiers pouring out, armor glinting, lances and spears and shields in hand.

Conrad approaches at a gallop at the head of his troop. His black-scaled armor reflects no light, indeed seems to soak it up, absorb it, drink it in. His helmet is on, hiding his features, the visor down, showing the visage of a vicious, snarling lion. He wields a lance, with a heavy shield in his other hand, and he's hunkered down behind his shield, body poised to absorb any impact. His men are spread out behind him in an arrowhead formation, angling right for Charles.

Charles is no fool, however. He is injured, and does not ride at the head of his men, but in the middle, protected. Coward indeed. I think Conrad, even injured, would be at the head of his men, would fight like the lion he is, would claw and snarl and battle to the bitter end with his men around him, behind him, rather than ever hide in the middle, thus.

I cannot look away as the two forces meet. The crash is deafening, mail and metal and flesh colliding with a brutal, battering impact. Blood flies, horses scream, men shout, and all is chaos. But as I watch one thing is certain: Conrad's men are the better warriors, as Conrad is the better warrior. His force slices through Charles's with the ease of a knife through butter, splitting the silver-armored foe apart into a unit divided. Conrad's calvary wheels, then, and the arrowhead formation breaks, forming two lines. Lances are abandoned and swords are drawn, and the men begin to swing, and now the battle begins in earnest.

There is no missing Conrad even amid the tumultuous fray. He is a fiend, a devil, death incarnate. His mighty sword swings like a scythe, smashing aside shields and rending armor, dealing mortal wounds with every stroke. Men scatter before him, toppling from their mounts, clutching injuries. He battles his way toward Charles, who remains at the rear of the scrum, shouting instructions, his sword in hand but engaging no enemies. Charles sees Conrad approaching and calls the retreat. Charles's men, upon the command, pivot and disengage, wheeling toward the still-open portcullis. The unexpected maneuver leaves Conrad's forces in the lurch, swinging at foes now absent.

And then the arrows fly.

I watch them arc in a thick black rain toward Conrad and his men, and my heart seizes with fear and worry.

The arrows impact with a clatter of metal on metal, most bounce harmlessly enough off the armor and shields, but a few find a gap and elicit cries of pain.

Charles underestimated Conrad's speed, however. The moment the retreat was called, Conrad shouted in turn for his men to press forward, to carry the attack after Charles and his men.

The arrows left a dozen or so of Conrad's men on the ground writhing, horses trotting loose, but most were left unharmed, their superior armor and oversized shields protecting them. Their speed is unchecked, and now they charge after Charles and his silver-armored soldiers, howling for blood.

Charles is through the gate and calling for the portcullis to be closed, and it starts to grate downward slowly, but it's not enough. Conrad is through, ducking beneath the massive black spikes of the portcullis, several dozen of his men behind him, and now the battle is in the courtyard.

Several of Conrad's men break off and throw themselves from their mounts to storm up the stairway, fighting toward the gatehouse. I turn my attention to Charles, waiting for him to give the command that would end my life. And indeed, the blade presses tighter as if the man wielding it anticipates the order as well. When the battle swings into the courtyard, the man at my back pivots us so I now face the interior of the castle, with both Charles and Conrad in view.

Charles is busy, however. Embattled, surrounded by six of his men, the rest cut off by Conrad's forces, he is desperately fighting for his life, and doing so one-handed, struggling to wield his heavy sword with any efficacy. The portcullis had been halted halfway down, and the men who'd stopped its descent are now cornered in that gatehouse and fighting off Charles's foot soldiers. Outside the walls, Conrad's men are pushing the stragglers of Charles's retreat into the courtyard, which is growing crowded indeed.

The tide has turned, that much is obvious.

Or, rather, the tide had never really run in Charles's favor. Poor tactics, desperation—against a foe of Conrad's caliber, such errors are only made once.

The battle grinds on beneath me, and I watch with bated breath.

Conrad is the same furious demon he'd been outside, charging his horse forward, sword crashing and swinging, helmet pivoting this way and that, blood running red on his blade. Charles watches his men fall in droves, and yet he fights on, sparing not a single glance for me.

And then, after what feels like an eternity of watching Conrad's men batter down their inferior foes, Charles sags back against the wall and shoots a glance up at me.

"CONRAD!" He shouts, pointing at me with his sword. "LOOK TO THE WALLS!"

Conrad fumbled mid-swing, the lion visor tracking up to me.

I watch him freeze, his sword dangling.

Charles lifts a gauntleted fist, and the knife at my throat presses tighter yet, and I feel the deep aching burning agony as the edge bites into my thin, sensitive skin.

Charles pauses, an evil grimace on his face, and then drops his fist.

I expected death, but it never came.

I tensed, eyes closed, not breathing, waiting for the cold dark to drag me under.

Instead, I hear a grunt, feel the blade at my throat quiver. I reach up, push the hand away, expecting resistance. There is none; the hairy paw flops aside, and the soldier stumbles backward.

Conrad's dagger is buried to the hilt between the ugly soldier's eyes. The same dagger that once sliced open my dress, and left me naked for Conrad's touch.

An impossible throw, it would seem to me. How far away is Conrad? Thirty feet? An easy shot with a bow, but with a thrown knife? It shouldn't have been possible.

But there's the man behind me, a blade through his skull, already dead.

I'm shaking all over, gasping. I fall to my knees, giving in to the panic. Letting the fear push through me.

I hear the sounds of battle, shouts, cries for mercy.

I hear Charles and Conrad.

I do not open my eyes, do not uncurl from the cold stone flags. I don't want to see any more.

I hear Charles shouting, hear the sounds of metal on metal, and then one final crunch, and Charles goes silent. I open my eyes, and see Conrad standing over his former friend, his sword buried to the hilt beneath the lower edge of the breastplate. Charles is gasping, blinking.

"Damn you, Conrad," he says, sinking to the ground. "Damn you."

Conrad hesitates as the light fades from Charles's eyes, and then yanks his sword free. He turns to look at me. He sees me lying on the walk, staring over the edge, and immediately he sheathes his sword. A few of Charles's men are still attempting to hold out, but the majority are already either dead or have surrendered, especially now that Charles is slain.

I'm dizzy, disoriented, panic still bashing through me. I'd denied myself the luxury of panicking while the knife was at my throat, but now that the danger has passed; I have no control over myself. My legs are jelly, I'm trembling, tears trickle down my throat.

I hear boots on stone, shrinking away from the sound, but it's Conrad. He bends, scoops me up, and clutches me against the scales of his armor. Gauntlet fingers brush hair out of my face.

"Hannah." His voice is low, careful. "Are you hurt?"

I shake my head. "A minor cut to my throat. Painful, but doesn't threaten my life."

"I expected treachery," Conrad says, "but this deviousness was callous even for him."

"He hated you more than he desired me, I think."

Conrad carries me down the stairs. I bury my face in the cold hard metal of his armor and refuse to look around. Men moan, weep, beg for help; I don't want to see any more. I don't want to see.

I hear a horse whicker, and feel warm fur against my cheek. "Can you ride, Hannah?" Conrad asks.

I open my eyes, see Conrad's massive white charger in front of me, ears twitching, nosing me curiously. I nod, and allow Conrad to settle me on the saddle before swinging up behind me.

"Take measure of this place, Edward," Conrad calls, and one of his men nods, slams his sword's pommel against his breastplate in salute. "Set your most trusted man as warder until I can find someone to govern. I'm off for the castle—I've had enough of this day."

"What of the prisoners, sire?" Edward asks.

Conrad shrugs dismissively. "Prisoners are useless to me. Loyalty to Charles does not mean hatred for me, so if they're willing, put them to work. If they're recalcitrant, put their heads on a spike. I care not which."

"As you will, sire. How many men do you wish as escort?"

"A dozen at most. With Charles defeated, I have no fear of ambush any longer."

We're off, then, hooves thundering, the horse moving powerfully between my thighs, Conrad at my back. He's doffed his gauntlets, and his hand is warm and strong and gentle at my belly.

It should be impossible to sleep on a cantering horse, but I somehow manage to drift beyond awareness.

It is nearing dusk when we reach the castle. The bridge is down, the portcullis up.

As soon as we're in the courtyard, I hear the clanking of massive gears and the rattle of man-thick chains, and the bridge jolts upward behind us while the portcullis lowers. Conrad leaps off the horse with lithe alacrity, energetic and powerful even after an entire day of riding and a battle behind him. He sweeps me off the horse, carries me into the castle. I allow myself to drift, as he walks with me through the long hallways and up the many stairs.

I'm drowsy, loose, weak, terror and fear having sapped me of strength.

I feel something soft beneath me—Conrad's bed. I curl gratefully into the blankets, listening as he removes his armor piece by piece, the quiet murmur of a servant assisting him.

The bed dips, and I smell the familiar odor of Conrad, the sweat, and the male musk. He is warm, huge, hard, and gentle. He lies down beside me, curls me in his arms, cradles me against his chest.

"Sleep, Hannah." His voice is soothing, close to my ear, buzzing against me.

I sleep.

I stir, wakefulness upon me but not yet thoroughly arrived. Dawn light is yellow and warm on my eyelids; I feel Conrad behind me, feel his breath on the back of my neck. I remain as I am for a time, content to bask in Conrad's warmth. His arm is low across my hip, his fingers trailing against my belly and perhaps even a bit lower. His thighs press against the backs of mine, and I can feel the stirring thickness of his cock going erect, even through the silk of my dress and the cotton of his breeches.

He hums, his muscles tense, his hand tightens on me, his hips flex forward; he's fully erect now, and pressing between the globes of my buttocks.

His lips touch the back of my neck, and I feel them curve in a smile. "Well. Quite a good morning, is it not?"

I moan, the feel of his cock rubbing against my ass cheeks igniting my libido like a flame touching tinder. "If there were fewer layers between us, I think it might be a better morning."

I feel his fingers untie the laces of his breeches, he shifts and wiggles behind me, and then he's tossing the garment aside and his hands are on me. I'm curled up in front of him, knees drawn up, and his hands begin at my ankles, finding the hem of the dress I'm still wearing, having been too exhausted last night to bother removing it. He caresses my thighs as he brushes the silk upward, and I lift my hip to allow the fabric passage further upward. I moan again as he return his touch to my hips, scouring the tautness of my buttocks, and then reaching around to dimple my thighs with his fingertips, pulling at my leg. I roll to my stomach, sit up, and yank the dress off, hurling it aside, and then lay down facing him.

His eyes are dark and hot and fierce, his skin radiating heat against mine. He smiles at me again, a brief sweet secret smile meant only for me, a smile I would bet no one else has ever even suspected him capable of. Then his fingers walk and trip and dance down my body, finding the juncture of my thighs. He leans into me, presses me to my back, and his mouth immediately goes to my breast, tongue flicking over my nipple, lips tracing damp lines and wet arcs across to the other peaked, sensitive mound of flesh.

I gasp, and then my breath catches entirely when his fingers find my slit and delve into me, spearing through my slick silken heat, scissoring, curling, withdrawing to smear my juices over my clit, multiplying the sensitivity of my clit infinitely. His mouth laves at my nipples and his fingers circle my clit, setting a slow pace at first, teasing me toward the edge, bringing me to the crest and then when I begin to buck and beg and whimper, he slows to pull me back away from the cusp of climax.

And all the while, his cock rests hot and thick and hard against my hip. He's beside me, levered over me, his bulk reassuring, his muscular form spread around me, over me. I caress him everywhere I can reach, slide my hands through his long loose black hair, trace the contours of his shoulders, the subtle inward curve of his spine, the taut hard bubble of his ass, and then finally I allow myself to curl my hand around his erection, moaning in pleasure at the rising burgeoning heat of impeding climax and the soft steely velvet of his beautiful cock.

"Conrad, please—*please*—" I whisper, my lips touching his ear.

I feel the rumble of his voice as much as hear it. "Please what,

Hannah? Speak it, and it's yours."

"I need you inside me, Conrad."

He nudges my thighs wider apart with his knee, settling between my legs. One fist buries in the mattress beside my face. He is huge and masculine and gorgeous and his cock is throbbing delicious heat as he guides himself to my slit, his fist hard around the base of his shaft, and then I'm unable to breathe or whimper or gasp or anything. I can only tremble with eyes wide as he slides into me, rocking home in a single powerful thrust.

"Oh fuck, Conrad. Fuck—how is it you feel so perfect?" I find my voice, the words bubbling up and pouring out.

He grinds with slow power, unhurried, taking me, claiming me, piercing me so perfectly, and I feel his many thick inches stretching my cunt open and filling me to the hilt, until I am glutted on his cock, and still I need more, more, more.

I cling to his neck with both arms, lift myself as close to him as I can get, wrap my legs around his pumping buttocks and moan in his ear and bite his earlobe. My fingers claw down his back as his thrusting erection pushes me from the cusp of climax to the teetering edge and then over. The orgasm blasting through me is a detonation of such potency I cannot even scream, can only sink my teeth into the firm muscle of his broad shoulder and whine in my throat as I am seized by a battering succession of twisting white-hot waves. They curl in my core, wringing ecstasy out of me.

I thrash beneath him, writhe under him.

And then I feel him grunt, feel his hips stutter in their rhythmic pounding against me, and I know his release is imminent.

I push him backward, sitting up with him. My thighs wedge around his waist, my ankles lock behind his back, and my fingers knot in his hair. I lift up, feel the slick, sex-coated length of his shaft sliding out of me, feel him tremble, holding back.

"Hannah—" his voice is a barely-audible snarl.

"Come for me, Conrad," I whisper, and slam my ass down on his thighs, impaling him deep within my cunt. "Say my name as you come.

Let go. Give it all to me."

"Hannah—" he growls. "Hannah…fuck—"

He loses control then, his powerful thighs and hips driving him upward, lifting me, rocking me, his cock filling me, fucking deeper and deeper. His muscles shift and sweat beads on his flesh. One of his hands knots in my hair and yanks to tilt my face up, his other hand curls around my waist and pinions me tight against him. We writhe together, then, his climax inciting another of my own, his wild passionate fucking driving me over the edge all over again.

"God, Hannah!" He breathes this, a desperate, disbelieving gasp. "What are you doing to me?"

His body bucks and writhes and heaves beneath me, and then his mouth slams against mine, his teeth bruising my lips, his tongue demanding and slippery in my mouth and against my tongue, his kiss a mad crush of need, as if he couldn't help but kiss me, as if some force woven through the fabric of reality itself demanded he kiss me.

I whimper, a tear sliding down my cheek as he kisses me.

He kisses me, and he comes inside me.

I feel it, a hot wet rush filling me, his hips tensing, flexing, his cock throbbing thicker and harder and deeper, spasming, and he groans into my mouth, his fist in my hair smashing my face closer to his, his lips moving furiously, his tongue dancing.

His cum fills me, a river spreading through me, suffusing me, and his kiss envelopes me.

My hands move, shaking, to his face, I cup his cheeks. I fall into the kiss, whimpering through it.

It is so a moment so beautiful it hurts—*please don't stop kissing me.*

He pulls away, and I resist the loss of his mouth, the absence of his hungry tongue. I shake like a leaf as he pulls back, my lips quivering, my hands trembling on his cheeks.

His deep dark brown eyes fix on mine, and he gazes at me as if truly seeing me for the first time.

He is still impaled fully inside my slit, hard, throbbing. His fingers uncurl stiffly from the tangled mass of my blond hair, but his hand does

334 Jasinda Wilder with Jade London

not leave the small of my back.

"I—" he whispers so low, so nearly inaudible I have to strain to hear him. "I don't—I wish—"

"What, Conrad? You wish what?"

He shakes his head, buries his face in the crook of my shoulder. His breathing is slow and deep. He clutches at me, as I'm being pulled away from him.

"Don't go, Hannah." His forehead touches mine. He's still so hard inside me we could fuck again and yet I'd still not be sated. "I wish you didn't have to go."

His words slice razor-sharp, sending a myriad of agonizing ripples throughout me. "I'm not leaving, Conrad. I won't. I'm here. I'm staying with you."

His forehead separates from mine, and his gaze swivels to the closed door of his chambers. "You can't."

"I won't go." I whimper this, desperate.

I cling to him. Squeeze around his still-hard cock. Claw at his shoulders, his back.

He falls forward, planting my back to the mattress. He stares down at me, and his hips flex. "God, Hannah. I hate this. I can't—"

I cry out as he begins to fuck me. But it's not fucking, now. It's something else. It's rough and desperate and wild and furious, but it's not fucking. I cling to him as desperately as I can, wrapped up in him, tangled around him.

"Conrad—"

"Hannah—"

It's all too brief, but in those moments, each of us clinging madly to the other, there is no him or me, only us, mingled, united, merged, and his breath and mine are one, his body melts into mine, mine into his.

His growl is agonized, the mournful wail of a wounded wolf.

We come at the exact same moment, and his arms wrap around me, and we tumble to the mattress together, his mouth on mine, rolling so I'm on top, both of us grunting and gasping, hips crashing together.

There's a secret eternity buried somewhere in that mutual orgasm.

He pulls away, ripping his body from mine with a pained snarl, as if removing himself from my touch causes him physical pain. He stands a foot away from me, chest heaving, jaw clenching and releasing, fists knotted at his sides.

Then he moves toward me, fists unfurling, and he lifts me from the bed, carries me the few short feet across the room and sets me, naked, leaking his cum, whimpering, trembling, in front of his chamber door.

"You have to go, Hannah. It's time." He sounds as if he can barely get the words out, but knows he must.

The door is solid dark aged wood, banded with black iron straps. Where a handle would be, there is a lion's head, nearly life-size, captured mid-roar in solid gold. It has a thick gold ring between its jaws.

I remember another like it, a lifetime ago.

An eternity ago.

A journey down a long stair, coming face to face with a haughty king.

Before that?

Darkness.

And I know, with a dread certainty, that when I pull on the gold ring, the door will open not to a throne room but to infinite darkness.

I do not want that darkness.

It is cold, there.

Lonely.

There is loss in that darkness.

"No, no." I whimper.

"You have to, Hannah." His breath is at my ear.

His lips touch the side of my jaw, and then his huge rough calloused paw cups my cheek with exquisite gentleness, and he kisses me, softly, tenderly, briefly.

"You must."

Tears drip down my cheeks, and I reach out a hand toward the door. The gold ring is colder than ice, biting, burning. I pull, because I must. I know it. I cannot resist this. My body obeys commands not my own.

I pull.

The door swings open toward me. The darkness beyond is a maw, cold and ravenous. I glance back, see Conrad behind me, hair a loose black cascade around his burly shoulders. He is naked, beautifully so, perfectly so, nude and masculine and massive, every angle and plane of his body rugged and hard and breathtaking. But his eyes…oh his eyes.

*Don't go*…they say.

But he doesn't reach to stop me, as if he knows he cannot.

I know he cannot.

Now that the darkness stands before me, I am called into it.

Drawn.

Inevitably.

My feet carry me, one step at a time, from the chambers of a haughty, handsome, powerful king into the unwelcome frigid embrace of darkness.

Ice bathes my flesh; shadows suck me into an inky pool. Here there is no awareness, no knowledge, no me, no Conrad, no drip of hot cum down my thighs…nothing.

I rage against the clutch of nothingness.

But it consumes me nonetheless.

So complete and thorough is the blank all-consuming expanse of dark that I cannot even weep, for there is no loss, no memory, only the shadows and the cold.

$* * *$

Silence.

Perfect, utter silence.

A drowning quiet.

Loss; the first sensation.

What have I lost? Within the confines of my mind there are only scraps and fragments of thought, shreds of memory. A man. A king? His body claiming mine. His relentless possession and protection. I am his. But now I've lost him.

I recall his name, now—Conrad Killian. Possession of his name; the second sensation.

He is a man of many guises. But his face is always the same. The essential quiet strength of him is always the same. His ready touch, his fierce, primal hunger is always the same. He is who he is. He is constant.

I must find him.

I must find...there is something else, but it is too obscured in shadows and slippery cold for me to grasp it.

I wake up, then. Fully. The black room surrounds me. The candle flame shudders beside me, perhaps three or four inches of white wax remaining. The candle is burning down—the thought of the candle guttering out frightens me, somehow.

I stand up, moving on silent feet across the empty space to the nearest door, the torch flickering in its sconce beside the frame. I go to the next door, the second to last. The green, familiar door with the plain brass knob, the keyhole scratched from a lifetime of keys hunting for the opening. I cannot bear to look at this door. Cannot. My heart twists painfully in my chest, beats fit to burst, aching and thundering behind my ribs. Tears squeeze at my eyes, looking at that door. I feel nothing more than the pain. No memory, no reason, just the blinding, horrible pain in my heart and soul.

The torch beside that door burns low.

So, too, does the torch at the last door, the plainest door.

The torches, the candle—they provide life, here. Awareness. Without that candle, without those torches, there will be nothing.

There is no time here, except for the measurement of that ever-burning candle.

My existence here in this black room is fleeting. I must find Conrad. He is beyond the doors—

Beyond each door—

I remember each one, now, each version of him. The boxer, the urban sophisticate, the gunfighter, the cunning card-sharp, the king...

Each one is Conrad, but none of them are truly *him*; the third sensation.

It is the true, real man I must find.

I find myself in front of the sixth door. I am eager, now. My heart trips and skips as I stand before the door. Like the others, the door itself is a plain unadorned black, the numeral 6 in plain silver at the center. But instead of a knob, lever, or even an ornately sculpted ring-pull, this door features a latch of ancient wood. It is a lever of sorts, but primitive. To lift the lever moves a bar from its housing on the frame, allowing the door to be opened. The wood is rough-hewn, hand-planed, and has been worn smooth by generations of hands.

I lift the latch, and the heavy door swings inward.

The smell of burning peat assaults my nostrils, thick, earthy, acrid.

There is heat, close and billowing.

I step through; find wood flooring beneath my bare feet. Some automatic instinct has me closing the door behind me and, as I do so, the darkness flees, retreats behind me, replaced by the warm orange glow of a fire in front of me, burning merrily in a fireplace made from huge rough stones joined by crumbling mortar, the interior of the fireplace black from countless generations of fires.

The ceiling is low, made of stout dark wooden beams, as rough-hewn as everything else.

I look around me: there is another door on the wall to the left, standing open, a bed beyond it. The room I stand in is tiny, but cozy. There is a loft overhead, accessible by a hand-made ladder—I can see barrels, bags, and various other supplies. There is a table near the fire, rectangular, wide enough for several people, with six crudely fashioned chairs around it. Crudely fashioned, yes, but well-worn, sturdy, aged. A clay pipe rests on the table, as does a large jar with a cork stopper. A plate, a fork, a small dagger. Along one wall is a bookshelf, handmade as is everything else, with several rows of tattered books, each one ancient and care-worn, the spines peeling.

This is a home. Rough, rustic, but everything has been made with care and love and an eye to last for generations.

And I am utterly alone.

$$* * * *$$

I'm startled by the opening of the door behind me. I jump forward, squealing in fright and shock. As the door opens, a blast of ice-cold wind and blowing rain spatters against me. The door swings open, smashes against the opposite wall, and I am immediately drenched by sheets of rain and skirls of knifing wind. I shrink away, toward the fire, putting the table between the door and me.

Between me and the figures standing in the doorway.

Three of them.

Tall, broad, shadowy figures filling the frame, cloaked in darkness.

Not for long are they obscured, however. They step through, into the small house. My heart skips a beat, and then thunders madly when they step into the glow of the firelight. Terror fills me.

Each man is clothed identically in thick white wool leggings or breeches, with heavy scarlet coats whose hems brush their knees, the edges trimmed with thick white bands that cross over their chests in a wide X. Belts of the same white color encircle their waists. Heavy gray greatcoats hang on their shoulders, open despite the blowing rain. Each man carries a long rifle in one hand, wears a three-corner hat on his head, and has a sabre at his side.

They merely stand staring for a long moment, and then a leer crosses the face of the soldier in the center. His pale blue eyes pierce me from his place across the room. Lank wet yellow strands of hair stick to his golden-stubbled cheeks, the rest queued at his neck. He is frightfully beautiful, a demon in angel's guise—a demon, I say, because his eyes give him away.

"Killian's bitch," he says, stepping toward me, "discovered alone. Quite a treat, I'd say, eh, Martin?"

The soldier on the left—Martin—grins evilly, his eyes raking me. "Oh quite, Charlie. A rare treat indeed, I'd say."

The man standing on the right speaks next, with a lick of his plump lips. "And she ain't wearin' nary a stitch, Charlie. Lucky day for us."

I back further away, until I bump into the wall beside the fireplace. The heavy stone of the wall is cold against my bare skin. I am, as the last soldier pointed out, totally naked.

Cold.

Wet.

Terrified.

And faced with three lecherous redcoats.

Charlie, the centermost, circles the table in a rush, his damp, cold, strong hand snagging my arm. "Martin, get over here and hold her."

Martin tosses his rifle onto the table and joins Charlie, circling behind me, taking my both my arms in his cruel hands, holding me. Pulling me backward. Forcing me to the floor.

Charlie stands above me, lips curving in a wicked leer, tongue sliding along his lower lip, hands working at the buckle of his belt.

There's a wet sound, then, behind us, a metallic squish and then a thump. "I'll run you through where you stand, Markham," a deep, grating voice snarls. "I've already got a price on my head. A few shillings more won't bother me."

Charlie freezes, his grin fading. "Conrad Killian. Thought I'd caught you away." He stands, re-buckling his belt.

"You had," comes the voice, that rough, familiar voice. "But I heard whispers of a certain trio of redcoats sneaking about the highlands."

"Whispers, eh?" Charlie says, his hand settling on his sabre. "If I find the whisperers, I'll cut their tongues out and feed them to the crows."

"Let her go, Martin," the voice rumbles. "You know my reputation. Neither of you will clear steel before I've separated your ugly head from your uglier body."

The hands release me, and I scramble to the side, find my feet, and scurry back against the wall as far from the redcoats as I can get—which isn't far in this cramped space.

Conrad, standing in the doorway, a sword nearly as long as I am tall gripped in both hands. A forest green tartan kilt wraps around his waist and hangs at his knees, with the tartan crossing his chest and over his shoulder. A heavy cloak hangs from his shoulders, and a thick black leather belt circles his waist, with a pouch at his belly—a sporran.

His sword is stained red, a redcoat dead at his feet. Conrad's face is a rictus of hate, knuckles white around the hilt of his claymore.

"Come to me, Hannah," Conrad murmurs. I scurry to his side, and he slings off his cloak and drapes it around me. "Out. On the horse."

I obey him immediately, trotting outside into the gale, gratefully wrapping the thick wool cloak around my naked body. A horse stands in the rain, head down, munching on grass, reins tied to the pommel. I climb up, not without difficulty. The saddle is blisteringly cold on my bare buttocks even through the thick wool, but there's nothing for it.

Conrad follows me out, backing slowly out of the house. He's got his claymore in one hand, and a musket tucked against his side in the other, aimed at the two men.

"You're a fool if you think you'll get away with this, Killian," Charlie says. "The price on your head will double. Poor George here is at least one of His Majesty's soldiers you've slain, that I know of. Then there's that bloke at the hanging—when was it? A year ago? You're making quite a name for yourself as an outlaw, Killian. Take your little slut with you, if you wish, and run to your friends. I'll find you."

"I'll be waiting when you do, Markham," Conrad says, standing at my knee.

"Oh, but I won't be alone, though, will I? I'll have an entire company of friends behind me." Charlie grins, and despite his handsome features, that grin is not a pleasant sight. "We'll have us a merry scrum then, won't we, mate?"

Conrad stuffs a foot into a stirrup and swings up behind me, leaving the reins tied to the pommel, and nudges the horse into motion with his heels. "I look forward to the meeting, Sergeant Markham." He lays the musket across my lap, his claymore held in one hand, the flat resting on his shoulder.

We're off at a fierce gallop. Rain dashes against my face, slides down my back, splatters in my eyes. The wind is razor-sharp and colder than shards of ice, but Conrad is warm around me, behind me, broad and hard and powerful.

"Where will we go?" I ask, trying to huddle deeper into the cloak that is my only protection against the elements.

"No worries, lass. I've a friend close by." We've slowed for a moment so Conrad can sheathe his claymore and strap it to his back; our best defense is now the musket, and putting as much distance between the Englishmen and us as possible.

We ride in silence for a time, the horse tireless, hooves squelching in the mud. Trees rustle in the ceaseless wind, the branches reaching and grabbing in the wild, seething, storm-tossed night.

Then, apropos of nothing, Conrad's voice buzzes in my ear. "Why were you naked?"

I hunt for an answer, come up with nothing. "I—" a certain truth strikes me. "I was waiting for you."

His deep voice is rife with amusement. "I see. A surprise I'd have enjoyed much more did we not have unwelcome company."

"Charlie...will he make trouble for you?" I ask.

"Trouble enough, piled on what I've already brought on myself. I've nothing but hate for the damned lobster-backs, and they for me. My sword swings a little too eagerly when there's redcoat blood to spill."

"What will we do?"

"I say again Hannah: have no worries. I'll keep you safe from the likes of that scum." A moment of silence, and then, in a darker voice that sends shivers down my spine, delicious, heated shivers, "Whether you'll be safe from me is another story entirely, though."

"If he comes for you with a whole company…what then?"

His voice is fierce. "Then I'll bring the ransom of an entire company's worth of English corpses down on my head, as I'll slay every man jack of 'em and piss on their corpses when I've finished."

A different kind of shudder runs down my back at the venom in his voice—I do not doubt him. Not his intentions nor his ability, nor his thirst for English blood.

"Can he muster that many men to hunt for only you?"

A bitter curse, then, "The bastard is dreadful well-connected. It may not be tomorrow, or even next week, but he'll come. A few well-placed messages to friends back to London-town will have a company of bloody-backs marching to his drum. And yes, they'll come for me."

"I'm sorry to have brought so much trouble down on you."

He nuzzles the back of my neck. "To fash is for fools, lass. I'd have had the trouble one way or another." He rests the musket across my lap and curls his arm around my waist. "At least this way, I get a moment with you out of the bargain."

"Only a moment?" I ask, turning my face to brush my cheek against his.

"As many moments as I can steal, *mo chroi*," he growls, "I'll spend showing you how worth the fight you are."

We ride across the highland through wind and driving rain. For an hour we ride, more perhaps, but when all one can see is darkness ahead and behind, when nothing exists but the thunder of hooves and the cold wet misery chilling down to the bone, time ceases to have much meaning.

Finally, after what feels like an eternity, Conrad slows our horse and gathers the reins tight in one fist. I hear him pull back the hammer of his musket and feel him tense, his body alert and straight.

"Expecting trouble?" I ask, keeping my voice low.

"Always. But on nights like this, it pays to take extra precautions."

A few hundred yards ahead, I can see the dim glow of a light burning in a window. Sitting in the middle of nowhere, the dwelling itself is little more than a patch of blackness, somewhat darker than the night around it, except for that tiny square of yellow-orange light. Conrad lets the mount sidle a bit further forward, and then he reins us in. We are close enough that I can make out the door, the low sloping roof, a hint of wet stone around the window. Conrad gives a low three-note whistle, and then waits, musket held casually at the ready in one hand. A tense moment, and I half-expect Charlie and Martin to emerge, guns blazing, from the door. I know this is not possible, given the wild speed of our journey here, but still, the fearful expectation causes my heart to thud as the door finally swings open.

I feel Conrad relax behind me as he uncocks the hammer of the musket. "Angus," he says, "I need your hospitality, old friend."

I can make out little of the man in the doorway except that he's wearing a kilt, is built broad and stout, and has a sword held in both hands, fully as large as the one on Conrad's back. "Hospitality, is it?" His voice is gruff and rolling. "Harbor from the lobster-backs, more like."

Conrad laughs. "True enough, but not just for me, this time."

"Who've you brought, Conrad?"

"Her name is Hannah. We had a bit of a run-in with Charlie Markham and Martin Ellis, and one other. You well know the reputation of that despicable pair."

Angus's laugh is mirthless, bitter. "Markham killed my nephew and raped his young wife. So, yes, I'd say I'm familiar. Martin was there that night as well."

Conrad swung down out of the saddle, tossed his musket to Angus and then reached up and lifted me from the saddle. "Well, I fear I've earned another bounty on my head. Martin, Charlie, and some other lick-spittle bastard they had with 'em, they had Hannah here cornered and were ready to take their hatred of me out on her. I slew the nameless one and then rode off here with Hannah."

"Should've ended Markham while you were at it," Angus said, ushering us into his home. "He'll have revenge on his mind now, and he's good at nothing so much as revenge."

"I'm well aware, Angus," Conrad says, a note of irritation in his voice. "I know Markham needs killing, but it's not so simple as just lopping his damned head off. You know as well as I that he's got too many friends in power. I'm not so worried about the poor bastard farmer's boy from the English countryside that I killed tonight, but they'll just add more to the price on my head. Eventually they'll catch me and stretch my neck, but if I kill Markham, it'll bring the power of the crown down on me, you, and everyone I know."

Conrad led me into the croft as he spoke, and I was glad for the warmth and safety it afforded us.

"You took his fun, killed his friend, and embarrassed him," Angus returns. "He won't let that slide, Conrad."

Now that I could get a good look at him, I could see that Angus was shorter than Conrad by nearly a foot and close to twice his width, but none of it fat—he's merely enormous, built of raw power. His hair is queued to mid-back, brown as rich soil. He wears a kilt in red tartan, his sporran left off, his claymore laying across the table, shirt loose and untucked. The interior of Angus's home is similar enough to Conrad's that it could have been the same dwelling: large irregular blocks of stone stacked and mortared, a big fireplace crackling with a blazing fire, hand-made furniture.

Conrad slumps into a chair at the table, snags the clay jug sitting near to hand, yanks free the cork and takes a generous slug of the contents. "Again, Angus, you're not telling me anything I don't already know."

Angus blows out a breath, takes a seat and drinks as Conrad did. "Keep growing the price on your head as you've been, eventually the price will be too much of a temptation for someone."

"I know this, too."

"We've been friends since we were wee lads, Conrad. You know I'll stand by you no matter what, but…you're making a hanging an inevitability at this rate."

"He threatened to bring a company of redcoats to find me," Conrad admits.

Angus snarled a curse. "Not an idle threat from a man of his connections."

I was left standing near the doorway, listening, dripping wet, naked under the cloak and shivering. I inched closer to the fire, sitting on the edge of the hearth to dry out.

Conrad shot a glance at me. "Shite, sorry, Hannah. You've got to be frozen." He turned to Angus. "Have you got any women's clothing about?"

Angus just blinks for a moment. "Women's clothing? Why would I keep such around?" He glances at me suspiciously. "And why hasn't she any of her own?"

Conrad hesitates. "She was…washing when Charlie and Martin showed up." A shrug. "I'm a fair hand with my sword, but so is Charlie, and Martin's no slouch himself. I thought it best to get shot of them quick as I could, which meant she's got nothing to wear but that cloak of mine."

Angus's fair skin reddens. "Ah. I see." He lumbers to his feet, shuffles to a thick wooden chest in a corner, opens the top and rummages. "I've little enough, but…aha. Here it is." He comes up with a wad of wool in his hand, dark, soft looking, aged. He hands it to me and I shake it out. I see that it's an old woollen underdress. "It's all I've got but my tartan and another old cloak and some clean shirts, I fear. But it'll warm you."

I eye the garment suspiciously. "Is it…clean?" I sniff it.

Angus is still red in the cheeks, shifting from foot to foot. "Oh, aye, it's clean. Been in that trunk for nigh on twenty years, but it's clean."

Conrad clears his throat, and when I glance at him, it's obvious he's holding back laughter. "That's—why Angus, that wouldn't happen to belong to Mary Ainslie, would it?"

Angus clears his throat a few times. "It's all I've got, damn you. Never you mind whose it was."

Conrad chortles, coughing to cover it. "It is! One tumble in the hay with a girl twenty years ago, and you've still got her shift?"

"'Twas more than once, damn your eyes. I was near to askin' her to marry me, you might like to know." Angus turns away, slugs at the jar of whisky. "Then that business with the Darroch clan swept us all up, and by the time I got back to her, she'd taken up with Murray of the Campbells, and that was that."

Conrad's laughter abates, then. "I'd no notion it was that serious."

Angus shrugs. "Was for me, at least. I always suspected it was rather less so for her. I'd no great place in my clan, nor aspirations for much more than what I've got now. She always had designs on a mite more than she figured I could provide." A wolfish grin, then. "But she was more than willing enough to dally with me of a night. Left that shift here, the last night we passed together."

I felt a bit awkward, then. "Are you sure you want me to wear it, then?" I asked. "I don't want to take anything from you that might have sentimental value to you."

Angus waves a hand. "Sentiment, bah. I held on to it because it seemed daft to throw it away, perfectly good shift an' all, y'ken? I stuffed it into the trunk and forgot it till now."

It was obvious enough that Angus was lying to me but I let it go, grateful at least to have something to wear. "Thank you, then, Angus."

I wait, hoping Angus at least would turn around so I could change into it, but he and Conrad both merely sat at the table, engaged in conversation.

Eventually I clear my throat, glance around for a separate bedroom like Conrad's home had, but there's only the one open space, and the loft. "Might I use your loft to change in, then?"

Angus shoots to his feet. "Oh. Right. I'll just…go check on the… um, outside."

He was gone in a blast of cold rain and a glimpse of darkness. Conrad tips back in his chair, eyeing me. "Like me to leave too, Hannah?" His voice betrays his own ideas on the subject.

I hesitate a moment, then unfasten the brooch holding closed the cloak, shrug it open, letting the heavy wet wool fall to the floor. I stand naked in front of Conrad. His intense dark eyes fasten on me, raking over my body. The cabin is warm, the fire hot at my back, yet my nipples pucker and tighten as he stares at me. My skin pebbles, and my breasts feel heavy. My long blonde hair is damp at my neck. Conrad slowly sets the front legs of his chair down, slides it backward, and stands up. His movements are slow, deliberate, predatory. I shiver as he approaches, but not from cold. Everything inside me burns, aches, trembles, and he's done nothing but take a handful of steps in my direction. I stand where I am, wait for him to step closer. He's all the cabin contains now. Him, his heat, the damp scent of him, wet wool and man.

He's an inch from me, then. The tips of my breasts brush his shirt, my erect nipples so sensitive that even the slight, subtle brush of my flesh against the wet linen of his shirt is almost too much. His eyes bore into mine, unblinking, impenetrable, a brown so dark they're nearly black. His hair is soaked, sodden, dripping down his back. I just stand there, silent, staring up at him, waiting.

He reaches then, his palms grazing my hips. "Hannah…you've always been troublesome, you know," he says, a tiny smile playing at the corners of his lips.

"Have I?"

His fingers tighten against my hips, digging into the flesh, tugging me nearer. "Oh, aye. All the trouble I can handle. Wherever you are there, too, is trouble."

I feel my breasts crush against his chest, feel his heart thudding. His fingers toy with the flesh at my hips, daring inch by inch toward my ass. My hands curl at his shoulders, my fingers clutching at his shirt.

"Yet here we are together."

He slides a palm up my side, to my ribcage, around to my back, between my shoulder blades, grasps my hair in his fist. "Yet here we are. I don't seem able to leave you to your trouble." He tugs my head backward, tipping my face up. "Can't stand the thought of anyone else with his hands on you. This pale, perfect skin of yours…I fancy it belongs to me."

"Doesn't it?" I breathe.

His lips touch my jawline, midway between chin and ear. "You're asking me?"

"I am."

His answer is…delayed, somewhat. His lips are busy along my jaw, then traipsing down my throat, and the hand cupping my hip moves and curls to knead into the generous flesh of my buttocks. I can't move my head for his grip on my hair, and his touch has me paralyzed, dizzy. There's no breath, no movement, no heat, no life, nothing but Conrad. I can only stand in his touch and wait, hope for more. My throat is bared for his mouth, and his lips touch and dance and slither down the column, stutter over my clavicle, and then I feel his tongue on my skin between my breasts. I manage to let out a breath, and that breath is a plea—

*kissmetouchmemoremoremore*

"We can't," he murmurs, pressing his face against my shoulder. "Not here, not now."

"Conrad—"

"I know, lass." He breathes against me, fingers clutching me roughly, desperately. "Soon, I swear."

Conrad holds me, a moment longer, and then crouches down and snags the shift I'd dropped and forgotten. He tugs it over my head, and I thread my arms through, and just like that I'm covered, but I don't want to be. I want to feel Conrad against me, I want to push him down to the bed and bring him to climax, want to feel him grunt and clutch at me and feel him dominate me, and feel him release inside me.

"Soon, Hannah," he murmurs in my ear.

Did I speak those thoughts out loud? I didn't think I had, but his words seemed a direct promise to my needs, to my thoughts.

Conrad backs away from me, a devilish glint in his eyes, then turns away and opens the door, calling out for Angus to return. Then it's Angus and Conrad and me sitting around the table. Angus had a stew on the fire and he serves some up, warming us from the inside out. The whisky goes a long way to warming us as well, the jug passed around generously.

All I feel is the return of the heat, the pressure of need. The brief moment together wasn't enough to sate me, was only barely enough to whet my appetite. I'm more ravenous than ever, I fear, having felt his touch—but it was only a tease, only a taste.

Conrad's eyes don't ever quite go to mine, but somehow I'm aware of his attention. He's biding his time, it feels to me. Chatting quietly with Angus, discussing old friends not seen in many years, other friends lost in one way or another, girls they once knew, skirmishes fought and won or lost. I'm content to sit near the fire and listen, drowse to the sound of their voices lilting in quiet murmurs.

"What are we going to do?" I ask.

Conrad and Angus exchange glances. "Well, I've a few notions, and unfortunately, most of them include riding for somewhere Markham won't easily go, not without a large troop along."

I'd ask more, but I'm drowsing with exhaustion, and my eyes close and I feel arms beneath me, catching me up, cradling me against a warm solid chest.

I'm limp, loose, warm, asleep but not enough to be unconscious, but too nearly so to be able to move.

"Take the bed, Conrad," I hear Angus say. "She'll need the rest."

"I'll not throw you out of your own bed, Angus," Conrad argues, his voice pitched low. "That's pushing hospitality too far, even for you."

"A night in the stable won't hurt me. I insist. 'Sides, the stable's no place for a lady."

"There's the loft."

Angus snorts. "Bah. Full of sacks of meal and a half a dozen generations worth of who knows what. I'd not let her sleep up there if she were an Englishman."

"Angus—" Conrad starts.

"No, you shut your damn gob, Conrad. You'll owe me a jug and the tale of how you came to know such a fine lookin' lass."

Conrad snorts, and I feel the huff of air on my cheek. "Fine, and be damned, you stubborn Scot."

"You're the elder of us, so where'd I learn such stubbornness, then?"

Conrad just snorts again, and I feel him moving with me to the bed. He lays me down on something soft, and I'm covered with thick, warm, scratchy wool. "Keep a wary ear, Angus. Markham's a canny one," I hear him say, moving away from me.

"Calum is out grazing, and he's the orneriest, meanest damned mule I've ever seen. He's an ill-tempered, evil son of a bitch, and has no tolerance for strangers. He scents an unfamiliar horse or man, he'll kick up an almighty loud fuss, and is like to start kickin' and bitin' as well. He's better than a dog for guarding in the night." Angus grunted a laugh. "That's the only reason I've kept the old bastard around, truth be told."

Conrad's laughter is low and rueful. "I bore a bruise on my thigh for a month the last time I got near him. I was there when you first got him—winnings from that card game."

"He heard you call him a nasty old fuck, and he resented it. He understands every word we say, I swear, and every damned bray he lets out is his laugher at us."

"You ever try to ride him?"

Angus's silence is telling. "Ride Calum? Are you daft? I can barely fit a halter to the wicked beast without losing teeth or suffering a broken bone and that's just from trying to move him to fresh graze, or to haul a boulder. If I tried to ride him, he'd toss me off faster than you can spit, and then dance on my bones for spite."

Conrad laughs again. "True enough. It'd be funny to watch, until I had to set your leg."

"You'd have to set more than my leg, I think. Arms, legs, ribs, maybe even fit me for false teeth. He's the spawn of the devil himself on four legs, I tell you."

I hear hands slap thighs, and then short strides thunking across the wood floor. "I'm for the stables, then. Be at home, and if you hear Calum honking, get your girl and ride for the winds."

"Thanks, brother."

"Aye, well, you always did have better luck with the lasses than I, and far be it from me to stand in the way of your conquest."

A short silence, then. "It's not like that with her, Angus."

"No?"

"No."

Angus harrumphs. "Never thought I'd see this day, I'll admit. Well, it's your business. There's wood by the hearth, and more stew. See you in the morning." The door opens and the scent of rain floats over me, and then the door thuds closed and a wash of cold damp air skirls in the room, and I hear Conrad moving about the room.

I'm beginning to drift deeper under when I feel the bed dip as he lays beside me.

"You're not asleep," he whispers, "and I wasn't done with you."

The blanket lifts, settles, and he's beside me.

Bare.

Hard muscle, warm flesh, his breath on the back of my neck. His hot hard hands smoothing over my waist. I breathe out, a soft sigh I cannot help. His lips, touching between my shoulder blades, curve in a smile.

"I knew you weren't asleep."

I'm on my side, facing away from him. I remain motionless, for the moment. Waiting. Wanting his touch, but wanting more to know his desires and make them truth.

His fingers brush and pluck at the thin fine wool of the shift and, bit by bit, it finds its way upward, and more of my flesh is bared for his hands. First my thighs, then my hips, then my belly, then my breasts, and then his hands are skating down my thighs and gently tugging at them. I allow him to part them enough to fit his fingers to the crevice between my thighs, as if I'm still too sleepy to capitulate to his touch. I'm fully awake, though, and aching to be touched.

He wiggles closer, and now I feel him. All of him. Ohhh....there's so much to feel. His lips on the side of my neck, his hand between my thighs, burrowing closer to my core, and his huge hard body behind mine, a wall of heat and muscle. And his cock, thick and throbbing, nestled between the globes of my ass.

"You think I don't know you're playing at sleep, Hannah?" His voice is at the shell of my ear, breath warm, words amused.

He curls his hand around my thigh and lifts my leg, spreading me wide. I gasp, then, because he's touched the tip of his cock to my entrance, and he's teasing me. Nudging, teasing.

I turn my head and blinking, my eyes open, ready to end my game, but he's already plunging into me.

I'm wet, slick, ready for him. But still I gasp in surprise as he drives into me, thrusting deep without warning. "Conrad—Jesus…"

"Oh, you're awake now, are you?" His voice is laced with heated amusement.

"I am *now*," I whisper, my eyes finding his.

He pushes deep, and his palm scrapes over my breast, cupping harshly as he fills me. I'm spread open, split, stretched. He's too big, too hot, too hard, too much, and it was so sudden and I'm gasping, eyes watering at the sweet burning ache of him inside me. Too much. God, too much. I want to weep from it, but it's not tears of pain, they are tears of overwhelming pleasure, feeling so much so suddenly. God, his cock. So fucking huge inside me, stretching my pussy so wide I can't breathe, so deep inside me I'm glutted on him, unable to feel anything but him, but this, his cock inside me is everything, everything.

I can't even whimper, I'm so breathless.

There's nothing but him, but this connection, his body inside mine, his hand griping my breast, his breath on my nape.

And then he moves.

Sinuous, slow, gentle. A nudge, little more. And then a bit harder.

"I need to come, Hannah," he whispers. "I rode the whole way fighting arousal. I've but to look at you, touch a fingertip to your skin, and I'm hard as the mountain stone."

"Come, then, Conrad." I manage this much, gasping each word.

"Right now?"

I push back against him. "Right now."

He grunts as he buries himself deeper. "Don't ask for what you don't mean, Hannah."

I writhe, then, coyness abandoned, needing only to feel that release, to feel him give himself to me. To take his pleasure as my own, to take his cum inside me and squeeze him as he throbs.

"Conrad...I need to feel you come."

He rolls with me, pivoting to his back so I'm laying on top of him, my spine to his belly, his cock still impaled deep inside me, but now his hands find my inner thighs and spread me wide apart. I draw my heels up against the backs of my thighs, though there's no need, because he's got my legs pinned as wide as they'll go. He thrusts deep, his breath on my neck, his teeth nipping at me.

"Can't promise it'll be gentle, Hannah," he whispers.

"Don't want gentle," I breathe.

He releases my legs, plants his feet in the mattress so his knees point at the ceiling, propping my thighs wide. I hook my legs around his, moaning as he withdraws and thrusts in, slowly, teasingly. His hands cup my tits, rough and callused palms scraping my sensitive nipples.

"Touch yourself, Hannah," he says.

And I do.

I spread my fingers around my clit, pulling apart the folds, and then use my other hand to circle two fingers around the hypersensitive bundle of nerves. It's an immediate zap of ecstasy, that simple touch, and it has me writhing on top of him.

"Oh fuck, Hannah. I feel you clenching around me when you do that."

I squeeze harder, clamping down with every ounce of strength I have, and he grunts wordlessly, and I know he's gone, then. His grip on my tits is mercilessly rough, and now his hips begin to move, pumping slowly at first. He uses my breasts as a handhold, only his hips moving. I lay my head against his shoulder, turn my face to the side, and find his cheek with my lips. His jaw. The corner of his mouth.

His thrusts are measured, the pace increasing slowly. Each slide out drags a moan from me, each thrust in a gasp, and I try to find the rhythm, my fingers swift at my clit, now, bringing my orgasm nearer and nearer, until my hips are moving on their own, and his are, too. We thrust at odds for a moment, his push timed to my withdrawal.

He takes over, then. Knocks away my fingers, guides my hand to my breast, and I pinch my nipple and toy with my breast, feeling the luxurious sensuality of the weight of my own tit in my hand, my erect nipple. His fingers at my clit begin to move in sync with his thrusting hips. I'm groaning, gasping, whimpering, and I'm helpless in his thrall, taking his thrusts with my legs still spread wide apart so he can bury himself as deep as possible.

I feel something clench inside me. Heat coils, tension tightens to impossible tautness. And his thrusts go mad in a wild pounding.

He's grunting, hips driving with a crazed rhythm, each thrust slamming his cock into me with enough force to bounce me on top of him.

I need nothing else, then, but this, but him.

I kiss his jawline and quest closer to his lips, and seek his hands with mine. His thrusts pound into me, squelching wetly, sliding slick. I find his hands, his palms, twine my fingers through his, and when his hands close around mine, something shifts.

We cling hand in hand, and I feel his body arch beneath mine as he moves. He thrusts, pounds, his voice growling wordless snarls as his thick wet cock slides into me.

The intimacy of his hands in mine doesn't last long.

He slides his arms behind my knees and tugs my legs apart and flattens them against my body, opening me further, and my hands develop desires of their own, one slithering down to my pussy, finding my clit and swiping, circling, and my other hand clutches at my tits, one and then the other, grabbing and kneading and pinching my nipples. His cock is slamming into me, and I'm lost.

He's growling as he thrusts, arching off the bed, fucking me with utter abandon.

And then his face turns, and his eyes meet mine, and something crackles between us, sparks. I feel as if this thing we have between us has always been there, but now there's also something new, this meeting of his eyes on mine, the blaze in those hard brown chips, the knowledge of something new thawing there.

He fucks me, as he's always fucked me. And I take it, as I've always taken it, because he fucks me so good, so perfectly I cannot exist without his body, without his hands on my flesh, without his cock inside me, without these thrusts, the ones he's giving me right now, hard and brutal and beautiful, slamming so hard each slap of his thighs against my ass is loud in the small room and his cock fills me and pounds into my cunt and stretches me wider.

"Oh fuck, Conrad, yes—yes—" I murmur. "Fuck me. Please, Conrad, don't ever stop fucking me, just like this." I've no control over these words, no way to stop them from slipping out. "Yes, god yes, fuck me, baby. Fuck me so hard."

He snarls and his thrusts increase to a manic, unsustainable pace, the slick wet sucking, squelching of his cock driving in and out of me wild and loud, and I'm groaning, whimpering at each crashing thrust. "Like this, Hannah?" He grunts. "This is how you like me to fuck you?"

"Just like this…" I breathe, and then I can't manage any more words because I'm coming, three of my fingers strumming my clit hard and fast to the rhythm of Conrad's tireless fucking. "Oh—oh—oh—God, Conrad, oh god—"

The moment I come, he does too. The way my cunt squeezes his cock is too much. My climax is his, and his is mine, and he's grunting savagely as he fucks me to completion, and something seizes me deep inside my soul, demanding something new, something—

I claw at his jaw and wrench his head over to face me, and his eyes drill into mine as we lock gazes. "Look at me while you come inside me, Conrad."

"Hannah, fuck—I—fuck…"

His words are lost in the snarl of his orgasm. I feel it unleash. I squeeze, clamping in spasms around his throbbing shaft, and feel his cock spitting seed into me. Wave after wave of hot wet cum spills into my cunt and he grunts and groans and snarls, but I have his face clutched in my hand and I refuse to blink, refuse to look away, and he doesn't either, and some portal is ripped asunder as we stare into each other through this climax, my body seized by wracking, wrenching waves of climax, heat and pressure breaking open, ecstasy smashing through me as he comes, as I come, and I don't know where his pleasure ends and mine begins.

He fucks me through our united climax, and I fuck him back, writhe on him, undulating on top of his hard body.

At the apex of our union, as I'm crying out and he's snarling, we're drawn closer, his movements pushing him closer to me, me to him, and the space between our faces narrows, and I know he's fighting it, because I am, too.

We don't do this; I know this instinctively. This union, this merged clash of pleasure and vulnerability, it isn't us. It just isn't, and I know it, he knows it. We fuck. We don't…mingle souls..

We're still fucking, but it's more than that.

And it's turned into something else entirely when the wringing waves of climax shudder through us and begin to subside, leaving spastic quakes in their place, aftershocks that shake each of us into trembling gasping throes of sated bliss.

And that's when it happens.

I fall into him, and his lips meet mine, and we smash together in a way we've never done before, his lips on mine, his tongue warm and strong and hungry in my mouth, and now a new need is born, and a fierce fury seizes both of us, and what was the end of fucking becomes the start of—

"Goddamn it," Conrad snarls, and rolls toward the edge of the bed, yanking himself out of me and away, stumbling off the bed, cock swaying and dripping strings of come. "Goddamn it, Hannah. What the devil was that?" His voice is low threatening snarl.

"I—I don't know, Conrad." I speak quietly, fearful, shaken from the potency of the moment.

"I feel…struck," he murmurs, wiping at his mouth with the back of his wrist. "Struck down to my very soul."

"Me, too," I whisper.

He doesn't take his eyes from me, his brows furrowed in consternation, as he wraps his tartan around his waist and shrugs into his shirt, stuffs his feet into boots, and then he's out the door.

• • •

Heartache alone isn't enough to keep me awake the whole night. Hope is there too, because even though my memory of our time together is hazy at best, I know that the kiss we shared was something totally new and utterly unexpected for both of us. Which means there's hope for another kiss. And another after that.

I want those kisses. The second, and the third, and the thirty-third, and all the kisses too numerous to count after that.

Does he want the same thing? I don't know. His behavior says not. But the remembrance of the kiss, its intensity, says something else to me. He lost himself in that kiss, for a moment or two, and Conrad is not a man to lose himself easily. Truly, he is a man completely assured of who he is, self-possessed, confident but quiet about it. Losing himself in something like a kiss? I am not at all surprised by his sudden departure, by the fact that he seemed so rocked to the core that he responded with anger.

Not surprised, but hurt.

So, yeah. Hope and heartbreak do not make the best bedfellows. They tend to keep a person awake all night, wrestling with a million unanswerable questions. Worry, too. He's out there, somewhere. Still.

It's well past dawn and he's not returned. He could be sleeping in the stable, but something tells me he's not. He's out there. Doing what? No way to know. Does he love me? *Can* he love me? Has he ever? Will he ever? If I were to kiss him again, would he curse at me and run again? Might he allow the kiss and collect another?

He can fuck me, but he can't kiss me?

The fucking wasn't as significant as the kiss, and the fucking was out of this world. Shockingly, violently perfect.

I *felt* him. Not just his body, but *him*. And I want more. I want all of him. More of the vulnerability, more of the softening of his hard brown gaze.

He'll kiss my jaw, he'll kiss my breasts, he'll kiss my cunt. Every inch of me has felt his lips. Every inch, except the millimeters of my mouth. Until just now. Why did that feel so significant?

I don't know. Answers feel so far away. It's as if I'm missing some essential part of myself. I look at Conrad, and I *know* him. I *know* his touch. It is as familiar to me as my own name, the sight of my hands, as real and vital to me as the blue of the sky, and the warm yellow of the sun, and the grass under my toes, and the taste of a long sharp winter wind with the tang of snow woven through it.

I know his touch. I know the sight of his naked body. The hard muscles, the planes and angles and masculine curves. The taste of him. His skin beneath my lips, the salt of his skin, the musk and tang of his cum as it fills my mouth. I *know* this. But I don't know *how* I know it. I just do. He's as part of myself as my own sexuality. As necessary to me as breathing, as eating, as fucking.

I don't exist without him.

But he won't kiss me.

And I don't understand.

I'm ruminating on Conrad and his inexplicable ways when the door slams open. Dawn is pink on the horizon through the doorway, framing the stout, burly form of Angus.

"Best dress and quick, lass," he says, sweeping in with the wind. "They've caught our Conrad, and will not long delay in separating him from his life."

"Who has?"

He snorts as he throws a cloak on and buckles his belt around his torso. "Who do you think? Markham, devil take him. How he found Conrad here I don't know. Maybe he has a tracker? I don't know. Fact is, he's got him, and we've got to get him back."

Angus is armed to the teeth within a minute. A basket-hilted broadsword on his right hip, his traditional dirk on his left, claymore unsheathed with the scabbard left on the table, a pistol hanging from his belt by a butt-hook, and a musket in his other hand.

I'm still laying in the bed, blinking in surprise.

Angus stomps a boot on the floor. "Well? MOVE! If you wish to see Conrad again alive, you'll get your pretty arse out of that bed."

I scramble out of the bed, tug the now-dry cloak on, and follow Angus out of the house. His horse is saddled, and Conrad's stands waiting beside Angus's. I'm still shoeless, but now at least I have a shift on. Better than nothing. I swing up into the saddle, and Angus does the same. He hands me the musket to hold as he nudges his horse into a trot, and I find it heavy, alien, and frightening.

He nods at me. "Now, ride hard, lass."

Another pell-mell gallop across the highlands, this one in the growing dawn. The storm of the night has passed, leaving a clear sky and sharp bite to the air, quickly turning my bare feet to ice. Exhaustion pulls at me, but worry pulls harder.

Markham won't be merciful, nor gentle. A quick death, I think, would be mercy enough.

I don't know where we're going, but Angus seems to, so I follow close behind him, struggling to stay on my horse as we slant across a rolling hill and down, through a damp, fog-shrouded valley. Past low stone houses, flocks of sheep, which bleat and scatter as we pass. Smoke wreathes from chimneys, and men stand in the grass here and there, watching our wild journey as they tend to their sheep.

Thankfully, our flight is brief. We climb a rise, and as we reach the crest Angus slows so we don't quite breast the apex. He dismounts, beckoning me to join him on the ground. He spends a moment staking the horses in place with enough slack to graze in a wide circle on the hillside, and then he sidles up the hill to peer over the edge. Watching for a moment, he carefully backs down.

"Beat 'em here, sure enough, but not by much."

"What did you see? Did you see Conrad?" My voice is shaky and I feel a kind of fear I've never felt before.

He takes a deep breath. "Yes, I did see him but I've no time to talk. You just stay here, lass. This could get ugly. Keep watch, and if ought goes amiss for us, you mount and ride for my place. Lock the door and don't let anyone in who isn't me or Conrad."

He unhooks the pistol from his belt and hands it to me. "Have this in case you need it. Don't use it unless you have to. It's primed and loaded and ready, all you've got to do is haul back the hammer and pull the trigger. I don't know if you've any experience with such things, but it's only going to hit someone directly before you. So...be sure of your shot." He has his claymore in one hand again and the musket in the other, an unwieldy arrangement if I've ever seen one, as the claymore cannot be swung with one hand, but he seems comfortable with it.

He eyes me, nods, and then he's over the hill. I shimmy up to peek over the edge, and watch as Angus quickly makes his way down the steep hillside, taking cover behind an outcropping of rock.

I look into the distance and, after several long tense moments of waiting, I see Conrad in the distance, approaching on foot, driven by the black mouth of Markham's musket barrel. Four men accompany Markham, those being Martin from earlier and three others I don't recognize, each armed with a sword and musket.

Given their greater numbers and firepower, I can't imagine how this is going to result in anything but quick deaths for both Angus and Conrad. Four muskets against one man? Even if Angus is the doughtiest warrior in the land, I don't see how he'll manage this without dying.

Angus waits until the small knot of men pass almost directly beneath him, and then he peeks up over the outcropping, tucks the butt of the musket against his shoulder, draws aim, and fires. The concussion is deafening even from here, followed by a detonation of white smoke and yellow flame. Then there's the scream of frightened horses and the howl of an injured man, a scrum of chaos.

I lose track of Angus for a moment, and then the wind clears the smoke and I see him, running down the hillside at a speed I wouldn't have believed possible were I not watching it with my own eyes. His huge sword, fully five feet long and as wide as a man's palm, is held in both hands, point skyward and scything in a crushing arc as he leaps the last few feet.

His blow hits a horseman's skull with a crunch that is sickening even from here, blood spraying. Angus yanks his blade free, kicks the horse of the man he just killed to send it into a mad gallop, and then he's darting forward to slam the tip of his sword in a thrust across the distance into a second man's belly. Mere seconds have passed since Angus fired his shot, and three men are dead or dying: the man he shot is on the ground writhing in agony, clutching his chest; the second is still on his horse, head lolling unnaturally to one side, connected by a strip of flesh to his body; the third—Martin—is toppling off his horse with a mortal wound to his gut.

None of the Englishmen have yet managed to get off a shot and it is clear they have been taken by surprise. Markham is off his horse, ignoring Angus, his musket leveled at Conrad who is sprinting for his life, his hands bound in front of him, deking and juking left and right, hoping to throw off the aim, or perhaps even dodge the musket ball that is surely about to whistle his way. Markham takes a knee, hesitates a split-second, and then his musket bellows fire and belches smoke, and I see Conrad stumble, twist, and hit the ground rolling. The second his shot is off, Markham drops his musket and rises to his feet, sword whickering out of the scabbard with a ring that echoes across the valley.

He darts forward, his officer's blade aiming for Angus's belly in a silver blur. I've yet to draw breath to cry for Conrad, who is on the ground writhing in pain, and the battle is already shifted to single combat. I don't see how Angus can move that mammoth claymore fast enough to parry Markham's much smaller and lighter one-hand saber. Angus changes tactics, from the moment he sees Markham move from the kneeling position, Angus tosses his claymore aside to draw his smaller broadsword.

The clash of blades rings like a bell, Markham's thrust turned aside with a neat parry, and then Angus is back-pedaling and desperately trying to parry a flurry of slashes from the English officer. Markham is wicked fast, his sword little more than the silvery blur of a striking serpent. Angus is on the defensive, backing, circling, dancing ever just of reach of Markham's faster, nimbler attacks. Indeed, it seems one-sided, with Angus sure to be on the losing side. It's only a matter of time, it appears. I know little enough about swordplay, but even I can see that Markham is far more skilled at this kind of combat. If Angus had his claymore in the wild heat of melee, it might be a different story, but like this? I fear for him.

I cast a nervous glance away from the sword fight to look for Conrad, but he's nowhere to be seen. There's a damp, trampled patch of tall grass where he fell, stained dark with his blood, but he's gone.

I'm about to leave my position on the ridge when I feel a hand clap over my mouth, a hard huge body pressed against mine from behind.

"Hush, Hannah. It's only me." Conrad's voice, close in my ear, a rough growl. "Do *not* scream."

I nod, and he releases me. I twist in place, and see that's he's shot, a red stain turning the entire left side of his torso red. "Conrad, you're shot."

He shoots me a grimacing grin. "I'd noticed, lass. It doesn't exactly tickle, I'll admit, but I'll live. Didn't pierce me, only grazed my side. 'Twas a close one, but for the now it's only blood." He looks me over, sees the flintlock pistol in my hand, and snatches it from me. "Stay here."

He's gone before I can respond, vaulting the sharp ridge and running slantwise down the steep hillside to where his friend and enemy are still engaged in fierce combat. Angus is bleeding from a slice along his ribs and another to his left thigh. He's slowing, his parries weighted with exhaustion and pain. Markham seems to sense imminent victory, and presses the attack, scoring another hit to Angus's off-hand arm.

Conrad fires the flintlock, and Markham jerks to one side, his red coat stained darker at his right shoulder just above his pectoral muscle. Conrad doesn't slow, though, but continues his mad rush, discarding the empty pistol and bending to scoop up Angus's claymore. He hauls the enormous blade around one-handed, pivoting his entire body to impart momentum to the sword, spinning in place as he catches the hilt with his other hand.

Markham, impossibly, manages to get his saber up in time to block the swing, but his smaller sword is broken in half by the crushing force of the blow. The claymore's momentum is slowed but not stopped, and the blade bites into the round of Markham's already injured shoulder, sending him staggering to one side.

His horse, battle-trained as it is, only trotted away a few yards after Markham hurriedly dismounted, and is now grazing on the grass with the reins trailing, unfazed by the musket fire. Markham turns his stagger into a desperate run, still clutching the hilt of his broken sword in a hand now painted red with his blood. He catches at the saddle and hauls himself into it, gathering the reins and giving the mount a vicious kick to the ribs with his heels. The horse bolts forward in a startled leap, and Markham discards the remnant of his blade in order stay in the saddle as the leap turns into a wild gallop.

Angus is leaning heavily on the pommel of his sword, the point jabbed into the dirt at his feet. He stumbles to one side, limping, and then topples to the earth on his back, gasping. Conrad is there immediately, kneeling by his friend, and I'm not far behind, gathering the skirt of my shift in hand and picking my way more carefully down the hillside.

"Angus, you with me?" Conrad says, as I approach.

Angus groans. "Barely. Markham is a damned fiend with that blade of his."

"Well I know it, having crossed swords with him once before my own self." Conrad gingerly pokes and prods at Angus's injuries. "Bah, you'll live. Shallow cuts, all. He was toying with you, I think."

"That the bastard was," Angus agrees, wrenching himself to a sitting position with a series of grumbled curses in Gaelic. "I wish your aim had been but a little better and we'd not have to deal with him again."

Conrad snorts in irritation. "I've been shot myself, and I was running downhill. Next time you try and see if you can do better."

"It was an idle wish, my friend, not a true complaint," Angus says.

Conrad waves a hand. "I wish the same myself, truthfully. A few inches to the left and that festering pile of English horse shit would be dead."

"Yet he's not, and now it'll be twice over you've wronged him." Angus uses his broadsword to lever himself to his feet, and hobbles toward the corpse of one of the dead redcoats.

Drawing his dirk, he cuts several large swaths out of the coat and shirt, ties them around his thigh, arm, and chest, and then cuts more strips and gives them to Conrad to do the same. Together, then, the two men raid the corpses for useful gear. Gunpowder, musket balls, a spare musket for Conrad, Martin's officer's saber, scabbard, and belt. Conrad makes his way up the hill and reappears a few moments later on horseback, leading Angus's mount. Martin's horse is nibbling at grass a dozen yards away, having stopped after Martin fell off, and Angus fetches the mount for me.

"We should make for Kilchurn," Angus said. "It's the closest to us. Neither of us are Campbells, but they'll not turn us away."

"Agreed," Conrad says. He glances at me. "Are you up for more riding?"

I can only shrug. "Do I have a choice?"

"Not unless you wish to experience the hospitality of the redcoats."

"Then we ride," I say. "But there'd better be proper clothing at the end of it."

I pull myself up into the saddle, flexing my bare toes in the chill.

And so we ride once more. This time, thankfully, it's not a desperate gallop, but a more leisurely canter. Time is still not our friend, however, as both Conrad and Angus are injured and still losing blood.

· · · ·

We ride the night through, each of us drowsing in the saddle. The sun is pinking the horizon behind us when we see Kilchurn castle dark against the rippling waters of Loch Awe.

Not long after, we're in the courtyard, surrounded by kilted, hard-eyed Campbell warriors, waiting for the laird to decide whether to let us in and give us respite from our travels.

It's a long quiet wait, still in the saddle, with Campbell hands holding our reins. After what seems the better part of an hour, a steward emerges.

"You have till tomorrow," he announces, terse and brusque. "Then you'll be on your way. We've no wish to share in your troubles, but the laird will not be so heartless as to turn you out."

"Our thanks," Conrad says.

"Servants are drawing baths, and the laird's niece has been so kind as to provide dress for the lady." The steward pivots sharply on his heel and precedes us into the main hall.

We're not given an audience with laird himself, but then we had no reason to expect this kind of courtesy. All Conrad and Angus are after is a few hours rest, someone to tend their hurts, and some refreshment.

And clothes for me. Even so, we are pushing the limits of hospitality, especially given the trouble we're courting—an English officer with a taste of blood and at least four soldiers slain by Scottish steel.

I find myself in a guest room, a hot bath steaming in a tub, a young girl waiting to assist me. After I've been thoroughly washed and scrubbed and my hair washed and rinsed and re-washed and rinsed once more, the girl vanishes to let me soak away the chill that has lodged in my bones.

The girl freshened the hot water before leaving, so the bath is hot once more, heat leaching the cold away and relaxing me into a grateful euphoria.

Perhaps it turns into a light drowse, warmth tugging me under the veil of wakefulness.

I'm not sure what wakens me. The scent of a man, wool and leather and whisky? The gentle swirl as water is scooped and poured over my breasts? A light fingertip tracing the dark circles of my areolae?

His breath on my ear?

His teeth nipping at my neck?

He's there, doing these things. They all rouse me, each one in turn. I wake with an aching core, thighs trembling, but I don't open my eyes, and I don't move.

"I know you're awake, lass," he murmurs, his voice a rough croon.

I blink my eyes open sleepily, a smile curling my lips. "How do you always know, Conrad?"

He scoops a handful of water over my breasts, watches it sluice over the floating mounds of flesh. Another, and then his hands replace the water, caressing, playing. "You give yourself away. A twitch, a murmur in your throat, a slight smile on these plump red lips of yours, things you can't quite hide. You always know it's me, do you not?"

"Always."

He's kneeling beside the tub, clad in nothing but his kilt. His hair is damp and loose around his shoulders, thick waves of black scraped backward from his forehead. Bandages wind around his torso, stained red where his side is still seeping a bit. There are bruises on his ribs and shadows on his jaw, and a swollen lump on his lip and a cut on his eyebrow. Gifts from Charlie Markham and friends, I assume.

He notices my gaze. "Don't bother thinkin' on my hurts, lass. I've suffered worse after a disagreement with Angus if we've been in our cups." His accent deepens. "Markham is a weak-fisted fart of a man whose only strength is behind that skinny blade of his, and the stronger men he knows. I'll have his head yet, worry you not on that score."

"You broke his skinny blade," I point out.

A fierce grin crosses his lips. "I hoped you'd seen that."

"How could I miss it?"

"I'd have cleaved him in half had he not gotten that blade up in time."

"What will he do now?"

"Retreat to his barracks and put together a hunting party," Conrad says, sounding far too casual about it. "Scotsman is on his menu, I do believe, and I'm his prime target. Angus too, now, and I regret that heartily."

"He doesn't seem to."

"I know, because he hates Markham near as much as I do."

"And why is that?" I ask.

Conrad's expression darkens. "A story for another time," he says.

"What will we do, Conrad?"

A shrug. "Try to stay out of Markham's clutches."

"What does that mean, Conrad?"

He sighs, a slow breath out as he thinks. "It means I'm not sure where we'll go, honestly. I'll have to consult with Angus, come up with something like a plan."

I search him. "You're worried."

"Markham is a dangerous enemy. I'd be a fool were I not worried." He pulls me closer. "But I've other plans for this moment than wasting my breath on Charlie Markham."

"Oh?" I breathe the word.

He doesn't need words to answer. He leans in, presses his nose to the side of my neck, inhaling deeply. His fingers tweak my nipple, sending a thrill through me, and then delve lower, under the water. He turns his face into my throat, lips touching, touching, touching. His finger teases over my belly, and then he touches the pad of a single finger to my clit, and lightning strikes. My back arches as that touch sears through me, sending need billowing hot and wild. As my spine bows, my tits leave the warmth of the water, and his mouth latches onto my flesh, his tongue laving away the water, circling my nipple. And that fingertip of his, it touches ever so gently, teasing in small light circles. Not enough, not nearly enough.

"Oh…Conrad—" I groan.

"Keep quiet, lass. All the castle is rousing."

I bite my lip as he moves his fingertip a little faster, nudging me closer to the edge. The water splashes and sloshes as he moves his hand, and I begin to grind against him, pushing my core against his touch.

Just the tip of his finger, barely brushing the tip of my clit, and it's enough to make me crazy, enough to make me writhe in the tub until water splashes over the side, until I'm gasping through clenched teeth.

Conrad's touch vanishes, and I wrench open my eyes to see him backing away from the tub. He lifts a rectangle of thick, rough wool from a nearby bench, holds it out for me. "Out, lass."

I stand up, water dripping down my body. My tits throb, my core aches. The need to come is a taut, desperate heated tension inside me. He beckons to me, and I step shakily out of the tub; he's there to wrap the wool around me, the loose, rough fibers wicking away the wetness. He scrubs me gently, pats my hair until it's merely damp, and then tugs me from the bathing room into the bedroom. I don't see much but the wide four-poster bed with a canopy, the walls rolled up. There's a window overlooking the loch, glassed in with thick, wavy glass, which is pushed open to let in a light cold breeze,.

He puts my back to the window, stands facing me, the wool wrapped around my back and open at the front, baring a slice of my flesh down my middle from throat to slit. I clutch the edges of the makeshift towel, stare up at him, pussy throbbing, and every fiber of my being desperate to return to the edge of climax and fall over it. His hands touch the upper swell of my hips over the wool.

"I left you wondering, earlier." His voice is low, a quiet, intimate murmur.

"Wondering," I repeat, knowing exactly what he's referring to and how he left me after our kiss. "Yes, that's one word for it."

He shifts his hands under the wool, to my bare flesh, caressing the curve of my hips. I need more of his touch, but I don't say so; I want to hear what he has to say.

"That kiss, though, Hannah. I've felt nothing like it in all my life. It took me by surprise."

"I find it difficult to believe that with all the women you've kissed, you've never—"

"There've been a few other lasses I've kissed, aye, and I'll admit it readily enough, but that kiss, last night—it was...it was singular, Hannah." He stumbles over his words in a way I've never heard from him before—he's not a man to trip up in speech. "It wasn't merely a kiss. The way you felt as I was inside you—all of it. It felt...*different*. And I don't mean the actual physical feel of you."

As I listen to him I trace the lines and ridges and grooves of his torso, the curve of his pecs, the sharp hard furrows of his abdomen. "Conrad, I—it felt different because it *was* different." My fingers find that V-cut and tease it gently. "It was *more*. More of everything. And it... it *meant* more."

"It's always meant something with you, Hannah. You've never been just some lass to me."

"I know. But last night, it meant more. That's why you ran off."

"Now hold on—"

I keep going, "It *meant* something, and that scared you. But it's all right Conrad, I understand. I wish you'd have stayed, but I know why you ran."

"I've never run from anything in my damned life, woman," he snarls.

"You're wrong, Conrad. You ran from me, from what you were feeling." I clutch his waist, leaning back against the stone blocks of the wall, the breeze ruffling my hair.

His touch roams lower and slides around to my backside, cupping, kneading, and exploring the generous swell of my ass. "Perhaps I did. Perhaps it was because I've never had a notion of settling, not for anyone, not anywhere."

"I'm not asking you to do that," I say, looking him directly in the eyes.

"All I know is that if a woman loves you, she wants you at home, a home that is warm and cozy and filled with comforts" he counters.

"You said it, not me." I lean forward, touching my lips to his breastbone; the wool falls off my shoulders, leaving me totally naked in the cool air; my skin pebbles, and my nipples harden to aching diamond points. "Settling has never entered my mind either. I like you *wild*, Conrad. I like you rough. I rode all but naked, did I not? Without complaint, I might remind you. Do I seem like a woman who needs finery and niceties?"

"No, but—"

"No but *nothing*, Conrad Killian." I unbuckle his belt, toss it aside, and tug at his kilt, loosening it slowly. "Take me as I am, or not at all."

"Oh, I'll take you alright," he rumbles, heat in his voice now.

I keep loosening, until the tartan comes loose, and then he's naked, the plaid on the floor around his feet. I take him in my hand and stroke his length. "Promises, promises," I tease.

I stare up into his eyes as I caress the enormous length of his cock. He doesn't move, just stands there with his hands on my ass, watching my small pale hand slide up and plunge down.

"Your hands are magic, Hannah," he murmurs.

"Are they?" I ask, quirking an eyebrow.

I sink to my knees, keeping my eyes on his as I tilt my face to one side and wrap my lips lengthwise around his dick. I can barely fit him between my lips, so thick is he. I taste each vein and slither my tongue over the tautened salty flesh, sliding my mouth from tip to root, tickling with my tongue as I move downward. He groans low in his throat as I repeat the wet stutter of my mouth up and down the side of his cock.

"Jesus, Hannah. The things you do…" he rumbles, scrubbing his hands into my damp hair.

"If my hands are magic," I ask, "then what's this?" One last time I meet his eyes, let him see the small, eager, pleased smile on my lips as I move up a bit further, tilt my head straight…and bury his cock in my mouth.

"Fuck, Hannah, holy fuck." He can't seem to help a thrust, an involuntary shuddering push of his hips, and his hands tighten in my hair. "No words, there are no words for that."

I open my throat and take his accidental thrust, then back away and focus on the broad springy tip of his dick, circling it with my tongue as I bob down shallowly. Then I back away and let him fall out of my mouth. "No? Not one word you can think of?"

He cups my cheeks in his hands, his brow furrowed, jaw clenched, chest heaving. Then his thumb brushes across my lips, as if remembering the kiss. Or perhaps remembering the feel of those lips wrapped around his erection. He slips the pad of his thumb between my lips, and I open for him, let him tug my jaw open.

"More," he whispers, and thrusts himself into my mouth. "That's one word I can think of."

I stretch wide and stare up at him, sitting on my heels, hands on my thighs, and let him slide his cock deeper and deeper into my mouth. His breathing goes shallow and hoarse as he thrusts gently into my mouth, pulls back, then thrusts in again. I palm his ass cheeks and pull him toward me, encouraging him to move. He groans, and his next thrust is deeper, harder.

"Fucking hell, Hannah."

"Mmmm-hmmm?" I hum, turning the question into a wordless encouragement.

He pulls back and now I can swallow properly without him in my throat and breathe for a moment, and then he's pushing in again and immediately pulling back out, and I dig my fingernails into the hard muscle of his ass and jerk him toward me.

He pulls back out completely, breathing hard, abs tensed. "Dammit, lass, you've got me ready to blow already."

I stroke him with both hands, one above the other, plunge my fists roughly up and down as he growls. "What if I told you to let go?"

He's struggling. "I want to come inside you, Hannah. In your cunt. I need to feel you clench around me as you come."

"Yeah?" I keep stroking with my fists, faster now. "You like it when I squeeze around your cock? You like it when I milk your cum out of you?"

"Fucking hell, Hannah, you're driving me mad."

"Good," I murmur. "Be mad. Be rough. Be wild. Don't ask, don't be gentle, don't be sweet, don't be my lover."

I let a string of saliva drip from my lips onto the plump pink round of his dick and then smear it hand over hand down his shaft. Now he's actively holding back, eyes closed tight, abs taut. I plunge my fists around him hard and fast, then, bring him to the edge, until he's gasping and growling.

I can tell he's seconds from coming, and that's when I stand up.

He glares at me. "Not how I thought that was going to end, Hannah," he says through gritted teeth.

"Oh, nothing's ended, Conrad." I reach up and grasp his shoulders, tug him downward. "But you left me unfinished in the tub. Fair's fair, after all."

He lets me tug him to his knees, and I lean back against the rough cold stone of the window ledge, spread my legs wide apart, and bury my fingers in his hair. I clutch the long black locks in my fists, and guide his mouth to my cunt.

"Make me come, Conrad," I say, my voice deep and husky. "Lick my cunt. Fuck me with your fingers."

He goes in, spreading my pussy open with his thumbs, his tongue slatherung wet and hot against my opening and flickering over my clit. I gasp, flexing my hips to push my cunt harder against his mouth. He moans as I writhe, and his tongue probes my slit, pushes in, withdraws and circles my clit, and now I'm helpless to do anything but move against his mouth and gasp.

"Please, Conrad," I groan. "Please."

"Please what?" he breathes.

"Don't stop." I grind into his mouth, clutch his hair and force him closer. "I need to come."

He reaches a hand up and finds my breast, pinches my nipple between forefinger and thumb, pinches *hard* and rolls it between the pads of his fingers, and then his other hand steals up under his chin and he slips two fingers into my slit. His tongue is wild on my clit as he curls his fingers inside my cunt and slides them out and shoves them back in and curls them, and when he crooks them in a come-here motion, he finds that spot high and deep inside me that sends me shaking and shivering and makes me moan.

I'm on the cusp within minutes, and he's relentless in the pursuit of that climax. He knows my body, he knows my cues. Knows when my gasping goes high-pitched and my teeth clench and my hips thrust forward and lock I'm close.

He fucks me with two thick fingers, grinding them in and out of my channel and rolls my nipple, the right one, the more sensitive one. He knows even that about me, which nipple is more sensitive.

"Oh fuck, Conrad, yes, *yes*…god yes, I'm there, Conrad." I grind and writhe and thrash and clamp teeth down on a scream as heat blasts through me and tension snaps into bliss, an orgasm barreling through me like a tidal wave.

My spine arches and my heels leave the floor, my head tips back, and my fingers claw at Conrad's scalp. He suckles my clit between his teeth and works it with his tongue and lips and teeth, and he's pinching my nipple so fucking hard it hurts perfectly, the throbbing a mirror of the suckling of his mouth around my clit and the thrusting fuck of his fingers.

And then, as I'm riding the apex of my climax, he stops it all.

He stands up, catches me up in his arms, his hands under my thighs, lifting me off the floor. We line up so beautifully, so naturally, so perfectly that he doesn't even have to guide himself into me, he just has to lift me up and cradle my core against his and his cock slides into my wet aching cunt so smoothly it makes me cry out in relief. He's inside me, filling me, stretching my pussy open so wide it burns, and no matter how many times I take his cock it still burns and makes me gasp as he fills me, makes me shiver around him, makes me tremble and quiver as he slides deep. Oh, so deep. So fucking deep. I cling to his neck and lean backward away from him, hook my legs around his waist and crush my cunt down around him.

"Oh fuck yes, Conrad. *This*—this is the magic."

"Jesus, Mary, and Joseph—" his cursing voice is raw. "How can you feel more perfect every single goddamn time I fuck you, Hannah?"

"Because this is what I meant, a bit ago," I say, tilting my head forward to meet his eyes, letting him see the ragged vulnerability I'm opening up just for him, because of this. "You and me, Conrad. This? How we feel, together? It's *everything*. It fucking *means* something, god-damn it."

He fucks me, then, his eyes on mine, his cock driving into me over and over and over, pounding into me, and it's so much, so hard, so fast that it's too much and I come apart there, holding on to him, clinging to him. I fall forward and bury my face in his neck, and he hooks his arms under my knees to stretch me even more wide open, so he can fuck even deeper, and then I'm gone, because the way he's fucking me now is glorious, incredible. His cock is drilling so deep his balls slap against my ass and he's driving in until there's no way I can take any more, but I do, and I'm coming, biting his neck and screaming as my second orgasm rips through me.

I'm barely aware of him moving. He drops me on the bed, on my back, and I'm staring up at him, gasping, shaking all over. He's so fuck-ing gorgeous. Long hair wild and loose around his broad, hard shoul-ders, abs taut and ridged with six-pack muscles, cock glistening with the wetness from my still-spasming cunt. His cock stands up straight against his belly, the tip just below his navel, the shaft curving ever so slightly back toward him. His balls are heavy and taut, veined. He's a god, this man. And he's all mine. I wait for him, gasping as the af-ter-shocks ripple through me.

"I need to come now, Hannah."

He climbs onto the bed, kneeling over me. Lifting my legs as he slips back into me, he tucks my feet into his armpits, spreading my thighs apart.

"Touch yourself, Hannah. I need to feel you come once more, while I'm coming."

I'm still throbbing and quivering from the last orgasm, but I press my fingers to my clitoris as he slides slowly home, filling me inch by inch until he's buried against me. He watches himself, watches his cock disappear into my pussy; I watch him. Watch his face contort as he begins to move, pulling back, thrusting in, and I shake as my fingers press just so and circle with a light fast pressure, and his cock hits me every time he thrusts in, hits just right against that magical spot inside me, and I think it's him fucking me that has me ready to come within mere seconds rather than my fingers. It's going to hurt, tearing through me, ripping me apart. I welcome it. My hand slides across my body and finds my nipple and now I'm pinching myself and fingering my clit and he's fucking me in slow hard thrusts, and I'm shaking, thighs quaking, mouth open, eyes wide, lip quivering, a scream stuck in my throat.

"Hannah," Conrad grunts, jaw clenched, brow furrowed, a snarl on his face, in his voice. "Come for me, Hannah. Clench me so I can come."

He fucks into me, and his cock hits that spot, and I come, and I can't stop the scream so I bite down on it and let it seep through the gate of my clenched teeth and I stare up at him, meeting his gaze, refuse to look away as I come, and as I knew it would, it hurts. This pain is beautiful, though, bright and sharp and clear and powerful, a knife slicing inside me, but the pain and the knife are pleasure so taut and exquisite and perfect that it shears through me as an agony of ecstasy.

"Conrad!" I cry, through gritted teeth.

His name becomes a sob, and the sob becomes another cry as the orgasm continues to rifle through me, because he's still fucking, and each thrust pushes me further and further into the climax. I feel my cunt squeezing, clamping, and I bear down as hard as I can, watching him, squeezing with every ounce of strength I have left.

He snarls like a wolf, releases my legs and falls over me. Plants his hands beside my face and I hook my heels around his ass and claw my hands down his back, raking him as I come and come and come, and now I feel it, now I feel him. He's coming.

Oh god, he's coming.

I feel the first spurt, and I swear the hot wet rush makes me come again, and I cry out and my fingers dig like claws into the flesh and muscle of his wide hard back, and I'm writhing under him, thrashing against him, clenching with my vaginal muscles around his driving cock.

He pounds into me, and another wave of his cum fills me, and now I feel it inside me, a wet ocean of his hot seed. Another thrust, harder yet, our flesh slapping together. His cum leaks out of me, again, and again, each time he comes.

He gives me his weight, then, gasping, still rock-hard inside me.

I'm still not sated.

I roll him away to his back, and I surprise him when I slide down his body and take his cock into my mouth and I taste his cum and my juices mingled, taste them together, taste his flesh. It's never enough, no matter how much of him I get, I want more. I need more. I wrap my hand around his cock, slide my fist on the sticky shaft and suck at the head, loving the taste and feel of him, of us, and he groans, arches.

"Jesus fucking Christ, woman, you're gonna make me come *again*."

I moan in my throat because that's what I want—I need it. I'm desperate for him, aching for him, for more, for everything he is, to taste him even as I still quake from the shocks of my orgasm, to taste his cum on my tongue and feel him send it shooting down my throat even as his cum drips down my thighs.

I fist his cock hard and fast and bob around the head with my mouth and suck, and he curses under his breath in Gaelic the whole time, spine arched, heels digging into the mattress.

"Oh fuck, fuck, fuck, Hannah, there it is, Jesus Christ, I can't stop it—fuck, it *hurts* to come this hard—"

I let go with my hands and fuck him with my mouth. Fuck him

desperately, taking his hot, hard erection as far as I can, as hard as I can, and I cradle his balls in one hand and massage them, massage the cum out of them, press a finger to his taint to make it better, make him feel it harder.

"FUCK!"

When I feel him throb and feel the beginnings of his orgasm, I back away so I can fuck just the upper few inches of him with my eager lips, stroke his root with both of my hands and caress the orgasm out of him. He's incapable of words, then, as the climax rips through him.

His cum spurts onto my tongue and I swallow it, lick the head with my tongue and pump more out of him until finally there's nothing left. He goes slack in my hands and I give his beautiful cock one last kiss and then lay his lovely spent member against his belly and climb up his body.

"Fucking Christ and all the saints, Hannah." He cradles me against the warm solid wall of his chest, curls his arm around my shoulders and cups my ass with the other hand. "I'd no idea that was even possible, to come so hard so soon."

I only kiss his chest and trail my fingers over the flat disc of his nipple.

"Hannah." His voice is soft, surprisingly tender and hesitant.

I tilt my face up to look at him. "Hmm?"

He rolls into me. Palms my cheek, thumb brushing across my lips, and then...

He kisses me.

My heart stops, my gut twists. Lurches. My eyes prick hot. I lean up into him, curl my arm around his neck and brush the stubble of his jaw. I kiss him back, and imbue the kiss with every last morsel of desperation I possess, pleading with him silently. My heart aches, twists, yearns. Hopes. Fears.

This time, he doesn't stop kissing me.

How long we kiss, there in that bed, I don't know. At once, for both forever and a moment. We kiss until neither of us can breathe, until we're gasping, panting. Until I feel him hardening at my thigh. I shift, and take him into me, and this time it's slow and languorous. We move together, kissing, his mouth warm and strong on mine, the slide of his cock deliciously slow. How long do we writhe together, thus? I don't know. Not long enough. So long I lose track of minutes, of kisses, of anything but his mouth and the joining of our bodies.

This…there is nothing of fucking in this.

We both come at the same moment, and he pulls me down and kisses me breathless.

He's everything and, here with him, it's so perfect and beautiful.

Yet…why is there a dull heavy throb of dread lodged deep in my gut?

Fear, dread. Loathing. It's there, and I can't deny it, can't shake it, can only push it away and drink in the luxurious, relaxed warmth of Conrad's arms around me, and the throbbing bliss of having just come yet again. I refuse to do anything but soak up the moments I have with him, kissing, making something together with our bodies that is deep and true and real and meaningful and fraught with a roiling sea of emotion.

It's all there is, and it's all I need.

I sleep again, and Conrad snores behind me, spooning me, wrapping me up in his strong arms.

Early the next morning, well before dawn, we prepare to leave. I've finally got some warm clothing thanks to the young woman I met yesterday. I wear a woolen shift, a fine cotton dress, thick stockings and sturdy boots, and a warm cloak fastened at my throat with a bronze brooch marked with the insignia of Clan Campbell. Conrad and Angus are armed for conflict once more, each of them with the Brown Bess muskets taken from the dead redcoats, Angus with his broadsword and claymore and traditional dirk, Conrad with a borrowed claymore—plain and rather more crude than the one taken from him but still sharp and serviceable—and the saber taken from the slain officer Martin, Markham's friend.

The Campbell's wary hospitality extended so far as to provide us with some basic foodstuffs and a small jug of whisky, which apparently is considered a necessary staple of survival.

And, indeed, as we ride in the blustering cold, the jug is passed around and when it comes to me I take a small slug of the fiery, smoky liquor and feel it slide down my throat and hit my stomach like a firebomb, and then the heat spreads through me, suffuses me, warms me. I cough and snort and wince the next time it goes around, but I do drink, much to the men's amusement. The warmth is worth the raw burn in my throat.

We're several hours into the day's ride when I ask again where we are going. This time, Angus and Conrad exchange meaningful glances before Conrad responds.

"Angus is a MacLeod," Conrad says, "so we're heading to the MacLeod laird's castle in Skye."

"How far away is that?" I see the men still shifting in their saddles uneasily. "Why the odd looks?"

"It's a long hard ride to the north and west," Angus answers, "and we've to pass through Fort William to get there. There is no much choice, given our lack of supplies."

"What's the problem with that?"

Conrad rattles the hilt of his borrowed English saber. "It's a massive garrison for the redcoats. If Markham's gone anywhere to lick his wounds and rally forces to find us, it's there. And we're walking right up to him."

"Oh," I say.

"Aye," Angus says. "Oh."

"Isn't there anywhere we could go that wouldn't take us to Fort William, then?" I glance at Conrad. "Your clan, maybe?"

"It's not quite that simple," Conrad says, his expression tight and dark. "Though I wish it were."

Signalling the discussion is at an end, he kicks his horse into a canter, his long black hair flying behind him.

I glance at Angus, who merely shrugs and says, "Touchy subject for the lad. He doesna really have a clan, you see. My own father raised him and I both from the time Conrad was just a wee little lad. We're brothers more than friends, but he's never been really accepted as a MacLeod. Not as such—he's too ornery, too difficult, too given to trouble for that. But he's no other family as such either, so it's Skye or nothing. Edinburgh? Inverness? We'd be alone there as we are now, and Conrad's got enough of a price on his head that it'd be rank foolishness to do anything else. We'd be sold out in a trice. And were he not my brother, I'd not blame them for it either, since his price is high enough it'd keep a family in food for a year. Hard to pass that up, even when it's giving one of your own over to the English for hanging."

"I see," is all I can say.

But, really, I don't see at all. I knew little or nothing of Conrad's past, and what Angus has told me gives me pause—it explains a lot about Conrad.

Angus harrumphs, and rides in silence a few paces. "I'm no so sure you do, lass. We're riding into Markham's very hands. There'll be talk. Which means there'll be a fight. We've few enough friends in Fort William that this could be suicide like as not."

"But *must* we go to Fort William?"

"Unless you've a wish to starve out on the road, yes. We know no one out here who could or would provide shelter. Conrad's name is too well known for that. The Campbells, the MacLeods, they've influence enough to weather the rumors of harboring him. A farmer with little more than a plow for defense? Even the villages we might pass...no, it's too dangerous for them. Markham could and would crush them and burn them out without rebuke." Angus shook his head and sighed. "No, it's Fort William, and we'd best hope we can keep Conrad's name from being uttered too loudly."

"What about you?"

Angus shrugs. "Bah. I've no worry. Markham can do no more harm to me than he already has and I welcome him to try. A price on my head? I'd sell myself to Markham if it meant I could put my dirk in his gullet."

We lapse into silence for a long time after that. Conrad rejoins us after a while and rides beside me, but remains silent, brooding. His hand is never far from his sword hilt. Neither is Angus's, I notice. They're wary, watchful. And, with Markham's tendency to simply appear when least expected, it's not an idle precaution, either.

We ride past dark, and then find the ruins of an old farmhouse on a hillside with just enough of a roof remaining that we can build a fire and hope for shelter from the elements. We sleep in our cloaks, all three huddled together in the corner near the fire, though I notice Angus's eyes glinting in the firelight, keeping watch, and then later I feel Conrad stir and rustle the fire to nudge the embers into life.

We spend days in the saddle, thus. Riding from before dawn to after dusk, sleeping beneath trees or in ruins, keeping watch the night through. Aching, cold, hungry. The provisions Campbell provided lasted us quite a long while with careful rationing, but we're still a day from Fort William when they run out, and hunger gnaws at our guts from then on.

Constant watchfulness, constant hunger, constant cold. The tension is weighty and wearying, expecting Markham at every turn. We speak little, and though Conrad always remains near me, there's little of the tenderness or affection he showed in the room at Castle Kilchurn. I feel his eyes on me, though, and feel the weight of his attention.

We ride, and we ride, and we ride.

I learn to hate the saddle, and the cold of the Scottish Highlands, and pretty much everything else. By the time we reach Fort William, I'm fairly certain I'd sell my soul for a hot bath and hot meal.

We enter the town of Fort William without issue just past sunset— Conrad keeps his head down and has his hood drawn and his hair pulled back in a tight queue. He's always scanning, though. I see his head swiveling constantly, scanning the crowds thronging the streets. There are redcoats everywhere, in singles and pairs and groups, in stomping-boot troops, muskets shouldered, eyes hard, bayonets fixed. Conrad keeps his gaze away from them, finds something to fix his attention on until they've passed.

We all expect to see Markham at every corner, and in every face above a scarlet coat.

My heart pounds in my chest like a hammer on a barrelhead, and I find myself watching closely, eyeing the redcoats, and shifting my gaze elsewhere as they pass by. Angus sits tall and proud, hood pulled back, red hair a flaming beacon, weapons proclaiming him a Highland Warrior. He accepts the attention, I realize. Claims it, and thus keeps it off Conrad.

It's a long winding journey through Fort William, turning here and there until I'm hopelessly lost, although Angus seems to know the way well, wherever we're going.

Our destination soon becomes obvious: an inn—though the word "inn" is a generous appellation. It's a small, dark, dirty, low-ceilinged place off an alley, which is itself well off any busy thoroughfare. There's a bar, with a hoary old man behind it rubbing glasses with a cloth that may have once been white. A few tables, only one of them occupied, and that by a person with a cloak hood drawn and his shoulders hunched, hands cupped around a mug of something hot. There is a booth along one wall and stairs on the other leading up to a short hallway with two doors on either side. If the hovel has a name, there was no sign proclaiming it.

Angus takes a seat one side of the booth, which is in a shadowy corner of the already dark common room, and Conrad and I take the other. The men spend a moment readjusting scabbards to sit out of the way, and I notice they each have their smaller swords easy to hand, with me sheltered on the inside of the booth. Angus slides a coin across the tabletop as the bartender approaches, ordering food and whisky and hot tea and requesting two rooms.

"None o' the rooms are let," the old man grumbled in a throaty, raspy voice. "Take your pick. They're all the same." And then he ambled away, shuffling on a game left leg, flipping the coin Angus gave him across his knuckles.

The food, when it arrives, is…edible, and hot, but of a similar quality as the rest of the inn. But then, the draw of the place isn't the finery of the accommodations so much as the privacy, and the lack of questions asked. The bartender didn't even really look at us as he took our order, nor when he brought it out from the kitchen.

We finish the food and the tea, and then Conrad leads me upstairs and we choose a room. It's the size of a closet, with a straw-filled mattress draped across a rickety makeshift frame taking up most of what space there is. There's a stand in the corner with a pitcher and basin, and a small window overlooking the dingy alley. Bugs scrabble in corners—or at least, I hope they're just bugs. Could be worse things, but I don't really want to know.

All I care about is the bed itself. Straw it may be, prickly and lumpy at best, but it's still a far sight better than the cold hard ground. I collapse gratefully into the bed, still fully clothed, and pull the thick wool blanket up to my neck, and promptly drowse.

Conrad kneels beside me. "I've got to go with Angus, take in some more supplies for the journey to Skye. Stay in here. Don't leave, not for anything."

I nod sleepily, and hear the door open and close, boots on the wooden floor and then, distantly, the door of the inn opening and closing.

I'm not sure how long I slept or what woke me. A sound? A voice? An instinct? All I know is that I wake suddenly and in full darkness. Many hours have passed, and Conrad should have returned by now.

I rise slowly, carefully, and peer out the window. I can make out the entrance to the alley and a bit of the street beyond. At first, I see only shadows, but then as I stare the shadows resolve into shapes. Bodies, male, moving stealthily on careful feet. Musket barrels gleam dull in the dim moonlight, the bayonets fixed. It is hard to tell for certain, but I know there are several men. While their red coats are hard to see in the darkness, the white stripes in an X across their chests is identifiable enough.

My heart thunders.

Have Angus and Conrad been caught already? Or did they spot the redcoats on their way here? What do I do?

Not sit here waiting to be found, that's the truth.

I'm still fully clothed, so I carefully, quietly open the door and peer out into the hallway. I can see nothing, and the inn is deathly quiet. I'm halfway out the door when I see that Conrad's left his claymore by the door, and I don't dare leave it behind. It's a marker of our presence, if nothing else. I move out into the hallway, carrying the huge, heavy sword, which is longer than I am tall. I see another door left partially open.I peek in and see Angus's claymore by the door, as well—they obviously knew it wouldn't be wise to go traipsing off through Fort

William lugging around such mammoth weapons, which is why they left them behind, thinking we'd be safe here one night. I add Angus's sword to my burden, and then close both doors tightly.

I tiptoe to the top of the stairs and peer down. All is silent and dark so far as I can see, so I angle down the steps on silent feet, two giant, enormously heavy swords in my arms. The fire in the hearth is banked, nothing but dull orange coals casting a dim glow on the common room. I hear snoring—the bartender is stretched out on the booth bench.

I hear voices then, English accents just beyond the door.

My heart is in my mouth and fear thrums in my veins, my pulse racing. They're out there, right beyond the door. What do I do? I'm hyperventilating, gasping. There's nowhere to go—no back door, only the stairs whence I came and they are a dead end, and there is a troop of redcoats on the other side of the main door. I'm guessing they have orders to take me.

Or, if they don't have such orders, I don't think I'd like what would happen to me, as a woman, if these soldiers get their hands on me. It's the dead of night and I'm alone, all but defenseless, and they're both the keepers of order and the source of the danger. I'd be raped a dozen times by dawn, no doubt.

The thought has tears pooling in my eyes, a knot in my throat, and bile at my teeth. No. No. I cast one last desperate glance around the inn, and see the bar. As a hiding place it is better than nothing, although surely the redcoats will search here as a matter of course.

I hustle behind the bar, crouching down with my back to the wall, keeping the two huge claymores angled so they won't knock or bump inadvertently.

There's a shelf built into the back of the bar, stocked with old jugs, dusty mugs, a few old rags, sacks of something or other, and a large dagger, the blade bare; unlike everything else under the bar, this blade is clean and dust-free, sharp, well-used and cared for. I won't let them take me without a fight, I decide, and set the swords down as carefully and quietly as I can, taking the dagger in both hands. It's heavier than I expected, the polished wood hilt cold in my fists.

The door creaks open, and a gust of wind blows through the common room. Silence, but for that creak of hinges. Then I hear boots on wood plank floor. There are too many footsteps scuffing and thunking to count, and I have to clap my hand over my mouth to keep from crying out as they pass mere feet away from my hiding place on the way to the stairs. The old innkeeper snores away as the soldiers clamber up the stairs.

I hear doors open, thuds against the walls, scuffles, and voices.

There are a few moments of this, as they search the rooms, then I hear a single pair of boots on the stairs.

"Sir," a young male voice says. "No sign of them. One of the beds is warm from being slept in recently, but no sign of anyone. Just the old innkeeper."

"My source said they'd be here," I hear, and this voice is close, so close, just above me—it's Charlie Markham. "He saw them enter. The girl, at least, should be here."

"I'm sorry, sir, but the rooms are empty."

"Damn. Double damn." Markham is angry, frustrated. "Look again, thoroughly." Louder, then, to the rest of the men. "They can't have gone far, spread out and watch the alleys and doorways. Five guineas to the man who finds them."

Footsteps carry Markham away from the bar, and then I hear snores choke and cease.

"Whass th'meanin' of this?" I hear the old man say, sleep muzzy and irritated. "Got no call to be here. Bugger off, English."

There is a ring of steel, and a hiss of pained surprise, then Markham's voice, "I'm looking for two Highlanders and girl. They were here. Where are they?"

"Dunno, English. Ate, drank, took two rooms. Came and went, coulda been back after I fell asleep. Dunno—dunno."

"They left? All of them?"

"I guess, I dunno. Didn't watch 'em leave. What my custom does is no concern of mine."

"You're lying."

"Why would I lie with a blade to my throat? I don't know nothin', I swear't . Two men were here, with a woman. Ate some stew, drank some whiskey, went up to sleep. Heard feet a while later, but I was—got old bones, right, and the whisky helps the ache, y'know? I like a tipple or two at night's end. Didn't see who left or where they were headed. I swear that's all I know."

"If I find you've harbored them, I'll have your head off myself, old man." A pause. "You know who you had under your roof?"

"No sir, swear I don't know nothin."

"Conrad Killian. Sworn enemy of the Crown, and wanted outlaw."

"I didn't know, sir, I swear I didn't."

Markham spits. "No, so you've said."

The footsteps move away, and then another set of feet can be heard trotting down the stairs. I'm holding my breath, hardly daring to believe they'd just waltz right out without checking behind the bar.

I hear Markham's voice once more, outside. "Smith, pop back in and have one last look. Can't be too thorough." I hear his footsteps recede, leaving Smith to do his bidding.

"Sir."

Feet clomp back up the stairs and can be heard on the ceiling over my head. Finding nothing, he comes back down again. I can hear him kicking the chairs aside, as if someone would be hiding under a table. And then, yes, at last I hear him approaching the bar.

I clutch my dagger in shaking fists, get my feet underneath me, ready to leap.

First I see tips of boots, black, scuffed and worn, and then white leggings. As I look up I see a red coat and a young face, barely old enough to shave. His hands clutch a Brown Bess, the bayonet fixed. His eyes are squinting in the darkness.

As soon as I see him, I leap. It's automatic, without forethought. The dagger is clutched in both of my fists, tip pointing at the ceiling. It scythes upward as I cross the few feet between us. He sees me as I'm leaping, and there's just time for him to register surprise, and to begin bringing his musket to bear, but it's too late. I feel myself slam into his thin body, knocking him backward. My arms jolt, and there's a hard thud and a wet squish, and warmth coats my hands. I stagger backward, and the young soldier is staring at me, blood staining his coat at belly level. He blinks at me, seeming more surprised than anything.

Then…he lifts his musket. The barrel wavers, the tip of his wickedly sharp bayonet circling dizzily, as if he can't quite make it fix on me. He steps toward me, and I shuffle backward with a squeal of fright.

He's not dead yet.

I…stabbed him, but he's not dead. I thought it would happen faster. Bile fills my mouth as I realize I'm not safe yet. I have to…I have to finish it. He'll shoot me, and even if he doesn't hit me, the noise will draw Markham.

I move toward him, but leathery hands snatch the blade from me. It's the old man. He steps in front of me, knocks the musket aside, and drives the dagger neatly into the soldier's throat with one hand, catching the musket barrel with the other and snatching the weapon away. There's a wet gurgle, and then I look away. I hear something else wet and then a heavy thud of a body hitting the floor.

I look, then. I have to. He's on the ground, the young soldier, eyes blinking, feet twitching weakly on the floor. Blood is everywhere. On my hands, on the innkeeper, on the floor.

"Go, girl." The innkeeper's voice is low, steady. "Go, before they send someone to look for young Smith, here."

"What will you do?" I ask, my voice quavering.

"I've friends who can deal with the body quick enough. Won't be the first redcoat to find his end on this floor, and won't be the last." He eyes me. "I knew Killian on sight, and I wish him God's own luck ending that bastard Markham." He waves at the door. "Now…*go.*"

I fetch the swords from the floor behind the bar and exit the inn with one last backward glance. The innkeeper is dragging the body somewhere, blood trailing in a thick dark wet smear.

What now?

I have to get as far from this alley as I can, before someone comes back for the missing soldier. But what if Conrad and Angus come looking me? I can't stay here, I know that much…but where do I go? I've got blood on my hands, wet, still warm and sticky. Fear pulses in my gut. I cast a glance around, see nothing but shadows and the alley walls. I creep slowly toward the main street, listening, watching.

Looking both ways as I reach the end of the alley, I see nothing to the left or right but the empty streets. The town is completely silent.

*Spread out*, Markham had said—which meant they must be everywhere. The redcoats were going to find me. There was no question of it.

I swallowed my fear and chose to turn right, trying to walk quickly and quietly. My footsteps sound loud in my own ears, echoing off the walls all around, surely sending my location directly to Markham's ears. I turn right at the next corner, and then left, and then I'm as lost as could be, with no way of even finding the alley-side inn again. I'm fighting tears and a hot hard knot fills my throat. My hands are shaking so hard the heavy swords rattle in their scabbards—and the damned things are so heavy I'm not sure how much longer I can carry them both.

I don't know how long I wander the streets of Fort William alone. The night is dark and cold and endless, and somehow I manage to keep hold of both swords, though they are a burden that only slows me down. They're a comfort though, a reminder on this endless futile trek on empty shadowy streets that Conrad is real, Angus is real. As I walk I see no one, nor any lights in any window. There is no sign of Markham, either.

I begin to despair as dawn burns dull gray on the black horizon beyond the rooftops. I'm on a side street somewhere, and I hear the lap of water against the docks. I can also hear voices. Many of them. Conversing in low tones in distinct English accents. I'm aware of boots on cobblestone, the rattle of metal. I hear a coarse laugh and smell the acrid scent of burning tobacco.

I halt mid-step, hunch lower and press back against the wall, freeze in my tracks. They're approaching, and there are at least four of them. They're taking their time, meandering slowly, joking, laughing, and smoking, on a patrol they've obviously deemed futile.

I must turn around and try to put distance between the patrol and myself without being too loud about it. The road ahead curves, and then joins another in a sharply acute angle—perhaps I can duck down the other street before they see me. I begin to move, my slow, careful shuffle becoming a tentative lope. I desperately try to keep my steps silent and keep my heels from clacking too loudly on the stone.

"Hush a moment, mate," a gruff voice mutters behind me. "Thought I heard somethin'."

I freeze again.

A second voice: "Bah, a rat most-like. Markham's got us on a fool's errand."

Third voice: "Might be, but this fool's errand means five guineas if we find 'em. Between us, that's a guinea and five shillings each."

"Two men and a woman, in all of Fort William? And none of us even know what they look like. Pair of these Itchland Highlanders, yeah? Whossat mean, then? Red hair? Kilts? And one of those men is Conrad Killian." This is the first voice again. "I've heard talk of that bloke. Right deadly with a blade, they say. I don't think much of our chances if we do come across 'em."

A fourth voice, then. "Stuff and nonsense. He's but one man. Even two of 'em, it's still them against the four of us. Don't be a coward, John."

John, then, the first voice. "You ever see what one o' them claymores does to a man? You're new to these parts, Harry—I'm not. I've seen it. Seen those bloody massive swords cleave a man straight in two, head and guts going one way and the legs another. You can call me a coward all you want, but I've no great eagerness to get chopped down like a damned tree. A guinea and five ain't worth it."

They're only a few yards from me now. I huddle back against the wall, trying to shrink into the doorway I'm hiding in.

I've stopped breathing. My heart has gone wild, thundering out of control. My hands shake, my knees knock, and my stomach is lurching. They're going to find me—they'll rape me and give me over to Markham and the whole night's flight will have been in vain. I'll never see Conrad again.

The footsteps come closer and closer, the soldiers discussing what they'd do with the reward money—most of the answers revolve around alcohol and a certain bordello in London.

I'm a statue as they approach my hiding place, such as it is, not breathing, lungs burning, fear turning my blood to ice in my veins, eyes squeezed shut, childlike, hoping if I refuse to see them they won't see me.

"Oi, mates." The voice is low, male, amused, rough. "Look what we have 'ere."

I open my eyes to see four tall redcoats with muskets in hand, faces rough and unshaven, hair greasy and wet under three-corner caps, white leggings dirty. Black fingernails. Rotting teeth. Foul breath even from two feet away. One clutches a clay pipe, smoke trickling from the bowl. As his companion draws attention to me, he knocks the pipe upside down on the heel of his palm, the cherry dropping orange and fading to the ground, then stuffs the pipe into a pouch on his belt.

"Think this is the slut Killian had with 'im?" The one who first spotted me asked. "I'd lay a heavy wager it is. Look, she's even got their swords."

"Means we must've just missed 'em back at that dodgy inn, then."

"Who cares about them?" Says the man directly in front of me. "We got us a wagtail right in front of us, and no molly officer to keep us off her."

"Markham said—" began the man who had the pipe.

"Bugger Markham. He ain't here." He lunges forward, grabs my arm and yanks me out into the street. "Take a gander at her, Harry. You want to scarper off to tell Markham we found her then have done with it—me and the other lad's'll keep her busy till you get back."

I'm shaking, too terrified to move at first. His grip is weak, thinking me too scared to move—and for a moment, he's right. But then terror turns to action. I pivot as hard and fast as I can, smacking the hilts of the two heavy swords into his ear with a loud clatter, sending him stumbling. As soon as I make impact, I jerk away and start running, still foolishly keeping hold of the swords.

I should've let them go.

I risk a peek behind me, see one of the redcoats on my heels, reaching for me. He catches the trailing end of my cloak and jerks me backward with it. The brooch chokes me and digs into my throat—I'm being hauled backward. I flick at the brooch and it pops free, letting the cloak billow away from me, giving me a few extra paces.

But it's not enough. I know it's not.

I turn a corner, scrabble to a stop, and toss one sword aside. Set the point of the other on the ground, put my foot on the scabbard and yank as hard as I can. The oversized blade rings free of the scabbard, and now I've got a naked blade in my hands as the redcoat rounds the corner.

He stumbles to a halt a couple feet away, grinning even as he pants for breath. "Oh-ho, gonna swing at me are you, love?" He lifts his musket, reaching at his side for the bayonet, circling me slowly as he fixes it to the barrel of his blade. "Come at me, then, if you can even lift that bloody thing."

He's not wrong. It's too damned heavy for me to even attempt to brandish it with both hands. But it's my only chance, my only defense. I back away from him, the tip of the claymore dragging on the cobblestone with a loud scrape. He's grinning at me, lecherous, amused. Just waiting for me to swing, knowing he'll turn the blade aside easily and then I'll be done.

It's then, as I'm backing and circling, that I notice the bottom of the blade where it meets the hilt is wrapped in a short length of leather. A secondary handhold, I realize, allowing better leverage in close range. I shift my grip, so my lower hand is near the pommel and my upper hand grips the leather just above the crossguard. The sword is still absurdly huge and impossibly heavy, but it's slightly more manageable now. I might just get in a hit before I'm taken. I won't make it easy, that's for damned sure.

I keep the point low to disguise my intention, let him close in until he's within range. And that's when I strike. I lunge forward as fast as I can and lift the point up. I feel it hit, and for the second time this night

I watch steel slice through flesh, watch as the palm-width blade scores through his gut. He lurches toward me, eyes wide, brows furrowed, gasping soundlessly. Instinct has me pushing harder, driving the blade deeper, and then he stumbles and the sword is jerked free of my grip.

His bayonet snags in my skirts near my ankles as he tries even still to strike at me, but he's too weak, too near death. He falls, and the weight of the sword drags him toward his belly but prevents him from rolling over. A good two feet of red-stained steel protrudes from his back. Bile touches my teeth and I turn my head aside, spit—but then I find myself bent over and retching, shaking, sobbing. I only allow myself a moment of self-pity, and then I put my foot to the dying man's chest and jerk at the sword. It only comes loose a few inches, and I've got to work it free with no small amount of effort, each jerk of my hands drawing a gasping groan of agony.

Damn me if it doesn't take a hell of a lot longer for a man to die than I'd thought. That was my final thought as I finally get the blade free.

I hear boots on the stone behind me and I spin in place, sword sparking on stone. Two of the remaining redcoats face me, blocking off the street, and then I spin again and see the third. They each have their muskets to shoulder, hammers drawn back.

"Put it down, girlie. You got poor John, and that's a shame. But that just means an extra guinea to split, don't it?" He gestures with the barrel of his musket. "Set it down. I'll shoot you, see if I won't."

I've no choice, then. I lower the sword to the ground at my feet, and immediately one of the soldiers darts forward and kicks it aside, and then I've got hands gripping my arms. I'm thrown to the ground and knees dig heavy and painful into my shoulders. Grubby, eager, dirty hands shove my skirts up. I kick, thrash, scream, but then a hand claps across my mouth, sour, vile, cutting off my scream. A fist plants in my stomach, knocking the air out of me, and then I feel the cold night on my bare lower half, blink against the pain to see leggings lowered to bare a hairy, filthy, engorged male member. I thrash and kick and scream and howl until another fist smashes into my stomach, harder this time, and now I can't breathe, can't even cry for the agony.

He's closer, closer—

I feel him against my thigh.

I try to bite the hand over my mouth muffling my screams, but can't find purchase for my teeth.

There's an odd pause, then. The man about to violate me freezes, spine arching forward, and then I see something red and silver at his chest, pushing through skin and cloth. A sword tip. The man pinning me to the ground with his knees looks up, then throws himself backward, scrabbling away. His hands find his musket and he lifts and fires in one motion. The blast is so loud my ears ring.

Boots plant on either side of my waist, and I cough through musket-blast smoke, glance up to see Conrad, saber in one hand and a dirk in the other, hair coming loose from the queue and whipping behind him in the breeze off the water.

Conrad is faced with two redcoats, one desperately rushing to reload, the other with his musket trained. Conrad hesitates a moment, head swiveling to track each man, assessing. I scrabble out from beneath him, hunker against the wall and watch, fighting sobs.

Conrad's hesitation lasts less than ten seconds, but it feels like an eternity.

The redcoat slams the ramrod down the musket barrel then withdraws. The musket is righted, and powder is poured into the pan.

Conrad's dirk-hand is at his side, and I notice that he's surreptitiously rotated the dagger so he's gripping it by the point of the blade.

The next twenty seconds happen in a blurred flurry.

Conrad hurls himself away from me, toward the reloading English soldier. His left hand flashes and there's a silver smear in the darkness, and then a concussive musket blast and the angry whir of a ball zinging past my face close enough that I feel and hear its passage.

At the same moment Conrad's saber is slicing forward, piercing the breast of the reloading soldier. His dirk missed a killing strike, burying itself in the second Englishman's shoulder, but it's enough to give him the advantage. A jerk to withdraw his saber, and then Conrad is sidestepping and pivoting to thrust.

I hear the wet slice of steel through flesh, and then Conrad is in front of me, lifting me to my feet, snaring me in one arm and crushing me against his chest. "Thank Christ, Hannah—you're alive." He pulls back enough to look me over. "Are you—did he…?"

I shake my head. "No, but it was a near thing." It all hits me like a ton of bricks, and I dissolve into sobs.

He holds me for a long moment, and then lets out a rough sigh. "You've earned a good cry, all you've been through, but we've got to move." He snugs his fist in my hair at my nape, gently but firmly tugs my head back and then his lips touch mine, a sweet, gentle kiss. "Can you run?"

I nod. "Yeah, I—I think so. Not sure I can carry your swords any longer, though."

He frowns at me. "What d'you mean?"

I point at the claymore on the ground, the other a few feet away up the street, opposite the way he came. "I couldn't leave them behind."

He sheathes the saber, snatches his dirk out of the dead man's shoulder and wipes it clean on the same man's leg, then sheathes it. He catches up the sword I'd used, lifting it easily, twisting it in the dim light of near-dawn. "It's blooded, lass."

I point further up the street at the man I killed. "I—he—I—"

Conrad laughs. "I'll be damned. It's no easy feat to wield one of these even with practice." He finds the scabbard and sheathes the blade, catches up the other, peeking at the soldier I stabbed. "Ran him through but good, you did. Impressive, Hannah."

I'm staring at my hands, the blood on them crusted and flaking. The killing of the young redcoat at the inn seems like a lifetime ago, this night has been so long. "There was another. Back at the inn. Markham showed up. Luck alone woke me up before they caught me in bed. I hid…they found nothing and were ready to leave, but…Markham sent a boy back to search one last time, and he found me. I had a knife, and I…I put it in his throat. There was so much blood, but he didn't die. Not…not right away."

402         Jasinda Wilder with Jade London

He's there immediately, arm clutching me close once more. "You did what you needed to, nothing more. Feel no guilt."

"I know, but—"

He squeezes me, and then pulls me into a fast walk behind him. "We have to go, and quick. The shots will have all of Fort William on us."

It's another run, then, through the streets, dodging and ducking and turning seemingly at random, although the unerring way Conrad turns this way and that tells me he knows where he's going.

We reach the outskirts quickly and without further encounter.

"Where's Angus?" I ask, once we're away from the city.

"Ahead."

"Think we lost Markham?"

A negative grunt. "For the nonce, perhaps, but not for long. He knows Angus is a MacLeod, so he'll eventually assume we headed into MacLeod territory."

However, it turns out Conrad was wrong.

Instead of Angus, we find ten redcoats stretched across the road with Markham at the center, muskets drawn.

"Enough is enough, Killian," Markham says. "Weapons on the ground, hands on your head."

Slowly, Conrad tosses his weaponry to the ground, and then places his hands on his head. His glance at me is sad, resigned.

# ❋❋

What can be done? Our hands are bound behind our backs, and we're marched away from Fort William. Not what I was expecting, and it worries me.

We spend hours walking, the English muskets at our backs. We walk past the break of dawn and into mid-morning. Once again the monotony of fear dulls its edge. It quickly becomes clear Markham has some other intention beyond merely putting musket balls in us and being done with it. Something…rather more nefarious, I fear.

Hours pass and time loses its meaning. Weariness accosts me, and when I slow my pace I feel the sharp point of a bayonet in my back. I have no choice but to keep pace.

The day begins to darken into evening, and that's when we reach what appears to be a small crofter's farm. Smoke rises from the main house, but not from the chimney…from the house itself. The structure itself is smoldering, the wreckage charred and ruined. I see no bodies anywhere on the ground outside the house, so I can only assume the worst about whoever the occupants were. Markham guides us to the barn, and then stops.

We turn, standing just inside the open door of the barn. It smells of hay and manure and age, not unpleasantly. There are three ropes dangling from the rafters, tied in hangman's nooses.

"Wasn't originally meant for you," Markham says, glancing at the nooses, "but for the stupid dirty sots who lived here. An old man and his two sons. Informants, you might say. Sold sheep's wool down in Fort William, and any information they might find useful. The old man in particular spent a lot of time in pubs, swilling and listening. We learned quite a bit from him, we did. Of course, he heard talk of you, nothing useful, but that you'd been sheltered up at Kilchurn. Earned him a shilling or two. But then I had myself an idea."

He snaps his fingers, flicks a finger at Conrad, and three of the redcoats bolt forward to press their muskets against him. No escape, no way to fight free...no chance to protect me, even at the cost of his own life.

Markham sidles over to me, draws a wicked, curved-blade dagger from a sheath at his side. He flicks my cheek with the tip, drawing a drop of blood and a pained gasp. Then, button-by-button, he cuts open my dress until I'm left in just the shift. His eyes flick to Conrad now and then, to gauge his reaction. I fight to remain still, stoic, strong.

"MacAllister and his sons were hated by most everyone," Markham says, using the tip of the blade to lift up the hem of my shift. "Including his own clansmen. He was a traitor, you see. So...it wouldn't be too far out of the realm of belief that he'd be killed to silence him. A torch thrown in the night? Quick and easy, and it puts an end to a known informant."

Conrad's chest is rising and falling quickly, heavily, as if he's readying himself for action. I shake my head at him. *Don't*, I plea, silently. Don't.

His eyes only narrow, and I see his muscles clench and tense.

"So then I'm presented with a unique opportunity. The King's justice is too good for you, Killian. Far too good by half. The reward is a pittance compared to the joy I'll have watching you suffer. Oh, I'll torture you well enough, have no fear on that score, but the suffering I'm speaking of?" He palms my breast over the wool of the shift, his grip rough and harsh. "It'll be her doing the suffering, and you watching."

He gestures at me, and two men grab my arms, dragging me toward a noose. I shake, fight, kick, scream, thrash, but it's useless. Futile. All I get for my efforts is a slap across the face.

Markham joins me and the two soldiers at the noose they've positioned me under. One of them lowers the noose a bit, and Markham fits it around my neck. Tightens it. Gestures again, and the slack is pulled taut enough that I'm forced up on my tiptoes or risk choking—it's tied off once Markham is satisfied.

"Once I've had my fill of her," Markham says, gesturing at me, "Well, it wouldn't do to deprive my men, would it? Oh, no. Wouldn't do at all. I imagine we'd all like a turn or two, wouldn't we, Miller?"

One of the soldiers at my side nods eagerly and paws at my buttocks. "Oh, quite, sir, quite," he drawls with an eager leer.

"And you?" Markham shrugs. "I'll finish you off once you've watched your woman here get raped a few dozen times. When I tire of the game, what then? Well, you're guilty of so much no will care I've hung you without trial."

I can't breathe. I can't stay on my tiptoes for very long either, or my calves and thighs will give way. It's a balancing act, a trade-off. Let the slack take over and choke, or fight to remain on tiptoe.

Markham tosses his coat aside, tugs at the laces of his leggings. "You don't mind if I go first, do you lads?"

It's a rhetorical question, of course, and no one answers.

He's in front of me, hands lifting my skirts, dirty fingers digging at my crotch, scraping sensitive skin. I clench my thighs together and try to twist away, determined to resist to the last, even if I die in the act. Markham's hand lashes out and he smacks me across my cheek in a vicious blow that spins me around and leaves me gasping and gagging as the noose tightens and digs into my throat. I'm off balance, choking...

The moment is broken by a shrill, piercing howl and the wild blare of bagpipes, and the air is rent by shouts and screams, and muskets fire and chaos reigns.

I'm dizzy from not being able to breathe, but I see a flash of kilts and red hair, and see Angus swinging his broad sword and stabbing with his dirk, and there are too many other Highlanders to count, a dozen at least, maybe twenty or more.

Claymores, broadswords, an axe, a long spear-like axe…they're all screaming, snarling madmen, these Scots, knees flashing in the evening light. I see more than one fall in a spray of blood as the redcoats gather wits and fire muskets, but the surprise attack has already won the battle before it's joined. The initial broadside of musket fire dropped half a dozen, and then the subsequent rush overwhelms the stunned English soldiers.

Markham is a devil, though, saber drawn in his uninjured hand and swinging and thrusting, turning aside blades, and dancing and dodging, skillful even with his off-hand, though not as deadly as he'd be had he the use of his sword arm.

I'm tripping and tiptoeing, trying to find my balance so I can breathe, so I can at least catch a breath, but I'm dizzy and the world is darkening, shadows snatching at the edges of my vision.

There are fewer and fewer redcoats with each passing second—and then there's only one remaining, Markham.

Angus is in front of me, dirk arcing over my head to sever the rope. He catches me, lowering me gently to the ground. "You're safe now, lass."

My throat is on fire, and I cannot answer, but I nod. Angus is bleeding from a dozen cuts to his arms and face and leg and torso, but none of them are mortal, or even dire.

Conrad, I see, when I finally catch my breath enough to look, is still bound with his hands behind his back, forced to stand in place the entire time…

…watching Markham.

"Wait." Conrad's order is a bark that cuts through the melee, and all goes still and quiet.

A Highlander has his sword pressed to Markham's throat, ready to cut him down.

"A quick death is…how'd you put it, Markham? Too good for you by half." Conrad's bonds are cut, and he shakes his hands out, and then approaches Markham.

His fist smashes into Markham's face, and blood sprays. Conrad seizes Markham by the hair and yanks him off balance, draging him across the barnyard by the queue. When Markham fights for his feet, Conrad stops and plants his boot in Markham's side, and then resumes dragging him across the yard to the nooses.

He hauls Markham to his feet, then fits a noose around his neck and yanks it taut so Markham gags. Then, as Markham did to me, Conrad pulls the slack in the rope tight enough to force the Englishman to his toes. Unbound, Markham can reach up and try to haul himself aloft enough to give himself some slack, but it's not quite enough…and not for long. The noose is too tight to get his fingers under it, too well knotted to be pulled loose; Markham made sure of that.

Conrad watches Markham struggle for a moment, and then he turns away. He walks over to Angus and pauses at his side, "Watch him die, Angus. And when he quits struggling, sever his head."

Angus nods. "Nothing would give me greater pleasure, brother."

There's a hay bale off to one side, tied with twine. Angus drags the hay bale across the yard and sits on it in front of Markham, crossing an ankle over his knee, pulls a small pipe and tobacco from his sporran. Tamps, lights, and puffs. Markham gags, struggles and attempts to lift himself. He begs, but the noose turns his words into unintelligible gargling.

Conrad scoops me up in his arms and carries me to a horse and sets me on it.

I sit and wait as Conrad converses briefly with the other men, clapping shoulders and nodding, and then he swings up behind me and we're off at a gallop. A few Highlanders follow behind us, obviously meant as an escort.

It's an hour before I can muster breath enough to speak. "How did we come to be saved?"

"Angus." Conrad lets the horse fall into a trot. "Those were Campbells and MacLeods. The clans might bicker between each other like so many squabbling children, but we all share a hatred for the English. How Angus got word to them I don't know, but he did, and they came."

"Thank god for Angus, then," I whisper, my voice hoarse. "And the Campbells and MacLeods."

"Aye, thank god for them."

I drowse in the saddle, Conrad firm and solid and warm behind me, his arms cradling me and we ride. Darkness falls and we do not stop, and when I wake again dawn pinks the horizon.

When I wake once more, the sun is making a rare and beautiful appearance from behind the clouds, and Conrad's little home is in front of us. Our escort waits until we're dismounted and then, with a wave, they wheel their mounts and gallop away, as if they haven't just ridden the night through.

Conrad lifts me in his arms and carries me inside and sets me on his bed. I hear him make a fire, and then he's beside me in the bed, curled up in front of me, between me and the door. He's so warm, so solid, so strong. I wrap my arm around his chest and cling to him, and shiver until his body heat warms me, and then I delve under the scrim of sleep.

$$* * *$$

To wake is to succumb to light. The darkness is my friend. Warmth. Peace.

I'm floating, drifting, and all is right.

But...no. All isn't right.

The darkness, the warmth, the peace...it's a lie. I don't want it. It's a prison, this darkness. It's not merely shadows, an absence of light— this darkness is utter nothingness. It's *wrong*. But it's deep and powerful and tempting, hypnotizing. The darkness wants me, it whispers subtle insinuations, plucks with invisible fingers, twines and tangles and twists and tugs.

The darkness wants me.

But I do not want the darkness—if only I could remember *why* I don't...

*Hannah...*

The voice is deep, musical yet rough, familiar and so beautiful—it's *everything*, that voice.

*I'm here, Hannah. I—I'm sorry. I'm sorry it came to this. There's so much I wish I could say to you. So much I should have said already.*

The sadness in that voice is unbearable. It's a deep, abiding, cut-to-the-marrow sadness. Despair. Resignation. Sorrow. He's…he's lost everything.

He *is* lost.

He is why I don't want the darkness.

*Come back to me, Hannah. Please—don't—don't leave me.* I hear sobs in those words. Ten words, eleven syllables, packed pregnant with sorrow. Ragged and raw.

Haunted.

*I—Hannah, I love—no. No! Not like this.*

I strain, push, but I can't reach him. Can't find him. Can't even really hear him, or feel him. I just…I *know* him. I *need* him.

If only I could touch him, see his face, hold him to my breast and whisper to him and cling to him…

If only—

I push against the darkness, but I am—

I don't know what I am.

The brutal bitter black sucks me under.

*Hannah—please.*

I'm trying. I'm trying, I swear.

But the darkness is too strong.

$$**** $$

Conrad.

I jerk upright, a sob in my throat.

Conrad.

I look around, and despair rifles through me, filling me to overflowing.

I'm in the black room once more. Sitting on the plain white cot, the candle flickering beside me. It's down to an inch of wax, now. Rivulets and rivers and puddles of wax cover the table, dripping down the legs. The thought of the candle extinguishing fills me with terror. If that candle goes out? All will be dark. I will be lost in this blackness, alone, forever in the darkness.

I throw myself off the cot, the sob in my throat now emerging. There is no echo. It is a loud, ragged guttural sob, but it does not echo, does not fill the black room. The darkness swallows my sob, as it will swallow me when that candle goes out.

The remaining two torches by the last two doors are both nearly extinguished, as well. Guttering, fluttering.

Conrad...

I stumble in a half-run across the empty, dark, featureless black to the second to last door. I stand in front of it and I shake all over. Everything in me rails against this door. I don't want to go through this door but, at the same time, somewhere within me is the knowledge that this door, somehow, is me.

I am on the other side of this door.

I *have* to go through.

Conrad is there.

I sob again.

God, Conrad. I didn't even get to say goodbye or get one last look. I remember…the flight across the highland, his arms around me, a fire crackling in a fireplace, his chest at my back, feeling at home and at peace and content and safe.

I would have stayed there, I think. I couldn't have gone through the door, couldn't have come back here, knowing I was leaving him behind.

The door in front of me is not black. It is green and very old. The paint is faded, chipped in places. The handle is plain brass, scratched by countless keys hunting for the keyhole. This door…the sight of it cuts me to ribbons and makes the secret, hidden places in my heart ache. I both hate this door and love it.

Trembling, I place my palm on the brass, let out a querulous sigh, and then turn the knob.

I push the door open and step through.

I'm standing in my living room.

This is my home. I feel the truth of this as precisely and deeply as I feel the reality of my name: Hannah Tavistock.

I blink a few times, and the ache in my chest swells to a painful throb. My throat is so tight I can barely breathe.

I look around and take in the features of my living room. The carpet is cream, faded, stained here and there—by the couch there's a wine spill, sprayed with stain remover a thousand times and scrubbed as many times; just inside the entrance from the kitchen is a coffee stain, also often sprayed and scrubbed to no avail; by the front door is a more nebulous brownish stain, from mud, perhaps.

The couch is old and much loved, pale maroon cloth, the cushions indented, the arms scuffed and worn. A side table to the right of the couch, dark brown oak with a single drawer, the top scratched and marred by coffee rings; there's a lamp on it, a glass tube with a cream shade, and the shade is torn in places.

A painting hangs on the wall above the couch, a still life: a bowl of fruit on a table, apples, bananas, pears, and a vase full of Gerber daisies beside it. It's not a very wonderful painting, but it's striking and lovely in its simplicity; in the lower right hand corner is the artist's initials: *HT*. Another painting on the wall opposite the couch, above the medium-sized flat screen TV. This one is a landscape, a lake, and mirror-smooth, reflecting the pine trees ringing the lake. In the center of the lake, the focal point of the painting, is a small rowboat, two figures in it, a man with a fishing pole and a woman with a parasol; there's an *HT* in the lower right hand corner, as well.

My feet carry me to the short hallway off the living room. A bathroom on one side, a closed door opposite, and an open doorway at the end of the hall.

I peek in the bathroom and see the tub and shower, veiled by a plain white shower curtain. The smell of a recent shower fills the bathroom. There is a dark wood pedestal with a freestanding clear glass sink and black faucet. A red blow-dryer sits to one side of the sink, a hairbrush on the other, long strands of blond hair tangled in the bristles. There is a cup with two toothbrushes, one blue, one pink. A tube of toothpaste sits behind the faucet, Crest Whitening, the end curled up. Old Spice Deodorant, Dove Dry Spray. An orange bottle of pills with a white cap, three little pills rattling around the bottom—*Sertraline, 50mg.*

I avoid the doorway opposite the bathroom for now and pad on bare feet into the bedroom at the end of the hallway. The bed frame is old, plain, just a flat rectangle of wood and a smaller one at the foot. Messy, unmade. Lots of thin blankets, a thicker comforter and a duvet folded and draped across the end. Flannel sheets. Only the right side is slept in, the left side is untouched.

There are nightstands on either side with phone charger cords, stacks of books, magazines. There is a man's watch, a Citizen, with a brown leather strap. I don't have to look any closer to know that there will be a thick gold wedding band nestled inside the curl of the strap.

I back out of the bedroom, because knowing that ring is hidden inside the curled strap of the watch hurts, even though I feel like somehow it shouldn't.

I can't avoid the art room any more. The knob is plain brass, worn, and it fits my palm as if made for my hand. It feels warm. It's soothing to hold that knob. I push the door open; the scent of paint fills my nostrils. Outside the window a huge oak tree fills the view, leaves transitioning from green to orange and red. I feel the cool breath of air from the window and breathe it in.

My easel stands in the center of the room. I step closer to it, hands shaking, knees knocking, lungs seizing, as if the easel and the canvas are things I should fear, things that could cause me pain.

I blink, and the ache shifts, sharpens, deepens. I blink again.

I'm dizzy. So dizzy. I close my eyes, feeling everything twist and warp inside me.

When I open my eyes again, everything feels different. Warped, oily, less real. Less true.

I'm disoriented, wobbling within my sense of self, my sense of reality.

I blink and shake my head—

The dizziness recedes, and the sense of reality reasserts itself. But it's still not…quite right. Not quite real. But that thought makes no sense to me even as I think it. Real is real, isn't it?

I don't know. I don't know.

I let out a breath, center myself. Close my eyes.

Tilt, shift, toss, spin; dice in a cup.

I open my eyes once more.

And I'm at my easel, in my art room. The window is open wide, even though it's fall outside and the air is chilly. I'm in an old white button-down of Charlie's, the hem hanging to my knees, the sleeves rolled up to my elbows to prevent them from dipping into the paint on my palette. The sleeves are crusted underneath with old dried paint, red and yellow and green and brown and blue and orange in a million layers. Dabs and drips and smears and smudges of paint cover my shirt. There's paint on the backs of my hands, under my nails, on the tops of my feet, and I can feel it crusted in my hair and on my forehead.

I've been in here working on this painting for so long I've forgotten everything except the brush in my right hand, the palette in my left, the table off to my left cluttered with tubes of paint and a chipped off-white mug full of paint water; "Arnes & Abel Hardware" is printed in blue lettering on the side of the mug. Another mug sits beside the paint water mug, this one much larger and contains coffee, now cold. This mug is my favorite. It was once white, but I painted it with a landscape, trees and a lake and ducks and geese and a moose; it was a project in a university art class I audited a few years ago, when I first got the painting bug.

The door behind me opens, and I feel tension pull at the base of my neck, sending an ache through my skull. I feel him approach, that hesitant shuffle he does when he knows I'm painting and knows how much I hate being interrupted when I'm in the zone.

"Hey, Hannah, sorry to bug you." His voice is low, almost a whisper, as if speaking quietly will give me my focus back. "I've gotta run out for a while. Hit the bank, a few other errands."

"'Kay." I speak through clenched teeth.

I don't turn around. Don't put down my palette. I dab my brush in the deep green I've been working on, trying to get that pine-tree shade of green just right. I place the flat of the brush to the canvas and drag it down an inch, then smear little dabs to either side to create the pine-tree shade.

"I'll—um, I'll be back later."

"Great." I feel him still there behind me, and I know he's working on what else to say. "See ya."

"Love you, honey."

"Mmm. You too."

"Need anything while I'm out?"

"Hmm? Oh, no." I'm faking preoccupation.

In reality, I'm utterly laser-focused on Charlie standing behind me. The feel of him there is like oil slicking the surface of my pristine lake. I need him to leave.

Instead, he shuffles closer, and I smell him, Old Spice deodorant and Polo cologne. Why cologne for errands? But I know the answer. I've known for some time, but I just refuse to face it. Easier and less painful to hole up in my studio and paint and pretend everything is hunky-fucking-dory. He's clean-shaven, I feel the smooth scrape of his skin against my cheek as he leans close from behind, touches his mouth to the corner of my lips. His left hand touches my waist, exactly midway between ribcage and hipbones. I glance down and see his hand. The dusting of hair on his knuckles, slightly darker than the blond hair on his head, which will be carefully and precisely slicked back and to the left. The scar on his index finger from when he was cutting onions and sliced himself open. The bluish-purple veins on the back of his hand. His ring finger, bare. A strip of skin paler than the rest.

I air-kiss. "I'm covered in paint, Charlie. You'll get it on you."

He backs off then and leaves, and I finally breathe in relief when I hear the door click, and breathe even more deeply when I feel the slam of the front door and the smooth clatter of the engine of his sensible, economic four door sedan. I hear him back out, hear him pause at the end of the driveway as he looks one way and then the other, and then backs out into the street. In my mind's eye, I can almost see him do it, that pause on the apron of the driveway, the tail of his little red Corolla just over the sidewalk. His head will swivel, and he'll curve precisely out into the tree-lined avenue. The moment he shifts gears into Drive, his hand will lift, his cell phone will be tucked against his left ear, and he'll call her to say he is on his way.

I wonder where they will meet? The Hilton on Third? The Olde Towne Inn on Main? That little bed and breakfast over on Mackie? The B&B, probably. That's his style.

Quaint, a little old-fashioned, cutesy.

The perfect place to hide his betrayal.

I shake my head to push Charlie and everything else out of my mind. I resume my work and touch my brush to the canvas. I paint a few pine trees, since I've finally got the green mixed to the right shade. Soon enough, I'm back in the zone, everything tuned out except the canvas, the brush, the palette, and the visual memory of the lake scene I'm painting.

I'm so preoccupied with my work that I don't hear the door open, don't feel his approach.

I just feel hands on my waist.

I hiss. "Goddamn it, Charlie."

"I sure as hell ain't Charlie." His voice, oh, it's a sweet sensual rumble that makes my stomach flip. "Watched him leave about twenty minutes ago."

I lean back, exhaling in relief and desire, eyes closing. "Conrad. I didn't hear you come in."

"You get so focused when you're painting." I hear the tiny, amused smile in his voice. "You wouldn't notice if a brass band went through here."

I twist my head to look at him. He's got a week or two of stubble on his jaw, not quite a beard. His black hair is messy, as always, strands dangling in front of his eyes, curling over the top of his ears, brushing at the base of his neck.

"What are you doing here, Conrad?" I hate myself for leaning so fully against him, for being unable to resist nuzzling his jawline. "We can't do this here."

"Yeah…we can."

He takes my brush out of my hand and dunks it into the Arnes & Able Hardware mug. Then he takes my palette from me and sets it on the corner of the table. He spins me in place then touches my chin with the knuckle of his index finger, tipping my face up.

"Take it off, Hannah." He speaks quietly, firmly.

My fingers tremble as I thumb open the top button of my painting shirt. The second, the third. All the way down until it hangs open, revealing a slice of my pale ivory skin, a hint of my core, the inner swell of my breasts.

His touch is rough and reverent as he pushes the shirt off my shoulders. It pools to the floor at my feet, and I'm naked in front of him. He's dressed gorgeously and simply in a pair of faded, ripped blue jeans and a white V-neck T-shirt that's molded to his perfect body. Scuffed Caterpillar boots, dried and caked with mud on the heel and toe. No cologne, no deodorant, just the smell of Conrad, clean and masculine and comforting.

He reaches out, touching a fingertip to the green on my palette then slowly drags it across my nipple, and then in a circle around it.

I shiver and clutch at his arms. He doesn't seem to care that I smear paint on his shirtsleeves. He dabs a different finger in the blue I was using for the lake and traces patterns on my other breast.

That same hand, another finger, is in the brown paint now, smearing and stuttering down the valley between my breasts, down to my belly. His other hand isn't idle, oh no. It finds me wet and ready, delves up into my core. He finger-fucks my cunt and finger-paints my body, but he doesn't kiss me. He simply watches me come apart, a paint-smeared mess, whimpering through clenched teeth as he makes me come.

And then he yanks open his jeans and watches as I fist his beautiful erection and bring him to my opening and he fucks me against the wall in my art room, fucks me so hard the canvases stacked against the wall topple over. Fucks me until I'm screaming his name and panting against his neck and biting his shoulder to muffle the screams.

He holds me, pinning me against the wall, both of us gasping and sweaty. His lips touch my throat and my jaw, but not my lips.

He tugs his jeans up and fastens them.

He steps back, eyeing me—I'm covered in paint, which means a long hot shower spent scrubbing the paint off.

He leaves, then, with my fingerprints in paint on his shirtsleeves and on his skin. There are physical reminders of me on his cheek, in his stubble, on his cock, on his ass, his spine, and his shoulders.

He doesn't *have* to wash away those reminders of my touch...of our coupling.

But I do.

And I hate it.

A seagull haws and caws somewhere overhead; another gull answers, cacophonous, raucous. Waves lap, lap, lap against my toes. Despite the grit under my cheek, I am lazy and content and free and warm and cozy—

A hand descends over my lower back, cups my ass. The hand is large, male, rough, callused. I know this hand. I smile before I even open my eyes.

"Mmmm. I love the way you touch me," I murmur muzzily.

He rumbles wordlessly as he continues to explore the curves of my buttocks. Memorizing them with touch, as if he didn't already know every last inch and curve of me oh so intimately. His hand caresses me across my lower back from hipbone to hipbone, and then his fingertips trace the fold under the bubble of my left ass cheek. His fingers run across the crack and follow the fold to the other side. Across, again, to my tailbone, and then he drags his index finger down the seam from top to bottom. I remain utterly still, eyes closed, a half-smile on my face. I'm just letting him touch me, and I'm enjoying every single second of it.

Now his palm is part of the equation, his huge paw cupping the

424 Jasinda Wilder with Jade London

right globe. Just holding, at first. And then a bit of pressure. Kneading, a thumb digging into the flesh and fat and muscle. A hearty squeeze. Then the left cheek, in an expanding language of touch.

Then his hand is smoothing across both sides, circling, squeezing now and again, fingertips tracing. He does this for a while, sating his appetite for touching my ass.

And then his middle finger brushes down the seam, back up. Down again, and this time he applies a bit of pressure, sliding that fingertip between the globes, just a little. A little more, and a little more, and then I start and gasp when his fingertip brushes against the tight knot of my asshole, and I wonder if that's what he's after.

I'd let him.

God, of course I would.

I'd give him every last part of me, no questions asked, no holds barred. I have, and I will.

Always.

He doesn't even have to ask. He just…*has* me.

I remain still, breathing slowly, trying to relax. But I need a little more build-up first if he wants to put his finger inside me back there. He knows this, though. I don't have to tell him.

He's smiling, I can tell without looking.

"Dirty girl," he murmurs, in that dark bass growl of his, so deep and so strong, like the voice of a mountain, all granite and miles-deep caverns. "You like it when I touch you back here, don't you?"

"Mmm."

"Mmm?" There's a hint of laughter in his echo of my response. "What's 'mmm' supposed to mean?"

I shrug one shoulder. "It means mmmm."

He smacks my ass, *hard*, sudden. The crack of his hand echoes across the lake, and my butt stings. "How about that? You like that?"

"Ow! You bastard!" I reach back to rub where he smacked me, but his hand is there first, smoothing over the spot.

Then he spanks me again, on the opposite side—*CRACK!*—and the echo ripples across the lake.

"Jesus, Conrad!" I open my eyes this time and twist to glare at him.

"You like that, don't you?" His eyes are twinkling.

He soothes the sting with gentle circles of his palm. I stare at him, tensed, waiting for the next spank, but it never comes. He just caresses my ass cheeks, one and then the other, until I'm lulled back into comfortable drowsing, forehead pillowed on my forearms, sand against my cheek.

And then, just as I'm beginning to truly relax into his soothing yet sensual caresses—

*CRACK!*

*CRACK!*

Both sides, one then the other, spanked in quick succession. I try to roll away from him, but he seizes me, drags me onto his lap, face down, my stomach over his knees, my ass in the air. My hands grasp at the blanket we're sitting on, but it's not going to help me. Nothing can, now. He's too strong. He's got me pinned down easily, his hand on my back enough to prevent my escape. And really, deep down, way down where I don't even really dare look too closely, I know I'm not trying to escape. Not really.

But I still put up a pretty good fight. I kick, scream and twist, but it's no good.

His hand cracks across my ass, one side then the other, back and forth, again and again—*CRACK!CRACK!CRACK!CRACK!*—until I'm squirming for real and fighting to get away, my ass on fire, stinging and aching and throbbing.

"Quit fighting, Hannah."

"Stop hitting me!"

"I'm not hitting you, I'm spanking you. Stop trying to get away."

"It hurts!"

He spanks me again, once on both cheeks, and the fiery sting is almost unbearable. But I know he'd never really hurt me—not *hurt* me hurt me—so I force myself to be still, to allow him to spank me. Fuck, it hurts. It stings so bad I can't stand it, the ache spreading through me like wildfire. The spanking continues, hard, god, so hard. I'm squirming despite my best efforts.

And then he tugs my legs apart, keeping me positioned over his knees. One hand goes to my ass cheeks and he smoothes and soothes in circles where the flesh is surely reddened from his palm. And his other hand? He slides two fingers against my slit and teases the lips apart, and then those two fingers glide in, and god, I'm fucking soaked, dripping wet with arousal, absolutely drenched and throbbing. I hear the wet squelch of his fingers going inside me and feel them spearing into me and I gasp a breathy whimper of surprise.

He slides those fingers in and out of me a few times, drags them through my essence until his fingers are coated, and then he brings them out and uses those two middle fingers to brush my clit, and now lightning sears through me at his wet, gentle touch and my hips pivot, pushing back against his touch.

*CRACK!CRACK!*

The spanks are harder than ever and come out of the blue, with his fingers circling my clit, and I'm so surprised I scream, but the pain has shifted, become something else, something deeper and darker. The touch of his fingers to my clitoris is constant and slow and perfect, just the right amount of pressure and speed.

His palm soothes where he spanked, and I fall into the lull of his fingers against my clit, topple willingly into the chasm of impending orgasm, whimper and shift and thrust and push against his fingers—

*CRACK!CRACK!CRACK!CRACK!*

Back and forth, left-right-left-right, and his fingers never slow, and the sting of his spanking becomes a throb that weaves through my trembling arousal, twines around the pulse of nascent climax.

More smoothing caresses again, and his fingers speed up. Faster, faster, his fingers circle my throbbing, diamond-hard clit until my hips are pumping up and down and I'm gasping against the blanket, fists clenching the quilted material.

"Conrad, oh god—" I gasp. "I'm so close."

The climax powers through me, twists and uncoils and seizes me. I begin to gasp and writhe harder, embracing the orgasm, dragging on it as if it were a hit of oxygen for my starved lungs, or a hit of a drug.

But he doesn't let me fall over the edge. He pulls his fingers away from my clit and shoves them deep inside my cunt and fucks me, and his hand spanks me so hard I cry out, his palm connecting across both cheeks, over and over and over, in time with the thrusting of his fingers, and I can't separate the fucking and the spanking, both become one sensation, and my cries are equal measure pain and ecstasy.

I don't lose the edge of the orgasm, even though I need direct clitoral stimulation to come. The spanking and the fucking take the orgasm and wrench it into something else, taking every sensation, every nerve ending, every shred of heat and pressure and multiply it all into a mind-melting, soul-distorting experience.

I'm arching away from his spanking hand and bucking into his fucking fingers, both equally, which means I'm thrashing like a wild animal caught in a trap, screaming, whimpering.

"Please, please, please, please—" I hear myself gasping.

"Please what, Hannah?"

"Come! Let me—fuck fuck fuck! Let me come!"

He stops spanking me, pulls his fingers out of my soaked, clenching cunt, and touches them to my aching clit. Instantly, I begin twisting and writhing and gasping, the touch of his fingers alone nearly enough to push me over the edge.

"Come for me now, Hannah." His words, a direct order, are like a button being pushed.

I obey.

He commands, and I obey.

*Come*, he says, and I hit orgasm instantly.

My scream of release is deafening, rippling across the water and echoing back to us, and the shrill caws of the seagulls mock me.

When I come, crushing and pumping back into his fingers on my clit, he spanks me one last time, and the climax breaks open and crescendos and I can't handle it, can't stand it. I'm coming so fucking hard it's perfect agony.

And that's when he presses one finger, coated with my essence, against my asshole. I'm still coming, still clenching and quivering, and I have no hope of resisting; I don't want to. I want everything he wants to give me.

I'm still coming when his finger delves into my asshole. Just the tip, slipping in.

"Touch yourself, Hannah."

"I just came. I can't—I can't, not so soon."

"Do it."

I shift backward, pulling my body over his lap and tucking my knees under me. I reach between my thighs and touch my clit. Oh god, oh god—it's too much. Too fucking much. I'm still shaking from my orgasm, my cunt is still spasming, and my clit is still hard, erect. I touch myself. And oh god, oh god, oh fuck, it's pure, beautiful torture.

"Make yourself come." His order is firm, brooking no argument.

"Yes, Conrad."

"Good girl."

"I need your cum."

"You'll get it."

"I need your cock."

"Baby, you'll get it. But make yourself come first."

So I find that rhythm, that pressure. No one will ever be able to touch you the way you touch yourself. Your pussy knows your touch, responds to it differently than a man's touch, or a woman's. It's just... different. My touch is firm and quick, yet light. Not quite touching my clit directly, but circling around. And then, when I feel the riptide of climax burgeon deep in my core and my hips begin to quake and thrust, I press three fingertips against my clit and increase the speed and grind against my fingers.

He has one hand on my ass cheek, just holding on, an affectionate, possessive grip. The other hand? He's two knuckles deep inside my asshole, and pushing deeper every moment. Slowly, gently. And then I feel his hand against my ass cheeks and I know he's all the way in, his long thick middle finger deep inside my asshole. Then he pulls out completely. I hear him spit, and then wet warmth touches my asshole and he works it against me and worms that finger into the opening, and now the lubrication of his saliva makes it go in easily. I'm on the verge of coming again and I'm clenching and releasing, and I feel him put his finger into my asshole, but it registers as a deep, perfect, beautiful aching pleasure.

God, yes.

Yes.

"More—" I gasp.

He glides that finger out, then back in.

"Yes, yes…" I whimper. "More."

I feel him add more saliva, and then he's got a second finger inside me and I'm whining in the back of my throat and grinding hard against my fingers and his fingers, and it's so amazing, so much, so perfect, so incredible.

"Take it, Hannah."

"I am, oh god, I am."

Everything is a riot of sensation, then. His fingers, two of them, fucking my asshole. My fingers, wildly circling my clit.

It all congeals and coalesces into a single incendiary infinite moment, a climax crashing through me with the force of a thousand suns going nova. I can't cry, can't breathe, can't scream, can't do anything. I'm seized and spasming violently, breathless, and his fingers fuck my asshole hard and fast and mine are moving faster and then my lungs squeeze and I can scream, and the sound of it startles even me, a scream so loud and so wild it's deafening.

And then I'm sobbing, just absolutely sobbing.

He pulls his fingers free of me and twists me and settles me on his lap and cradles me against his chest.

I cling to him and shudder through the quaking aftershocks.

When they pass, I feel him shifting beneath me. Feel his erection against my hip. I wrap my arms around him and press my face into the side of his neck. I lift up, settle astride him, knees in the sand, toes digging in. I wedge my core against his belly and slide down until I feel his cock nudging me. His palms cup my cheek, his fingers bury in my hair pulling my head back and his eyes fix on mine, fierce and intense. I clutch the back of his neck, writhe my hips until I feel the head of his beautiful cock align with my slit, flutter and roll my hips to settle him deeper, deeper, until he's splitting my pussy open.

"Hannah."

I kiss his cheek. Just below his ear. His temple. Then pull away to meet his eyes, and I pause just like that, his cock almost but not quite inside me.

I hold my breath, lower lip caught between my teeth and then, keeping my eyes on his, I sink down, impaling his thick, throbbing cock inside me.

He groans, and his fingers shake and his eyes widen. "Holy fuck, Hannah."

I settle onto his lap, his dick deep in my cunt. "Don't make me wait, Conrad. Just give it to me. Give me your cum."

He thrusts into me, driving upward with all his power, and his eyes fix on my tits as they jiggle.

"Make them bounce," I murmur. "Fuck me so hard it hurts."

He groans again, long and low. I squeeze around him, and he hisses, and that's his undoing—that squeeze of my pussy around his cock. He claws at my tits and drives with his hips, once, hard, watching my tits bounce. And then he's fucking me, no restraint, no technique, no gentility, just my Conrad fucking me as hard as he can, teeth gritted and groans scraping past those clenched jaws, eyes on mine and on my tits, which he is indeed making bounce, the heavy mounds jiggling to the rhythm of his cock slamming up into my slit.

"Yes, Conrad, god, yes. Just like this. Don't stop. Fuck me until you come."

"Hannah, god, honey…you feel so fucking good. Why does it always get better every time I fuck you?"

"Because you were made to fuck me." I cling to him, lean close and bite his earlobe and then his shoulder. I whisper in his ear. "We were made to fuck each other. You and me, Conrad, just like this. The way you fuck me is so perfect, every single time. You're what I need. *This* is what I need."

"God, baby. Me, too." He wraps his arms around me, one around my shoulders, his hand clutching my nape, the other arm low around my waist, gripping the crease of my hip where my leg bends. "I'm gonna fill you with my cum."

"Oh...*please*, please—fill me until I can't take any more. I want it all. Come inside me. Come all over me." I tangle my fingers in his hair and ride him, my ass hitting his thighs with a loud *slapslapslapslap*, and his cock drives into my cunt with a wet squelch and he's groaning and I'm whimpering and I feel him throbbing inside me, he fits me so perfectly I can feel him tense as he starts to come.

"Oh—*Jesus*—" he snarls, "Fuck, fuck, fuck!"

"Yeah? You're gonna come now, aren't you Conrad?"

"So fucking hard."

"Do it, baby. Fuck me. Come for me." I grip his hair with a rough yank, drive down onto him. "Right now, Conrad. Come inside me."

He obeys me. My command is his undoing. He unleashes, then, driving up into me and spurting deep into my cunt. I groan in relief and delight as I feel his cum fill me, wet warmth spreading through me. I squeeze around him and keep riding him as he tenses and stiffens and loses the capacity to even thrust.

"Oh—my fucking god..." he groans.

But he's not done.

I lift up off him and fall backward to the sand and reach up, grip his thick slick throbbing dick and pull him forward to straddle kneeling over me.

"Paint me with your cum, Conrad."

I pump his cock with my fists and he arches his back and I watch his eyes close in bliss and his hips thrust forward. Cum spurts out of him and splatters on my stomach. I caress his erection, lift up and lick my own essence off his shaft and then he's gasping and more cum drips onto my face, onto my chin and my tongue and my lips and my cheek, hot and wet and sticky and dribbling everywhere.

"Holy shit, Hannah. You're so fucking hot like that."

"Covered in your cum?" I ask, smiling up at him.

"Yeah."

He lifts me up and settles me on his lap again, cradling me against his chest. He tips my chin up with a finger, and my heart hammers. He wipes a thumb over my lips, and then fits his thumb into my mouth; I taste his cum, salty, smoky, musky, *mine*.

He leans down and cups my face in both of his hands, and his eyes are deep and dark and intense and passionate.

His thumb brushes across my lips again, and this time his mouth isn't far away. Closing in, his lips brushing mine.

I close my eyes, tears of happiness trickling down my face as he kisses me…

And then the darkness shifts and coruscates and my awareness tilts forward and tumbles and I'm lost for a heartbeat, for a timeless moment when there is no heartbeat, no me, no heat or cold, or up or down. There are no kisses, no lips, teeth, or tongues, no limbs covered in salt and heat and sweat.

I am aware of nothing at all but a deep, twisting, and razor cold darkness.

• •

Charlie is across the bedroom, fingers laced together on top of his head, shoulders rising and falling rapidly, raggedly. His ass is bare and pale in the moonlight, hips trim and back rippling with muscle. He's staring out the window. I can't see in the gloom and shadow of our bedroom at three in the morning, but I know his jaw is clenching and releasing, clenching and releasing.

A long moment passes in silence. Not even the ticking of a clock breaks the fragile quiet between us. Not even the sound of our breathing, his or mine or ours.

"Charlie, I'm sorry. I don't know—"

"Save it, Hannah. I don't want to hear it again." He doesn't turn around. "You're sorry. You don't know why it keeps happening. You can't control it. It's nothing I'm doing, or not doing. We've gone in circles a million times about this."

And we have, too. So many times. No resolution, no change. Just the same old problem, over and over and over.

"Well I don't know what else to say. What to do."

"Neither do I," he says, still facing away from me, still staring out the window.

I know what he sees, beyond that window: A lake, the far shore nearly out of sight, rimmed in pine trees. The water will be silvered by the moon, gentle ripples distorting the reflection of the waxing half-moon. A thick curtain of pine trees lines the shoreline near our house, framing the one hundred feet of beachfront just off our back deck.

Out in the lake a quarter mile or so is a tiny island. No more than bump in the water, but there's a gazebo on it, white-painted wood. After so many years, and so many generations of people, along with constant exposure to the elements, the paint is fading and shredding off the hand-planed wood. There's a bench in the gazebo, just right for two people to sit on. An iron spike is driven into the big rock at the water's edge, used for tying off a rowboat. Sit out there at night, the sky is a black endless bowl sprinkled with a million, billion stars.

He turns back to me, eventually. He's still hard, rock hard, achingly hard. His cock sways as he walks back to the bed.

"I just wish I could—" He groans as he throws himself onto the bed beside me, on his back, cock jutting away from his body at a shallow angle. "I wish I was better. I wish I knew how to—"

I roll toward him, feel my breast drape against his ribs. "It's not you, Charlie. I've said it—I don't even know how many times. I love the way you touch me, honey. You make me feel *good*." I touch his chest, let my palm linger, drift lower. "I love our lovemaking. I really do."

"I know, Hannah. You say all that, but I just—it's never enough. You never come. I do, and you say it's okay and it felt great, but you just...never come. And no matter what you say, I can't help feeling like it's my fault somehow. My shortcoming."

"But it's not, Charlie."

"You're just saying that to make me feel better." He eyes me as I let my hand drift lower yet. "It's what you always say."

"Because it's always the truth."

Sort of. Mostly.

I think.

I don't say that, though, because those doubts are harbored in the very pit of my belly, under a layer of fear and hope and desperation and heartache. I just want him to…fuck, I don't know. I want to be able to come. I want to be able to come *with him*. I want to be able to lose myself in him. But, in truth, a thousand little things all piled up over the years, making an orgasm ever more elusive.

Even alone, it's hard to get there.

But fucking hell, I don't want to think about any of that. I just want not to be in this moment again with Charlie. I wish I could just… *change* it. Make it not…this.

I want to forget it all.

I want this stupid endless fucking argument to be over.

And I hate the hurt on his face. The frustration.

God, frustration. That's the refrain of my life. It's *everything*. I *am* frustration. We kiss, and it's beautiful; the man knows how to kiss. He's so gorgeous, my Charlie is. My husband is fucking *hot*, and I love that. Fine perfect blond hair, Brad Pitt hair. Pale blue eyes, a sculpted jawline. Muscular, but lean and sharp. Hands that love to roam my body. He kisses me, and he touches me, and I drown in it. He undresses me, and I revel in it. I kiss him and I feel him respond. I yank his clothes off, touch him, caress him, feel him hard and ready for me.

He kisses me and when we're both naked he levers over me and stares down at me with that soft tender affection in his eyes and he fits his hips between my thighs and he's *there* and it's perfect and he feels so good. My belly twists with anticipation and I sigh in happiness as he pushes into me and it's *beautiful*—it's *us*.

And I love the way he moves, the sinuous undulation of his back and the slow stroking of his shaft in and out of me. I cling to him and memorize the way his hair falls over his eyes and the way dots of sweat bead on his forehead and upper lip, and it's such beautiful connection, our physicality, his hands caressing my breasts and twisting my nipples and he's kissing me now and again and thrusting so powerfully and I feel things shift and pulse inside me and I move with him, move with him, push against him—

And then he's groaning, face buried between my breasts, his sweat smearing on my skin, and he's filling me and moving raggedly, blissfully, and that ache inside me is thunder and wildfire and I'm close to some kind of edge and if only he'd move a bit more and touch me and kiss me and turn that thunder and wildfire into—into something *more*—

But he doesn't.

I experimented a little, I learned to touch myself, to bring myself there. But I don't *want* to bring myself there, I want *him* to do it.

And he wants that same thing.

But we never get it.

I never get it.

And the ache never leaves. It's a quiescent but fierce tension low and deep inside me, a quiet desperation, and a need, a yearning for something.

And he notices. He sees the ache building, the frustration mounting.

And then, like tonight, he throws himself off me before release, angst-ridden and full of self-deprecation and self-doubt, and he's hurting and confused, and I'm a complicated tumult of chaotic emotions, too many to name or sort or understand even with myself. The only thing I feel for sure is the frustration, the yawning hunger down deep inside me, so deep it's the very maw of my soul opening and crying out for that thing, that immaterial impossible *something* that I just need down in my bones, in my heart, throughout every fiber of me, and I'm not getting it and he can't give it to me.

But fucking hell, I *love* Charlie.

And I hate the hurt on his features, and I hate the obvious frustration he feels. I can't relieve mine, but maybe I can relieve his.

I cup his erection. "Let me help you, Charlie."

He groans. "Goddammit, Hannah."

"No reason for both of us to be frustrated."

"But—"

"I love you, Charlie. I hate seeing you upset."

"I hate seeing *you* upset. And I just—it's not fair to you—"

"We'll figure it out."

"Will we?"

I quiet him by stroking him slowly, root to tip. One hand. I take my time. Just the one hand, slowly, until he's thrusting into my hand and groaning.

"Be still, Charlie. Just let me do it."

He throws an arm over his eyes and stills, hips ceasing their movement. Curious, I watch my hand slide up and down his cock—almost idly, curiously, almost outside of myself—and see my small hand around his long thick shaft. Slow strokes, my fist burying at his root and then gliding up to the head, squeezing, and sliding down.

"Oh god."

"Yeah?"

"Yeah." He tenses, his fists knotting in the flannel sheets.

His hips lift off the bed, ass flexing. I stroke in the same slow measured gliding movements as he groans through clenched teeth, and then, when I feel him begin to thrust helplessly into my fist, I give him what he needs, the short hard fast jerks, and he hisses and curses under his breath. Cum spurts out of him and stripes across his belly in a thick white line, pooling in his navel. I keep stroking until cum is dripping from him and he's gasping for breath.

He lays there a moment or two, then gets out of bed on unsteady legs, and goes into the bathroom just outside our bedroom. I hear water running, then silence.

I roll over, close my eyes, one hand on the pillow next to my face. I feel Charlie get into bed beside me, but he doesn't cradle in close. He's on his back, arm across his eyes. He's clean, breathing slowly, asleep already.

I know this without having to roll over and look at him; this is what happened last night and the night before that. It's what happened last week, last month.

I stare at my hand. There's a little sticky dot of his cum on the knuckle of my index finger, just enough to maybe cover my fingernail. I watch it, stare at it. I'm curious. It looks like a droplet of pearl in the moonlight. Almost...beautiful, against my skin. Warm, wet. I like it there. I touch my tongue to it, taste it, and I'm shocked by the flavor, the musk and salt and tang.

My mind twirls and whirls and wonders as I drift to sleep, and when I go under, I know there'll be dreams half-remembered, dark erotic things dredged from the deep unexplored recesses of my soul, the dirty filthy places I know nothing about.

Even as I drift into sleep, I ache. I throb. I am deeply unsatisfied.

• • •

"Hannah."

"Mmmmm. Not yet."

"Hannah, babe. Wake up."

"No."

"God, you're cute when you're cranky. You need to get up, Hannah."

"Do not. And I'm not cranky, I'm sleeping."

"It's after midnight. We've been out here all night. You need to go home."

"You're my home."

"I wish I was, honey. I wish I was."

The sadness in his voice is what brings me around. I blink, and see the sky over my head is silver and scintillant with stars, and there's a tiny crescent of the silvery-white moon.

The steady sound of the waves against the big rock—*clup…clup… clup* lull me to the edge of sleep again.

Just as I'm drifting off I hear the *thumpthump…thumpthump… thumpthump…*of Conrad's heart beating under my ear.

He's there, beneath me. His arms are around me and his hands are on my bare ass, possessively. His nose is pressed against my ear, and his voice is a near-inaudible murmur. I feel it rumbling as much as I hear it.

He stirs, and I sit up. We're on a fleece blanket, something I found at a second-hand shop for cheap. It's big enough that we can both lie on it together and have enough leftover material to pull over us if it gets chilly.

We're on the island, the tiny little bump of rock in the middle of the lake behind Charlie's and my house. The gazebo is behind us, and the house can be seen from the other side of the island. Conrad and I always come to this side of the island, out of habit, or superstition, or caution, or all three. It's a private lake—well, not truly private, as in we don't own it, but we're the only house with beach frontage, the rest being owned by the state so, in effect, it is private. Meaning, we don't have to worry about neighbors with telescopes. Probably a good thing, since Conrad and I aren't exactly…discreet about our meetings out here. There's no point in discretion in our case, though, since Charlie is always gone, either working or indulging in his own indiscretions.

Indulging in his own indiscretions… god, what a mess. What a fucking mess.

"I hate this," I say, apropos of nothing.

Conrad hauls me against his chest. "I know, babe. I want better for you. For me. For *us*."

"For us?"

He nods. "I want an *us*. I want you in a bed—a bed that is ours. I don't want to hide or be your secret anymore."

"I want that, too."

"Only you can give that to us, Hannah." His voice is sad, hesitant, as if he's wary of expressing that thought.

And indeed my heart twists at his words. "It's not that simple."

"I think it could be. You don't love him. He doesn't love you… *I* love you. I don't know what's so fucking complicated about it."

I sigh, deeply, and shift away from him, tug my shirt on over my bare breasts, slide on my yoga pants and wiggle my feet into my favorite pair of Toms.

"It's because you're not married, and you never have been," I tell him. "I've been with Charlie for ten fucking years, Conrad. Since I was sixteen and a virgin. I've never known anyone else, never dated anyone else, never...*been* with anyone else—except you, now. And, I'm sorry, but you're wrong about me not loving him. I did. I still do in some weird way. I just—it's complicated."

He stands up, naked. He looks at me and his expression is, as usual, unreadable. He's a hard man to read, Conrad Killian. He lets out a slow, soft, tense breath. Almost a growl.

"It's not really all that complicated, honey—you're *making* it complicated. And I get it, I do. But it's pretty damn simple from where I'm sitting. He doesn't love you. Maybe he did, I don't know. But he doesn't anymore, because if he did, he'd give a shit that he's never made you come. He'd give a shit that he's never made you scream the way I make you scream. He'd give a shit that he doesn't know how wild and crazy you are. It's pretty fucking obvious he doesn't care about any of that. Why? Because he *doesn't love you*. I'm sorry, honey, I hate being blunt about it, but it's gotta be said."

He moves behind me, puts his big hands on my hips. "You've given him too much, Hannah. He doesn't deserve to get any more of you. He hasn't earned you. Maybe you did love him, maybe part of you still does but, honey...you gotta let that go and take what's in front of you, what's good for you, what makes you happy."

He spins me around, tugs me against him, flush, chest to chest, hips to hips, nose to nose.

"Me, Hannah," he murmurs. "*I* make you happy. *I* make you scream in pleasure. You sleep in my arms better than you sleep anywhere else. Fuck, Hannah, everything about us is *perfect*. You're just scared because it's different, and leaving him will be hard. It'll hurt. But it'll be worth it."

I rest my forehead on his chest. "Will it?"

He nods. "Yeah, babe. It will be."

"You promise?"

"I swear on everything I am. I'll spend every single moment of every single damn day making you happy."

"Okay, okay. I'll leave him. Just…give me time to work it all out. To…I don't know. Do it right. I can't just pack a bag and vanish."

"Sure you could. I know a lawyer. It's simple—we get papers drawn up, sign 'em, leave 'em where he'll find 'em, pack a bag, and we just leave. Why not?"

I step back, flush with anger. "Because I'm not that kind of person, Conrad! I'm not going to just…just *vanish* on him! Like I'm ashamed or embarrassed, running off in the dead of night. If I'm going to leave my husband, I'm going to do it my way. I'm going to confront him. I'm going to tell him what's happening and work through the consequences like a goddamn adult."

He sighs, rubbing the back of his neck. "All right, all right. You have to do this your way, on your time. I'm sorry I'm pressuring you."

I step up against him, palms on his chest. "I wish things could be different, Conrad, I really do. But this is what we have, for now. It won't be this way forever."

"It's already been forever," he murmurs.

"I know. For me too." I rest my head on his chest again. "I hate this whole situation. I hate feeling like this. I just want to be with you, but…I already feel guilty and dirty because of this. I hate feeling like a liar and a cheat."

"How do you think I feel, being your lie, being your secret?"

"It's shitty," I agree. "And honestly, I'd be leaving him for making me feel this way even I didn't have you. I'd leave him for pushing me aside like he has. For…discarding me, and not even having the balls to own up to it."

"As well you should."

I push away from him and head toward the rowboat. "I have to go."

He growls. "Tomorrow, babe. Be here."

"I will if I can."

I step from the rock into the rowboat and sit facing the island. I reach forward and untie the bowline, dip the oars into the water and begin pulling. Conrad stands where I left him, still naked, watching me. After a few moments, he folds the blanket and hides it under the gazebo bench. I pull at one oar to turn away from the island and point toward the house, and the dock. Conrad is out of sight and, as always, I have no idea where he lives—he's always just there when I show up. I don't know, and I don't want to know. Not knowing where he comes from or where he goes is part of the mystery, part of what feels so…daring, so thrilling.

It takes me ten minutes or so of rowing to reach the dock alongside our property. I tie up, make my way unhurriedly to the house. Charlie's car isn't in the driveway, so he's still gone. Honestly, he may not even come home tonight. There've been nights when he hasn't come back. "Working late" is always the excuse. He pulled all-nighters fairly frequently before we got married, but had mostly stopped staying all night at the office until recently. Until *her*. Now…he stays out all night, calls it work, and hopes I don't know the difference.

I do. Of course I do: I smell her on him, I see her in his eyes, in the distance between us, how he's stopped trying to touch me pretty much altogether. I just…*feel* her. I don't know her name, don't know what she looks like, or how they met. I don't want to know, either.

Or…maybe I do. Maybe I do wonder, deep down, why I wasn't enough for him.

But it's not me, is it? I gave him everything. Always. And still it wasn't enough. But…why not?

The screen door on the back porch creaks and squeals as I pull it open, slams as I let go and step through. The house is dark and silent, heavy with emptiness. I flick on the lights, illuminating the kitchen. Pale yellow walls, a laminate floor that is old and peeling and warped. Deep, double farm sink. Old, dented, scratched butcher-block countertops. White cabinets, tarnished brass pulls. The refrigerator rattles as it hums. Ice clatters from the icemaker in the freezer. The faucet drips, as it has for years—*dripdripdripdripdripdrip*—each droplet plunking noisily. Two steps in from the door and the floor groans as I step on it. If I was trying to be quiet, to hide my steps, I'd skirt around the slight depression where the floor creaks, but I don't care.

I shower, taking my time in the hot stream. Scrub, lather, rinse, and then spend a few minutes just luxuriating in the relaxing heat. I towel off, wrapping the towel under my arms, and then twist another around my hair. I go back to the kitchen and pour myself a glass of cabernet.

I'm about to take the glass back to the bedroom with me when a shudder runs down my spine.

Conrad steps through the porch door, wearing nothing but a pair of sopping wet swim trunks. Water drips down from his hair to his chest. His breath is coming hard and fast, and his eyes are dark.

"I tried to leave," he growls. "I couldn't."

"Conrad—dammit." I stand in the middle of the kitchen, watching Conrad drip lake water onto the floor.

We stand staring at each other for a long tense moment, and then he moves. Slowly, languidly. As he reaches me, he takes the glass of wine from my hand and touches the rim to my lips. I drink three long swallows, and then he takes it and drains the rest. It goes to my head almost immediately. I clutch the towel at my chest. I'm breathing hard, as if I was the one who'd just swum a quarter mile instead of Conrad. He reaches up, untwists the towel wound around my hair, slowly and gently. Taking it, he towels off his body then tosses it aside.

"Stop me, Hannah." He brushes aside my hands. Nudges a limp wet strand of my blond hair away from my eyes and tucks it behind my ear. "Tell me no. Tell me not here. Tell me not now."

I can't breathe. God, what does he do to me? What is this power he has over me? I just spent hours with him. In his arms, wrapped around me. But yet here he is, not even thirty minutes since I left, and I need him all over again, just as desperately as if it had been a day, or a week. I just...*need* him.

He just stands in front of me for a long moment, staring at me; not for the first time I wish I could read his thoughts, understand how his mind works. He wants me, he needs me as much as I want and need him...that much, at least, is obvious.

His fingers pluck at the folded towel and work it free. I shiver and shudder as the towel falls open and pools around my feet. My nipples harden, my belly tightens, and my core dampens. I meet his hot hungry stare, and I don't miss the way his swim shorts tent as he becomes erect. I untie the string, pull his swim shorts down, and stroke his cock into a full erection.

I expect him to…I don't know, pull me to the floor, or set me on the counter to wrap my legs around his waist. Instead, he turns me around, walks me backward to the counter, runs his hands down my arms from shoulder to wrists, tangles his fingers with mine as he presses me up against the edge of the counter. He sinks to the floor behind me, his nose trailing down my spine, and kneels in front of me. I stare down at him, gasp as he lifts up to lick at my nipples, one and then the other, as they hang over his face. He licks, sucks, and bites them until I'm gasping, and then I feel his fingers slip inside my pussy and I'm writhing for him. It takes but a moment, and I'm aching for him. Ready, needy.

His tongue touches my clit and I'm gone, crushing my core against his mouth, clutching the counter for dear life as his tongue lazily slithers against my cunt. I could reach orgasm in a moment, but he knows me, knows my body. He teases me. When I'm reaching the edge, he moves away, finds his feet. Spins me around so I'm facing the counter, bent over, my hands gripping the edge, ass pushed out. Palms skate down my spine, and then he caresses my ass.

"I'm gonna take you here," he whispers, his voice soft and reverent. "Soon."

"Is that a promise?"

He growls, wordless, feral. "Fucking right it is. You want that?"

"I want everything you have to give me, Conrad." I push against his touch, undulating sinuously.

"We just fucked, Hannah," he says, sounding as disbelieving as I feel. "How do I need you this badly already?"

He lines his cock up against my slit and nudges in. I gasp as he penetrates me, and then whimper as he fills me.

"Because it's not just fucking," I whisper, between whimpers and moans. "It's…more."

"I know, babe."

He shuts me up by slamming deep without warning, so hard I cry out, rocked forward. I push back immediately, arching my back, feeling him fill me so completely I could cry for the fullness, the bliss, and the heady dizzying beauty of being united with Conrad. It's everything, this, with him. Absolutely everything.

I groan low in my throat as he pulls away, hesitates, grips my hips and yanks me back against him. I move with him, grinding into his thrusts, aching, throbbing, desperate to reach the edge. Desperate even more to feel him topple over into orgasm, to feel him come, to feel him lose control. I squeeze around him with my cunt, clamp down as hard as I can and push against him and moan his name and take his cock deep, again and again and again.

"God, Hannah," he groans, "I'm gonna come."

"Do it, Conrad. Come for me. Come inside me."

"I can't stop it."

"Good," I whisper. "Don't. Just let go."

He leans forward, kisses between my shoulder blades, and I feel the moment he decides to let go and just come. Sometimes he draws it out, drags two or three or more orgasms out of me first. This time, though? It's about him. And I want it that way. I grind against his thrusts, undulating, writhing, moaning breathlessly, whispering his name, squeezing around him. He slams into me, faster and faster and faster, until his hips slap against my ass and I'm not moaning for him anymore, but because the way he's fucking me just takes me there with him, the way his big, beautiful, thick, perfect cock hits me just right so deep inside my pussy. I can't help it.

"Oh fuck, fuck." His voice is ragged, and his thrusts falter, and then crash harder. "Hannah, god—"

"Yeah? Gonna fill me with your cum, Conrad?"

"Fuck yeah I am." He slams deep once more. "Right *now*."

And he does. I feel it spurt into me. Feel it feel in wave after wave as he resumes fucking through his orgasm, and I have no choice but to join him, to come with him, to come apart for him. I cry past gritted teeth as my climax rips through me, gripping the counter edge so hard my fingers ache, pushing back against Conrad to feel him fill me deeper.

He finally goes still, falls forward to lean over me, reaching under to cup my swaying tits. "Better every time," he says. "Don't know how that's possible, but it is."

He pulls out, straightens. I feel his cum inside me, a wet warm pool, and then it drips out of me. A droplet slides down the inside of my thigh. He's still behind me, and I feel his hand smoothing and caressing my ass, then delving down and between my thighs. He wipes at my slit with a finger. He touches his finger to my lips, and I lick his cum away, tasting him and me together.

I stroke his slackening cock, wet and slick and sticky with our mingled essences.

He backs away slowly and steps into his shorts. He turns away, pulls at the back door. It squeals as he opens it. I'm aching, but in a different way, now. Needing him. Needing him to just…stay with me. To not leave.

I clench my eyes shut rather than watch him leave.

*Slam.*

The bang of the screen door closing is definite, final.

My heart judders and cracks, and I open my eyes.

Instead of an empty kitchen, I see Conrad. Standing in front of me, palm ascending to cup my cheek.

Leaning in.

Something breaks inside me as he touches his lips to mine, soft, wet, warm, familiar, comforting, arousing, making everything inside me twist and contort and go wild and cry out and plea and sink into bliss.

He's kissing me.

I could weep with joy, and indeed I feel a tear slide down my cheek.

I lean into him, cling to his wrist with both hands, a physical plea to keep his hand there on my cheek, cradling, fingertips behind my ear, thumb on my cheekbone, lower edge of his palm at my jaw.

Kiss me, kiss me, kiss me and never stop—

●  ●  ●  ●

It is three twenty-one in the morning, according to the red digital read-out on the stove in the kitchen. The house is dark. Silent. Empty, but for me.

I can't sleep, so I get up and wander around the house, staring out the windows at the warm, clear May night.

The front window of the house faces the street. To the left is the reflective yellow diamond sign with thick black lettering: DEAD END. To the right, the dirt road stretches away, ending at the two-lane high-way. I can see a pool of dull yellow-orange light bathing the transition from dirt road to old highway blacktop. Across the street are trees, thick and impenetrable, a new-growth forest, elm and alder and ash and oak and maple, the underbrush gnarled and tangled beneath them.

On this side, at our house, one hundred and fifty feet of space is cleared of trees from street to lake. Thick green grass rolls gently down to the water's edge. Our house, small, white siding fading and dirty, concrete porch with a wrought iron railing. Green door, aged, faded, pocked, dented. No screen, no storm door. The driveway, twin ruts in the grass leading up to the low carport. This is home, where Charlie and I have lived together for eight years.

Abruptly, I can't breathe, can't think, can't move, can't do anything. Surely I'm seeing things.

I'm not here, I don't exist, I'm not seeing this.

I'm not seeing this.

But I am.

I see him out there, right now. Charlie, I mean. His car, his sensible red compact sedan is in the driveway, the engine is turned off but is still ticking. There's another car out there, too, a red convertible, far less sensible. It's exotic, expensive, the wheels black, the tires oversized, red brake calipers peeking between the wheel spokes. The interior is probably a creamy tan leather with a glossy walnut finish and digital readouts.

*Her* car.

Bitterness seethes inside me. It wells up, vile and burnt and acidic, in my gut, in my throat.

I see them.

They are shadows and profiles and silhouettes—I would recognize Charlie anywhere, but I don't know the woman.

I can't turn away. They are in her car and he fills the frame of the window. I see her on top of him, in the passenger seat. Her hair is long, wild, and loose. His hands slide up her back, grip her hair, tug her head back, and I see her in profile as she cries out, hand on the ceiling of the car, the other on him as she rides him.

Right out front of our house.

I keep watching. I can't help it.

God, it's all on display for me, the two of them. I can see her tits bouncing, the peak of her nipples, his hands clutching them. I watch him latch his mouth around them.

It lasts for...I don't even know for how long, but I watch every minute of it.

I'm wrapped in my robe. Made of thin T-shirt cotton, dark gray, with a long belt I only loosely knot, it has a tendency to fall open even if I tug the edges closed and tie the belt. I tug the knot tighter and cross my arms over my breasts and watch, my heart in my throat, as she climbs off my husband. He gets out of the car, bathed in the interior LED lights. His jeans are still open as he exits the car, and his T-shirt is in his hand. He doesn't bother fastening his pants or putting on his shirt, he just waves at her and walks toward the house.

She gets out and circles the car, says something I can't hear, and he stops. He goes back to the car, and she leans her butt against the front quarter panel, the interior light illuminating her. Sharp, exotic, beautiful. Thick lustrous red hair, a vivid bottle scarlet. She's wearing a little black dress, or rather, a Little Black Dress, worthy of the caps. It leaves little to the imagination, especially since she hasn't bothered to even pull the garment back into place. It's still rucked up around her hips to reveal that she's not wearing underwear, and the strapless top is out of place as well, leaving her breasts all but bare.

He pushes her back against the side of her car, flattening himself against her. He kisses her. His hands roam, hers explore, and I begin to wonder if they're going to start all over again, this time out in the open. But then he pulls back, a little shakily perhaps. Wipes his mouth with the back of his wrist.

My gut aches.

The way he looks at her…the way she leans back against the side of her exotic sports car, lounging like a contented feline, yet still managing to look somehow…wistful.

It hurts so fucking much, seeing that.

Loneliness guts me. I have no one. Nothing. Just this damn house, the lake, my little island where I go to get away when I need solitude. But I'm alone. So fucking alone.

And he has her, at least, but who do I have? No one.

He's approaching the house now, t-shirt in hand, jeans still open, unzipped, unbuttoned. I leave the living room and climb into bed in my robe. I face away from the doorway of our room. Listen to him putter around in the kitchen for a while. As he steps over the transition from the hallway to our room I hear the slight creak there.

He sits on his side of the bed, shucks his jeans, and leaves them on the floor at the foot of the bed. He rolls toward me.

I smell him.

I smell *her*. I smell their sex.

"At least take a fucking shower, Charlie," I snap.

"Goddammit." A long slow sigh. "It's not what you think."

I only laugh, bitterly.

"What are you going to do?" He asks. "Leave me?"

"And go where?" There's no bitterness in this, only resignation. I've wrestled with this for weeks.

"Exactly." He leans toward me. "For what it's worth—"

"Nothing," I interrupt, "whatever you're about to say is worth nothing."

"Whatever." He sighs, stands up, and the bed shifts as he leaves it.

I hear his step, then the shower running. I pretend to be asleep when gets back in bed, but I'm not.

I'm seeing her. Her hair, her breasts, her effortless sex appeal. The way he looked at her, the way he touched her.

As if he couldn't get enough. As if he was just…drawn to her.

He doesn't look at me that way. Doesn't touch me that way. Doesn't *see* me that way. Doesn't want me that way.

I don't even have the courage to cry. I want to, the tears are building up inside me, but it hurts too much to even cry—

There's paint everywhere. The window is wide open, letting in the cold, late fall air. Tarps are tacked on the walls and draped across the floor. But they are not those blue plastic tarps—these are white painter's drop cloths. There are buckets of paint in every corner, in every color, the tops off, pools of paint mixing on the floor. Green, red, yellow, orange, blue, black, white, taupe, mauve, olive, maroon, sienna, canary, azure, all the colors and shades mixing merging smearing mingling in a lake of pigment.

In the middle of it all, naked, are Conrad and me.

Skin to skin. Hot flesh on hot flesh, cooled by the sharp bite of the November wind from the window.

We roll, twist, kick, and flail. His hand stutters down my spine, dragging five colored trails from shoulder blades to tailbone, each trail a different smear of a dozen mixed shades. His thigh presses against mine, leaving a green splotch, and then my toes scrape his calf, spreading a splash of blue across the muddy coral-yellow-green already there.

He's inside me, moving, sliding, gliding, pushing. Slowly, unhurriedly. Pausing now and then, letting the need build, pulling us both back from the edge.

I fall to my back and he's levered over me, and I cling to his waist with my thighs, hook my feet together behind his back. The paint on my toes is actually toenail polish, ten ovals of vivid red applied moments before Conrad appeared in my bedroom. His hand covers my breast, pressing an imperial purple palm print onto my pale flesh, and then his mouth covers mine and I feel tears start in my eyes and trickle down my cheek, and he feels them and knows them and allows them and doesn't wipe them away or shush them. He just kisses me until I'm sobbing and the paint on my cheeks is swirled with tears, turned to Picasso-like abstractions. He lets me sob while he kisses me, and kisses me, and kisses me, and fucks me with delicacy and gentility.

I clutch him with one hand, slashing forest green smears from the round of his shoulder to his nape, and then I've got two handfuls of his taut hard ass. I smear my hands in the paint at my sides and push at the floor to roll him away and onto his back so I can straddle him, gathering ochre on my index finger and gliding it in rune shapes on his chest, nonsense lines and whorls, his cock seated deep inside me and throbbing and I'm content to sit on him like this and feel him inside me and just hold him there and feel the stretching wondrous aching perfection of him and paint on his body. He holds still, hands tucked behind his head, uncaring of the paint matted in his hair. He watches me, and for once I can read his expression:

LOVE.

It's there and clear and obvious, and we both know it but neither of us say it or even address it. He just lets me see it. I smear my palms across his chest to wipe away the designs I've traced. I swirl my hand through a puddle of charcoal on the floor to my right and then glop it on his chest. Spread it around. Find a puddle of red and drag it through the white to make pink, like I would on a palette.

I draw a heart on his chest.

It's a ragged, uneven heart. Intentionally lopsided, angular, broken.

His brows furrow, and his hands grasp my waist and he thrusts up into me, and I cry out.

Umber on my hipbones. Cerulean on his wrists. Amber streaked

454           Jasinda Wilder with Jade London

with black down the valley between my tits. Orange becoming purple on his belly below his navel, low, where our bodies meet, where I can't help but begin to move, to roll my hips, to slide my ass against his thighs, slathering a dozen shades together in those few points of contact.

Our hands meet, palm to palm, fingers twining, and I crush his hands with mine, cling to him until my knuckles whiten beneath the paint. He moves with me, and our bodies find the rhythm, the roll and crush. We writhe together and our eyes are locked, and then my core muscles tighten and shift and everything inside me crashes into an explosive orgasm and I'm grinding on him hard and fast and using our joined hands for balance until the climax becomes too much and I have to fall against his chest and cling to his neck. Coming apart with sobbing whimpers of ecstasy, I smell the paint and him and us.

He leans over to the side, gently depositing me on my back. He pulls out and sits with his knees astride me.

His hands are at his sides, waiting.

His cock is stark clean white against the whorls of paint covering the rest of his body. From head to toe, we are both creatures of paint and sex and desire, except for where our bodies were joined, and there we are both clean, his cock and my cunt.

I take him in my hands, smear paint on him there too, now. Stroking him slowly from root to tip, I pause to add more paint, smearing and streaking the pigment on his erection until it, too, is covered in paint. He rumbles in pleasure as I glide my touch along his shaft, cupping his balls and massaging them, stroking him until he's thrusting into my hands.

His breathing goes harsh and ragged and his hips flex and his cock grinds through my fist. Pink at the tip, green-blue around the glans mingling into yellow and gray and a touch of white further down. I slide my fist and the colors merge and mix, shades eddying.

He doesn't warn me, doesn't say a word, but I know when it's coming, though. I watch him, and I know his body and I know when he's about to explode. His lip curls into a snarl and his jaw tightens and he growls low in his throat. He lifts up on his knees and reaches down to tweak my nipples, one last greedy touch, and then his eyelids flutter and his abs tense and his cock throbs in my fist.

Cum gushes out of him in a thick white stream. It splashes onto my paint-slathered tits, flowing in a line down to my belly. I stroke him and squeeze at the base and he grunts and spurts again, and this time I aim it to splash onto my face. I open my mouth and taste his cum on my lips and feel it on my chin and in my hair and I keep sliding my fist on his cock and take another load of his cum on my chin and down my throat and on my extended tongue. I swallow his salty musky viscous cum and drag my fist down his cock until he's finished coming, and then he collapses off of me and rolls me into his arms. The paint is sticky on his shoulder. Drying, going tacky.

We laze in the drying paint, content in each other's arms.

"Take a shower with me," I whisper.

He doesn't answer, but we stand up and I lock the door to my paint room. The art we made on the floor there is sacred to me and I won't change it, won't clean it up, won't let Charlie even see it. It's *mine*, that whorl of body painted sex art, fuck art, love art. It's ours.

He lifts me in his arms, carries me to the bathroom and starts the shower, getting it hot.

By the time we're both clean, and all the paint scraped and scrubbed away, he's hard again. I sink to my knees in the tub and the water beats down on my head and neck and back, and I suck his cock until he comes down my throat, and then he trades places with me, kneeling in front of me and hooking one my legs over his shoulder and burying his face between my thighs and licking my cunt until I come with a shuddering sigh. I come so hard I barely keep my balance.

Clean and wrapped in towels, we avoid the fact that he needs to leave. It's getting late and who knows when, or if, Charlie will come home. I still haven't faced him, can't face him, because I don't know what to say, not after all my raging and accusing, not now that I've taken Conrad in every room in this house a dozen times on every surface, in the kitchen, the bathroom, my art room, on the couch, on the back porch, on the dock, in the grass, up against the siding. I've fucked Conrad a hundred times in this house, in every room except my bedroom. Never in there, never in that bed.

He refuses to do that, and so do I.

I can't face Charlie. I can't tell him I've been fucking another man, and that I feel more for Conrad than I've ever felt for Charlie in the ten years we've spent together. That fucking Conrad is utter heaven, every single time, and that he can make me orgasm a dozen times and I'll still need more, that I could fuck Conrad all day every day, all night every night, and never ever tire of the feel of his body, never need rest, never get enough.

I don't know how to tell Charlie that our inability to share intimacy is part of the reason I'm fucking another man. Not the whole reason, but part of it. Charlie's infidelity drove me to it, gave me the excuses I needed to justify what I'm doing. But at the heart of it, it's Charlie and me. It's that he doesn't excite me, doesn't make me come, can't make my heart race, can't push me into desperation. He never did, and he never will, and then I met Conrad, and he does. Conrad gives me all that.

And now it's gone on for too long for me to know how to tell Charlie about Conrad.

The lie is too easy, because there is no lie. Charlie and I are two people living two separate lives, only occasionally meeting here and there, but yet I am still Charlie's wife by law, and I do care about him, in some way. It's just that I'm terrified, petrified, absolutely fucking horrified at the prospect of leaving Charlie for Conrad and discovering that

love isn't real,

mystery doesn't mean romance,

sex isn't love,

there is no us outside of our fucking.

If these things are true, I'll have no one and nothing and Conrad is just

fucking

*everything* to me.

And I wish we could just fuck and ignore love, and pretend this is normal, and just occupy this totally fucked up thing we've created that we're calling life.

"Hannah. You're brooding." Conrad wraps me up in a hug. "I can feel you thinking."

"I don't know if I can do this any longer, but I don't know how to *not* do this."

"Just come with me," he murmurs, for the thousandth time.

I dissolve into a sudden paroxysm of sobs, and his arms tighten around me. He doesn't try to shush me or tell me it's okay, he just tilts my face up after I've cried myself out and touches his lips to mine and kisses me as if kissing me is the only balm that can soothe my pain.

And he's right.

He kisses me and I just want to sink into the kiss, live in, bathe in it, and soak up the memory of it into my soul—

"I don't know where we go from here." Charlie sat on the closed lid of the toilet, elbows on his knees, leaning forward, fingertips pressed together, right toes tapping a nonstop staccato rhythm.

"Me either." I'm in the tub.

The bubbles are up to my throat, the water steaming—almost too hot to stand—and every so often I nudge the hot water knob open with my big toe, slide the drain lever aside to let out some of the lukewarm water and let the hot water fill the tub again.

Charlie lets out a sigh. "Who is he?"

"Does it matter?"

"Yes."

"First, answer me this, who is *she*?"

"I met her at a coffee shop on the way into work."

"And did you fuck her that day? Or was it the next?"

"It wasn't like that." He shifts, leaning back, crossing his ankles out in front of him. "It's not like that."

"What's it like, then, Charlie? Because that's how it seems to me." I slide lower in the water, close my eyes so I don't have to look at him. "I've seen you with her."

"And I know you're seeing someone."

"So? You're the only one who gets to cheat?"

"That's not—"

"Bullshit, Charlie!" I shoot upright, stabbing a finger at him. Suds slip down my chest, and I sink back down under the water once more. "Don't even try to act like you're not jealous."

"So there *is* someone?"

My heart hammers in my chest, and my stomach twists and lurches. "Yes. There is someone."

"Who? How'd you find him? Where—where do you—?"

"Uh-uh. Nope. You don't get to ask me jack shit, Charlie." I hear him huff in anger. "That's not how this works. You cheated first. I would never have cheated if you hadn't."

"And what—that makes it okay?"

I laugh bitterly. "No, it doesn't make it okay. Nothing makes it okay. Cheating is cheating, and I hate myself every single fucking day, and I blame *you* for that."

A long silence, and then when he speaks his voice is low and almost venomous. "You know why I cheated, Hannah?"

"I'd love to know, Charlie."

"The sex was awful between us. It was always awful. For years I kept hoping it'd get better but it never did. You were always just…cold, a dead fish. Like it was chore for you. You'd just lay there and wait for it to be done." He pauses. I glance at him, but he's not looking at me. "You didn't want me. You didn't enjoy what we had. How long was I supposed to just…hope it got better? Ten years, Hannah, and it never got better."

"So you found someone better?"

"It didn't happen like that, but, yeah."

Laughter bursts from me, a harsh bark of pained disbelief. "Wow, Charlie. Just…wow."

I sit up again, this time not caring that the soap bubbles slide down and bare my breasts; we don't have that kind of intimacy anymore, but it does feel like I'm cheating on Conrad by letting Charlie see me naked now. Weird but true.

"Did you ever stop to think that maybe you were at least partially at fault for the awful sex?" It hurts to say all this, but these are things I've been harboring for years.

"I was a virgin when we met, Charlie. That means for our entire relationship, I never knew sex with anyone except you. How was I supposed to know better? And let's get down to the real dirty stuff, shall we? You didn't make me come. How am I supposed to enjoy sex when I never reach orgasm? You always got yours, but I never got mine. I could get there by myself, so it's not like it's impossible to make me come—and yeah, now I'm realizing how much it is your fault, because now I'm with someone who *can* make me come.

"I'm not trying to rub this in your face, really I'm not. It's just the truth. So, yeah, I agree the sex between us was awful. So why didn't you—oh, I don't know—talk to me about it? Divorce would have been better than this. That's where we're at anyway, but now we've got all this bullshit between us. We've both put ourselves and each other through all this bullshit we didn't need. You should have been up front about things instead of sneaking around behind my back and acting like everything was normal."

"Now hold on one damn second—"

"How long were you fucking both of us, Charlie? Because the moment I met…him…I realized I wouldn't be able to stop what was going to happen. And that was the last time I touched you, or let you touch me."

"It wasn't *like* that!"

"You keep saying that, but I fail to see how it wasn't exactly like that."

"It was…complicated."

"Un-complicate it, then."

"It was just harmless flirting at first. We'd be waiting for our coffees at the same time, and we'd talk—"

"If you're married, there's no such thing as harmlessly flirting with another woman. But continue."

"Why do you want to hear this, anyway?"

"Because I'm curious, I guess." I lay back down in the tub and close my eyes. "Honestly, I'm not even really hurt anymore. Now I'm just... vaguely angry and a lot apathetic."

"Apathetic?"

I shrug, sending a series of ripples through the bathwater. "Yeah. I just...don't really care all that much about our relationship anymore. I'm angry with you for being a cheat and a coward, and I'm sad that our marriage is ending like this, but I've found someone who makes me happy and I just want all this bullshit to be done with. I'm tired of feeling guilty, tired of acting like the way we've been living is normal or okay, or anything but completely fucked up." I wave my hand. "So... continue."

He sighs, long and frustrated. "Like I said, it started out as just talking. Then one of my meetings got canceled so I went down to the coffee shop for a refill, and she was there. We sat down and had coffee together. Then we ended up, by coincidence, in line together at Qdoba for lunch. So we ate lunch together, and that turned into a regular thing, coffee in the morning and lunch in the afternoon."

He leans forward again, this time scrubbing his face with his hands. "And for two months that's all it was, just...talking. She's fun to be around, easy to talk to, we get each other's sense of humor, and it—it was just...easy.

"Then...I was leaving work late one night, legit—I got roped into finishing an account and didn't get done till like nine or ten or something. Anyway, she was there. She works in the same building as me, two floors up. I was signing out and so was she, and we went out for drinks. Drinks at the bar led to drinks at her apartment, and...then we slept together. After that—" a shrug, a sigh, hands lifting up in a *what are you gonna do* gesture, "—we just couldn't stop."

"Sounds like how you start dating someone...only you were *married* at the time."

"I know, I know." He passes his hand through his hair. "I didn't know how to stop it."

I glare at him. "Really? Oh, I don't know, how about something like 'I'm sorry, but I'm married so I can't see you anymore'?"

"It wasn't that simple, Hannah."

I think about Conrad, and I sigh. "I know. I get it, I do. When you fall in love with someone, you can't really help it, can you?" I shake my head. "But you were married to me. You owed it to me—to *us*—to end things with me before you started anything with her. That's just common decency. And that part *is* that simple. You may not be able to help how you feel, but you can help what you do about it, Charlie. And *that's* what I'm mad about."

"Yeah, I guess you're right."

The question still hangs in the air, unanswered—

*Now what?*

I mean, it's fairly obvious. I'm already thinking of Charlie and I in the past tense. *Were* married, not *are* married. But who files first? How is either of us going to pay for lawyers? There are so many things to consider, and all of them are painful.

I lied to Charlie: it does hurt. I'm in pain. But it's deep, dark, drowning pain, the kind that wakes me up in the middle of the night, the kind that hits hardest in the most unexpected moments. Shaving my legs, and I remember being eighteen and a brand-new wife to Charles Markham, and him watching me shave my legs and it felt so grown up, living with him, being his wife, having a house together, a life together.

Or remembering Charlie watching me put my bra on. He thought it was so weird that I'd hook the clasps together in front of me so the bra was backwards, the cups at my back, and then when the clasps were fastened I'd spin it around and slide my arms through the straps and then stuff my tits into the cups. He thought the process was fascinating.

The memories hurt. It all hurts.

In the bath, facing him, the reality of our crumbling marriage set out in stark and unavoidable relief, I lift my hand out of the water and stare at my ring finger. There is a thin strip of slightly whiter flesh where my rings sat for eight years. Those rings are on the vanity counter. The engagement ring is a small diamond solitaire, white gold. The wedding band is plain, a narrow circle of thin white gold, unadorned. It sits on an angle, resting on the engagement ring.

"Hand me a towel, would you?" I ask.

Charlie gets a towel from under the sink and hands it to me. I stand up and wrap the towel around my torso. I step out of the tub, dripping on the tile and on Charlie. I grab the two rings from the counter, hold them up, and stare at them.

I hand them to him, placing them gently in his open palm. "I'm leaving."

He stands up, watching me leave the bathroom. "Hannah, wait."

I stop, turn around, and meet his eyes.

"I—I'm sorry." There's genuine sorrow in his eyes, along with pain. "Me too."

He reaches for me and tugs me into a warm embrace.

We're both exhausted, but relieved. We know things are at an end for us, but we've acknowledged what we had. We slip into bed together, uncomfortable and awkward. Charlie falls asleep right away. As he sleeps, I think about the family I lost, and I'm reminded about why I was adamant about not taking Charlie's name when we married.

$$* * *$$

"My name is all I have left of my family, Charlie."

He cradles me closer; we're naked, in the afterglow. I stare at the small diamond and thin silver band on my ring finger, placed there by Charlie a week ago in a courthouse wedding the day I turned eighteen.

Rain hammers on the roof and beats against the window. "I know, but—I just…it's important to me."

I stifle a sigh of irritation. "What about what's important to me? I'm an orphan, Charlie. I've got no one except you. Literally no family at all."

"I know, Hannah, I know. But you're my wife now. You're supposed to take my name."

"Lots of women keep their name. Celebrities do it all the time. It doesn't mean they're less married or anything, they're just keeping their name."

"But you're not a celebrity. They do it because their name is part of their brand. Angelina Jolie didn't suddenly become Angelina Pitt."

I can't answer for a while because I'm too upset.

After a few minutes of tense silence, I state it outright. "I'm not changing my last name, Charlie."

"Hannah, come on."

I sit up, pressing the flat sheet against my chest. "You can get mad all you want, but I'm not changing my mind. I've been telling you this since you asked me to marry you—I told you then and I'm telling you now, I'm *not* changing my last name. I'm not hyphenating it, either. I'm Hannah Tavistock, and that's not going to change. And if that's such a big deal to you, then you shouldn't have married me."

"I thought you'd change your mind."

"Well…you thought wrong," I say. "Listen, *please*, Charlie, listen to me. I love you…but me not taking your last name isn't—it's not about you. It's about me needing some kind of connection to my past. I'm eighteen years old, and I've been on my own since I was nine. I have basically no memories of my family at all, just…vague impressions my parents, that's it. All I've got is their name. Please try to understand. I've already lost them, and I just—I have to try to hold on to some part of them. I *have* to."

He's silent for a long, long time. If it weren't for the fact that he was staring at the ceiling, blinking now and again, I'd think he had fallen asleep. Eventually he lets out a slow breath. "Okay. All right, babe. I get it."

He sounds bitter.

"Do you?" I ask.

He glances at me. "As much as I can, yes. I know you said it's not about me, and it's not. But it still hurts. I always thought of us getting married and of you becoming Mrs. Hannah Markham."

"I married you, Charlie. I have your rings on my finger. We live in a house we picked out together. I'm your wife; that's important to me. I chose you. Not taking your last name shouldn't lessen the importance of that. It doesn't to me, at least. We've been together for two years… you're the only person I've ever even kissed, so I hope to god you understand by now that I fucking *love* you. I'm just…not taking your name."

He pulls me against him, and I listen to his heartbeat and I wait for his words, for his comfort, for him to tell me that it doesn't lessen the importance to him either—I'm waiting for words of affirmation.

But they never come.

Tears prick my eyes, but I don't let them fall.

Even after he's snoring—that gently snuffling inhale and sudden puffing exhale—I don't let the tears fall.

He loves me, I love him; that's enough.

Or…it should be.

Shouldn't it?

（

"It's not your place to make that fucking decision."

"Yes, it is. I'm her husband."

"No, you're not. You gave that title up a long fucking time ago, asshole."

"We've had our problems, but I'm still legally her husband. We never agreed on anything, legally or informally. Nothing was finalized. So I'm still her husband. She wouldn't want this, she wouldn't want to live like this, if you can even call this living."

"You wouldn't know what she wanted even if she fucking told you—and oh, wait, she DID tell you. You just didn't care."

"Fuck you. I DO care."

"Not about her, that's for damn sure."

"Gentlemen, please. This isn't helping. If you can't remain civil toward each other, I'll have security escort you both out, and that's not in anyone's best interest. She needs you, both of you. She needs to know you're here. I know it doesn't seem like it, but she's there. She needs support, and love, not the two of you arguing like this."

)

Light, dark; up, down; through, beneath, above, beyond;
It all twists, tangles, breathes, morphs,

Chaos, despair, sleep, terror, pain, joy, love

Darkness

Existence is filtered through distortion. Memory, fantasy, reality,

What is true?

There is light. There is darkness. There is sound, and there is si-
lence. Alternation, variation, replacement, it all twists in on itself, an
ouroboros of reality and nightmare and truth and fantasy and darkness
and light.
I—
I—
I—
Sense of self is tricky, disorienting. I am, and I am not. Cold. Thirst.

Pain.

NEED.

Conrad?

✳ ✳ ✳ ✳

He smells like her.

Why does that still hurt?

I don't know why, but it does. I never wanted anything but a simple, happy marriage. To belong to someone. To just...*belong.*

I don't know where it went wrong, where I went wrong, what I did wrong, what I lack as a woman. Was it that I didn't know what I was doing? That I didn't know how to fuck? That I never sucked his cock? I would've, had he asked me to. Our sex was always one thing, one way, because I thought that's what it was—how you did it.

Until I married Charlie, my limited exposure to sex was tainted by surreptitiously watching my foster father watch porn. I saw ugly, grunting, cursing men with absurdly oversized dicks shooting their loads all over women who were obviously pretending to like it. I never wanted that—to look like those women, faking enjoyment in demeaning positions. To me, it was all false expectations, something that could never exist.

And then there was Charlie, who showed me that life could be different. He was gorgeous and he held my hand and kissed me and charmed me and took me places I'd never been before. He took me away from foster homes and group homes and stints on the street, and he treated me like I was a girl in a romance movie. He touched me like I was a woman and not a broken, lonely, confused girl. His touch put a fire inside me, made me wonder, made me want. Made me curious.

Somehow just kissing wasn't enough for me; the drug of sex was in my veins once Charlie's exploring fingers fired my blood. My bra loosened as the clasps came unhooked under his fingers, and my jeans opened, and I felt things. Hot, deep, incredible things. And he let me indulge my curiosity, touching and exploring. Taking a peek at his cock, then touching him, feeling him. A glorious slide into sex, one molasses slow moment at a time.

Together.

Being naked with him for the first time and feeling so grown up, feeling heat in my belly and fire in my veins and a trembling between my legs. Feeling him above me, his hair in his eyes and his gaze intense and his cock at my entrance, and his hesitant query—*are you ready? You're sure?*—and then he was inside me and fuck, it hurt at first. But then we were moving together and it felt different—not like I'd imagined—but still good. The heat quavered and expanded and I *needed* something; I needed *more*.

That was the start, and I always edged so close to *more* with Charlie, but more never came, and I thought it was me, but then the need for more became desperation. I started giving myself more, with my fingers in the dark after Charlie was asleep beside me, a brand new thing for this lonely orphan girl, and the privacy to do things in the dark that I never dared do before.

When I first gave myself an orgasm, I cried in the darkness, alone, for an hour: I knew then that it wasn't me. I needed more, and Charlie never gave me more. I wanted that with him, goddammit, and I loved him and knew we deserved to find that together.

And now, lying beside him as he snores, I can smell another woman's pussy on his fingers, on his breath, on his skin. He stinks like sex.

What hurts the most, I think, is that he doesn't wash her off before coming home to me.

That feels like complete and utter disregard.

Makes a lie of every time he ever said, "I love you."

Makes a lie of his kiss, his touch, the tenderness in the quiet moments together.

It makes a lie of fucking everything.

His hand lays on top of the comforter, over his belly. His ring finger is bare. Curious, I lean close to his hand, and sniff; ring finger, middle finger—they smell of pussy. I sniff his mouth—pussy.

He eats her out.

Did he ever do that for me? No. He never did. Not once. That was the only thing in that foster father's porn movies that looked like something I wanted, a man putting his mouth between my thighs and licking me until I screamed and thrashed.

But I never asked him to do it, and he never offered, never tried.

But he eats *her* out?

What the fuck?

I wonder about her quite often.

I know she has red hair, bottle scarlet locks tumbling down to midback. Long legs, big tits. A sharp profile, foreign looking. Maybe a piercing in her lip, or tattoos on her skin. I don't know. She's not ordinary, that's for sure. No blonde hair and blue eyes and confused fumbling in the darkness for the *more* that never quite materializes.

She's exotic, with a sports car and scarlet hair and a pussy that he licks and fingers.

And I lay here, awake at 3:23a.m., my pussy aching, my core twisting, my heart thundering. He's never eaten me out.

What would he do if I woke him up and told him I wanted him to lick my pussy like he does hers?

I want to feel that.

Would I wrap my legs around his neck and arch my back and scream? Or would I writhe off the bed and clutch at the sheets and gasp?

I wonder about her. What is her name? Why her? What is it like for her when they fuck? Is it passionate? Does she claw his back, scream his name? Does she suck his cock? When he eats her out, does he use his fingers too? Does she clutch and grab at his hair and rock her pussy against his face?

Desperation blazes inside me. I need—fuck, I *need*. I need to feel something like that.

My phone is plugged in, resting on the nightstand beside me. I unplug it. Sliding carefully out of bed, I tiptoe from the bedroom, closing the door behind me, careful to let the latch click slowly and quietly.

Once outside, I go down to the dock. I'm totally naked, but I don't care. The night is cool, but not cold, and I'm alone.

I unlock my phone and bring up the browser and type in a single word: *porn*.

The results are predictable, and nothing I'm interested in.

I scroll through the results until I find something. It's a thumbnail image that captures my attention: a woman on a couch, her head thrown back, mouth open, hair wild. A man kneels on the floor in front of her, his head between her thighs.

I click play, adjust the volume down as the opening scenes come up. No time is wasted on set up or pretending it's supposed to be part of a story. The woman is already naked, sitting on the couch, waiting as the man enters the room. He grins at her and falls to his knees in front of her, and she snags him by the back of the head, yanks him forcefully, roughly even, to her pussy. God, that's hot, the way she just...*took* what she wanted.

I want to do that, to jerk a man between my thighs, to shove his face against my pussy like that. He begins licking her, slowly at first, and she watches, mouth open, sighing quietly. And then he slides his fingers inside her and she whimpers—I up the volume a bit, so I can hear the noises she makes. My core aches as I watch. He works his fingers in and out of her slit a few times, and I can hear how wet she is, hear his fingers squelching noisily.

God, my own pussy is dripping now, imaging that man between my thighs. He's ugly, but if his face is between my legs, I wouldn't have to look at him; shame bolts through me at the way my horny thoughts are objectifying him, but I'm too caught up in my own need-fueled fantasy to care.

The man on my phone screen is sliding his fingers in and out of the woman while licking her clit in ever-quickening circles, and she's moaning loudly now, spine arched, head thrown back, and her hips are swiveling, bucking. Faster and faster, and the noises she's making are mewling whimpers of desperation, not faked but cries and sighs of real of pleasure.

My fingers are between my thighs, rubbing around my clit, and I'm starting to feel the boiling rise inside me. I slip my fingers inside my cunt and fuck myself with two fingers, and then smear my juices on my clit, and then circle again. I lose myself in it, until I don't need the porn anymore, because I'm caught up in the feeling, caught up in the fantasy of a man with his tongue on my clit instead of my own fingers.

I hear a splash, but I ignore it; probably a fish.

I work myself into a frenzy, closer and closer to the edge of climax.

The next splash is louder, and closer, and there's a sound of something hard—metal-on-wood—and I open my eyes.

I see a rowboat gliding toward the dock. The half moon is bright, and the endless bowl of stars even brighter, reflecting on the lake, turning the night silver and luminous. There's a man in the rowboat. He's shirtless and barefoot, wearing only a pair of shorts. He twists to look at me as he pulls the oars once more.

I'm at the end of the dock, laying on the old, smooth-worn wood, knees drawn up, heels against my ass, fingers on my clit, breath coming in short sharp gasps, an orgasm moments away.

And then, out of nowhere, at three in the morning, a man in a rowboat appears at my private dock.

He's fucking gorgeous. His hair is a wild black mane, breeze-ruffled, loose. Beginnings of a beard. His body is heavy with muscle, a slight gleam of sweat on his skin. His eyes, my god, those eyes. He's less than three feet away as the boat catches up against the side of the dock—he grabs one of the pillars to stop the boat so he's directly parallel to me. His eyes are deep, dark brown, almost black, liquid, hard, but they betray him. They flick over me, touch on my breasts, my pussy.

THE BLACK ROOM—door seven

His tongue touches his lips, and then vanishes.

"Keep going," he murmurs, a hot grin tipping the corner of his mouth.

Fuck.

I should go inside, tell my husband a stranger is at our private dock, on our private beach, that I was masturbating and he just appeared. That he wants to watch.

At the very least, I should I go inside.

But his voice…I shudder at his voice. It's so deep, so smooth, humming with power, raw with arousal.

I don't move. Not to cover myself, nor to finish my orgasm.

"I won't move," he says. "You were close, so finish it."

"While you watch?" I ask, startled that I managed to find my voice.

"While I watch."

"I don't know you," I say, sitting up.

"That's why it'll be hot." He gives me that grin again, a subtle slight tipping up of one corner of his lips. "For both of us."

"I don't know."

"I get to watch a sinfully fucking gorgeous woman give herself an orgasm, and you—you get a little bit of exhibitionism. Your own little secret. You masturbated, and let a man you've never met watch."

*Sinfully fucking gorgeous?*

"You have to stay in the boat," I say.

I'm shocked at myself, that I'm saying this, that I'm even considering this.

"You have my promise that I will not leave this boat."

I close my eyes, slip middle and ring finger between my thighs, slowly and hesitantly. It's not the same, now. Not even Charlie has even seen me do this. I always felt guilty doing this at all, touching myself without telling Charlie, but it's the only way I could get an orgasm.

And now this? A mysterious, gorgeous man? A total stranger?

Jesus.

Embarrassment wars with excitement and fear.

I try to block out the man in the boat, focus on finding the rhythm.

Circle, gently, slowly, not quite touching my clitoris directly.

"Turn this way, so I can see that beautiful cunt." His words are not a suggestion—they're an order.

And they're erotic as hell. They send heat sizzling through me. I shiver, but my body obeys him. I pivot, stopping when I'm looking at him between the V of my upraised knees. He's got a full, open view of my pussy, spread open for him to look at. My tits are squashed between my arms as I reach between my thighs with one hand and use my fingers to spread open my pussy lips, flicking the fingertips of the other hand against my clit.

I close my eyes, but I hear him grunt a negative. "No. Keep your eyes on me."

My eyelids whip open of their own accord. He's tied a rope to the dock, and he's sitting sideways on the bench, thick arms across his broad, hard chest.

Oh god, oh god, oh god. What the fucking hell am I doing? Why am I doing this? This is foolish, stupid, and dangerous.

He's watching, his jaw clenching and releasing rapidly.

My heart is beating so hard and so fast it actually hurts, and my skin is tight and tingling. I'm vibrating from head to toe, frightened and aroused and unable to stop myself. Unable to even *want* to stop. Just the way he's looking at me, watching me is enough to send heat and need billowing through me, enough to make me feel...shit—like he wants me.

That is more addictive to me than any drug could ever be.

I keep my eyes on his as I plunge my two middle fingers inside my pussy, and his eyes flare, his jaw grinds, his bare stomach tightens. I lay down on my back, work those fingers between my labia, in and out, scissoring them to spread the wetness around, and then draw them out and smear my juices over my clit. Back in, then, and the sound of my fingers entering my cunt is noisy, wet...just like that squelch on the porn.

"Fuck," the man growls. "So hot."

His breathing is quickening. He's gripping his biceps so hard the skin dimples and whitens under the pressure of his fingers.

My eyes flicker over his body, his bulging biceps, his huge shoulders, that trim waist, those brick-hard abs. I look down and I realize then that his cock is visibly tenting the fly of his shorts. He's hard.

Watching me.

My fingers fly into motion. Circling, flicking. I find the rhythm easily, the perfect pressure. His eyes never leave mine, nor mine his. The heat and the wetness of desire congeal, meld, burgeon. Need becomes pressure, low and deep in my core, a hot, sharp, taut live wire buzzing and tightening inside me, centered on my hard, throbbing clit.

"Pinch your nipples," he orders.

And I do it. Fuck, why do I obey him so instantly? Why do his words, his simple instructions work on me like this, unbidden and without thought? My hand flies up to my tit, and my fingers roll my nipple back and forth, pinching hard.

"Oh—oh god," I gasp, then, because it's all too much, the orgasm is rising inside me like a tsunami approaching shore, gaining size and power and intensity the closer it gets.

"You're gonna come, aren't you?" He asks.

I nod, my eyes fluttering, but I still can't quite look away from him. I'm laying down on the dock, staring at him over my body, fingers at my clit and on my nipples, and my breathing is ragged and harsh, and I'm there, riding the edge.

"Goddammit," he growls. "You're killing me."

My hips move out of my control then, flying up and down, and my voice is a whining gasp through gritted teeth, and my fingers are a blur, swiping around my clit hard and fast and relentless.

I think of Charlie just inside, sleeping. He could hear me and come out at any moment, see me masturbating while a man I don't know watches, mere feet away.

He could touch me, the man in the boat. If he were to reach out his arm, he could run his hands along my leg. Leaning forward just a little bit, his fingers could replace mine. If I shimmied toward the edge of the dock, he could do so many dirty things to me, things nobody has ever done before.

"Quit looking at me like that, goddammit," he snarls.

"Like what?"

"Like you're afraid I'm gonna do something I shouldn't." He shifts on the bench. "Like touch you.

"I'm not...*afraid*...of that, necessarily," I hear myself say.

"Fuck." He slides across the boat bench, closer to the dock, arms uncrossing. "No? Then what?"

"More...wondering."

"Wondering what?"

"What I would do if you did."

"You really shouldn't wonder that."

"Why not?"

His hand extends, and his index finger touches my kneecap, circles, and then slides down my shin. "Because if I did touch you..." He trails off, his fingertip skating up the side of my calf.

"If you did touch me...what?" I shouldn't be wondering that, shouldn't be thinking that, and shouldn't be saying that.

I'm all but begging him, daring him, inviting him.

"Because if I did touch you, honey...I wouldn't stop until I'd made you come so hard you'd remember that orgasm for the rest of your fucking life."

"Dammit, dammit, dammit." I growl this through clenched teeth, angry at myself for being so weak, so needy. But I'm coming—it's happening, and I can't stop it and he's watching and I need to be touched.

"You're coming, aren't you?"

"Yeah—oh...oh yeah..." I sound like the girl in the porn, all breathy and horny and erotic and whining high-pitched whimpers.

My eyes are narrowed to slits, my hips pumping, my fingers flying. I'm there, oh god, oh fuck, it's hitting me like a freight train, blasting though me so hard I can't bite down on the brief, shrill cry.

"*Fuck!*" he snarls.

And then I feel his hands on my ankles, right as I'm coming. Pulling me.

Toward him.

I'm terrible, a horrible person, a dirty girl with sinful needs, but I shimmy on my ass across those old boards, to the edge of the dock. He pulls a little more, and now I'm nearly hanging off the edge, my ass mostly in the air. He plants my feet on his shoulders, and he's a solid, immovable wall of gorgeous man.

I can't help but watch, then, as he runs tickling fingers tripping and traipsing up the insides of my thighs, stopping at my pussy. He touches me then, and I flinch, gasp.

"Sensitive?"

"Like crazy," I whisper.

His finger glides down the seam of my swollen labia, and then back up. He finds the hard bead of my clit and flicks it, and I jerk.

"Holy shit," I cry out.

I'm so, so sensitive from having just come that any touch is too much, but his touch…like this? I almost move away from how completely overwhelming it is. I don't know him, not even his name, and I'm on my dock, alone, naked, in the middle of the night, and I'm *married*.

I'm a terrible, terrible person.

But I'm not going to stop. If Charlie can cheat on me, I can cheat on him. Shitty logic, but there it is.

But as the man's finger teases down the slit of my cunt again, still tracing the seam of my lips, guilt hits. I don't want the fucking guilt, goddammit. I want to feel good, I want to feel wanted, and this man's touch gives me that. His eyes give me that. The way he's taking his time, just staring at my pussy as if he's memorizing it, touching it as if intending to make this moment last in his mind forever. As if he's sure he has only this one single moment with me, and he's going to make the most of it.

"I shouldn't—" I start. But then he flips his hand so his palm is facing up, and he curls his long middle finger into my cunt, and I cut off with a gasp. "Oh *fuck*."

"What?" He leaves his finger inside me, the backs of his other fingers flush against my pussy, and then crooks the finger inside me and touches something that makes me writhe up off the dock and cry out. "You shouldn't what?"

"I shouldn't let you do this to me." I whisper, propping myself up on my elbows and watching his finger move inside me.

"Too late now, beautiful. I *am* doing this to you." He watches his hand, too.

We're both watching him slowly, sinuously, curl and straighten that middle finger inside me, and each time he curls it just so, he touches that spot and I whimper, and my hips start to flex.

"Oh god—what the *fuck* are you doing to me?" I sound desperate, wild, confused, almost in pain.

Because what he's doing feels so incredibly good it almost hurts. No, it *does* hurt.

And then he changes tactics. He pulls that finger out my cunt entirely, stares at it, and lifts it to his mouth. His finger is glistening, wet with my essence, and he puts that finger in his mouth and licks it clean. I moan, watching him do it.

"What does it taste like?" I ask.

His lips curve. He slides that same finger back into me and swirls it around my channel, then withdraws it. I sit forward, knowing what he's going to do, and I want it. Dirty, shameful, but I want it. I want to know what my own pussy tastes like. He fits that long, thick finger into my mouth, and I close my lips around his finger and lick it with my tongue, and I taste the salt of his skin and something else, something tangy, almost sweet, musky.

He pulls his finger out of my mouth and I go back to leaning on my elbows. He looks me over, eyes lingering on my breasts, on my wide dark areolae and thick, erect dark nipples, so hard, so sensitive.

"I could spend an entire night on your tits, you know that?"

"Doing what?"

He laughs, a low, amused, aroused sound. "*Everything.*"

"Oh—*god.*"

I fucking want that. What would he do? Lick them? Kiss them? Pinch them? That's as far as my imagination goes, but the look on his face tells me he has a much more vivid imagination than I do.

His hands reach for me, and I shudder all over at the sight of those big, rough, strong hands closing around my hips—

My brain misfires, and I'm seeing him grip my hips like that, but it's a…a memory, a memory of this man, whom I've never before met in my life, grasping my hips and pulling me like he's doing in this moment, pulling me toward himself, but it's not now that I'm seeing, it's some other time…the past, or the future, or an alternate reality, or I don't even know.

I see his swarthy, sun-darkened, work-roughened hands on my pale white flesh, cupping the generous bell of my hips, pulling me across lily-white sheets. I see his knees, he's sitting on his shins, and my ass slides up his thighs and his cock is erect and thick and veiny and there's a slight, trimmed smattering of curly black pubic hair around the base and a dusting on his heavy balls. The head of his cock is a broad mushroom, the groove of the glans ridged and puckered, the flesh beneath lightly pebbled and dark and stretched taut. God, it's so fucking huge, this cock. Perfect, so, so perfect. Straight as a rod, so thick there's no way my fist will close around it. And he's pulling me toward it, gripping my hips in those big, rough yet so exquisitely gentle hands—

The boat rocks as he pulls me. The vision is erased, and I don't understand it, because I *felt* it, felt him, and I knew it was him even though all I could see was his hands, it was like I was seeing myself from a bird's eye view, from above, out of myself, looking down on this man and me.

He was about to fuck me in that vision.

I shudder, and I'm on the dock, completely suspended now, my lower half off the dock and in his hands. My legs are curled around his neck and his hands are under my ass, holding me up, cupping my buttocks.

I blink, disoriented, and then I watch him open his mouth and his flat pink tongue extends and touches my clit, and I jerk, shudder, cry out—it's so strange, that feeling, the wet slithering pressure of his tongue against my clit, but it's bliss, it's euphoria, it pleasure beyond the ability of words to capture.

I watch him, don't even blink, don't dare breathe as I watch his mouth close around my pussy and feel his tongue warm against my clit. Then I feel him suckle, and lick. I crane up to see more, and he backs away and extends and licks my cunt from bottom to top, again and again and I feel each lick shuddering through me like earthquakes. He licks me and licks me, slowly, taking his sweet time, and I can't prevent the whimpers from seething past my clenched teeth.

He pauses between swipes of his tongue and glances up at me. "You...woman, you are the single most beautiful and erotic creature I've ever encountered in my life."

My heart twists, squeezes, contorts. "I'm not."

He laughs and sucks my clit between his teeth. "Yes, you are. So fucking sexy, so gorgeous. The sounds you make? Jesus. You're killing me."

Then he can't talk anymore because he's eating my pussy like it's a last meal, tongue laving madly, and his left arm hooks under me to take my weight and his right hand slides around to fit two of his fingers into my cunt. Index and middle, driving in. Fucking heaven, I'm in heaven, I've died and gone to a place of utter ecstasy. I moan and whimper and reach for him, bury both hands in his thick and loose and wild hair, and then I let myself go. I keep my eyes open and watch, curled forward as far as I can to watch his mouth move and his fingers move, fucking me in and out.

My hips become pistons, driving me against him, grinding, and my teeth are clenched so hard they ache but if I don't keep my jaws together I'll scream. As it is I'm barely containing myself, barely able to stop from screaming even with my jaw locked. My voice is hoarse and ragged and raw, breathy moans and gusting shrieks. And he's nonstop, tireless, fingers fucking and mouth kissing my cunt and I'm—

fuckfuckfuck—

"Come. Give it to me, right now." I hear him growl the command, feel his lips moving against my pussy.

It's like his words flip a switch.

I come.

Oh god, fuck—Jesus, I come so hard everything goes dark, dizzy, twisting, shattering, collapsing, flailing, writhing, too breathless to scream. I come and I come and I come, wave after wave of driving piercing orgasm, climax without end. And his mouth is there on my cunt licking kissing, eating, devouring until the climax shatters and becomes something else. It's too much, and I'm outright sobbing, shuddering all over, muscles contracting helplessly, searing euphoria like jagged shards of distilled, crystallized pleasure replacing my blood and bones and thoughts and needs.

"Fuck, fuck, stop, stop," I gasp, pleading with him. "Please, stop. It's too much."

"No." He lets me down onto the dock and his fingers leave my cunt and I blink and look and see those two fingers are coated with my cum, my essence. Seeping, dripping, liquid desire is leaking out of me, his fingers are coated in it, dribbling down his knuckles. "Not enough."

He wipes all that essence onto my clit, and I jerk at the wet contact. He dips again into my pussy and scoops out that creamy moisture and slathers my clit with it, and then that becomes his rhythm: in, circle, in, circle. Fucking, smearing. I feel his other hand on my hip, then my belly, then my ribs, and my heart—already hammering so hard it hurts—pounds even harder as I force open my eyes and watch as his palm skates up over my breast, cupping my tit.

He touches my breasts reverently, one then the other, over and over, and all the while his fingers fuck my pussy and then smear my wetness over my clit. The orgasm hasn't stopped, hasn't lessened, and everything he's doing is making it worse, better, deeper, harder. I can't stop shuddering, shaking, can't stop gasping and cursing, can't stop watching what he's doing.

I know, without a doubt, this is the best thing I've ever experienced in my entire life.

And I know I won't end this when I stop coming.

I'll touch him.

I'll fuck him.

I'll suck his thick hard cock and I'll swallow his cum.

I'll ride him from moonrise to sunrise and take his gloriously perfect cock a thousand times and a thousand different ways.

Because he is…

He's *everything*.

I know this, and it's not because I'm—fuck, *fuck, FUCK!*—coming again, coming harder than the last time, putting my knuckle between my teeth and biting down on the scream—it's *him*, it's the way he touches me, the way he looks at me, the way he does everything.

This is meant to be.

He moans as I orgasm around his mouth. I feel his tongue drive between my labia and he's licking away the dripping juices and licking my clit and he's lifting me up with both hands again and his tongue is wild, manic, mad.

And fucking hell, it's so incredible I don't want it to ever, ever, ever stop.

I want to come on his mouth and never ever stop.

"Jesus Christ, you come like a goddess." His voice breaks my orgasmic reverie. "You *are* a goddess."

His words, my god, his words. They hit me like a fist, slice through me like a knife. They make the after-shocks ripple harder.

I collapse back against the dock, gasping for air. Quivering, shuddering, shaking.

I open my eyes, and he's breathing almost as hard as I am, his mouth and chin and upper lip glistening. A grin on his lips. Eyes gleaming, aroused, amused, self-satisfied.

"Holy shit," I whisper.

"You're fucking amazing," he says. "I could spend all day and all night making you come and never get tired of watching you."

He shifts back onto the boat bench, flexes his hips, plucks at his zipper. He's still hard. He winces as he adjusts himself, as if he's in pain.

"That was…god. Thank you, I—I didn't know it could be like that…" I trail off, because he's grimacing, jaw clenched, fists squeezing until his knuckles go white. "Are you okay?"

He shrugs. "I'm about to come in my pants like a damn teenager, that's all."

No.

No.

Don't. Don't do it.

Don't go down that rabbit hole. You'll never stop yourself. You can stand up and walk on your shaky stupid legs back up to the house and pretend this never happened.

But I can't.

He was right. He did exactly what he said he would: give me an orgasm I'll never fucking forget for as long as I live.

And I need another one.

Look at him, though. Gorgeous, male perfection. My cum on his face, on his fingers. Zipper stretched from the hard arousal behind it. Pain on his face, aching, shifting uncomfortably, barely holding it back.

*I want him.*

I want to touch him.

Once Charlie and I went from making out and fumbling at each other to actual sex, we never just…touched each other. He fucked me, I didn't come, he fell asleep, and I finished myself off.

This…

This man, this is different.

I *need* to touch him. I have to.

"Don't come in your pants," I say.

I sit up, facing him, and dangle my legs off the dock, feet kicking a little. I look down at him, at the bulge in the zipper of his khaki cut-off shorts.

"No?"

"No." I lick my lips, knowing I shouldn't do this, and knowing I'm going to. "Let me…help."

"Help, huh?"

I nod, and then feel a bolt of daring shoot through me. "Let me touch you. Like you touched me."

He leans back, unbuttons the fly of his shorts, and lowers the zipper. Commando underneath. His cock springs free, huge and erect and thick and dark. My gut twists at the sight of it, my heart stops beating. If I could come again, I would, just from the sight of his cock, from the aching desire to touch it, to have it in my hands, to see him come. To know I made him come as hard as he made me.

I reach for him, and he grabs my waist, lifts me down to his level, the boat rocking gently from side to side. His strength has me marveling, the way he lifted me so effortlessly, set me down as easily.

There's another bench in the bow of the rowboat, but I ignore it. I sink to my knees as he pivots to face the bow, and me. His shirt is on the floor of the boat, providing a cushion for my knees. He wiggles, shimmies, and tosses the shorts toward me. I put them beneath me for added cushioning and move toward him, until I'm between his knees.

I'm trembling at his proximity. His nearness is intoxicating, nerve-wracking. This is wrong, forbidden...and thrilling. I've never been so scared and nervous and excited in my life.

I've never been here before, kneeling in front of a man, his cock in front of my face. With him, like this, somehow...I don't feel like being on my knees is demeaning, but rather...powerful. He wants me to touch him, he *needs* my touch, and I'll only give it if I want to.

And fuck, I want to.

He opens his mouth, but I shake my head. "Don't. Don't say anything. Just let me touch you."

"Okay."

I just stare for a few moments, because god, he's so beautiful, so perfect. But I can't just stare. I need to touch. I reach out, trace a single fingertip down the underside of his cock, from tip to balls. He shudders, letting out a growling breath.

"You're killing me," he murmurs.

"Sorry. I just..."

"The good kind of killing me," he clarifies. "Do whatever you want. But you keep doing that, I'm not gonna be able to help making a mess."

I grin, because that was kind of what I had in mind. But I don't say that. I just return my finger's journey back up from root to tip, and then as I trace over the very top, I close my fist around him and plunge it down.

He groans long and low, throwing his head back, and then jerks it back forward to watch me.

I slide my fist up, feeling my heart hammering in my chest. I'm touching him. A total stranger. I have my hand around his cock, and it feels dirty and naughty and delicious and perfect all at once.

I know this is wrong, that two wrongs don't make a right, but I don't care. Not right now. All I care about right this moment is this man's dick in my fist. How hard it is, how long it is, how thick it is. My fist doesn't close around him, my middle finger and thumb don't quite connect; my hand is small and pale and his cock is huge and dark. His thighs are tensed and hard as rock, his stomach pulled inward, his fists gripping the sides of the rowboat so hard the wood creaks under his powerful grip.

I've stroked his length twice, and he's losing control; I'm giddy at the knowledge that I'm making him feel that way, that my touch, my hand on his cock is enough to eradicate his self-control. I glance up at his face and meet his eyes. His brows are drawn, his forehead furrowed, jaw clenched tight, lips curled and parted in a snarl.

I add my other hand, now. Slowly, I caress his length from top to bottom and back up, rubbing my thumb over the slit at the top, twisting my fist around the head and then plunging back down. And now, on the next journey of my hands from glans to root, his hips twitch. Flex. A soft groan leaves his throat.

"Goddamn," he moans. "I can't hold out much longer."

"I don't want you to hold out," I hear myself say.

"You want me to come all over your hands?" His eyes meet mine as he asks this.

"Yes," I breathe.

Fuck, I want that. I remember having the tiniest droplet of Charlie's cum on my hand and feeing a tiny, illicit thrill at the sight of it. Now, my entire existence is hinged on this man's orgasm. I *need* more than anything to watch him come, to watch him lose control, let go, to spray his cum everywhere...on me and on my hands. I remember touching my tongue to Charlie's cum, tasting it, and feeling a similar bolt of excitement. But now, in the moonlight of a stolen moment with a nameless stranger, caressing his massive, beautiful cock, I want to taste more, taste *his* cum. I dare to want things in this impossible fantasy made real that I've never even dreamed of, never dared want with Charlie.

I cup the weight of his balls in my palm, massage them, and feel their softness in my hand. Stroke his length slowly, unhurriedly, exulting down to the very pit of my soul in the way he feels in my hands.

"I'm—shit, *shit*—I'm gonna come." He thrusts his hips, powering his cock through my hand.

"Hold still," I say. "Let me do it all."

He leans backward against the back edge of the rowboat, head lolling over the side, stretching out, flexing every muscle as I continue caressing his cock. His whole body is rigid, hips levered off the boat.

"I'm there, Jesus, I'm coming." He snarls, wordlessly. "Fuck, that feels incredible."

My fist is on the upward journey, nearing the head, and that's when he comes. It's a fountain of cum, jetting straight up into the air and drenching my knuckles and my wrist. I need more, need to feel more of him, need to make *him* feel more. I want to give him more pleasure, make him come even harder.

It's...instinctual. Automatic. Desire bypassing my brain, pushing straight through my body to force me into action.

I gather my hair to one side and bend over him. I part my lips and feel the head of his cock on my lower lip, then my tongue, and then I have his shaft in my mouth. Taste his skin, taste something muskier, tangier, saltier. He groans, twitches, and I feel him shift his weight.

"Your mouth feels fucking perfect."

I hum in response, and he groans and his hips flex forward. His cock fills more of my mouth, the head nudging at my throat, and then I feel something wet and hot hit the back of my throat and I swallow it. I take more of him, and then I have to open my throat and breathe through my nose, but this feels right, it feels amazing, it's perfect because it's *him*, and his cock is so perfect it deserves this, *he* deserves to feel me take his cock this deep for how hard he made me come. I feel him spurt again, and I'm still taking more of him, choking on the thick presence in my throat. I back away until just the head of him is in my mouth and I kiss it, suck it, fuck it with my mouth. He leaks cum. I taste it on my tongue. Lick it away without removing him from my mouth, stroke him at the root as I suck and fondle the head with my lips, flutter my tongue against the soft springy roundness of the tip.

"Fuck fuck fuck fuck—" he growls.

Finally, he's done coming, and I feel him softening in my hands and mouth, and I let him pop free.

I still taste his cum on my tongue, and I lick my lips. Lifting my right hand, I admire the cum coating my skin, the way it drips and slides from knuckle to knuckle, over my wrist. He stares at me as I lift my hand to my mouth and lick at the dribbling pool of cum. It's thick and viscous, salty, pungent, but not overpowering. I meet his gaze and don't look away as I lick away every last drop of his cum.

"Fucking hell, that's…" he shakes his head. "Who *are* you?"

Dawn is pinking the gray on the horizon. I have to go, have wash the evidence of him away and pretend to sleep.

His cock, now mostly slackened and still impressive, has a droplet of cum at the tip.

I lick it away, and then climb back onto the dock. "My name is Hannah," I say.

I stand up, conscious of his eyes on my body, scouring my naked curves. I let him look, revel in the fierce, fiery gleam of lust I see in his gaze. His eyes are on my breasts, my hips, my pussy—then up to my face, memorizing my features.

"Hannah," he repeats. "I'm Conrad."

I grab my phone, walk back along the dock, self-consciously letting my hips sway a little extra, because his eyes are on my ass. I make it to the end of the dock when I hear his voice, pitched low.

"Hannah."

I stop, glance back at him over my shoulder. "What?"

"When will I get more of you?"

"Tomorrow night," I say, knowing I'm unable to resist, unable to even *want* to resist. "The island. Midnight."

"Perfect." He lets out a breath, and I wait, knowing he's going to say something else. "If you meet me at the island tomorrow night, or tonight or whatever you want to call it, you have to know I'm going to fuck you. I'm going to fuck you like you've never been fucked before. I swear to you, you'll never forget the way my cock feels inside your cunt, and you'll never want anyone else."

"That's the problem," I say, "I already don't."

I walk away, then, because if I don't, I'll fuck him right here on the dock, and Charlie is an early riser.

I go into the house, avoiding the creaky floorboard in the kitchen. I close the bathroom door behind me and turn on the faucet in the sink. With hot water that's a little too hot, and a bar of soap, I scrub my pussy and wash my hands and my face. I dry off, slip on my bathrobe and sneak into bed.

"What're you doing, Hannah?" Charlie slurs, half-asleep.

"Couldn't sleep," I whisper. "Took a walk outside."

"Naked? In the middle of the night?"

"We don't have any neighbors," I say, "so why not? The air feels nice."

Charlie goes quiet again, and I hear him snoring.

I tingle everywhere. My heart is drumming in my chest.

I have no hope of sleeping, not now. Not ever again. I have *him* on my mind, now. Conrad.

Memory of his cum on my skin, his cock in my mouth. His lips against my cunt, his fingers inside me, his tongue tasting.

More.

Fuck, I want *more*.

I want things I don't know the name of, fantasies I don't have images for.

I pretend to sleep until I hear Charlie wake up, take a shower, fix coffee and breakfast. When I hear his car start and hear him leave, I fling away the covers and stare at my hand, as if I can still see Conrad's cum.

I pull up porn on my phone, watch with renewed interest as women take face-loads of cum with eager, open mouths, watch as they deep-throat impossibly huge cocks and watch what they do and how they do it, and I watch how they go on their hands and knees to take it from behind, how they straddle the men to ride them facing their feet, asses bouncing. It's still obviously fake and patently ridiculous, but now, with Conrad in my mind, I picture myself doing those things with him. Taking him from behind. Sucking him until he's about to come, and then letting him shoot his cum on my face and on my tits—the thought should disgust me, but it doesn't…what does that say about me? I don't know, don't care. All I know, all I care about, is that I want that. I want him, and I want everything with him. *Everything.*

I touch my pussy and make myself come as sunlight pours through the bedroom window, and I cry Conrad's name as I come, picturing his fingers, his mouth, his cock—

The island; the gazebo. Moonlight bathes the lake silver, only the occasional ripple marring the mirror surface.

Our quilt is spread out on the floor of the gazebo. Four large white candles burn brightly at each corner; beside each candle is a slender fluted vase containing a single perfect crimson rose. To one side, a small Bluetooth speaker sits on the bench of the gazebo, emitting soft solo cello music, slow, languid, and expressive.

I'm standing just outside the gazebo, staring, tears in my eyes. Conrad stands on the center of the quilt, surrounded by the candles and the roses and the silver moonlight. He is more beautiful than everything else around him, capturing my attention, setting my heart to thundering. Faded blue jeans, no shirt, no shoes. Bare chest rippling with muscle, taut and toned and blocky, bare feet. Wild thick black hair, loose and damp and curling against his neck and around his ears and dangling in perfect strands across his eyes. Hands at his sides, watching me.

"You deserve romance," he says, as I step up onto the gazebo and onto the quilt and into his arms.

He kisses each of my cheeks, kissing away the tears. Then his lips move to capture the corners of my mouth, one, and then the other.

"I don't know what to say," I whisper.

"You don't have to say anything."

His tongue tangles with mine, slips between my lips and scours my teeth and steals my breath, and something sears between us that should be termed a kiss but is simply too much to be contained by such a flimsy thing as language.

It is elemental. Spiritual. Deeper than souls, beyond lips and tongues, more than romance or sex. It is…fusion.

Union.

We've fucked too many times to count, in nearly every way there is to fuck. But this? I shudder, twist in his arms, clutch at his shoulder blades, gasp against his lips.

I never thought of sex as anything other than sex, or fucking. There are a dozen words or terms for it, each cruder and baser than the last, and sex has always been those things. Something you do, a physical act, necessary, inevitable, pleasurable. But with Conrad, it was always…*more* than all that. Not emotionally, not at first. It was fucking, but fucking as it should be. Fucking done right. Every moment with Conrad has taught me how limp and weak and empty every sex act I've ever had before was, because each moment with Conrad is intense and fiery and wild and unpredictable and exponentially more powerful than I ever understood anything could be.

I gave into this thing with Conrad because I needed to feel wanted, and he gave that to me. I needed to feel…well, I'll just stop there. I needed to *feel*. And good god, does he make me feel.

Too much, I think.

That's why I'm always so afraid with him, because what I feel with him and for him…is overwhelming. So much so that I don't know how to contain it, or how to express it, except by fucking him as intensely as I can, as much as I can. And that's what we do. He feels the same way—I know, because I can feel it in the way he touches me, the way he can't help but to kiss me, despite his own rule that we wouldn't kiss until I could be his in every way. But he can't help it. He's as overwhelmed as I am by this thing, by the enormity of it, by the all-pervading power and intensity of it.

The connection between us consumes us completely.

And yet, for all that, until this very moment…I couldn't grasp what it was, what it meant or how deeply it was rooted into the soil of my very existence.

It is love.

Not comfort, not attraction, not reliance, or co-dependency, or even need. No, love is all of those things, but it is far more than the sum of its parts.

Words are useless and empty.

Love…

Is.

It just *is*.

It makes itself known, makes itself understood, and it cannot be denied. Cannot be refuted, or mistaken.

And when it arrives with the concussive impact of a meteor slamming into soft loamy soil, you will very swiftly realize that anything before it was the light patter of rain, the feather light touch of a gentle breeze.

True, deep, real, furious love is a hurricane.

Conrad kisses me, and I know then that I am his. Utterly, irrevocably his.

.

.

.

I'm on the quilt, on my back. He is above me. I am naked, bare for his touch. His hands roam my every curve, sliding possessively and wonderfully over my flesh. He cups my cheeks and kisses me breathless, and traces the line of my bicep and the tender angle of the inside of my elbow and down the underside of my forearm. Lips touch my cheek and the corner of my lips, and his fingers dance along my diaphragm and toy with my nipples and caress the weight of my breasts. He tickles and traipses his touch down my ribcage and over my belly, dipping his kisses into my navel and over the hard knobs of my hipbones and into the hollow where thigh meets core. He elicits a muted whimper from me as he touches his tongue to my slit and tastes the weeping dampness of my desire and continues the exploration of my body. My thighs, my shins. Kisses behind my knee and along my calf. The arches of my feet.

Where he is not kissing, his hands touch and caress.

His mouth and his tongue, and his fingers and palms elucidate what his terse nature cannot reveal.

I am too full of fire to remain still. I reach for him, grasping his nape and demand his mouth on mine, biting his lower lip until he growls and lick his lips as I grind against him. Crush myself to him. Revel in the hardness of his body, the iron of his muscles and the softness of his skin. Touch him. Smoothing my hands down his back, I roam the bubble of his ass, the thick trunks of his thighs. The mountains of his shoulders and the silky, inky thatch of his hair. I run my fingers over the stubble on his cheeks, not quite a beard. Between us, his cock. Erect, a steel rod begging for me, for my hands, for my mouth, for my cunt.

There is no guiding him into me, no fumbling for entrances. I curl my legs around him, cradle his waist with the V of my thighs and cling to him with my feet and clutch at his spine and his biceps and his hair with my clawing fingers. I breathe his name onto the breeze. Tilting my hips, I writhe against him, and that's all it takes.

He shifts, and I tilt, and we are one.

He slides into me in a slow hot glide, stretching me apart and filling me to glutted ecstasy. I whisper in his ear, but I am too crazed with the fullness of him to even know what I'm saying.

"Hannah—Jesus Christ, Hannah." His growl in my ear is the rough primal snarl of a creature barely evolved.

Our candlelight is the blaze of the entire universe, the sun in four parts. His body above mine anchors me to this place, into this reality, and that's all I want. This moment, forever.

*Hannah—Jesus Christ, Hannah.*

I hear it and I hear it and I hear it, that gutted grunt of awe.

He moves in me, burly arms beside my face blocking everything out, his heart thundering against my breast, sweat sliding slick against my flesh and merging with mine, his heartbeat and his sweat both mingling with mine. I cannot breathe, don't, can't, no need, no breath but his mouth on mine, not quite kissing anymore but sharing oxygen, teeth against teeth, lips quivering.

He moves in me, and I squeeze around him, begging him to stay inside me like this forever. Beyond sunrise, beyond sunset, beyond the turning of the world from spring to fall to winter to summer. Stay here. Fill me. Hold me. Kiss me.

Fuck me breathless.

Love me to overflowing.

I've been empty all my life and now I'm full. I'm more than full, I'm bursting with you, taking you inside me, taking your cock into my cunt and your tongue into my mouth and your heart into my heart and your soul into my soul—did I say that? Think it? Feel it? Hear it? Was that from him or from me? I don't know, don't care, because it's raw truth put into words.

"*Yours*," and this isn't even a whisper, perhaps he didn't even truly speak it out loud but I heard it all the same.

*Yours*

*Yours*

And it echoes back—

"*Mine*,"

*Mine*

*Mine*

*Hannah—Jesus Christ, Hannah.*

We move together, endlessly. Limbs sliding and tangling. Hands palm to palm, fingers twined. My breasts are crushed against his chest, nipples scraping against his chest hair. His thighs press against my hips, pushing, moving. He groans, and I kiss that sound away.

He moves, thrusts.

I feel his cock gliding wet between the lips of my cunt as he pulls back and I ache and ache and ache, and then my moan is almost a sob as he pushes back into me and I feel that sweet stutter of slick hardness against my pussy as he fills me.

Again,

and again,

and again,

Until I am sobbing with the ecstasy of it.

He licks away my tears and claims my shuddering lips.

My entire being goes fractal, crystallizing into fragments of rhapsodic detonation, euphoria flooding through me, taking me over.

My screams echo off the lake.

I'm clawing and clutching at him and biting his shoulder. His hands tangle with mine and force my arms up over my head and he pins both of my outstretched hands with one of his, and with the other he's cupping my nape. My entire lower body is levered off the quilt and he's thrusting into me and I'm coming so hard it hurts, every muscle contracting at once, my core spasming around his cock,

and then he comes,

and I am utterly undone.

Because he doesn't roar, doesn't grunt or curse or yell my name or stare intently down at me while he fucks me through his climax.

He touches my lips with his and cups my nape in one hand and pins my arms over my head and his hips slam against mine and the sound he utters as I feel him orgasm is…raw and ragged and shattered.

"Yours," he whispers.

And I feel his cum pour into me and I'm wracked all the harder.

I claim the kiss, then, as we both come, breaking apart together, lifting up to take his mouth with mine, helpless beneath him—perfectly, beautifully so.

*Hannah—Jesus Christ, Hannah—*

Where am I?

Darkness.

Floating, coruscating shadows within shadows. Hints of images, scraps of memory, shards of light. Fragments of skin. Palm pressed to palm, fingers tangling, trembling. A hand on a breast. Lips on lips. Inky hair on dusky skin. A droplet of cum pearling on pale flesh in the silver moonlight.

Conrad.

I feel him. I feel his arms around me, his chest under my ear. I hear his heartbeat. Feel his fingers trail along the curve of my hip.

"I need you," I whisper, and my voice shivers, echoes—

*need you need you need you need you*

—I cling to him, clutch at his broad, hard shoulder. Nuzzle into his warm solid flesh, inhale his scent. Curl against him, breathe him in. Fill my lungs with him, crush against him. Refuse to let go.

He's prizing at my clawed fingers, but gently, reluctantly. Touching my chin with a fingertip.

"No." I shake my head, murmuring my denial, my refusal pushing against his pectoral muscle.

I feel his insistence. Pulling at me. Untangling.

"I don't want to go."

*You have to.* A thick, tragic pause. *You have to.*

"Don't make me."

*I'm here, Hannah.* I feel his palm on my cheek, his chest against my breasts. *I need you.*

His lips brush my lips. I feel them move as he whispers. I feel the dampness on his cheeks. Or is it on mine?

"Don't cry, Conrad. Don't cry. It's okay. I'm here."

*I should have said this before. I shouldn't have waited so long.*

Said what?

"Tell me!"

*tell me tell me tell me tell me tell me*

**I love you, Hannah.**

"I love you, Conrad."

*loveyouloveyouloveyou*

He didn't hear me; I can feel it. I can feel him, hear him, but I can't make him hear me. We're having two separate conversations. I'm stuck. Or he's stuck. Lodged in ice, shadowed and marbled with light and cold and darkness.

I reach for him. Strain for him.

For the light.

"Conrad!"


*conrad conrad conrad conrad conrad conrad*


*I love you, Hannah. I fucking—I love you.*

His sadness is a razor blade to the shredded mess of my soul, my identity. His sadness is too much, too deep…it hurts, hurts, hurts.

It hurts—

The darkness is hungry.

It wants me.

It is so strong, alien, reaching for me with too many invisible arms, hands pulling me under.

LET ME GO LET ME GO

I want out.

Let me out.

Conrad.

He's there, I feel him, hear him, smell him, know him.

I know him.

But the darkness is too strong.

I scream, but make no sound.

Rage, but leave no scars on the blackness.

Desperation is a searing flameless heat within me, incendiary, alive, magma in my veins.

Release me.

Let me go.

LET ME GO.

LET ME GO!

# Let

# Me

# Go!

I scream and thrash and rage and push against the darkness with all that I am—

●

There is darkness, because there is always darkness. There is only darkness.

But now...

I sense I'm not alone.

Yet I cannot see, cannot feel, cannot breathe or move or shift or walk or cry.

I simply *am*.

But then the black void dissolves, or resolves—and it's like stepping back from a pointillist painting.

I'm surrounded by emptiness. Only vaguely do I feel corporeal, in possession of an I, of a body, an awareness.

There is nothing, only a sense of me, and a need to move forward. Am I moving? I don't know.

Slowly, the shadow lightens and gathers form. Not light, not illumination, but an *other*, something outside the point of awareness that is...

*I.*

I sense movement, like floating in a current on a river, but the river is so warm I feel at one with the water, and the current is so gentle that movement is imperceptible.

I'm not alone.

I *know* this.

But I see nothing, feel nothing.

The shape solidifies, and the darkness becomes lighter…silvers.

The shape becomes four-sided with two long vertical edges and two short horizontal edges. A familiar shape, this rectangle. Memory, awareness—it's fuzzy, slow, thick, and sludgy and slippery.

A door.

It is a door.

There is more to this notion of a door, but I've lost it.

All I know is…I must go through it.

Silver. Old, dented, scratched, cheap steel. Plain metallic knob. No features, nothing. Just the door standing alone in the darkness. It calls to me. Beckons me. Pulls me forward.

I am powerless to resist.

I'm not me, I'm not anything, just a spark of awareness in a vast shadowland; but that door…beyond it… is more.

And I have to go through, or this darkness is all there will ever be. And I want more.

But what do I want, what is it that is *more* beyond the silver door? I don't know. But whatever it is, I need it. I need it so bad the need becomes desperation, which is familiar. The desperation becomes something else too, a wild dizzying universe of emotions. The little spark that is

# I

cannot contain or fathom or express anything but to do what I must:

go through the door.

I push gently against the aged metal.

It opens, silent and smooth.

I move through, over the threshold—

I'm not alone, and this reality is comforting. The darkness is the darkness of deepest night, and the room is bathed in the shadows of beyond midnight. A real darkness, a soothing warmth, a knowledge of myself, of...

*Him.*

I twist, roll, and I find him. Feel him.

I cannot see him, but I know him as well as I know myself.

I stretch my hands out and find his flesh. Muscle, hardness. A smattering of hair, the protruding hardness of hipbones. His belly, steely with muscle, his chest like a wall, then his face. I touch his cheek and his chin and his angular jawline, and I know each plane, know him by feel. I don't need to see him to know this is Conrad.

"Hi." His voice is low and deep and slow and happy and sleepy.

"Hi." Mine is breathy, giddy.

"Been missing you."

"You have?"

He laughs. "Babe, of course I have. You're gone for ten seconds and I miss you. You get up to take a piss and I miss you before you're back."

I laugh with him. "Good thing I pee fast, huh?"

"Good thing."

Sober, now. "How long have I been gone?"

A long pause. "Too long, sweetheart." His hands close on me, cup my ass and my shoulder. "Too damn long."

"I'm back now, though."

"Yeah." But he doesn't sound as happy about that as I'd thought.

"Conrad?"

"Yeah, babe."

"Why don't you sound happy that I'm back?"

His hand explores the broad curves of my generous ass, tests the bounce and firmness of it, and then delves down, down, seeking the sensitive flesh between my thighs. "Kiss me, Hannah."

I move up his body, feeling his hardness and solidity beneath me, his fingers teasing my slit, his other hand buried in the loose wild mass of my hair. I'm crushed against him, lying fully on top of him, thighs to thighs, hips to hips, belly to belly. His cock is a hard thick ridge wedged between us, and my breasts are flattened, cushioned against his chest. He moans deep in his throat as I move up his body until my mouth finds his chin. I kiss him there, then underneath, and then down the column of his throat. I press my lips behind his ear and he shivers. I run my tongue around the spiral just inside his ear and blow a hot breath. He shudders, his grip tightening on me.

"Fucking *kiss* me, Hannah," he demands, harshly.

"I *am* kissing you, Conrad." I'm teasing him, riling him.

"Not what I meant, goddammit."

He palms my cheek and guides my mouth to his, and his kiss is brutal at first, lips smashing against mine so hard I taste blood, and I welcome the sting as evidence of reality. Then the kiss softens, deepens. Gentles. His tongue probes my lips, parts the seam, steals past my teeth and tangles with my tongue.

There is no time, then, except the endless, eternal measurement of a kiss, of love exchanged lips to lips, tongue to tongue, mouth to mouth, soul to soul. This is that kind of a kiss, chasm-deep and infinite.

I feel him moan, and my hand sneaks behind his head, pulling him closer. His fingers test my cunt, tease the entrance, and I splay my thighs apart and draw my knees up, lift my hips an inch or two—a welcoming, an invitation. He slides a long middle finger into my silken wet heat and draws it out and spreads my desire over my clit. Yes, yes, yes, just like that—I move my hips to tell him how good it feels, silently begging him to keep going, to do that again. And I don't stop kissing him, just devour the love he's offering and give it right back.

It's not long before his fingers bring me to the shuddering brink of climax, and I'm breathless, unable to kiss him through the waves of orgasm as they crash through me. I can only cling to him and shudder against his mouth and whimper his name and—

"I need you inside me, Conrad."

He bites my lower lip. "Then take me inside you."

I reach between us and grasp his erection and guide the head to my slit, taking the opportunity to caress his length as I put him where I need him—inside me. We moan in unison as I slowly, agonizingly, lower myself on him, fill my tight cunt with his massive cock. I'm so tight around him, squeezing and clenching from my orgasm, and he's so big, throbbing and hard he fills me, stretches me, completes me, he perfects me as he drives deeper and deeper. His hands grasp the heavy globes of my ass, lifts and separates so he can go that much deeper.

"Oh fuck, fuck, fuck, Conrad—*Conrad!*" I whimper, breathless and aching.

And then we're moving, our thrusts synchronized, my down stroke meeting his up thrust. My ass slaps loudly against his thighs, bouncing hard and fast off of him, and his cock drives into me and slides out with a sucking wet squelch, and he's growling and I'm screaming—

I come, come so hard dizziness twists me into spiraling disorientation, everything heightening and going dissolute—

——

There's a shift and a movement—

The darkness is altered, and I feel Conrad beneath me, still. His cock is hard inside me, filling me. His hands caress my ass, soothing, possessive, familiar.

But there's something different.

I need *more*; dark, dirty thoughts spread through me. I'm desperate with the need for *more*.

There's a movement beside me.

Hands touch my back, and drift up my spine. They are familiar, gentle hands—they are Charlie's hands.

Oh…

*Yes.*

I can't see; there's nothing *to* see. There is only touch. Indulgence in physicality, and giving in to the need, the want, the desire. Whatever has been hidden in the darkest, dirtiest, most sinful and hidden corners of my soul, this darkness brings out and makes real.

Charlie.

He's near me, beside or behind, I don't know, don't care. He's there. His touch is familiar. Soothing and familiar, a touch I'd know anywhere, any time. The way he slides his palm up my spine is just so Charlie. He buries his hand in my hair at the back of my neck, and I feel the heat of his body, the warmth of his breath. His lips touch my shoulder, hesitantly, in that way Charlie has. I reach for him: he's naked.

I move my caress to his cock. Long, hard, not quite as thick as the one inside me, but pleasing to touch and hold and stroke all the same. I stroke his length and appreciate the way his breath catches at my touch.

I slide off Conrad so he's on my left, push Charlie to his back on my right. And then I have Conrad in my left hand, and my heartbeat is a wild syncopated tattoo behind my ribs. This feels…so fucking good, to have both of these men beside me. I groan in pleasure at the sensation of it, Conrad's massive cock in my left hand, Charlie's long, slender shaft in my right. I stroke them both, one then the other, then in union.

Charlie flexes his hips and sighs as I stroke him. Conrad is silent, but I can feel his pleasure. All that exists in this moment, for me, are these two cocks, each perfect in its own way, each familiar yet so different.

There's so much pleasure in the touch.

But it's not enough.

*MORE.*

I lean over to my left and take Conrad into my mouth, tasting my essence on his shaft. I slide my fist slowly along Charlie's hard length, and swallow around Conrad. I back away, releasing him from my lips with a loud *pop*. I sweep my hair to one side and find Charlie's cock with my lips, swirling my tongue around his glans while plunging my fist down Conrad's shaft. Alternate stroking and deep-throating Conrad and Charlie, until they're both groaning deep, masculine grunts of arousal.

"Get on your knees," I say, and they both obey me.

I keep my grip on their cocks as they move to their knees side by side, in front of me.

Giddiness shudders through me. How erotically indulgent is this, to have so much hard male arousal all for me? All mine.

I stroke their cocks with each hand, Conrad on my left, Charlie the right. God, god, I love the way Conrad's cock slides through my hand and I love the way Charlie tastes; I keep my mouth around his head, sucking, licking, bobbing shallowly, and stroke Conrad with long fast gliding pumps of my fist. Then I switch, taking Conrad down my throat, and spreading my lubricating saliva along Charlie's length with my fist.

Again and again I switch, filling fist and mouth until the men are both grunting and cursing and thrusting helplessly.

Whose cum do I want first?

Conrad.

God, yes. Of course—always; there's an implicit bias there, but it's buried deep beneath the rampant raging white current rapids of lust.

Here and now, there's only lust, only need, only the wildfire of my libido.

I feather slow, gentle caresses along Charlie's throbbing cock and give him a lick and a kiss, a promise, and then turn my attention to Conrad. I keep stroking Charlie, but slowly, intermittently.

Conrad has my focus now. I plunge my fist down his length, run my tongue around the glans, across the tip, and then mouth the entire head. Down the shaft, until he's at my throat. I fist him at the root, short fast strokes, and he groans, pumping his hips. I release his cock to grasp his ass and pull him toward me, encouraging him to move, to fuck.

He obeys.

I keep a slow gentle pressure on Charlie, keeping him at the edge; I can read him like a book, I know exactly how close he is, and when he gets too close and starts moaning in a certain way, starts flexing his hips, I know it's time to back off and slow my pace and lighten my touch.

Conrad is grunting. "Fuck, Hannah. Fuck, I'm gonna—"

"Mmmmm. Mmmm-hmmm. Mmmm." I moan in pleasure and that only encourages him.

I cup his ass and pull at him to increase the strength and speed of his thrusts. He's fucking my throat and it's perfect, the way he throbs between my lips and grunts and snarls. Beside me, I can feel Charlie losing the ability to hold off.

Conrad is done, though. I feel him getting ready to come. He's thrusting hard and fast, snarling. Throbbing, thickening. More, more. I hum as I take as much of his cock as I can, until my lips reach his base and I'm gagging and glutted on him.

"Oh fuck—" Conrad grunts.

And then he comes. I feel the burst down my throat, back away so I can feel his cum fill my mouth. He spurts and my mouth is flooded; I taste his cum and I swallow it all, move away and stroke his length with my hand and feel his cum spray all over my lips, on my extended tongue and on my chin, and I swallow it and keep stroking and he grunts again and thrusts into my fist. Thick warm wetness splashes onto my tits and puddles hot and trickles down the slopes, and then I turn to Charlie.

I caress his length, slowly at first and then faster and faster, using a light, loose touch. He groans low and soft, and his hips flex. I take him into my mouth, fist his shaft beneath my chin and bob my head to fuck him with my lips. He'd never fuck my throat, not like Conrad. So I fuck him, then. Fuck him with my mouth until he's spasming and his hips are taut and flexed forward and fluttering, ass tightened.

I back away, then, and slide my fist up and down his long, hard cock until he comes with a curse. I moan at the feel of his cum splattering on my tits and puddling with Conrad's and sliding down between them in a hot wet stream. I have to taste him, and I take his next spurt in my mouth and swallow and suck as he comes. Charlie's cum is tangier, saltier, sharper, thinner, while Conrad's is a little sweeter and thicker.

Both men are groaning as they finish their orgasms, my fists on each of them, stroking sticky, slackening cocks, smearing cum down their lengths. I lick my lips and taste the commingled flavors, Conrad's and Charlie's. I wipe my face with my palms until the cum is gone, and then I lie on my back and reach for Conrad, find his neck and pull him toward me. Then I gather Charlie to my tits and smother his face between my heavy breasts. There's a river of cum coating the mounded flesh, sliding down in thick warm rivulets, dribbling, drying in crusty patches. Charlie's lips close around my nipple and his tongue flicks and his teeth saw gently and he suckles until I gasp and then he switches to the other breast and does the same.

I guide Conrad's face between my thighs, letting my knees fall apart and welcome his tongue on my clit, welcome his fingers into my channel. All is pleasure, then. Conrad's tongue begins slowly, long fat swipes of his tongue up my slit from entrance to clitoris, then back down, and then a fluttering as far into my cunt as his tongue will go, and then another slow lick back up. Fingers in, two of them, curling in and finding my G-spot with that unerring accuracy he has, and his tongue starts a quickening side-to-side flick, which sets my hips into motion.

And Charlie...oh Charlie. He's devouring my tits as if he's been starved of them. Licking, sucking, biting, sliding his tongue along the undersides.

Sensation overload—

All I can feel is tongues and lips and teeth on my erogenous zones, flinging me into climax. It's immediate. I grip Conrad's hair and hold him in place and ride his mouth, palm Charlie's neck and writhe my tits against his mouth.

Come.

Scream as loud as I can, let go utterly.

But they don't stop. Conrad's tongue pushes me past the orgasm and into the throes of the next, adding fingers this time, driving into my slit and curling for my G-spot, and now he doesn't pull them out as he licks my clit, but continues to fuck me with his fingers, and Charlie pinches my nipples, somehow just hard enough to make it hurt so good I gnash my teeth and whimper as my second orgasm rises within me.

I lose myself in the climax, forget who's who and who's where, forget everything but the spastic waves blasting me into paroxysms of bliss.

"Oh—oh god. Oh god…" I gasp as the orgasm leaves me shuddering, thighs trembling.

Charlie's lips stutter up my breastbone and scatter tender kisses along the side of my neck and I can't fucking help it, can't help it—

I turn my face to the side and kiss him—

———

Charlie is pressed against my ribs, not quite hovering over me. He's kissing me breathless in the pitch black. His lips move and his tongue slides on mine and he caresses my breasts, toys with them, flicks my nipples and then teases his way down my ribs and across my belly and finds my cunt. I gasp against his mouth and spread my legs apart for him, take his fingers inside me and he gets me writhing with a few wet strokes into my slit, but I need *him*, need more than this, more than his fingers.

I pull him on top me, moaning in anticipation as he kneels between my thighs and grasps my ankles and fits my feet into his armpits, levering my ass off the mattress and spreading my cunt open for him. I reach between my thighs and find his cock, guide him to my slit, moaning again as he nudges in. He hesitates with the head of his cock splitting open my labia.

And then fucks into me.

He's so *long*, driving in and in and in, the tip scraping against my G-spot as he fills me. His strokes, as he pulls back and fucks, are slow and measured and sinuous, so smooth I lose track of whether he's driving in or withdrawing, until there's only the slide of his cock, the wet glide, the glut of fullness and the ache of absence.

I clutch my tits and moan as Charlie fucks me.

It's endless and beautiful. I shudder on the ragged edge of climax, where it's so beautiful, caught up in such wild ecstasy, in that perfect place right before I topple over the edge, where I've always wanted to be, just like this, with him.

I let him fuck me and fuck me and fuck me, never coming, just the grinding gutting wonder of his cock moving inside me, hitting that spot. His hands are on the insides of my thighs, holding my legs apart, his hips flexing against my thighs.

I want to stay just like this, just lay here and moan, drowning, in heaven, letting myself be beautifully and perfectly fucked into oblivion.

I don't need to scream or thrash, all I need is to let the fucking take over. Moaning, whimpering, I lift my hips to meet his thrusts letting the orgasm build and build and build, denying myself the release.

"God...Charlie—*Charlie*—" I gasp.

"Hannah. I wish it was always like this."

"Me too, Charlie."

"You feel so good, wrapped around my cock."

"Don't stop, Charlie. Don't come. Keep fucking me, just like this."

Charlie obeys me.

He just fucks me, never coming, never quite giving me the edge I need to come, and the orgasm I'm denied builds into a raging inferno inside me, and Charlie just keeps fucking me like he's never fucked me before, giving me so much pleasure just by the way his cock feels driving in and out of me—

but it's not enough—

the need to come grows and grows and grows, and memories

assault me, memories of him, of a woman with red hair bobbing up and down on him in the car outside our house, her huge pale breasts bouncing as she rides him in the passenger seat, and I gasp from the poignancy of the memories, and of the secret shame I feel from knowing what I did, late one night, after watching the red haired beauty suck Charlie's cock:

I stood at the window and finger-fucked myself while watching them; I brought myself to a whimpering, weak-in-the-knees orgasm while watching her slap up and down on his cock, and the orgasm was made all the more potent because I was wondering what *she* would feel like, what her tits would feel like in my hands, what her pussy would taste like, what her cunt would feel like around my fingers, what it would be like to kiss her lips…and I wondered what it would be like to suck his cock and finger her pussy, or lick her clit and make her come while his cock drove into my throat…I made myself come imagining all that, watching them—

———

—long hair slides between my fingers. Slippery, silky. It's utterly dark, but I just know this hair whispering between my fingers is red, a vivid scarlet. Soft flesh presses against me, a thick, strong, soft thigh against mine, a long lithe arm drifting across my belly, fingers tickling, long nails scraping my flesh. A delicate nose nudges the outside of my breast, and then plump tender lips close around my nipple. Those fingers, those long nails…they scrape and tickle and tease, dancing torturously from my ribcage to navel, thigh to hipbone, across the upper swell of my pussy. Then, oh—*then*…then a fingernail scrapes my clit, and I jerk, gasping.

Feminine laughter echoes, a dark, amused, erotic tinkle; she's pleased with herself.

"You like that, do you?" she asks, her voice a low silky murmur— if a voice had a color and a texture, her voice would match her hair, shimmery, vivid, lustrous, smooth, exotic, bordello-scarlet. "You like it when I do...*this*?" She scrapes that fingernail against my clit as she emphasizes the last word.

"Yes..." I breathe.

She runs her fingernail along the seam of my cunt, not quite sliding in, a slow shuddersome rasp. I shake so hard my tits quiver, and I gasp in anticipation. She's teasing, torturing; she *knows*. My every weakness is laid bare; the knowledge of precisely how to make me a writhing, begging mess is obvious to her. A flick of her tongue against my nipple, another long, slow rake of her fingernail along the soaked, dripping slit of my cunt. Her hair drifting over my breasts and throat, cool and slippery, and then her mouth on my other breast, not going directly for the nipple but licking and nipping around it, her tongue stuttering over the tiny bumps on the areolae. Her fingernail scraping up and down, up and down, up and down, teasing, never quite penetrating, never quite touching my clit.

I'm at the cusp of orgasm, I've been teetering on this verge for an eternity, but I can't fall over into climax, I can't come. I know she can make me come in an instant—one flick of her finger, one touch of her tongue, and I'd come apart screaming. But she denies me. Instead, she pushes me closer and closer, her fingernail starting to spread apart my cunt just a bit now, as she continues to stroke the slit.

She leans over me, her breasts crush against mine, hers huge and soft and squishy, her nipples hard little nubs rubbing against mine. I feel her grin as she flicks my lower lip with her tongue, and then brushes my mouth with her lips. I move in to feel her mouth against mine, but she denies me again with a laugh.

"Ah-ah," she admonishes, "not yet."

She teases my lips with hers, again and again, rubbing her lips on mine, pretending to kiss and then taking it away, touching my upper lip with her tongue, then licking my lower lip, then darting her tongue against mine. And all the while, her fingernail scrapes and rakes and rasps up and down my clit, penetrating incrementally deeper between the labia with each swipe up and down. I'm shaking and shuddering, needy, moaning, but she continues to tease and deny, and I've already been denied this release for so long, and I *need* it, but she won't give it to me.

"Gimme," I whisper, leaning in for her mouth, flexing my hips into her finger.

She pulls away just before I get what I want in both places, with that same breathy erotic laugh. "Gimme what? What do you want first?"

"Both," I say, writhing, fists clenched and trembling. "Both, please."

She teases me another few moments, her tongue sliding slowly along my upper lip, her fingernail ever so slightly inside me, just barely splitting open my pussy, teasing both sets of lips with tongue and finger.

I'm aching, throbbing all over, my skin coated in a sheen of sweat from rocking on the edge of orgasm for so long—

And then, all at once, without warning, she plunges her finger into my cunt and covers my mouth with hers, and I…

*…COME.*

I'm screaming so loud my ears ring. My entire lower half arches up off the bed and her finger is inside my pussy and her tongue is writhing against mine and it's bizarre to feel such sweet tender feminine lips against mine, such a thin delicate finger inside me, and the kiss is not masculine clashing with feminine, not a war for dominance, not showing me alpha possession, not affectionate emotive mingling of souls via mouths. This is…something else. I don't know what. But fuck, it's incredible. She sucks my tongue into her mouth and her fingernail grazes that place deep inside me behind my clit, where a single touch incites madness.

It is madness itself, this orgasm.

Utter chaotic detonation.

She stretches that finger inside me, scratching that G-spot, and then she presses her thumb to my clit, and the orgasm shatters and twists into something higher, deeper, hotter, *more*. It's an orgasm both vaginal and clitoral, turning me into a mewling screaming writhing puddle. And all the while she's kissing me, kissing me, kissing me, her lips sliding and moving, tongue skittering and toying with mine.

She doesn't stop until I'm quivering and panting raggedly. I catch her wrist to stop her because it feels so good, too good, so much it hurts.

"My turn," she announces.

She stretches away from me, straddling me, sitting on my hips. I feel her pussy against mine, an erotic thrill of clit on clit. She grinds there for a split second, but then moves up my body—all too soon. I would have liked more of her clit on mine, but now she's above me, hovering, balanced, and I smell her desire inches from my face. I lift up, flicking my tongue out. I taste pussy, feel the plump lips on my tongue, shaved bare. Oh god, god. Sweet female musk, tang of her juices.

"Mmm, yeah," she murmurs. "Lick my pussy."

I don't tease her. No need, no reason—she's already on the edge. All I have to do is plunge my tongue into her cunt and she's gasping, shuddering. She uses her fingers to spread open her pussy for me, and I press a fingernail against her clit, scraping like she did mine, and I'm rewarded by a shrill shriek and a jerk of her hips. I do it again, licking into her entrance, and she jerks again and writhes.

"Like that?" I ask, my breath huffing hot on her flesh.

"Yeah—fuck yeah. Just like that." Her voice is rougher now, not so smooth, not so collected. "Make me come." This from between clenched jaws.

Her whole body shudders as I switch mouth and hand, sliding my finger into her pussy and flicking my tongue against her clit, and the shaking of her thighs, a helpless quiver accompanied by a long low groan, tells me how close she is. I know what I'd want right now, so I give it to her—another finger deep inside her, both curling to massage her G-spot, my tongue fluttering against her clit in rapid circles. She cries out and grinds her cunt against my face, and I feel her come, then, feel the wetness spread against my tongue and smear on my lips, feel her pussy spasm and squeeze around my fingers. I moan with her as she comes, fucking her tight clamping cunt with two fingers and sucking her throbbing clit between my teeth, letting her ride my face and hand.

"Not the same as coming around a big hard cock," she mumbles, gasping, "but *goddamn*, that's amazing."

She's sliding down my body, her shaking hands smoothing over my tits, mine on hers. God, her tits are huge. Her nipples are thick, standing tall and hard as I pinch and roll them, getting a quaking shudder and a gasp from her. Our hands are everywhere, then, body on body, soft flesh on soft flesh, her cunt against my thigh, our legs scissored and then, god yes, her pussy against mine, clit to clit, hands on tits, mouths on mouths—

———

—And Charlie is there, somewhere, somehow. His hard body is a contrast to our soft curves. His hand is on my thigh, and a gasp from her tells me he's touching her somewhere. His back is to me—she's on the other side of Charlie, and I curl against him, stroke his arms and his ribs and lean closer, run my hands everywhere, feel her hand reaching over Charlie to find me, caressing my ass as I pinch her nipple. I hear kissing, mouth on mouth, breath on breath, I feel movement.

I find their hands between their bodies, her fist around his cock, his on her cunt. Placing my hand with hers, around his cock, we stroke him together. She pushes and I pull, and he rolls to his back between us. Her hand is on top, stroking and pumping around the head, and mine is on the bottom, plunging at his root. His hips flex and push, and he's groaning and grunting, and still kissing her. So I press in, join the kiss, and then it's three mouths all colliding as she breaks away from Charlie to kiss me, and then him, and he does the same, transferring from her mouth to mine, and then all three of our mouths somehow find each other all at once, and her tongue is sliding on my lips and his tongue tangles with mine, our hands stroking his cock in unison.

God, it's too much, so much. So fucking much. His hands find us. Fingers in my cunt, mouths all confused. I feel fingers pinch my nipples, and realize it's her tweaking my tits, sending surges of heat through me, spastic bursts of pain-induced pleasure.

She moves first. Slides astride him, sitting upright on her knees. I have my hand on the root of his cock, and I feel her lowering herself onto him. I slide my fist up his length and my knuckles touch her cunt, and I seek her opening with my thumb, guiding him into her. I feel him tense and hear him groan, hear her moan. She glides down, and I feel their joining with my fingers, feel his cock sliding through my fist and into her, between the lips of her pussy.

He pulls me closer to himself then hooks my leg over his shoulders so I'm straddling him. He uses both hands to settle me on my knees above his mouth, facing her. His tongue finds my clit, his fingers sliding into me. I hear her huffing gently, whimpering as he fucks her; I reach out and she finds me in this all-consuming darkness. Her mouth finds mine, her hands clutching my tits, and I feel her movement, feel her grinding up and down, and hear the wet squelch of his cock driving into her. She shudders and moans, an erotic gasp against my mouth, and I slide my hands down her body, find her clit and finger it in quick light circles, bringing her to breathlessness, and I'm gasping right along with her as Charlie eats my pussy with a skill I never knew he had, his tongue wild against my clit, his fingers drilling in and out hard and fast, pushing me to climax all too soon. I come with a whimper, grinding on him, her fingers pinching my nipples until it hurts, her teeth catching at my lips.

I swing off Charlie, because it's not another orgasm I want right now. I reach for her, and I find that she's pivoted on Charlie to ride him reverse, so she's facing his feet. I push her so she's laying on her back on top of Charlie. I palm her tits and slide my mouth across hers, then to Charlie, and we're all kissing again, and I feel Charlie moving, feel him fucking her. I cup his balls in my palm and massage them as he fucks her, then I move down their bodies.

I press my mouth to her clit, lick her to shrieking paroxysms. Charlie's cock slides against my chin as he slams into her, the noise of their fucking loud in my ears. I tilt my head, take the sliding shaft between my lips and taste her pussy on his cock, and he groans, growls, and she whimpers as I press a fingertip to her clit. Just like that, then, Charlie fucking her, my mouth on him as he drills into her, my fingers on her clit, both of them going wild, cresting the rise of climax. I feel her tense and I move my mouth to her.

She comes first, screaming as Charlie fucks her, as I eat her. She's wild, a feral thing, slamming down on Charlie and writhing against my lips at the same time, clawing at my hair to keep me against her.

And then Charlie groans, and his thrusts go staccato. Her screams turn to gasps as he slams hard and slow against her cunt, their bodies meeting with slaps and wet squelching. My palms are on her thighs, which shake and tremble with her orgasm, a second one, or a continuation of the first, and she's breathless, unable to even gasp as he fucks her and fucks her and fucks her, and I feel it all, feel his cock sliding into her, feel her body tensing, contorting, arching as the climax rips her into shattered bliss.

"Oh...*fuck*—" I hear him grunt.

And then he's coming. I know those sounds, those desperate grunts he makes, the way his thrusts go deep and stay there, fucking deeper without pulling away.

And then she does something unexpected—she slides up his body and yanks his cock out of her, and pulls at me and guides me to him. She's got his cock in her fist and my hair in her other hand, and she pushes me onto him. I open my mouth and feel him slide between my lips, tasting her essence on his cock, and then he's spurting a stream of cum into my mouth, and driving into my throat and backing away, unable to slow his thrusts, more cum filling my mouth, and then before I can swallow it she's smashing her lips against mine and his cum drips down my chin and her tongue is in my mouth and she's licking his cum away as she kisses me. Then he's in her mouth, fucking her throat, and then mine, and then he's thrusting between our mouths and cum is sluicing down his shaft and she's sliding her mouth down the side and I'm sucking around his glans and he's a grunting cursing snarling helpless creature caught in the throes of orgasm, torsion wracking his body.

She pulls me away from him, and her hands glide all over me, cupping my tits and palming my cheeks, and she wipes clean my chin and lips, and kisses and licks away the last of his cum from my skin and I taste him on her.

———

And then it's just her and me, wrapped up together, skin to skin, my face against her breasts, her breath on my hair, her hands all over me. Her body is so lush, her tits huge and high and firm and full of bounce, and her ass is tight and juicy, and her hair wraps around my fist, and her lips are soft and pillowy and eager, and her hands are skillful.

I get it, Charlie, I get it…

…but it still hurts.

It fucking hurts that it's her and not me. The way you fuck her as you never fucked me, the way you devour her cunt as you never did for me. She's wild and eager and willing, and when she comes she's spastic and loud and erotic. But I couldn't come, not with you.

But was that because you didn't fuck me like this?

———

You didn't cling to me and grip my hair in your strong fist and kiss me dizzy. Instead, you slide into me easily and beautifully, because I'm wet and I'm already so close, your mouth brought me there, your fingers got me there, and now I've got your cock inside me and it's beautiful, the way you slide in and our bodies meet and line up and your lips are nonstop against mine. This is how it should have been, just like this, your cock moving perfectly, gliding in and out, hitting me just right. You brace yourself on one hand and fit the other between us and finger my clit as you fuck me, and that's all it takes, foreplay to put me on the edge and your mouth on mine and your fingers on my throbbing clit and your cock inside me, thrusting, hitting my G-spot with that gentle curve of your cock.

God, god, god, the orgasm is a shuddering series of gasps as heat blasts through me and pleasure seizes me and you fuck me through it, waiting, waiting, waiting until I've come.

And when I reach up and cup your jaw with my palm and bite your lip, when I whisper—*come for me, now, Charlie*—you pull out of me and flip me over onto my hands and knees and drive into me from behind. Your hands grip my ass and you slam in, hard and rough, and you fuck me with abandon, and I scream through it because it feels so goddamn good to have you fuck me like this, my orgasm making me so wild and hypersensitive and needy that I—I—come again, and then you grunt and squeeze my ass cheeks so hard it hurts and slam in, pull out, and I hear those desperate grunts you make when you're about to release. Cum splashes onto my ass, and you groan through it, spurting a thick, tacky, hot pool of seed onto my flesh, sliding down between the heavy globes—

"Shit, Hannah…" you gasp, and your voice is deeper, rougher than it used to be— "why was it never like this before?"

Because this isn't real.

You never fucked me like that, never ate my pussy, never pushed me to orgasm, certainly never fucked me from behind, never gushed cum onto the outspread roundness of my ass as I knelt on all fours in front of you.

You never fucked me like that.

That wasn't you—

· · ·

"Conrad?" My voice is querulous, echoing in the dark.

No answer.

"Conrad?"

I can't see, can't see, can't see. The darkness is all pervading. All-consuming. It's a drowning kind of dark. I'm bathed in utter blackness. Reaching out, I find nothing.

"Conrad!" A sob breaks my voice, then. "Conrad...*please*. Where are you?"

Alone.

I'm alone.

Alone in the dark. I've been alone in the darkness for so long, so fucking long. I hate the darkness, hate the aching loneliness.

"Hannah?" His voice is close, beside my ear, his breath warm on the shell of my ear. "I'm here, Hannah."

I reach for him, but I have no limbs. Or if I do, they're too heavy. Trapped in sludge, frozen in place. No way to reach, to find, to touch. He's there, I feel him, hear him, sense him, but I can't reach him. I can't feel myself, my body; I'm stuck, trapped, and I can't see.

"Conrad?" My voice echoes.

*Conrad?*

**conradconradconrad**

No…no, no.

He can't hear me. Am I speaking? Am I here?

"Hannah, I—fuck, I hate that it took this for me to finally own up to how I feel about you. I hate seeing you like this, hate talking to you like this, but they say you can hear me. I don't know. It's so fucking hard, baby. Being here, it's—it's hell. I just want you to—"

What? Anything you want, Conrad, anything—I'll do it. Anything. Just tell me, so I can make the sadness in your voice go away, so I can make the pain go away.

"—Wake up, Hannah." His voice echoes, now.

*wakeupwakeupwakeupwakeup*

Wake up.

Wake up, Hannah.

● ● ● ●

I'm in the living darkness, the hungry black.

I feel myself, feel the prickling of the hairs on my arms, the smooth slide of my legs brushing each other, the way my breasts are pulled by gravity as I lay on my side. My hair is splayed out. My heart beats steadily, rhythmically.

I sense him.

"Conrad?"

"Yeah, babe." He's beside me, suddenly, his body warm and huge and hard and naked.

"Hi."

I hear the smile in his voice. "Hi, sexy thing."

"You think I'm sexy?" I ask.

"Fishing for compliments, Miss Tavistock?"

"Why, yes, I am, Mr. Killian."

He levers himself over me, his proximity palpable even though I can't see him, or anything at all. I don't need to see, only feel. His breath is on my cheek, and then I feel his knees wedge between my thighs. I feel his hands brace above my shoulders, beside my face. Then his lips touch mine, and his tongue slides along my lips.

"Hannah, you are the most beautiful woman I've ever known. You make me crazy, you're so goddamn beautiful. I just— I can't fucking stand how much I want you all the time. I think about you whenever I'm not with you."

"You do?"

"Yeah."

"What do you think about?"

His lips touch the peak of my left breast and then the right. "This. And this."

"Oh?" I barely manage to squeak the word out, because his kiss leaves me breathless. "What else?"

"What else do I think about?" he slides down my body, his palms cupping my tits, squeezing, kneading, massaging. His lips stutter and slip over my belly, kissing, kissing, and then brush the seam of my pussy. "This. I think about this a lot."

"Oh really?"

"Nonstop." He licks the slit, breathing on the wetness. "Literally, all the fucking time. I think about licking you and kissing you here. Sliding my fingers inside." He suits action to words, pushing two long, thick digits inside me. "Feeling how wet you get for me."

He withdraws his fingers, and smears them over my clit; his fingers are soaked in my juices.

"Anything else you think about?"

"Hannah, babe...I think some pretty dirty things about you. Sometimes, when I'm at home alone, I think about you, and I imagine all the things I'd like to do to you."

"Just...*think*...about doing them?"

He laughs, a low erotic grumble. "No, Hannah, I don't just think about them. I picture you, just like this, naked, and I think about what I'd like to do, and I imagine myself doing it to you, and I jerk off."

"You jerk off thinking about me?"

"Fuck, yeah. Do you?"

"I touch my pussy and pretend it's you." He dips his fingers inside me, pulls them out, touches my clit, alternating in that way that I love so much, that makes me so fucking hot and wet and horny. "Just like you're doing."

"God, that's hot, thinking about you making yourself come, thinking about me."

"What do you picture yourself doing to me, Conrad?"

"Everything."

"Tell me. Tell me everything. I want to know. I want—oh, oh *god*—I want to do it all with you." He has me on the edge already, within seconds.

"Everything?"

"Everything."

He stops when I'm a heartbeat away from coming. "God, where do I even start? I think about this, making you come. I think about the way your eyes close and your mouth falls open, and your thighs shake, and you can't be still, and the way you moan my name." He touches my clit, and I jerk, the orgasm teetering, wobbling, about to topple through me. "I think about the way your pussy tastes." His mouth covers my cunt, his tongue sliding up my slit and dipping in, then flattening against my clit, and I can't stop it, can't hold it back. I come with a scream, and he moans as he tongues me through the climax. "This, Hannah. I think about this, all the damn time. You, coming for me."

"God, Conrad. I don't know how you can make me come so hard, so fast."

"Because I know your body. It was made for me."

"Do you think about me doing things to you?"

"Fuck yeah, I do."

I roll toward him, push him to his back. "Like what?"

He brushes his fingers through my hair, rubs my cheekbone with his thumb, and brushes the pad of that thumb over my lips. "I imagine you putting this mouth on my cock."

I slide down his body and cradle his massive, throbbing erection in my hand. I cup his balls, and then stroke up the shaft to slide my fist around him and then pull it away from his belly until it's standing perpendicular to his torso and can't bend any further. I stroke my other hand down all those long, thick inches. He groans as I let my hair drift over his belly. He gathers the sheaf of my hair in his hand, and wraps it around his fist.

Parting my lips, I touch them to the broad soft springy head of his cock. "Like this?"

"Mmmmm—yeah, just like that."

"Tell me, Conrad. Tell me how you picture it, how you want me to do it. Tell me what you want, and I'll do it. *Anything*, baby—I'll do anything for you."

He groans, long and low. "*Anything*, Hannah? I've got a dirty, wicked imagination."

"I'm a dirty girl, Conrad." I keep him bent away from his belly and caress the hard veiny silky shaft. "Haven't you figured that out by now? There's nothing you could want that I won't want to do with you, or to you."

"God, Hannah. What the hell did I ever do to deserve you?"

"I ask myself that all the time about you." I lick the tip of his dick with the flat of my tongue. "Now…please, tell me everything you want me to do to you, so I can do it. I want to make your dirtiest, darkest fantasies come true."

"*You're* my fantasy, Hannah."

"I'm serious, Conrad. Anything. Just tell me."

He sighs. "You're so fucking amazing, Hannah. That mouth of yours, Jesus." He pushes me closer to his cock. "More of your mouth. Take me into your mouth. Use your tongue."

I kneel between his thighs and bend over him so my throat is open, and I start slow, start shallow. This isn't new, I've done this to him before, and I know exactly how much he likes this. But…this time it feels different—sweeter, more tender. I bob on him, taking the glans between my lips, licking around it eagerly. Then deeper, sliding my mouth down the shaft inch by inch, slowly. I'm holding him with one hand at the base, keeping him tilted straight up, and my other hand is cupping his heavy balls, delicately, gently cradling them, caressing them.

"Shit, yes, honey—just like that. Keep doing that."

"Mmmmm-hmmmm?"

"Oh yeah. I dream about this. Then I wake up and it's not real, and I have to jerk off. But this time it's real. You're real."

I'm real. Yes, I'm real.

This is Conrad, beneath me, his cock between my lips, sliding toward my throat. I taste him, that familiar male musk and the salt of his skin. His cock stretching my lips, so thick my jaws ache. I back away and suck on the head, and then bob back down, and this time, without warning, I take him all the way, gagging and breathing through my nose as I swallow him down my throat, deeper, deeper, until his balls are at my chin and my nose bumps against his belly.

"Fucking hell, Hannah."

"Uh-huh?"

"Fuck, that's incredible." He groans as I back away, let him pop free of my mouth. "You know what else?"

"What?" I ask, wiping my lips.

"The way you sometimes just…put your mouth on the side of my cock, going down. And then you put your mouth on my balls, and use your hands on my cock."

I give him exactly that. Tilting my head sideways, I take his shaft between my lips and flutter my tongue along the veins and ridges, tasting him as I slide down, down, to his sac. I kiss and lick the tender globes of his balls, and then take the whole sac into my mouth and suckle, back away, tease them with my lips and tongue while stroking his cock with both fists, hand over hand. He groans and thrusts into my hands, and then cries out helplessly when I close my lips around his balls again and take them into my mouth. Stroke, suck, lick, and he's gone, moaning, fist in my hair.

"Okay, stop, stop. I'm gonna come, and I'm not ready yet."

"You're not?"

"No, god no. I don't want to come in your mouth. Not this time."

"Where do you want to come?"

"Inside you." He lifts me, sets me astride him. "Ride me, Hannah."

I straddle him, kiss him. I lift my ass in the air and clutch his cock, nudging him between the lips of my pussy. Flutter my hips to tease him, not quite letting him push in. My palms rest on his shoulders, my tits smashed against his chest, my mouth shuddering against his. I tease him, rolling my hips in tiny circles so just the upper few inches of his cock grinds in and out of me, and then, when I'm as desperate as he is, I nab his lower lip between my teeth.

I plunge my hips down, my ass slapping against his thighs, his huge, beautiful cock stretching me to a dizzy burn, sliding into me.

His hands grip my hips and yank me down onto him, then he releases the pressure so I can lift up, and then, together, we slam me down on him, and I scream his name as he spears into me, filling me to glutted ecstasy, spreading my cunt apart, driving in deep—

—there's no stopping this, no way to hold out, no way to hold back. I can only hold on to him, my knees on either side of his waist, my hands clawing into his broad shoulders, my teeth nipping his hard chest. He fucks me with raw abandon, hips pistoning hard and fast, slamming his cock into me over and over and over, battering my cunt with bruising, beautiful power. My screams of pleasure are shaken by the force of his thrusts. He shifts his grip, his palms cupping my ass cheeks, spreading me apart so he can ram in deeper.

And then, abruptly, he stops. I feel him tense, feel him pulling back from the brink of release.

"I thought you wanted to come inside me?"

"I do."

"Then why'd you stop?"

He palms my ass, smooths and caresses. Spreads the globes open, and his finger brushes over my asshole. "Because I want you here."

I moan against his chest. "Then take me there, Conrad."

"Need you ready, first."

"So make me ready."

He thrusts slowly, angling to hit my G-spot. "Touch your pussy, Hannah. The more you come, the better it'll feel when I touch you back there."

So, together, we make me come. He fucks me slowly, grinding

smoothly in and out, hitting that magical place deep inside me that makes me so crazy, that makes me come so hard, but even when I'm wailing in ecstasy and writhing against him, he doesn't stop, doesn't let up, so neither do I, and together we make me come again, and this time, as the climax rips through me, he pulls his cock out of me.

He rolls me onto my belly, and I gather my knees beneath me and draw them up to open myself for him. His fingers guide mine to my clit, and he silently urges me to keep touching myself, so I do. I finger my clit even as waves of ecstasy continue to assault me, one after the other, each more potent than the last. I feel him touch a fingertip to the tight rosebud of my asshole, massaging gently. His lips touch my ass cheek, kissing all over, closer and closer to where he's touching, and then I feel his breath. I gasp a surprised shriek as his tongue touches me there, a light wet warm tickling that turns darkly erotic in an instant, tumultuously thrilling, sending pangs through me, low, sharp, and deep. And then I feel moisture pool against my asshole—his saliva. He presses a finger to me, and then, as I whimper with a wracking wave of orgasmic pleasure, he fits that fingertip inside me, and the gasp turns to ragged moans as I'm penetrated by his fingertip. God, it's so good. So dark, so full, so filthy. I'm coming still, or again, coming nonstop, and he slowly, gently glides his finger deeper into me, millimeter by millimeter, and then his knuckles bump against my buttocks. He pulls his finger out, and I moan in agonized bliss as he pushes it back in. Again, and again, and each successive wave of orgasm is hotter and deeper than the last, and each time I come, he moves his finger in and out faster and faster, until he's fucking my asshole with that single finger.

But it's too much. "I need—shit, Conrad, I need a minute. I need to stop coming for a minute. It's too much."

He presses a kiss to my back, his finger buried deep inside me. He lifts up behind me, and I feel his cock at my slit, begging to slide inside me. "How about this?" he whispers.

"Oh, yes," I gasp, "god, yes. Please, please. Fuck me until I can come again."

He's inside me before I've finished speaking, driving in. And god, it's too good, his cock inside me, and his finger buried all the way into my ass. I'm so full, too full, and it feels too fucking good. It's heaven. Or whatever is better than heaven, this is it, being like this with my Conrad. Taking him, all of him.

"More," I whisper.

It's all I have to say; I'm ready. My fingers go to my clit, and Conrad drives his cock slowly in and out of me, and he drags his finger out, slides it back in, fucking me both ways. An orgasm wells up, sending spasms bursting through me, and he feels it in the way my cunt clamps around his cock. I feel more saliva drip onto my asshole, lubricating me for the second finger he adds, and then I'm even more split apart, more full, and my voice breaks as shudders wrack me.

I writhe against him as he fucks me, as he glides those two fingers in and out of me, and it's so good, so amazing, so much…

Yet not enough.

I want *him*.

"*More*, Conrad," I beg. "Fuck me there."

I feel him pull out of my pussy, hear him spit and hear the slick slide of his fist on his cock as he smears his saliva on himself.

"Ready, Hannah?" He slowly pulls his fingers out of my asshole and nudges the opening with the head of his cock.

"God yes. Yes." I writhe against him, my fingers slowing on my clit, keeping myself teetering on the brink of an orgasm. "Put it inside me, Conrad. I want it all."

He spits again, and now my asshole and his cock are wet with saliva, slippery and ready. He pushes, and I focus on opening for him, moving my fingers against myself faster now. The climax builds, and I feel his cock press into my opening, beginning to stretch me apart. God, so slow. Then it's an eternity of hovering on the edge of orgasm, gasping as Conrad gradually, carefully splits me open and fills me, inch by inch. I'm groaning as he slides in the last few inches, shuddering head to toe, tits shaking, sweat dotting my skin, pussy clamping as a strange dark new ecstasy rifles through me.

"Okay, honey?" he asks.

"Fuck yes. So much fucking more than okay." I've got all of him inside me, then, stretching me and filling me. It hurts, but it's such a beautiful hurt, the kind of pain that translates into jagged euphoria, utter rapture. "Fuck me, Conrad. Fuck me until you come."

I push back against him, and he remains still, his hands gripping my ass cheeks in a rough, desperate squeeze. He needs to move, but he doesn't want to hurt me; I need this, need it. *Need* it.

So I fuck him.

I brace my hands in front of me and lower my chest to the bed and push into him until my ass squishes flat against his hips. Then I pull forward, a ragged whimper scraping out of my throat as I feel his cock slipping through the spasming ring of muscle. My jaw clenches on a grating scream, and I keep pulling forward until he's nearly out of me, and his grip on my ass cheeks tightens. I begin pushing backward, then, taking him into me, and the scream I'm biting down on escapes in a shrill burst. Conrad snarls, and thrusts the last few inches.

"Yes, *yes*," I breathe, meeting him on the in-thrust, "Like that, baby. Give me that, please, *please*—fuck me, Conrad. Please fuck me."

"Jesus Christ, woman," he groans, "you're too much. You're too perfect."

"*We're* perfect."

"I can't hold back anymore, but if I let go, I won't stop."

I pull forward, knowing I'll have to help him past his desire to not hurt me when he lets go of his control...

I scream as loud as I can as I slam my ass back into him, hard and fast. "*Good!*" I snarl, "don't stop. I want it. I can take it. I *need* it, baby. Fuck me, *please*."

He loses the battle with a primal growl. He lets go of my ass, caresses gently, and then spanks me, *hard*, and I squeal and lurch away in surprise, and that's when he gives in, thrusting into me. My squeal of shock at the spanking morphs into a groan of delight as he glides in. He takes hold of my buttocks again, gripping a handful on each side. Drives in, hard, and I scream again.

He leans over me, his chest against my spine, and cups my tits, grinding while buried as deep as he can go. Resting his forehead between my shoulder blades he thrusts, kneading my tits and pinching my nipples, and then he gathers both breasts in one hand and slides his fingers down to my clit. Brushes quick circular touches to me, thrusting, kissing my spine, biting the skin, groaning as he moves.

"You're holding back," I murmur. "Don't."

He leans back, stretching away, taking hold of my ass once more, and pulls almost out.

"Yeah," I murmur, as he drives in. "Like that."

"God...*damn*," he growls, feeling me writhe back into his thrusts. "Gonna lose it in about ten seconds."

"God, yes," I breathe. "Lose it. Lose it inside me, Conrad. Give it all to me."

He starts fucking, then, no longer the scraping, slow, grinding single thrusts. Instead he's pushing into me in a slow, deliberate rhythm. "Like this?"

"Yeah—yeahyeahyeah," I gasp, shrill, breathlessly whimpering the last three syllables in a single rush. "Oh god, yes. Don't stop, Conrad, don't you dare stop now."

He's picking up speed, clutching my ass in a harsh, crushing grip and pulling me back into his thrusts, snarling each time he slams deep. I can feel his balls swinging and swaying, tapping against my cunt on each thrust, feel his body flexing behind me, feel his power. I can feel each ridge and vein of his cock as it slides into me, again and again, and I'm lost in moans, gone for this, drowning in it.

"Conrad!"

"Fuck, Hannah—Hannah—"

The orgasm that's building now is...a different beast than anything that's gone before. It's just entirely *more*. I press my ring and middle finger against my clit, face buried in the bed, ass in the air, taking Conrad's cock hard and fast, and I grind my touch against my clit the way I like it best, pushing myself to the edge, but waiting, waiting for the moment Conrad lets go.

"Come with me, Hannah," he growls.

"Now?"

"Now, baby. Come now." He grunts wordlessly, gasping, groaning, fucking my asshole with all the primal power he possesses. "Jesus—fucking hell, I'm—*god*, I'm coming…Hannah, I'm coming!"

My fingers are circling so fast my forearm aches, and I'm writhing on him, slapping back against him, crying out as my own climax seizes me in a giant fist, wringing me into sobbing, shaking convulsions.

I feel him come, and it's the most violent release I've ever felt from him. He slams as deep as he can go, and I feel cum shoot out of him and fill me, and he pulls back and rams back in, more cum spurting into me. Again, and again, and again, each driving thrust pouring more and more cum into me, until it's pooled inside my asshole and being forced out by his still thrusting cock, squirting out of me, dripping out of my asshole, sliding wet and warm down the outside of my pussy. God, so much cum. And he can't stop fucking me, groaning, snarling, cursing. My asshole spasms around him, clamping down on his softening cock.

Finally, he pulls out of me as slowly as he'd pushed in.

When he flops free, I feel empty, aching, but wrung out with ecstasy, utterly spent, utterly sated.

He collapses to his back beside me, rolls into me, cradles me in his arms, rolls back so I'm nestled in his arms, my head on his chest, his heart beating under my ear. We're both panting hard, gasping for breath.

"Holy shit," he breathes.

I smile against him. "Yeah, baby. Holy shit."

Silence. Drowning, drowsing, liquid silence.

Except his heart beating under my ear: *da-DUM da-DUM da-DUM*…

I'm melting into him.

But he is becoming part of the darkness, and it's not Conrad's brawny arms I'm melting into, but the darkness itself.

"No," I whisper. "No. No…no-no-no, please no, god, please—*no!*"

It's too late.

I'm losing the reality. Losing the skein of truth. Losing Conrad.

"You have to come back to me, Hannah," he whispers.

And it's that low, close, hot, buzzing whisper again, so close, yet on the other side of some barrier.

Barely a whisper.

He whispers in the darkness.

"You have to come back to me, Hannah."

"I'm trying."

"Squeeze my hand if you can hear me."

I squeeze, with all my might, but I'm the darkness, I'm floating amid the whispers in the endless night and I can't squeeze, can't even feel his hand. I can hear him, but I can't feel him.

I need to feel him. I need to hold him, need to touch him. I want that back.

The dark rises up, surrounding me, preparing to drag me back under where the oil-slick puddle of reality and fantasy and truth and dreams all merge, where touch is real but I'm not, where Conrad can touch me and hold me and fuck me and I can give it all back to him, but it's all in the darkness, it's all muddied and muddled, and I want the *real thing*, not the transportive secret euphoria, not the black drowning bliss, but the simple pleasure of just *him*.

The rough scrape of his sandpaper stubble against my thighs. The calluses on his palms brushing the silk of my breasts. His lips on my jaw. His hair tickling my belly. His hands holding my legs open for him.

Just holding his hand.

His arms around me, cradling me close.

His body warm and solid and *real*.

The darkness slides up slick around me, eddying.

"You have to come back to me, Hannah."

*I'm trying.*

God, I'm trying. I want to come back to you; I need to come back to you.

I'm lost in a shadowland, trapped under an endless sheet of black ice.

I want to come back to you, Conrad. I hear you. But I, I can't—I can't reach you. Can't find you. Can't find my way out.

*The waves chuck against the pilings, a boat rubs against the dock, oars clink in the oarlocks. Wind skirls warm on bare flesh. The moon bathes us, silvering our skin. We're twisting, writhing, our flesh tangled and our sweat mingling.*

*"Hannah," he murmurs. "You feel so good, Hannah."*

*He presses me down on the dock, my hair splayed out on the aged wood, his hips moving between my thighs, sinuous, sensual, slow. The wood is smooth and worn, splinterless from age, and still warm from the sun.*

No, no. He never fucked me on the dock. I wanted him to, but he never did. We explored each other in different ways, but he never left the boat. I learned how to deep throat him in that boat. I learned how delicious his stubble felt on my thighs as he ate me out until I was a shuddering puddle on the dock, my legs draped over his shoulders. I learned how much I loved the sight of his cum on my skin, how I loved the sticky wetness of it, knowing it was his, that it was him marking me. This was always in the rowboat. He never fucked me on the dock.

I'm being pulled back down.

*What's true?*

Memories tumble through me, a million of them.

Doors. A candle. Torches. Doorknobs, and always him behind them. Him, in all the ways I love him, primal, masterful, wild, dark and dirty, sparing with his words and free with his touch. Always teaching me new ways to enjoy my body, new ways to enjoy his. Never shaming me for my desires, but rather always exploring them with me. Horses. A castle. A condo. Bodies tangling in sunlight in a big bed. The bite of wind and the white expanse of snow and a horse warm behind me and him in front of me, taking me in the cold. A sword gleaming in the moonlight. Men's eyes, men's touch, but always him, all of it always him.

They flash and flit and flicker through me, bright and vivid and utterly real, not just memories, but each one an experience momentarily real all over again. Him, him, him, again and again, in all the ways he owns me.

Him.

I remember all that.

I cannot escape it.

It is the darkness, the claw-grip of the feverish dark. It's pulling me under, into the shadows.

I don't want all that anymore.

I want the truth. I want to be free.

"Come back to me, Hannah. Please." His rough, deep, beautiful voice is fainter, now. Farther away.

I'm trying, Conrad.

*Come back to me, Hannah.*

I'm trying, I'm trying, goddammit, I'm *trying!*

It's like drowning, feeling the water close over nose and mouth and eyes and being unable to break the surface, unable to claw back up, unable to breathe. I fall under the scrim of the dark, tumble down under a meniscus of shadow, and I cannot stop myself, cannot paw for air, for light, for breath.

I can only rage against the swallowing black.

*Remember what is real*, I order myself.

*Remember the real.*

*Remember the real.*

*Remember the real.*

The sky is a bright brilliant endless blue. Not a single cloud, just a wild expanse of azure. The lake is a mirror of the sky, crystalline, utterly still. Around the edges are the trees forming a carpet of vibrant green, reflected in the lake and standing silent on the shore.

A crow wings across my field of view, black on blue, cawing raucously.

The gazebo is white, faded paint chipping in places, aged wood showing through in places. The rock on which the gazebo is built is gray, made darker by the occasional lapping of the water.

The rowboat is brown, old, faded, smooth-worn oak. The oarlocks are tarnished metal, the oars long and thin, with wide, dripping blades. There's a green and blue-checkered flannel blanket on the middle bench of the boat, folded into quarters, the edges hanging over the front and back of the bench. On the floor of the boat is a wicker picnic basket, showing the remains of a lunch: an uncorked and empty bottle of Malbec, two wine glasses with smears of red at their bottoms, a small block of Dubliner cheese and a red-handled paring knife, a plate with scraps of cold cuts and cracker crumbs and a few browning apple slices, a quarter loaf of baguette with the end ragged from being torn rather than sliced.

I'm on the floor of the gazebo, wrapped in our fleece blanket. Shivering. Aching. Teeth chattering. "I'm cold, Conrad."

He frowns at me. "It's July, Hannah. It's eighty degrees out here."

A shiver seizes me, wracking me so hard my bones rattle inside my skin. "I know. But I'm cold." Another violent shiver. "Everything hurts."

I've been feeling shitty for a few days, but it was nothing I could put my finger on, just a general malaise. By turns I'd feel confusion, nausea, a low-grade fever and then, yesterday, a headache; yucky, but nothing I couldn't push through.

Then, today, after lunch, feeling shitty turned into something worse. At first, I thought maybe the wine was bad, or that I'd had too much, even though we'd only split the one bottle, and I'd not even finished mine, nor eaten much. But the longer I sit here shivering, the more I realize it's not bad wine, or having had too much to drink, or even food poisoning.

This is...something worse. The headache is debilitating, an excruciating onslaught of vicious pain, accompanied by a stiffness and soreness in my neck.

"I think I need you to take me home, Conrad." I wrap the blanket more tightly around me. "I have to lay down."

He kneels beside me, and then helps me to my feet. He tucks the blanket higher around my shoulders, and his fingers brush my neck. His frown deepens, the worry lines at the corners of his eyes and between his brows sharpening. He touches the back of his hand to my forehead.

"Fucking hell, Hannah, you're burning up."

"Fever."

"Yeah, and I'm thinking it's a high one." He scoops me up in his arms.

With exquisite care he carries me out of the gazebo, across the rock and sets me in the boat, and then climbs in after me. I can tell he's worried; he doesn't show emotion on his face very easily, so the worry written clearly on his face scares me. He rows vigorously, putting his whole body into the work, leaning forward and then pushing back with his legs and hauling on the oars with his entire upper body. We're back at my dock within minutes, and he's dripping sweat, breathing hard. Climbing out of the boat, he leans down and scoops me up in his arms again and jogs with me up to the house and in through the back door.

Setting me in my bed and covering me with blankets, he touches my forehead and cheeks with his wrist, and lets out a gusting sigh.

"I'm seriously worried about you, Hannah."

"I'll be okay," I say. "I'll sleep it off. Take some Tylenol, maybe."

"Tylenol is in the bathroom?"

I nod, and he ducks out of my room and into the bathroom. I hear him poking around the medicine cabinet, hear pills rattling. He comes back with a tiny Dixie cup of water and two white pills.

"Here. Take these." He hands them to me, but my arms are heavy, and my sight blurs, and I'm too exhausted and weak to get the pills to my mouth.

"Help?" I try to sound like it's funny, but it's not. It's terrifying, to be this exhausted, this suddenly.

My head is full of heat and thickness and dizziness. My whole body is heavy. I'm freezing, shaking, shivering. He takes the pills from me, puts them on my tongue, and helps me drink from the cup to swallow them.

"Jesus, Hannah." His jaw clenches and releases spastically. "You have a thermometer?"

"Back...of the cabinet." It's hard to talk, to think, to put words in order.

He leaves again, comes back with the thermometer. It's an old one, the kind with actual mercury in it. I open my mouth as far as I can, and he sticks it under my tongue. Waits a minute, maybe two, and then pulls it out.

"Fuck," he whispers under his breath. "It's one-oh-four, Hannah. That's dangerously high."

"The Tylenol will help," I whisper. "I just...need to sleep. You should go."

He stares at the thermometer. "I can't. I'm not leaving you. Not when you're this sick."

The headache intensifies with every passing minute, becoming so excruciating that nausea batters through me from the agony, setting my stomach to heaving. "Gonna…shit—I'm gonna puke."

Conrad barely gets the trashcan from the bathroom back to me in time; my vomit is thin and sour and wine-tinged.

"Just leave the—the can," I say. "I'll be…I'll be okay."

"Fuck that, babe. I'm staying here." Conrad perches on the edge of the bed at my feet.

"Ch-ch-Charlie will—be home…s-s-s-sooon."

"Don't care. Not leaving you." He touches my head again, hissing. "Goddamn, you're seriously on fucking fire, honey. It's scaring me."

"Just a f-f-fever."

"Maybe, but anything over one-oh-four is dangerous. If that medicine doesn't take the temp down soon, I'm taking you in to the hospital."

"No. No hospital."

"Babe—"

"I—I watched my p-p-parents die…in a hospital. Got put…put into the sys—system." It's so hard to think, and my teeth are chattering so hard I can't speak. "Left the hospital with a social w-w-worker. I ha-*hate*…hospitals."

"I know, but…you may not have a choice." Compulsively, he lays his wrist on my forehead yet again. "I don't like this. The way it hit so suddenly, how hot you are. Doesn't feel right to me."

"I've been feeling shitty for a f-f-f-ew d-d-days. Then it got worse today."

"I'm just saying, Hannah, like it or not, if your fever doesn't go down, or if it goes up, I'm taking you in. I won't risk it."

My eyes close, then, and I can't open them. I feel like I'm being sucked out of the light and into the darkness. Out of the world and into the shadows.

Everything is heavy.

I hurt.

I'm cold.

Something hot touches my forehead, lies across my head from temple to temple. Hot? Or cold? I don't know, I can't tell the sensations apart; it feels hot, but I think it's cold.

It vanishes after a while and is replaced, but again, I can't tell if it's hot or cold.

"Hannah?"

I hear him, but he's far away. I try to wake up. "Mmm."

"I'm gonna take your temp again, okay?" He sounds...scared.

"Mmm."

I feel something small, thin, and cold at my lips. I open as far as I can, and the thermometer just barely slides between my teeth. I manage to put my tongue over it, and that's all I have the strength for.

A minute, an hour—some indistinguishable amount of time passes, and then the thermometer slides out of my mouth.

"*Fuck.*" His voice is a low growl, panicked. "One-oh-five. Fuck, fuck, fuck!"

"Mmm." I want to tell him it's okay, but I can't.

I'm scared, but the fear is deep down, under the layer of shadows skirling inside my head. Or maybe the fear *is* the shadows. Or above them. I don't know. I just don't want Conrad to be afraid.

"I'm taking you in. You could die if it gets any higher. Brain damage, comas, seizures, all sorts of shit can happen when it goes this high."

He vanishes, and then he returns and I feel him scoop me up. I'm wrapped in something piercingly hot or cold that envelops my whole body. I fight to open my eyes, and it takes every last shred of energy I have to squint through my eyelashes.

"Cold."

"I know, baby." His voice is tight, hard. "It's a wet towel I put in the freezer. We've gotta try to get your core temp down on the way to the hospital." He kisses my forehead, and I feel his lips tremble. "You'll be okay. They'll help you at the hospital."

The pain and the nausea and the exhaustion are too much for me to protest the hospital.

He lifts me in his arms and carries me. I'm laid down on what feels like the leather bench seat of a vehicle. The towel is laid over me, and it's at once icy cold and scorching hot. A wave of pain sears through me, but this is pain like I've never felt before, not just intensely, viciously, blindingly painful, but…different.

It feels decentralized, a throbbing agony in my entire head, as if my skull is going to explode. This sensation is quickly followed by a sudden spear of nausea hitting so fast I don't have time to do anything but heave, gag, and puke again. I'm on my side, and I feel it trickle down my cheek and pool on the leather under my face. I hear Conrad cursing, feel him wipe the vomit away, and then the door closes at my feet. The driver's door opens and then I hear the tires squeal. I'm aware of movement that pushes and pulls at me. Bumps in the road send agony lancing through my head.

I vomit again, but there's nothing to bring up but burning strings of bitter bile.

Darkness grips me.

I fight it, but it's futile.

Sensations wash over me, too far away and foreign and sludgy, they don't even seem to be happening to me.

Voices.

"—Just suddenly started getting sicker—"

"Can you tell me what her symptoms are?"

"—Seems like meningitis to me …"

"…Possibly fatal but…tests to be sure—"

———

"—have to put her in a coma to protect her brain, to reduce the swelling."

"Will she come out of it?" This is not Conrad's voice. Is it Charlie?

"It's impossible to say at this juncture, sir. If she does, there is a distinct possibility that she could be in a vegetative state. She could also make a full recovery, or she could suffer any number of various disabilities. This is a very complicated and dangerous disease, Mr. Markham. Her...um—Mr. Killian undoubtedly saved her life by getting her here as quickly as he did, but she has a long road ahead of her."

"How—how long will she be in the coma?"

"Hard to say, unfortunately. A few days, possibly more."

"It doesn't seem like you know very much at all, if you ask me." This is Conrad.

I know his voice—it's inside me, part of me. I yearn for him, strain for him.

"As I said, sir, this is a very tricky illness to deal with. It hits hard, it hits fast, and it disguises itself as the flu until it's nearly too late. We're doing all we can to help her, I assure you."

"Why are you even still here, anyway?" Charlie's voice, harsh and angry.

"Because I saved her life, and because she'd want me here?"

"Yeah, well, I'm still her husband, asshole. The fact that you got her here is the only reason you're still here at all, so keep your goddamn mouth shut or I'll have security make you leave."

I hate hearing them talk to each other like that. Hate the anger. Hate Charlie's pain. Hate that he found out about Conrad this way.

———

dark

cold

a swelling thickening susurrus of white noise,

which resolves through a stifling impossible floating eon into something—something—

a sound, a quaver of sensation—

**BEEP...BEEP...BEEP...BEEP...**

crackling, a squeak, a cough, a muffled voice somewhere above me— "Doctor Reed to the ER, Doctor Reed to the ER please..."

movement, the dark cold thick burying cavern of shadows that is

*I*

being rolled to one side, something cool and wet sliding along something that has no name, that isn't attached to anything, disconnected sensation, disorientation, movement to the other direction, more wet cool sliding,

***BEEP…BEEP…***

"BEEP…BEEP…"

***…BEEP…BEEP…***

"BEEP…BEEP…"

───

"…That you face reality, Mr. Markham. She may not ever wake up. The fever may have damaged her brain. Scans show that she may also have suffered a seizure while Mr. Killian was en route with her. He wouldn't have and *couldn't* have noticed, not if she was already unconscious and he was driving. I know the situation is…uncomfortable, but I feel it is my duty to report the truth of the facts so no one is held accountable for something unpreventable."

"So what are you saying?" Charlie, his voice slow, dark, rough. "About Hannah, I mean."

A long, exhausted sigh. "Just that you need to begin thinking about a DNR."

"A what?"

"A 'do not resuscitate' order."

"Like, if she's dying, just let her die?"

"It's been over a week, Mr. Markham. We've weaned her off the medication which put her into the medical coma, so she should have woken up by now." Another of those sighs, which communicates somehow a soul-deep pain, a mortal exhaustion from having to say this. "There's simply no way to know if she'll ever wake up, if she can survive on her own without the ventilator. This could be the way she'll be, kept alive by machines, constantly rolled and washed to prevent bedsores, fed through tubes…it's no kind of life, Mr. Markham. It is entirely your decision, however; I'm merely giving you the facts."

No.

No.

NO.

I'm here.

I'M HERE!

I can hear you, Charlie. I hear the doctor. Don't, don't.

I don't want to die.

I don't want to die.

But I exist only as the ability to hear. I can't blink, can't wiggle fingers—don't even *have* fingers to wiggle—can't rage, can't protest…

I'm trapped.

"I'll leave you to think over your options, Mr. Markham. And…I'm sorry. I promise you, we've done everything we possibly can, but sometimes these things are simply out of our hands."

"Thanks, Doctor."

Shoes squeaking, the sound fading.

Silence, except for the beeping of the heart monitor.

I hear Charlie breathing, then.

"Hannah, god, I'm—I'm so fucking sorry, Hannah. I just—I wish—fuck. FUCK!" The last word is shouted, suddenly loud, and full of anger and agony. "I hate this, Hannah. I hate everything about this. What am I supposed to do? What do I *do*, Hannah? Keep you alive on fucking machines? Let you just—die?"

He sobs, then, a raw, ragged, broken sound.

"Goddammit…*goddammit*." The last three syllables are spoken so low, so soft, with such palpable agony that they're nearly inaudible, nearly unrecognizable as human speech.

Oh Charlie, Charlie. Don't. Please don't.

Silence again, then, except the monitor beeping and Charlie sobbing.

I hear him moving, more silence, and then a female voice.

"Yes, Mr. Markham?"

"I need to talk to Doctor Abernathy."

"I'll get him for you, sir."

"Thanks."

"Of course."

More silence, and now Charlie isn't sobbing anymore, but I hear him sigh every now and again.

The other male voice from before, the Doctor. "How can I help you, Mr. Markham?"

"I…I don't think she'd want to be like this. To…just sort of…exist."

"You want a DNR, then?"

"Yeah."

A brief silence. "I—ah…perhaps I'm speaking out of turn here, but…I wonder if you should offer Mr. Killian a chance to voice his opinion? The legal right to choose for your wife resides with you, of course, but…it was quite clear to me that Mr. Killian cares very deeply for her."

"He doesn't get a goddamn vote."

"I think he might disagree. This is, obviously, a painful and difficult situation to navigate, and…the decision you're making, sir, it's… it's very—well, it's final. There's no going back. You have to try to think what she'd want, more than what you want for her."

"She's a goddamn vegetable!"

"I never said that was one hundred percent the case, Mr. Markham. Just that we have to be ready for that eventuality, as tragic as it would be." Another pause. "I would like to encourage you to consider all aspects of this. She could pull through—it's happened before. It's just that the longer she remains unconscious, the less likely a full recovery becomes. The decision may lie with you and you alone, but the consequences and effects of that decision are not limited to you."

Charlie groans, and I can almost picture him clutching his hair and tugging on it as he does when he's deeply upset. "I'll talk to—to Killian."

"I truly do feel that would be wise."

"Did he say when he'd be back?"

"I believe the nurse said he just went down to the cafeteria."

"Thanks."

"Whatever I can do to help, Mr. Markham."

Silence, long and profound.

I feel the darkness swallowing me, pulling me under. I fight it. Fight to remain where it's a little lighter, where there is sound and reality that makes sense, even if it hurts.

But I'm powerless.

Helpless.

━━━

Conrad's voice is a fishhook, lancing into me and jagging deep and pulling me upward, out of the deep cold impenetrable blackness and into lesser darkness where I'm able to hear—and only hear.

"What are her chances?" His voice is careful, quiet, but I hear the pain he's masking. He can't hide it from me, even when I'm like this.

"Only that the longer she's under, the less likely it becomes that she'll ever wake up and, if she does, she could be a vegetable. Basically no more alive than she is now." Charlie is reluctant, resentful.

"But she *could* make it?"

"He said others have."

"And…what—um. What are you thinking?"

"I can't stand seeing her like this, a shell of herself. It's not…*life*. It's just existence. How long can I sit here, waiting, hoping she'll just… miraculously wake up? What if she never does? Or what if she wakes up, but she's just a—a fucking potato?"

"Forever." Conrad's voice is low, and I think Charlie almost missed it.

"What?" Quick anger. "What'd you say?"

Conrad repeats himself, but louder. "Forever. I said fucking *forever*, Charlie. That's how long I'd sit here waiting. That's how long I'd hope."

"She's not in there, man."

A sudden scrape of chair legs. "Yes—she—*fucking*—is!" The words are punctuated by scuffling, and then a loud thump.

"Leh—leggo." Charlie's words are garbled. "You're choking me—" this, again, is mangled, as if he can barely get the sounds past a throat caught in a vice-grip.

Shoes on tile, a hard female voice. "Let him go, Mr. Killian, or I'll call security. Let him go *NOW*."

A pause, and then Charlie gasps raggedly. "It's fine…I'm fine."

Another silence. "She's in there. I feel her. I can't explain it, but I feel her." Conrad is close to me, so close I can *almost* feel him. "You can't give up on her, Charlie. You—you *can't*." Conrad, strong, powerful, fierce, vibrant Conrad…his voice breaks on the last word.

And my heart breaks with him.

Because I *am* here.

"God…*dammit*," Charlie's voice grates. "You gonna pay the hospital bills, Killian?"

"Yes." This is quiet, calm. "I'll take care of her, take care of everything. You don't have to ever come back here, if you don't want to."

"Hey, man, don't make it seem like I don't care—"

"I'm not. I'm just…saying. I'm not leaving her side. Not until her heart stops beating. Whether she's a fucking vegetable or not, I'll never leave her side."

Conrad, Conrad, Conrad…

The pain I feel, the emotional agony, the searing turmoil, the grief, the longing…it's too much. Too fucking much. It hurts, it hurts, it hurts.

Don't leave me, Conrad. Don't give up on me.

I'm here.

I'm here.

———

I—

I can't let him hurt anymore.

I can't stay here.

I can't stay in this darkness anymore.

I have to—

I—

I have to wake up.
I have to wake up.
Darkness tries to pull at me, and I fight it, fight it.
Cold seizes me, and I fight it.
The shadows pluck and pull and grab, and I fight it.
I have to wake up.

**∗∗**

Wake up.
   Wake up.
   Wake up.

   WAKE UP
   WAKE UP.
   WAKE UP.

**WAKE UP.**

**WAKE UP.**

**WAKE UP.**

*WAKE UP.*

*WAKE UP.*

*WAKE UP.*

*WAKE UP!*

*WAKE UP!*

*WAKE UP!*

$$* * *$$

Indelible darkness inhabits all of me.

But...there is a spark.

Tiny, fragile, and precious. That spark is all I have. It is everything. *Everything.*

I breathe into it, cling to it, and give myself over to it.

The spark is not small, I realize, nor tiny...it is merely far away. I yearn for it. Strain for it. Reach, reach. I must, I have to—that spark is the fire of my soul. It is the only weapon against the darkness.

What is beyond the black? I don't remember. But there's something, some reason, some vital, all-consuming, all-compelling reason I must reach beyond the black, must exit these shadows, must find the spark and fan it into flame.

What is it?

Why can't I remember?

I can't remember. But there's...something.

Drifting. Cold, empty, vast.

No, no. No. Not that, not any longer. I have to push, push for the light, for the something, for the spark.

The spark…what is the spark?

I don't remember.


Warmth.

There is warmth. It soothes. It is peaceful, delicate, breathing through me, spreading through me. I like the warmth. It…it reminds me of something skin

stubble, a caress, a whisper

a breath in the silence, a muffled sigh, a constricted sob
a voice
a sound which resonates through every last particle of my being

Conrad

\*\*\*\*

Conrad is the spark. He's the something. He's the reason, the push, the essence, the fury.

He's the light against the darkness, the agony within me driving me to chaotic, weltering, screaming rage against this darkness.

Conrad.

The warrior. The king. The gunslinger standing in the snow, breath hanging like frozen fog in the crystalline golden evening light. The master of my body, the owner of my sexuality.

Breath.

I feel...I feel his breath.

I dare not let even the flimsiest shreds of hope flutter through me.

But...I *feel*.

Heat, warmth of breath on my...my shoulder. I'm *aware* of my shoulder.

My shoulder is real.

*I* am real.

**I AM.**

My name is...my name is Hannah Tavistock.

I have a shoulder, and Conrad is breathing on it. He's here. He's close.

CONRAD!

But I have no voice, no strength, no eyes, no throat, no hands. All I have is that fragment of sensation, the curve of my shoulder, and the warmth of Conrad's breath on it, and the sound of his breathing soughing in and out slowly, rhythmically; he's asleep beside me.

Hope, nascent and delicate, blossoms slowly, gradually, like sunrise.

And I cling to it. I cling to that sensation, his breath on my skin, and his sleeping presence beside me. It is all I have, and it will be my strength.

Floating, drifting, like a cottonwood seed in a long slow breeze.

There's…something. Another sensation, a new one. I still feel the outside curve of my shoulder, though Conrad is no longer beside me, sleeping. But now…now there is something else. What is it? I *feel* it, but I can't identify it. Can I…move it? I send an impulse, and even that effort is exhausting, debilitating, but I do it anyway, fling the impulse out into the emptiness…

And I feel something in return, a distant echo of the impulse I sent out. A toe? Yes, a toe. Pinky toe, and all I can do is send the impulse and feel the echo. But—I think…I *think* I'm wiggling it. Maybe just a tiny bit, not enough for anyone to notice, but it's real.

Then I'm floating again, back in the emptiness. It's not darkness, now, though, but real true emptiness, a nothingness. But the nothing-ness nonetheless still somehow contains the spark that is me, and I can feel the fractal crystals of me floating in the nothingness. But maybe, just *maybe* I can gather them, cobble them into a larger sensate existence.

The effort is endless and tiring. But I cannot, do not, do not dare stop trying. It is like trying to gather handfuls of sand and grip them as tight as possible, hoping to reform them into a block of stone—only I do not have hands, only a fragmentary semblance of I.

There is...a lightening. A slight, vague filling of the void with some kind of...reality. Light, truth, I don't know. Just...something. Yet as vague and insubstantial as it is, that something heartens me, gives me renewed hope.

If awareness is a sunrise, then I am the subtle tinge of gray staining the blackness on the horizon. No pink yet, just a lifting of the complete darkness of night.

I struggle in the void, yearn for more, aware of Conrad and of his existence, if not his presence.

I have to wake up for him.

"—And then he—he fucking jumped! Can you believe it? He fucking jumped, the dumbass. And wouldn't you know, he made it? Cleared it like it was nothing. Must've been, oh, at least three or four feet. Doesn't seem like all that much until you have that gap in front of you and the cops are behind you. Then three or four feet might as well be a fucking canyon. But the goddamned asshole didn't even slow down, just fucking jumped across. He got away, and I got arrested. Spent three days in juvie lockup before my aunt showed up to get me out. She knew I was there the whole time, but figured I needed a lesson, so she let me twist. I learned a lesson, all right. Learned that you can't trust anyone, not anyone. Nobody. And I never did after that. I found the so-called *buddy* who ditched me and let me get arrested, and I broke his goddamn jaw. Used a cigarette punch. Know what that is? It's when you offer a guy a smoke, and when he's got his mouth open and relaxed, you nail him in the jaw. Breaks it easy as you please. That was…kind of the beginning of it all, for me. Or maybe the end, I guess you might say."

A silence, and then his voice continues; he's close, speaking just above a whisper.

"Figured out I could hit like a Mack truck, and figured out I didn't mind getting hit all that much. Get popped as much as I did when I was a kid, before the state took me out of there, you don't feel pain quite the same way as others might. A crack across the jaw isn't a big deal when you've taken a dozen hits like it from a full-grown man. I was a brawler, plain and simple. Not proud of it, but there it is.

"I quit going back to Aunt Sue's about a year after I got arrested. Didn't see the point, you know? She didn't want me there, and I didn't want to be there. She was probably gonna kick me to the curb at some point anyway, so I just quit going back.

"This was the South Carolina coast, so being out on the streets was a different prospect than it might be somewhere like New York or Chicago. No winter to speak of, you know? I'd sleep in alleys, under bridges, wherever the cops would have a hard time finding me to kick me out. I had this one spot under a pier, man…that was the shit, that spot. Ocean breeze, stars on the water, and the sound of the surf…it put me to sleep like magic. I couldn't stay there every night though, or the fuzz would get suspicious and I'd lose it. They figure out your spots, you know? And they make you leave, they'll show up while you're sleeping and make you move, usually by the oh-so kind method of a boot to the ribs. 'Get a move on, kid. Can't stay here,'" his voice turns into a gravelly growl, then goes back to his smooth, silky midnight voice.

"You wanna know how I got off the streets? Pure luck, that's how. Kind of a Hollywood story, you ask me. Kinda thing you'd see 'em make a movie out of. I held up this old man, right? Stuck a knife in his face and told him to give me his money, or else. I probably wouldn't have stabbed him, but I figured he wouldn't know that. I was wrong, though. He knew. Man, he *knew*. Dared me to stab him, and when I wouldn't, he slapped the knife out of my hand and told me to follow him. So I did.

"Not sure why, even now, but I followed him. He took me to this junkyard, like a real deal junkyard, full of scrap and old cars and just piles and piles of old useless shit. And he gave me a job sorting through the shit, taught me operate the cranes and the tow truck and the front loaders, showed me how to itemize useful parts and how to find those useful parts for guys rebuilding junkers or whatever.

"I worked in that junkyard for six years. The old man gave me a bed in the back of the office, and there was a shower there, so I just lived there. Sounds like shit, but it was heaven to me. Safe, solitary, work to do, a little money in my pocket. Well, after six years, the old man died and left me the junkyard. Managed to turn the profit from the junkyard into enough cash to invest in a cube van, and I started another business hauling people's junk away for them, like the shit too big for garbage trucks.

"I cleaned out garages, towed cars out of yards, hauled away broken fridges and whatever else. I made a career out of actual, literal junk, babe. Never told you what I do for a living because it isn't pretty, it isn't romantic or badass or whatever. But it pays good, you know? I got my own house, a nice truck, a big old TV. I got fifty guys working for me. I own three scrapyards, and got four teams of guys serving most of the state."

A pause, silence filling the space, except for the *beep—beep—beep*.

Then he starts up again. "I'm thinking of buying a restaurant. Did I mention that yet? I don't think I did. It's this shitty dive bar up the coast a ways, not much to look at, kinda dirty, kinda sketchy. But the guy in the kitchen makes these killer fucking burgers, right? Like, just the juiciest, thickest burgers I've ever had in my life. Clean it up a bit, redecorate so it don't look like a failed biker hole, fix a few things, get a decent bartender? Man, I think it could make some bank. It's right on the highway, looking out on the ocean. Decent spot, lots of potential. What do you think, babe?"

Silence, brief, expectant.

"Yeah, I think I should too. You'll love it there, once I fix it up. I'll paint it light colors, so it looks bigger. Make it like an old beach bar, you know? Ropes and boat steering wheels and fishing poles and shit. Keep the old wood floors, except maybe replace the ones that squeak. Bust a few new windows to let in some light—or maybe—maybe even open the whole front wall and put in one of those indoor-outdoor decks, you know? Where the walls slide apart and it's all open? I think that'd be cool.

"The bathrooms, though, those are important. People will judge a place on the bathrooms. If they're small and dirty and smell like old piss, folks aren't gonna come back, no matter how good the food or booze is. I've noticed this. I do the same thing myself. Nobody likes to piss in a smelly-ass pit where you don't have room to even turn around, you know? So I gotta invest in nice bathrooms."

Another silence, this one long, and this silence feels...tense. Painful.

"It's hard to keep up these running monologues, babe. I'm not one to talk this much, usually. You've probably figured that out by now though, right? I think I've spoken more all at once over this last week or so than I have the rest of my entire life. They say, if you're in there, that you can hear me. I like to think you can hear me. It's fucking hard, babe. I'm trying, but I'm...I'm running out of shit to talk about. Maybe I'll bring a book, read it out loud to you. That might be easier than trying to work up what I'm gonna talk about all damn day.

"What do you like to read? We never talked about that. You like classics? Shakespeare and shit? Or newer stuff, like romance, maybe. What do they call 'em...bodice rippers? Nah, that's not you. I bet you like sci-fi. Ha, I'm just kidding. Maybe I'll start with something cool, like...Hemingway. I know I don't seem the type, but I love to read. Hemingway, man, that dude was the shit. You'll like him. You're smarter than I am, so you've probably already read it, but...what are you gonna do, complain?" He groans. "Too soon? Yeah, definitely too soon."

He groans again, and the sound is muffled, as if he's scrubbing his face with his hands. "I'm going crazy, Hannah. I'm sorry, shit—I'm sorry. I shouldn't crack jokes. It's not fucking funny, I know it's not."

Actually, that *was* funny, Conrad. And I'm not smarter than you. I've never read Hemingway, and I do like sci-fi—I like space opera. It's kind of a guilty secret of mine. And I'm not a fan of Shakespeare. I mean, everybody raves about Shakespeare this and Shakespeare that, but...*Romeo and Juliet*? It's so stupidly tragic—it was all so preventable. Like those stupid romantic comedies where the whole thing is predicated on a simple misunderstanding which could have been fixed if they'd just talked things out like rational adults.

I wish he could hear me.

Conrad?

CONRAD!

Wiggle your toe, Hannah.

I think of that movie—*wiggle your big toe—wiggle your big toe*—

I'm not as badass as Beatrix Kiddo, but if I can wiggle my pinky toe, maybe he'll notice. Maybe he'll know I'm here, I'm here, I'm in here, I'm listening.

Impulse.

Wiggle your damn toe, Hannah.

I feel an echo of sensation, and his breath catches.

"Hannah? Babe?" His voice cracks. "You—you moved your toe."

Conrad. Keep talking to me, Conrad. I'm here, my love. I'm here.

"Can you do it again?"

I try. TRY. I focus on that echo of the impulse, and this time the echo is louder, closer. I feel—more toes. More movement. Not quite all five toes, but nearly. The four smaller ones, I can feel them twitch.

"Babe...I—what do I do? Do I get a doctor? Shit." He sounds panicked, excited. "Okay, Hannah, babe, listen. If you're in there, if you hear me, wiggle those sexy little toes of yours for me again. Twice, can you do that? Wiggle 'em twice."

That's so much harder than you know, Conrad. You don't know what you're asking. But for you...I'll do anything. For you.

It takes an eternity. The void reaches for me, but I deny it.

I wiggle. Wiggle.

And Conrad laughs, but the laugh is a sob. "You're there. You're there! You hear me!"

I hear you, Conrad. I fucking hear you. Keep talking to me, sweetheart. Read me Hemingway. Tell me about your aunt. Tell me about your scrapyards. Tell me—tell me about all your girlfriends, so I know how to love you better than any of them ever did. Tell me everything.

Commotion then. Male voices, female voices, a flurry of sounds and activity. More sensation, now. Things happening...to me. I feel it! I feel it. Touching, poking.

A male voice—the doctor?—asks me to move my toes again, and I do.

But it's too much, then.

Too much; I'm tired. So tired.

But this time, oh…this time what pulls me under isn't the cold hungry darkness, or the empty void, but rather…

Sleep.

Precious, normal, peaceful sleep.

The difference between sleep and what had me in its clutches before? It's…impossible to describe, even to myself. But I feel it, I know it, I recognize the touch of sleep as I sink into it. Sleep is sweet, delicate, and temporary.

I sleep…and I do not dream.

"What are you doing here, asshole?" Conrad's voice, angry.

"I...I wasn't in my right mind, before. The doctor, he made it sound like—"

"Charlie, listen. There's no love lost between you and me, right? We both know that. So I'll just be blunt: you had your chance, man. Ten years worth of chances, actually. And then, when she needed you the most, you were just gonna, what...let 'em shut off the ventilator? Let her fuckin' code out because you don't have the fuckin' balls to stay by her side when shit gets rough? You don't deserve her, Charlie. You don't deserve to be here."

"I—I just—shit. You're right. I know you're right. But I didn't come back for that. I had to see—"

Poor Charlie sounds so confused, so disoriented.

My brain wobbles, tilts, and I have flashes, fleeting glimpses and visions of Charlie, but not this Charlie, not *my* Charlie. A different Charles Markham. A Charlie Markham with a six gun and a leer, hauling me through the snow. A Charlie with a saber and a musket, arrogant in a scarlet coat. A Charlie dressed in a suit, blond hair slicked back, winning a hand of cards, kneeling between my tied-open thighs with a cocky sneer.

So many versions, all Charlie but none are *this* Charlie. Which one is real, though? Did the real Charlie ever love me? The nights spent awake, alone, desperate for release, while he snored beside me…was that real? The sightless, fever-flesh moments suspended in darkness without time, his mouth on mine, his hands on me, touching me like I always wished he would…was that a dream, too? Or was that reality? It's all tangled together.

"Had to see what?" Conrad says, his voice low and grating. "Whether she died or not? Whether she's a vegetable?"

"I don't know. I just had to see her." Desperation in his voice, and then an attempt at bluster. "I *am* still her husband, you know. I have every right to be here."

"The fuck you do. I don't give a shit about your legal rights. Get your look, and get out of here."

I hear him, sense him. I smell him, that cologne he prefers. And then…I *feel* him. His hand in mine—I feel it, but I can't find the synapses to move my fingers, can't find the impulse to squeeze his hand.

I try: ten years together—I owe him that much.

I loved you, Charlie.

I feel his hand cover mine, and it feels both wrong and right at the same time. Ten years of familiarity; I know his touch, know his hand, I know this is his hand on mine even without sight. But yet…it's not *right*. That's not us, anymore. Not Charlie and Hannah. His hand on mine feels uncomfortable, awkward. Because it's Conrad and Hannah, now.

"Can I just…can I have a couple minutes alone with her, please?" Charlie asks.

"Sure."

Conrad didn't tell Charlie that I'm…not awake, really, not fully conscious, but…*here*. That I've wiggled my toes. That I'm finding my way back.

I hear a door close, and then I know I'm alone with Charlie. I can't feel it for certain, but I think he's perched on the edge of my bed, holding my hand. Staring down at me, probably, with those pale, ice blue eyes. I can almost see the confusion and the hurt and the distance in his expression.

"Hannah, I—I don't know if you can hear me, or not."

I can, Charlie, I can; I don't wiggle my toes—can't. Also...won't. Not for him.

"I really did love you, you know. I hope you know that. I don't—I don't know what happened, between us. How did we get here? I mean, if you were awake, if this hadn't happened to you, we'd still be...in this fucked up mess we're in. You have Conrad, and I have Arelia, but you and I are still married. My feelings for you...they're not gone.

"I don't know what happened, honey. I never set out looking for anyone, it just—happened. I mean, I know that's bullshit. You don't accidentally sleep with someone, I know that. I'll never excuse it. But once...once Arelia and I started, we just—we just couldn't stop. I think you probably kind of understand. But it never meant I loved you any less, or that I just...stopped having feelings for you. I just—I feel... *more*...for Arelia. And...I just—fuck, I don't know *how* it happened. I don't know how to explain it to you. Or even to myself, really."

A long, ragged sigh. "I don't know. They say couples that start out in high school, as young as we did...that you can just...sort of grow apart. You grow up, you become who you're supposed to be, and that person you are now just isn't compatible with the person your partner has become, not like when you were both sixteen or eighteen or whatever. I mean, it makes sense, doesn't it? We change so much between sixteen and twenty-six, don't we?"

I don't know what you're trying to say to me, Charlie.

"I'm sorry we're here. That we're dealing with this is. That we got here. We can't go back, I know we can't. And...if I'm being honest, I don't want to. That's probably kind of terrible of me to say, but... it's just true. I loved you, but we can't go back, and I think it would be foolish to try."

I agree with that. There's no going back. Not now. Maybe there never was. I can't forgive the things I saw you do with Arelia, especially since you never did them with me. Am I more upset that you did them at all, that you cheated on me, or that in cheating on me you gave her things I never got? I don't know. That there's even a question is pretty fucked up in itself.

"But...despite the fact that we can't go back, that we won't go back...I can't just walk away from you. Not now. Not with you like this."

You *did* walk away, you bastard. You don't get points for changing your mind and coming back.

"I have to know you're going to be okay. I know things are fucked up between us, honey, but...I'll still be here when you wake up, and when you start getting better. We'll figure the rest out later, okay? I still care about you."

It hurts, Charlie. Everything hurts. You hurt me, and I know I hurt you. That you cheated first doesn't negate my guilt.

I fade, then. It's hard to remain above the surface of conscious for this long.

———

I don't know what brings me to the surface, this time. There's silence, except the incessant beeping of the heart monitor.

Nothing—*nothing*. Where is Conrad? Where is Charlie? I don't hear either of them, no snores, no breathing.

Being alone brings panic. My heartbeat pounds frantically in my chest. Did they leave? Did they leave me here?

Conrad? Don't leave. Don't go. I can't do this. Not by myself. How do I wake up? How do I push through this?

I'm weak. I hurt. I'm confused. Weak. So weak. Dizzy.

My throat hurts.

There's a dull but constant throbbing in my lower back.

I have a wicked headache.

Wait...pain? There was no pain, before. I think this is some kind of cruel improvement, where pain means I'm waking up, getting better.

But god, what pain. Deep, dull, constant, inescapable, all pervading, a wild variety of pain.

Where's Conrad?

I hear the heart monitor beeping faster as my heart rate increases with my rising fear of being left alone in this hospital. I can't be alone, not now. Not here. I can't, just can't. I can't wake up without Conrad.

Then there's a squeak of shoe soles on tile, and a human presence. "It's all right, Hannah." A calm female voice. A cool, small hand on my forearm—I can *feel* it, I can feel her hand on my arm. "You're okay, Hannah. You're in the hospital. You're going to be fine, okay? Mr. Killian just stepped out for a few minutes, but he'll be right back. And your—Mr. Markham...he said he'll be back in the morning."

He'll be right back. Conrad will be right back; this sends a rush of calm through me, and my heart rate slows, the fear draining.

"That's good, Hannah. That's right. It's okay." Her voice is hypnotic, soothing. "I'm going to move you around a little, okay? Just to give your arms and legs some exercise."

I feel—I *feel*. She takes my left leg in her hands, her cold, small hands, and lifts it, pushes against me to bend my leg at the knee, extends it, bends it, brings my leg out to the side and back in, then holds my calf in one hand and rolls my ankle this way and that.

"I heard you can wiggle your toes, Hannah," she says, "can you do that for me? Don't want me to feel left out, do you?"

Focusing on my toes isn't as hard, this time. I can feel them, sense them at the end of my leg; I send the impulse down my body, through my leg, and I feel my big toe twitch. I try again, and this time I feel all my toes curl at the same time.

"Good job, Hannah, that was great! Big improvement. Now, how about the other leg?" She sets my left leg down, picks up my right and puts it through the same series of movements. When she finishes rolling my ankle, she pokes my big toe. "How about this side, Hannah? Can you move any of these piggies?"

Piggies? What am I, a child? Irritation zings through me, but I can't express it, can only focus on my foot, my toes, on moving them. This is harder, and I don't know why. I thought I could only move the toes on my left side, until now. It requires strain, effort, intense focus, a supreme effort...and all I manage is a slight twitch of my big toe.

"See? You can do it." She takes my left arm, puts it through the same series of movements, bend at the elbow, side to side, up and down, roll the wrist; this time she massages my hand, my fingers. "Can you move your hands, Hannah? Twitch a finger or two?"

Not for you. For Conrad, maybe.

She massages my fingers more, rubbing them from knuckle to fingertip, pressing the center of my palm with her thumb. "Come on, Hannah. Try it for me." I sense humor in her voice. "See, I think you're not trying. You gotta try, Hannah. Give me a finger wiggle."

I feel oddly, intensely stubborn about this. I want Conrad to feel me move my hands, not this nurse.

"Okay, well, if you don't want to, you don't have to. But the more you practice, the more it'll all come back," she says as she works my right arm, and then massages my fingers on that side.

"Doctor Abernathy will be in later this morning, and I think he'll be pleased with your progress. We might even be able to get you off the oxygen."

———

"...Tracheal extubation...stoma will heal on its own...assess her neurological status..."

"—Thought she was waking up, Doctor Abernathy, she was moving her toes." Conrad sounds so sad, so frustrated.

I try to stay with him, struggle to push above the surface, but I'm just so tired, so weak.

"She's been through a lot, Mr. Killian. I know this seems like a step backward, but really, it *is* improvement. This isn't a comatose state any longer, just very deep sleep. Her body has experienced significant trauma just in fighting off the meningitis. Add in complications from the extreme fever, possible seizures, and nearly two weeks in a coma? She has every right to be exhausted, don't you think?"

"I guess you're right. It's just…hard."

"Of course it is. Watching someone you love suffer, and knowing there's nothing you can do…that's it's own special kind of hell." A sigh. "I know you've heard this a dozen times by now, Mr. Killian, and I know it sounds…trite, possibly, but I promise, just being here with her, talking to her, that's huge. It really is the best thing you can do to help her. I've tended to dozens of coma patients, and they all say they heard their loved ones. Sensed them, at the very least. She knows you're here, and she needs you."

I do, oh I do. Listen to him, Conrad.

"So what's next, then?"

"Like I said, we'll look into weaning her off oxygen."

I'm fading, now. Conrad is speaking, but I can't follow it, and I want to. I need to hear his voice. I need him. Need him. Need him.

Sleep claims me, then, and I sink and twist and drift.

——

Everything is different.

Harder. Deeper. Sharper. Brighter.

Darkness, still, but I sense light beyond my eyelids.

Sounds, close and far, muffled and detailed, layered—voices in the hall and shoes on tile, a distorted voice on the PA, the heart monitor beeping, a slow soft snoring off to my left.

I *feel*.

I feel *everything*.

Myself, a thousand kinds of pain, aches, throbbing, thirst, discomfort, all mixed and muddled.

Disoriented.

The dreams in the darkness, they're layered throughout memory. They're all there, fresh, real, vivid, both the truth and the fiction, the dream of reality, the remembered fantasy, the fantastic reality. I don't trust my memory, because it's been…tainted, fragmented, twisted by fever dreams, coma dreams.

    It hurts to breathe.

    I feel a mask over my nose and mouth.

    IV in my right forearm just below my elbow.

    My toes are cold.

    My eyelids are so heavy.

    It hurts to be awake.

    Not yet…not yet.

    I'm sorry, Conrad, but I can't. Not yet.

"'…On the second and final day of their descent into the down deep,'" I hear Conrad's voice, but it's metered, paced, reading rather than speaking, "'the novel gradually became the habitual. The clank and thrum of the great spiral staircase found a rhythm.'"

I don't recognize the words, don't know what he's reading.

An oddity: out of all the desperation and heartache and pain and love and desire and need, it's curiosity that opens my eyes.

Blurry at first. Flickers and distorted, eyelash-filtered glimpses, then my eyes shutter once more.

Again.

This time I get a full snapshot of reality: a window frame, glass and steel beyond, a gray sky; close in the foreground is Conrad, feet kicked up on the table beside my bed, feet bare, toes wiggling idly, long denim-sheathed legs, plain gray T-shirt over his hard beautiful torso, his inky black hair long and shaggy and loose and messy and greasy, a thick, untrimmed beard on his jawline; in his big strong hands a paperback book. The cover is a spray of fiery orange sparks over a black background with one word in white capital letters at the center: *WOOL*. Beneath, in slightly smaller letters: Hugh Howey.

God, what a perfect vignette to wake up to. My Conrad, reading to me. So sexy, a fantasy made real in jeans and bare feet, a book in his hands.

I close my eyes—take a test breath, discover I can breathe on my own, no tubes—and I open my eyes once more.

And then, for a time I do not care to measure, I just luxuriate in Conrad reading to me from this book, *Wool*, and I watch him read, watch the way his eyes flick over the words rapidly, listen to the sonorous, soothing sound of his voice steady and clear and smooth. Watch his thick fingers turn page after page.

After a long while, he sets the book face down on his thighs, rubs his eyes, stretches, his back popping.

And his eyes fix on me and…

Find mine.

He stands up abruptly, the book tumbling to the floor with a noisy flapping and a thump. "Hannah?"

He darts forward, finds my hand and takes it in both of his.

I swallow; my throat is sore. I try to speak. "Hi." My voice is raspy, hoarse.

He blinks rapidly, and I don't miss the tears pooling in his eyes. "You're awake."

I try to smile, and manage a small, weak curve of my lips. "I think—I think so."

His palm cups my cheek. He doesn't try to hide the tears in his eyes. "You scared me, Hannah."

"Sorry."

He laughs, blinks, and a pair of tears trickle down his cheeks and drip off his jaw onto the shoulder of my hospital gown. "You were in a coma, and they—they weren't sure if you'd—if you'd ever—"

"I dreamed of you." I'm so tired, achy, sore, weak; words must chosen carefully. "I heard your voice."

"God, Hannah—"

"I came back for you."

"You dreamed—of me?" His voice breaks. "You heard me?"

I nod. Words are too much, now, and my throat hurts. "Read more. Please?"

He kisses my cheek, my jaw. "I'll read to you forever, Hannah."

I frown at him. Purse my lips. "You...missed."

He laughs. Leans close, cups my cheek in his paw, thumb caressing my cheekbone.

And he kisses me.

Kisses me.

Kisses me.

On the lips. Slow, delicate, and careful, but I feel deep, thrumming emotion in the meeting of our lips, feel his worry, his fear, his need...

His love.

When he pulls away, I close my eyes to savor the memory of his lips on mine, the dampness from our joined mouths, the tingle.

The coma dreams batter through me, memory after memory after memory. Being forced back through the doors again and again, away from him. Never kissing him. Never quite knowing him, never quite having him, not all of him. Knowing, deep down, that he wasn't real, that none of it was real, even though each time it felt so real, *was* so real.

But now...it's finally, truly *him*.

And I can't help the tears then, and I don't try.

"Oh, Hannah."

I nuzzle into his hand. "You're real. You're finally real." It hurts to sob, but I can't stop.

"What do you mean?"

"I dreamed of you. But it wasn't ever...*you*. It was a dream. Always a dream. And now—and now—" I can't continue, can't finish.

He holds me, clings to me, and cradles me to him. He lets me cry, doesn't shush me. After a while, he brushes away my tears with the pads of his thumbs and stares down at me.

"I'm real, Hannah. I'm here. You're awake, now."

"Promise me—"

"What, honey? Anything."

I have to pause, gather strength to speak past the ache in my throat from the tracheostomy. "When I can go home, when I'm better…you'll take me to bed. Make love to me. Kiss me….and never—never stop."

"God, Hannah." A shuddering breath. "Of course. I promise, love. I promise." He laughs.

"Don't laugh at me."

He only laughs harder. "What the hell did you dream about, Hannah?"

I blush, and he doesn't miss it. "You," is all I say. "I dreamed…of you."

He isn't laughing anymore. His gaze is hot, fierce. "I think I'm gonna have to get you to tell me about these dreams of yours."

I'm in a hospital gown, with a tracheostomy stoma, IV tubes, monitor leads. I've been in a bed for two weeks with only sponge baths to clean me. But yet…his eyes tell me clearly that I'm beautiful.

To him, at least.

His eyes communicate that he needs me.

Wants me.

That I'm his.

I shiver, and meet his gaze with a heated one of my own. "Maybe, when I can, I'll just…*show* you."

His nose nudges mine. His beard is rough against my cheek. I feel his body heat, smell his masculine scent.

His lips brush mine, but instead of kissing me, he whispers to me:

"I love you, Hannah."

I've found what's real.

# Jasinda Wilder

Visit me at my website: **www.jasindawilder.com**
Email me: **jasindawilder@gmail.com**

If you enjoyed this book, you can help others enjoy it as well by recommending it to friends and family, or by mentioning it in reading and discussion groups and online forums. You can also review it on the site from which you purchased it. But, whether you recommend it to anyone else or not, thank you *so much* for taking the time to read my book! Your support means the world to me!


My other titles:

Preacher's Son:
*Unbound*
*Unleashed*
*Unbroken*

Delilah's Diary:
*A Sexy Journey*
*La Vita Sexy*
*A Sexy Surrender*

Big Girls Do It:
*Boxed Set*
*Married*
*On Christmas*
*Pregnant*

Rock Stars Do It:
*Harder*
*Dirty*
*Forever*

From the world of *Big Girls* and *Rock Stars*:
*Big Love Abroad*

Biker Billionaire:
*Wild Ride*

The Falling Series:
*Falling Into You*
*Falling Into Us*
*Falling Under*
*Falling Away*
*Falling For Colton*

The Ever Trilogy:
*Forever & Always*
*After Forever*
*Saving Forever*

The world of *Wounded:*
*Wounded*
*Captured*

The world of *Stripped:*
*Stripped*
*Trashed*

The world of *Alpha:*
*Alpha*
*Beta*
*Omega*
*Harris: Alpha One Security Book 1*
*Thresh: Alpha One Security Book 2*

The Houri Legends:
*Jack and Djinn*
*Djinn and Tonic*

The Madame X Series:
*Madame X*
*Exposed*
*Exiled*

Standalone titles:
*Yours*

Non-Fiction titles:
*Big Girls Do It Running*

Badd Brothers:
*Badd Motherf\*cker*

Jack Wilder Titles:
*The Missionary*

To be informed of new releases, special offers, and other Jasinda news, sign up for Jasinda's email newsletter.

www.ingramcontent.com/pod-product-compliance
Lightning Source LLC
Chambersburg PA
CBHW030840030726
47495CB00005B/1310